OF BEASTS AND BEAUTIES

FIVE FULL-LENGTH NOVELS RETELLING BEAUTY & THE BEAST

MIRANDA HONFLEUR   RYAN MUREE

EMILY ALLEN WEST   EMERALD DODGE

KATHERINE BENNET

Cover art by Patricia Lira

Proofreading by Patrycja Pakula for Holabird Editing

ISBN: 978-0-9994854-7-7

www.enclaveauthors.com

CONTENTS

NO MAN CAN TAME

MIRANDA HONFLEUR

Editing by Laura Kingsley

Proofreading by Patrycja Pakula for Holabird Editing

A human princess. A dark-elf prince. A kiss of fire and powder.

After a failed courtship in an ally kingdom, twenty-one-year-old Princess Alessandra returns home to a land torn apart by mutual hatred between the humans and the dark-elves. The "Beast Princess," as Aless is known by courtiers, confidently sets her mind to ways of making peace, but her father has already decided for her: she is to marry one of the mysterious and monstrous dark-elves to forge peace, and go on a Royal Progress across the kingdom to flaunt their harmonious union. While she intends to preserve the peace, the Beast Princess has plans of her own.

Prince Veron has been raised knowing his life is not his own, but to be bargained away by his mother, the queen of Nozva Rozkveta, to strengthen the dark-elf queendom. When his mother tells him he is to marry a self-absorbed, vile human, he is determined to do his duty regardless of his personal feelings. After arriving at the human capital, he finds the "Beast Princess" rebellious and untamed—and not to be trusted.

Aless and Veron face opposition at every turn, with humans and dark-elves alike opposing the union violently, as well as their own feelings of dissonance toward each other. Can two people from cultures that despise one another fall in love? Can a marriage between them bond two opposing worlds together, or will it tear them apart for good?

Genre: Fantasy Romance
Heat level: Sensual

CHAPTER 1

*T*he raven leered down his long, black beak at Aless as she twirled, his gaze so intense it burned.

A blur of bodies in jewel-toned silks and brocades circled her and Bianca in three-quarter time. Ravens, cats, bears, peacocks, wolves… The animal kingdom had come to their king's call beneath arched ceilings and canopied swaths, or maybe to catch a glimpse of the notorious Beast Princess back from her worldwide hunt.

Tonight she'd donned a lion mask with a full, voluminous mane and a grotesquely painted facade. If she was to be gawked at anyway, the least she could do was make it count.

No, she wasn't beside herself with excitement over yet another party. And no, she wasn't pleased to be home. She wouldn't be, not until Papà properly heard her out about finally building Mamma's public library. Books were always a sore spot with him, and so was Mamma—since her death—an even sorer one, but maybe enough time had passed and he'd finally listen.

But in the meantime, well, she could hardly be faulted for fitting in some entertainment, now could she? Just a little. If Papà refused to build the library, well, then he should know what idle hands were wont to do.

Signore Raven leaned against a pillar and raised his chin, peering at her through his mask. Oh, he'd been looking at her all evening with those hungry, dark eyes. And not in the aghast gawking of most of the nobiltà. He wanted something—and considering he definitely wasn't royal, he wasn't a man Papà would approve of.

All the more tempting to give Signore Raven what he seemed to want so badly.

Signore Cat next to him was the same, ogling Bianca as if she were a plump, unwitting canary. Bianca hadn't been sent around the world by Papà in offering, so she would no doubt know who they were.

"Don't look now," Aless whispered from behind her lion mask, "but the cat and the raven have been struck dumb."

Bianca giggled and spun, her slippered feet clicking on the parquet floor to the music of the harp, the flute, the drums, and rebecs, amid a chorus of practiced laughter and effusive tones of conversation. No matter the spectacle and gossip, Bianca could always be counted on to stay by her side. A loyal sister, and a trusted friend.

Bianca adjusted her elaborate tabby-cat mask and tucked a lock of shining onyx-colored hair behind her ear. "The Belmonte brothers."

Ah, so the raven and the cat were none other than Luciano and Tarquin Belmonte. Their reputations preceded them. Especially Luciano's—Bianca hadn't stopped talking about him for months.

The taller of the two, Signore Raven, had to be Tarquin, the younger brother and general of the Belmonte Company of mercenaries; the older of the two, Signore Cat, was Luciano, and after their father's passing, now visconte of Roccalano.

Morally fluid, physically fit men, who were good dancers and—if rumor held true—vigorous lovers, but lacked the blood and moral obligation of royalty. These were men intended to be beneath a princess—for a night or two—not at her side. At least in the Sileni court.

Aless guided Bianca off the dance floor to the nearest trestle table heaped with marzipan torte, custard tarts, and colorful berries. She popped a grape in her mouth and held out a goblet until the telltale splashing of poured wine ceased. After a sip of the bubbly white, she handed the goblet to Bianca, all the while keeping her gaze locked on the Belmonte brothers.

"Maybe *Luciano* will finally become your latest entertainment?" she asked Bianca, who hid her face in a goblet of wine. "Not that I'm complaining," she whispered, giving Tarquin a slow—*very* slow—once-over, "but what are they doing in Bellanzole?"

Bianca leaned in. "The Belmonte Company has been handling our... issues with the Immortali. The army didn't have the expertise to clear the harpy nest in the cliffs, but ever since Arabella Belmonte, their sister, disappeared a couple months ago, Luciano has been studying them and Tarquin has been handling them. They've become experts on the Immortali, so Papà hired their company."

She'd been reading about the Immortali, even more since the Rift had torn the Veil a few months ago, when they had re-entered the world as if stepping from the pages of myth and legend. Some were peaceful here in Silen, like the light-elves, the dark-elves, and the fae, and others were monsters who killed with impunity—harpies, wyverns, basilisks, and more.

Still, despite the variety among them, there was a general distrust of the Immortali among her people—and since most couldn't read or write, there would continue to be until that changed. The dark-elves, especially, had been the subject of wanton persecution, since their looks were so terrifyingly outlandish.

The Immortali were unusual, yes, sometimes even repugnant, but not universally evil. Most just wanted to survive peacefully, raise families, live *quietly*. Everyone in Silen—human or Immortali—deserved that chance. No one had to marry a dark-elf, but treating them fairly was the right thing to do.

She'd been reading a newly transcribed copy of *A Modern History of Silen*, its new additions. But like every copy of the book, it contained ample blank pages at the end, just like the ones in the older copy Mamma had given her. Ones she hoped to fill with an account of the peace forged between her people and the Immortali. Maybe the new library could become a place for humans and Immortali alike to learn together.

As for the monsters... Papà had deployed many of his forces combating piracy ravaging the coasts and his trade routes, and the rest had to be stretched thin fighting enemies no one understood—no one except the Belmonte brothers, apparently.

"Say a prayer for me, Aless." Bianca gripped the goblet tightly. "I think I love him."

"I know you have your heart set on him," she replied, "but maybe you could... adjust your expectations a little."

Bianca gulped the wine, then upturned the goblet and drained it entirely. Liquid courage? She glanced over her shoulder at the Belmonte brothers.

"I'm already twenty-three," Bianca insisted, "with no other prospects, so perhaps Luciano could be more? Papà may be keen on sending you to every eligible royal bachelor in the region, but not me."

"Two. *Two* royal bachelors in this past year—"

"In this *past year*." Bianca raised her chin. "And they *are* all the eligible royal bachelors. All the others are already married or betrothed." She frowned, her eyes meandering up and off to the side. "Or little children."

"Papà is only keen on sending me around because he wants to get *rid* of me. Unlike his favorite daughter." Since she'd reached marriageable age, Papà had sent her to maybe... a dozen or two royal bachelors. Although this year, he'd only sent her to one prince and one king. Maybe it was a sign that he was giving up and would finally leave her in peace with her books.

Bianca set down the goblet. "It's only because he finds you so meddlesome. Once you decide something must be, you don't let up. It can make you... difficult."

Was that bad? She straightened. Mamma had spent her life teaching the paesani to read, and when she'd died, all that had stopped. For nearly a decade, Papà hadn't just stalled Mamma's plans to build a public library—a center of learning for all—he'd actively avoided it. Hadn't even allowed her to revive Mamma's program to teach the paesani to read and write.

It was *meddlesome* to want to dedicate her life to seeing the library built, to want to teach any and all who wanted to learn, just as Mamma had wanted?

"I want to do more than just be foisted onto royal bachelors," she declared. "Is it so wrong to have dreams of something more?"

Sighing, Bianca shook her head. "Difficult. And that's why you're still the Beast Princess." With a final shrug, she sashayed back onto the dance floor.

Heat spread across Aless's skin, climbing over every inch until she burned. But she hadn't been the Beast Princess all her life without learning to tame her temper.

So it was fine for Bianca to have dreams of marrying beneath her station, but it was *not* fine for *her* to dream of teaching people to read and write? She sighed through her nose.

To any woman of the Ermacora royal line, Luciano was forbidden fruit when it came to marriage. Still, in her wistfully recounted daydreams, Bianca always seemed to find herself in an orchard of forbidden fruit anyway, with a ladder just tall enough to reach anything she wanted.

Trying to ignore the rapid pulse in her ear, Aless popped another grape into her mouth and eyed the dance floor as she cooled. At least Bianca had found something to *do* instead of squabbling. There was wisdom in that.

All of the palazzo's ballrooms dazzled, but this place, the Sala di Forza, was a tribute to one of the Terran faith's greatest heroes, Forza, son of Nox and a mortal woman, a demigod of great strength. Painted with his exploits, great hunts and battles celebrating strength, war, and masculinity, it was Papà's favorite.

It was suffocating.

With Papà, it was *always* strength, war, and masculinity. Lorenzo was a master swordsman and could hit a target with his throwing knives from thirty yards—so no matter his shortcomings, Papà favored him. And since Papà didn't allow her to learn any of the martial arts—and she loved books as Mamma had—there was just no way to win with him.

Masked guests dressed in the height of Bellanzole couture mingled and danced. The nobiltà and the nuovi ricchi devised this adventure, preened for one another as usual, their eclectic fashion diverse—within an allowable variation, of course.

Except for Tarquin Belmonte. No, he'd thrown the *allowable variation* to the winds and had come here to shock. To arrive cloaked in death was to object. In his raven mask, black brocade doublet and trousers, and a feathered mourning cloak, he filled out couture well, and he had a lot of nerve showing up to a masquerade at the Palazzo dell'Ermacora dressed in funereal garb. As much nerve as a princess in a grotesque lion mask.

She grinned. A man with a spine. Good. At least one courtier who didn't fall all over himself bowing and scraping before Papà. Yes, according to court custom, such a man was beneath her—and he *would* be, tonight.

Eyes locked with his through her lion mask, she turned, rearranging her ample costume mane behind her, and glided through the crowd with ease, mingling, brushing off eager courtiers as she stalked from the Sala di Forza and out onto the balcony. He'd follow, of course. The perfect moment to come together—about their objections to Papà's policies. She traded brightly colored silks and paintings of Forza's many mythical victories for the faraway diamonds dusting the black velvet sky.

Gripping the stone balustrade, she closed her eyes and took three deep breaths. The soft, fresh scent of roses embraced her, surrounded her, as it had countless times in her dreams and fantasies. The same dense, overgrown courtyard of vining roses in full bloom sprawled before her, mysterious and lovely, exhaling the most spellbinding perfume in the clearest, purest air. She reached out a fingertip and could almost feel the velvety soft, shimmering petals—

"The lion's den is the balcony, is it?"

Next to her stood a vision in black feathers, nearly six feet tall and built like a gladiator. Tarquin Belmonte. She blinked, and that spellbinding perfume faded. She gave him a coy once-over. "Don't you have a carcass somewhere to peck at?"

A half-laugh. "I have sight of better game."

Suppressing a grin, she shook her head. "Bold as a raven."

He rested his hand on the stone balustrade, too, his warm skin just barely touching hers. "Nothing less than bold can be expected to win a princess."

"Is that what you came here for?" Nobody dealt in boldness like the Beast Princess. She turned to him, covered his hand with hers, and reached for his raven mask. "To 'win' me?" When he didn't move, she took it off.

Carnelian-brown eyes gleamed in the starlight beneath black lashes and matching close-cropped hair; the lines of his coarse jaw were strong, and the corners of his mouth turned up mischievously, as if he knew something she didn't.

She hadn't expected a handsome face to match the tall, well-muscled physique. But then, she hadn't seen Tarquin Belmonte in years—since before he'd taken over his father's mercenary company and grown into that role. And my, had he *grown*.

"Princess Alessandra," he said sotto voce, his Roccalano accent melodious, "I have come here for anything you wish of me."

She should have laughed, but no part of her could muster anything like it. Not at him. Not at those bold words.

His gaze stroked over her once and again. "I know it is a masquerade, but why a lion? And a grotesque *male* lion, at that?"

She smiled, reaching for borrowed words. "Telling you would reveal the answer in the most unexciting way."

He quirked a brow. Let him sweat a little.

Lively notes plucked on the harp inside—a quessanade corrente.

"Then shall we begin the revelation with a dance?" He offered her his hand.

She took it and replaced his mask upon his head. One night. He could be one night's entertainment, and he needn't be more.

He tucked her arm around his and led her back into the grandeur of Sala di Forza.

Across the room, Bianca danced with Luciano, two matching masked cats, but Papà's willowy page, Alvaro, approached them. He bowed and spoke to Bianca, who smiled, nodded, then promptly bid Luciano goodbye before gliding to the hallway.

Only one thing could drag Bianca away from her forbidden fruit.

And now Alvaro, his young face lined grimly, made his way to her. He bowed. "Your Highness, Princess Alessandra, His Majesty requires your presence."

She spared Tarquin a disappointed shrug. Their *revelation* would have to wait.

"It must be the Immortali again," Tarquin said darkly. "A corruption that must be eradicated from the kingdom."

A corruption? He had to mean the monsters *among* the Immortali? The harpies, the basilisks, the wyverns—not the peaceful Immortali people?

She frowned, but such fire smoldered in Tarquin's eyes that it burned the question from her lips.

"Your Highness," Alvaro prompted.

With perfect form, Tarquin inclined his head to her, and she acknowledged him before turning to leave. It couldn't be the Immortali. Papà had summoned her, and what Tarquin didn't know was that Papà would never desire her presence for input regarding an *important* matter—such as conflicts with the Immortali. No, when it came to what really mattered, Papà preferred she be like a paladin under a Vow of Silence.

As she followed Alvaro, she shivered. Papà wanting to see Bianca was nothing new, but he could barely stand to look at his other daughter. His Beast Princess. Everyone knew that.

Especially me.

In the dimly lit hall, Bianca offered her a thin smile. A pitying smile.

Papà had only one use for his Beast Princess.

Aless shook her head and swallowed. *Not again.*

He would send her away again for another courtship. So soon.

But to whom?

ALESS GLARED UP AT PAPÀ, seated up on his throne beneath the high vaulted ceiling. He'd left the masquerade right after she'd arrived—because he'd been *so* pleased, no doubt—but he looked the epitome of regal, dressed in expensive violet silk brocade and wearing the jeweled crown on his coal-black hair streaked with ash. Royal Guards in purple cloaks lined the room, standing in perfect formation, immovable, intimidating.

He'd called her here, and Bianca, to show them exactly where they stood—far, far below—and who *he* was. King.

But for once, he'd actually detailed the kingdom's dire need to her and Bianca: piracy had depleted the navy, and while the coast needed defending, the heartland was rife with Immortal beasts attacking the paesani and unrest between humans and the Immortali.

"That scoundrel Sincuore and his pirate rats have all but devastated our navy. Our resources must be diverted to replenishing it, meaning we need protection *and* peace in the heartland." Papà stroked his close-cropped beard. "The Belmonte brothers have both come here expecting marriages in exchange for their services, but I have only one daughter to give to the Belmonte family, and she is going to Luciano."

Bianca smiled at her. So she was getting her Signore Cat. The orchard of her daydreams was coming true, and it had never been so wonderful to have been so wrong.

But why had Papà called them both here?

"We are making peace with Nightbloom." He leaned back in his throne.

The dark-elves? Papà was going to stop the hatred after all—

He'd said he had only *one* daughter to give to the Belmonte family. That meant…

By marriage.

To the dark-elves.

Her blood ran cold.

He's offering me up to Nightbloom?

Holy Mother's mercy, he wanted her to marry one of *them*? They had claws and fangs, lived in underground caves where not a single rose would grow, and they ate lizards and lichen. Her skin crawled. They had creepy yellow irises, ghostly white hair, and blue skin like a snake's.

She cast her gaze aside, at the massive tapestry of Forza slaying the hydra. That mythical monster was about as attractive to her as a dark-elf male. She didn't hate them, but she definitely didn't want to marry one of them, kiss one of them, sh-share a marriage bed—

She fought back a gag. Those clawed hands on her body, fanged teeth in a mouth kissing hers—

A shudder rattled her bones. Peace was a worthy end, but Papà couldn't expect her to—to *wed* one of *them.*

She didn't want to. She would never.

"Bianca, you will be wedded to Prince Veron of Nightbloom," Papà declared, and her gaze snapped back to him. "And Alessandra, you will be married to Luciano."

Unbelievable.

Bianca's smile faded like a pappose dandelion in the wind. Her olive skin paled, and the sheen of her agate eyes dulled.

No, it was all wrong. Everything.

"Papà." Aless shook her head and rubbed her sweaty palms into her tulle gown. "How can you do this? Surely you know Bianca fancies Luciano?" She wrapped an arm around Bianca's trembling shoulders.

He breathed deeply. "This is what's best for you."

"*I* know what's best for me." She glared at him.

"*Bianca* can be trusted to do her duty. *You* cannot. Luciano will know this by now"—her reputation, of course, preceded her, too—"but Prince Veron is not a Sileni. He won't understand your... *spirit,* and this kingdom needs a peace with Nightbloom to succeed. We're fighting wyverns, harpies, basilisks, and all manner of beasts—we can't afford to fight the dark-elves, too. Their numbers could help us quell the Immortali beasts in the heartland, help relieve the burden on our military. There will be a wedding ceremony here, then another in Nightbloom, and the peace will be sealed."

She stomped her foot. "I refuse to marry Luciano. You must release Bianca from this... this nightmare of a betrothal." She took off her lion mask and threw it onto the marble tile.

Papà dropped his forehead into his hand. "Alessandra, this wedding will happen with or without you. You can either appear in person or be married in absentia, but you *will* be married, and Luciano *will* take you to Roccalano, with or without your assent. You will do this, or you will be useless to this kingdom."

Useless. He'd called her that before, a long time ago, although she was certain he hadn't known she'd been listening. When she'd been eight years old, Mamma had been lamenting the latest physician's torture devices.

Must we put her through so much suffering? This treatment must be agony, Mamma had said. And yes, that back brace had been extreme, too rigid, too tight, painful to tears.

We must, Papà had answered sternly. *Unless her spine is fixed, she'll be useless in this world.*

In the hallway outside the solar, she had covered her mouth, hidden her tears, smothered her sobs. Even at eight years old, she had resolved to learn everything she could about running a kingdom, even if she had to do it alone. And to never be *useless*, no matter what Papà thought of her.

And here she was. Boxed into the only purpose he had for her.

Or so he *thought.*

Bianca sobbed into her shoulder, and Aless rubbed her back gently.

"And Bianca?" she asked. "She clearly doesn't want to marry that dark-elf male. Will you see her dragged away to their... their *cave?*"

"If that is what is required." He regarded Bianca, her downturned mouth, and his gaze softened. "But Bianca has always understood the burden of royalty. I have faith she will not disappoint."

What a man of honor, this prince! He'd drag Bianca kicking and screaming to his hole in the ground? "Such a *moral* and *kind* man you've chosen for her."

"He is," Papà answered, unperturbed. "He's mending the rift between our people. He's a paragon among his kind."

"Maybe *you* should marry him, then."

"He and his people have been mercilessly attacked by humans for months, and he's followed orders not to engage, not to fight back at all. He has an iron will and a disposition toward diplomacy."

Humans had been attacking him and his people for *months*, and he'd been under orders not to fight back? "So before he's even met Bianca, he'll already *hate* her because she's human."

Brilliant. Even better.

Bianca swept her forearm across her eyes and rested a hand on her arm. "Aless... It's all right. I'll... I'll do what Papà says." She sniffled. "And haven't you been saying how much you've wanted to do something important for our kingdom? Luciano is... a powerful man, and I'm... I'm sure you'll be a good influence. This is your chance."

Bianca was in love with Luciano, and Papà had just announced her betrothal to a dark-elf! How could Bianca stand there and say this was all right? Bianca had been waiting for a marriage since her sixteenth year; she was twenty-three now, had finally fallen in love with a man, and was to be married off to some... dark-elf?

Papà was right; Bianca would do her duty. But in doing so, she'd utterly destroy her life. How could she just accept this?

If it were me, I'd fight tooth and nail. I'd find a way to make him release me, even if no one helped me. I'd do it on my own.

If it were her...

If.

Bianca offered her a sad smile and a nod as she turned toward Papà, but Aless grabbed her arm.

Her heart thudding in her ears, she met Bianca's gaze. She wasn't going to marry her sister's love. She wasn't going to let Bianca live a bleak life. She could make it right. She—

Bianca drew in a sharp breath and shook her head. It didn't matter. She didn't need Bianca's permission.

"Papà," Aless said, sweeping up her tulle skirts as her heels clicked up to the first step of the dais. "Offer me instead. I'll wed Prince Veron."

Behind her, Bianca gasped. "Aless, you can't! You don't know what you're doing! A dark-elf—"

"No. I do know what I'm doing." She watched Papà's face for any sign he agreed, but it betrayed nothing. "Please, let Bianca marry Luciano, and I promise I will marry Prince Veron."

Papà rested his chin on his fist. "Alessandra, you know I love you. But if we are being honest, you are willful, short tempered, sharp mouthed, and presumptuous. You are everything a man *does not* want in a wife. You try to hire street urchins for your household, donate your coin to peasant rebellions, find every opportunity to show the nobiltà you *disagree*—"

It was on the tip of her tongue to object, but he did say *sharp mouthed*.

She sighed. Yes, she'd done all those things. He had no reason to expect anything like silent obedience from her.

Silent...

Maybe there *was* a way to persuade him, an old tradition among the most devout of Terrans—something the priests and paladins of the Order of Terra still did, designed to create circumstances for introspection and self-reflection. "I won't say a word to him. I will swear the Vow of Silence until the wedding."

A vow not to speak to the groom. Many parents in Silen demanded this of their daughters for arranged marriages among the nobiltà—both a show of piety and a way to ensure loose lips didn't beget unfortunate slips.

A grin tugged at the corners of Papà's mouth. What amused him more? Her keeping her peace now, being married off to one of the Immortali, or promising to keep her mouth shut?

Maybe all of it. "This is an easy choice. Make Bianca happy," she said, squeezing Bianca's hand, "and get rid of me. All in one sweep."

Papà sighed with heavy shoulders, no doubt weighed down by two decades of her disappointing him. "I'm not trying to 'get rid' of you."

She shrugged. He could couch it in whatever words he chose. He'd decided he'd had enough of her, and that he'd needed to sacrifice Bianca. Each of them knew this truth, hard as it was, no matter what else he said.

But his silence stretched, and Bianca's hand went limp in hers.

"With this marriage"—Papà stood—"you will be making peace between two nations. There is no greater thing anyone can do for our kingdom, Alessandra."

He'd agreed to it!

She wanted to grin, but... she'd just won a wedding to one of the dark-elves. Maybe there was something more she could add to the bargain. "And the library? I want to teach in Bellanzole like Mamma did."

He looked away. "I gave your mother too much freedom, and that is what killed her," he said softly. "If she'd only *stayed* in the palazzo instead of venturing among the rabble, she would still be alive."

And that was it? Because Mamma had been killed, no one could ever do anything again?

After years of research, she'd worked tirelessly on the proposal, but he and Lorenzo hadn't replied. He could at least give it serious consideration. "I handed you plans for the library, and lists of all the masters to build it, and suggestions to finance—"

"That was what your mother wanted, and look what happened to her!" Papà shouted.

She shuddered. Mamma had died, but she'd devoted her *life* to sharing knowledge with others, teaching everyone willing how to read. She'd always been known as the wild heart no man could tame, but Papà had loved what she had loved and had done the impossible—or at least he'd *pretended* to support her. Mamma had wanted to build a public library, more than anything, and after her death, everyone had forgotten that. Just as they had forgotten her.

But I haven't. "Papà, please—"

"Libraries mean paesani who can read, write, and think, who can write pamphlets and treatises, and protest instead of working. Find new ways to destroy us." He heaved a sigh. "This is a volatile time. The kingdom cannot take such a risk."

"Papà, that's—"

"The truth. And Alessandra, do you have any notion of what it costs to build a library and keep it maintained?"

"Yes. It was all there in the—"

"Not monetary cost. You laid out a tax plan to see it done. But the non-monetary costs of taxing our signori, especially *now*, when many of them are stretched thin or deep in debt to finance defenses against the Immortali? There's another *harpy* nest just outside of Stroppiata! We have bigger concerns right now. By enacting your plan, I'd be sowing the seeds of rebellion myself.

"Our survival has not come without sacrifice. Your sister, Giuliana, she married Emaurria's Prince Robert to become queen, to help protect our kingdom and forge favorable trade terms when her time came. And she was killed. We lost not only our precious Giuliana, but the boons she would have granted our kingdom. And you failed to captivate the new king."

Captivate? The king was in love with another woman; there had been little else to do but leave gracefully. "He was already—"

Papà held up a hand. "Whatever the reasons, you failed. This is a responsibility you must accept and now account for. The terms are set, and fulfilling your duty now will mean no more paesani lives lost to battles with the dark-elves, no more money spent on it by signori for defenses against them, and it will mean a military ally against the other Immortali, knowledge of this new world, and valuable trade."

There was no use trying to convince him. He'd already made up his mind; she and Bianca were no more than pawns.

Her library, a place where she could help anyone who wanted to learn and grow, nobiltà or paesani, human or Immortali—it had only ever been a dream, just like the courtyard of overgrown roses and its spellbinding perfume.

But she—she would do what was required to make peace between her people and the dark-elves. It didn't necessarily have to be *marriage*.

I'm not useless. But I won't let you define my purpose.

She'd agree to this arrangement, but as soon as Bianca and Luciano were married, she'd find a way to persuade this dark-elf prince to release her, to let their *friendship* show the peace between their nations. Marriages had solidified peace for millennia, but these were modern times. Surely consensual, honest friendship could demonstrate a partnership without resorting to a marriage neither party desired?

In fact, the entire kingdom could stand to see the point: it was time for a change.

She crossed her arms and lowered her gaze. "Fine."

"Good." He descended the steps and placed a hand on Bianca's shoulder. "Your wedding will be three days after Alessandra's. Congratulations, *luce dei miei occhi*." He cupped her face in one hand. "You will make a beautiful bride."

Bianca smiled as he dabbed at her tear-streaked cheeks. Her large, agate eyes were soft. "Thank you, Papà."

He grinned back at her, then raised Aless's chin with an abrupt finger. "Alessandra. Try not to destroy the peace. I know it is difficult. But try."

She scrunched her face, and his eyes gleaming, he walked away, his guards trailing him.

Her life could be over, and he *jested*? Holy Mother's mercy.

She'd agreed to wed the dark-elf prince, and to say nothing to him until their marriage vows, and so she would. She would complete the wedding in Bellanzole and say no words until after that.

No *words*. She smiled. But there were other ways to get a point across.

CHAPTER 2

*A*s the tree he perched in swayed in the raging storm, Veron held his bow at full draw, tracking the hind through the wind-battered foliage. He'd been here for hours and was not going home empty handed. Not today.

His people had been starving for several months, scraping by on small game and what sustenance they could find in the Deep before the crops could stabilize in a couple months.

He couldn't afford to miss, but if he couldn't get a good shot, he wasn't about to let the animal flee and suffer until she died. A waste of a life.

There would be a good shot. Deep, Darkness, and Holy Ulsinael, there would have to be.

As the hind picked her way through groaning trees and fluttering shrubs, she paused every so often, swished her tail, swiveled her ears irritably. *Not yet.* So agitated, she'd jump at the snap of the bowstring. *Not yet.*

His arms ached as he held the excruciating full draw weight, twisting his position to keep her in his sights, and she emerged past the enormous trunk of an old oak, halting in the howling wind, and as his tree swayed, he timed the shot—

The distant, roaring call of his fellow *volodari*. Short, sharp—a warning.

He loosed.

She balked.

More calls from his team answered, their longer, acknowledging roars closer—Vlasta's, Dhuro's, Rút's, Gavri's—

His arrow lay in the undergrowth battered by the storm. The hind was gone. He'd shot too late. Just a second too late.

And for that, his people would continue to starve.

The acknowledging growls repeated, and he roared back, listening to the calls return all the way to Vlasta's distant one.

He stashed his bow, dug his claws into the bark, and rappelled down the trunk. His boots slopped into the mud—they still didn't fit right, and now they'd slosh the length of the way home.

Other than the storm, all was quiet, with not a single person in sight, much less an enemy. But still, he drew his *vjernost* blade. Made from the magic-nullifying metal *arcanir*, it could also kill most Immortals, on the chance a basilisk or a wyvern had attacked.

But it wasn't basilisks or wyverns that had been the most pressing threat recently. No, it was the *human* Brotherhood that had been hunting him and his people for months. Entire parties of volodari from other dark-elf queen-doms had disappeared while hunting or foraging. A few from his home, Nozva Rozkveta, had evaded them with only injuries, but if nothing changed, it would soon come to deaths on one side or the other.

The echoing roars led south, and staying low in the concealment of the shrubs, he made his way through the stormy forest. A crack ahead, high in the canopy, and a long scratch—Gavri.

Like a living and breathing shadow, she splashed into the mud in her black leather *kuvari* armor, her long braid sopping wet, and she shook out her hands, throwing scraps of bark off her claws. Her deep-amber eyes fixed on him, and she cocked her head south.

He nodded. Given her call, Vlasta must have sighted an enemy. If she was in trouble, they had to get to her.

They retraced their steps toward the tunnel Gate they'd emerged from—Baraza Gate, where Vlasta had taken the first hunting stand. They passed the second stand—where his brother Dhuro should have been—but it was already empty.

By Deep and Darkness—

Voices rang out, human voices calling out in Sileni—near Baraza. Gavri tugged his sleeve southeast, toward another Gate.

Wordlessly, he followed her lead, and as the shouts neared, he and Gavri quickened their pace to a run, leaping over deadfall. If they didn't make it to a Gate before the humans caught up to them, there would be no re-entering Nozva Rozkveta at all. They'd be stranded.... and likely killed.

Gavri's heel hit a pile of soaked leaves and slipped into the mud—he caught her arm and yanked her up. The humans' shouts increased in urgency. They were gaining.

Ahead, a dark-elf bore another over his shoulder—Dhuro carrying Vlasta, a broken arrow shaft protruding from her side, buried in her gut.

No. *Not* one of his people. *No.*

She was still breathing, whimpering. Alive. A shot like that wouldn't have killed her—at least not quickly. It was meant to end her slowly, *painfully.*

Goose-feather fletching. A human's arrow. The Brotherhood.

He and Gavri caught up to Dhuro, who heaved a breath of relief as they continued to the nearest Gate—Heraza.

"The others?" he hissed to Dhuro as they ran.

"Already home," Dhuro bit out from beneath low, drawn eyebrows, and bared his fangs. Dhuro hadn't agreed with Mati's orders not to engage the Brotherhood, but he'd obeyed as a proper subject to the queen first and as a son second. A rage, however, had simmered in Dhuro from the first attack—a narrowing of his eyes, a clenching of his jaw—and now, while holding a bleeding huntress in his arms, that rage bubbled far too close to the surface.

It was a rage he knew as keenly as Dhuro did.

Just get home. Holy Ulsinael, just let us get home. Because if we meet the Brotherhood, orders or no orders, I can't promise not to kill them. Just let us get home...

The Bloom thicket tangled ahead before Heraza Gate. He took Vlasta from Dhuro carefully, whispering to her as she groaned, as her face creased. The Bloom parted, letting them through to the locked stone door, then wove back together behind them.

Smearing wet hair from her face, Gavri frantically tapped the Nozva Rozkvetan knock on the stone door.

Nothing.

As she did it again, Dhuro stepped up next to her and joined her, both of their hands beating the rhythm.

No answer.

The human shouts closed in.

In his hold, Vlasta whimpered as her blood ran down his leathers, mingling with the mud while Gavri and Dhuro continued.

"We're almost home, *volodara,*" he murmured to her, and she nodded weakly, raindrops rolling down her face, or tears.

The door creaked open.

They scrambled inside, and the two kuvari guarding Heraza barred the stone door after them. Danika and Kinga.

"*Where were you?*" Dhuro shouted as he cornered them.

Both Danika and Kinga immediately bowed. "Your Highness."

"Dhuro," Veron said, prodding him with an elbow, still holding Vlasta. "We need to get her to the mystics. Come on." He headed down the tunnel toward Central Cavern with Gavri as she shook her head.

"Where were you?" Dhuro repeated, snarling the words. "The Brotherhood nearly *caught* us."

Danika stayed bowed. "Captain Riza recalled the kuvari to reinforce Baraza, but when Your Highness and Prince Veron didn't show up there, the Stone Singers sang it shut and we were ordered back to posts."

"Dhuro," Veron called over his shoulder, and Gavri took a deep breath next to him as they headed to the mystics' lifespring with Vlasta.

Dhuro could hardly shout at Mati about his frustrations over the Brotherhood; as their queen, her word was law. But taking it out on two kuvari, especially when Riza had given the order—that wasn't helping either. Dhuro could take it up with Riza later, who'd lay him out on the stone—with Mati's implicit approval—if he so much as barked at her.

As they made their way, the lavender glow of the bioluminescent mushrooms high above on the stalactites lit the enormity of Central Cavern, tempered by the soft white light of the glowworms and the sprawl of flora that had always bloomed here, even without the sky realm's sun.

Below, the blackstone dwellings spread among the interwoven pathways and shining streams high above the Darkness's embrace. Stone Singers crowded smaller walkways, singing stalagmites into dwellings in their deepest and darkest bass tones, beseeching stone to meld together and form to their collective will.

Nozva Rozkveta was serene, even as the Brotherhood thirsted for dark-elf blood just outside the Gates.

He and Gavri had almost reached the mystics' lifespring with Vlasta when Rút caught up to them, breathing hard, her face lined as her wide eyes fixed on Vlasta.

"No," she breathed, reaching out to touch Vlasta's hand, one of her claws broken. "When I heard the call, I-I tried to lead them away, so she could escape. But even then, I could feel her weakening, and—" She covered her mouth, running alongside them.

"Your claws," Gavri said with a gasp, and Rút curled her fingers.

Damaged claws meant weakness, and the weak were seen as a disgrace to their families. But to mention that now? Really? He scowled at her.

Gavri cleared her throat. "She'll be all right," she offered to Rút. "And Queen Zara won't let this go. You'll see."

Rút and Vlasta had made the Offering to each other and had been lifebonded for eight years; they shared anima. If one weakened, the other would strengthen her, and if one died, so would the other...

"We're almost there." He plunged through the dark entryway and into the mystics' lifespring, where Xira—the oldest dark-elf among them at nearly four thousand years—ran to meet them, her dark-purple robe trailing, and apprentices huddling around her.

NO MAN CAN TAME 21

"Take her to the waters, Highness." Her long, white hair shimmering beneath the lavender glow, Xira led them to a brightly lit pool, and he climbed the shallow stairs to gently lay Vlasta inside while Xira checked her and removed the arrow, eliciting a pained cry from Vlasta. "She's still breathing. Good." Xira cocked her head to Rút. "You, too. In with her. You'll both need the strength of the lifespring to fortify you."

Because if Rút's anima wouldn't be enough, Vlasta would die. And if Vlasta died, so would Rút. Such was the danger of the lifebond.

Chewing her lip, Rút nodded several times as she held Vlasta close in the lifespring waters, stroking her short, wet hair and whispering words of comfort. Here, seated on a large Vein of anima, Nozva Rozkveta's life was stronger than any other queendom's, and the lifesprings were concentrated with anima, places they'd used for recovering since before recorded history.

This would work. It had to.

He braced on the warm, smooth stone while Gavri patted his back. Vlasta and Rút would survive—both of them. A lifebond was an act of absolute love, rare in its complete and utter devotion because with one death, it could claim two lives instead of one. Queens and their most valued kuvari among the Quorum rarely lifebonded, as their loss would leave a queendom weakened.

It was, in a way, fortunate that his own father hadn't been lifebonded to Mati when he'd betrayed his family and gone to his death. A kind, placating grin as he'd secretly left them for the last time, given his life away.

Veron lowered his gaze to the stone. He'd never weaken Nozva Rozkveta that way. Ever. At twenty-seven, he hadn't even contemplated making the Offering to anyone, let alone the death sentence that was lifebonding.

Heavy footsteps echoed into the lifespring's cave.

"Will she be all right?" Dhuro asked. "I swear by Deep and Darkness, if—"

"She will recover, Your Highness," Xira said, meeting Dhuro face to face as he dripped rainwater and mud onto the gleaming blackstone. "But"—she turned back to him and Gavri—"they'll need to have something substantial to eat to recover their strength."

Something more than the individual rations of small game, cave fish, and shellfish, and wild bits of edible flora.

The humans had the entire bounty of the sky realm while *his* people had to scrape and scrounge for the smallest of meals to share—and they couldn't even hunt in peace.

"They can have my rations," he said.

"Your Highness," Rút breathed, sitting up, but he held up a hand.

"It's done, Rút." He'd just redouble his efforts hunting in the coming days.

"Mine, too," Dhuro said, thumping a fist to his chest. "The Brotherhood will pay for this. They have to."

Xira rested a gentle hand on Veron's shoulder. "I'm certain Her Majesty will be relieved to know Vlasta and Rút are safe."

In other words, *Get this raging prince out of my lifespring.*

He nodded. "Come, brother. Mati will want to know what happened."

"I'll report to Captain Riza," Gavri said, her eyes soft as she parted ways. After having loved his brother Zoran for eight years before he'd left, she knew *exactly* how Dhuro could get.

Heaving a sigh, Dhuro left the lifespring with him, and they headed toward the black crystal spires of the palace in the heart of Central Cavern.

"The volodari of other queendoms are dropping like flies to the Brotherhood." Dhuro forced a breath out of his nose and shook his head. "It won't be long before they focus more of their attention on us."

"Mati said she's handling it. It is not our place to question." A queen spoke and her subjects obeyed. Every last one. And Mati had said she would resolve the crisis, and to trust her.

"I know. I know." Dhuro ran a palm over his damp mass of shoulder-length hair. "I just wish she'd trust us enough to tell us what's going on."

They passed the kuvari at the entrance and headed down the main corridor, their boots sloshing.

I just wish. That was Dhuro. Always Dhuro. Pushing for more, for privilege, instead of obedience. He'd spent some time among the humans before the Sundering, and had returned with *I just wish* and *Why can't she just* and *I think that* instead of the stoneclad obedience he'd been born to.

More like Ata. Their father had thought he'd known better than Mati, and had betrayed her and given up his life for that rebellion.

He shook his head. Unthinkable. Unacceptable.

Dhuro strode toward the glaive-bearing kuvari guarding the doors to Mati's quarters, but they barred his path.

"Prince Veron *only*," one of them—Lira—said to Dhuro. "By Her Majesty's order."

Crossing his arms, Dhuro stood his ground, staring down at her a moment before grunting and stepping aside. "Figures. Share the knowledge, will you, brother?"

He eyed Dhuro. Of the many things that could happen, sharing anything a queen said in private wasn't a likely one. "How about a sparring session later instead?"

A corner of Dhuro's mouth turned up. "That'll do." With that, he took off.

Lira and her partner opened the doors and stood aside. "Your Highness."

Riza emerged first, fixing him with sharp eyes that soon gentled. Resting a palm on his shoulder, she breathed deeply and gave him an encouraging nod. If Riza of all people was trying to encourage him, then whatever Mati had to say to him wasn't going to be good.

"Gavri is looking for you," he said, breaking the silence.

She gave his shoulder a final pat before donning her usual stone-faced expression anew and passing him by.

As soon as he stepped inside, Lira and her partner closed the doors behind him.

Within, bioluminescent *roza* vines twined around pillars, climbing and sprawling across the ceiling, casting a soft white glow inside. Roza had always been plentiful in Nozva Rozkveta, and some had already begun to bloom.

Mati strolled back and forth across the roza-vine rug, bobbing baby Dita in her arms while his sister Vadiha slept on Mati's bed. When everyone had awoken after the Rift, Vadiha had still been with child, thank the Darkness, and she had given birth to Dita not five weeks ago. After Mati, Vadiha was Nozva Rozkveta's strongest warrior, and she'd scarcely had the energy to stay awake to feed Dita, let alone train. The food shortage had been especially hard on her, and even with increased rations, and the volodari—her husband and their sisters among them—hunting at all hours, she still wasn't getting enough nourishment.

His hands clasped behind his back, he waited while Mati lulled Dita into a shallow sleep, then glanced at him and toward a bench, where he sat down.

"Anything today?" she asked quietly, her voice low and even as she kept her gaze on Dita's little slumbering face.

He shook his head. Coming home empty handed was always difficult, but all the more when he looked at Vadiha and Dita, who relied so desperately on the volodari teams' success.

"You didn't engage the Brotherhood."

"On your orders, we did not," he answered. "Vlasta took an arrow to the gut, but Xira said she and Rút would recover."

Mati nodded softly, brushing a wisp of fine baby hair off Dita's brow. "The conflict with the humans—and this famine—will soon be ended."

She had said it would. And it *would*. Of that he had no doubt.

"I have been in negotiations with the king of Silen via correspondence," she said, rocking Dita gently.

Negotiations? So that had been why she'd ordered them not to engage the Brotherhood. All this time, she'd been negotiating. And the other dark-elf queens must have known as well—there had been no word of dark-elves fighting back.

All for this.

If there was a bloodless way to end the conflict with the Brotherhood, then it was worth pursuing.

"Until our crops are stabilized, the Sileni are going to deliver food, both to Queen Nendra and to us, which we will distribute among the allied queen-doms by way of the tunnels. This will begin as soon as the agreement is finalized in Bellanzole. And we have devised a diplomatic means of handling the Brotherhood."

Good. As keen as he was to end the persecution, as good as it would feel to spill the Brotherhood's blood... blood would only beget blood. This was the whole of dark-elf history. Spilling blood only to spill more. It had to end somewhere, and if they could make peace with the humans—and survive—then he would do everything in his power to make that happen.

And if they couldn't make peace with the humans... then he'd make certain *his* people would be the ones to survive. The humans were numerous, but his people had trained for battle from the moment each of them could walk on toddling legs—if it came to war, the humans would fall.

"In return, they want our assistance in keeping the Immortal beasts at bay."

That was simple enough. All the volodari were trained in combat against all beasts—Immortal or otherwise. "Is that all?"

She met his gaze and held it. "I've agreed to give them one more thing."

If it meant food for Vadiha and an end to the conflict with the Brotherhood, then that was worth almost anything.

"You."

CHAPTER 3

*V*eron swept out an arm and caught the stone before it could hit his
fey horse, Noc.

Good catch, wasn't it? he thought to Noc, who only snorted. *Come on. It
was good.*

Good, Noc thought back. *Yes.*

"Get out of our kingdom!" an elderly human woman wailed at him from
the small crowd, spittle flying from her mouth.

"Divine take you!" another cried. "And all the rest of the monsters!"

Monsters.

"Silence!" Riza spat from beside him. "You human filth dare attack Prince
Veron? Danika, Gavri"—she cocked her hooded head toward two of the
kuvari guarding him—"cut out their tongues. Now."

Danika and Gavri dismounted, boots thudding on the summer grass, and
drew their vjernost blades. The small crowd shrank away.

"Captain," Veron warned, muffled through his face mask. Danika and
Gavri halted, though they stood ready to attack.

Riza turned to him and inclined her head the merest fraction. "Your
Highness."

One of the human children ogled them wide eyed. Veron chuffed softly
and tossed the stone to him. The Brotherhood merited all of Riza's anger, but
these humans? There were peasants—agitated, but not murderous. Even now,
they shrank away, some looking to him with big eyes.

He pulled aside his leathers at his chest to expose the royal black sun tattoo over his heart to the humans. "No harm was done, Captain. They did not know me."

Her eyes narrowed. "Highness—"

"No harm was done." Firmer this time.

Mati's orders to them all had been clear: *Keep your peace, but do not allow any harm to come to the prince. Harm none unless he is harmed.* And even Riza wouldn't dare to disobey his mother, queen of Nozva Rozkveta.

"Highness." Riza nodded coolly. "Mount up!" she bellowed to Danika and Gavri, then turned on the humans, scowling. "Remember this day, humans. You keep your tongues at the mercy of Prince Veron u Zara u Avrora u Roza, Valaz u Nozva Rozkveta, Zpevan Kamena, Volodar T'my. But disrespect His Highness again, and I won't be able to hear his mercy over the sound of your blood spraying."

Subtle, Riza. Very subtle.

The crowd scattered, some humans sprinting away, others running with occasional glances over their shoulders. The human child stood frozen, grass-green eyes wide as moons, clutching the stone to his chest. The boy could only be a few years older than Dita. He'd always liked children, and human ones were no different, even if they didn't recognize royalty.

"Hyah!" Riza urged her horse forward.

He sighed inwardly, smiling behind his face mask at the human child as the cavalcade moved once more, continuing down the cypress-lined road to Bellanzole and the soaring Palazzo dell'Ermacora.

Humans probably hadn't seen one of his kind in millennia; their ignorance was understandable, if inconvenient. Dark-elf royals did not adorn themselves in the golden crowns and circlets to which the human peasantry was accustomed to seeing on theirs; dark-elves knew their royalty by their bearing, their demeanor, their faces, and as a last resort, by their black sun hearts, tattooed by royal *czerni* ink at birth.

Nozva Rozkveta's scribes had been working tirelessly to bridge the gap between Old Sileni and the modern tongue, and although he, his party, and many of the other dark-elves spoke the modern tongue now, that didn't cure the ignorance.

Mati had sent him—and the entire host of dark-elves—on a mission of peace, leaving camps of dark-elf troops in his wake to help keep the peace for themselves and the humans against the beasts, all part of the bargain struck between Nozva Rozkveta and the kingdom of Silen.

He rode up to Gavri, who eyed him peripherally and hissed.

"I don't question my queen's wishes," she said, shaking her head vehemently and sending her braid swinging from side to side, "but you, one of our most valued princes, are doomed to make the Offering to one of *them*? It's a sad fate."

"Do *not* question Queen Zara," Riza hissed at her, and Gavri inhaled sharply but nodded.

He'd known both of them his entire life; they were as much his friends as they were kuvari. They could always be trusted to tell him the truth.

He gazed out ahead, at the humans' world of lush green, so different than home. Human mages shaped this sky realm with magic like the Stone Singers shaped the Deep with song, spelling buildings and roads like the Stone Singers sang stalagmites, stalactites, columns, and pillars. He still had memories of sketching sky-realm flora and fauna with Ata as a boy, when he'd been training to become one of the volodari. But after Ata's death, he hadn't sketched much of anything.

The humans and their sky realm were different, but difference was not inherently bad. He'd brought a myriad roza blooms grown from the Vein of Nozva Rozkveta's power, a gesture he hoped would demonstrate the bridge that could exist between their realms.

"It's what I was born to do, Gavri," he replied, and her head perked up. "I've been raised knowing my life is not my own, but to be bargained away by my mother, to strengthen Nozva Rozkveta and our people."

Riza nodded. "And you perform your duty with honor and valor."

Gavri bit her lip. "But they… they are just so *ugly*."

He laughed under his breath while Riza hissed at her again.

Oh yes, humans were ugly. Their women weren't taut and toned like dark-elf women; human women were soft like the very livestock they raised for slaughter. They had no fangs or claws, which even dark-elf *children* had. And their skin—thin, delicate, so easily broken.

By Deep and Darkness, what he'd give to be in a hunting stand now, in a raging storm, instead of on his way to make the Offering to one of *them*. It was enough to make him shift in his new boots, which fit even worse than the old ones. Ata had been a skilled hand with leatherworking, and no pair of boots had fit right since his… death.

Too picky, Noc chimed in.

You don't wear boots. If you did, you'd be picky, too. Trust me.

The human, Noc clarified. *You both live, both walk on two legs. Man. Woman.*

As if that were the whole of it.

But he didn't have to *desire* the human. He just had to make the Offering to her. With this agreement, Vadiha, Dita, and all his people would no longer starve—that alone gave it merit. And there was far more to Offering than mere desire. There was trust, partnership, encouragement, companionship. And any human woman who'd agreed to make the Offering to him had to be open minded; that alone gave her potential as a partner. In any case, there was nothing more important than doing Mati's will, for the peace of Nozva Rozkveta.

He drew in a deep breath. He was only twenty-seven—unless he counted the 2,372 or so years all the Immortals had been petrified since the Sundering... which he didn't—and by the end of the week, he'd be making the Offering. To a human.

By her agreement to it, she welcomed him into her life. That much was certain. And it meant this peace between them would succeed; and once it did, the peace between their people would, too.

As long as she was honest, he could trust her, and as long as they could trust each other, they had a chance.

"We will do what's right. This Offering will go smoothly," he assured them both. Besides, Riza had helped him choose an impeccable Offering gift for the princess. "And once it does, all of this unrest will dissipate."

Riza scoffed, then shrugged. "I pray to the Deep for it, Your Highness." Hesitating, she lowered her gaze for a moment, her brow furrowed. "But... Gavri's objections aren't entirely without merit. If there's one thing I've learned about the humans, it is that they can never be trusted, especially when it comes to doing what's right."

～

BENEATH THE LATE-AFTERNOON SUN, Aless held still in the courtyard, her spine straight, her shoulders back, her chin high. The summer breeze riffled the rosy-pink silk brocade of her gown and the carefully styled curls cascading down her back. The jeweled circlet was warm against her forehead, but Papà had left specific instructions with her ladies-in-waiting and maids. They had decorated her like a horse for dressage.

"You really won't speak to him, my lady?" Gabriella, her friend and lady-in-waiting, whispered, tucking a lock of black hair behind her ear.

She'd already promised Papà she wouldn't. And it really didn't matter, did it? Her choice didn't matter, so why would her words? This prince would probably arrive on his mother's orders just to look her in the mouth and check her gait. A chattel didn't need to say a word to be *useful*.

He'd simply place her in his cart, take her to the dark-elf cave, and shelve her like some trophy to present whenever the need arose to prove peace with the humans. They'd say, *We have no quarrel with the humans! Look, one of our princes has a human wife.*

And because the dark-elf women ruled Nightbloom, she would never have a say in anything, never make herself useful there, just remain a pawn as she had here, except in an alien culture that spoke an alien tongue, and surrounded by strangers who had no reason to be friendly with one of her kind.

Mamma's library would never be built, she'd never help anyone learn to read, nor Immortali and humans learn about one another in a place of peace and knowledge.

Surely this dark-elf prince didn't wish for this fate any more than she did, and yet they both had to do this dance at the behest of their parents and rulers.

Which didn't make it any better.

A bee lazily flew by. *Sting me. Please, please, please sting me. Anything to avoid this meeting.*

Hooves clopped beyond the iron gates, and a cavalcade of riders trotted into the courtyard, ringed by the Sileni Royal Guard. The strangers were cloaked and hooded in black, shadows but for their unsettling yellow irises and ghostly white hair. The occasional glimpse of slate-blue skin peeked over the face masks covering their mouths and noses.

The dark-elves.

Each of them had to be at least six feet tall. As they dismounted, they revealed leather-armor-clad muscle on lean, athletic frames.

The tallest of them—on a massive, mesmerizing destrier, its ebony coat gleaming in the sun—was bulkier, with broad shoulders, thick biceps and thighs, a muscular chest. A male.

He hitched the blade at his side and dismounted nimbly, rubbed his hand and wrist, and took in the courtyard with narrowed, searching eyes. They settled on her. Intense. Eerie.

Different from the rest. The only male among them. It had to be *him*.

But neither he, nor any of his party, were dressed in a manner befitting royalty. They all wore mere black leathers and plain cloth, like any common soldier. Maybe a sign of how special he considered this meeting.

He would have already met with Papà at Bellanzole's walls for escort into the city. Papà had met this Immortali male and, despite his obvious insult, had allowed him entry to this courtyard.

But would anything have deterred Papà from this bargain? He'd sold Bianca's hand in marriage, sight unseen, to this Immortali male. He could be ugly, disfigured, beastly, utterly disgusting—even beyond being a dark-elf—and would that have changed Papà's decision at all?

Of course not. He'd bought his peace already. Cheaply. And hadn't even tried anything else.

She stiffened as the male approached her, escorted by one of his own and a Sileni Royal Guard. Maybe her Vow of Silence was for the best, as her words would have been just as frozen as the rest of her.

He inclined his head. "It is my honor to meet you, Princess Alessandra," he said, his low voice like velvet over honed steel, muffled through the black cloth face mask. "I am Veron."

That voice—deep and flowing like the mirror-black rivers of the Lone.

Holding her breath, she looked at his hand—gloved—his fingers pointed, but he didn't offer to take hers.

"It is your custom to take hands," he said, matter of fact. He removed the gloves and passed them to his companion, a sharp-eyed female standing at attention, a soldier by the look of her. He extended his hand, slate blue, with long fingers capped in points.

Claws.

The moment had almost passed when she shakily offered hers in return.

Callused skin closed around her fingers as he raised her hand gently, pulled down his face mask, and lightly pressed his lips to her knuckles.

The barest touch, and a shiver tingled down her spine before she could stop it. He could kill her. With little more than a sweep of his hand.

As he straightened, she covered her reaction with a smile, which he returned.

Fangs. Sharp, pointed fangs, like a lion's. She held her smile, kept it plastered on her face. Hopefully it would keep any other reaction from showing.

"It is the first time you have seen one of my kind in person." His eerie eyes stayed fixed on hers, unwavering, his callused hand still wrapped around hers.

Nothing moved in the courtyard. Holy Mother's mercy, even the breeze didn't dare blow.

She nodded. That smile was still plastered on her face—she returned her expression to some semblance of normalcy.

Like the rest of him, his face was hard, all brutal planes and angles, with even harder eyes. As a statue, he might have been terrifyingly beautiful, but living, breathing, he was simply terrifying. Like a nightmare from a children's fairytale.

At any moment, he could lunge at her, pin her to the ground, sink his fangs into her flesh and tear it open. Drive his clawed hands through her body. Rip her apart. He could do all that and seem completely natural.

"It is my hope that, in time, you will find us familiar despite our differences."

Familiar? Maybe. Any less terrifying? Likely not. But she nodded again.

"Would you care for a walk around the courtyard? I will answer all your questions to the best of my ability. Perhaps we might become better acquainted before the ceremony tomorrow."

She turned to Gabriella and pointed to her own mouth.

Gabriella's hazel eyes flickered between her and the prince. "Princess Alessandra wishes me to tell you that she has sworn the Vow of Silence and cannot speak to you before the wedding, Your Highness."

Aless faced him once more. Or rather, his scowl.

"A vow of silence?" His face tight, he clasped his hands behind his back, and his companion narrowed her smoldering yellow eyes. Like glowing embers. "Your people expect such things from their women?"

Did Papà neglect to mention that he wouldn't agree to the marriage until she'd offered the Vow?

She nodded.

His hiss punctuated the quiet, and his companion hissed, too. Their eyes turned hard, fierce, like those of lions ready to pounce. He'd hidden his hands —his claws—and who knew what they would do?

Shivering, she took a step back. But if he disliked the Vow of Silence, then he wasn't as bad as Papà. Maybe even reasonable.

He looked her over and relaxed his posture, revealed his hands from behind his back and let them fall to his sides.

Her gaze fixed on them, on their sharp claws, until he inclined his head.

"There are preparations before the ceremony tomorrow," he said, his voice wooden. "I take my leave, Your Highness. Good day to you."

She matched his gesture, and with that, the Royal Guard escorted him and his companion toward the palazzo.

Still as stone, she stood, watching until they disappeared inside and the doors closed.

"My lady?" Gabriella rested gentle fingers on her forearm.

Another shiver wove through her. Her heart pounded, so hard and so fast that surely Gabriella heard.

"Come, my lady. Let's get you inside." Gabriella took her arm and led her in the opposite direction, another entrance into the palazzo.

She walked alongside her lady-in-waiting, but the surroundings were a blur. Those eerie eyes. Sharp claws. Pointed fangs. Slate skin. Steely velvet voice. Ghostly hair. The way he hissed, the lithe way he moved—

Trembling, she shook her head, shook out her hands. There was no choice. Unless she married him tomorrow, Papà would not keep his end of the agreement either. She had to, or else Bianca would.

Finally, Gabriella helped her into a suede armchair next to a large, mysterious box, and within moments, Bianca sprang away from where she'd been looking out the window, with a swath of sapphire brocade skirts trailing as she ran and laid her head in Aless's lap.

"I'm so sorry!" Bianca cried, taking her hand.

Aless stroked her hair softly and dismissed Gabriella with a wave of her hand.

"You're really going through with it?" Bianca's voice broke.

She had to. Kind-hearted, daydreaming Bianca could never handle a marriage to a dark-elf, but she could, for her sister's sake.

"Come on, Aless," Bianca urged, nudging her. "Never mind the Vow. Speak to me. *Please.*"

She sighed. After Bianca's wedding, they'd be parted; Bianca would go to Roccalano, and she would go to Nightbloom. The idea of spending most of their remaining time in silence was... painful. "I... will go through with the *wedding.*"

Bianca raised her head, frowned, and sat back on her haunches. "What do you mean? Is there another way?"

There might be. She'd go through with the wedding in Bellanzole as promised, because it was required for Bianca's sake. For her sister, she would marry him. For three days, she would endure—whatever she would have to endure—and then she would witness Bianca's wedding to her beloved Luciano. Bianca and Luciano were both human, and once they consummated their human marriage, their bond would be unbreakable. But after that?

She would do more good for peace bridging the cultural divide and teaching than being kept as some trophy in a cave. Even if Veron didn't approve of the Vow of Silence, she could never be one of the dark-elf women, those who truly had power in Nightbloom. She'd just be... a token.

This dark-elf marriage wouldn't be complete until the second ceremony in Nightbloom. And after meeting the prince today... Yes, he was intimidating, but he'd also been well spoken, polite—considerate, even.

In fact, she had the perfect wedding gift for him: her new copy of *A Modern History of Silen.* She still had Mamma's copy, and the parallel gift would have meaning. It would show her willingness to share this new world with him and his people, and to welcome them as a part of it as he filled the remaining pages with the peace she hoped their people would forge together.

After their wedding here, Papà had said they were set to go on a Royal Progress throughout Silen to Nightbloom to show off their harmonious union and inspire peace among the paesani, the nobiltà, and the dark-elves. What if, along the way, she really *could* convince him they didn't need to be married to achieve a peace? Maybe she could suggest the library as a joint venture, earning goodwill for the dark-elves from the paesani.

With him on her side, they might convince Papà and the Queen of Night-bloom to reconsider. And she and Veron could still act as ambassadors of peace, as friends, demonstrating that relations between their people could be good.

And if he didn't agree... Well, she wasn't the Beast Princess for nothing. She'd find another way to persuade him. "After this wedding, there's still the second ceremony in Nightbloom before this agreement is sealed. I'm going to use the time in between to try to convince him we don't need to be married for there to be peace between our nations. I'm sure he doesn't want to marry a human any more than I want to marry a dark-elf. Maybe he'll listen."

Bianca sniffed, blinking away tears. She swabbed her face with the sleeve of her sapphire frock. "And if he doesn't?"

She shrugged. "I'll find a way."

Bianca looked away, her eyebrows drawn, and bit her lip. "Luciano told me that Tarquin is an influential member of the Brotherhood, hoping to find justice for Arabella. With their help, and the Belmonte Company, your freedom can be assured."

The Brotherhood? Tarquin was involved with that hateful group? What he had said about the Immortali... *A corruption that must be eradicated from the kingdom.*

No, he wasn't like her at all. He was one of *them*. The Brotherhood.

Shortly after the Rift, the Brotherhood had come together to "advance human interests." Somehow "advancing human interests" always seemed to involve violence against the Immortali. For every perceived injury to humans, the Brotherhood retaliated twofold. Thankfully the Immortali seemed less prone to such violence, as no such faction had emerged on their side—that she knew of. "But Luciano isn't a member?"

Bianca shook her head.

"Good. Anyone involved with the Brotherhood has sunk too deeply into hatred." As much as she didn't want to go through with this marriage, she didn't wish the prince, or the other dark-elves, any ill.

"But they'd liberate you in a heartbeat—"

"No." She took Bianca's hand. "I appreciate your care, but I'll think of something." She smiled. "Don't worry about me. Let your only concern be your wedding, your honeymoon, your happiness."

"How can I think about that?" Bianca's smooth brow creased.

"That's why I've done all this. So you must be happy. Promise me." With any luck, she and the dark-elf prince would achieve peace through alternate means, both be free of each other and this arrangement, and Bianca would get to stay with the man she loved.

Bianca's lovely agate eyes hardened, and she gave a determined nod. "I promise." Her gaze lowered. "But what about your library? Maybe Papà will still help?"

There had been no hope of that earlier either; she knew that now.

But she wouldn't give up. She'd never give up. Books had been Mamma's life and had changed her own, given her companionship and escape when the Sileni court and even Papà himself had been ruthless in their treatment of her, of a deformed child, a useless pawn. Books had power, the power to defeat hopelessness with escape, ignorance with enlightenment, fear with knowledge. And she wanted every person to have access to that power, to harness it, for peace, understanding, and better lives.

And they would have it, just as Mamma had wished before she'd died.

Maybe a Terran shrine would take her in, a High Priest or Silen's Paladin Grand Cordon himself—Sir Massimo de' Nunzio—could hear her out about wanting to build a library, to care for their paesani. The Order of Terra was known in Silen for its dedication to charity and peace; Nunzio would hear her out. He would. And the Order, so instrumental in forging peace, would no doubt be open to letting the dark-elves take part in the venture.

Veron seemed like a reasonable man. Maybe he'd support the idea to his mother.

"I'll find another way," she said to Bianca. "I have all the plans finished. It's only a matter of finding the right investor." And the Order would have the funds. Maybe she could send the library plans ahead to Nunzio and meet with him in Stroppiata during the Royal Progress to discuss it. But Papà would have her correspondence watched.

"Luciano and I could help." Bianca perked up. "We could write to wealthy potential investors, find someone who's interested."

Her mail would be watched... but Bianca's? Luciano's?

"I'd love your help. I'd like you to send something for me, if you could."

Bianca nodded. "Of course."

Later tonight, she'd have Gabriella deliver the plans to Bianca with instructions.

"Oh! Your gown arrived." Bianca darted toward the large, mysterious box and opened a flap. "It's bittersweet, Aless, but the gown is at least beautiful."

Papà had been planning to marry her off for years, and no doubt the gown had taken almost as long to make. "I won't be needing it."

Bianca's mouth fell open. "But... Then what will you wear?"

Oh, she'd given plenty of thought to that over the past few days. When Mamma had given her *A Modern History of Silen*, she'd written inside, *Be brave, my rose, and fill the remaining pages with your deeds.*

I will, Mamma.

Fortunately, her bellani d'oro were still good with some of her dressmakers. The ones who didn't fear Papà. "I will wear my thoughts, Bianca."

Papà had bargained them away like chattels—in this day and age. *Let the signori know exactly what I think about that.*

AFTER PULLING OFF HIS BOOTS—THESE new ones still didn't fit right—Veron paced the dim bedchamber barefoot. Silence. They'd *silenced* her. He rubbed his chin. "Why? Why would she be expected to swear such a vow?"

Gavri shrugged at her post in the doorway next to Riza. "Perhaps her voice is like claws on limestone. Or perhaps she's a twit, and her father doesn't want you to find out."

He snarled. "That is my soon-to-be *bride* you are insulting." His gaze locked with hers in the lengthy silence before she looked away.

He drew aside the heavy window drapes and peered into the courtyard. A storm. Dark clouds had shrouded the heavens, and the world below darkened with them; heavy drops pelted the lush green leaves, the grass, the stone walkways and benches. Umbrella pines swayed in the unrelenting wind. The sky realm changed with the hour.

It was hard to get a fix on Princess Alessandra's personality. What mattered to her? What did she enjoy doing? What did she think? Her wide eyes had answered none of those questions. Their meeting had only revealed her fear and the troubling notion of her silence.

"You suspect she is unwilling," Riza said quietly.

He did more than suspect.

"What?" Gavri snapped. "Prince Veron is an exemplary—"

"She's a human, Gavri," Riza shot back, earning a groan from Gavri. "They see things differently."

Princess Alessandra was unwilling. What else could possibly be so damaging that would require a vow of silence? "I came here believing that my bride had agreed to this."

Gavri grunted. "This human king substituted one daughter for the other. Perhaps there is some defect she would otherwise confess to you, if not for this vow."

King Macario had explained that, much to his embarrassment, Princess Bianca was in love with another man and marrying—making the Offering to —him, but that Princess Alessandra was equally beautiful, willing, and younger. Humans prized the youth of their brides—more childbearing years.

"No, the king swore Princess Alessandra was healthy, fertile, not with child, and willing." Before the meeting, it truly hadn't mattered to him which human bride he had to—as they called it—"marry," as long as she had agreed and was honest. There had been no reason for him to interfere with a love match.

Riza stood taller, raising her chin slightly. "With all due respect, Your Highness, even if she *is* unwilling, does it matter? Queen Zara gave you her orders."

Thunder rolled, then lightning flashed white into the room.

"Does it really matter *what* the human wants?" Gavri added.

He stiffened and glared at her. By Deep and Darkness, of course it mattered. He was bound to obey Mati's orders, but not without care.

And yet both Riza and Gavri seemed to be in agreement. He forced himself to relax.

"Duty must supersede honor, Your Highness." Riza clenched her *vjernost* blade's pommel. "Sometimes, to save thousands, one must be sacrificed."

Gavri nodded, her brows drawn.

The peace. How many dark-elves and humans had died to this conflict?

And how many more would?

Their parents had already sacrificed him and Alessandra for the sake of those lives. Could he do the same? The Brotherhood's attacks had to end. The famine had to end. If he wavered now, how could he return and look Vadiha —and Dita—in the eye?

His duty was to Nozva Rozkveta, its queen, and its people. All else came after. Riza and Gavri were right. Even if Princess Alessandra was unwilling, his hands were tied. As were hers.

But there would be *two* ceremonies. If he was right about everything, then there would be the entirety of the Royal Progress back to Nozva Rozkveta for him to elicit her assent. They *had* to marry, but whatever her fears were, he could allay them. If she could never see him as a lover, Princess Alessandra could live her life as she wished, to the best standard he could deliver, and he could live his. A practical arrangement.

He could never defy Mati's orders, so he would find a way to persuade Princess Alessandra on the way to Nozva Rozkveta.

He heaved a sigh. The hunting stand in a storm only seemed more and more appealing as the days went by. "I'm going to bed."

"Sweet dreams, Your Highness." The corner of Riza's mouth twitched—a grin, for her at least.

Gavri eyed her with an impish grin and puffed a breath, blowing a wisp of hair off her face.

They both well knew he'd barely get a wink in. At least with this on his conscience.

But he rounded the canopied bed, out of their line of sight, and undressed, then parted the bed curtains and settled in. The soft mattress yielded under his weight, and he stretched out, curling an arm behind his head. It had been a long time since he'd slept in a human bed. They were far more luxurious and intricate than the practical dark-elf beds, but he missed the pleasing give of moss filling and the coolness of plant-fiber bedding. No doubt Princess Alessandra would prefer something like this instead—he'd have to arrange one for her.

Everything in Nozva Rozkveta was prized for its practical value. He'd have to explain that to her. An Offering—a wedding—celebrated not just a union, but what each partner could offer the other. And he'd been raised his entire life to become a person of worth: a capable hunter, swordsman, archer, and rider; well educated; strong, honorable, and valorous. A prince Mati could trade confidently when the time came.

And the time had come.

Tomorrow, he would make his Offering to Princess Alessandra of Silen. He'd never been to a human wedding, but they wore armor, carried weapons, and rode horses everywhere else, so weddings were no exception, right?

CHAPTER 4

*a*less dismissed all her servants from the private chambers outside the nave of L'Abbazia Reale. She smoothed the wrinkles from her wedding gown, yards of Pryndonian white lace and intricate pearl beading. It was a gorgeous gown, one any happy bride would eagerly wear down the aisle.

Any *happy* bride.

She paced the gray rug, whipping the gown's train about her. No matter what happened after, today she would be officially *married*. Even if she could persuade Veron not to complete the second ceremony in Nightbloom, they would always be married by Sileni law.

But if they didn't live as husband and wife, that wouldn't matter, would it? And it wasn't as though she'd *need* to remarry for love. As long as the Paladin Grand Cordon could help her see the library built, as long as she could teach there, she didn't need a thing more. For the rest of her life, she'd be making a difference, just as Mamma had.

This would all work out. Terra willing, everything would go as planned.

Tradition had ruled over so many lives, including her own, for long enough, and other voices had chosen for her. Maybe standing up to that today, even a little, would make a difference.

Yes, she would marry Prince Veron and she wouldn't destroy the peace, but she would speak her mind on it, in the only way left to her. Papà may have given her no other meaningful choice, but she still had this.

A soft rap came to the door, then one more. She opened it. "Bianca."

Bianca gave her a wide-eyed look, her mouth falling open, then cleared her throat and hastily waved in two servants with a trunk.

"Were you seen?" After they entered, Aless glanced out into the hall, left and right, but no one else was about other than the Royal Guard. Good. No one to tell Papà.

"No." Bianca nodded to the servants, who set down the trunk and left. "Are you sure you want to do this?"

"Of course. We have the dress ready and everything." Aless pulled aside her hair and bared the lacing down her back. Bianca's quick fingers began undoing all of Gabriella's hard work.

"I didn't mean the wardrobe change." Bianca pulled the last of the laces, and Aless slid the gown off her shoulders, stepped out of it, and threw open the trunk.

Blood red.

Smiling, she took out the gown and handed it to Bianca, who helped her pull it over her head without disheveling her hair.

"I told you I'm doing this for you." Aless slipped her arms over the bust line, and Bianca began lacing the back and then rearranged the tulle netting carefully. The bodice fit like a glove, and the skirts flared out in dramatic fashion, with a ten-foot train worthy of a princess.

"But this statement of yours," Bianca said carefully, "won't this sabotage your marriage?"

Being thrown together like two horses in a pen would have already sabotaged this marriage. She sighed. "Yesterday, when Gabriella told him about the Vow of Silence, he seemed... enraged."

Bianca's hands paused in their work, and her footsteps retreated. "Enraged? As if he would get violent?"

"Not exactly." She held up her hair again. His reaction had seemed almost —almost protective of her. "At least not toward me."

Bianca settled the black raven-feather funereal cloak about her shoulders and arranged the twelve-foot train over the gown while Aless let her hair fall free, and clasped the front of the cloak.

"He had this expression of fury, and he hissed... It was as if the very notion of me being sworn to silence offended him." A good sign. She turned to Bianca, who settled the white-lace wedding gown into the trunk.

"The dark-elves' royal line is matriarchal, right?" Bianca closed the trunk. "It is their women who hold power. Maybe he agrees that others shouldn't dictate the course of your life—nor silence your voice when it comes to your future."

Yes, dark-elf women didn't "meddle" in politics—they ruled. "Maybe."

"Well, the entire nobiltà will hear your voice today."

Be brave, Mamma had said. She would. And ensure her voice was heard.

The familiar, overbearing notes of the pipe organ invaded through the walls and door; she stepped into her black jeweled slippers, checked her diamond earrings, then gathered her pearly-white wedding cloak.

"It's time." Bianca hitched up her periwinkle silk-taffeta gown, then opened the door.

Veron would be waiting beyond the corridor and outside the entrance to the nave of L'Abbazia Reale.

The pipe organ summoned her there, and she went as bid. The way from the side chamber to the entrance was quiet, only her heeled steps and Bianca's fighting the silence as they passed the purple-clad Royal Guard at their posts.

No one waited outside the massive entry doors.

Was he coming? No doubt he had as much *eagerness* for this marriage as she did.

But she took up her position, and Bianca fanned out her train behind her.

A rhythmic clopping on marble echoed from the opposite corridor.

Her head swiveled to face the sound.

The massive ebony destrier filled the corridor, muscles rippling, copious mane and tail flowing as it trotted closer.

Inside the abbazia.

Royal Guards circled the enormous horse, hissing clipped words to one another, while a stoic Veron sat astride the beast, all six and a half feet of him clad in fine black-leather armor.

A bow hung across his chest.

A saddle quiver full of arrows.

A long sword and a scroll strapped at his side.

A round shield on his black-cloaked back.

Knives sheathed in his knee-high riding boots, in a baldric, and on his gauntleted wrists.

Her mouth fell open. He looked armed for war.

"Your Highness"—a Royal Guard stammered— "horses... are not allowed inside L'Abbazia Reale."

His gaze locked on hers, Veron dismounted nimbly and handed the reins to the guard, then gave the beast a pat before approaching her.

No part of her would move. Not her gaping mouth, not her feet, not her hands. To stare was her only ability.

He wore no face mask nor hood today, his blue skin bared for all to see. His ghostly white hair was adorned with braids that met, intertwined, and hit to mid-back. With the Rift so recent, most of the people here today would have never seen a dark-elf, much less an unmasked one.

Was he... was he making a statement, too? Going through with this, just as she was, but not silently either?

With a confident, regal gait, he strode to her, then lowered to a knee, bowed his head, and looked up into her eyes.

"Alessandra Ermacora, princess of Silen, I, Veron of Nozva Rozkveta, offer you power"—he rested a hand on his sword pommel—"survival, skill, defense, wisdom, and partnership"—then on his bow, his knives, his shield, the scroll strapped to his belt, and he took her hand—"to harness for your ends or ours, as we walk our lives together from this day forward for as long as the Deep allows."

His yellow irises stayed locked with hers, making her heart pound, and a breath escaped her open mouth as she remembered to breathe.

"This is my people's tradition," he said quietly and stood. "We call being wed 'making the Offering.' We give ourselves to one another, offering all we can do and all that we are."

Did... did he expect her to respond in kind?

She swallowed, her gaze wandering the many offerings he'd brought. "Veron, prince of Nightbloom, I..."

She blinked. What was she offering him? Could she truly offer anything, when her heart hadn't even been in this? When, more than anything, she wanted to follow in Mamma's footsteps? "I..."

A huff came from behind him; his companion from the day before. The sharp-eyed female guard. She wore fine leathers today, too, and no face mask nor hood to cover her midnight-blue skin and short, spiky white hair.

The footmen opened the doors, and the pipe organ's volume was almost deafening as it blasted forth.

Veron offered her his arm, and remembering to close her mouth, she took it. They entered L'Abbazia Reale's nave on the long, crimson runner leading to the front, compressed into its lengthy, narrow path. A susurrus mounted as they entered, wide-eyed guests eyeing Veron as if he were Nox himself, come to claim their souls and drag them to the Lone.

Light poured in from the unattainably high windows, crowning the massive statue of Terra that held court at the front, overwhelming and breathtaking. Imposing. Demanding quiet obedience.

Not today. From *either* of them. With her dressed in a blood-red gown and a funereal cloak and Veron in black leather armor and weapons, all of Silen would believe that while they swore vows, neither of them did so without objection.

But Veron, by his words, had done this from a cultural perspective. Had Papà not mentioned human wedding customs? Assumed that the dark-elves did the same?

Despite his sincerity, Silen would see a different symbolism in his attire today. Unintended, certainly, but the people wouldn't know that.

As they proceeded to the time of the pipe organ, she pulled the clasp on her wedding cloak and let it fall from her shoulders, revealing her raven-feathered statement.

Gasps rippled from the nobiltà crammed into the pews. Veron's arm contracted slightly, just a soft creak from the leather armoring his bicep. But no more. They did not stop.

No reaction from the royal box up in the right balcony, removed from the abbazia proper and separate. No shouted orders. No Royal Guard closing in.

Success.

The music continued, and so did they.

Padre Graziano, the former High Priest of Monas Bellan, awaited at the front, towering on a dais just below the massive statue of Terra looking down at them all. His wide eyes speared her blood-red gown, the shock wrinkling his lined face even more than old age already had.

Good. This was a royal wedding. News would spread far and wide, the nobiltà and the paesani would talk, object, and this would have to stop. At least for the *next* generation.

When she reached the front, she knelt, as did Veron. While Padre Graziano shook his face to alertness, Veron's gaze meandered toward her.

"Willing?" he whispered, so low she wondered if he'd spoken at all.

It was a simple question, but the answer wasn't so simple. To spare her sister a walk through fire, she would walk it herself. But was that willing? Veron seemed kind, reasonable, and if she had to marry a strange dark-elf, there could have been far worse men. But if she *had* to, was that "willing"?

Padre Graziano cleared his throat. "Please join hands."

Veron held out his palm, and she placed her hand on his.

Padre Graziano wound a golden ribbon about their hands. "As your hands are joined, so your lives, as you support one another, protect one another, strengthen one another."

He then offered the vow to Veron and bid him repeat.

Veron turned to her, his pale eyebrows drawn as he assessed her. "I, Veron of Nightbloom," he said hesitantly, "promise you, Alessandra of Silen, that from this day forward, I will be your husband, your ally, and your friend." His uncertain look lingered as Padre Graziano offered her vows.

"I, Alessandra of Silen, promise you, Veron of Nightbloom, that from this day forward, I will be your wife, your ally, and your friend."

She met his gaze. No, she hadn't desired this marriage, but she did partici-pate in this ceremony willingly. For Bianca's sake, and for the sake of future Ermacora women. Hopefully Veron would be open minded about finding another way to forge the peace between their peoples instead of the second ceremony at Nightbloom. She nodded to him.

The tension in his bearing visibly lessened, and his expression softened.

"Veron of Nightbloom and Alessandra of Silen are now bound to one another. What Holy Terra has bound, let no man sever," Padre Graziano announced as he removed the ribbon.

Veron helped her up, and holding hands, they faced the nobiltà, who clapped softly and stared—at Veron, at her gown, some craning their necks to look into the royal box.

She followed those looks to Papà's seat. The white of his teeth didn't show, nor even a smile that she could discern. Just a hard, expressionless mask.

He wasn't happy. Good. Then he was beginning to understand how she felt, how Bianca would have felt, probably how Veron felt. Even if Papà hadn't wanted to see her as more than a chattel, he'd have to now.

Down the aisle, they passed Luciano and Tarquin Belmonte, and Tarquin —rigid as that statue of Terra herself—stared a hole through her, his carnelian gaze fixed upon her with such intensity that it felt like he looked *through* her. What was he seeing?

She shivered as they walked past him.

Veron walked her out of the abbazia and out to the cobblestone drive, where a grand white coach-and-six awaited.

He stepped in front of her, barring her path with his arm.

The sky darkened, enormous shadows cast upon the cobblestone streets, and a wave of gasps and withered cries rolled through the crowd outside.

Veron reached for the shield at his back as two winged creatures soared overhead, bright sunlight glittering on iridescent violet and tan scales.

"Don't move," he ordered, and Holy Mother's mercy, she couldn't even if she tried. Every part of him was rigid, focused, honed to the point of a blade as he kept his eyes fixed on the creatures.

"Th-those a-are..."

"Lesser dragons," he answered quietly. "En route toward the sea. Uninterested in us, by the looks of it," he whispered, "so perhaps on some Dragon Lord's order."

Lesser dragons... Dragon Lord...

Her entire body trembled, like a mouse under a broom, and there was no stopping it.

The shadows passed, and Veron's bearing relaxed, his arms slowly falling to his sides as he stepped away from her.

"M-maybe it's g-good you wore armor," she offered, trying to swallow past the lump in her throat.

"I'd love to think so." His mouth curved as the footmen opened the doors to the carriage. "But if they'd wanted us dead, armor or no armor, we would be."

A nervous laugh escaped her as Veron helped her into the carriage and then sat across from her. Bianca and the sharp-eyed dark-elf guard entered after them, eyeing each other silently.

Dragons. They'd just seen *dragons.* Beings she'd only ever known from books.

But the door closed, the driver called, and just like that, they were on their way to the feast and their wedding night.

AS THE COACH jostled over cobblestone, Aless stole a glance at Veron sitting across from her. His keen eyes scanned their surroundings beyond the window, and with his many weapons, he was as intimidating as any guard. More so, even.

While the entire crowd had gasped and trembled, he'd stood firm in the face of dragons. The next time those dragons appeared, they might not ignore the city, and if her people were fortunate, the dark-elves would help them.

Veron didn't need weapons to be intimidating... That imposing physique made him strong, as strong as any guard—no, stronger. He rested a clawed hand over a knife sheathed at his wrist. Those claws—and those fangs, although she dared not look at them—meant he never needed a weapon.

He'd come to the wedding ceremony armed like a warrior. He'd said it was a dark-elf tradition, but... had he known how it would appear to humans? The dark-elves seemed to know vastly more about human society than humans knew about theirs.

But then, she hadn't considered how her own statement would appear to the dark-elves. At all.

She'd made her point to Papà, and to everyone, about choice. But... she clenched the tulle fabric of her blood-red gown in fists. It hadn't been her intention to oppose Veron, but that was how it might've looked.

No doubt the whole of the nobiltà already gossiped about her unwilling bridegroom armored from head to toe. Rumors would be spreading far and wide about how even a dark-elf only reluctantly wed the Beast Princess.

Considering the rumors about her, too, it would serve her right. She bit her lip.

The sharp-eyed guard next to Veron was glaring at her, and mustering the confidence to say anything to him beneath that glare was a losing battle. Maybe her statement had gone over even worse with the dark-elves than she'd thought. Later on, once she and Veron were alone, she would have to apologize to him.

Maybe he'd be relieved once she told him they didn't have to wed. She'd lied in her promise, but maybe he'd overlook the lie in favor of freedom for them both.

A squeeze of her hand—Bianca intertwined their fingers and didn't let go until the coach pulled up to the palazzo's main gate. A crowd had already assembled, clapping and cheering to the bright fanfare of brass horns and rain of colorful confetti. Footmen opened the carriage door, and the sharp-eyed guard exited first, then Bianca, and then Veron, who held out his hand to her.

Those exotic eyes met hers, yellow like a lion's, and she shivered, but he didn't waver. Her heart pounding, she extended a hand to his, and he helped her exit, a sharp claw just barely grazing her wrist with a scratch. She suppressed a wince and schooled her face, willing no reaction to show.

The crowd pushed in, even against the line of Royal Guards, cheering and shouting and staring wide eyed, but Veron's form was regal, and he held her hand as they ascended the crimson carpet into the palazzo.

Inside, shimmery bright-red roses gladdened the cavernous foyer, the loveliness of the blooms too beautiful for reality; she had seen their like only in dreams, and even then, they hadn't reached out with color so vivid it could touch her, a scent so embracing it wrapped her in familiarity and comfort. Where had they come from?

Next to her, Veron seemed unaffected, looking only ahead toward the distant figures of Bianca and his sharp-eyed guard, but his hold on her hand wasn't cold—it was warm, gentle.

Even if neither of them had wanted this, he'd given her no reason to deserve the rumors she'd caused.

"I wanted you to know," she whispered, and he eyed her peripherally, "that I was trying to make a point to my father about choice. With the red dress and raven feathers. I wasn't trying to offend you, although it occurred to me that that's exactly what might've happened. I'm sorry."

"What point was that?" he answered, just as quiet, looking ahead.

She exhaled lengthily. "That we should have a say in our own futures."

He stiffened. "You didn't have a say." That steely velvet voice was low, icy.

A dreaded conclusion?

Willing? he'd asked during the ceremony.

He had cared. Maybe more than she'd assumed.

Her face turned abruptly toward his, then she looked away again, wiping a damp palm on her gown. "I... I did. Although not in the way you might expect. My father betrothed me to my sister's love. I offered to trade places with her."

Those vivid yellow eyes widened, infinitesimally, for just a moment.

She could imagine him summoned to a throne room much like Papà's, his towering figure lowered, kneeling before a dais where his mother held court, surrounded by dour, silent subjects bearing witness from the shadows. His head kept bowed as she decreed her orders that he marry a woman so different from him, so undesirable. Orders he refused to disobey, no matter his feelings on the matter.

"Did your mother ask you whether you wanted this?" she thought aloud.

"No." The answer was matter of fact, as if there could only ever be one answer. "The queen does not *ask*. She expects. And we rise to those expectations. Such is the life of a prince, and of any dark-elf. Ready to sacrifice for the good of the Deep, for the good of all dark-elves."

"Sacrifice," she whispered, repeating the word, and her voice trembled a little.

He would never have been eager for this marriage, and that suited her plans—her plans to convince him that they didn't need to complete the second ceremony in Nightbloom—but there was something so very sad about him having no say in his happiness, something that squeezed at her heart. He was bound up, wrapped in duty like a curse, one he couldn't break.

In this, they were the same.

His hand tightened around hers, just a little. "Forgive me," he said deeply, quietly. He leaned in, toward her, his nearness making her quiver as those vivid eyes met hers and softened. "I spoke without thought."

So near, so close, that terrifying, if alien, beauty was hard to ignore. The slate blue of his skin was the color of distant mountains, blue-gray behind a veil of mist. The color of ancient rock formed in the earth before she had been born, before humans had.

Before she could reply, the doors to the great hall opened, and both Bianca and the sharp-eyed guard stood aside as she and Veron entered. The guests had not yet arrived, but the hall certainly wasn't empty. Servants bustled back and forth, carrying all manner of platters, bottles, glassware, and viands. The musicians were already setting up in the corner, and massive floral arrangements adorned the outskirts of the hall, matching ostentatious centerpieces on tables.

Veron took in everything with a narrow gaze, as if such preparations were foreign to him. Maybe they were. What, exactly, was a dark-elf wedding feast like? She turned to him, but Bianca's soft grip closed around her arm.

"Come," Bianca said with a subtle smile. "Let's get ready for the feast."

The sharp-eyed guard murmured something to Veron, inclining her head.

"See you at dinner, Alessandra," Veron said.

She offered him a smile. With the briefest of looks exchanged, she and Veron parted ways. It wouldn't be long before the guests would start arriving, and she would have to return to the great hall long before Papà could arrive—at least if she wanted to avoid his further ire.

And then... the consummation.

CHAPTER 5

*I*n her dressing chamber, Aless stroked a finger over the swath of crimson chiffon spread out on her chaise longue, ethereal and romantic. A nightgown for later tonight. Bianca had selected it, along with a dazzling array of rubies and gold.

"You make it look like I'm trying to seduce him," Aless muttered.

Behind her, Bianca pinned the train of the red gown. "Maybe that'll make things easier tonight?"

Tonight.

She shivered.

After the feast, she and Veron—along with a host of lords and councilors—would depart to her bedchamber. For the *consummation*. The bed curtains would be drawn, and in the presence of these officials, she and her new dark-elf husband would have to—to—

"Are you scared?" Bianca asked softly.

Scared. Oh yes, she was *scared*.

That is, she had been with many a lover, many a *human* lover. All men she'd chosen herself, strong and handsome, well bred, alluring. With those men, she had been bold, fierce, confident. She had pursued them and seduced them and played with them as she'd pleased. There hadn't been a single worry in her mind, no more than the pulse-pounding mystery of whether each would prove capable and worth her time.

But Veron...

Veron. She ran a fingertip over the scratch on her wrist.

She hadn't even become accustomed to just *looking* at him without holding her breath or shaking. Even his voice rippled shivers down her spine. They'd only just met, were so different from each other—*too* different. Maybe two dark-elves weren't concerned with claws and fangs, as their skin seemed firmer, too.

But one of his claws had only *grazed* her wrist as they'd exited the carriage, and it had left a scratch. Stroking a finger over it, she knitted her eyebrows together. So commonplace a thing, helping a lady out of a carriage, and he had left a mark.

Even if they… overcame their differences, how careful could he be? How much control could he have? Being raised a dark-elf, how much could he know about the limits of a human? In the throes of pleasure, even humans forgot themselves, gave themselves over in mind and body to sensation, and what would happen to her if he did?

The scratch was shallow, almost beneath notice, but if he forgot himself for just a moment—

"Aless?" Bianca stood before her, face pale and creased with worry, and took her hand. "I'm touched that you want to do this for me. I am… and thank you for stepping in. But you don't need to do this. The marriage hasn't been consummated yet, and we could still—"

"I'm—I'm just nervous." Holding a smile in place, she embraced Bianca. There was no way she could even consider sabotaging her sister's happiness. Not when Bianca actually loved Luciano. "Don't worry about me. I'll be fine."

Bianca struggled in her hold. "You're just saying that, and —"

"No," she said, tightening her embrace. Her heart fluttered in her chest, but she had to make Bianca believe everything would be all right. "The witnesses will be there tonight, remember? And after that, I have my plan, right?" Her voice broke, and along with it, her composure. No matter how hard she tried to hold everything in, a couple of lone tears escaped.

She closed her eyes and took three deep breaths.

Never had she wanted to fade away into that sprawling courtyard of overgrown roses more than she did now, surrounded by them and their tangible air of magic, in that place of dreams where she knew she belonged. A thicket of tangling vines, wild and winding, reigning there and yet making a place for her, clearing a corridor through the green and letting her inside.

"I don't want you to do it," Bianca whispered. "I know I said—"

"It's done." Pulling her shoulders back, she moved away and smiled at Bianca, who sniffled softly. "It'll be fine. You'll see. You'll get to marry Luciano, and Veron and I will come to an agreement. Neither of us wants this, so I think he will be motivated to work with me. And then…"

She would still technically be married in the human realm, and Papà would never let her return if she reneged. She would find herself as the

Order's ward, at best, and she'd ply every ear among them until the public library was built. A place where she could make a difference.

Her eyes overbright, Bianca gave a small nod. And there it was—an understanding. She had resolved to do this, and Bianca wouldn't fight her.

Good. At least one of them could be happy.

In the mirror, her cloak of raven feathers was gone, and the dramatic wedding gown was pinned up, perfect for dancing. Did the dark-elves dance? Did Veron dance?

"Did you see Papà's face in the abbazia?" Bianca asked with a half-laugh. "I've never seen his eyes so wide. And Lorenzo, his eyebrows shot up so high, but his eyes were half-moons, as if he'd been smiling." Bianca tried to hide a smile herself, but she failed.

Lorenzo was Papà's firstborn son and heir, but for years he had bucked that yoke, struggling in vain for a simple life that he could never have. Oh, if only they could have traded places—she would have gladly accepted the responsibilities he wished to shirk, and he could have as simple a life as he wanted being traded away like a pawn.

"Maybe he'll put in a good word for you with Papà," Bianca added. "Help you get back into Papà's good graces."

"I think he has no more good graces to spare for me." She narrowed her eyes at her own reflection before turning toward the door. There was nothing left for her here. Ahead of her, she had only negotiations with Veron, and a life outside the palazzo, whatever she could make of it. "Come. I think my wedding feast is about to begin."

Bianca joined her as she exited the dressing chamber and headed for the great hall. Tonight, she and Veron would find a way to survive the consummation, but before that, there was an entire hall filled with courtiers, some of whom belonged to the Brotherhood, who were here for a human–dark-elf wedding feast. No doubt Papà had already prepared the Royal Guard, and she would have to prepare herself. As much as she wanted out of this marriage, nothing about her exit strategy could ruin the peace. She wouldn't allow it.

The herald announced her and Bianca, and as they entered, all of the guests seated at the many tables stood, including Veron at the head table, wearing a finely tailored black jacket with silver rose buttons—one of Lorenzo's—form-fitting trousers, and his own boots. Lorenzo must have spoken to him—helped him.

A kindness. *Fine of you, brother.*

Veron's gaze rested on her, even but purposeful as he clasped his hands behind his back, cutting a strong figure. He didn't look at her with the intensity of the men who had desired her—it didn't take a lot of thinking to realize *why*—but even a serene look like this was unsettling in how perfectly controlled it was. As a child, he must've feared to even have a hair out of place and risk his mother's disapproval. Even now, the shadow of that risk had followed him here.

She and Bianca moved to the viand-laden head table, where a sweetly smiling Luciano pulled out a chair for Bianca as Veron did for her. Those two. They probably already had adorable pet names for each other like *kitten* and *tomcat*.

As she inclined her head to Veron and took a seat, a chill slithered down her spine, and her eyes meandered toward the direction of Papà's gaze.

He was *smiling*.

He raised a goblet to her, glanced past her toward Bianca and Luciano, then leaned back.

Her heart pounding, she stared at the spot he'd leaned into before, at *nothing* now. The low hum of the hall faded in favor of the pulsing thud in her ears, loudening and loudening.

Holy Mother's mercy, he'd—he'd *played* her.

The way he had called both her *and* Bianca into the throne room to announce the marriage arrangements—

He had—he had *manipulated her* into this.

She had never been able to ignore an injustice, not when she could do something to fix it. And Bianca...

Bianca had pined after Luciano for *months*, and Papà was a lot of things, but not ignorant, especially where his *favorite child* was concerned. He could've predicted her exact reaction and planned for it, expecting her to submit for Bianca's sake.

And she *had* submitted.

But not completely, not while she still had moves to make that wouldn't jeopardize Bianca's happiness. Papà wouldn't get away with this. He *couldn't*.

Her hands had gone numb, and there they were in her lap, fisted so tightly her blood wouldn't flow.

Her gaze tracked Papà again. If he'd thought he could play her, *deceive* her, and think her so *stupid*, then he should've thought of the consequences.

These consequences.

Of being outed publicly for his treatment of her, as he'd be right now.

She scraped the chair back, but a hand closed around one of her fists. A slate-blue, clawed hand.

Glaring at Veron, she was about to demand he release her, when she met that even gaze. That even, tightly controlled gaze, which panned toward the dance floor, and back to her.

He raised his white eyebrows once, as if to encourage an answer.

An answer to what? Had he spoken?

She swallowed, and music filtered in, a prelude—an *extended* prelude. Her clenched hands slowly relaxed.

"Alessandra?" that steely velvet voice asked, but there was a softness there, a gentleness.

"Hmm?"

"The dance." He blinked. "Do you—"

"Oh, yes," she said quickly. The first dance.

Surrounding the dance floor, myriad faces followed her every movement, the collective whole of the nobiltà watching her carefully, watching the *peace* carefully. She'd seemed to oppose Veron during their wedding, and he her, and she still needed to show the semblance of acceptance, if only a little longer. And then hope to transition to genuine, clear friendship.

If she didn't play her part well, the symbolic peace between her and Veron would fail, and along with it... the peace between their peoples.

I won't let that happen.

No matter what Papà had done.

Forcing a smile, she rose with Veron, allowing him to guide her as the musicians yet again extended the prelude, wary of those sharp claws. It would begin with a quessanade.

The quessanade... A human dance. She drew in a sharp breath, and Veron's eyes swept toward her briefly.

"Do you know how to dance the quessanade?" she whispered.

His pale eyebrows drew together, his lips pressed into a thin line. "I know the human dances well—"

Thank the Mother.

"—but I haven't danced in over two thousand years," he answered, not a muscle moving out of turn.

Two thousand—

"Do you trust me?" he whispered, as they approached the center and assumed the position.

Two-thousand-year-old human dances? "You haven't—"

"Do you trust me, Alessandra?" His voice was soft but firm as his hand clasped around her waist, just the barest scrape of claws against tulle.

Either she would have to lead, or... or she would have to trust him.

No, this could go completely—

But as the first movement of the dance suite began, he drew her in close, just barely apart from his chest, and led her in a gliding step, in a whirling rotation that flowed from one turn to another and another. A dazzling array of colors spun around them, but those shimmering golden eyes stayed locked with hers in unbreakable focus, intense, determined, and he kept perfect form, his hold strong but guiding.

This had to be how her ancestors had danced thousands of years ago, face to face, eye to eye, close enough to breathe in that blend of fresh earth and the scent of the purest water, like a forest stream so clear that the smooth stones at the bottom were perfectly visible, their surfaces honed by hundreds of years or more to the sleekness of glass. Her fingers brushed their hardness—but no, it was his shoulder through black brocade. *Holy Mother's mercy, so awkward—*

Those eyebrows pulled inward, and those pale eyelashes shuttered, his unbreakable focus glimmering a moment as he glanced down at her mouth and back to her eyes.

"Good dance," she breathed.

A corner of his mouth turned up. "They called it the rotante. The young adored it, and the old—"

"Were appalled by it?" she offered, as he led her into a turn.

An amused inclination of his chin as other couples took to the floor, following his lead to attempt this *rotante* themselves. Excited voices and giggles surrounded them.

The closeness of this dance would have been scandalous, no doubt, but by today's standards, it was quite tame compared to the sarabande or the volta. "Unafraid of scandal, Your Highness?"

"Veron," he corrected, searching her eyes. "I... chose the most modern dance I knew."

A two-thousand-year-old dance? She held back a laugh, but when a smile played on his pinched lips, she allowed a grin. If she had succeeded in leading, this would have been a disaster. "How do your people dance at weddings?"

A glimmer. "We don't. We do dance for a few occasions, but for most, we have games."

Games?

Lorenzo cut in, beaming like a debutante newly revealed, and Veron joined their hands with a smile, the point of one of his fangs peeking. *Fangs.*

"Spare your worry, sister," Lorenzo remarked with a broad grin. "I won't keep you long tonight."

Tonight. She breathed deeply as Lorenzo led her, and Veron took Bianca's hand. The dancing had gone well, but tonight—*that* was an entirely different matter.

"This will be the newest trend at court," Lorenzo drawled. "What is it called?"

"The rotante," she answered.

Tonight, she and Veron would be in a bedchamber, surrounded by officials. She'd be wearing that... *nightdress*—no, that flimsy swath of chiffon that could barely be called a *garment*—and would he ask her to trust him then, too?

"Once you look past all the"—Lorenzo frowned—"*differences*, you might like him, Aless."

Like had nothing to do with it. She *liked* plenty of people well enough, or at least didn't hate them, but that didn't mean she chose to *share a bed* with them.

And what about Veron? No doubt he wasn't interested in her either. Did anyone care what he chose? What either of them chose? Or did tradition stand in for choice when Papà or the queen of Nightbloom deemed it so?

Bianca laughed nearby as Veron turned her, his movement controlled, smooth. How much time had he spent learning this dance, and all the others? He had put in more thought and effort as one person learning human culture than the whole of this room had probably spent on his.

And that dark jacket, those tailored trousers—they fit him well, if a bit tight. His build was a bit larger than Lorenzo's, who had a big frame but spent less time training it. He worked enough to hone his skills with the dueling sword and throwing knives, but he'd always preferred beds over training yards.

"Thank you," she said to him, "for the wardrobe change."

With a crooked smile, Lorenzo tilted his head. "Careful, Aless. A kind word or two like that, and rumor may spread that you're going soft."

"Holy Mother forfend," she deadpanned as Lorenzo looked away.

Tarquin cut in before she could object, dark-brown eyes gleaming in that too-handsome face. After what he'd said the night of the masquerade and his rumored membership in the Brotherhood, she wasn't interested in learning any more of him and his hatred. She followed his lead, but her entire body had gone rigid.

"Even a lion can be afraid sometimes," he said carefully as he glided into step.

"That is when they are most dangerous." She didn't meet his eyes. Wouldn't. He didn't merit the respect.

"A sole lion may be defeated with ease," he replied, not missing a beat, "but only if it forgets its true strength. The pride."

The Brotherhood? "This lion has no need of a pride," she bit out.

"You don't need to wear a mask, princess," Tarquin whispered. "Not with me. The pride is watching. Only say the word, anytime, anywhere, that you protest, and our strength will… relieve your solitude."

She shivered. Anytime? Anywhere? How could—

He was already gone, and Luciano was in his place, smiling. "Well, Your Highness, what do you make of this dance?" He led her into it.

This dance was becoming dangerous. And now, more than ever, with the *pride's* eyes on her, she'd have to watch her step.

CHAPTER 6

*V*eron paced the length of the bathing chamber, disrobed down to his shirt and braies. Pausing, he yanked off his boots—well made, but too tight—and resumed his circuit.

They waited in there—the human councilors and lords, their holy men— to know this marriage would be completed.

That was a problem.

To the humans, a marriage was incomplete without what they called the *consummation*. The first act of lovemaking between a bride and her groom. For royals, especially, as oftentimes such massive consequences relied on marriages, it was imperative that the consummation be viewed by credible witnesses and its performance marked in documents. He well knew this, as it had been so even two thousand years into the past.

Alessandra's attire had been a statement, she'd said, and it had had an effect, based on the humans' gasps in their shrine. Or perhaps arriving in full armor on horseback with all one's weapons was not the marriage custom here.

But she hadn't stopped. Her arm had remained wrapped around his, and she had proceeded down the aisle. Whatever statement she'd been making, it hadn't been a refusal. Nothing good, but… not a refusal.

They hadn't spoken the entire ride to the palace, and hardly at all during the feast. Instead, they had just danced, then eaten the humans' food silently while the guests had drunk themselves into a stupor.

And then… this.

Riza had been right; even if both he and Alessandra had been unwilling, this ceremony had needed to happen. As right as she was, everything inside him right now didn't care.

There would be a woman in the next room, his new bride, with whom he would have to consummate this marriage. His likely *unwilling* bride.

To do so would be—

Dishonorable. Unconscionable. Vile.

An answer. He needed to find an answer.

A door clicked shut in the other room. Alessandra.

He stared at his own door. How long had it been? He shouldn't have left her to be the first one out. *He* should have awaited *her.*

First, they'd exchange gifts, and then—

He eyed the long, flat wooden box on the nearby table. There had been no way to know whether she was a skilled archer or not; if she was, she'd appreciate the Nozva Rozkvetan rosewood bow, and if she wasn't, he'd teach her everything she needed to know. But would she like it?

With a deep breath, he rolled up his sleeves, tucked the box under one arm, then opened the door.

In the scant candlelight, she stood on the other side of the room, wearing a long, flowing red sheer nightgown that pooled on the floor, with a wrapped parcel in her delicate hands. She wore jewels on her fingers, wrist, ears, and around her neck in a ruby-encrusted golden necklace. Her hair was loose and voluminous, a warm brown like rain-dampened cypress bark, a shade lighter than her dark eyes. The nightgown hung by thin, delicate straps, leaving her long, elegant arms bare.

He suppressed a shiver. Every part of her looked so *soft.* There was no hardiness to her, just give... Give that would have never survived the difficult conditions in Nozva Rozkveta, nor any queendom in the Deep for that matter, if she were on her own.

But now she had *him.* Together, they'd survive anything.

She moved to the window, as far away from the hovering group of humans as possible, and he joined her. Nearly shoulder to shoulder, he looked out at the dark city with her, glittering with lights as far as the eye could see, beneath a starry sky.

What could he say to her?

Mati had ordered this. He trusted her completely, had pledged his allegiance to her. Whatever she ordered, he would do.

And Alessandra, she had orders from her father, too, didn't she? Neither of them wanted this, but for the sake of the peace, they had to show a united front.

Just before the dance tonight, the way she'd gone rigid in her chair—something had angered her. Made her livid. She'd had that wild look about her, like a volodara about to go berserk, and he hadn't been certain whether his touch would quell that wildness or unleash it.

One of the humans in the group cleared his throat impatiently.

"Alessandra," he whispered, placing the box on the ample windowsill, and she peered down at it, eyebrows raised, then eyed him. "Accept this gift as a token of my commitment."

With a soft smile, she grazed the length of the box with a fingertip before gently flicking open the brass closure. She lifted the lid, revealing the deep reddish-brown Nozva Rozkvetan rosewood short bow. Her eyes flashed bright as reverent fingertips smoothed over the wood. "It's beautiful," she breathed.

"Only the royalty and kuvari of Nozva Rozkveta are permitted bows of our rosewood. Its perfect balance of density and strength make it the most sought-after bow wood in the land." Or at least it *had* been two thousand years ago. "Do you know how to use a bow?"

A light blush. "Papà forbade it. I've only attempted it once, and I can't say I was very good."

"If you wish to learn, I will teach you," he said, brushing the rosewood. "I will always do my all for you, and that includes helping you hone skills to hunt for and defend yourself, should you ever need to."

For a moment, she didn't move, didn't speak, just watched the bow with a dreamlike intensity, and then finally she nodded, breathing in lengthily as if awaking. "Thank you. I'd love to learn, Veron."

It would be something they could do together while they got to know one another. Perhaps, in time, they'd be friends.

She extended her own wrapped parcel to him brightly. "This is for you."

By its shape, it was clearly a book. About what? He accepted it and cut through the twine with a claw, eliciting a gasp. Her hand covered her wrist, but not before he glimpsed a hair-thin scratch. Fresh, recent—

No. Had he—?

He hadn't meant to, but at the feast, or—

When I helped her out of the carriage.

"Alessandra, did I—"

"It's fine." She grinned, *beamed*. Forced it.

By Deep and Darkness, he'd *hurt* her. He hadn't even known, and he'd caused her injury. "Forgive me, I—"

Only her eyes indicated the direction of the human officials, and she gave the slightest shake of her head.

So she didn't want them to know about this. If the humans found out, they might call him—and all dark-elves—dangerous. Violent. Incompatible with human society.

All dark-elves had claws, their look and sharpness a point of strength. A clawless dark-elf would be like a toothless lion, weakened, devalued, seen as lesser—something any child of Mati's could not do, so as not to reflect poorly on her or Nozva Rozkveta.

But Alessandra—

Smiling, she nodded toward the parcel. "I hope you like it, but if—"

He drew away the paper wrapping with a rustle, revealing a thick tome. *A Modern History of Silen.* Well, he could certainly stand to learn what had transpired in two thousand years of stone slumber.

On the title page, in elegant calligraphic script it said, *To Veron: Silen would be honored to create history with Nightbloom as these final pages are filled with the peace we will forge together. Aless*

These final pages? A thrill wove through him as he glanced up at her sparkling eyes and turned to the back of the tome. Of its thousand pages, perhaps two to three hundred were blank at the end.

He huffed his amusement softly. A thoughtful gift. She intended for him to write in their peoples' shared history into this Sileni tome, a symbolic gesture. The last time he'd written in a book, it had been sketching with Ata, as he'd taught him about the sky realm and its exotic flora and fauna, before Ata had—

"It was newly transcribed," she said, eagerly thumbing the gilded pages, "and the bookmaker left space to continue recording, just like in the copy my mother gave me." Her eyes brightened. "Actually, the latest Magister Trials from a few weeks ago were just added, and only this edition—maybe only *this* first new transcription—has it. The Emaurrian candidate, in the second trial, she looked the Grand Divinus in the eye, and, well, you'll see, but—"

He grinned at her over the tome, and she bit her lip. So books excited her. A *lot.* Something they could share. "Thank you. I look forward to filling up these remaining pages."

As she reddened, another throat-clearing came from the councilors. They were beginning to grate on his nerves.

Alessandra glanced over her shoulder, then back at him. "It's time," she said quietly. Gravely. They left the bow and the book together on the windowsill.

Steeling himself, he offered her his hand, and with a swallow, she took it. He ignored the crowd as he escorted her to the curtained bed, pulled aside the ethereal fabric, and helped her up. She sat stiffly, her olive skin pebbled against a chill, and fidgeted with the sheer red fabric of her nightgown. He didn't look at it too closely, didn't dare, especially when she seemed so nervous.

But that wasn't what tonight was about, for either of them. It was about trust. They had both been ordered into roles they'd never desired, and for the sake of the peace, for the sake of their peoples, they wouldn't buck these roles, even if they were neither attracted to one another nor in love. So they had to build trust, a friendship, a partnership. If any of this was to succeed, those bonds would be crucial between them. And at least a foundation.

She would have every honor, and more. She would have everything she needed, everything she wanted, anything on this earth that he could provide.

There was a washbasin nearby, and he took it—and a towel—to the edge of the bed, placed it on the floor by her feet. She eyed the basin curiously, and another human in the group cleared his throat again.

Alessandra lowered her gaze.

By Deep and Darkness, not only were these humans to *witness* this "consummation" they demanded, but they intended to hurry it along, too? And to interfere? Such blatant disrespect, for him, and worse, for *her*. The night of the Offering, the acceptance, was *private*. A time when a couple calmed after feasting and games, comforted one another, affirmed their vows in private—and, if they so chose, made love. It was a sacred moment for two, and two only.

Another throat clearing. "Your Highness, if we could—"

"No." He speared the elderly little human with a glare and strode to the exit doors. Enough was enough.

He pulled them open, then gestured to the humans. "Out. Now."

They all stared at him, then exchanged glances with one another.

"Your Highness," the same human objected, "it is this kingdom's custom that—"

"It is not *my* custom, nor that of my people, nor was it part of the marriage agreement that this 'consummation' be witnessed. Leave. Now." He stood firm, his glare at them unwavering, steeling through his uncertainty.

Mati knew the full details of the agreement; he didn't. She had told him what he'd needed to know, and she hadn't mentioned this specifically. It was possible he was wrong.

But he had to try.

One by one, the group of humans trickled out into the hall, until only the one who had spoken remained. The little man stared back at him defiantly.

Whispers came from the hall. "What will he do to her?" one asked. "Perhaps we should call a healer," another suggested.

Veron didn't break eye contact with the little man. This was the sort of idiotic ignorance they aimed to defeat. And as much as he wanted to *defeat* it right in its bulbous nose, *defeat* it until it shrieked in fear and then fled, instead he took a breath.

Finally, he closed the distance between them—the man cowered—and baring his teeth, Veron shoved him out into the hall, where Riza and Gavri were posted. He shut the doors on the whispering gossip and wide eyes, and turned the lock.

A cough came from the bed.

He turned, and Alessandra was observing him over the rim of a wine goblet as she drank.

"What will you do to me, dark-elf prince?" she mocked with a nervous laugh, then took another sip before setting the goblet down. "Will you chop me up into little pieces and eat me? Will you skin me alive and wear my hide?"

He shook his head, and a grin rent free. "I don't know. Perhaps we should call a healer."

Another nervous laugh. Hopefully he could put her mind at ease.

He moved back to the bed, back to the basin. Her curious gaze followed him, the mirth still glimmering there as he lowered to a knee and rolled up his other sleeve. He gestured to her foot. "May I?"

She frowned, a small, puzzled one, but nodded.

Silky fabric brushed against his fingertips as he lifted the hem of her nightgown, baring her feet. They were narrow, small, unblemished, as if she hadn't ever walked barefoot on the stone. Perhaps she hadn't.

He gently bathed one in the warm water, smoothing his hands against her too-soft skin.

She shivered, then smiled. "Is this a dark-elf custom?"

"It is." He patted her first foot dry, then grasped the other delicately and repeated the process. "On the night of the Offering, it says to a bride, 'I am not too proud to serve you. I will never be too proud to serve you. It is my honor and pleasure.'"

She held her breath as he poured water onto her skin from his cupped hand. Slowly, sluggishly, she blinked. "Things are quite different where you're from."

He laughed. He could say the same to her. The outlandish things that had happened today alone could fill an entire tome. "Different... in a bad way?"

She shook her head. "Just... different."

After toweling her other foot dry, he set the basin and towel aside. She moved over in the bed, and he went to the hearth and put another log on the fire.

His heart pounded as it never had. It wasn't fear, exactly, as he'd had lovers before this and knew what happened between a man and a woman. This was required for her human kingdom to acknowledge the marriage.

But no part of her was anything like a dark-elf woman, not ferocious, nor intimidating, nor dangerous. No claws, no fangs, no muscle nor combat prowess to speak of. Was human lovemaking anything like the fierce, raging, unrestrained madness that was a night with a dark-elf woman?

There had been a gleam in her eye, when she'd taken off the white cloak in the abbazia, that could have rivaled that of any queen of the Deep. Heat flushed in his chest. That look had been ferocious, yes, but fleeting. Then the wildness smoldering in her at the feast... as her fists had clenched tightly enough to break.

But to her, he was little better than a beast, wasn't he? Nothing like a human man. Not someone she desired nor envisioned herself with.

There were no witnesses here. Not anymore. Would it really *matter* if this consummation happened?

With a silent exhalation, he turned back to the bed, offered her what he hoped was a consoling smile, and joined her, careful to keep his distance.

He sat next to her as she lay deathly still, barely moving but to breathe. Staring up at the bed's canopy with intense focus, she looked as though she were preparing herself mentally for an amputation.

He suppressed a laugh. No, he really oughtn't laugh at her when she was making such an effort to bear this indignity. "Alessandra, I do not share *their*"—he nodded to the door—"expectations for this night. You need not fear me."

Only her eyes moved in his direction, wide and a chatoyant tiger's-eye brown. "But the consummation—"

"Is not a custom required by my people." He kept his bearing loose, open, unthreatening.

She blinked, her breath coming faster, harder, shifting that sheer red fabric of her nightgown in folds. "Then you don't wish to"—she closed her eyes—"to..."

"No." He watched the tension melt from her body. "This arrangement is new to both of us."

She sat up, leaned her back against the pillows, and nodded, bunching up the covers at her chest.

"Neither of us wants that tonight, but I don't mean to close the door on this, either. I want you to know that I'm open to your wishes, and that you shouldn't fear rejection should you express them to me." Now that they'd made the Offering to each other, she would never be heartsore with him, ever, not if he could help it.

She reddened. "But you don't find me desirable?"

Raising his eyebrows, he looked away. She'd asked that directly? Admirable, and... difficult. "You're intelligent and bold, but we only just met yesterday. I am yours and yours alone, but this... will take some time."

She laughed. "So then you don't."

"I don't need to ask you the same." He hid a smile.

She slapped the duvet. "You're the first dark-elf I've ever seen face to face!"

"So then... you don't." It was his turn to laugh.

She waved him off and sighed. "Good. I'm glad we cleared the air."

"So am I. Trust is the one expectation I have," he answered.

A long silence. "Veron, I... There are many things I want to discuss with you, but I don't wish to offend you. Well, to offend you more than I already have."

He huffed. It would take more than a style of clothing to offend him. "You haven't. And you can discuss anything with me."

She bit her lip, stroking the duvet. "Maybe after Bianca's wedding?"

That was in three days. It seemed as though she planned to attend.

There was only one problem: he was under strict orders from Mati to leave with her tomorrow. "Alessandra, we... we can't stay."

Her eyebrows drawn together, she stared at him. "What?"

"We're scheduled to leave tomorrow." Had her father not told her about the schedule for the Royal Progress? The famine in the queendoms?

She threw off the covers and knelt on the bed, angling to face him. "Veron, my sister is marrying in three days. My *sister*."

"I know," he said gently, but even so, her eyes were widening, glistening. "I'm sorry, but—"

"It's my sister's wedding. I can't—won't—miss it," she said with a vehement shake of her head.

"I cannot disobey a direct order, Alessandra." No matter how much he wished she could stay. "Not even for this. And we have a strict schedule—"

"Please," she said, her voice breaking. "I'm begging you. I can't miss her wedding—I can't. She and I, we've always been the closest of all my brothers and sisters, and she's in love with him, Veron. This will be the happiest day of her life, and you and I are moving away. I have to be there, please, just for her wedding, so could we just delay our departure, just a little, shift the Royal Progress arrangements, only until after Bianca's wedding, and—"

Tears rolled down her cheeks as he shook his head.

Her father really hadn't told her anything. Had let her hold out hope.

Holy Ulsinael, he wanted to take her in his embrace, comfort her, but what could he say? He had orders from Mati. Vadiha and Dita were *starving*, as were the rest of his people, who awaited them and *food* on specific days. Nothing would change that they had to leave tomorrow. "People are expecting us, expecting we'll bring—"

With a sob, she covered her mouth and scrambled from the bed.

"Alessandra, let me just—"

She stormed out to her dressing chamber, then slammed the door behind her.

CHAPTER 7

*I*n the palazzo's courtyard, Aless stood before Papà in the weak morning sunlight. Even after manipulating her into a marriage, he still hadn't been done trying to break her. He and the queen of Nightbloom had set the Royal Progress schedule, and everyone involved had known about it but *her*.

Papà had *known* she'd miss Bianca's wedding, and he'd said nothing. He'd even left Veron to break that bitter news.

Ever since Mamma's death, Papà had looked at her differently, and a distance had grown between them, and grown and grown. Everything she cared about was wrong, and anything she did was punished, and it seemed he was never done punishing her. She hadn't fit in here, not in a long while, and now she was leaving, for maybe the last time.

Bianca had finally gotten what she'd so long carried a ladder for in that orchard of daydreams.

And Papà couldn't have even given *her* the sweet farewell of witnessing Bianca's wedding. Not even that.

"You are so much like her," Papà said, his dark-brown eyes dull. "This will be best for you."

So like *Mamma*. Mamma, whose entire palazzo library and every book he'd had destroyed.

No, this was best for *him*. Getting rid of her, like he'd gotten rid of Mamma's memory.

"Remember your promise," he whispered.

"Goodbye, Papà," she replied, before moving to Lorenzo, who wrapped her in his arms.

"I sent some things along with you for Veron," he said, "so you two can match in equally... haute couture. Despite the piety of Stroppiata, Duchessa Claudia is a fashion snob."

"Thank you." With a half-laugh under her breath, she pulled away from Lorenzo as he gave her a soft smile.

"You're getting away from the palazzo," he whispered with a twinkle in his eye. "Make the most of it."

Unlike him, she'd never wanted to escape the palazzo, but rather to become a more useful part of it. Maybe that was what she had carried a ladder for, only for her, it would ever remain a daydream.

"Make the most of being here, too, brother," she whispered back, giving his stubbled cheek a goodbye kiss as she at last turned to Bianca.

Veron clasped arms with Lorenzo as she took Bianca's hand and met her eyes, red and welling with glistening tears. With a lace-trimmed white hand-kerchief, Bianca dabbed at her face, her lower lip trembling, then shook her head sadly.

Aless pulled Bianca into her arms, holding her tight. Next to her, Veron said his goodbyes to Lorenzo.

At their wedding, Veron had said, *I, Veron of Nozva Rozkveta, offer you power, survival, support, defense, wisdom, and partnership, to harness for your ends or ours, as we walk our lives together from this day forward for as long as the Deep allows.*

Papà had kept this from her, yes, and he bore the brunt of the blame. But she'd begged Veron, *begged* him to delay their departure, shift the Royal Progress arrangements, just until after Bianca's wedding.

But his *mother* had given him a direct order, and that had been that.

What was important to her was supposed to be important to him, too, wasn't it? What would life be like if even this hadn't merited some compromise?

Bianca wept softly into her shoulder. "We've sent the package to Nunzio."

Good. Then she could discuss the plans with him when she arrived in Stroppiata, where the Order of Terra was headquartered.

All the more reason to persuade Veron against the second ceremony, if he'd listen. If he'd even be *open* to viewpoints other than that of his mother and queen, that is.

Honesty is the one expectation I have, he'd said. Fine words. But what good had her honesty done her about Bianca's wedding? She'd tell him her plan once they were on better terms, once she'd proven she could deliver a peace before the second ceremony.

Bianca sniffled. "I just wish—"

"I know. I'm so sorry, Bianca," she whispered, stroking Bianca's hair softly. "I wish I could stay."

"I'll visit you," Bianca cried. "I promise."

A lovely thought. She pulled away and smiled softly. "You'd better. I'll want to hear every detail."

Bianca beamed through her tears and nodded, swiping a muslin-clad arm across her face, a smiling, weeping, loving face against the backdrop of lush green and the white stone of the palazzo.

This was it. Goodbye, as no matter what happened from here on, she'd never live under Papà's roof again.

Papà, standing first in line, raised his chin and met her eyes. He'd been the first to bid her goodbye, reminding her of her promise. She remembered all right. She'd promised to *wed* Veron, which she had done, and the rest was up to her and Veron.

Papà tipped his head toward the waiting cavalcade just as Gabriella took her arm, leading her away. With food, coin, her belongings, and picture books for the children along the Royal Progress, the number of carts had grown.

"Come, Your Highness," Gabriella said. "We've a long road ahead of us."

A long road indeed.

She fisted her gray skirts. Just as she was about to turn away, Veron approached Bianca—and bowed. Low.

In the ensuing silence, he remained utterly still, his powerful form as if sculpted from stone, ready to endure for centuries, millennia.

He'd bowed. Apologized to Bianca.

Bianca's perfectly sculpted eyebrows shot up.

So did hers.

ALESS PULLED ASIDE the curtain in her carriage. All was verdant and beautiful outside—the cypress trees lining the road, the fields of grass, the umbrella pines in the distance, and the occasional fields of artichokes or orchards of lemon trees. So bright and cheerful. Maybe Bianca was airing out her wedding dress right now, smiling and laughing with her ladies-in-waiting, preparing for the big day.

Veron had apologized to Bianca, but he'd still gotten his way, hadn't he? Could he be trusted, or did he only wear a mantle of earnestness, beneath which only his mother's will lived and breathed? Begging him had been awkward, but being rejected had been even more awkward.

He rode just ahead, his hooded figure nevertheless identifiable by his broad shoulders and bearing, atop that massive beast he called a horse. She narrowed her eyes.

He glanced over his shoulder in her direction.

With a huff, she yanked the curtains shut and crossed her arms.

"I'd hoped he'd find a way for you two to remain for Her Highness's wedding," Gabriella whispered from the seat next to her.

At least Papà had sent *one* familiar face with her.

"Will his mother always have the final say over everything?" Gabriella asked under her breath.

"Too early to tell." Aless exhaled slowly, stroking the cotton batiste of her gray skirts. But it seemed Veron didn't have a disobedient bone in his body. He'd been reasonable and kind, and because of that, she'd hoped he might soon hear her out about a friendship instead of a marriage.

But now she wasn't so certain.

If his mother had ordered this union, then to alter that, it would take more than simply *asking* in order to convince him. She'd need to sort out the library plans with Nunzio and present Veron with an idea for a joint venture, something to symbolize their peoples' new peace and ongoing friendship. A place where humans and dark-elves could unite.

It would start with this one place, the library, and then grow. Maybe someday, Silen would be a land where humans, dark-elves, light-elves, and other peaceful Immortali all lived together in harmony.

Once she and Nunzio spoke and planned in concrete terms, she could bring their ideas to Veron and hope for the best.

Gabriella patted her hand, imparting warmth with a gentle hazel-eyed look. "I wish they weren't so cold to you, Your Highness," she said. "Perhaps it would be better if the Brotherhood helped you escape? Would they do that, or would it have to be violent?"

The Brotherhood—no. She did not want any part of that. As much as she wanted freedom from this marriage, she didn't wish for the Brotherhood's plan of fire and death to succeed.

"Before we left," Gabriella continued, "there was word that they sacked a light-elf settlement near the coast. People were saying the Brotherhood put all of them on a ship to Sonbahar in the dead of night."

Sonbahar? For what? The slave markets? Unthinkable. "Are you certain?"

"That's what they're saying, and that now the surrounding villages will be 'safe.' They seemed just fine before."

Safe? Safe from what?

There had been rumors that sick or misbehaving children were light-elf changelings, that any maiden or child that disappeared was abducted by the light-elves or the other Immortali. That light-elves cursed crops, stole random trinkets from people's homes, poisoned livestock...

But surely no one had believed such farfetched tales? Light-elves had no magic and rarely if ever ventured out of their forests. They placed no value on jewels or precious metals, let alone worthless trinkets.

Human women fled their husbands, children got lost, crops failed, livestock died. It was easier to blame the Immortali than to accept the cruelty of everyday life. And the Brotherhood encouraged it.

"Where was this?" she whispered back to Gabriella.

"Near Portopersico, I think."

A small village on the coast just east of Bellanzole—there had been a light-elf settlement nearby?

Tarquin and the Belmonte Company had been clearing out harpy nests near Bellanzole. Had he led this attack? He and his watchful "pride"? Where would they strike next?

It would be days before she and Veron would arrive at Stroppiata, their first stop, where they'd be presented to the duchessa, to earn a promise of her friendship. Too long of a time to go without news. She'd have to tell Veron about the Brotherhood and—

"Just how many trunks of silks and baubles do humans need to cart around?" the dark-elf guard with the braid asked outside the carriage, in *Sileni*, no less. Clearly wanting to be overheard.

The sharp-eyed guard shushed her, but Veron grunted in reply. It was about as much as he'd said all day since their argument last night.

The dark-elves had gaped at her luggage—really, it was only ten large trunks or so; she'd packed light for *moving her entire life*. What did they expect, for her to bring just one change of clothes and nothing else?

Besides, the cavalcade had left Bellanzole with dozens of carts bearing food and coins, all to distribute to humans and dark-elves alike along the Royal Progress. No complaints about *those*, it seemed.

"They have no respect," Gabriella muttered. "You are a princess of Silen. You travel and dress in the style befitting your station."

Nothing she was and nothing she had was acceptable to the dark-elves. Everything she owned was extravagant, unnecessary, indulgent. They wouldn't be pleased until she wore a burlap sack and tied her hair with a daisy chain. "Fortunately, I don't care what they think."

Gabriella smiled and gave her a nod of encouragement. "Besides, all that leather can't possibly be comfortable. Their fashions don't have to be ours, do they?"

She smiled back. Her dresses won over leathers any day, but especially Sileni summer days.

"And what an insult," Gabriella added, pursing her lips, "to provide you with no household."

That had been the least of her concern. Even if Veron agreed to her plan, she'd never have any wealth to speak of ever again. All of her wealth had come from Papà, and by his choice. He'd never welcome her back after this, so... so she'd have to learn to do things for herself.

She had what she needed for camp. Papà's household had packed an elaborate silk tent, and naturally, he had sent no one to pitch it.

No one but her.

"We'll make do," she answered. Compared to dealing with Papà, it wouldn't be hard at all. Not like telling Veron about the Brotherhood—and Tarquin—would be.

CHAPTER 8

$\mathcal{V}$eron pounded his tent's first stake into the ground while Alessandra and Gabriella rifled through the countless packs and chests from Bellanzole. "Has the princess been given one of our tents?"

Gavri huffed under her breath. "Yes, she has. I saw to it myself. No doubt she's turning her nose up at it. Typical human."

Stubborn, spoiled human princess. Dark-elves *and* humans were dying daily, fighting over senseless reasons, and Vadiha and Dita were *starving* waiting for this food from Bellanzole. He and Alessandra were tasked with sowing peace, ending the famine, and she'd wanted to let them keep suffering longer for a wedding? Of course she'd wanted to be there for such an important day in her sister's life, but delaying the Royal Progress for that would have had negative consequences for so many more people—starving people—that Alessandra either didn't seem to notice or didn't concern herself with. He set another stake and hammered it.

"How dare she treat you with such disrespect," Gavri added, but Riza glared at her. "You don't need to appease her, Your Highness." When Riza snarled at her, Gavri held up her hands and backed away before taking her leave.

It didn't matter. Disrespect? He didn't care about that. There was far more at stake. Their union and this Royal Progress through the realm was their one chance to stop the flow of blood before all-out war, and Alessandra couldn't see past her own immediate family. Even beyond Mati's orders, there was sound reason she ignored because it suited her.

She paid lip service to peace, but did she even understand what war truly was? The stench of blood and entrails after combat, the screaming widows and crying orphans? The disease that came after, and the famine resulting from the loss of able-bodied people and the bankruptcy of the powers financing it all?

Had she ever looked any of them in the eye, or had she only heard news from her lady-in-waiting and seen paintings of battles in the grand human ballroom, while faceless servants filled her goblet and brought platters of cakes and fruits?

He moved along the tent's round edge, and Riza handed him another stake.

"Give her time, Your Highness," she said nonchalantly as he hammered.

He speared Riza with a peripheral glare as he moved along. Could time fix this?

"She is young. Very young. And has been kept sheltered," Riza said, handing him the stakes as he needed them. "Now that she is touring her own land, her eyes will open to many things. Be patient." Riza stepped back and admired his work, then hmphed under her breath. She nodded toward the carts, where Alessandra and Gabriella were removing a large, bundled tent.

A *yurta*, or at least similar to what his people used for more permanent camps. What about the smaller tent Gavri had given her?

"Perhaps you may need to be a little *more* patient."

Alessandra's *yurta* was about six times the size of this tent, twice as tall, and made of purple-and-white-striped canvas. That monstrosity would take at least three people and two hours to assemble.

"Humans are drawn to ostentation like harpies to anything shiny." Riza tsked and brushed a hand through her short hair. "That thing, for one night's camp? At this rate, she'll be sleeping outside."

He rubbed his chin, then sighed. "No matter how we disagree, my bride will always have a place to sleep." He'd suggest the tent Gavri had given her; hopefully Alessandra would see reason.

Riza nodded, a faint smile on her lips. "You treat her like a dark-elf bride, Your Highness—albeit a very inadequate one."

"She *is* a dark-elf bride, Riza."

She raised an eyebrow, then her mouth curved wider. "Her Majesty would be proud of you."

Deep, Darkness, and Holy Ulsinael willing. But this wasn't just for Mati's praise; he and Alessandra would now be living a life together. He needed to make amends, and she... well, *she* needed a tent pitched.

Rubbing his face, he headed toward the heap Alessandra was now digging through. Her skirts in the dirt, she burrowed under the purple-and-white stripes, muttering while Gabriella held the canvas. As soon as he took hold of it, Gabriella released it, inclined her head, and excused herself.

"Raise it higher, Gabriella. It's suffocating in here," Alessandra said. Except Gabriella was making her way across the camp.

Suppressing a grin, he did as she bade.

Wood thudded against wood and ropes hissed while she shuffled around inside. "Yours looked so simple, but this one is—*not*. I'm definitely not going to ask *him* for help. Are you certain there are no instructions?"

He schooled his face. "None that I saw," he answered, unable to hold back the amused lilt.

No answer came as she froze beneath the canvas, then scooted completely under it.

"Alessandra…"

A heavy sigh. "I suppose you're here to tell me you have *orders* that we must share your tent."

He took a slow, deep breath. A *very* slow, deep breath. "I'm here to ask you whether I can pitch the tent Gavri gave you."

"Who?" she shot back. "No one gave me anything."

He rested a hand on his hip. "One of our tents. She gave you one."

"No, she didn't, whoever *she* is. I think I'd remember that."

Then what? Gavri had made it all up? Why? She wouldn't betray him. *Ever.* As one of his best friends, Gavri *knew* his father had lied to him once, just *once*, and had never returned to Nozva Rozkveta. Gavri would never—

"Besides, I have my own, thank you."

He scoffed. "Even for three experienced people, this tent would take at least two hours to put together."

She hmphed. "Oh, *now* you want to help me?"

This again. "I already told you—there are greater concerns than—"

"No, there aren't. That's what you led me to believe. That when it came to making an Offering, it meant there were no greater concerns." A tremor shook her words. "But I suppose my understanding doesn't matter, only your mother's commands."

He shook his head. "Our first stop is the city of Stroppiata in two days," he said gently. "Did you know they've planned our reception for weeks now?"

"A reception can be postponed," she shot back.

"How about a parade route, a banquet, and the feast the duchess promised her people? Those people are waiting for us to arrive in *exactly* two days." When she didn't reply, he added, "And then three days after that, we're going to Dun Mozg—you may know it as Dunmarrow—a small dark-elf queendom farther inland. Queen Nendra's people are starving, and they're expecting us *that day*, will be celebrating us *that* day. My own sister barely has the energy to feed her newborn daughter, and we are bringing her food in Nozva Rozkveta. How long should she wait while we postpone for a wedding?"

A barely audible throat clearing came from the tent. "Why didn't you tell me that sooner? That the people were expecting us on specific days?"

"I told you we had a strict schedule, that people were expecting us." But even as he'd spoken the words then, she'd stormed out in tears and hadn't wanted to listen to another word.

And he shouldn't blame her for it. At least she seemed of a mind to listen now.

"I didn't know about your sister. I didn't think the people were looking forward to the specific day. I thought..." A deep breath. "I don't know what I thought."

To people who barely survived on rations, the distribution of plentiful food was everything. She had to know that. Didn't she notice the suffering of people now living in her own land?

The canvas shifted as she slowly wriggled out from under it, her brown eyes big as she eyed him, dusting off her dirt-marred hands. When there had been no servants to pitch her tent, she'd gotten her own hands dirty. She'd tried to do it herself. Perhaps she wasn't as spoiled as he'd thought, just... hadn't been allowed beyond the walls of the world she knew.

"You were thinking about your sister," he said softly and crouched to meet her at eye level. "When my mother told me the schedule, I didn't realize my bride's sister's wedding would be a few days later. If I'd known..." He would have wanted to speak up, to ask Mati whether he and his bride would be allowed to stay, perhaps send some food on ahead. "I'm sorry."

Kneeling in the grass, she rested her smudged hands in her lap, centered on the gray fabric. Errant dark curls had escaped her elaborate coiled hairstyle, framing her face, spilling over slender shoulders. She bit her lip. "I should have heard you out. I'm sorry, too."

There was so much more to discuss. The night of their wedding, she'd also mentioned wanting to talk to him about something. But this... unfortunate situation with Bianca had thwarted everything.

He rested a hand on hers. "Come with me. I'll find you another tent."

As he began to rise, she took his hand. "Wait. Can I sleep with you tonight?"

The question stopped him—stopped him completely—but he swallowed and helped her up as he stood.

"I mean—" she whispered. "Won't it look bad if we sleep apart? As if we don't agree, as if there's disharmony between us."

She was right, but there *had been* disharmony between them.

He'd assumed separate tents, but... "As long as it doesn't make you uncomfortable."

"It doesn't." Her brief smile lit up her face with its brightness, just for a moment. It reached her eyes, their beautiful darkness gleaming, like moonlight over rippling night waters.

He hefted her pack and her bedroll, then led her toward his tent, nodding greetings to the faces that turned to them. What he'd wanted was to keep looking into those eyes, so different than the ones he was accustomed to, all in shades of amber and gold. But the surface of those night waters had rippled, and there was something lurking there that she hadn't revealed. Until she did, the risk of drowning, no matter how small, wasn't worth the consequence.

He'd already trusted a liar once. Watched Ata leave their family. Only to be crippled by the news of the truth.

Never again.

And Gavri—if she'd lied—

No, there was no excuse.

He settled Alessandra into his tent, and then went back to the heap of a *yurta* they'd left behind and packed it up. Unlike human royalty, he didn't travel with a legion of servants; dark-elves were expected to do nearly everything for themselves. Of course she wouldn't have known that.

Humans had such different values, but Alessandra... She was to spend her life in Nozva Rozkveta. It wasn't easy being a newcomer to a strange place; if he had been tasked with living in Bellanzole, no doubt Alessandra would have helped him find his way among the humans. And he could do no less—*would* do no less—for her.

Once he'd finally put the bundled tent back in the cart, he dug through his pack for his pipe and glanced back to check on Alessandra.

Outside the tent, Gavri stood, arms crossed, her brow creased. Her firebright eyes smoldered, every inch of her battle hard. What did any of this matter to her?

It clearly did, though.

She'd done it. She'd lied.

When she finally looked away, he caught her gaze. That battle hardness softened, her gaze cooled, and her mouth dropped open a moment before she closed it anew.

He jerked his head to come hither, and biting her lip, she approached.

"Your Highness, I only meant to—"

Scowling, he held up a hand. "You lied."

She met his eyes, wouldn't look away, that crease returning to her brow as she crossed her arms. "She put on that *show* in her ignorant human city and made you look like some barbarian, abducting her from—"

He leaned in. "*I. Don't. Care.*"

Gavri had known him for his entire life. She should've known better. She had known better.

And this was about some minor hiccup in his arranged marriage? It had been a few years, but maybe she was still sore over Zoran making the Offering to Queen Nendra.

"Everyone at home is just suffering so much, and she throws these little fits over her whims. Rebellion. Disobedience." She ran a hand over her hair, down the length of her braid, and exhaled a sigh through her nose. "You deserve—"

"I am not Zoran," he hissed, "and Alessandra is not Nendra. She has done nothing to you."

Gavri's eyes widened a moment before a scowl creased her face. "This has nothing to do with Zoran! This is about some *human* disrespecting—"

"You're dismissed."

She scoffed and shook her head, then turned away.

"From my guard."

She whirled back around, eyes wide. "*What?* I was defending you!"

"By *lying* to me?" he bit out, stepping to her. "You are *sworn* to truth. But more than that, I *trusted* you. And you try to sabotage the peace your queen worked so hard to build? To sabotage my marriage before Alessandra and I have even gotten to know each other?"

Her lower lip trembled as she breathed hard. "I know, I know it, but I was just—"

"Don't let me see your face again for the rest of this trip. And once we're back in Nozva Rozkveta, you'll be transferred from my guard."

With a sharp breath, she grabbed his wrist. "Veron—"

He shook her off and strode to his tent, fists clenched. Gavri was like a sister to him, but if she was going to betray his friendship, endanger what they were doing here, *disobey* Mati's orders, then she had no place among his inner circle. The cost of her recklessness could be catastrophic.

Outside the flap, he took several deep breaths. Relaxed his hands. Finally, he drew the flap aside.

Alessandra was already scrubbing her hands in a small basin of water she'd gotten from... he didn't know where. And two plates of Bellanzole bread, cheese, and figs sat between two neatly laid-out bedrolls.

"You don't waste time." When her dark eyes met his, he added, "Will you be—"

She moved the basin aside and, sitting stiffly, nodded him inside. "Please, this can't wait. We need to talk."

Talk? That was cryptic. Drawing his eyebrows together, he ducked into the tent, pulled off his too-tight boots, and lowered onto the bedroll across from hers, trying to roll the tension out of his shoulders.

On their wedding night, she'd mentioned wanting to speak to him about something, perhaps the same matter lurking beneath those night waters in her gaze. Was this it?

Rubbing her palms on her skirts, she faced him. "Veron, there's this group called the Brotherhood, and they're—"

"A rogue human army devoted to ousting all Immortals. I've... come across them before."

Alessandra nodded gravely. "I don't suspect Luciano is involved—"

He took a slow breath. Thank the Deep, the Darkness, and Holy Ulsinael. Calling one of those bigots *family* wasn't one of his life's goals. Besides, King Macario had sworn to Mati that he'd finesse the Brotherhood as part of the agreement.

"—but his brother, Tarquin, has given me reason to believe *he* is," she said, wriggling closer. "Veron, I think he might be... watching us."

"Tarquin," he said, testing the name as his claws bit into his palms. There had been a man in the abbazia who'd stared lances through him, the same man who'd cut into Alessandra's dance with her brother Lorenzo.

"His sister Arabella disappeared, and he blames the Immortali. Before we left, there was an attack on a light-elf settlement in the night, not far from Bellanzole," she said, wringing the gray fabric in her hand. "I don't know whether it's isolated or part of a greater plan, but I needed you to know in case..."

In case the Brotherhood came after the *monsters*. In case they *rescued* their human princess. In case they chose to *make an example* of him and his entourage, staking them out in the sun and starting the all-out war the Brotherhood so desperately seemed to want.

Her bearing tight, she watched him, those small, clawless fingers fidgeting. She blinked dark lashes over dark eyes, beneath a furrowed brow. "In case..."

"In case they come for my blood, and that of every dark-elf here."

CHAPTER 9

The early morning rays hit the distant red clay roof shingles of Stroppiata as Aless rode alongside Veron. She adjusted her right leg in the sidesaddle, spreading out her rosy-pink brocade skirts. The pink softened her look, a subtle contradiction to her infamous intemperance... or so her sister Giuliana had once said.

In less than an hour, they'd be inside the city walls. Normally, she was accustomed to riding inside a *carriage*, but today wasn't about comfort—it was about being seen. If it went well, it would set a good tone for the rest of the Royal Progress. If it went poorly... the best case would make this entire maneuver a failure, and the worst would see her, Veron, and countless others dead.

She exhaled. Too bad those thoughts couldn't leave with her breath. *No pressure. None whatsoever.*

She'd been on a Royal Progress once, when Lorenzo had come of age. Just outside each city's gates, Papà, Mamma, and Lorenzo had mounted horses, while she, Giuliana, and Bianca had stayed in the carriage. Smiling faces had lined the streets, eyes wide and shining, as cheers had drowned out all but the clink of coins and clop of hooves.

The people need to see Lorenzo, who'll be their next king, Giuliana had whispered, leaning in. *They need to see us, their monarchs, up close. It makes us real, creates connection, gives us the chance to show them who we truly are... or who we want to be.*

Giuliana had gone on a Royal Progress in Emaurria with her husband, Crown Prince Robert, several years ago after their wedding. No doubt she'd been the perfect princess, claiming space in every Emaurrian's heart as she'd shown them who she'd truly been. Talented and strong, beautiful and charming, a singular person capable of taming conflicts with a well-placed compliment or just the right laugh. If only Giuliana were here. If only she'd survived. If only—

No. There would be no useful thoughts in that direction. Not today. She sighed.

Golden eyes narrowed, Veron peered into the distance at the city, his face masked in black but for his eyes. His head hooded, hiding most of his ghostly white hair. The first time she'd seen him, back in the palazzo's courtyard, he'd been masked, hooded, cloaked—a black rider on a black horse, mysterious and intimidating, like some phantom hunter fallen to earth from the Wild Hunt.

The people need to see us.

"Veron?" she asked, and those golden eyes found her before he turned her way.

"Hmm?" A gruff sound, but soft.

Behind them, the cavalcade stretched so far back she couldn't tell where it ended, but she and Veron needed to speak. Even if he chose to ignore her, as Papà always did, she needed to try. This first visit was crucial—it would set the tone for the rest of the Royal Progress, and if it went well, maybe Veron would agree that they could maintain the peace as friends... and she could see her public library built. "Could we stop for a moment?"

He nodded and held up a hand.

The sharp-eyed guard bellowed, the first of a series of shouts down the line as it drew to a halt.

Veron dismounted that enormous beast of a horse, his motion practiced and fluid, and three guards followed suit as he extended a gloved hand to her. She removed her foot from the stirrup, then lifted her right leg over while turning in the saddle to the left.

It wasn't her first time dismounting a sidesaddle, but she took his hand anyway and hopped down. Ever since her... fashion statement at the wedding, it was more important than ever that she and Veron appear at peace. Especially with Tarquin's *pride* out there somewhere, watching.

Veron offered her his arm, and when she looped hers around it, he walked her to the blue-green maritime pine forest. A few feet into its concealment, he paused among some myrtle shrubs, his guards several feet behind and scanning the area.

When she'd told Veron about the Brotherhood and Tarquin, he'd taken the news calmly and said the Brotherhood wouldn't launch an attack in a human city, that she'd be safe in Stroppiata.

That had made sense, as all the previous attacks had taken place in Immortali settlements, and yet the entire dark-elf cavalcade seemed on edge, every guard more responsive, more watchful.

"I'll wait for you here," he said, his deep voice muffled through his mask as he nodded toward a farther patch of shrubs.

Wait for—? "No." She smiled, shaking a ladybug off her rosy-pink skirts. "Not that." With a glance at his nearby guards, she took his hand and led him behind a thicker orange-red trunk, where he looked down at her with glimmering half-moon eyes.

She reached up and brushed a finger along the edge of his black hood. "Do your people always wear masks and hoods?"

He looked away. "In the sky realm, yes." A matter-of-fact answer.

"Why?"

A pale eyebrow quirked. "People fear us."

People did fear them. Their imposing size. Those golden eyes, like those of predators in the night, with sharp canine teeth to match. Hair pale as a ghost's, come to drag them to the Lone. Blue-gray skin, so different from their own, its hue cold and stony. And claws... she well knew those.

Biting her lip, she slowly raised a hand toward his face, and when he didn't move, simply kept those golden eyes fixed on her, she tugged down the mask, revealing his sculpted jaw, the slate-blue of his face.

So close, his scent of earth and fresh water soothed its way to her nose, like a meadow after a summer storm, maybe, and she breathed in deeply, rising on her tiptoes to draw back his hood. Her finger brushed against smooth, pale hair, and for the briefest of moments, he closed his eyes, exhaled through parted lips.

For a second, everything paused. The breeze rustling through pine needles and myrtle leaves, the nearby whisper of a guard, the distant calls among those in the cavalcade, and everything waited as that slow, quivering exhalation rolled through him.

His eyebrows drew together as his eyes found hers once more, searching, questioning, but only a muscle twitched in his jaw.

No part of her would move while those eyes held her in place, not her hands, not her lips, not even her tongue. Her pulse raced her breathing, and which was faster, she couldn't tell.

Dark-elves kissed, didn't they? That's what this felt like, almost a kiss...

Only... he dropped his gaze between them, and both her pulse and her breathing—thank the Mother—slowed. He, too, had been frozen, but had it been in repugnance or discomfort? Unsettled that she might have been trying to kiss him? It had only been a few days since their wedding night, when he'd made it very clear he hadn't found her attractive in the least.

Had that changed, even a little? Or were his reactions a courtesy, so his human wife wouldn't feel like a fool? Or maybe a show.

Or duty.

There was no order of his mother's that he'd refuse. Even on his wedding night, utterly repulsed by his human bride, he would have done his duty if she'd demanded it. He'd been ordered to marry her, and any warmth, if that's what it was, would be in service of that order.

When he looked at her, he'd only ever see a human. Someone unappealing he'd been forced to wed. That's all she'd ever be.

Obedient as he was, he'd been kind to her. Sympathetic. Understanding. Patient.

And to her, now, the thought—of kissing him—

She sucked in a breath.

It didn't fill her with repugnance or discomfort. It didn't unsettle her. It—

She shook her head. This wasn't why she'd led him here. "People fear the unknown."

He blinked, those eyebrows still drawn together.

"The people need to see us up close," she said, repeating Giuliana's wisdom. "It makes us real, creates connection, gives us the chance to... show them who we truly are... or who we want to be."

The breeze picked up, and a lock of hair wisped across her face, but supple leather grazed her cheek as he tucked it behind her ear with a gloved hand. "Alessandra," he said softly, his brow creased, "the people don't *want* us to be real. It's not the same. It's why we cover ourselves."

She took his hand. "But you *are* real. And the nightmares we imagine behind the masks and the hoods are more terrifying than the reality."

He grinned, but then suppressed it. "*More* terrifying?"

"That is..."

That pale eyebrow quirked again, and she laughed.

"You know what I'm trying to say!" She averted her gaze as her cheeks warmed. "Our people are more alike than they are different, and once the reality is *known*, there won't be as much to fear. Nor *anything* to fear, I hope."

He tilted his head, working his jaw. "What do you suggest?"

"No masks. No hoods. You're distributing food and coin, so let the people associate that with your looks. Smile—"

He did, exposing those longer, sharp fangs.

"—but maybe not too broadly," she said, wincing, receiving a huff in reply. "And if people give us flowers, bouquets, take them. It's hard to fear anything covered in flowers."

"Sound logic," he said, a smile still on his lips as he squeezed her hand. "But the gloves stay on."

She hadn't realized she'd still been holding his hand. "Why—"

He let her go, and the smile faded. "Because I hurt you," he whispered, and swallowed. "I—we—might not yet possess the awareness required not to hurt anyone else... anyone *human*, and avoiding any—"

"Accidents," she provided.

"—would be for the best."

"Veron," she said gently, "you didn't mean it."

"Not everyone will be so understanding."

As much as she wanted to, there was no arguing that. Not when people like Tarquin were looking for excuses to dehumanize Immortali like the dark-elves. "We'll need to show a united front. Hold hands, smile at each other, stay in close proximity—that kind of thing."

"Like this?" A deep, low murmur. He glanced from himself to her and back again. "Pretend a deeper intimacy?"

Her cheeks warming, she nodded. *Pretend.* That's what this was, after all.

The world knew so little of dark-elf culture that maybe the pretense wouldn't be held to Sileni standards. She hoped. But for a few moments in the public's eye, they could be like players on a stage and pretend affection for each other, couldn't they?

"Very well." Excusing himself, he spoke to the sharp-eyed guard, who acknowledged him and then headed toward the cavalcade. The other two remained behind while Veron offered her his arm.

She took it, keenly aware of his thick forearm and thicker bicep, of his broad shoulders and towering figure, of his summer-storm scent and the shiver it stroked up her back.

It *excited* her.

He excited her.

No, the last thing she needed would be to fall for her dark-elf husband—and end up a trophy his mother would lock deep inside a cave somewhere. It would be the life Papà had always wanted for her, the life she could never stand to live. She'd never see Mamma's library realized, nor live her dream.

And worse, Veron didn't find *her* attractive. This was all still pretense for him, wasn't it? Developing genuine feelings for him would be...

She bit her lip.

No, they both had roles to play today, and that was all. They'd have to garner a positive response from the paesani during the entry, as well as the promise of friendship from the duchessa and the support of the nobiltà tonight at the banquet. She'd see Paladin Grand Cordon Nunzio there and discuss her plans for the library.

It would all go perfectly.

It had to.

Veron went utterly still next to her.

She froze, too. *Holy Mother's mercy*, not dragons again. This time, they would—

"Alessandra," he whispered, and leaned in, tipping his head slowly toward the heart of the forest.

She followed his line of sight, where something so impossibly immaculate hid among the pines. With a coat of pure white, it was a large, four-legged creature not unlike the enormous horse Veron rode, but with a long, flowing snow-white mane and tail, and with a pointed, spiraling horn peaking from its forehead. It bobbed its head, eyeing them with gentle, sable eyes.

Mamma used to read a book of myths to her when she'd been little, and this was—this was a *unicorn*. Gentle creatures devoted to peace and serenity. "We didn't scare it away," she whispered.

"He wants to be seen," Veron answered softly. "We've entered his domain, and he is greeting us. They normally stay hidden, keep to themselves, but something compelled him to emerge."

Greeting them? "How do you know?"

"Noc," he said, keeping his eyes on the unicorn. "He's a fey horse, a being not too different from *him*"—he nodded toward the unicorn—"and Noc has told me many things."

"Told?" she asked, and the unicorn tossed its head and swished its tail.

Veron's horse *told* him things?

He eyed her peripherally, a glimmer in his eyes. "I suppose you haven't been properly introduced. We'll have to remedy that," he said, a corner of his mouth turned up. "But like fey horses, unicorns are descended from the shapeshifting dragons. They once *were* dragons. Dragon Lords have guided other beings, often with a heavy hand, bending them to obedience, controlling them so they wouldn't err.

"But there was a group of pacifists among the dragons who dreamed of a world where every being would be treated like every other, and when at last they voiced their protests to the Dragon King, he cast them out of his kingdom. He took all memory of dragon society, and how to Change into a dragon, and gave them the shape you see. They wished to live peacefully and not to wage war, not to control others, and he made them so."

The Dragon King cast out his people, punished them, simply for disagreeing with him? "What about their dream?" she whispered.

His gaze fixed on the unicorn, he drew his eyebrows together. "One day, you might ask them. Young unicorns must Change with the fullness of the moon and take the form of other lesser beings, but older, stronger ones—if they choose—can Change as they will, even turn other lesser beings, but only the purest of heart. Just like any shapeshifter, if they survive the fever, they become an Immortal." When she gasped, he smiled at her. "But what do you think?"

She watched as the unicorn blinked long lashes at her before snorting quietly and turning to disappear into the forest. He'd trusted them, enough to face away, and that meant a lot. *Thank you. I pray we meet again.* "I think... I think when terrible things happen, it's easier to do nothing. I'm sure they knew the likely costs, but they did a hard thing, a brave thing."

A gentle breeze blew, swept Veron's pale hair as he looked at her, eyelids drawn, a subtle smile playing about his lips.

If this was pretense, then he was the world's best player.

∼

AT THE CITY'S GATES, Veron sat taller astride his horse as Riza presented their documents, provided by King Macario himself. Beyond the gate, distant crowds were already gathering, and massive tapestries hung from buildings lining the main thoroughfare.

He'd already briefed Riza on Alessandra's idea; he had only to give a sign, and everyone in the cavalcade would remove their hoods and masks. For the wedding, he'd gone unmasked... but only in the presence of some of the human nobles. Not out among the general human public. It wasn't the dark-elf way.

He shifted his feet in the stirrups, his boots too tight over the bridge of his foot.

Calm, Noc teased.

The calmest, he mocked in reply.

Noc's tail smacked his back. *Swatting flies.*

Of course, he thought with a grimace.

But for this peace to work, the humans couldn't fear them. Alessandra's idea was smart, and he never would have thought of it himself; had she been a dark-elf, any queen would have been fortunate to have her among her Quorum. He'd trust her in this.

Next to him, she had her shoulders back, her chin raised, a pleasant smile on her lips. Confidence, composure, joy. That was what she projected.

And he—he had to be nonthreatening. *Peace, sincerity, altruism.* An open, relaxed bearing. Making brief but genuine eye contact. Subtle—not fanged—smiles. He and the rest of his entourage would distribute food and coins.

As harmless as that was, every dark-elf would be watchful for Tarquin Belmonte and the Brotherhood. They wouldn't mount an assault in a human city—of that he was certain. The city was surrounded by open plains but for cliffs to the west. No sane commander would lead his troops down those steep cliffs to be picked off by the city's archers.

But there were other options besides full-scale assault.

The city guards opened the gates. Riza's gaze met his, and with a nod, he slowly removed his mask, and then his hood. It was time.

Riza signaled to Danika, and then did the same, and there was a rustling of leathers and wool behind them.

None of the city guards started—one gawked, but only for a moment—so Deep, Darkness, and Holy Ulsinael willing, this would work.

Danika and her unit preceded him and Alessandra, distributing boules and confections to the first families crowding the route. Eyes wide, they looked over him and his people, mouths gaping—but only for a moment before Alessandra waved.

"Terra's blessings upon you!" she called, her voice sweet but carrying far. She'd mentioned the piety of Stroppiata; the Terran shrine here was famous.

"And upon you!" came the shouted replies.

A woman raised a little boy bearing a bouquet of white flowers, and at Gavri's nod, Alessandra accepted them with a smile, handing out gold coins to beaming people.

As she brought the white blooms to her face and inhaled, cheers rose up from the crowd, more densely packed the farther in they rode. Behind the front lines, heads popped up over shoulders, gazes locking on Alessandra's face, her gown, him, his fellow dark-elves. The wide-eyed shock was ephemeral, quickly chased away by grins, laughter, and cheers as he distributed gold coins.

Danika and her unit stayed in formation, gently guiding the crowd back. Tossed flowers graced the path before them, a welcoming carpet leading them toward the castle in the city's northern district.

"Veron," she said, like the softest moss feathering down the back of his neck, like warm breath on his skin, and he faced her.

Her eyes were the dark embrace of home, the bloom of night and beauty of shadow, and when she smiled, his breath caught.

She held out the bouquet, and when he took it, her touch lingered on his hand. "Nothing to fear," she whispered, for him and him alone.

With a nod, he smiled back, but restrained it before his teeth would show. *No teeth. Nonthreatening.*

A little girl with dark curls like Alessandra's squealed her delight, and Alessandra unclasped her pearl bracelet and handed it to Kinga, another of his kuvari, to give away. With a happy little laugh.

No, she wasn't spoiled. Her father had adorned her with luxury, but she didn't seem to hoard these things.

She called out to Gabriella, who removed several books from her horse's pack, and distributed them to older children.

Alessandra's fondness of books—he'd have to note it in *A Modern History of Silen.*

She didn't look like the fiercest dark-elf women, the ones young men dreamed of—equals in battle, ambitious subjects, the strongest among their people. Fiery lovers. But...

Honest, generous, wise, brave, kind... That anyone should find such traits in a partner was a blessing. One he'd never expected. All he'd been allowed to expect had been a marriage Mati deemed beneficial to Nozva Rozkveta. As was proper.

In the forest, Alessandra had been close, her perfume of some sky-realm flower so near he could've almost tasted it. Her fingers had stroked against his hair, a whisper of a touch, and he'd had to fight the desire to lean into it. As his heart had pounded then, there had been something in that dark embrace of her gaze. A curiosity. A question. An invitation...

One he'd been tempted to accept. Very tempted.

But did she feel the same? After her utter terror on their wedding night, he wouldn't push. If he misread her, it would only frighten her more, and trouble her. No, he'd have to confess his feelings to her. And he would. No hiding. No dishonesty.

The final time he'd seen Ata, he'd only been a boy, not even old enough to go hunting alone with his father. *Can't I come, Ata?* he'd asked.

Ata had crouched to eye level, smiled, and patted him on the shoulder. *Not this time, son. But I'll be back before you know it.*

With a beaming grin and a nod, he'd watched Ata walk to his death. To end the war between Nozva Rozkveta and Lumia, Ata had willingly turned himself over, and had saved many dark-elf lives with his sacrifice, but he'd betrayed the love of his own children, of Mati. The stillness Mati had gone through, like living death... all because Ata had betrayed their love when he could have—

Dangerdangerdanger. Noc's fey-horse mind invaded his own.

Shadows cloaked them as they neared an arch, and he could still hear the flap of funeral shrouds, vast and heavy, the beat of each shake—

And gasps, horrified screams—

He blinked, and the flapping came from above, the beat of great, black wings that blotted out the sun.

CHAPTER 10

*E*normous wings spanned fifteen feet wide above them, two dozen harpies with too-wide mouths and razor-sharp talons.

A few swarmed the top of the arch, while the rest dove for the crowds. The humans would be slaughtered. Alessandra would—

"My bow!" Veron leaped off Noc's back and pulled Alessandra from the saddle, wrapping his cloak about her as the crowd dispersed in screams.

"Veron, why are they—"

A harpy swooped low, talons out, and Alessandra screamed. He shielded her. Nothing would harm her. *Nothing.*

Gavri rushed in, drew her bow, and the first harpy wailed as it hit the cobblestones before them.

"Hide anything that shines!" Riza bellowed in Sileni. Someone handed her his bow and a quiver full of arrows, which she tossed to him.

"Shines?" Alessandra shouted, ducking along with Gabriella.

Gavri's unit ringed them while Danika's covered the crowd ahead of them, and he shuffled Alessandra and Gabriella behind him to the narrowest point of the alley as he took aim.

One through the neck. Down on the cobbles.

Another in the eye, and arrows pierced its wings as it fell.

Riza's kuvari cut heads with vjernost blades—the only way to ensure the final death—and the arcanir caught the sunlight. Sharp, screeching cries pierced the air.

He took aim, burying arrows in wings and bodies, but—

Noc bucked, then kicked at a harpy—coins jingling in his saddlebags.

No.

"The coins!" Alessandra called. "If we could just—"

Get them on the street.

"Gavri," he snapped, taking his glove between his teeth and yanking it off. "Cover me!"

As soon as he sprang forward, arrows hissed through the air above him.

"Your Highness!" Riza growled, her vjernost blade meeting talons.

Hold still. He caught Noc's reins, then cut the girth free. The saddle and its bags tumbled to the street as he clapped Noc on the rump, sending him to Gavri and Alessandra.

Blood rained onto his head and neck—a harpy thudded to the cobbles, an arrow in its gaping maw.

He grabbed the bag of coins, opened it, then tossed it to the empty street ahead of them. Gold exploded on the stone in a chaos of clanging and clinks, bright sunlight glinting off hundreds of shining facets.

A dozen harpies descended over the glittering metallic sea.

Over fifty bows angled as one, myriad arrows burying in shrieking targets. Riza gave the kill order, and vjernost blades cut heads from bodies.

Booted footsteps hurried in. Two squads of city guards, whose commander Riza met with a blood-spattered scowl and recounting of the attack.

He wiped the blood off his own face… with a blood-soaked sleeve.

Hooves clopped behind him—Noc neighed his location as Alessandra led him.

She was all right. Thank the Deep, Darkness, and Holy Ulsinael—she was *all right.* At the first sign of the harpies, he thought she'd…

A sigh left him and, with it, the rigidity claiming his body. He took a step forward before she held out a handkerchief.

He paused. What had he been thinking? To throw his arms around her, feel her safe against him, to kiss her? No, he had to tell her how he felt first.

With a murmur of thanks, he took it and swabbed his face, then patted Noc's neck. *Thank you for the warning, old friend.*

Noc only nickered. He always had been a fey horse of few words.

City guards combed the streets, although there seemed to be no human casualties. A couple kuvari nursed wounds, but Riza already had their mystic, Xira, tending them.

The commander of the city guards, wearing a mermaid emblem, approached. A middle-aged man with graying black hair, he bowed low to Alessandra. "Your Highnesses, have you been harmed?"

Still wearing his cloak, Alessandra seemed uninjured. "I'm all right. Veron?"

"The only injuries are two of my kuvari, but you'll have to check with Captain Riza."

The commander's throat bobbed. "Please accept my deepest apologies for the bad luck. Her Grace had us take every precaution."

Every precaution would have included clearing the nearby harpy nest before the Royal Progress, or at least issuing a warning about reflections. But unlike the humans he remembered, these had a lot to learn about Immortals.

And *bad luck* would have meaning that would ripple throughout the human kingdom. That their human gods disfavored the peace, the marriage, *them*.

Alessandra took his hand, then with a deep breath, turned to the commander. "It wasn't bad luck, Captain…?"

"Scianna," the commander supplied. "But I don't understand, Your Highness—"

Alessandra handed Noc's reins to Gabriella, then walked with him back toward the alley he'd led her to, with Captain Scianna following. Gavri waited there attentively, but when he passed her, she lowered her gaze.

She'd fought bravely, capably…

But she couldn't be trusted. The first betrayal had been small, almost harmless, but the next could mean a life, or more. She couldn't be trusted. He turned away.

"Harpies are drawn to shining objects," Aless said, catching his eye for a moment, "like coins. Jewelry. Blades. Anything that might catch the sun, and their eye."

True enough. And she'd clearly been listening. Her idea with the coins had been brilliant. What was she planning now?

She reached the spot where he'd left her during the attack, the narrowest point of the alley, then turned toward the arch. Her finger pointed upward, to the top, where as the clouds cleared, a shine reflected, blinding white and large, toward the cliffs. As they'd approached from the south, they wouldn't have been able to see it. But from her vantage point in the alley, she had.

"I believe that's a mirror, Captain," Alessandra said. "What seems like bad luck was actually sabotage."

∾

ALESS EYED Veron surreptitiously as a squad of city guards escorted them, Gabriella, and his guards into Duchessa Claudia La Via's castle. The duchessa waited in the great hall, where she and Veron would have to earn the duchessa's support and that of her nobiltà. If by the time they left, the nobiltà was all smiles and the duchessa extended a promise of friendship, their objective here would be a success.

But the duchessa had instructed Captain Scianna and her household to lead them inside discreetly to freshen up first.

Which was good... because next to her, Veron's ghostly white hair was a deep, dark crimson, stained with blood, which was smeared all over his pale, slate-blue face and neck, and soaking his leathers. Utterly chilling. Combined with his coiled rigidity and the grim set of his jaw, he looked like a demon warrior, made of wrath and malice, a thirst for blood in his narrowed golden eyes and not a shred of mercy to be found.

Phantom hunter from the Wild Hunt indeed.

The conspirators responsible for the attack weren't worthy of his mercy, and to her mind, deserved every ounce of wrath and malice he had. Even aside from the repugnance of trying to spark a war—that mirror had been left behind—there had been *children* in that crowd. She'd even given a little girl jewelry—which could have drawn the harpies. Thank the Mother none of the children had been harmed.

The attack needed a response.

Out the window, the garden was serene, a colorful geometric knot, but the window reflected her and Veron over its greenery.

Someone had planted the mirror on that arch—likely the Brotherhood. They hadn't openly attacked a human city in their war on the Immortali, but they'd been willing to let one breed of Immortali kill the other, even if humans would have been caught in the middle. Even if *she* had been caught in the middle. So much for Tarquin's promises.

This union had been about securing peace, but safety had gone. She was no longer the palazzo's Beast Princess, deflating oversized egos and raising eyebrows at court. She and Veron were now a symbol—a symbol some would try to use, and others would try to destroy.

Not without a fight.

"Veron," she whispered as they ascended the carpeted stairs behind a chamberlain, and Veron's hold on her hand tightened, ever so slightly, as his narrowed eyes eased, settled on her. Warmth, comfort, the calloused roughness of a grip that had wielded bows and blades. That could protect her.

Somehow, from the streets of Stroppiata to the stairwell of this castle, she'd held his hand the entire time.

And he'd let her.

"Are you all right?" he rumbled, his voice low and his brow furrowed as he looked her over.

"I am. That is, I'd... like to start learning the bow." To start protecting *herself*, and him, and anyone who'd need it. It was past time. Papà had always forbidden it, but Papà wasn't here now.

Veron's mouth curved for just a moment, then he inclined his head. "We'll start tomorrow morning."

Those quiet words, offered freely, with the hint of a smile, warmed her, but that furrowed brow returned. Although he walked alongside her, held her hand, he was still out on the blood-drenched streets, still eye to eye with the harpies, among the screams and fighting.

It's all right, she wanted to say, but... no. It wasn't all right. Not in the least. But she'd find a way to make it so.

Thank the Holy Mother that the dark-elves had had their blades—made of arcanir—which seemed to disrupt certain abilities of the Immortali, and had ended the harpies.

The chamberlain led them to quarters, and the sharp-eyed guard, along with two others, swept the rooms before giving the all-clear. While she and Veron entered, Gabriella excused herself to oversee the delivery of their luggage.

The rooms were opulent—the ducal apartment, no doubt—with fine white silk upholstery, blackwood furnishings, and high ceilings. Veron approached the windows, peering out with a discerning eye. A wary eye.

After what had happened, what could she say to him?

The Brotherhood had risked much, and this wouldn't stop.

Revealing the setup could turn the public against the Brotherhood, but it would also shift national attention from the peace to the rebellion. And with the Immortali openly fighting in human cities, there was too big a risk that the Brotherhood would enjoy vocal support, whether it would deny planting the bait or not.

Publicizing the unrest could be *exactly* what the Brotherhood wanted. The entire purpose of the Royal Progress—spreading the message of peace—would be frustrated. Hushed. The focus would once more return to the *threat* of the Immortali.

But did it *have* to?

"Not without a fight," she murmured.

Veron, his arms crossed, turned to her with a raised brow. She'd start protecting him, herself, and everyone else—for now, with the only methods she knew.

"You think we failed." She moved toward him as servants entered with pails of steaming water for the bath, poured into a tub behind her.

He grunted. "We did fail, whether I think it or not."

"Everything was going well until—"

"The attack. And that's all anyone will remember." His low voice became practically inaudible. He lowered his chin, and his gaze dropped to the floor. His eyes shut, he stood in the window's sunlit radiance, covered in blood and gleaming, terrifying and bright.

As the winged shadows had sailed in overhead, she'd been frozen to her saddle, unable to move, unable to think, staring at gaping mouths with sharp teeth, at frenzied eyes, at razor-like talons. Seeing a vision of flesh torn and blood rain, an unholy feast in the sky above an anguished city. And then she'd been pulled from the saddle, wrapped in sheltering black, and moved to a tight alleyway.

Veron. The low rumble of his voice, the rainwater and fresh earth of his scent. His shielding arms, his dauntless form, his implacable mettle. He hadn't hesitated. Hadn't frozen. Hadn't panicked.

He'd saved her life.

She reached up to him, to where his long hair swept over his shoulder, and she pulled the tie binding his braid, slowly, gently. His eyes opened just a sliver, pale lashes catching the sunshine's luminance, and his breath slowed.

The coppery tang of blood was overpowering, and with his arms crossed, those sharp claws rested on his biceps.

But she pulled that tie down and off. Looped her finger through the weave of his braid, undoing it, unbinding it, freeing it.

He didn't move, simply watched her through those slitted eyes, let her do as she willed.

I'm open to your wishes, he'd told her the night of their wedding. *You shouldn't fear rejection should you express them to me.*

He'd saved her life—and she could kiss him just for that. But when she did, she'd want him to kiss her back. And not just because of his mother's orders, nor because of duty, but because he wanted to. Which at worst was an impossibility, and at best, a challenge.

But challenges were made to be answered.

"Alessandra," he breathed, and she wanted to hear him say her name again, a hundred times, a thousand times. To call her the name she only allowed her loved ones to call her.

"Aless." She smoothed her hand from his hair to his leather-armored chest. "Call me Aless."

"Aless."

The smooth sound was a bare stroke, an intimacy, but she wouldn't close her eyes, wouldn't let herself descend deeper into the moment, read her hopes into his words, that he might see her as something more…

She wasn't more.

She was—how had Papà put it?—*willful, short tempered, sharp mouthed, and presumptuous.* Disobedient.

Everything a man didn't want in a wife…

On their wedding night, Veron had led her to understand that if she wanted more, he'd give it to her. Was that what he was doing? Giving her what she wanted, no matter how *he* felt?

But her fingers pressed against the leather.

He caught her hand, his hold careful, his claws well away from her flesh.

Brushing his thumb over her fingertip, he smudged the bloodstain already on her skin, from the armor. "The blood."

Something thudded behind her, and she glanced over her shoulder. The last of her luggage, including the trunk Lorenzo had given her.

She turned back to Veron.

There was the blood, yes, but even more pressing, the duchessa awaited them. "There's a bath ready," she whispered.

With a deep breath and a nod, he looked past her and back again. "Will it offend you if I...?"

"Not in the least," she replied too quickly. "But if you wish me to leave, I'll—"

"No." He straightened. "Stay."

Before she could reply, he released her and passed her on his way to the tub.

"Lorenzo had me take a few things for you, since we would find ourselves among the nobiltà," she said, among the rustling of leathers and fabric.

"That was generous of him. It was a help at the capital."

Holy Mother's mercy, he was removing his clothes, right behind her, and her heart was in her throat, as if she'd never been around an undressing man before.

So instead she opened the trunk from Lorenzo and removed an assortment of men's couture. "I think the clothes will help bridge our people's differences. Sort of like the flowers."

A soft splash of water, and she was wringing a shirt in her hand. She cleared her throat. "Speaking of the flowers, I don't think we failed today."

"Aless—"

"No one died. None of the attendees were even injured. If anything, we proved that your people can deliver exactly what you promised—help against the other Immortali." She chose black velvet for him, a well-tailored jacket and trousers, without the color and ornamentation that would seem as though they were trying too hard.

He sighed. "It was inauspicious."

"If we leave things as they are, that will be the story." She laid out the clothing on the sprawling bed, to the soft slosh of water behind her. The Beast Princess would have strode before him, undressed, and slipped into the tub before he could remember to close his mouth. The Beast Princess would be bold, daring—

The *Beast Princess* was nowhere to be found.

Instead, here was this quivering, awkward mess, barely able to function in the mere *presence* of this one man. Some smelling salts would do her good.

This attraction—it would go nowhere. All he felt for her was *duty*, and she wouldn't be the pathetic wretch longing for a man who didn't long for her.

She'd meet with Nunzio today, discuss her plan for the library, and no matter how it was done, she needed to live her dream, to help in any way she could. She'd explain it all to Veron. He didn't deserve this mess—he *deserved* the truth, to know her plans, even if it would upset or anger him. A decision had to be made, and soon.

Soon... That is, not right this instant. Tonight they had to sway the Strop-piata nobiltà to support the peace—with both human and dark-elf lives at stake, that had to take priority. But after that...

She heaved a sigh. After that, she'd tell him, and he... he'd understand her desire to cure the ignorance driving this rebellion, and if she helped solidify the peace during this Royal Progress, there would be no need for the second ceremony, for the marriage. With his mother's goal fulfilled, he wouldn't want to marry a human anyway, so he'd be free. He'd understand. He'd—

"That was our one chance," he said quietly. "The schedule has us spending the rest of our visit here with the nobiltà."

"Then the Brotherhood wins. They choose the impression we leave the paesani with, and we make no effort to change it, and appear resigned or, worse, afraid."

A loud splash and rustle of fabric. "What do you propose?"

"That we set the narrative. Let's keep Silen focused on the positive. On *us*." As footsteps approached the bed, she turned away. "We'll ask the duchessa to have her people spread word of your heroism, and your people's, during the *rescue* today. And tomorrow, let's plan an impromptu visit to the Terran shrine. I'll make an offering before the Mother of Stroppiata for a blessed union, and we'll do our best to seem affectionate and unified." It wouldn't be too big of a challenge, at least on *her* end.

"Will that work?" Velvet swished behind her, Veron changing, casting an interplay of sunlight and shadow stretching before her.

"Stroppiata is Silen's most pious city. It will be seen as an act of respect." They had the advantage of the public eye; while the Brotherhood hid and slinked in the shadows, she and Veron could use their visibility to win the public's favor, if they proceeded wisely. If they won that, the Brotherhood's cause would fail.

A brief silence.

She glanced over her shoulder as he buttoned a shirt beneath the open black jacket, over a sculpted, hard body, blue-gray like Carrerra marble from the North. Dreaming Sileni artists had built gods and heroes, powerful ideals of myth and legend, with such form. And he stood before her now, real and breathing and beautiful and strong, the godly and the heroic driving him in his earthly deeds. Layers of rumor and presumption and mystery that had hidden him before now swept away like dust, and he'd been here, beneath it all, this entire time.

"I'm glad it was you, Aless."

Her heart skipped a beat. Blinking, she fixed her gaze upon the parquet floor.

"Glad it was me?" she whispered, daring to meet his eyes as he now fastened the jacket's golden toggles. Holy Mother's mercy. Seeing him only confirmed her misplaced attraction.

But he'd said he was *glad*. Maybe it wasn't misplaced?

Holding her gaze, he abandoned the toggles midway and took a step closer.

Her heart pounded. Had he noticed her awkwardness? Was he teasing her? She swallowed.

He carefully took her hand, her shaking hand, and raised it to his chest, pressed it there, over his heart. "When I arrived in Bellanzole, I'm glad it was you."

Her eyes widened, but he didn't waver, just held her hand there against the pulse beating in his chest. His golden eyes, soft and warm, held her speechless, breathless, and his hair, clean and damp, begged for her touch. The toggles on his jacket, halfway done—she couldn't decide whether she wanted to finish fastening them, or—

"Am I alone in this, Aless?"

He blinked, and for a moment, she couldn't breathe. She shook her head slowly. No, he hadn't misread her. He wasn't alone in... "I think there may be something here that—"

A soft rapping on wood came from the hall.

Veron's mouth curved as he searched her eyes. "It's time to meet the duchess."

It was time, and their discussion had been cut short, but it didn't matter —he *knew*.

He knew, and he felt the same.

CHAPTER 11

$\mathcal{A}$ corner of Veron's mouth turned up as he escorted Aless to the great hall, following a footman. By Deep and Darkness, he could scarcely stop himself from smiling.

Aless spoke not a word of Elvish. Didn't worship Holy Ulsinael. No combat prowess whatsoever. Couldn't hunt, nor even pitch a tent reliably.

But she was devoted to peace, generous with her things, loved her sister fiercely. She was determined, a strategic thinker, passionate about knowledge, and eager to learn new things. Charismatic and inspiring. Above all, honest. The more he learned about her, the more he liked her—something he hadn't expected in this arrangement.

Next to him, she practically glowed, darkly gleaming ringlets cascading over her shoulders, drawing his gaze down to the neckline of her silver-trimmed purple gown, plunging just past the curve of her breasts.

He shouldn't look, but—

Human fashion had certainly changed in two thousand years. Drastically, *gloriously* changed. Just like the sheer red thing she'd worn on their wedding night. A sheer red thing that now lingered in his thoughts.

With a sharp breath, he looked away.

The softest of giggles came from her, quickly stifled. "Something the matter?"

Quite the opposite. "Just an uncommon sight."

"Breasts?" she teased.

He cleared his throat. "The *dress*."

Her dark eyes gleamed as she blinked, long black lashes fluttering. How had he not noticed her strange beauty? She had dark hair, dark eyes, olive skin—outlandish among his people. No fangs, no claws, a soft—*too* soft—body. She was *human*. So different from dark-elf women, from the most beautiful of them, but...

It didn't make her ugly. No... Among a sea of stars, she was the moon. It was as though he hadn't looked up until now.

Those dark eyes weren't the amber of his people, but how they gleamed as her mind worked, sparked when she had an idea, softened when she looked at him, held mystery like the holy Darkness. And her hair wasn't white, but its shade was like the Deep, mystical and mesmerizing, and contrasting with the olive tone of her skin.

Her skin—sometimes when he looked at her, it pinked, turned such a delicate shade of rose on her cheeks, and she didn't have to speak her thoughts when they were so clear on her face. No shades of blue and purple and gray, but pinks. Like the Bloom protecting Nozva Rozkveta. The more he looked at her, the more she reminded him of home.

Her arm, looped around his, curled closer as she stroked his bicep softly. He carefully covered her hand with his as two men opened the tall double doors, and a third announced them.

"His Highness, Prince Veron of Nightbloom, and Her Highness, Princess Alessandra of Nightbloom."

The low din of conversation in the great hall quieted as he led in Aless, the crowd parting and every face turning to them. Wide eyes blinking, manicured eyebrows rising, painted lips parting. A spectrum of colors swathed the hall, where on the other end, a woman sat in a throne-like chair behind a massive head table. Dressed in a golden gown, she had a little emerald adhered high on her cheek, and blond hair pinned elaborately with a peacock feather adorning it.

This woman would have clad herself in all the wealth of Nozva Rozkveta's mines, and yet her smile seemed entirely genuine. The duchess. It was the promise of *her* friendship that they'd have to earn here tonight.

Beaming brightly, she stood and began a slow but confident clap, which the rest of the assembled guests joined.

"Prince Veron and Princess Alessandra," the duchess said with a ringing pleasantness. "You are most welcome. I thank you both for your bravery in defending my people." She curtseyed gracefully, and a ripple of bows and curtseys followed.

"We are honored, Your Grace," he replied, inclining his head with Aless as befitted their station.

"To the happy couple." The duchess raised a goblet of wine, as did everyone, except for a tall, large man near the duchess, who raised a glass of water and nodded to Aless, tattoos peeking out from under his sleeve.

Aless smiled warmly, inclined her head, and then tightened her hold on his arm. Someone she knew, then.

The duchess motioned to the musicians, who struck up a winding tune, and the hall's conversations resumed as she approached them.

It was already a far warmer reception than he'd expected.

A troupe of vividly dressed dancers filed in, claiming the hall's center in an elaborate routine of swinging hips and fluttering silk.

At any dark-elf queendom, now would be when the traditional games would begin, light sparring testing one another's prowess. There was honor in challenging formidable opponents, in accepting, in winning, and even in losing, but above all, it was *fun*, and sometimes—as in the case of the humans' dances—a courtship.

"Some entertainment to celebrate your visit and your union." The duchess's green eyes twinkled. "There will be dinner, dancing, fireworks in the garden, and then a private party in my salon until the sun rises."

"The promise of the famous Duchessa Stroppiata's parties does not disappoint," Aless said as a young man brought them two goblets of wine. She must have spent a lot of time partying in the royal court. Vibrant, energetic, curious, witty—she had no doubt shone brightly.

"I am an admirer of all things beautiful," the duchess said, looking him over with a slow smile. "It is not every day that I have the unique privilege of hosting dark-elf royalty. Hopefully not the last."

He could have laughed. Such attention wasn't unusual among dark-elf women, but he hadn't expected it here. "The privilege is all ours."

The duchess held his gaze, a smile on her lips. What would it take to win her promise of friendship?

Flames shot high above them—a pair of fire-breathers weaving through the crowd.

Aless started, her eyes wide. Perhaps she hadn't quite recovered from the harpies.

The duchess laughed heartily. "Do you like them? I invited them from Zehar. They're quite talented."

"They are," he said to the duchess as he stroked Aless's hand gently. "Your gardens, too, were beautiful from the window."

The duchess swept a jewel-encrusted hand toward the doors to the courtyard. "Allow me to show them to you properly."

He followed her, and Aless swallowed next to him and flashed a fleeting smile, holding his arm close. Did the harpy attack still affect her? Some air might do her good.

The silence was not like her at all. He'd become accustomed to battle, but that had been a lifetime of training with the kuvari and fighting alongside them, many of whom had made it into Mati's Quorum. Aless, however, had been kept from all training and fighting, and today's events had to have shaken her.

Footmen opened the glass-paned doors out to a colonnade. Beyond its arches, a scrolling pattern of hedges and flowers stretched far, lined by a border of trees, their dark-green foliage silvered by the stars. At its end lay a shimmering pool, steps cascading into its placid waters.

"My mother loved all things green," the duchess said, leading them on the paths among perfect hedges, and she nodded to the abundant purple flowers. "Lavender was her favorite. When I married the duke, he was twenty-six years my senior, and we had nothing in common. I spent my time here, with the gardeners, planning this—my sanctuary. Even now that he's gone, this garden is still where I find solace."

By her face, she was still young, in her early thirties perhaps. The way her eyebrows creased together spoke volumes of her late husband, none of it good.

"It's beautiful," Aless whispered, releasing him as she curled over the lavender and inhaled, closing her eyes. She held still for a moment—one he wished to commit to memory.

The duchess watched her, that crease fading, and joined her. Her hands clasped, she cleared her throat. "I won't mince words. Someone had the audacity to plan an attack in my city. That alone would have spurred me to side with the enemy of my enemy. But your heroism today, when you could have fled, makes me proud to offer you my friendship."

She placed her right hand over her heart and bowed to them both gracefully. "Should you ever require assistance, you have but to ask."

"Thank you, Your Grace," Aless whispered, as he inclined his head.

The duchess searched Aless's eyes, then glanced at him. "Enjoy the garden. Join me at your leisure for the feast."

With that, she nodded to them, gold dress trailing past them as she strolled back to the hall.

As soon as the door shut, quiet settled in once more, only the muffled tune and voices from the hall, along with the trilling of insects and the occasional bird call playing the music of the night.

"My mother had a library. That was where she found solace," Aless said softly, her eyes still closed. "I spent so much of my childhood there, with the scent of leather, paper, candle wax. Sometimes just opening a book will take me right back there."

A special place to her.

"I'd like to see it someday," he said.

Aless's eyes fluttered open, and she gave him a watery, sad smile as she straightened. "Papà had it destroyed."

"Destroyed?" He shook his head.

Aless stroked gentle fingers over the hedges, meandering the path for a few steps.

"Tell me," he said to her, and she looked over her shoulder with a half-smile, her gaze dropping, then shrugged half-heartedly. A fragrant night breeze swept through the trees' canopy, curling the flowers to its direction, and she shivered as her dark ringlets swayed.

Undoing the toggles on his jacket, he approached her, then took it off and settled it about her shoulders. She covered his hand with hers, holding it there a long moment, and he pulled her to him, slowly walking the path.

"My mother adored books," she said with an ephemeral smile. "They lined the hall to her heart, you see. My father built her a library and proposed to her there. She filled it with stories and ideas from around the world, from all time periods and cultures.

"She wanted to share that joy and knowledge with the world," she said, her voice breaking as her eyes teared up, shining in the lambent starlight. "Every week, she and her ladies-in-waiting would read to the local children in Bellanzole, and then teach anyone who wanted to learn. Many women learned, and they took new jobs and traveled, bettered their lives. A few years ago, a man came, saying he wanted to learn, but while she was teaching him, he blamed her for his wife leaving him... He had a knife... She died before anyone could do anything."

He held her closer, and she stopped, rested her head against his chest. Humankind had changed, in every way but the ones that mattered.

"Papà banned her ladies from returning to read or teach," she whispered, muffled against his shirt. "He destroyed every book in her library, and the place itself, blaming it for her death. I cried and begged him not to, but he had the Royal Guard restrain me while it was done. My copy of *A Modern History of Silen* was the last book she gave me."

Tucked into his embrace, she went utterly quiet, leaning into him, brushing his chest with her cheek, so small and slight. Not the woman who'd ridden at his side with her head held high, regal and formidable, indomitable.

Those were walls she'd taken down for this, for him, allowing him to see the little child inside whose father had destroyed not just a library but the precious memory of her mother. That loss still had to hurt, and so did her own father's coldness to her in doing what he'd done.

He shielded her from the breeze, his shoulders taut. He wanted to meet that coldness with warmth, that loss with comfort, destruction with creation. Nothing would harm her like that again, not while he drew breath.

Against a field of lavender, she gazed up at him, her face tear streaked, and he brushed the wetness from her cheek with a thumb, and leaned in. She raised her chin, and his lips met hers, so soft, her skin the smell of salt and summer flowers as she relaxed in his arms. Her palms glided up his back, her fingers pressing, no prick of claws, just her touch, her wanting.

She leaned into him, opening her mouth to his, the sweet bloom of a dark red wine on her exploring tongue, slow, sensual. Her breaths warmed his mouth as they fell into rhythm, longing, urging, and by Deep and Darkness, it was all he could do to cup her face, deepen his kiss, meet her tongue's sensual taking with his own.

The muffled music from the hall stopped, and he pulled away just enough to watch her open her eyes and lick her lip, then smile as her cheeks flushed. He took her hand in his.

"I'm glad it was you, Aless," he whispered as she held his gaze, "because I've fallen in love with you."

She beamed, the smile reaching her eyes, but it began to fade. "Veron, I…"

He shook his head. "You don't have to answer yet. Take your time."

Her eyes brightened, and she nodded. "I will. But, Veron…"

Little lights blinked into existence around them, glowing all around them. Pixies.

She gasped. "There are… There…"

"Pixies," he said softly, savoring the wonder illuminating her face. "Little winged people, no taller than your thumb. They love gardens, and live in the healthiest of them, thriving on nectar and pollen."

Her lips parted, she very slowly reached up toward a tiny glow, and the pixie flitted closer to her hand, just out of reach, casting a gentle light on her skin.

"They feel a kinship toward those who love gardens as they do, will even fight to save them."

"So little," she whispered, her eyes wide.

"No one is ever too little to fight for what they believe in."

She turned back to him then in his embrace, beaming a smile, her eyes shining, reflecting the ethereal glow in the starlit night.

His breath caught. He loved Alessandra Ermacora. Through and through. He loved his wife and would do anything for her sake. And he knew it as clearly as the stars shone above them.

She lowered her gaze, her smile fading. "Veron, about the ceremony in Nightbloom…"

He raised her hand to his lips and pressed a soft kiss to it. "We'll discuss it after the party." Whatever she feared about the ceremony, he'd allay. It was different from human celebrations, but he'd prepare her. "Will that be all right? I think we're due for the feast."

"If you keep the duchessa entertained, I think it'll go very well." A brief glimmer in her amused eyes, and she nodded, turning to the hall with him.

So she hadn't missed the duchess's look. Of course she hadn't. And she wanted to use it to their advantage. He wouldn't expect any less.

And it would go perfectly.

His bride was human, he loved her, and she now knew it. Nothing could ruin this night.

CHAPTER 12

*A*less tried to slow her racing heartbeat to no avail as they entered the great hall, each step echoing in the vastness. It was as though she could feel every hair on her head, and every swish of fabric against her skin, every individual thread. Where Veron's hand held hers, the barest touch, the merest stroke of his skin against hers tingled, warmed.

Holy Mother's mercy, she *loved* him. She *loved* him, and she was about to meet with Paladin Grand Cordon Nunzio.

She wanted to hide, go back to that moment outside and tuck her face against Veron's chest, shut out the world, shut out everything but him, and live there, in that moment, forever.

Nunzio probably wouldn't even agree to her proposal about the library and teaching there. The Order of Terra didn't want women so involved anyway, did they? It had been everything she'd wanted, and she'd been willing to try convincing Veron that they didn't need that second ceremony in Nightbloom, that they'd be better as friends, but...

But she wanted him. Veron *and* her dream.

Say a prayer for me this time, Bianca.

Holy Mother's mercy, if her dream had already been higher than she could probably reach, trying to take both would mean she'd need a taller ladder. A *much* taller ladder.

She'd just have to make one.

Maybe she could talk to Veron, and they could stay together *and* find a way to make the library happen together near Nightbloom? Maybe he'd be passionate about this, too.

And Veron... when she'd tell him tonight what her plan had been, he'd forgive her, wouldn't he? She'd planned all this before she'd truly known him, before she'd fallen in love with him.

There had to be a way for her love and her dream to coexist. She would just have to find it.

Against a backdrop of myriad mirrors, the duchessa sat at the head of a long configuration of elaborate place settings, with two empty seats at her side. For *them*.

Her reflection caught in one mirror—a betrayer, a *liar*—and it reflected in the next angled against it, and the next, and the next, and the next, a crowd of betrayers, of—

"Are you all right?" Veron whispered to her as they approached.

Can we please just leave? Can we disappear into our quarters, into each other, and never emerge?

But even as the thought surfaced, it was impossible. They had the duchessa's friendship, but they couldn't abandon her party and her nobiltà without consequence. It was a victory lap, but a necessary one. She glared at her reflection.

As long as Nunzio didn't approach her about the library while she was here with Veron, she could keep the situation from spiraling out of control.

She cleared her throat and forced a placid expression. "I'll be fine."

With a warm smile, he led her to the table, seated her, and then himself between her and the duchessa, who had taken an obvious interest in him earlier. That would work to their advantage. He could describe Nightbloom to her, his culture, his people, and as long as the duchessa's curiosity held, the nobiltà would take her cue and support them as well.

A servant between them poured some bubbly white wine, and she tasted it.

"Princess Alessandra," a man's deep, gravelly voice greeted from her other side. "I received the plans you sent for your library."

She froze. *Holy Mother's mercy.*

No, not him. Please, not him.

As she caught the man with a peripheral glance, his eagle-sharp blue eyes met hers. That aquiline nose, full head of graying hair, cleft chin, and a build like Forza's, wrapped in sigil tattoos.

Nunzio.

She swallowed the wine already in her mouth. "Paladin Grand Cordon," she greeted, cordially but softly.

Slitting those eagle eyes, he leaned back in his chair, his gaze raking over her as if she were some ruffian he'd taken in for questioning. "Your proposal was quite... *passionate*."

For a moment, she paused, listening to Veron telling the duchessa about his brother in Nightbloom. As long as Nunzio kept his voice down, this night wouldn't turn into a disaster.

"Maybe we could discuss this another time," she said softly. They could find a way to move forward on the project. Somehow. Maybe the Order would agree to help build the library elsewhere, closer to Nightbloom?

"Are you no longer passionate about literacy and cultural exchange?" Nunzio tilted his head. "Of building peace through shared knowledge and education? Those were your words."

Keep your voice down.

"Of course I am," she whispered, then sipped her wine. The rest of the nobiltà were deep in their own conversations. Thank the Mother for small favors.

Nunzio leaned in. "Then give me a name, any name, of a person who can manage the implementation of your plan," he said, "because I cannot in good faith meddle in this country's political agreements. How did you mean to both oversee the construction and management of a library while marrying and residing in Nightbloom?"

Each word elicited a shiver, even as she struggled to stay still. There was a lull in the conversation next to her, and she dared to look at Veron.

His eyes were wide beneath furrowed brows. He gave a slow, disbelieving head shake.

He'd heard it.

He'd heard it all.

No, no, no, no... She opened her mouth, but he raised his chin, went still—unnaturally still, the wideness of his eyes narrowing to icy, metallic gold.

Coldness.

With a deep breath, he was smiling again as he turned to the duchessa and said something about stone-singing.

What was—?

He—

Her chest tightened as Veron chatted with the duchessa, his steely velvet voice smooth with charm, his quiet laugh lofty.

She'd disappointed him, completely and utterly, and he had bottled it, continued trying to keep the duchessa and her nobiltà entertained. Inside, he had to feel...

"Princess?" Nunzio asked, and he continued speaking, but the sound of his voice faded as a high-pitched ringing found its way to her ear, grew louder and louder until she could hear nothing else.

Her gaze dropped to her lap, to her hands on the violet tulle of her gown, hands that had held Veron's not even an hour ago.

ALESS STOOD WHEN VERON DID, and although he guided her from the hall with a gentle hand at the small of her back, there was nothing gentle about his expression.

He bid the duchessa goodnight with an elegant smile and inclination of his head, called good-natured goodbyes to certain members of the nobiltà he'd chatted with. But beneath that charm was that cold gaze, the chilled gold of his eyes, and the look he'd given her at the table.

The night had been a blur. It still was. She'd eaten tonight and drunk, she supposed, and maybe even danced. Probably with him. But it was just a mess of colors and murmurs and laughs, and then a walk to an empty corridor.

She'd betrayed him. Before they'd ever met, she'd already been resolved to go back on her word.

No matter how badly she wanted to see Mamma's dreams realized, she'd sacrificed Veron's trust to pursue them. Now he knew. And hated her.

"I'm sorry," she said, as he walked her up the stairs, past the windows to the gardens where her life had changed. "I wanted to tell you tonight, but then the Paladin Grand Cordon was there first, and he had questions, and…"

And Veron didn't even look at her. Didn't waver from ascending the steps. Didn't seem to have heard her at all.

"Veron, please," she pleaded, gripping his arm tightly, but he didn't react.

She squeezed her eyes shut as they reached their quarters, where the sharp-eyed guard stood sentinel, along with another. Veron greeted them, and even those brief words were like balm to her wounds.

Inside, he closed the door and released her, then took off his jacket as he headed to the starlit window, where earlier today she'd seen the beauty of him, terrifying and enchanting. In his love, he could be gentle, shimmering in the sunshine of quiet moments. In his malice, he could be terrible, drenched in the blood of their enemies. And she wanted him. All of him.

And he'd brought her into a new world, his world, full of beauty and magic, and had shared it with her. She wanted to live in that world of beauty and magic *with* him. As his love, his wife, his partner.

She had to try to fix this. She *had* to. "Veron—"

"I only had one expectation." His voice was low, cold, lifeless.

She took a step forward. "Please, I—"

"Do you remember, Alessandra?"

Trust is the one expectation I have, he had told her, on their wedding night.

She wrapped her arms around herself. "Trust."

"And all this time, you had this… plan." He clasped his hands behind his back. "All this… nearness. Affection. Was it all just so I wouldn't suspect?"

"Of course not," she replied quickly, rushing up to him. She reached out to touch his arm, but he didn't budge an inch.

Swallowing, she stared out the window at the darkness, letting the silence settle.

A sprawling courtyard of tangled rose vines lay below, bathed in starlight, shimmering—

Ripped away.

She shook her head.

No, a dream.

Below lay the knot of hedges in the night, rows of lavender, the rectangular pool. She took a deep breath. "I didn't expect we'd fall in love, Veron. I thought we'd always have an aversion to each other, but that we could become friends. Inspire peace through friendship. That you could be free to do as you wished, and I could see to the library, teach our people, keep fostering this peace—"

"This *peace* is built on the concept that a human and a dark-elf could bind themselves to one another even in marriage," he replied. "Even if only in semblance."

"I know that."

He turned on her. "And you thought separating would be conducive to that? I expected better from you, Alessandra."

"No, it would only mean that we still want to be friends but are on different paths—"

"That the symbol the peace is built on, our marriage, can't work. We'd be setting an example that would take root in every heart across the nation. We'd be doing the Brotherhood's work for them."

She reached out for him, but he avoided her grasp. "But our parents *forced*—"

"The two of us were sacrificed for an entire realm of peace," he said, his voice low. With a hand to his forehead, he sighed. "The worst part of it all is that I would have understood. If you'd just told me in Bellanzole that you wanted to be released, I would have understood."

"I don't *want* to be released."

He stared at her coldly. "I have orders. Even if you wanted me to, I couldn't. Even if I do understand."

He's the one who wishes he could release me. She exhaled sharply. "So that's it? One misstep, and you hate me forever?"

"I don't hate you, Alessandra, but I can't love someone I can't trust."

"I made that decision before I ever knew you, Veron. You didn't deserve to be betrayed, but did I deserve to be married off against my will? Traded like some pawn? Was that to be the sum of my worth?"

He squeezed his eyes shut, then ran a hand up over his face and back over his hair. "I can't blame you for that. But the lying? Trust means everything to me. We could have come to an arrangement. But if this had come out some other way, had…" With a shake of his head, he strode to the bedchamber, and she followed. "You don't even see it, do you?"

What was he talking about? "See what?"

He plucked a pillow off the bed and a folded blanket off the chest at the foot of the bed. "Alessandra, tell me where Gabriella comes from."

What was he getting at? "She's my lady-in-waiting. She's from… the royal court."

He marched right back to the parlor, tossed the pillow and blanket on the sofa, then began removing his boots with a grimace. "Her *home*." The sofa cushion dipped under his weight. "Where is she from?"

She shook her head.

"Gabriella takes care of your entire life. Where is she from? Does she have any siblings? What's important to her?"

"I—I don't know."

He rested his elbows on his knees and leaned forward, his cold gaze boring into her. "You've never asked, have you?"

No… she hadn't. She should've, but… but…

She lowered her chin, scrutinizing the crimson and sable rug, its fringe, broken in places.

"You don't even really know her. And she lives for you, Alessandra. But this—your plan to refuse the second ceremony—would have rippled and caused destruction for so many, those who live outside the tunnel of what you choose to see. Your father might have seen this as reneging, might have pulled the aid he'd given us, and do you have any idea what a baby's starving cry sounds like?"

A chill wove through her. She… She hadn't considered that.

Without the marriage, would Papà have trusted the dark-elves enough and keep sending them aid? Or would he have looked for an ally elsewhere?

And while Veron had mentioned how much people were looking forward to the aid from Bellanzole, she hadn't realized that people were… really starving. That babies were…

Those golden eyes speared her own a moment longer. "I don't blame you for fearing what this marriage would be. Nor even for not wanting it. But did it ever occur to you that, for the good of both our peoples, we might discuss alternate arrangements? That maybe I didn't feel too differently than you did? Was planning to betray me, to run away without a care for the treaty, really the best course of action? Or just the easiest?"

He looked away with a sigh and stretched out on the sofa, arm tucked behind his head.

Wringing her tulle skirts, she waited, but he wouldn't look at her. He'd said he didn't blame her, but that wasn't what this felt like. Their people expected so little from one another, and maybe he'd expected little from her, too. And despite a couple brief, glowing moments, she'd fulfilled those low expectations... instead of defying them.

They'd spent every night since Bellanzole together.

Not tonight.

She left for the bedchamber, where she shed all of her clothes, hairpins, and washed her face, donned her nightgown, found her old copy of *A Modern History of Silen*, and nestled into the bed, cocooned herself in the bedding. Such a wonderful night had been destroyed, and it was all her fault.

Veron was angry about the lie, but even more so about the betrayal.

Cradling the book close, she opened to the first page, traced her finger across Mamma's script. *Be brave, my rose, and fill the remaining pages with your deeds.*

As a child, she'd written in minor things. Things most people would deem trivial. Saving a cat from cruel children. Making a statement. Winning an argument.

Over the years, she'd set her sights higher. So high, the view blurred the sight of individual people, the ones she wanted to save, and even the ones around her. She'd worked so hard for peace, for realizing Mamma's vision, that she'd lost the instinct to see those around her.

She saw Veron now, or was beginning to. She'd see Gabriella. The dark-elf guards with them. And the people she intended to save. She wouldn't be anyone's pawn, but in her pursuit of Mamma's vision, she wouldn't sacrifice the lives of others by destroying the peace. Not the Sileni, not the dark-elves, not even the Brotherhood if it could be avoided. Enough lives had been lost.

And Veron might have given up on her, but she... she wouldn't give up on him. He was right about her not thinking through the consequences for his people, and even her own. He was right that she shouldn't have lied.

But not being able to love her after this? When it came to that, he was dead wrong. And she would prove it to him.

Tomorrow he'd begin to see just how stubborn a so-called Beast Princess could be.

CHAPTER 13

*B*efore Veron could properly open his eyes, there were already sounds coming from the bedchamber. Quick footsteps, the slosh of water, rustling fabric, and creaking hinges.

The sun hadn't even risen yet, and she was already up. He shook his head. The sun had to be mistaken.

He was on his feet and stretching when Aless walked in, wearing a form-fitting but utilitarian purple dress and holding the Offering bow. With a raise of her eyebrows, she met his gaze.

"I'm ready for an archery lesson, if you're going to the range." She sat in an armchair while he began his morning routine.

He nodded an acknowledgement, then washed up. All this time, from the moment he'd met her in Bellanzole until last night, she'd been lying to him. There had been moments when she'd wanted to confess—on their wedding night, and in the garden, at the very least. But she hadn't, in all this time.

He wanted to trust her, but if she was prone to hiding things, could she be expected to change now, for the rest of her life?

But they were still married. He still loved her.

And in the garden, there had been no lie in her kiss, in her embrace. The touch of her hand had borne no deception in its warmth. And the tears in her eyes hadn't welled with betrayal.

She did love him, too. She would have told him the truth eventually, but that wasn't trustworthiness.

Where did that leave them?

He dressed, eyeing his own bow in the corner. Even if he and Aless didn't see eye to eye right now, he *had* promised to train her, and he wouldn't go back on his word. But he couldn't forget last night either.

He grabbed his bow and headed through the parlor and out in the hall. Her light footsteps fell in behind him, along with Riza's and Danika's.

Some of the kuvari were already in the training yard, practicing with their vjernost blades, and the duchess's men were somewhere between sparring and gawking. Seeing the kuvari in combat—honed for decades or centuries— was a thing of wonder, mesmerizing and deadly. One of them in Mati's Quorum, his sister Vadiha included, would someday take Mati's place. Their skills had to be impeccable.

At the range, Gavri was already shooting, and moved to retrieve her arrows—clustered in the center, per usual—before her gaze snapped to his direction. She bowed, removed her arrows, and quit the yard.

Staying out of his sight, as he'd ordered.

He swallowed over a pain at the back of his throat.

With a tilted head, Aless eyed him, but he only took her bow and strung it for her. He didn't need to talk, not about this.

In the sword ring, one of the kuvari disarmed another, and whoops rose up from the Sileni guards clustered around them. He nodded to the victrix— Lira, who smiled knowingly. Only Mati and Riza could take her when it came to swords, and she well knew it.

After he gathered some supplies, he met Aless fifteen yards from a target, where she crouched, plucking clover. He pointed his chin downrange. "You said you've done this before."

She grimaced. "Poorly."

"Show me." He took a step back and crossed his arms.

She held out a partially braided clover chain until he reluctantly took it. Then, with a heavy sigh, she faced the target, nocked an arrow with her shoulders high, aimed, then closed her eyes as she released. The arrow landed on the ground five feet away.

She winced at him.

Poorly had been right. "Give it another try."

She puffed. "Veron, I…"

He only fixed her with a stare. No one was perfect without practice.

With an even heavier sigh, she turned back to the target again, but this time, he grabbed her shoulders—eliciting a gasp, but no objection—and turned her to stand at a right angle to the target. Using his foot, he tapped her feet shoulder-width apart.

Her shoulders were tight as a bowstring.

"Relax," he told her, patting her shoulders gently, and she smelled like… like—he frowned—like the lavender last night, and it soothed, made him want to close his eyes, breathe slow and deep.

With a nod to herself, she nocked another arrow, and he readjusted it under the nocking point on the string. As she extended her bow arm, he pressed her shoulders down.

"You're at full draw. Transfer the weight of the bow from your arms to your back. Now aim." As she did, he added, "See the string line up on the top bow limb a little to the right of the sight ring. Now pull your shoulder blades closer to each other as you relax your right hand's fingers, and keep aiming. Your relaxed left hand will let your bow drop a bit. Let it. And don't move until the arrow hits the target."

She released, eyes open, and the arrow missed just shy of target.

Her eyebrows drew together, but then she glanced up at him, lips parted, purple dress battered by the wind. Like the lavender last night, when they'd...

Just a blink, a flutter of dark lashes, and he was in the garden again, his shoulders tensing as he wanted to wrap her in his arms, shield her from the wind, feel those soft lips against his once more...

He cleared his throat. "Not bad. Keep practicing."

Before she could reply, he headed for a target of his own, far from hers.

BEFORE A MIRROR, Aless rubbed her shoulder as Gabriella put the finishing touches on her hairstyle. She shifted in the chair, rubbing against smooth mahogany armrests, and flinching. Both of her shoulders hurt, and her arms, and her fingers... but she and Veron still had to make an offering at Stroppiata's shrine before they left the city. Although she felt like a mess of soreness and fatigue, she'd have to be perfect. Ideal.

Or at least *look* it.

Veron had kept his word and given her an archery lesson today. If she'd been a better person, she would have released him from the promise. Let him keep his distance. Let him forget all about her. Not worn the lavender dress. Not used the lavender perfume. Not seized the opportunity to get close, as she'd once seen another courtier do.

But she *wasn't* better. His touch, even through his mask of coolness, had been like a comforting whisper, telling her all hope wasn't lost. Maybe it wasn't. But whatever his feelings for her became, she'd heard him clearly last night: she hadn't examined too closely the things and people she hadn't wanted to see.

She would today.

And for their sakes, she wouldn't disrupt the peace in any way, even if Veron hated her for the length of their marriage. There had to be another way to realize her dream, one that didn't involve abandoning the marriage—and she'd find it.

"Well, what do you think?" Gabriella asked, smiling in the mirror as she evaluated the elaborate hairstyle, with warm hazel eyes.

The princess in the mirror didn't look like a cold-hearted liar or betrayer. She had shining hair, half of it up in soft twists with pearl pins, with the rest flowing voluminously in gentle brown waves. A delicate pink stained her lips, and the daintiest blush enlivened her cheeks.

Gabriella had suggested a yellow taffeta dress with gold-threaded embroidery, and it was bright and happy, with long, flowing sleeves that softened the look even more. The color of the sun, of the Goddess's bounty each harvest. Fitting.

"You've outdone yourself," Aless whispered as Gabriella laughed and fastened a strand of pearls.

"Today is important, so you have to look the part." Gabriella adjusted the pearls, keeping the closure at the nape of Aless's neck.

So much effort. "I thought you didn't like the dark-elves?"

Gabriella's hand rose to her chest. "I don't think anything of them—I—"

"Just with the talk of the Brotherhood, it seemed—"

"I only thought you wanted out of the marriage. That day we left the palazzo, you looked so... so..." Gabriella's round face sank in the mirror. "I just want you to be happy."

In the years she'd known Gabriella, there hadn't been a hateful bone in her body. Maybe there still wasn't. "Well, today I look it, thanks to you."

With an uneasy smile, Gabriella took a step back, clasped her hands, and gave a pleased nod in the mirror. Gabriella's dress was a plain but well-tailored mauve satin overgown with a white cambric kirtle beneath, feminine and cut fashionably. Always taking great care in her appearance.

"Have I ever asked you where you're from?" Aless whispered, meeting Gabriella's eyes in the mirror.

Those beautifully shaped eyebrows shot up. "Vistadelfino. Our fathers grew up together, and His Majesty made him the conte there. My mother was one of Her Majesty's ladies before..." Gabriella lowered her gaze and breathed deeply.

One of Mamma's ladies... before she was murdered.

"I became your lady shortly after..." Gabriella swallowed. "And you never asked me, but... you hardly spoke then."

After Mamma's death, all she'd done was read. About ancient wars, myths, and world-spanning romances. About women who fought, women who ruled, women who married for love. About mothers and daughters being strong together, and idealistic heroes bettering people's lives. About anything and everything that could take her from the misery of her own life then. Gabriella had been there with her, side by side, and had never pried or pushed. Just accompanied her when she'd most needed someone.

"Thank you," she whispered, and Gabriella raised a hand, shaking her head. "No, really. Mamma's been gone a long time, and I should have gotten to know you better—"

Arms closed around her, and she gasped, blinking, wrapping her own arm around Gabriella.

"Your Highness, it is *my* duty to take care of you, not the other way around."

"I'd like for us to take care of each other. You've been my friend for as long as I can remember, and I... I want to be your friend, too." She breathed in the gentle lilac of Gabriella's long, sable hair. "I want to know what's important to you."

Gabriella pulled back, beaming. "We're more alike in that than you think, Your Highness." She half-laughed under her breath. "My mother loved books and teaching with Her Majesty, helping the poor in Bellanzole. And when His Majesty forbade it... it broke her heart. She wants to see us doing that again. And so do I."

All this time, Gabriella had quietly supported her. As she'd helped distribute books and discuss plans, it hadn't merely been as a lady-in-waiting, but as a dreamer herself.

"I promise you that I will realize it. Even if it's with my dying breath."

"I know you will. And I'll be there to help," Gabriella whispered, just as the hall door creaked open.

"His Highness awaits you downstairs," a low, feminine voice called.

"We'll be right out," she replied. When the door shut, she stood and stepped into her matching yellow taffeta shoes.

She bit her lip. "Gabriella, do you know who that was?"

"Her name is Gavri, I think. She had a falling out with His Highness a few days ago."

AFTER SAYING their goodbyes to the duchessa, Aless let Veron help her into the carriage, where he sat across from her and Gabriella, who held the offerings of lilies, peacock feathers, honey, and pomegranates in a myrtle-wood basket.

He wore another of Lorenzo's gifts, a gold-embroidered black brocade overcoat, fitted from the shoulders to the waist, and then split and flowing from the hips to the ankles. It had an elegance to it, a drama that Lorenzo no doubt had loved, and a cut suited to strong shoulders and a fit physique.

Veron, and the other dark-elves, remained unmasked, unhooded. None of the duchessa's household seemed fazed, and hopefully their luck would continue with the paesani.

The carriage set out, and the castle's verdant, manicured grounds moved past the window, the standard of the Sileni nobiltà. Everything ordered and uniform, nothing like the sprawling wild roses in her daydreams. Not the variegated, messy, beautiful chaos of vines and blooms and ruins.

Leaning back against the seat, Veron rested an ankle on his opposite knee. He looked her over, and when his eyes met hers, he nodded toward the offerings. "What do they symbolize?"

She cleared her throat, trying not to seem too excited by the notion of him merely speaking to her. But it was progress. "They are Terra's offerings. The lilies are for loyalty. The peacock feathers for longevity. The honey is for abundance, and the pomegranates for fertility."

He raised a pale eyebrow and tilted his head.

Swallowing, she lowered her gaze to her yellow-taffeta skirts and clasped her hands. This was their one chance to leave a peaceful and positive impression in Stroppiata, instead of the harpy bloodbath of their arrival. But it was also her sincere prayer, for blessings she very much wished the Holy Mother would someday bestow upon her.

By the time they stopped at the shrine, a crowd of paesani had already gathered, watching as Veron helped her and Gabriella out of the carriage with an escort of dark-elf royal guards—kuvari—and cheering as dark-elves distributed food. More and more people moved closer, and the crowd grew and grew, voices shouting, hands reaching, bodies pressing closer, tighter.

"We have to move. Now," the dark-elf guard with the braid—Gavri—hissed to her. "On foot, we can't control this crowd. The situation could deteriorate quickly."

She'd trust Gavri's expertise—they would only stay long enough to fulfill their purpose. With a nod, she headed toward the shrine with Veron and his kuvari.

Along the way to the monumental bronze doors, Gabriella handed her the basket of offerings, and holding it with one arm, she clasped hands with an old woman, then two young women, and little girls. They'd all come to give their thanks at Terra's shrine, and in this, they were the same.

"Terra's blessings upon you!" an elderly woman offered.

"And upon you," she responded, the same response every Terran always gave to the blessing.

For his part, Veron smiled kindly at her side, offering cordial greetings and thanking the people for their blessings. His nearness was warm, comforting, and without even looking, she could feel his big form beside her, his watchful eyes glancing at her every so often.

As a pair of guards opened the bronze doors, Veron's gloved hand took hers, and they entered.

Some of the crowd filtered inside—as expected, to view this moment, to spread the word. Gavri and the other guards kept the crowd at a distance, while she and Veron faced the marble altar and the enormous golden statue of

Terra beneath the saucer dome. She'd seen it before, hand in hand with Mamma, craning her neck to see to the very top and following Mamma through the prayer and ritual.

Maiden, Mother, Crone; She of the Heights; Protector of All. The Goddess towered before them in shining gold, a crown upon her head, a peplos draped about her, bearing a spear in one hand and a phiale in the other.

With one hand offering, and with the other fighting.

Her hand in Veron's, Aless approached the altar, knelt, then placed her offerings upon it. "O blessed Mother, worshipped and adored, called by women in tearful need and in rites at ancient shrines, please accept these humble offerings. Revered among the Eternan pantheon for the realms you protect, for the bounty you offer, for the life you bloom, we ask You to watch over us as we journey this path together toward Your guiding light."

A hush had settled over the shrine.

Holy Mother, please let us succeed in sowing this peace, in stopping a war no one needs to fight. She kept her head bowed, as did Veron at her side. *Please guide me and let me be stronger, braver, more compassionate. Grant me the strength to follow your teachings.*

At long last, she made to rise, and Veron helped her to her feet. He'd been by her side, supporting her as she'd prayed.

"What do you pray for?" he asked, looking her over, his eyebrows drawn.

"Peace. Strength," she whispered back. And when it came to the peace, they could use all the help they could get. Especially the Holy Mother's. "But mostly just giving thanks."

When she grinned out at the crowd, some faces beamed back, but others faced away, murmurs spreading.

They hadn't been here long, but clearly long enough to allow doubt to enter, and questions.

"Monsters," someone whispered.

"Dangerous," said another.

No. She had to save this—*now*. The only way she knew.

She cleared her throat. "People of Stroppiata," she called out, "we thank you for opening your city and your hearts to us, and allowing us to share in our worship of the Holy Mother." She looked out over the people gathered as they quieted. "I have offered prayers for as long as I can remember, and today, I stand here blessed—with a husband both kind and strong enough to defend our people, and a new family, as both Sileni and dark-elves join together against the Immortali that would threaten us, and for the righteous cause of a lasting peace." *Both for survival, and our own betterment.* "We follow the Holy Mother's guidance—sharing our bounty with one hand, but with the other, defending one another against any dangers that would seek to destroy us, or to divide us. And together, we are strong. Terra's blessings upon you all, my brothers and sisters."

"And upon you," came the harmony of replies, the response every Terran instinctively gave, ingrained from early childhood.

She inclined her head, as did Veron next to her, but his golden gaze rested on her, intense, but softening as his mouth curved. That look remained as they exited the shrine, boarded the carriage, and headed for the city's western gates toward the dark-elf queendom of Dunmarrow.

Arms crossed, Veron leaned against the carriage's window, a smile on his face and a gleam in his eyes. "You were amazing in there, Aless."

So she was back to being *Aless* and not *Alessandra*. A step toward earning back his trust, maybe?

Don't put the cart before the horse.

Next to her, Gabriella grinned, but covered it and looked away. Nice of her.

"It was just some words," she answered, tapping his boot with her shoe. "Nothing like battling harpies."

"No," he said, with a slow shake of his head. "You know your people. You see them."

It was nice of him to say, but their argument had inspired her to look closer. And she would continue doing so. But... "I won't argue with that."

And so she didn't.

CHAPTER 14

*S*itting on a blanket, Aless steeped passionflower tea before the campfire while watching the chestnuts roast. The late-afternoon sun peeked through the canopy of turkey oaks, sparse but a vivid green. Some of the dark-elves picked through the undergrowth and climbed a massive sweet chestnut tree, gathering more that Gabriella helped collect.

"Are they any good?" Gavri asked, nodding toward the tree.

Over the past couple of days, they'd spoken from time to time, as Gavri seemed to guard her when Veron wasn't around. She wanted to befriend Gavri if she could, but hadn't caught her for more than a few minutes at a time.

"I've had chestnut creme in desserts before. Very sweet. Tasty." *Crème de marrons*, as the Emaurrians called it. "I've read about soldiers in ancient Silen eating chestnut porridge the morning of battle."

Gavri grunted. "I'll take that creme thing over the porridge. But considering we're going to Dun Mozg, maybe preparing for war isn't such a bad idea."

She frowned. "Why is that?"

Gavri leaned in, her braid falling over her shoulder. "Veron didn't tell you?"

She wiggled aside on the blanket until there was enough room to sit, and then she motioned to Gavri, who looked about warily before lowering.

"He told me about Queen Nendra, who's the most famous warrior among the dark-elves," she said, preparing another cup of passionflower tea.

"She is," Gavri replied, but with an exhaustion that could be a decade old.

"And her queendom sits on the largest arcanir mine we've ever known. A really important one, worth almost any sacrifice to gain access. Dun Mozg prides itself on its weapons, and its soldiery."

Arcanir? That certainly was useful against the Immortali beasts. She handed the ready cup to Gavri, who accepted it with a raised eyebrow. "He also said his brother Zoran was chosen as her consort because of his prowess among your people in Nightbloom."

Gavri inhaled deeply, turned the cup in her hands, and nodded slowly. "Oh, yes," she said. "Zoran's... *prowess*... is well known to me."

It didn't seem like Gavri meant *battle* prowess.

She swallowed, pouring the boiling water.

It overflowed, and Gavri caught the kettle's handle.

"Y-you and—" she stammered.

Gavri set the kettle down. "Once upon a time." She sighed. "I was a very ambitious kuvari recruit. And he was one of Nozva Rozkveta's most accomplished warriors. The math told me I needed to best him to prove myself. I did, and..." She shrugged a shoulder.

Frozen, Aless stared and stared. Never had a sentence needed finishing more than Gavri's. "And *what?*"

"And for eight years, we tired each other out in the training yard and in the bedchamber," Gavri said with a grin, then took a sip of tea.

"*Eight years?*" How had they been together for eight years, eight *long* years, and yet he'd ended up Queen Nendra's consort?

Gavri nodded and took another sip. "What's in this?"

"Passionflower," Aless blurted, then motioned for her to continue.

"Passionflower? Like the aphrodisiac?" A skewed stare. "Are you—"

"No! Holy Mother, no!" Aless cleared her throat, gathering her composure as some glances turned her way. She was not drinking it for *that*. "While it *is* a mild aphrodisiac, it also soothes the nerves."

Grinning broadly, Gavri shrugged again. "Whatever you say."

"So what happened?"

"Nendra bested the previous queen of Dun Mozg, and she needed a consort. Queen Zara offered her the best." She sipped her tea. "You know, this stuff is really starting to grow on me."

"Just like that, and he was gone?"

Gavri nodded. "He was. As a prince, he would never be able to make the Offering to anyone but royalty." She sighed. "But then Prince Veron found me in the training cavern and asked me to spar. And then the next day, and the next. We became friends, and then Queen Zara assigned me to his guard."

So Veron had seen Gavri after losing someone she loved, and he'd befriended her. That sounded like him. She smiled warmly.

A gentle shiver stroked up her back, and when she looked across the camp,

Veron was looking at her while he brushed Noc. She'd been earning Noc's trust lately, at least, with a couple apples here and there, and fables Mamma had read to her about unicorns and fey horses. If only Veron's trust could be recovered so easily.

Gavri followed her line of sight and started. "I... I should go."

She rested a hand on Gavri's knee. "No, stay, please."

Across the camp, a long, silky black tail smacked Veron in the face. He eyed Noc sheepishly and mumbled something to him.

As she smiled, a soft laugh bubbled next to her. Gavri's. But it soon faded.

"What happened between you and Veron? You don't speak to each other anymore."

Gavri set the cup down, tucked the braid over her shoulder, and fidgeted with its tip, her gaze downcast. "I... violated his trust." She took a deep breath. "I lost Zoran in an instant. And when Veron was betrothed to you, I expected... a lot. After the wedding, after your... dress... the reaction from your people wasn't invisible."

She lowered her own gaze. "I know. I regret that."

"It was between the two of you. I know that. But... I just wanted him to rebel against the marriage, too. I didn't want him to be understanding and reasonable and diplomatic as he always is. I wanted him to fight back," she said, clapping a hand on her thigh. "He wouldn't, so I... intervened. I badmouthed you and told him I'd given you a tent when I hadn't, just so you could seem spoiled. Well, *more* spoiled."

A half-laugh escaped her before she could stop herself, but Gavri met it with a fleeting grin.

"I probably deserved it, Gavri."

"Oh, you did. But *he* didn't. He didn't deserve me betraying him. He's not Zoran, and you're not Nendra. And you're—you're not what I expected." She chewed her lip a moment. "A bit spoiled, yes, but you actually care about nurturing peace between us and the humans. You tried to get them to accept us in Stroppiata, first with the mask thing, then at the shrine. I judged you too soon, and I was wrong."

Speechless, Aless could only give a nod.

"Veron doesn't let people into his heart easily." Gavri drained the tea and placed the empty cup before her. "Nozva Rozkveta was once at war with the light-elf queendom of Lumia. Veron's father, King-consort Mirza, killed the light-elf consort in battle, but we lost, and Lumia took many of our people as prisoners. Lumia threatened to kill them all unless Queen Zara delivered Mirza in exchange. Before the message got to her, Mirza had already decided to deliver himself. Regardless of the queen's wishes. Veron caught him leaving, and Mirza smiled. Told Veron he was going hunting and would return soon, so there would be no commotion, no fight. And then he left for Lumia, where he was executed before the light-elf queen released our prisoners."

The words, though spoken aloud, felt like air. Thick, dense, suffocating air, pushing in closer and closer until she could barely breathe.

Veron's father had gone against his wife and queen, had sacrificed himself for her, for their queendom, for Veron... But in doing so, he'd hurt his son, to the core, leaving a wound that had lasted for years, and maybe a lifetime.

"Veron was destroyed. Utterly destroyed. To his mind, Mirza had betrayed him, his entire family, because they'd loved Mirza and he'd ignored that to turn himself over. I don't think Veron ever forgave his father, and his trust, once broken, is unrecoverable."

Unrecoverable. The word hit her like an arrow, and she shuddered.

Gavri moved closer. "But he sees something different in you," she whispered. "Something special. And I... I see it, too."

Aless eyed her. "Too much passionflower tea, Gavri?"

A hearty laugh. "Not that. Although I'm certain it would help." She waggled an eyebrow.

Holy Mother's mercy.

"I mean... You think in an unusual way. At first, in your capital, you were using it selfishly. But then... on the way to Stroppiata, and when we were leaving, you handled matters in ways we usually don't. And Veron is a warrior, too, but he wants to see more peaceful means, diplomatic means, all he ever seems to dream about. And then here you are, as if you'd stepped right out of one of those dreams." Gavri pulled away, biting her lip. "If you'd been a dark-elf, you would've been perfect." A wink.

Smiling, Aless elbowed her. Every now and then, Veron looked at her for a while, contemplative, but kept his distance other than during their daily archery lessons. To his credit, she could now sometimes hit the target. *Sometimes.*

But what they'd had in the garden... That hadn't returned. And despite his contemplative looks, it might never return, no matter how much effort she put in.

But I won't give up. She'd earn back his trust no matter what it would take.

"I'm going to go see if I can help with that chestnut mush thing." Gavri rose.

"Porridge."

"That." Inclining her head, Gavri took her leave.

Well, if they were having chestnut porridge for breakfast, at least they'd be prepared for the queendom of arcanir and soldiery tomorrow.

~

VERON WATCHED Aless in the Dun Mozg tunnels, her staring, her gasping, her awe. She was impressed, and she would only be more impressed when she arrived in Nozva Rozkveta.

Perfectly circular, the rippled tunnels stretched through countless miles of solid rock, linking the dark-elf kingdoms. No one but a Dun Mozg dark-elf knew about direct Gates between the queendom and the sky-realm, but the tunnels were used by every queendom, and he well knew how to get to Dun Mozg through them, even if it was taking them an hour so far on horseback.

"They're massive," Aless whispered, and her voice carried. "How can you be sure the—the *earthmover wyrms*—are gone?"

He laughed under his breath. She was right; the tunnels were massive, and they were but small ants in them. "Although the earthmovers created our tunnels and territories, we know they're here no longer because there haven't been earthquakes."

"Earthquakes?" Aless's dark eyebrows knitted together before they rose high. "Aha. *Earthmovers.*"

Soon, the tunnels began to twinkle in the light of their torches and lanterns, and she squinted. "What are…?"

"Gemstones," he supplied, and she gasped. "Arcanir isn't the only material found here, although it's one of the few *useful* ones."

Her mouth fell open. "But gemstones are—"

"Very valuable to humans." He smiled at her. "They barter timber, leather, food crops, livestock, and other valuable items to us, and in return, they want *shiny stones.*"

She cocked her head. "When you put it like that, we all sound like idiots."

He shrugged happily. "Not all of you, but if the jewelry fits."

She stroked fingers over her pearls. "You know, it's not just the *shiny* aspect. Rarity means a lot, too. It means we've had to sacrifice to obtain something. An entire city crafting an icon of Terra out of gold means they sacrificed a great deal for the sake of the Holy Mother."

A little defensive. He bowed his head, hiding a smile. "Saffron is rare, isn't it?"

She pursed her lips. "A statue made out of saffron *might* not last very long, Veron." Despite her prickly tone, her eyes gleamed.

That gleam made his poking all worthwhile. There was something about her that just lightened his heart, made him feel almost weightless. The way she made him feel—that couldn't be possible if she were malicious, someone who'd betray love freely given. Perhaps he'd misjudged her.

People had always been difficult for him to read, ever since Ata. How could he have gotten his own father so wrong? And other volodari, kuvari, and former lovers.

He loved Aless. Perhaps even trusted *her*, but not himself, not his ability to understand her well enough to predict when things could go wrong, and to stop them.

"So does Nightbloom get arcanir from here?" Aless asked.

He breathed deep. "Dun Mozg supplies us with arcanir weapons, yes. We, in turn, provide food and spices, since they're scarce here," he explained. "They've had to hunt a lot more than we have, and they've lost volodari to the Brotherhood. When we woke from the Sundering, all our farms had long since withered or been overgrown, so we couldn't supply ourselves yet, let alone Dun Mozg. While we re-establish our food crops and spice caravans, we need the trade Silen could provide."

Nozva Rozkveta had been starving, but Dun Mozg had suffered an even greater food scarcity; they'd deployed more volodari to address that, and had lost many to the Brotherhood. That would make them either happier about the treaty or more embittered toward the humans as a whole. Hopefully the former.

"Your help against the other Immortali for our food," she whispered. "And then you provide food and spices to Dunmarrow for weapons..."

He nodded. Now she understood the basics of their trade with Queen Nendra.

Before long, they came upon the circular set of Dun Mozg's stone doors, where Riza dismounted, took one of the hammers provided, and pounded Nozva Rozkveta's knock. She replaced the hammer and stepped back.

"That sound was..." Aless whispered to him, her head tilted.

He urged Noc closer to her. "Each dark-elf queendom has its own. It's how we identify ourselves to one another."

She tapped her fingers against her thigh, the same rhythm Riza had pounded. Nozva Rozkveta's rhythm. Again and again, as if she were practicing it.

He leaned forward, watching the movement of those elegant, tapered fingers as they sounded like home, his home, *their* home, and when the doors creaked open, minutes must have passed... or seconds. Clearing his throat, he straightened.

Zoran, Noc thought to him, with a swish of his tail and a rolling, blowing snort.

We'll see him soon. Veron patted him. Zoran had always visited the stables every day in Nozva Rozkveta, before becoming king-consort to Nendra, and had been fond of Noc in particular.

Once the doors were open, two kuvari stood in light arcanir armor, bearing halberds.

Riza stepped forward. "Hail, kin of Dun Mozg, blessed of the Deep, the Darkness, and Holy Ulsinael," she called out, and every dark-elf in the cavalcade saluted. "We of Nozva Rozkveta come as kindred, in the service of His

Highness, Prince Veron u Zara u Avrora u Roza, Valaz u Nozva Rozkveta, Zpevan Kamena, Volodar T'my, and Her Highness, Princess Alessandra u Aldona u Noor u Elise, Valazi u Nozva Rozkveta, Valazi u Silen."

Aless leaned in. "Those are the names of my mother, my grandmother, and my great-grandmother," she whispered, her voice high.

Was she surprised? "My mother wanted to know everything about you," he whispered back. *And I wanted to know everything about you...*

"Dun Mozg bids you welcome," came the Dun Mozg kuvari's reply. "May the Deep, Darkness, and Holy Ulsinael guide you in our queendom." The two stepped aside, standing at attention as the cavalcade passed into the open doors. "Her Majesty, Queen Nendra, awaits you in the grand hall. Enjoy the games."

"Games?" Aless asked him. "Like you mentioned at our wedding?"

He nodded. "Our festivities include games, where anyone can challenge anyone in the ring to a light hand-to-hand match."

"Anyone?" Her voice broke.

Closing his eyes, he brought a hand to his face. It was so commonplace a tradition among his people, he hadn't even thought about it.

He should have.

He cleared his throat softly. "Yes. Anyone."

~

ALESS TIGHTENED her quivering fingers on the reins. There would be games tonight, and she—who'd never trained in combat a day in her life—could be challenged?

Gentle warmth rested on her hand, Veron's palm on her skin. Riding close, he dipped his head, meeting her gaze with his shimmering golden eyes.

"It's only light sparring, but there is no honor in challenging someone unskilled," he said delicately.

"Yelena," the sharp-eyed guard said with a cough, earning a glare and a hiss from Veron.

That couldn't be good. "What's Yelena?"

"Not *what*. Who," the sharp-eyed guard answered, while Veron waved her off.

"Don't listen to Riza. Yelena won't challenge you."

The sharp-eyed guard—Riza—scoffed, the sound echoing in the enormous dark tunnel.

Aless grasped Veron's fingers. "Who is she?" A rival? An old flame? An enemy?

He closed his eyes a moment and exhaled lengthily. "Yelena is spoiled—"

"Strong," Riza interjected.

"—and selfish—"

"Ambitious."

"—opportunistic—"

"And your former lover." Riza scowled at him. "She'll feel an instant rivalry."

Veron grunted. "Her people are starving and getting picked off by the Brotherhood. She knows better than to jeopardize this treaty."

Former lover...

What kind of woman was she, this Yelena? Strong, ambitious...

"She doesn't have to harm Her Highness," Riza said. "A challenge will be enough for everyone present to witness Her Highness decline. Dark-elves will never respect Her Highness after that."

So she couldn't fight, and she couldn't decline.

There had to be other moves to make. She just had to find them.

"I'll talk to her," Veron bit out to Riza.

"When has that ever worked?" Riza asked derisively. "Just ignore her. Completely."

"That might anger her enough to goad her," he replied as they neared the end of the tunnel.

"It's your best chance," Riza shot back, and they continued arguing, but it didn't matter.

She had no control over what this Yelena might do or not. All that remained was gathering what facts she could to determine a course of action. The *right* course of action, to both earn the dark-elves' respect while staying out of Yelena's way.

The tunnel opened to an unimaginably enormous cavern, so vast its end wasn't visible, washed in a soft green glow that illuminated buildings below. The cavern walls bloomed with green—

"Bioluminescence," Veron whispered in her ear, his steely velvet voice making her shiver. "Fourteen types of bioluminescent mushrooms grow in our queendoms."

Mushrooms? They looked like flowers, almost. Like petals. But beneath them was a city like black glass. Buildings with jagged edges, spikes, hard angles, but glossed and shining like mirrors. People wandered the black stone paths, chatting and laughing, while others disappeared into caves branching off from the main cavern. At the center of it all was the largest building, like a budding black crystal cluster, beautiful and majestic, surrounded by a glowing teal waterway that overflowed to the depths below.

Her heart froze, then pounded. "It's breathtaking."

Veron chuffed quietly, his eyes glittering. "Wait until you see Nozva Rozkveta."

It was like this, too?

But the cavalcade was already moving, and he cocked his head for her to follow. She urged her horse after him and Noc, a line leading up to a long building, where whinnies and nickers greeted them.

Veron helped her dismount and personally led Noc and her horse inside, through the bustle of people.

A man with long, unbound hair stood before one of the stalls, rubbing a horse's nose. Strapping, with long, flowing hair, a smile curling the corners of his mouth—it looked almost permanent. And the same shade of slate-blue skin Veron had, just a little darker than most.

"Zoran," Veron called. "I knew I'd find you in here."

Zoran? The same Zoran that Gavri had mentioned?

"Brother!" Zoran turned to him, those same golden eyes wide, and tackled Veron in a hug, patting him on the back. "It's been an age!"

Zoran had the same chiseled features Veron did—the high cheekbones, prominent chin, angular jaw—and yet they were louder somehow; Zoran's grin was broad and his laugh hearty, his movements sweeping and large. He himself was slightly taller than Veron's six and a half feet, and wider. Whereas Veron was quiet and intense, she could already hear Zoran's guffaws and booming voice.

"I knew that where horses were near, you couldn't be far." With a lopsided grin, Veron eyed his brother, clapping him on the shoulder. They stabled her horse and Noc, with a pair of stable hands coming to help.

Zoran gusted a heavy sigh. "Better here than the fortress. Nendra is occupied with her current favorite. A werewolf alpha."

Current favorite?

Veron's grin disappeared as he shook his head, earning a shrug from Zoran. "She'll tire of him soon enough. Too moody."

Wasn't the queen married to Zoran?

He looked past Veron to her. "And you must be Alessandra!"

Clearing her throat, she curtseyed, but he blazed right past Veron and hugged her.

"Glad to make your acquaintance, King-consort—"

"*Zoran*," he corrected, his arms tight around her. "We're family now!"

Despite his volume, his embrace was genuine, and he smelled familiar, of horse—she couldn't dislike him.

"Nice to meet you," she replied, meeting Veron's sparkling gaze as he stood, one arm crossed over his chest, and the other hand curled and covering his mouth.

He looked ready to burst out laughing himself, which would be a new sight for her.

Zoran released her and leaned against a stall, his face bright. "So how do you like my brother? Is he too quiet? Too severe? With his obedience and duty and peace and all that?"

Something like a bark of laughter came from Veron before he bowed his head and coughed.

"He's..." *Wonderful.* "I..." *Love him.* "We..."

"Say no more." Zoran held up a hand. "Or it'll all go to his head."

She grimaced.

"Ah, so she does have a humorous bone in her body."

Veron elbowed his brother.

"What about the boot thing?" Zoran continued. "Does he still do the boot thing?"

A wry look from Veron. "I do *not* have a 'boot thing.' It's not my fault most boots are just not in the least—"

"You *so* have a boot thing." Zoran fixed him with a stare.

"Boot... thing?" she asked. If there was one man who could make a perfect pair of boots, it was Lorenzo's cobbler. She'd have to write home.

Footsteps padded behind her, and the mirth faded from Zoran's gaze as he looked past her.

She glanced back, where Gavri had entered with a horse. Gavri quickly tried to back up, but there was nowhere to go.

Zoran bridged the distance between them, leaning in close. "Gavri." The word sounded like a greeting, a whisper, an apology, and an admiration all in one.

"I need to leave. Could you—" Gavri pushed through a trio of kuvari and their horses, but Zoran caught her hand.

"Meet me here later, during dinner," Zoran whispered to Gavri. "There's so much I need to tell you."

Gavri twisted in his grip, her hand going to her braid. "I—I can't. I have guard duty." She turned and picked through the crowded stable, but his glittering eyes followed her as she left.

Gavri really wasn't going to hear what Zoran—the man she'd loved, to whom she'd given *eight* years—had to say?

She moved to follow Gavri out of the stable, and Veron caught up with her.

"See you at the games," Veron called back to his brother, then helped her clear a path.

The games... the ones where—unless she got an idea in the next few hours—she would let down all of her new subjects with a single word.

CHAPTER 15

*A*s Veron entered the training cavern, Yelena was already there in her kuvari robes, practicing the sword. Her hair was up in the braided circlet as it always had been, and her movements were lithe and agile as ever.

"Did you miss me?" she asked with a sweep of her blade, smiling impishly.

"Two thousand years passed in the blink of an eye," he murmured, leaning against a blackstone pillar. Two thousand more could pass before he'd miss her—no, not even *then*.

Dark-amber eyes darted to him as she stepped into a lunge. "Look at you, all decked out."

He was already dressed in his combat leathers, ready for dinner.

"So your mother finally married you off. And to a human."

He crossed his arms. He loved Aless, but rubbing it in Yelena's face wasn't going to win him any favors here. "I do as my queen commands."

She forced out a laugh. "I certainly would have used that to my advantage."

"It was never going to be yours to use."

Setting her jaw, she practiced a block. "You just couldn't see my vision."

Oh, he had seen her vision, all too clearly. An ambitious, royal-blooded kuvari who had known she could never have defeated her own mother in single combat… and so had used a love affair with him in Nozva Rozkveta to try to learn *Mati's* weaknesses, in a bid to seize the throne of Nozva Rozkveta. Her plan had relied on making the Offering to him, then dueling to join Mati's Quorum—but he'd learned about Yelena's lies first and had told Mati.

Instead, Mati had betrothed Zoran to Yelena's mother. And that had been the end of that.

"Your... 'vision' was a pack of lies," he said casually. "And I wasn't about to let you try to overthrow my mother."

"Try?" A deep laugh. "I would have succeeded."

Yelena was a skilled warrior, but not Mati's match, whom even Nendra would have struggled to best. But for a person desperate to step out from her mother's shadow, Yelena truly seemed to believe in what she was saying.

"You don't have anything to prove," he said. "Everyone knows you're one of the strongest kuvari. And not just in Dun Mozg."

She rolled her eyes, slashed low, and then high. "I don't need to be told that."

"Because you already know. Everyone already knows."

She blew a sharp breath from her nose. "Your point?"

He stepped in front of her, and she stopped a blow just short of his arm. Her eyes wide, she looked him over, and he rested a palm on her sword-hand.

"My point is that Alessandra is a human," he said, keeping his voice low. "There's nothing to be gained from challenging her."

With a sneer, Yelena straightened, pulled away, and sheathed her sword, her pale kuvari robes dark with sweat. "Is that what you predict I'll do? Challenge your little human?"

"I know better than to try predicting what you'll do, Yelena." He peered down at her, at the wheels turning in her gaze, in her expression. "But our peace with the humans, our trade—even the food this queendom is getting—rely on my marriage with Alessandra."

"They're weak. Helpless. At the slightest challenge, they scurry like salamanders. No strength at all."

"Not in the ring. Not combat strength. But Alessandra has a different kind of strength," he shot back. Aless *wasn't* weak. *Wasn't* helpless. In a test of wits, Yelena would find herself vastly outclassed.

"There is only one kind of strength that matters, Veron," she hissed.

This was going nowhere. "I'm asking you this as a favor, Yelena."

"A favor? For old times' sake?" Raising her eyebrows, she looked away with a shake of her head, then crossed her arms. When her eyes met his once more, they were narrowed and dancing mischievously. A look he'd seen from her countless times. "Maybe one last roll in the moss, then, for old times' sake?"

He groaned under his breath. There was no sense in trying to reason with her when she would only toy with him for her own amusement. Yelena was determined to issue the challenge and embarrass Aless in front of everyone present, send a ripple through the queendoms about the new Nozva Rozkvetan *human* princess refusing to fight and thus having no honor.

No more toying. He'd simply beat Yelena to the ring and challenge her *first*. Once he defeated her, as victor he'd be able to choose his next opponent, and that would be that. Yelena would never even get the *chance* to embarrass his wife.

It was the right move.

He turned away and strolled to the exit. "Nice talking to you, Yelena," he deadpanned.

"See you at dinner," came the jesting reply.

~

ALESS ROSE from the stone bench in the chamber she shared with Veron. Decorated in smooth stone and metal, its surfaces were hard, sharp, softened only by what appeared to be undyed silk, a soft, cottony white. Silk bedding, cushions, curtains. Even a silk rug, woven in shades of white and tan. The room was a marriage of soft and hard.

In the mirror, she wore her dark-blue satin dress—one of her best—fitted through the richly embroidered bodice, with boots beneath, and the strand of Mamma's pearls around her neck.

She couldn't fight—true—but she was still a princess of Silen. And everyone who looked her way tonight would know that, and know that with her station came the aid they all enjoyed. And that if any harm came to her, they'd be without it.

Gabriella tightened the braid she'd coiled at the nape of her neck. "There. Perfect."

"I approve," Gavri commented from her post at the doorway, swirling the tip of her own braid around her fingers. "There's something I love about that hairstyle, but I can't quite put my finger on it."

As casual as Gavri seemed now, her meeting with Zoran had shaken her. She'd practically run from the stable after all.

"Very funny."

Both Gavri and Zoran had things they needed to say to each other, it seemed, questions that needed answers, wounds that needed healing. Maybe it would be better if they said them instead of keeping them bottled up inside. Easier for them to move on.

She strode up to Gavri and jabbed a finger at her. "You are going to meet him in the stables later."

"I am?" Gavri stared down at her finger. "I can't. What about guarding—"

Aless shook her head. "You need to hear whatever he has to say to you. You two have loose ends."

Sighing, Gavri leaned her head back against the door. "If Queen Nendra hears of it, even if nothing hap—"

"You can't help it if I need to get some air and require my guard to accompany me, can you?" With a grin, she breezed out the door.

"Good plan," Gavri said in a high-pitched voice, sidling up to her. "I like it."

In the hall, Veron strode toward them, over six feet of black-leather-clad muscle, the hard angles of his terrifyingly beautiful face tight, eyebrows drawn, golden eyes hard. Riza followed him with a scowl.

Had he spoken with Yelena, then?

But when he looked up, met her gaze, those hard angles gave way to a soft smile. One she'd put there.

He gave her a once-over, and the curve of that smile was unmistakable as he took her hands. "You look beautiful."

"All Gabriella's work," she said, rubbing her thumb over his hand.

He gave a friendly nod to Gabriella, who curtseyed. When his gaze wandered to Gavri, she bowed her head and looked away.

This disagreement between them would have to end. Maybe they could discuss it later tonight.

"How did your talk go?" she asked as he wrapped her hand around his arm and led her down the hall.

"Swimmingly," Riza snapped, shaking her head.

Veron hissed at Riza, then turned back to her, rubbing warmth into her hand. "She's eager to rule—"

"That's *one* way of putting it," Riza mumbled under her breath.

"—but is frustrated in her mother's shadow."

"She's frustrated, but she's not stupid," Gavri said, despite Veron's glare. "If she embarrasses Her Highness, when Queen Zara hears about it, that could affect relations with Dun Mozg. She won't endanger the alliance."

"You don't know her as well as I do," he snapped.

"*No one* knows her as well as you do," Gavri shot back, then her eyes went wide as she swallowed.

Veron went rigid, but Aless stepped in.

"How do the games work?" she asked as they crossed a corridor in the black crystal palace, their booted footsteps echoing.

"The first warrior may challenge until she or he loses," Veron said. "When the first warrior finally loses, the victor issues challenges until she or he loses."

"How do you win?"

"Get your opponent out of the ring, or until your opponent taps twice," Gavri supplied, and Veron nodded, but a frown slowly furrowed his face. "No blood drawn—it's bad form."

"What about the ring? What's in it?"

Veron jerked his head back. "*No*," he hissed, stopping near a stone bench.

"Sand." Gavri raised an eyebrow at him.

Sand... That wouldn't hurt too much. "It's light sparring, right?" she asked. "What if I accept the challenge?"

"*Absolutely not*," Veron said through clenched teeth.

"Not a terrible idea," Gavri replied while Veron scowled at her. "Hurting Her Highness would destroy the peace. She wouldn't use the games to truly injure Her Highness."

"If she endangers the peace, that could mean her people don't eat." She took Veron's arm with both of her hands until he looked at her. "If she wants to rule and she's intelligent—which I expect her to be, if *you* were fond of her—then she won't starve her people just to make a stranger look bad."

"She's passionate about leadership," he said with a sigh, "just extremely impatient, and sometimes myopic."

That sounded all too familiar. With a fleeting smile, she lowered her gaze as they walked endless stretches of gleaming black floors reflecting the light of mushrooms, glowworms, and torches.

Yelena—as a woman among the dark-elves—had a real chance, no matter how small, of ending up a true leader. When a dream became tangible, the temptation to reach for it became nearly irresistible. What had Yelena done?

Nothing too repugnant, if she was still free, still an heir to the throne here. She might have been impatient, but not deranged.

Soon, the din of myriad voices muffled through two heavy stone doors.

"If she challenges you," Veron whispered, "just decline. There's no good reason for you to take such a risk."

Two kuvari, armored in sage-tinted arcanir plate, opened the doors, revealing a sea of people crowding long stone tables and benches. Some of whom had arrived with her and Veron—her people.

Every reason for her to take such a risk.

"His Highness, Prince Veron u Zara u Avrora u Roza, Valaz u Nozva Rozkveta, Zpevan Kamena, Volodar T'my, and Her Highness, Princess Alessandra u Aldona u Noor u Elise, Valazi u Nozva Rozkveta, Valazi u Silen," a herald shouted, and every voice in the room hushed as Veron escorted her and Gabriella in, along with Riza, Gavri, and ten other kuvari. Every dark-elf stood, tall and straight, arms at their sides.

Floor candelabra and massive crystalline girandoles lit up the grand hall, reflecting firelight off surfaces like black glass, with an empty ring of sand at the center, outlined in white etchings. Their steps were the only sound, and as they passed several empty spaces on the stone benches, most of their entourage stopped but for her, Veron, Gabriella, Riza, and Gavri.

The air was thick with the savory spice of roasted sausage, and the lemon, olive oil, polenta, and rice-flour pasta. The aroma of Bellanzole's viands—human foods.

Veron led them to the farthest table, where a well-built, statuesque woman waited in a gleaming black throne, her long hair secured high, surrounded by four men, Zoran among them. No one else here seemed to have more than one partner, but this queen did. She wore impeccable plated black leather, and armor over her fingers.

"I am Queen Nendra. Welcome to Dun Mozg, Prince Veron, Princess Alessandra." With a measured smile, Nendra inclined her head, and she and Veron responded in kind. Nendra gestured to the men surrounding her. "This is my king-consort, Zoran"—who grinned and nodded—"and my concubines—"

Concubines?

"—Kral, Ivo, and Cipriano." A grim-faced muscular dark-elf in armor, a pale and slender well-coiffed man in a black coat, and a black-bearded, green-eyed man, olive-skinned just like her. Sileni?

Human? No, Zoran had mentioned a werewolf lover, hadn't he? What about Ivo?

But she greeted each in turn with Veron until Nendra gestured to the spitting image of herself, with her white hair braided in a circlet about her head.

"And this is my firstborn daughter, Yelena."

"A pleasure, Your Highness." She inclined her head to Yelena.

Yelena smiled, but it didn't reach her tawny eyes, and every shred of her brown leathers was pulled tight. A muscle twitched in Yelena's clenched jaw. "The pleasure's all mine."

Queen Nendra glowered at her, then glanced at a young girl seated next to Yelena. "And my youngest, Karla."

Karla, her voluminous hair tied in a high ponytail, met her gaze squarely, even while partially hiding behind Yelena's hip. A bold little girl, she could be no older than five or six, if dark-elf children aged as human children did. But even for a child, she was thin. When Veron had told her about the starvation, she hadn't wanted to believe him, but he'd been right.

Nendra turned to her people, arms raised. "Our honored guests have arrived," she bellowed. "After Kral saved two of our volodari yesterday, he has the honor of first match. Let the games begin!"

Cheers rose up from the crowds, who then seated themselves at the stone benches once more. A musician in the corner began a beat on a large, reso-nant drum.

Scowling, Veron gestured her to a nearby space, where she sat between him and Gavri on the cold, hard surface, with Gabriella beyond, and Riza at the end.

"What's wrong?" she whispered to him.

He shook his head. "I didn't realize anyone would have the honor of first match."

At least it wasn't Yelena.

The spread before them was colorful, with dishes of steaming pasta and sausage placed among Sileni boules, greens, fruits, and cakes. The entire table was laden with human food.

"Please tell me there's *butter*," Gavri murmured under her breath, patting Gabriella's arm. "Gabriella put some in my chestnut mush earlier today, and Holy Ulsinael, *she changed my life.*"

She laughed, and across from her, Cipriano was hiding a smile as he buttered a roll.

"Some things are worth the two-thousand-year wait," he remarked, his voice deep and gravelly.

"I'm going to need that. Really, really *need* that," Gavri said, her eyes fixed on the block of butter.

Nendra tipped her head up to Cipriano. "With this new alliance, you can have all the butter you want. Just don't get fat, eh?"

"If I don't, it won't be for lack of trying, my queen." They shared a grin that would have been sweet if Zoran hadn't been sitting between them, blinking lazily.

"Would you pass the, er, gigantic human bread loaf?" he asked Veron, waving a fork around, and Veron obliged with narrowed eyes, sliding the boule over to him across the table.

Yelena observed the exchange with an aloof glare, her gaze raking over the spread of Sileni food. Karla sat next to her, her little pale eyebrows drawn together as she looked out at the dishes. Yelena gathered some pasta and bread onto her plate, whispering words in an encouraging tone.

As she offered her little sister human food, Yelena had to know what the peace meant. She *had* to.

While Zoran tore off a chunk of bread and buttered it under Gavri's avaricious gaze, Kral stood and took to the empty ring. At its center, he clasped his hands behind his back and faced toward Yelena, who still sat with Karla.

A series of whoops rose up and rhythmic thuds of hands pounding on the stone, until Yelena looked over her shoulder at him, thumped her chest twice with a fist, and stood to raucous cheering.

"And so it begins," Veron said on an exhale.

"Why fight during a celebration?" she asked quietly. "Why not just dance?"

"It can be like a sort of dance," Gavri said, her mouth full of buttered bread. "When two warriors are attracted and then equally matched, it's... probably what you humans would call a seduction."

Swallowing, she nodded. Dark-elves chose their mates by their strength, choosing equals.

And never in her life would she ever be equally matched to Veron in combat.

Kral and Yelena circled one another, exchanging jests and feints, before Kral threw a punch, his massive physique the charge of a bull. Yelena misdirected his arm and evaded, dodging an elbow before landing a knee to the gut, then the face.

She backed away, grinning at Kral, who rubbed his jaw. As they circled, he moved her closer and closer to the white ring, until she tried to dart left.

He blocked, enclosing her in his enormous arms, but she slammed the top of her forehead against his face. His grip loosened, and she grabbed his arm, twisted it, and with her foot to his back, shoved him out of the ring.

Cheers rose up from the crowd while Yelena held up a fist, grinning.

No blood—Yelena had to have pulled her punches?

"Is he going to be all right?" she whispered to Veron.

"Nothing the hot springs won't cure," he whispered back.

Prodding at his face, Kral headed back to the table, where a dark-elf in gray robes and bone necklace rushed to tend him. All the while, Ivo and Cipriano and even Nendra herself patted him on the back while others shouted calls of support.

When they quieted, whoops staggered across the sea of tables, and that rhythmic thumping on the stone began again, and in the middle of the ring, Yelena stood, her hands clasped behind her back—

And staring right here.

CHAPTER 16

*A*less shivered.

Holy Mother's mercy. It was happening. It was actually happening.

She just had to decline and—

Next to her, Veron stood, staring down Yelena with an unwavering ferocity, and thumped his fist twice against his chest.

Yelena shook her head and looked over at her.

Gavri stood, thumping her chest.

Another shake of the head.

Across the table, Kral sat, having lost but nonetheless earned the respect of his family, friends, and subjects. There was no dishonor in losing. Only in failing to rise to the challenge. And then not only would she disappoint the dark-elves of Nightbloom, her own people, but she'd also humiliate them in front of an allied queendom.

"Your Majesty," Veron declared, turning to Queen Nendra, "I ask your permission to take my wife's place in the ring."

Queen Nendra leaned back in her throne and scowled at Yelena, who still stared right here. The crowd had gone utterly silent, as if three hundred people had stopped breathing.

"The games are tradition, Prince Veron," the queen replied in an even tone. "They must be fought by those who are issued a challenge, or not at all." The queen's gaze shifted to her, widened just slightly.

Even Queen Nendra invited her to decline.

"Princess?" Queen Nendra asked. "You must accept or decline," she said slowly, "unless you are blessed by Holy Ulsinael."

Blessed?

The queen's gaze lowered to her belly.

Oh.

A way out? It would be easy to lie, the easiest thing in the world, but in a few months, the odds were that everyone would know it. She could lose their respect anyway.

But as the dark-elves sat around tables of human food, as their queen celebrated a human and dark-elf marriage, Yelena would have to be insane to harm her. And an insane person wouldn't so lovingly have tried to feed her little sister.

As Veron stood, fists clenched, his eyes met hers, intense, pained, and as committed as he'd been to the truth before, that intensity suggested the opposite now.

What about the consequences? How would this reflect on Veron, on his mother, on the people of Nightbloom? And would his mother retaliate over the embarrassment, as Gavri had suggested?

Even if Yelena was willing to risk her people's wellbeing—*Karla's* wellbeing—*she* wasn't. Wasn't willing to risk anyone's wellbeing just to keep her own backside unbruised, especially when Yelena had every reason not to hurt her.

With a swallow, she stood. "Your Majesty, I am not in a holy state."

A ripple of gasps spread through the hall.

Veron took her hand. "Aless, no," he whispered. "Please."

She curled her fingers into a fist and thumped it twice to her chest, but the silence didn't break.

"Your Majesty," Veron called out, turning back to Queen Nendra, "I won't—"

Queen Nendra raised a hand. "The challenge has been accepted."

Yelena bowed elaborately.

"*Yelena,*" Veron snarled. "*So help me Ulsinael,* if you—"

Riza and Danika rose to grab Veron's arms and forced him to his seat while he bucked their hold. Even Zoran approached to help, and they finally wrangled Veron onto the bench as Zoran murmured reassurances.

Two taps. A step out of the ring. That was all it would take.

She took Veron's hand and offered him a look she hoped was reassuring. "Please. I have to do this."

His eyes locked on hers, blazing and furious as he heaved forceful breaths. "If she touches you, Aless, I—" A madness creased his features before he shook his head.

But she hadn't miscalculated.

Yelena wasn't insane, and if she did someday want to rule her people, destroying this peace and starving them was not conducive to that. What were weapons in the hands of emaciated soldiers?

She'd wanted to embarrass the human. Maybe even frustrate Veron. But her bluff had been called, and in two taps or just a couple steps, this would all be over.

She rested a palm on his cheek. "Trust me in this, Veron, won't you?"

As he stared at her, she stroked his cheek softly before she kissed him. Then, with a nod to him and another to Gavri, she stepped over the bench and made her way to the ring.

In the center, Yelena waited with a bitter smile, her eyebrows raised. "That was foolish of you, human."

Aless stepped into the ring but stayed on its fringe, close enough to step out quickly if she needed to. "I married a dark-elf, and this is part of his people's traditions. I want them to be *our* people, and that means stepping forward. Joining."

"Brave words, human." Yelena lowered into a fighting stance, narrowing her eyes. "But how brave are *you*?"

Inside of her, everything trembled, but she kept her fists clenched, stood her ground. She couldn't fight, not in the least, but this wasn't about winning a fight.

She would do her best to take it as Kral had, and then sit down and be welcomed. Avoid an incident that could affect so many people.

Yelena circled her, feinting occasionally, laughing, but Aless didn't move. Couldn't move. It was either fear or determination, but as long as it kept her standing, she didn't care.

A kick breezed by her face—just inches past her nose—

Her heart threatened to explode from her chest as the crowd heckled Yelena, shouting her name in disappointed tones.

Yelena's steps surrounded her, and growls, grunts, hissed words. The blow could come from anywhere—from behind, from the side, from above, from below. It could hit her anywhere, and for the life of her, she couldn't *move*.

Yelena circled to the front, her face contorted, and Aless chanced a look at Veron, who leaned forward at the table, both of his hands on it, with Gavri, Riza, and Zoran clamping down on his shoulders. The intensity of his gaze pierced her—

A lunge forward, then Yelena swept her legs out from under her.

Her back hit the sand.

Air whooshed out of her lungs.

"*Yelena!*" Veron shouted from across the hall, his voice echoing.

She wheezed, trying to catch her breath, while Yelena pinned her, took both of her wrists in the grasp of one hand, the clawed fingers of her other hand poised.

"No attempt to fight me?" Yelena snarled, tensing those fingers.

Holy Mother's mercy, she couldn't move even if she tried. But if Yelena had wanted her dead, then she already would have been. This was something else.

She held Yelena's gaze. "I didn't come here to fight you."

Yelena bared her teeth. "Then this could be your *end*."

Searching Yelena's eyes, she gave a slight shake of her head. If that were so, her end would have come as soon as she'd entered the ring, but Yelena had pulled all her strikes, had tried to get a rise out of her. Refusing the challenge would have shown fear. And cowering in the ring would have, too. Maybe *that* was what Yelena had tried to elicit. Fear. And assert all humans were cowards by association.

"No," she said quietly. "I'm your ally, and I trust you."

But even as she said the words and closed her eyes, a coldness swept over her, claimed her, raising every hair on her body.

Maybe it hadn't been *bravery* but bravado. Maybe she'd miscalculated, fatally, and Yelena would kill her.

She won't.

A hiss cut through the air, and a crunch hit, rippling impact through the sand and floor beneath her head.

She sucked in a breath, shaking, willing her hands to move, but Yelena's hold on her wrists was too tight.

The shadow over her shifted—Yelena—freeing her up to move a little.

Aless tapped her foot twice on the sand.

When she opened her eyes, Yelena was still above her, eyes narrowed, her brow creased.

"You—you don't belong here," Yelena snapped, then with a sharp breath, pulled away.

Minutes passed by, or hours, as she looked up at the black stone ceiling, waiting for her pulse to slow, for her breath to even out. Firelight flickered reflections in the mirror-like surface, and voices began to filter in. Cheers.

She pushed up to her elbow, her tailbone and her back sore as she brushed off the sand, and there was a sea of smiling faces, calls of encouragement. As she stood properly, Veron became visible between other people, held down still, his eyes wild as they met hers.

Yelena already stood at the center, paying her no mind, so she headed back to her spot at the table, nodding acknowledgements as others patted her on the back and offered kind words, and a dark-elf woman offering her treatment that she turned down. She was just a little sore, that was all.

Gavri winked at her, then she, Riza, and Zoran released Veron, who shot up from his seat.

He gathered her up in his arms, holding her tight, inhaling a sharp breath over her head before lowering his mouth to hers. Her heart raced anew as his lips pressed hard against hers, his kiss passionate and deep, his body taut and leaning into hers.

He pulled away, far too soon, and held her face cupped in his hands, searching her eyes with his own, his chest rising and falling in short, fast breaths. "Aless, that was—"

"A success?" she offered.

"—dangerous," he said quietly, before pulling her in once more. "And a success," he added, and she could hear the smile in his voice.

His arms around her weren't just warm and safe, but they soothed a loving familiarity into her, a feeling she wanted to wrap herself in and never leave, to fall asleep in and wake up in, to feel every day and every night, for as long as she wanted, whenever she wanted. She closed her eyes and breathed him in, the smell of leather and that forest stream, and something deeper, primal, that she couldn't get enough of.

Soon the whooping and rhythmic thuds sounded again, and when she turned back to the ring, Yelena stood at its center, arms clasped behind her back, staring down Veron.

"She picked the wrong day," he growled under his breath, then stood aside and thumped his fist to his chest. With one last glance at her, he rounded the table, cracking his knuckles as he strode to the ring.

"They were always evenly matched, but today, mark my words, by the time he's through with her, she'll be no more than a glorified mop," Gavri remarked, her voice low among the din.

She sat down, and her bottom rebelled, but she'd give it a hot bath later as a peace offering. Gavri patted at her hair, shaking out the sand, and she grinned in quiet thanks.

As Yelena and Veron circled one another in the ring, their gazes locked, their movements perfectly synchronized, it really *was* like a dance. Yelena met his ferocity with a quirked brow and a mischievous gaze, and he matched her every move with a countermove, their bodies turning to one another's whims without even touching.

It was as if they'd done this a hundred times before, a thousand times before, and knew everything about each other, a sort of natural intimacy that would take years to build, or more.

Yelena threw a punch, and he spun away with a kick that she ducked. She countered, and he caught her foot, then hooked her heel out from under her.

But her legs closed around him, and she arched her back, her palms hitting the ground as she tried to throw him. He spun sideways, but caught the floor with a palm and swept a leg low that she leaped to evade.

They knew each other's moves, every single one, and flowed around one another like winds in a cyclone.

Evenly matched.

She started, lowering her gaze to the table, and her half-eaten plate of food. No, Veron didn't care about that, not with Yelena, but every moment she watched them together only reinforced how perfect they looked, what an ideal couple they made, and how she could never be his equal like Yelena could. Never as strong or as skilled. Never a dark-elf warrior. And this dance, this seduction, would be something she could never do.

As for what he *did* see in her—could it be enough? Could it ever be enough?

Had he forgiven her for the lie?

Someone walked past—Zoran—and left the grand hall. In the ring beyond, Veron and Yelena battled blow for blow, with Yelena's face lit up in a broad grin.

Yelena looked confident, but Veron would handle her. He won small engagements, and bit by bit, he weakened her.

With Zoran at the stable, all that remained was getting Gavri there, *not* alone, so Queen Nendra wouldn't suspect anything. And nothing *would* happen—Gavri knew better—but they'd finally have a chance to talk.

She stood. "I think I'll take some air," she said over Gavri's head to Gabriella and Riza. "Will you tell Veron I'll be right back?"

"Your Highness," Riza said, rising. "I shall accompany you."

"No need," she said with a happy shrug. "I'll take Gavri. We'll be back shortly." She nodded to Gavri, who rose as well.

Riza eyed the two of them, then glanced back at the ring. "Very well. I will inform His Highness."

Riza inclined her head and waited. Veron and Yelena were still fighting when Gavri escorted her out of the grand hall, into the ample glowing green light of the bioluminescent mushrooms.

"Thank you for this," Gavri whispered to her as they headed for the stables, traversing the black causeways over waterfalls and dark depths.

"You haven't seen each other for two thousand years," she replied softly. "I think a private conversation is the very least you deserve."

Gavri nodded, slowly brushing a fingertip over her lip. "By the way, what you did in there..."

With a shrug, she shook her head. "Now there will be no misunderstanding that my fists are useless."

Gavri grasped her wrist. "Strength isn't just in your fists. Strength is

relying on your knowledge in the face of danger. It's standing up to a challenge with courage and dignity. Not running away."

She'd wanted to do right by Veron's people—now *her* people, too. If
Veron had possessed any remaining doubt of her commitment to him or
their people, he could now cast it aside. She would do whatever it took to
protect them, to keep them safe, and to maintain the peace. Whatever
it took.

Gavri lowered her gaze. "Actually something I needed to be reminded of."

Aless cocked her head toward the stables. "Then let's go see Zoran."

With a smile, Gavri escorted her there, where a quiet whinny came
through the open doors. At a nearby stall, strapping Zoran was feeding Noc
an apple.

"We're all feasting on human foods," Zoran said softly, "so why should he
be left out?" He looked over his shoulder with a pensive grin, fixing Gavri
with a soft gaze.

Gavri stood still, chewing her lip a long moment before she exhaled
sharply and ran to him, threw her arms around him. He gathered her up in his
embrace, held her close.

"I'm sorry I never said goodbye," he whispered, resting his cheek on
Gavri's head. "There was so much I wanted to say, but—"

Clearing her throat, Aless meandered to Noc's stall and opened it. "I think
I'll take Noc for a walk and give you two some time."

Gavri glanced over her shoulder with teary eyes and nodded. "I'll come
find you in a bit. Stay close, Your Highness."

She smiled. "I will."

While Zoran and Gavri whispered to one another, she strapped a halter on
Noc and attached a lead. "You could use a little walk, couldn't you?" she whispered, rubbing his nose. "Let's go."

He snorted softly and nuzzled her before heading with her to the open
doors. Outside, a few horses were corralled in dirt-laden paddocks, clustered
around water and feed troughs, but Noc led her past them... despite *her*
holding *his* lead.

Maybe a not-so-subtle message that he didn't need one.

A tunnel abutted the paddock area, not as large as the one they'd entered
Dunmarrow through—no, *Dun Mozg*. Why did the Sileni call it *Dunmarrow*
when the dark-elves called it *Dun Mozg*?

Or *Nightbloom*, for that matter? *Nozva Rozkveta*.

Sparse floor candelabra lit the tunnel as they entered, casting firelight on a
million shining colors.

She gasped.

Every surface was embedded with veins of gems, glittering in a kaleido-
scope of colors, reflecting their vibrancy on one another, and on her and Noc.

"You're a romantic at heart, aren't you?" she joked softly, and he swatted her with his tail.

She petted his neck, gazing at the beauty around her, unable to decide where she should look. The jewel-studded tunnel continued on an upward incline, and she neared the edge to smooth her fingers over the many treasures.

It was strange. Dark-elves claimed not to value things like this, and yet, if that were true, surely they would have bartered all these jewels away by now? But here they were, preserved in their natural beauty, a joy for all to look upon.

Noc tossed his head. She grabbed his halter as he pulled her backward. "What's wrong?"

The ground beneath their feet quaked. Dust rained from above, and bits of rubble thudded to the ground as something heavy crashed down behind them. Distant shouts rose up.

Noc dragged her up the incline—

Veron—

"Where are you going?" She tugged on Noc's halter to no avail. "Do you know a way out? We need to go back. Veron—"

Safe.

The word appeared in her mind, more like a feeling than a voice, and the world slowed around her as she looked at Noc, really *looked*. He eyed her as he led her, and those dark eyes—there was something reassuring there, in that deliberate gaze, in that slow blink.

He really wasn't just some horse.

With a resolute nod, she kept up with him, and the scent of fresh forest air filtered in while the crack and collapse of stone rumbled behind them.

Holy Mother's mercy, this tunnel was coming *down*.

Noc pulled to a halt, and she reached forward, her palms finding a bar. A barred set of doors!

Grunting with effort, she pulled at the bar, trying to lift it, and it rose—

A little more, a little more—

Finally over the hooks, it crashed to the floor. She pushed at the solid stone before her while the ground bucked, and Noc leaned against it until it finally started to grind open.

They pushed through leafy overgrowth into a dark grove of tall turkey oaks, with the waxing moon casting its glow overhead. The rumbling echoed from the tunnel, no louder than before, as Noc led them to a grassy clearing.

Veron—would he be all right? Would Gavri, Zoran, Gabriella, and Riza? Everyone? Veron was still back in the palace, still in the city, where she couldn't go.

She clutched at the satin over her chest, trying to catch her breath. The dark-elves had lived underground long before, and they had to have shelters of some kind.

"What was that?" she asked, and Noc rested his head against her.

An earthquake? Veron had said since there were no earthquakes, the earth-movers had gone. If there had been an earthquake just now, did that mean—?

"Holy Mother's mercy," she whispered, clutching Noc's mane.

He squealed, an unsettled sound, and began to back up.

"We have to go back." She headed for the doors again, and whatever it took, she would—

Dark figures waded in from among the trees. Three of them, in long coats, with swords at their hips and crossbows in their hands.

Her pulse quickening, she stepped back, pressed herself against Noc.

As the three walked into the clearing, beneath the moon's light, they were men. Sileni men.

"Well, well. Look what our geomancer chased out." A crooked grin from one of them, a man with a mass of black curls.

"Your Highness," the second one mocked with an elaborate bow. "The general will be glad to see you unharmed."

The general. Tarquin Belmonte.

They closed in as Noc kicked out with his hind legs.

CHAPTER 17

*V*eron caught Yelena's kick and shoved her out of the ring when a great rumble trembled through the hall.

People leaped from the benches, and Yelena moved to his side.

"Earthmovers?" he asked, frowning as he tried to isolate the sound.

Yelena shook her head and looked toward Nendra. "Mati?" she called out.

"Witches," Nendra answered, standing at the head of the table, her voice echoing. "Dun Mozg's heart is arcanir. They will not get through to us."

No magic could penetrate arcanir, so they would be safe here. He looked to the section where he and Aless had been sitting, but only Riza looked back at him, her face grim. Where Aless and Gavri had been, only two empty spaces remained.

While the floor shook, he ran toward Riza, and she strode to meet him.

He grabbed her armored shoulder. "Where's Aless?"

"She went to take some air and took Gavri with her," she replied, grasping his forearm.

Behind her, Gabriella caught up to them. "Your Highness, I think she might be at the stables."

"The stables?" Why would she go there? But as he looked toward Nendra and her concubines, her consort was nowhere in sight. *Zoran.*

He marched up to Nendra and bowed his head. "Your Majesty, I must take my leave—"

"Find your wife, Veron." With a raise of her hand, she dismissed him, and he raced across the grand hall with Riza and Gabriella, and all of his kuvari followed in his wake.

Outside the grand hall, dust misted from the ceiling, and everywhere people scrambled for purchase as tremors wove through the rock. Gavri and Zoran wouldn't let anything happen to Aless. They'd keep her safe. No doubt everything was just fine.

Even knowing all this, he ran for the stables and didn't stop until he dashed through the open doors. Horses squealed in their stalls, but Aless was nowhere in sight. Neither was Noc.

Some horses circled restlessly in the paddock, but—

"Your Highness," Riza called.

He followed the sound of her voice to a pile of rubble at a tunnel opening, where Riza, Gavri, and Zoran pried debris off the pile frantically. Deep, Darkness, and Holy Ulsinael, if Aless was—if she was under the rubble—

His heart hammering in his chest, he was already running before he could think to. He tore chunks of rock away from the rubble, clawing through it wildly.

"Your Highness," Gavri said shakily, "she left with Noc, only for a few minutes, and—"

He threw a slab of rubble aside. No words mattered right now. "Just find her," he snapped, and they all dug through the debris.

Holy Ulsinael, keep her safe. Deep and Darkness, cloak her in your sanctuary.

His hands bled, but he didn't care. Let them. Let them break, if it meant finding Aless safe, but there was nothing. Nothing.

Finally two of the kuvari cleared away a large piece of rubble. Behind it, two slabs formed a passage, and he darted into it.

"Brother!" Zoran called after him. "It's too dangerous! They could collapse if that—"

Rubble crashed behind him and voices shouted, but he squeezed through and picked a path until finally a night breeze blew in.

A doorway. A Gate.

He ran for it, and through, where the undergrowth gave way to sparse forest in the dark.

A loud neigh—Noc—and a scream followed.

Aless.

His heart caught in his throat, he bolted toward the sound, cutting through the foliage. In the clearing ahead, two men dragged Aless, kicking and screaming, south. Noc clamped his teeth down on the lanky one's shoulder, eliciting a cry.

Just ahead, a bearded man lay in the grass, groaning, with a crossbow nearby. Veron seized it as he passed—

Aless struck and kicked at Lanky, locked down by Noc.

"Just kill the horse!" Lanky shouted to a grim-faced third, who drew his sword.

Veron took aim with the crossbow and shot the bolt twenty yards directly into Grim's chest, making him stagger backward.

"Veron!" Aless shouted, repeatedly hitting Lanky, who struck Noc on the nose and dragged her away.

He closed in, grabbed Lanky by the coat, and threw him backward. Aless tumbled to the ground as Grim ripped the bolt from his own chest and slashed at him with the sword.

Lanky shot up to his feet, and Veron pulled the man to himself, catching Grim's sword with Lanky's gut.

"Behind you!" Aless shouted, laboring to her feet.

He snap-kicked Lanky's back, sending both him and Grim to the ground as footsteps crunched from behind.

A blade slashed across his arm before he could dodge as Beard pressed his advantage. A cut—he ducked—a lunge, and he evaded, caught Beard's sword-arm, and yanked him forward before burying his claws in Beard's neck.

Blood sprayed his face when Aless screamed, and a set of arms constricted his neck. He clawed at the gauntleted hands, grabbed for the man's head—

A sharp cry, and blood gushed over the side of his face.

The arms released, and he leaped away, spinning to face the man.

A body thudded to the ground.

Aless stood over Grim with wide, bulging eyes, gulping in breaths. The crossbow bolt was buried in Grim's temple, his face stained with blood, his eyes frozen in death.

"I… I—" she stammered.

She'd killed a man.

She'd killed a man to help *him*.

"Are you hurt?" He grasped her upper arms, but her haunted gaze remained fixed on the dead man. "Aless," he said, giving her a little shake. "Please, are you hurt?"

With a shiver, she looked up at him, wide eyes shining, lips parted, and covered her mouth with a hand before exhaling a huge breath. She began to fall, but he caught her, held her tight, rocked her gently.

"They were going to take me away," she blurted, her voice breaking. "Veron, I was so—I thought that—"

"I know," he whispered, stroking her back softly. This was where she belonged, safe in his arms. Loved. And never in his life, in centuries, in millennia, would he allow her to be taken. Ever. If she was in danger, he'd follow her to the end of the world, to the end of life itself. Because this was where he belonged, too. With her.

She'd looked so soft, so fragile, his human bride, but tonight she'd killed a man to save his life. The woman he loved was tough—tougher than he'd ever imagined.

Her plan to leave him didn't matter. The lie didn't matter. Nothing else mattered but this, her, here. And she *had* to know how much he loved her.

"Your Highness!" Riza bellowed from a distance, quieter voices and footsteps accompanying her.

Still holding Aless, he looked over his shoulder. Riza, Gavri, Zoran, and the rest of his kuvari paused in the clearing, splitting to check the perimeter.

"Dispose of these three," he said to Riza.

She approached, glowering at the bodies. "Brotherhood?"

He nodded. "Scouts. They must be using a witch to try to force us out, then using scouts to pick over the area and find a way in."

"When these don't report in—" Riza began.

"Let's make sure Nendra is prepared."

Riza gestured to Danika and two other kuvari, who moved in on the bodies.

"Is Her Highness all right?" Gavri asked, taking a step forward with Zoran.

He glared at her.

"Veron," Aless whispered, "it wasn't her fault. I was just outside the stable and—"

"She should have been *with* you," he shot back.

"But the collapse separated us. If not for Noc leading me outside, I'd be..." She lowered her gaze as Noc trotted up to them.

I'm never done thanking you, my friend.

Noc bobbed his head.

But now it fell to him to tell Nendra battle was at her doorstep, and Yelena's harsh stance on the human and dark-elf alliance would only grow in popularity. "Come. Let's help Queen Nendra prepare as much as we can. We're together in this."

He ushered Aless past Gavri and toward the tunnel while Zoran took Noc; he'd have to lead him by way of another entrance.

"Veron," Aless whispered with a wince.

He slowed. "Are you all right? Are you hurt somewhere?" he asked, looking her over.

"It's my..." She blushed.

He suppressed a grin. He'd seen Yelena throw her onto her bottom. "I know just the thing for that."

A long soak in Dun Mozg's hot springs would soothe that ache... although he wanted—*really* wanted—to see to that himself.

Low, deep Stone Singing came from the Gate, singers asking the stone to remain stable.

Two kuvari rushed ahead of them into the tunnel, then called the all-clear. He and Aless crept through, squeezing through the tightness, back into the heart of Dun Mozg. Nendra's kuvari were already there, along with the Stone Singers, *stavbali* who built, and an *inzenyra* who designed.

"Veron," Aless began again, "I think we should send a message to my father."

He stopped, watching the rest of his kuvari exiting the tunnel.

"He won't want to risk this peace, not after all it cost him publicly to achieve it. And if a threat to my life isn't compelling enough, he can always be counted on to defend his pride," she added quietly.

"But your father isn't a direct ally of Dun Mozg," he replied. Would King Macario risk his soldiers and his reputation without a formal alliance between Silen and Dun Mozg?

Aless nodded. "You said dark-elves travel between queendoms by way of the tunnels."

"I did."

"What if we send a message to your mother, too, and most of our cargo to Nozva Rozkveta by way of the tunnels," she said, "and then we travel light, by land, with our forces and lead the Brotherhood away from Dun Mozg?"

He crossed his arms, pacing before the paddock. If they stayed here and the Brotherhood laid siege, it could sour the people's view on the human and dark-elf alliance, but it might also risk terms between Dun Mozg and Nozva Rozkveta.

But if they did what Aless suggested, if they could stay ahead of the Brotherhood, it would mean leading the enemy to a prepared Nozva Rozkveta with —ideally—King Macario's army flanking. Strategically advantageous. And it would mean preserving favorable views of both the alliance with the humans and between Dun Mozg and Nozva Rozkveta.

And Mati would never want him to bring their problems to an ally's doorstep if it could be avoided. She'd back this plan.

"I like it," he said to her at last, and she rubbed her hands together—blood-stained hands. "I'll brief Riza and have her work out the details with Nendra. We'll set out before the rising call." He approached Riza at the tunnel entrance to do just that.

"What about you?" Aless called after him, following in his wake. "Us?"

He turned back to her, took her shoulders gently. Her large, dark eyes gazed up at his. She was brilliant, clever, brave. But tonight, she was completely and utterly his to care for, in every way she needed for as long as she needed, until she felt safe again.

"You were attacked tonight. I won't leave your side."

"I... I need to know..." She took a deep breath. "Have you forgiven me?"

Yes, he wanted to say instantly. He'd felt it as clear as a lifespring, only moments earlier.

She'd gone into this marriage under duress and had hidden that from him from the moment he'd met her in Bellanzole, and that... had been aggravating. Thinking they'd been allies, friends even—perhaps something more, when she'd been forced into this and planning to leave all the while. Would she have even said goodbye? Or would it have been easier to just leave with a smile on her face?

But it *had* been aggravating. *Had*. They'd spoken about it, and she'd made an effort time and again to prove her commitment. Sometimes to the point of recklessness, like tonight in the ring.

And although she'd hidden the circumstances from him, when he thought of it now, he had no resentment in his heart toward her. None whatsoever. It hadn't been a betrayal, malicious and sharpened to hurt. She'd been a scared human, sacrificing herself in marriage to a person she'd never met, from a culture she'd known nothing about—or worse, had been misinformed about. If she'd been weak, despite all that, she would have resigned herself to it.

But that wasn't the woman he loved. His Aless was strong. When someone told her there was no way out, she made her own. She hadn't resolved to be with him because her father had told her to; she'd made up her own mind, and for that, he loved her even more. There was no betrayal in her affection now.

"Yes, I forgive you," he answered.

CHAPTER 18

*A*s Aless watched Veron speaking to Riza, everything else seemed to fade, to disappear. Colors blurred around her, sounds muffled to unintelligible vibrations, and her gaze wouldn't be lured away from her husband, who passed on instructions—her instructions—in an important matter.

He'd *listened* to her, heard her out, considered her input, and it wasn't the first time. He'd listened to her in Stroppiata, too, about the entry, when they'd fought the harpies, about the shrine…

It would have been easy for him to wave her off, walk away, ignore her "meddling" and tell her not to worry her pretty little head over such complicated matters, as Papà had always told her.

But to Veron…

To Veron, she wasn't just a *pretty little head*. She was *someone*. A person with ideas, with a voice, with a need to help and contribute, valid opinions, and he'd listened.

And then, tonight, he'd *forgiven* her. Finally, that hasty plan from before the wedding didn't stand between them.

She would still follow her dream, but she couldn't imagine it any other way but with Veron at her side. Together, they'd see the library realized someday. She'd propose it to him, to his mother, to anyone who'd listen until it existed.

As Riza saluted and strode away, Veron glanced back over his shoulder, met her eyes with his own warm, golden gaze, and she had to remember to blink.

He returned to her, over six feet of warrior, strong, deadly, *hers*. Blood stained his jaw, his neck, his leather armor, and some of his hair, but she wanted nothing more than to wrap herself around him and kiss him until she forgot where she ended and he began.

With a smile, he offered her a hand, and she took it. He rubbed a thumb gently over the drying blood on her skin. "Let's get cleaned up."

He walked her toward their quarters across swaths of shining black pathways, past babbling streams and cascading waterfalls, shimmering with the soft sage glow of the bioluminescence.

A faint tremor shook the surface of the water, and she tightened her grip on Veron's hand.

"Magic can't penetrate Dun Mozg." He cupped her cheek. "It's encased in arcanir. You're safe."

She drew a slow, deep breath through her nose. Thank the Mother.

Veron pressed a gentle kiss to her forehead, and then to her lips.

Her fingers ached for him, and she moved closer, rested them on the broad expanse of his chest, let them slip slowly to the sculpted hardness of his abdomen. The rhythm of his breath changed, deepened, slowed.

Another tremor, and she blinked, meeting heavy-lidded, darkening eyes. He skimmed her jawline with his fingers, raised her chin, held her gaze. Her lips parted, and a shaky breath escaped them.

A couple of passersby smiled at them, and she became very aware of just how this looked. And how it *felt*.

Veron tipped his head in the direction of their quarters, and she nodded. The sooner they cleaned off all this blood, the better.

Once inside, she pulled off her boots as he did his, then began unfastening her bloodied dress. Veron lit a candle and then headed to the basin, where he dipped his hands and began to scrub them and wash his face.

Beneath her dress, she wore a short challis chemise tucked into trousers— her *stained* trousers, so she pulled those off, too. She moved to the basin next to Veron, washed her face and then her own hands together with his, using the olive-oil-and-rosemary soap she'd brought from Bellanzole. She soaped up his hands, too, careful of his claws, as he smiled.

"It smells like you," he said, raising a palm to his nose. "What is it? This flower?"

"It's an herb. Rosemary."

Closing his eyes, he made a low, rolling sound in his throat, and warmth rippled into her, made her tingle all over. It was a sound she'd never tire of hearing, that would grace the best of her dreams—the ones she hoped not to wake from.

He set down the soap, rinsed his hands, then set about unstrapping his leather armor. She reached for the straps, too, stroked her palms over smooth leather, helped him until he was down to his clothes, just a shirt and braies. There was a cut on his arm, and she took hold of his hand, examined the wound.

"Veron, you're hurt."

With a shake of his head and a smile, he pulled off his shirt and presented his bicep. The slash was already partially healed.

"We recover quickly," he said, although she dabbed at it with a clean washcloth. He took her hand. "I'm fine, Aless. Really."

He gazed down at her, his mouth curving, and there was a playfulness there. A teasing.

So he thought she was overreacting. Maybe she was. But the notion of him being hurt—at all—made her worry so much that she didn't know what to do with herself. Apparently fussing wasn't the answer. She smiled to herself and glanced away, to his bare chest, strong and smooth, and the black sun tattooed there.

"It's beautiful," she whispered, stroking it with her fingertips.

"You'll have one, too, Aless," he said, his voice deep and flowing as he covered her hand with his, "if you choose to go through with the second ceremony in Nozva Rozkveta."

"I *do* choose to. Veron, I made that desperate plan before I ever knew you. Now that I've gotten to know you, I love you. I want to pursue my dream *with* you. And I want to marry you. As many times and in as many ways as you want."

Slowly, he leaned in, unbearably slow, then tipped her chin up to his and kissed her, taking her in his arms. His hair brushed her cheek as she opened her mouth to him, pressed herself against his hard body. Holy Mother's mercy, he *had* to know, *had* to understand that she'd never leave him, *ever*. That she loved him, with everything she was and everything she had to give, no matter what she'd thought before knowing him.

With every breath, she inhaled the forest-stream scent of him, and that something deeper, something primal, that she couldn't get enough of. *Veron.*

His tongue claimed her mouth in slow, sensual strokes—strokes that made her whimper, made her heart pound. She wanted him. More than anything or anyone she'd ever wanted before, she wanted *him*.

I want you to know that I'm open to your wishes, and that you shouldn't fear rejection should you express them to me, he'd said to her once, on their wedding night.

She swallowed. As she leaned into him, against the hard, solid length of him—she gasped. His thoughts couldn't be too far from her own.

"Veron," she breathed between kisses, "I want to... I wish to..."

She'd been bold her entire life, had said things to lovers that would make a courtesan blush, but here, now, with *him*, she couldn't even bring herself to form a coherent sentence, and Holy Mother help her, if he *laughed* at her right now, she would just die, instantaneously, of embarrassment.

He pulled away, just enough for his soft golden gaze to lock with hers, and then intertwined his fingers with hers. Candlelight flickered, its warm glow cast against his skin. Her heart skipped a beat as he searched her eyes.

"I want to make love with you, Aless," he whispered, making her shiver. "I want to know you, as closely as one heart can know another, and I want you to know me."

Every inch of her tensed and trembled in equal parts, and there was a good chance she was about to tackle him no matter what he said next.

"Do you want me to, Aless?" A teasing smile tugged at the corner of his mouth as he peered down at her with gleaming eyes.

She nodded—more than once—and threw her arms around him, rose on her tiptoes to kiss him, and he took her mouth, grabbed her bottom, and scooped her up. The spot was tender, but she didn't care, not right now, not until the need coursing in her veins got its due.

Her mouth never leaving his, she locked her legs around his hips, let him take her to bed, where she threw off her chemise as he pulled off his braies.

In his nakedness, he was the most beautiful sight she'd ever seen—as if his god or hers had sculpted him from marble, chiseled his fit physique to the perfection standing before her now. Her *husband*. He was big, strong, *hers*, and he would know it to the core of his existence by the time she was through with him tonight.

He gave her a slow once-over, devouring her with his eyes, his chest rising and falling with every powerful breath, and she would have given anything —*anything*—to know what he was thinking right now, looking upon a human woman, *his* human woman.

He took her in his arms, claimed her with his lips, his kisses roving down her neck as she buried her hands in his long, soft hair.

"Teach my hands how to touch you, Aless," he whispered, and his touch was gentle curiosity, unbinding her hair, raking through her curls; he brushed lightly over her breasts, and when she gasped, he firmed his touch, rubbed them, kissed them. He stroked along her ribcage and over her waist, down her thigh and all the way to her ankle, which he grasped and pressed to his lips.

"Teach my lips how to kiss you," he whispered, his kisses fluttering along her skin, so light she squirmed as they graced her quivering inner thigh.

"Endlessly," she answered softly, and he smiled before pulling her to the edge of the bed and descending to her. He kissed her belly, her hip, and lower, lower, until his lips met her core, making her gasp. Slowly, he pleasured her, his passionate, deliberate strokes coaxing her breaths out in erratic puffs while her hands clutched the bedding in tight fistfuls. Pressure rose in her, and built and built until she writhed beneath him, close, so close, tension rising, rising until it crested, peaked, bursting from her in cries as she reached for him.

"Please," she said, wiggling farther up the bed as he braced over it, teasing with feather-light strokes over her thighs, across her belly, over her breasts. The tips of his long hair tickled her stomach before he kissed her chest, lavished her sensitive spots with a playfulness that made her back arch off the bed.

She buried her fingers in his hair, urged him up to her face, and his mouth met hers anew, reclaimed her needy lips. As she angled to him, whimpering for union, heavenly, wonderful, *glorious* union, he was ready against her. *So* ready, but when she rocked against him, a sharpness skimmed her bottom where his hand gripped her.

Just a graze—no matter—she didn't react, kept kissing him, her own hands roving the corded musculature of his back.

"Aless," he whispered between kisses, "teach me to love you the way you wish to be loved."

She moved against his hardness, gasping, pushing, and Holy Mother's mercy, if he didn't take her now, right now, she would die of want.

"Show me," he said to her, his usually deep voice an octave lower.

He didn't want to hurt her, maybe didn't want to presume, to lose control —he wanted to please her, to be who she needed, to provide what she needed. As she wanted to do for him.

"On your back," she whispered.

His mischievous gaze locked with hers, he did as bidden, and she sat astride him, held him at her core, watched his mouth fall open and his entire body go taut as he hissed an oath to his god.

With a gasp, she took him slowly, so carefully, until at last they were completely, utterly one, and despite his tense muscles rippling, he stroked her softly, her thighs, her hips, with perfect self-control. His eyes followed every-where he touched, heavy lidded and intense, taking her in with a boundless hunger. There were a thousand things she wanted to tell him, a thousand memories she wanted to share, and millions more she wanted to live with him, to learn with him, to create together.

He wasn't afraid to hold her gaze, to watch the truth on her face, just as she watched his, the love there, the desire, and not just for this moment, but for countless more, and for her.

She knew in that moment, in those eyes, that he would never betray her. That he would always love her. And that he would always hear her voice, and listen.

As she moved, she held his gaze, too, looked into his eyes, adoring and awed, his eyebrows drawn tight. A frisson rippled through her lower belly; the hard fullness of him inside her was pleasure, unbearable pleasure, and with every movement, she trembled, breathed shakily, the heat of his every touch pooling at her core, where it only wanted, and wanted.

His slow, rough breaths, rhythmic and primal, began to quicken, and her own surrender was just there, within reach, and she took him harder, faster, chasing it, chasing it, until at last she caught it, cried out, again and again, waves of hot sensation cascading through her, throbbing through her veins, pulsing at her core. As he groaned, low and deep, she didn't stop, kept going until his eyes pressed shut and his mouth fell open, need claiming his face with creased determination that—with a hiss—pleasure freed and freed and freed with every panted breath. Warmth filled her up, heat spreading through every part of her, kindled by his touch, his care, and the love they made together.

Veron, *her* Veron, lay beneath her, gazing up at her with stars in his eyes, and she reached for his face, gently stroking along his jaw, over his lips, and down over the chiseled beauty of his black-sun chest and his abdomen.

With a grin, he urged her down to him, tucked her curls behind her ear, and kissed her. She took his lip between hers, explored his mouth with her tongue, teased it with playful strokes as he rubbed her bare back with firm, sensual pressure.

"Was it worth the wait?" she breathed.

He smiled. "*You* were worth the wait, Aless."

Completely serene, he watched her, and she leaned in to kiss him again.

"So is that how the dark-elves do things?" she asked with a grin. "Because I approve."

He laughed in his throat and shook his head. "In essence, yes," he drawled, "but with us, everything is a test of strength. Even lovemaking."

She tried to picture pinning him, gasping as he rolled her over, dueling between the sheets. If that was how things usually went, then with her, he'd been exceedingly cautious, had submitted himself completely to her whim, to her ways, and let her do as she'd pleased while he'd resisted his instincts, restrained his body. He'd been so taut, muscles rippling, quaking, and it had been *restraint*.

The day she'd first met him, he'd clasped his hands behind his back, but when she'd taken a step away, he'd revealed them, held them at his sides, shown her he'd meant her no harm.

"I love you," she said, and his embrace around her tightened. She lay down at his side, nestled into the crook of his shoulder, into the warmth of him, as he caressed her arm. She hadn't told him, had she, since he'd confessed his love for her in Stroppiata's garden? "Did I wait too long to answer?"

"You already answered," he said softly. "With that purple-flower perfume and your eagerness to learn the bow. With your friendliness toward Gavri and

Noc. With your courage when you fought out there against the Brotherhood—"

"Aha," she replied. "And the ring?"

"—which I'm still frustrated about," he finished with a laugh. "I've felt your love in all these things, Aless, but... yes, it's good to hear the words, too."

She poked him, and he laughed again, then nuzzled her head with his nose before kissing her lightly there.

"I love you, too," he said softly, slowly, and urged her onto her back. There was no laughter in his eyes now, only rapt attention, and he reached out to brush her lips with his thumb before taking them with his own again.

His hands explored her gently, slowly, roving over her bottom, and then he went rigid. Froze. Pulled away.

He stared down at his palm, glanced at her, and left the bed.

Wriggling to the edge, she eyed him. "Veron?"

He rubbed his face with his hand, pacing the room, then held up the other. Blood.

CHAPTER 19

*B*y Deep and Darkness, he'd *hurt* her. Again.

As desire had claimed him, he'd remembered to be gentle, to keep his touch light, to avoid injuring her—and it had happened anyway.

"Veron?" she asked again, rising from the bed. She tried to embrace him, but he pulled away.

He shook his head. No, he couldn't touch her like this, not again. Not with his claws.

"It's all right," she whispered, rubbing his back. "It was only a little scratch." She kissed his shoulder. "Come back to bed."

Every dark-elf of worth had claws—sharp, strong, battle-ready claws. Claws he had defended her with just earlier tonight. If they were broken, taken in battle, or deformed, it was dishonor. Weakness.

Aless locked her arms around him from behind, her delicate, slender arms, with her supple, fragile skin. His lover, his partner, his wife. His *human* wife.

He wouldn't risk hurting her again, not for all the honor and strength in the Deep. Never again.

He could never give her lavish human celebrations, with new dances every season and theatre and opera and fashion and excess. He could never give her a legion of servants in her household to pamper her as she'd been in the palace. Nor could he give her a place in the sun, in the sky realm, among her kind and sunshine and light. He could never impress her or court her the way a human man would.

But the very *least* he could do was never hurt her. Keep her safe. The very *least*.

As he approached the table of toiletries, she let him go, and he searched through them until he found her nail file.

"Veron, what are you doing?" Her voice quavered.

"What I should have done before our wedding," he murmured, then began filing down his claws.

She grasped his hand, her eyebrows knitted together. "But won't your reputation—"

He raised her hand to his lips, kissed it. All his life, he'd guarded his reputation fiercely, never wanting to be anything but a credit to Mati and Nozva Rozkveta. But Deep, Darkness, and Holy Ulsinael, what did his *reputation* matter in comparison to her wellbeing?

"I don't want to hurt you, Aless, ever," he whispered, lowering her hand. "And if anyone questions my battle prowess, I won't need claws to trounce them in the ring."

He had been trained by Mati and Zoran—the best—and he didn't need claws to fight.

He started filing them again, as short as her human nails, shorter even. They'd grow back in a month, but he'd just file them down again, and the month after, and the one after that, for the rest of their lives.

Backing up toward the bed, she tossed her long, dark hair over her shoulder and raised an eyebrow. "Are you certain you need to do this now?"

He'd already taken several steps in her direction before he realized it. With a shake of his head, he continued filing while she giggled. Their first night together, and she already knew the power she held over him—and she wasn't afraid to use it. If she ever brought out that sheer red thing from their wedding night, he wasn't certain there was anything he wouldn't do.

"Not sure I've ever seen anyone file their nails so fast in my life," she teased, hopping onto the bed and kicking her legs playfully. She leaned back, propped a foot upon the bed, and eyed him over her round, bare breasts.

She parted her thighs, only a little, and Holy Ulsinael, the nail file clattered to the floor.

Veron held Aless's hand, leading her down the passage to the hot springs.

"Where are we going?" she asked with a tilt of her head, tightening the sash of her robe and looking around. "I can barely move."

He huffed a laugh under his breath. So far, they had spent the entire night in bed, and he would happily spend the rest of it there, but Aless couldn't leave Dun Mozg without visiting the hot springs—especially considering they had a couple of days on horseback ahead of them.

"After that landing in the ring earlier, I think you'll like where we're going." He smiled at her over his shoulder.

The air turned balmy right before the entrance, the soft splash of water babbling nearby. He led her inside, and she gasped.

Silvery moonlight peeked in high overhead, refracting off jeweled veins in the stone, flowing down to the steam rising off the vivid teal water. Streams cascaded from the rock into the spring with a pleasant, continuous sound. It was, thankfully, empty.

"I thought you could use some hot—"

She threw her arms around his neck and kissed him, then kissed him again... deeper, slowly; untying her sash, he moved toward the water, unwrapped the towel from around his waist before wading into the soothing heat. She let the robe fall to her feet—and Holy Ulsinael, he'd never tire of seeing her naked—and then she followed, entering with a lengthy, quiet moan.

Broad steps descended into the sultry water, and he sat on one, submerged to his chest, and she sank in next to him.

"Can we stay here forever?" she murmured, her eyes closed as she settled into his arms.

He sighed. "We can stay here... a little less than an hour."

With a quiet whine, she rubbed her cheek on his chest before resting against him.

To make their plan work, they'd be leaving Dun Mozg before dawn. As it was, they'd be traveling on little to no sleep, but he'd already planned on letting her sleep in the saddle while they rode.

"Veron," she said, lightly stroking his abdomen, "can we talk about Gavri?"

Clearing his throat, he straightened. No, they absolutely could *not* talk about Gavri while she touched him like that.

She giggled and settled her arm around him. "Sorry."

He rolled his eyes and sighed. "What about Gavri?"

As much as he cared for Gavri, her decisions hadn't exactly been brilliant lately—from betraying him, to carrying on with Zoran, to *derelicting her duty* to guard Aless.

She was quiet a moment, nuzzling his chest with her cheek. "Gavri told me that once lost, your trust is unrecoverable."

Gavri *would* say that, because up until recently, it had been the truth. After he'd lost Ata, he'd never wanted to go through it again. "One betrayal has the power to destroy everything. And I'm tired of losing things."

"But you forgave me."

He had. And it had happened through none of his own making—clearly his heart knew better than he did, and he wasn't about to complain.

Aless sat up and looked at him, her palm pressed over his heart. "People might sometimes betray your love, Veron, and you might lose them. But if you choose not to forgive, you don't have to worry about losing them...

because you've already pushed them away. It's still loss, but of your own making."

He blinked.

"Do you really want to lose Gavri?"

Even though Aless had lied, he'd fallen in love with her, hadn't want to lose her... had forgiven her.

He lowered his gaze to the water, watching its steam rise. But wasn't it better to lose someone knowingly, by his own choice, than to wait for a worse betrayal? Watching them walk away in deception, while he, without knowing the truth, was helpless to do anything about it? Wasn't it worth the years of wondering *what if*?

What if he hadn't let Ata leave that day? *What if* he'd followed him? *What if* he'd learned of Ata's plans?

Would he have been able to stop him? To save him? Would his father be alive right *now*?

"She told me about what happened with your father," Aless whispered. "You were just a child, Veron. It wasn't fair, but there was nothing you could have done."

He shook his head. "You're wrong. He was my *father*. I loved him, and I should have known him better than anyone. But I didn't." That day, he'd accepted Ata's smile without a second thought. "I have forgiven you, but there's a reason I don't forgive. I see people, Aless, but I don't understand them. I can know someone my entire life and not realize they're going to betray me. I can be in *love* with a person, and not know she's plotting to kill my mother. When it comes to understanding other people, I... I can't even trust myself."

If he trusted those who betrayed him, if he forgave them, would the next betrayal leave Aless dead? Or Mati? Or Riza? Or any of his sisters and brothers? His people?

He knew Aless would never betray him again, that she'd never hurt him or anyone he loved, and so he'd been able to forgive her. That had to be why.

But anyone else? He'd trusted Gavri after her lie, at least enough to let her continue performing guard duties, and what had happened? Aless and Noc could have been *buried under rubble*.

There was a reason he couldn't forgive betrayers. And it wasn't because they were terrible, or selfish, or evil. It was because he couldn't trust himself to understand them. And that could mean losing someone he loved... again.

Aless turned to face him, slowly brought her knees down around his hips, and settled into his lap. She wrapped her arms around his neck, and as hot as the water was, the warmth inside of him wasn't from the spring, but the soft look in her eyes as she leaned in and lightly brushed his lips with hers.

"People you love will let you down, Veron," she said softly. "I've been let down and I've let down others more times than I can count. But no one is perfect. Everyone makes mistakes. If you don't forgive, the only difference is that they'll make their mistakes without you. Is that really what you want?"

Those mistakes hurt. But never laughing with Gavri again? Or losing her, Aless, or any of his loved ones?

"And may I remind you," Aless said, kissing him lightly again as she leaned into him, "that if not for your forgiveness, we probably wouldn't be right here, like this, right now?"

A solid point. A very solid point.

"You might not be pushing away just the bad, but the good, too." Her mouth fell open as she rocked against him, water lapping about them.

Just the thought of her caring enough about his friends—and *him*—to broach this was enough to make it worth considering. "I'll think about it, I promise," he replied.

"Good," she said with a smile, and he held her close as he lifted her from the water. "Because we have a long ride ahead of us."

And a few days' worth of traveling, too.

CHAPTER 20

*a*s the rain started to fall midafternoon, Veron tucked Aless's copy of *A Modern History of Silen* inside her cloak, into her belt. Riding double with him on Noc, she'd been reading it aloud all morning since they'd left Dun Mozg, and the trip had been far less dull with her animated voice spinning tales.

She was fast asleep now, her head resting against his arm, and Noc's gait had become all the smoother.

You're fond of her, he told Noc.

So are you, Noc answered.

He laughed under his breath. It couldn't have anything to do with the apples she'd brought in their pack, which had mysteriously disappeared after their rest stop. Even for that short reprieve, she'd been eager to learn the bow, and could even hit a target now... sometimes.

"You spoil her," Yelena murmured, riding up to him, hooded and cloaked.

He sighed. Queen Nendra had insisted that Yelena and some of her kuvari accompany them to Nozva Rozkveta, saying she wouldn't risk Queen Zara's son and a Sileni princess being killed on the way home from her queendom.

"She was attacked last night, in case you forgot," he shot back. "By fanatics and, earlier, by *you.*"

She scoffed. "You know my mother would have me given into the Darkness if I destroyed the peace." She rolled her eyes. "Besides, let's not pretend this is about her little tumble in the ring, or the human scouts you killed." She gave him and Aless a stern once-over. "You were seen all over each other on the main thoroughfare. It was the talk of the cavern this morning. And then you"—she curled her upper lip—"*disfigured* yourself like that." She cocked her head toward his hands. "No dark-elf woman would have you now."

Aless nuzzled his arm sleepily, and he held her closer. He didn't want a dark-elf woman, or any other. The only one he needed was right here, would always be right here. "All that matters is she does."

Yelena shook her head.

"Let me guess—you disapprove."

A huff. "Well, she's no dark-elf." Yelena's eyes fixed on Aless. "But I heard she killed one of those scouts last night. A crossbow bolt through the head, *by hand*." She whistled softly. "She may not be a warrior, but she's not the typical scurrying salamander, either. I still don't like her, though."

From Yelena, that was a glowing endorsement.

"And I don't believe a word about those human deeds in her tales," she added with a grunt, "except the parts about all the dying and fleeing."

He suppressed a smile. So she'd been listening to Aless reading.

With the rain coming down, the day dragged traveling in the sky realm, but at least in the tunnels their cargo caravan wouldn't be slowed by it. No doubt the food and supplies from Bellanzole and Stroppiata would arrive in Nozva Rozkveta well before he did. He and Aless had also sent Gabriella with Danika to deliver the message to King Macario; with any luck, they'd take the tunnels as far as they could and stay out of the Brotherhood's reach.

Without carriages and cargo, his group made good time, even in the mud, moving fast enough to keep ahead of the Brotherhood's army while leading them away from Dun Mozg. He and Yelena had made sure to leave behind easily found tracks, so if the Brotherhood wanted him or Aless, they would follow.

Despite being faster, he and the rest of the group still took precautions— short rests only and sleeping in shifts. Scouts to make sure they weren't cut off by a forward team—Riza was out now with Kinga. With any luck, they'd be in Nozva Rozkveta tomorrow night.

Unlike Dun Mozg, however, Nozva Rozkveta wasn't encased in arcanir. While nestled on an enormous anima Vein, its only protection was that any magic used on it would mean the witch risking convergence—or what today's witches referred to as "fureur," according to Aless. Tapping into the earth's life force, its innate magic, would mean certain death for a witch. That and potentially upsetting the earth's anima.

It would be enough. Deep, Darkness, and Holy Ulsinael, it *had* to be enough.

Gavri rode nearby, and he'd promised he'd think about forgiving her.

One betrayal did have the power to destroy everything, but pushing someone away was destroying everything with his own hands. He couldn't predict others' actions with perfect accuracy, couldn't account for mistakes or betrayals, but when it came to people he loved, he wanted to be there for them through the bad *and* the good. When they made mistakes, he wanted to be there to help them, to support them, to save them if he could, instead of isolated, away, alone.

He was tired of losing things, but that meant he needed to stop pushing everyone away.

"Gavri," he called, and she looked over her shoulder, her wet braid swinging, and slowed. "I... I wanted to say I'm sorry. I overreacted."

Her eyes widened, and she glanced down at Aless before meeting his eyes anew. "You don't need to apologize to me, Veron. I understand."

He took a deep breath and brushed his fingers through Noc's mane. "No, I do. I want to. Your friendship has been... I can't even tell you how much it means to me. But one wrong move, and I just... I failed you."

She shook her head. "No, *I* failed *you*."

He huffed a half-laugh under his breath. "Malice doesn't hide in every untruth. One betrayal, one argument, doesn't have the power to destroy a friendship unless I let it. And I nearly did." Gavri's lie hadn't come from a malicious desire to betray him, but from a place of love, of care, for him. In her own—mistaken—way, she'd tried to defend him. "People are more than the sum of their mistakes, and you mean a lot to me. In spite of any mistakes —maybe even because of them—I want to be there for you. With you. Can you forgive me?"

With a subtle smile, she bowed her head. "Already forgiven. And I'm sorry I let things with Zoran interfere with my duties. I promise not to let that happen again."

The thought of Aless being under the rubble threaded rigidity through him, but she was right here in his arms. He sighed. Gavri had neglected Aless to do who-knew-what with his brother. *That* was not so easy to brush off, but she'd acknowledged her mistake and promised not to repeat it. He'd trust that.

"How did things go with you and Zoran?" he asked.

She rolled her eyes and heaved a sigh. "I'd resolved to lock up my heart, to keep him out. And then in Dun Mozg, he told me I was the love of his life, that it had been so hard to leave that he couldn't bear to say goodbye, and that we could never be together."

That much was true. Zoran's Offering to Nendra had sealed the alliance between Nozva Rozkveta and Dun Mozg. For as long as Nendra remained in power, Zoran had to stay by her side as king-consort if he wanted to protect that alliance. Zoran and Gavri had loved each other—did love each other— and could never be together.

And I get to be with the woman I love. In his arms was everything he'd never known he'd wanted, but if he'd been a little more skilled, a little more talented with a blade, he might have been the strongest of his brothers and been bargained away to Nendra instead of Zoran. That was an unjust twist of fate he felt keenly, that he should have love in his life when Zoran couldn't. "I have no words, Gavri. Would that the Darkness had shadowed your lives differently."

Her gaze downcast, she lifted a dispirited shoulder. "We serve at Her Majesty's pleasure."

As she looked back at him over her shoulder, she raised a fist.

The entire group came to a halt. She gestured behind them, where two riders tore up the muddy ground at a steady clip. Riza and Kinga.

They rode up, and Riza slowed her horse to a trot, approaching him.

"Your Highness," she said, heaving tired breaths, "a forward team. Less than half a day behind us."

They'd relied on the likelihood that the Brotherhood would follow, but a forward team made the situation vastly more dangerous.

"At this rate, they'll catch us tomorrow afternoon," Kinga added, panting.

"Send Gavri and Valka to keep an eye on them. And as for us, no more long stops," he bit out. They couldn't risk them. If they were pinned down, and the Brotherhood army caught up to them—he shook his head. "We pick up the pace."

Riza gave a curt nod. "You heard His Highness," she called out to the group. "Move out. Now!"

~

ALESS WOKE from dreams of vining roses and Veron's touch. As she blinked her eyes open, the sun was setting, and she was still in the saddle with Veron. She glanced around for Gabriella—but no, she'd sent Gabriella with Danika through the earthmover tunnels to Bellanzole, with letters for Papà, Bianca, and Lorenzo, and even Duchessa Claudia along the way. *Holy Mother, keep her in your light.*

"Are you hungry?" Veron whispered in her ear, his voice a low rasp. He handed her some bread and cheese they'd gotten in Stroppiata.

"Thank you," she said softly, and nibbled on the food.

When had he last slept? Their pace had only picked up since news of the forward team, and it was taking a toll on everyone. They had to stay ahead, but they couldn't take much more of this. *Veron* couldn't take much more of this.

She'd woken a few times during their travel as they'd paused briefly to feed and water the horses, to rest them and switch to fresh mounts, but Veron had told her each time to go back to sleep. She was saddle sore and tired, but if they hadn't stopped for long since yesterday, he had to be exhausted. "Is there a way I could stay awake and you could sleep?"

He kissed her cheek. "We're almost there. Only a little more, and then we'll both get some rest. Promise."

His optimism was heartwarming, but she could hear the exhaustion rasping in his deep voice. He was tired. Beyond tired.

Next to them, Riza pulled up on her horse. "Your Highness..." Her voice drifted.

Riza wasn't one to mince words, at least not in the short time she'd know her. This had to be bad news.

Veron stiffened. "What is it?"

"Gavri and Valka should have returned from scouting by now, Your Highness." The words were quiet. Uneasy.

Maybe they'd gotten lost. Maybe one of their horses had lost a shoe. Or maybe...

"Could they have gotten lost?"

Veron took a deep breath. "Not out here. We know these wilds well—sometimes our hunting or scouting takes us out this far."

Which meant...

We have to look for them, she wanted to say.

But it was the wrong thing, and she knew it, deep in her bones. If the Brotherhood had captured them, then they *wanted* Veron to come looking. *Wanted* to capture him, and maybe even her, and do who-knew-what to everyone else here.

She and Veron needed to negotiate for their release—only... they had nothing but themselves to offer. And Gavri and Valka would only be leverage until Tarquin got what he wanted—vengeance for his sister, Arabella.

But Queen Zara would be in a better position. And yet... "There has to be *something* we can do, Veron," she whispered. "It's Gavri."

"Gavri and Valka know what it means to be kuvari," Riza said, sternly but not bitterly. "They are prepared to give their lives for our prince, and for Nozva Rozkveta."

"It doesn't need to come to that," Aless replied, twisting in Veron's hold.

"There are no other options," Yelena said from next to them. "We're in no position to negotiate, and the humans would be waiting for a rescue mission if we tried that."

As much as she wanted to argue for Gavri, none of what Yelena had said was incorrect.

Veron's grip on the reins tightened, and next to them, Noc, unburdened and resting, blew out a breath and tossed his head.

Veron nodded. "No more scouts. We make for Nozva Rozkveta, then I'm certain my mother will send a messenger for terms."

"It's the right call," Yelena said.

It didn't feel that way, but getting themselves caught or trading themselves in wouldn't help Gavri or Valka. They had to handle this carefully, with Queen Zara.

Riza passed on Veron's orders, and the cavalcade picked up the pace, pushing their horses to the limit. Noc ran alongside the others, spurring them on, and she couldn't help but glance around Veron's arms from time to time, searching the darkening distance for Gavri and Valka.

After hours of more riding, night had fallen, and she could barely see her hand in front of her face, let alone the path ahead, but Veron and the rest of the kuvari picked their way confidently. She wanted to ask him about it, but her backside and thighs were so sore, her entire body so achy, she couldn't even muster the words anymore. Her thoughts lingered on Gavri, and praying for her safety and swift return, along with Valka.

Her eyelids were drooping when something glowed faintly ahead. Like fireflies, lights winked in the darkness, flowing in lazy curls and scrolls. Pixies.

A fresh, alluring scent filled the air—roses—its density surrounding her, so powerful she could close her eyes, reach, and touch the velvety petals. A dream—no, a hallucination?

The glow of the pixies gently illuminated vines twining old ruins, climbing the stone, claiming it in sprawling, verdant green—an ancient courtyard—and bright crimson blooms unfurled amid a thicket of green, roses so large, so vivid, as if they'd grown from her dreams and fantasies. In full bloom, mysterious and lovely, exhaling that most spellbinding perfume in the pure air. So tangled, wild, and yet they shimmered in the glow, dazzled with an otherworldly beauty.

The only roses she'd seen even *approximating* their brilliance had been at the palazzo, during the wedding, but they hadn't glittered as these.

"Veron," she breathed, and her voice was no more than a thin, tired whimper. "These roses..."

Warmth met the top of her head in a kiss, and his tightening embrace pulled her closer. "We brought many for the wedding in Bellanzole, but once cut, they begin to lose their luster. They shimmer here, wild and free, because this is where they belong, where they can thrive."

As they approached, she gasped. For a lifetime, she could take in their beauty and never get her fill. These roses weren't like the trimmed, manicured gardens of the nobiltà, but an unfettered, chaotic beauty that nothing tried to contain.

Ahead, a thicket of them knotted in a massive bramble, thorny and breathtaking.

"Nozva Rozkveta is seated over the largest Vein of anima in the land, the force from which all life and magic springs. And for as long as we have existed here, so has the Bloom, cocooning our home from all who would do us harm, allowing in only friends to our kind."

It was as if the land itself protected Veron's people—now *her* people— enshrining them from danger.

Soon, Veron halted the cavalcade and everyone dismounted. He helped her down onto her sore legs, and it took some waddling while braced against him before she could even move properly.

They approached a Bloom thicket, knotted and twisted chaotically in vines and roses, but Veron didn't stop. The tangle parted for him, reshaping into an arched colonnade that he entered without hesitation. All around them—on the sides, above them, even below—vines writhed in living form, held that shape, as she accompanied him, as the others followed behind with Noc and the horses.

At the end of the Bloom's colonnade, the path lowered to a large stone door, ancient and massive, etched with runic script. Still holding her hand, Veron approached it and tapped a rhythm on its face, the Nozva Rozkvetan knock.

The massive door opened, ground against its stone frame, revealing a tunnel inside and two kuvari in leathers.

"Your Highness," they greeted in unison. "Nozva Rozkveta bids you welcome."

He thanked them as he entered, stroking her hand softly, and the rest of the cavalcade followed.

The tunnel was dark, but at its end was a lavender glow. As they approached, Veron raised her hand to his lips and pressed a gentle kiss to her skin.

"Welcome home, Aless," he whispered, and they stepped into a vast space.

Bioluminescent mushrooms climbed the cavern walls, bathing the realm below in that lavender light, along with radiant white glowworms and glittering vines of the Bloom sprawling as far as the eye could see.

She gasped, looking everywhere at once, at gleaming dwellings of mirror-like black stone and glistening streams weaving among shining paths. On the outskirts, fields of green shoots peeked up from ebony soil.

"H-how can they grow here, when—"

Veron grinned at her, his golden eyes soft. "The Vein. It seeps life into everything here. Into everyone."

Groups of singers ringed unfinished structures, their tones impossibly deep, their songs unlike anything she'd ever heard. Passersby stopped to bow and offer cheery greetings.

Veron nodded toward the tall, black towers peaking above a building like a cluster of crystals. "I wish we had time to stop at the lifespring first, but we need to tell my mother what's happened."

"Let's get Gavri and Valka back first," she said with a nod, and then she could ask what a *lifespring* was.

Riza joined them as they strode toward the palace, and every muscle in Aless's body rebelled. The long ride had been difficult, painful, but they'd made it here before the Brotherhood could catch up to them.

Nozva Rozkveta would have time to prepare for the attack, and by the grace of the Holy Mother, hopefully the food had arrived by way of the tunnels.

Four kuvari guarded the palace entrance, and they stood aside as Veron entered and proceeded straight down the main hallway to a set of massive doors.

Two kuvari opened them, and inside, the grand hall yawned, massive, the Bloom vines climbing its walls, ceiling, and stalactites and adorning them in glittering green and crimson roses that radiated a vivid glow.

This place *breathed* life, teemed with it.

At the end, a regal woman sat atop a translucent crystal throne, its peaks fanning out behind her. She had a diamond-shaped face, elegant and smooth, slightly lighter than Veron's, and voluminous platinum hair, cascading in curls sectioned with beads, a futile attempt to contain the wild tresses. Her clothes were a robe and peplos of the finest silk she'd ever seen, and Papà's imports had not been inexpensive. Her feet were bare and clawed, their points shorter than the sharp ones on her hands, where she wore a pair of arcanir bracers.

Every part of her was lithe, sleek, and even as her crossed leg bounced lightly, it did so with a catlike grace, and yet her arms and shoulders were muscled, toned. The queen sat upon a throne now, but her physique said she could have anyone pinned to the gleaming black stone within seconds.

Her eyes were a warm amber, gentle and placid, and yet they glittered with innumerable facets of jeweled wisdom so deep those eyes could be infinite.

Veron's mother. The queen. Queen Zara.

This was her husband's *mother*, and meanwhile, she'd arrived with Veron in wrinkled, dirty, rain-and-sweat-soaked clothes, looking like something feral and smelling... well, "worse" was putting it mildly. Clearing her throat, she swept some stray horsehair from her rain-damp riding habit, her other hand in Veron's warm hold.

The queen smiled as her gaze landed on Veron, genuine, sweet, in a way that lit her face radiantly. She stood from her throne, pushing off with a limber little leap, and strode the length of the distance between them.

Veron bowed before the queen, and Aless followed suit.

"Welcome home, Veron," the queen said evenly, her low voice mellifluous, pleasant. "And you, daughter"—a gentle hand touched her shoulder, and Aless slowly straightened to face a smiling queen—"I welcome with a glad heart."

The queen was so beautiful that it was difficult not to stare.

"Thank you, Your Majesty," Aless breathed. "I'm honored to finally meet you."

The queen glanced down to where Veron's hand still held hers, and somehow, the queen's radiant smile widened. "I hope in time you'll come to call me Mati." Turning to Veron, she added, "I am overjoyed for you, Veron."

A corner of his mouth turned up as his gaze turned to her briefly, soft and loving, shining and pleased, before he looked back to his mother, that gentle smile fading. "Mati, I wish we came only bearing good news."

"The supply caravan arrived by way of the tunnels earlier today, and we've already begun distributing food," the queen replied. "And they brought news of the Brotherhood army and your plan."

If only that were the only bad news.

Veron took a deep breath and nodded. "They've taken Gavri and Valka captive."

CHAPTER 21

*V*eron walked with Aless to his quarters, her hand in his, and stared at the floor. He'd brought home his bride, and his mother and queen already approved of her. He'd be making the Offering to Aless at the second ceremony in three days.

In those three days, they might already be embroiled in a war.

One of his best friends and another of the kuvari could be held by a radical faction determined to annihilate his people.

Mati had said she would be sending one of her kuvari to the Brotherhood army to discuss terms. One had already volunteered, even knowing it was likely a suicide mission.

If only they could send in a small team to rescue them—but that would have no chance of success. If Tarquin was smart, he was holding Gavri and Valka in the heart of the camp, and a dark-elf team would have no chance of making it through the outskirts. Gavri or Valka or both would be killed, along with the team.

The convergence of such keen anguish and the most ardent joy he had with his wife weighed like the sky of stone upon his shoulders. He held the hand of the woman he loved, and allowing himself to feel even a fraction of that joy came with the sting of Gavri held prisoner, possibly hurt, possibly suffering, and their people stepping into what could be an impending war.

"Papà will come to our aid, Veron," she said, rubbing his arm. "He wouldn't make this alliance unless he was prepared to defend it. And we've already demonstrated its validity. Dark-elves defended humans in Stroppiata. We earned the duchessa's friendship. People embraced us. The Brotherhood alone is left, an embittered old radical on the back foot. Papà will snap up the chance to rid his land of it."

The lives and wellbeing of Gavri, Valka, and all their people rested with a man who had traded Aless—his brilliant, brave, wonderful Aless—away with not a care to her unwillingness, in the coldest, most unfeeling way imaginable.

"I wrote to everyone. I wrote to Bianca, and to Lorenzo, too," Aless added, giving his bicep a squeeze. "Lorenzo won't give up on this—unlike Papà, he actually cares about us. And maybe Bianca could have a word with Luciano, convince him to talk his brother down." She gave him a nudge. "We have multiple plans in place. Something will work in our favor. You'll see."

Those hopes were remote, but she was right in her optimism, in her *morale*. They had to believe in something, or else the battle was already lost.

"Besides, your mother already said she had a plan."

In an hour, Mati expected them over for a midnight supper with Vadiha, Dhuro, and Yelena. Before he and Aless showed up, he'd have to muster the requisite morale. Mati had given her orders. It was time to support them.

"You're right. I know you're right," he said, pulling her in to kiss her temple. "We'll find out more when our messenger returns." Not *if*, but *when*.

She gave him an encouraging nod as he opened the door to his quarters. Not much had survived since the Sundering, but he'd never needed much.

Inside, the space was bare but for his blackstone tables, laden with bowstrings, fletching, arrowheads he'd been making, and a boot brush and leather balm. Aless flitted to it and lifted the brush, grinning. "You really *do* have a boot thing."

He cleared his throat. "Taking care of your boots is just being responsible."

She lifted a brow, her grin broadening.

"If you don't, the leather can be hard, too stiff, unforgiving, and—"

That brow lifted higher, and she leaned against the table. "I'd say 'go on,' but I have the worst case of saddle soreness known to humankind."

Shaking his head, he smiled and closed the distance between them, grazing her cheek with his fingers. It was a surreal pleasure to stroke her without worrying about his claws harming her, and he couldn't get enough of her smoothness, of touching her, everywhere she wanted, in the way she wanted.

"If you're sore"—and he was, too—"I have the perfect cure for that."

Shuttering her eyes playfully, she tilted her head. "I am all for curing, although I should warn you that after days of riding in the rain, I reek like a farm animal right now."

He suppressed a smile. There was a possibility that something more amusing than Aless existed in the world, but it had to be slim. "I meant the lifespring. It has restorative properties."

Those eyebrows shot up and her mouth fell open before she tried to turn her face away. But no, he would get full view of this. Blushing, she looked everywhere but in his eyes until at last she relented and bit her lip.

"I'd love to hear all about this 'cure' you *thought* I meant," he teased, holding her gaze.

Her long, elegant fingers toyed with the fastenings on his jacket as that blush was soon joined by a coy smile. "Well, it would involve you, me, and..." She glanced toward the bed, then gasped. "Veron!"

He followed her line of sight to the enormous human-style mattress sitting on the platform below his blackstone headboard. *Her* mattress. "Someone must have brought it in from the tunnels."

She darted to it, ran her hands over it, then pressed a palm into its springiness. "This really is... How did you..."

"I thought you might like it," he said, "so I had it brought over from Bellanzole with us when we left." Along with all its bedding and pillows and countless other things that had adorned the beds in King Macario's palace—somewhere, in one of the carts.

Her eyes were wide but, when they met his once more, took on a mischievous gleam. "Oh, Veron... This bedchamber will see a lot of 'curing.' *A lot.*"

He burst out laughing before he could help himself, and she only grinned back at him. He offered her a hand. "But first, the lifespring?"

Taking it, she nodded. "And supper."

~

ALESS RUBBED her neck as Veron led her into the smaller, private dining chamber of the queen. The ache she'd felt there—and everywhere else—had disappeared, along with every trace of soreness ever. A short soak in the lifespring, and she was completely renewed.

They'd met two women there, Vlasta and Rút, who'd thanked Veron profusely for his help.

He'd explained that they were *lifebonded*, a dark-elf ritual that somehow joined two lives as one. They made each other stronger, shared life, but if one died... they'd share death, too. An oddly frightening and yet romantic concept.

The mystic at the lifespring, a healer named Xira, had given her robes that the other dark-elves seemed to wear outside of special occasions and traveling or combat. Soft and a neutral off-white, they wrapped her comfortably, with matching trousers that tucked into boots. It was strange not wearing her usual garments, not to mention wearing the same clothes as Veron, but she wanted to make an effort to fit in. These were her people now, too, and her family.

The queen wanted to have a private meal with her, Veron, his brother, and his sisters, but there was so much happening that it seemed impossible to just focus on getting to know her new family.

And there was the matter of the library. Paladin Grand Cordon Nunzio hadn't seemed averse to the plan, and she had to strike while the iron was hot, but with the Brotherhood threatening all-out war, it would have to wait.

She took a deep breath. Tonight was about making a good impression.

"They'll love you," Veron whispered to her as they entered the queen's quarters, where glowing Bloom vines wrapped pillars and climbed across the ceiling, like something out of a daydream. Veron led her off to the side, through a large archway into a dining room with a round blackstone table ringed by benches.

A number of people were already there—a stern-faced woman with long, tousled hair, carrying a little baby, and a man with her, the sides of his head shaved and his hair tied back.

There was a tall man with shoulder-length hair, his face simmering under a taut brow, and three women with wild hair only barely tamed into thick braids—clearly they'd taken after the queen. The three of them wore face paint, one with black smudges over her eyes, another with a strip across them, and a third with a line across each cheek.

All eyes turned to her and Veron as they entered, with the stern-faced woman holding the baby and the man with her rising first.

"Everyone, this is Aless," Veron said with a smile. "Aless, this is my sister Vadiha; her husband, Arigo; and their daughter, Dita."

Dita had large, sunny-yellow eyes with long lashes, chubby little cheeks, and little pointed ears, with fine white hair wisping off to the side.

"She was hungry, so she's up a little late," Vadiha said as she approached with Dita in her arms, who reached out a tiny hand for Veron's hair. He gave her his finger to clutch instead and kissed her forehead lightly.

"Veron," Vadiha breathed, her eyes wide as she stared at his hand. Her husband's eyebrows shot up, too. "What's happened? Did you—did you do that to *yourself*?"

His claws. He'd said they were a point of respect, hadn't he? This was a shock to his family, because he'd changed for her. But that change... had meant everything. It had meant they could *both* set aside fear, and love each other, without worrying about accidents. He'd done it for the sake of their marriage. Even faced with his family's shock, she wouldn't take that back. Even if that made her selfish.

Veron gave his sister a cavalier shrug. "I'm happy, Vadiha."

But Vadiha's gaze meandered to her, blinking long, pale lashes.

Veron leaned into his sister's line of sight, blocking her. "Vadiha. I mean it." His carefree voice had firmed.

But his sister's eyes only hardened as they met his.

"Love," Arigo whispered to Vadiha, "it's not self-harm. Some things need to change when two worlds collide." Arigo offered her an encouraging smile and a nod as he accepted Dita from his wife. "It's great to meet you, Aless. Welcome to the family."

"Thank you," she said, with a smile and a nod in return. "I still have a lot to learn, so I appreciate any help as I find my footing here."

Dita cooed, blinking wide amber eyes at her, and reaching for her hair with tiny, clutching hands.

Arigo laughed. "I'm sorry. She seems to be in a hair-loving phase."

"I kind of want to touch it, too, though. I've never touched a human's hair," one of the women said as the trio approached, a strip of black face paint across her eyes like a blindfold. She pursed her lips. "Is that weird?"

"Playing with each other's hair? Not weird at all," Aless answered. She wasn't all that different from them, but if they were curious, she wouldn't shut them down.

"I'm Amira," she said, offering her hand. "You humans take each other's hands, right?"

"We do," she said, taking Amira's hand.

"Gentle," Veron warned his sister.

"I know, I know. Their skin is silk thin. I know." Amira's fingers were stiff as she kept her claws away. "Veron, how do you keep from accidentally hurting her? Even without the claws, I mean, the skin, you know—"

Pressing his lips together tightly, he gave Amira a slight shake of the head.

"It's not *that* fragile," Aless cut in. "I mean, I can get thrown on my backside in a ring and not explode."

A bark of laughter burst from one of the other two women.

"This is Zaida and Renazi," Amira said, cocking her head toward them as they inclined their heads to her, the one with the lined cheeks laughing to herself. "We're volodari, and actually headed out on a hunt shortly, but we didn't want to go without meeting our new sister."

The one with the smudges over her eyes took a deliberate step forward, the rest of her body perfectly controlled. "Amira's mouth runs away with her, but we are glad to meet you, Aless. I'm Zaida."

Her voice was a night-quiet, misty whisper, grave, the kind that could silence an entire room. Well, except for her sister Renazi, who still seemed to be laughing to herself.

"A hunt, given the situation?" Veron asked.

Zaida looked toward him, the rest of her countenance unmoving. "Mati has us in territory farther out, by way of the tunnels."

Amira nudged Veron's shoulder. "We'll be safe, Veron. Don't worry!"

"Just because we have aid doesn't mean we should stop our way of life. You know that, Veron." The man with the simmering frown approached, nodding to her, every part of him taut and clenched. "Dhuro," he said, looking her over before meeting Veron's gaze a moment, his own speaking a thousand words she didn't yet understand. Dhuro seemed ready to pop like a bubble himself.

"Nice to meet you," she said, inclining her head.

His eyes narrowed. "I wish I could say the same."

"*Dhuro.*" Veron stepped up to him, every part of him rigid as he leaned in. "Apologize. Now."

Dhuro leaned in, too. "The kuvari and Yelena *talk*, Veron. Did you know *her* sister has married into the Brotherhood's general's family? How do we know this isn't all a human ploy to sack Nozva Rozkveta? She could be biding her time, waiting for a chance to open the Gates—"

"The ring. Now," Veron hissed, and cracked his knuckles.

Dhuro thought she was a traitor waiting to turn on them? And Veron wanted to *fight* him? She touched his shoulder, but he didn't budge.

Footsteps approached from behind, and everyone turned as the queen walked in, wrapped in her flowing white silk robe and peplos. "There will be no challenges tonight," she said firmly. "Veron, take a breath."

Forcing a harsh breath from his nose, Veron leaned away, fiery eyes still spearing Dhuro as he shielded her from his brother's line of sight.

"Dhuro, sit down and keep your mouth shut until I give you permission to speak." The queen looked down on Dhuro, her stance ready—would she attack him? Her son?—until he sighed and plopped onto the bench, slapping his palms onto the table and raising his eyebrows.

Amira, Zaida, and Renazi greeted their mother before saying their good-byes and heading out on the hunt, and Arigo excused himself to put Dita to bed.

And just like that, she stood with Veron, facing Dhuro and Vadiha, neither of whom seemed fond of her right now. At least Vadiha didn't call her a traitor to her face, so that was a win.

"Get the food, Vadiha," the queen said, jerking her head toward the archway, and Vadiha obeyed, but as she passed Aless, scowled at her.

"Aless, overlook my family's poor manners," the queen said to her, brushing her upper arm with a light touch. "They seem to forget that they have food on the table thanks to you, and that you and Veron have been standing up to the Brotherhood from the moment the peace was signed."

Behind her, a muscle flexed in Dhuro's jaw.

"I understand," Aless replied, fidgeting. "I'm new here. No one knows me yet. Trusting a stranger is a lot to ask."

Veron took her hand and rubbed her fingers gently. "But they all know me. And I love you. Trusting me isn't a lot to ask of my family."

Dhuro rolled his eyes as Vadiha brought in platters of food. The queen gestured them to the benches, and they all sat. Across from Dhuro, Veron glared at him, eyes wild and intense, narrowed. She held his hand, giving it a squeeze every so often, hoping to break that intensity. To no avail.

Dhuro glanced at her from time to time, over the dishes Vadiha laid out. When she finished and everybody was seated, the queen took a deep breath, sweeping her voluminous unkempt tresses back over her shoulder.

"I'm only going to say this once: Aless is our ally and part of our family." She looked from one face to another at the table, meeting Vadiha's stern face and Dhuro's simmering frown unequivocally. "Dhuro, repeat that to her and apologize."

His face hard, Dhuro looked away, ran a palm over his mass of shoulder-length hair, and turned back to her. "You're our ally and part of our family. I'm sorry for accusing you of betrayal," he gritted out.

The queen looked to her. "Do you accept? If not, it won't be Veron thrashing him in the ring, but me."

What, *really?* The queen would fight her own son—no, *thrash* him? Well, Queen Zara certainly ruled her family with an iron fist. And... perhaps it was best to remain on her good side.

Aless cleared her throat. "I accept. Thank you, Dhuro. No hard feelings."

He raised an eyebrow but said nothing more as they ate the spread of human food with some stew made from small game the volodari had hunted. The queen asked about the ceremony in Bellanzole and their trip, while Vadiha asked about the attack in Stroppiata and their skirmish outside of Dun Mozg. While Veron cooled, she answered most of their questions, playing with Veron's fingers.

After a brief lull, the queen's kuvari announced Riza, who entered and saluted.

Queen Zara gave her leave to speak, crossing her long, elegant legs as she perched on the bench.

"Your Majesty, Halina returned with the Brotherhood's answer," Riza said, breathing erratically. Had she run all the way here? "It's... They're being difficult."

Queen Zara waited.

"My queen—"

"What was the message, *exactly?*"

Riza bowed her head, her eyebrows drawn together, and for a moment, she shot a pained glance at Veron, and then at her, before looking back to Queen Zara. "It said, 'If you do not comply by dawn, our geomancer will collapse all tunnels leading from your queendom. We will lay siege until you wither and die. If you wish to live to see the dawn, return our princess to us and you may have your two beasts alive.'"

Return our princess? She started, but Veron took her hand in both of his. With a grave face, he shook his head slightly at her.

The queen didn't move, simply stared evenly into space. "It said 'live to see the dawn.' There is nothing there about suspending hostilities beyond that."

"You're not actually considering giving Aless to them?" Veron demanded, a low growl riding his question.

"Of course not," Queen Zara hissed. "But I have to determine whether this is a good-faith starting point to begin negotiations before I issue a counteroffer. It sounds, however, as though even if we were to comply, it wouldn't mean anything but a ceasefire until the dawn."

"What about Valka and Gavri?" Dhuro spat. "We're leaving them to die? I say we do the trade."

Queen Zara twisted so fast that she grabbed Dhuro's throat before he could evade. "You *have* no say." She tapped a claw to his neck. "And you forget yourself, *child*."

Livid eyes held the queen's.

"Your Majesty," Aless squeaked, even as Veron shook his head at her, "with all due respect, he's not wrong. My life isn't worth more than anyone else's. Especially not two. Their general is the brother of my sister's husband. He's wrong, but... they won't kill me. I'm certain of it."

Even the scouts outside Dun Mozg hadn't hurt her—they'd only tried to capture her and bring her to Tarquin.

Queen Zara still gripped Dhuro's throat. "I appreciate your valor, Aless, but like Dhuro, you have no say in this." Queen Zara's gaze slid to hers, and the queen smiled softly before shoving Dhuro away. "Supper is over. I will summon the rest of my Quorum and prepare for the dawn. Veron, Aless, you will stay in your quarters. The next few days will be difficult, but we are well supplied and we will persevere, as we always have." With that, she nodded toward the archway, and everyone but Vadiha rose and headed out.

No say. Every part of her rebelled.

His hand at the small of her back, Veron guided her out, leaving Queen Zara with Vadiha and Riza.

Queen Zara planned to wait out the dawn.

And if she stayed in her quarters as Queen Zara had ordered, the Brotherhood *would* kill Gavri and Valka, without hesitation. Two lives—one of which was her friend—would be lost.

Not without a fight.

CHAPTER 22

*A*less was already pacing the room as soon as Veron shut the door. Her stomach fluttered, but she rubbed it through her robes. This was no time to get nervous.

The Brotherhood would kill Gavri and Valka at dawn. Once they did, the war would begin. Hundreds or thousands would die, and not just here, but across the country, as like-minded people rose up to take sides. If nothing changed, that was inevitable.

But the Brotherhood wanted *her* in exchange. There had to be a move there. Something.

There was no question that the Brotherhood would kill any dark-elf without hesitation. There was no way any of them could mount a rescue mission. But *her*?

You don't need to wear a mask, princess, Tarquin had whispered to her the day of her wedding. *Not with me. The pride is watching. Only say the word, anytime, anywhere, that you protest, and our strength will... relieve your solitude.*

The Brotherhood *wanted* her, but they wouldn't harm her. Tarquin wouldn't harm her. No, that first night, and even at the wedding ceremony, Tarquin had *wanted* her for something, had even tipped his hand to offer her protection. This was a man waging a war of hatred, but also Luciano's brother, Bianca's brother-in-law. And if he killed a princess of Silen, that egregious move would never go unanswered, as it would create a dangerous precedent. Papà would not only annihilate him but his entire family into obscurity.

No, Tarquin Belmonte would not hurt *her*.

And although Papà might not get involved with two dark-elves on the line, if *she* were captured, it would force his hand. He'd have to intervene and help stop the Brotherhood.

There was only one person who had a shot at freeing Gavri and Valka, and it was *her*. The most unskilled, worst candidate to do it, but the only human among them. If she got caught—and odds were high that she would—no one would die. Tarquin had promised to release Gavri and Valka in exchange for her. So she'd either successfully free them both and escape with them, or she'd be caught and demand the exchange. Either way, Gavri and Valka would live.

And unskilled as she was, being a human gave her an advantage. There were no women among the Brotherhood soldiers, but every army had camp followers. Silen's military often had wives and children among them, but the only women who'd accompany the Brotherhood anywhere would be cooks, nurses, sutlers, laundresses, and prostitutes.

She could disguise herself as one and slip in among the camp's outskirts. From there, no one would give a Sileni woman—a human and camp follower —a second glance as a threat. She could search for Gavri and Valka even at the heart of the camp without garnering much notice.

But if she were caught—

If she were caught, the Brotherhood—no, Tarquin—would never release her back to Veron. If she left tonight, she might never see the man she loved ever again.

If she told him, he'd never agree to her going. Not only because he'd worry, but because his mother had forbidden it, and disobedience was unthinkable to him. He'd be furious, hurt, but if no one did anything and Gavri and Valka were killed, there'd be a war. A war Nozva Rozkveta might not win. One he might have to fight in, maybe even *die* in, along with count-less other innocent lives. No. If there was a bloodless solution, she had to try, even if he hated her, even if he never spoke to her again. This was to save his life, to save their people, and she'd vowed in Dun Mozg that she would do whatever it took to protect them, to keep them safe, and to maintain the peace.

Queen Zara had confined her to quarters, and nobody disobeyed her orders. Nobody. But as much as she wanted to fit in here, fitting in had never been more important than making a difference. And she wasn't about to sacrifice countless lives just to stay in her mother-in-law's good graces.

Come what may, she had to try.

Veron's arms closed around her from behind, and he tucked his nose into her hair and took a deep breath. "I'm sorry about Dhuro and Vadiha," he whispered.

She stroked his knuckles. "I wasn't expecting them all to love me right away. Even you took some convincing."

A soft laugh puffed against her ear. "You took more convincing to love me."

After arriving in Nozva Rozkveta, she knew better than that. Far better.

Smiling, she shook her head, swaying in his hold. "What you don't realize is that I have loved you long before I ever laid eyes on you."

He turned her, his eyes heavy lidded as he raised her chin. "How's that, my love?"

"I have dreamed of these abundant, sprawling, vining roses, wild and beautiful, even their scent," she whispered. "And when I came here, saw the Bloom—it can't be possible, but I dreamed of this place long before you ever brought me here."

He stroked her face, swept gentle fingers into her hair as he tucked it behind her ear. "We are on the land's biggest Vein of anima, a wellspring of the life that courses through everything and everyone. We walk toward the Bloom, and it parts for us. We sing to the stone, and it reshapes. Nothing is impossible, my love, and I believe your dreams, too, because you dreamt them and we are standing here, right now, together."

She trembled, all over, and it wasn't out of disbelief or fear or nervousness; it was everything inside of her willing her to him, to hold him, to kiss him, to stay with him forever and never let go, and she listened to it, listened to it all in this moment, and clung to him, pressed her mouth to his, undressed him with hands that couldn't move fast enough, never fast enough, frantic, desperate.

Holy Mother's mercy, there wasn't enough time to get her fill of his love, of his passion, of him. To live as his partner, to realize the library together, to raise a family. There weren't enough hours, enough lifetimes, and if the cruel hands of fate parted them at dawn, then she wanted to live a hundred hours, a thousand lifetimes, in his arms tonight. "Love me, Veron," she whispered. "Love me tonight, like a dark-elf bride."

"Aless..." he hissed against her lips.

"I want to know what it means," she said softly between kisses, "to be yours in every way." She clutched him close, and his brow furrowed, he nodded against her, claimed her lips hungrily.

He pulled at her robes, seams tearing and fabric ripping until it was all on the floor, and when his fang grazed her tongue, she bit his lip, and he snarled, taking her mouth with renewed zeal as she pushed him toward the bed, her urging stronger and stronger, but his steps were even and slow, playfully resisting against her while his eyes gleamed. The amused smile he'd worn when she'd teased him here earlier had returned, playing on his lips.

When he reached the edge, she hooked his ankle with her foot, just as she'd seen him do in the ring, and he let her, lowered to the bed. She brought her knees down around his hips, raised his mouth to hers, and he twisted, tossing her onto her back, and pinned her to the bed.

She fought, just enough to rile him, to stoke his ardor, and the determined intensity in his gaze was enough to make her gasp, to make her stare, to make her want to immortalize that look in her mind for the rest of her life, and as he took her, she did, memorizing the set of his jaw, the lines of his brow, the blaze of fire smoldering in the warm gold of his eyes, and the rapturous dance of wildness and passion that was being his in every way.

As tired as Aless was, she didn't let herself sleep, not completely, instead waiting until Veron's breathing evened out, until he slept soundly. After days of traveling, he needed it, and he'd had no reason not to trust her.

She tugged a lone blanket they'd found in one of her trunks over him gently and resisted the urge to kiss him. Even so, he only stirred a moment before resuming those even breaths.

This would hurt him. Deeply. But if she told him, he'd never agree to her going. But there was no living with the thought of Gavri and Valka dying for her sake, of a war beginning, of countless lives being lost, maybe even Veron's... when she could've saved them simply by stepping outside. She had to try.

It was the right thing to do. The only thing. But as she slipped from the bed, all she could think of was of Veron waking to find her gone, to realize she'd abandoned him, just like his father had.

I'm sorry.

It would hurt, but with this, she'd save lives. Maybe even talk Tarquin out of this course of action altogether. Now that she knew the dark-elves, she could meet his hatred with knowledge.

She bent for her robes. They were slightly torn in places, but not too noticeably. And besides, Veron's were huge—not an option. But if she wanted to be inconspicuous in Nozva Rozkveta, she'd get far less attention wandering around in dark-elf robes than in her clothes.

She carefully creaked open one of her trunks and looked for something suitable to disguise herself in. She had no commoners' clothes, but the best among the prostitutes might wear something approximating some of her plainer things.

With a wince, she hastily grabbed a bustier, white chemise, and as plain a blue overdress as she could find, low cut and laced in the front, but made of fine velvet. She stashed them in one of Veron's knapsacks, similar to ones she'd seen other dark-elves carry.

Her copy of *A Modern History of Silen* sat on Veron's table, and with a wary eye on him, she slowly dug out her quill and inkwell. She had to leave, but she couldn't leave without saying goodbye, without letting him know how much he meant to her in case she didn't make it back.

She opened to the first blank page. What could she say that would ease the sting of this? Was there anything?

I love you.

Maybe he'd hate her, maybe he'd curse the day he'd met her, maybe he'd never want to see her again. But she couldn't do this, not even to stop a war, without telling him that one last time.

She left the book open, set her quill on the page, then at the door, turned to gaze at his slumbering face one last time.

Veron, prince of Nozva Rozkveta, I, Alessandra Ermacora, princess of Silen, offer you love—she rested a hand on her heart—*peace, and a life here, quiet, safe from the Brotherhood, and every enemy I can protect you from... to harness for your ends or ours, as we... as we walk our lives together from this day forward for as long as the Deep allows.*

Wiping at her cheeks, she took three deep breaths and slipped out into the hall.

All was quiet, and there was no one about. Everyone had to be sleeping at this hour. She could find her way to the lifespring, and from there, the tunnels were not far. There were clothes at the lifespring, including kuvari leathers, masks, and hoods, which she could use if she managed to sneak them, but from there on, she still needed a way to make it past the kuvari guarding the Gate.

Gavri and Valka were kuvari themselves, so perhaps she could use that to talk her way past.

As she headed out of the palace, no one stopped her. In fact, the few passersby she met greeted her warmly, by the proper form of address. The main part of the city—Central Cavern, as everyone called it—was empty, and she crossed its gleaming blackness toward the lifespring. Through the dark entryway, the lifespring pools glowed a bright teal, and the clothes would be in a small cave off to the side of the pools.

Inside, one of the violet-clad mystics spoke with a woman in one of the pools with her hair braided in a crown about her head.

Yelena.

Backing up, she turned to leave, but Yelena twisted and met her gaze. "*You.* What are you doing here?"

She straightened. "I could ask you the same."

Yelena huffed. "I'm practicing the sword. What does it *look* like I'm doing?"

"Convalescing."

"Those human eyes work after all. And you had the same couple days in the saddle I did." Yelena looked her over with appraising eyes. "Your robes are all tattered. Rough night?"

She cleared her throat. "You could say that."

Yelena smirked and swept an arm wide. "Well, then. Come and *convalesce*, human princess."

She took a step forward, but... there was no time for this. Was there even any sense in trying to disguise herself in a mask and hood? She'd probably be caught anyway. "I..."

"What? Is my company not good enough for you?" Yelena quirked a brow.

"No, no, it's not that—"

"What exactly are you up to? What's in the bag?"

Shifting the knapsack, Aless looked over her shoulder, and the mystic had gone. *I need a mask, a hood, and leathers, and I want to save Gavri and Valka and stop a war*, she wanted to say, and then... blurted it all out.

Yelena's brow furrowed and stayed furrowed a long while. Her head bobbed before she drew in a deep breath. "Well, if you need help getting rid of yourself, you've come to the right person."

CHAPTER 23

Outside the Gate and beyond the Bloom, Aless shifted in her borrowed leathers, the knapsack over her shoulder, and removed her hood and mask, then began changing into her bustier, chemise, and blue velvet overdress.

"What are you doing?" Yelena hissed in the dark. Confident and gruff, Yelena had led her through the earthmover tunnels disguised as one of her kuvari, and since Yelena wasn't a citizen of Nozva Rozkveta, no one had even tried to stop her.

"In there"—smoothing her hands over her velvet skirts, Aless tipped her head toward the Gate—"I need a mask and a hood to blend in. Out here, I might be killed on sight. Better they see that I'm human."

Yelena eyed her from beneath a frown, then took a deep breath. "Are you sure about this?"

"I thought you were pretty keen on getting rid of me?"

Yelena shrugged a shoulder and looked away. "Do as you will. I'll keep Veron's bed warm when you die."

Veron.

Holy Mother's mercy, just thinking of him right now, about leaving him like that, made her hands tremble, but she fisted them. This was to save him, to save everyone from war and death, and even if she failed and got caught, at least it would force Papà to intervene and stop this.

To do what she needed to do, she'd have to shove down that trembling feeling, the memory of Veron's passionate face, the sight of him sleeping soundly as she'd left. *Shove it down.*

She shook out her hair into an unbound curly mess, cleared her throat, and nodded to Yelena. "I'm sure he'd rather a harpy kept his bed warm than you, but thanks."

Yelena crossed her arms and shot her a sheepish grimace. "I'll wait here until dawn. If you're not back by then, I'm going back in there to tell everyone you're probably dead."

Yelena's words were harsh, but her help had been invaluable.

"Thank you, Yelena. Really."

Yelena gave her a final nod.

This is it. She turned south and headed toward the Brotherhood encampment.

The forest was dark and quiet, with the rare animal call interrupting the silence. The only light came from the faint glow of the Bloom vines and flowers, and the little star-like twinkles of the pixies fluttering in the night air.

After walking for a while, the quiet and the dark hadn't abated—she should've found the Brotherhood encampment already, shouldn't she? The Gate she'd exited from wasn't the same one as the Gate she and Veron had arrived by.

A pixie flew alongside her, and she sighed. "I don't suppose you can help me find Gavri and Valka? Two dark-elves in a human camp?"

The pixie flitted about, darting erratically, then took off toward the side.

Is a pixie actually helping me? It was ridiculous, really, but if she was lost, then following a pixie wasn't any more ridiculous than milling about in the wrong direction.

Her skirts clenched in her hands, she followed the pixie's dimming glow, and soon, sparse firelight flickered between the trees and the undergrowth, and a sea of tents.

She suppressed a gasp, hiding behind an oak.

You really did help me? She eyed the pixie, who hovered next to her behind another trunk.

Thank you, she mouthed, keeping a wary eye on the camp.

It was quiet, with very few Brotherhood soldiers—or anyone—about, but considering the hundreds of tents, that could easily change with one alarm. Most on the outskirts were little tents, with the bigger ones toward the center of camp.

A few sentries walked a circuit, which would have been no problem if she'd been Yelena or Veron. But right now, even *one* was one too many. There was no possibility of walking in unnoticed here by blending in. They'd be waiting for someone to try a rescue from the trees here.

But toward the back of the camp, there was movement to and from a well-lit area, and she stalked through the undergrowth, keeping behind trees as best she could, to get a closer look.

Makeshift bars dotted the back end of the camp, along with some tents where soldiers entered and exited, smiling and laughing.

The camp followers.

If there was any chance of getting to the center of the camp, this was it. It would have to be from there.

As a chorus of crickets chirped, she crept as near as she dared in the forest's concealment, fluffing her hair and pinching her cheeks, rumpling her gown, even dirtying its hem a little.

The pixie flitted closer, landing on her shoulder.

"Your light's going to give us away," she whispered, and the pixie's light dimmed down to almost nothing, a barely audible little chime coming from it. Speech?

With the light, the pixie looked like a tiny winged person the size of a butterfly, a pink-haired woman wrapped in a leaf. An utterly *adorable* little pink-haired woman.

Her chest fluttered, and if this were any time and place other than sneaking outside a Brotherhood camp, she might have squealed with delight.

The pixie darted into her unbound hair, clinging on with the slightest tug. Unexpected, but somehow, this wouldn't be as terrifying when there was someone with her.

She watched the movements of the camp, with two tents close to the edge completely dark, with no movements in or out. A lone man strolled down a lane and then ducked into a nearby, lantern-lit tent.

Be brave.

With a deep breath, she strode out of the forest confidently, with only the clothes on her back and a pixie in her hair. No one was about, and she only needed a minute or so to cross the clearing between the trees and the camp.

Just a little more.

If she ran, that would draw attention. At least walking, she might seem like a prostitute returning from relieving herself. Her heart pounded as she neared the first tent, and voices laughed from nearby.

Just a little more. A little more.

She peeked into the first tent—a woman was sleeping—and a belt buckle fastened and coins clinked nearly just as she peeked into the second.

Empty.

She darted inside and drew the tent flap closed as booted footsteps emerged from the one next to her.

Holy Mother's mercy.

She gulped in breaths, trying to slow her racing heart, and looked around the dark tent. The stench of the bedroll was enough to make her gag. Wine, queen's lace, the bitter herbs…

A moment to gather her composure. She'd go to the center of camp, and if anyone stopped her, she'd say General Belmonte had requested her services. At best, she'd be left to go where she pleased, and at worst, she'd be taken to him—and of everyone here, Tarquin was still her best chance at not getting hurt, at the very least for fear of Papà's wrath.

She grabbed a bottle of red wine—holding something would at least make her feel better and give her trembling hands something to do—and then counted to three before emerging.

No one was outside, but as she headed toward the center, a few soldiers walked past, paying her no mind aside from the rare whistle and kissing sounds.

Thank the Mother.

An otherworldly scream came from the outer ring of the center, unlike anything she'd ever heard. That couldn't be Tarquin or any of the Brotherhood. Were any other Immortali being kept prisoner?

It's our best chance.

She headed toward it, and the line of tents here was utterly quiet, and the stench—

Swallowing past the lump in her throat, she peeked past tent flaps, finding posts, ropes, chains, and bloodied rags.

Holy Mother's mercy, had they *killed*—

No. She shook her head. They wouldn't have killed their only leverage against Queen Zara; the Brotherhood was hateful and violent, but Tarquin was not stupid, and underestimating his intelligence instead of accounting for it would only lead to failure.

A grunt came from the large tent ahead.

Everything inside of her wanted to freeze to the spot, but if the person emerged, that would only look suspicious.

A man in a white tabard with a clasped red hands insignia left the tent, smirking, his flinty eyes settling on her as his smirk abdicated in favor of a frown. "What are you doing here, whore?"

The harsh tone was accusatory, but as he approached, he looked her over, and the furrows lining his face faded.

Her heart pounding, she plastered a seductive smile on her face, relaxing her posture as she put a hand on her hip and gave the bottle of wine a shake. "It must get very lonely out here. I thought maybe you could use some company."

The smirk returned as his palm landed on her waist and traveled upward. "I wouldn't think a face like yours would need to work so hard."

Holy Mother help me. "Just trying to do my part."

He reached for her chin—

The pixie dashed out of her hair and past him—

He whirled, and she swung the bottle of wine toward his head. It connected, shattering glass and spilling wine as he tumbled to the grass.

Her heart in her throat, she grabbed him by the tabard and struggled to drag him into the tent he'd emerged from while he groaned.

It had been too quiet, the contact too loud, and someone would've—someone had to be coming—

"Aless," Gavri hissed, tied to a post across from another dark-elf woman—Valka? They were dirty, their leathers tattered, faces bruised and bloody. "What're you—?"

She ran to Gavri, scrabbling for the ropes binding her wrists, and frantically cut at them with the broken bottle. They weren't—it wasn't—not sharp enough, not fast en—

That otherworldly scream pierced the air again.

"Behind you," Gavri snarled.

She spun as the man grabbed for her, and both Gavri and Valka yanked at their bonds. The pixie darting at his face, he pulled her ankle and tumbled her to the ground, dragging her beneath him.

"You—" he snarled, but a foot crashed into his face, sending him flying off her.

Gavri snatched the broken bottle from her hands and buried it in the man's neck, spitting at him. She took his short sword and cut Valka free, who stomped on his head.

The otherworldly screaming resumed.

"What is that?" Aless breathed, laboring to her feet as Gavri stripped bits of the man's gear and his weapons.

"They have a unicorn here," Gavri said, tossing her a sheathed hunting knife.

She tried to catch it, but it fell to the ground. A unicorn? Was it the one from outside Stroppiata? They had it here? She picked up the knife and tucked it into her boot, and the pixie fluttered past her face and landed on her shoulder.

"Thank you, Tiny," she whispered.

"Come on," Gavri said, nodding toward the tent flap. "That commotion won't have gone unheard."

Valka nodded, holding up the broken and bloodied wine bottle, and swept aside the flap. "No one's here yet," she said. "We make for the trees."

Gavri followed.

"What about the unicorn?" Aless whispered as it continued its screaming. What would the Brotherhood do to it? Torture it? Sell it? Kill it?

"No time," Gavri said.

No time? Something tightened in her chest, her breaths coming in short, quivering gasps.

"I'll follow you soon," she told Gavri, and then headed toward the screaming.

"Aless," Gavri hissed after her.

"Go," she whispered in reply. "I'm human. I'll be fine."

Eyes wild, Gavri stood frozen, but Valka grabbed her wrist and dragged her away as Aless cut through the lines of tents.

They *had* to leave. As dark-elves, they'd be identified and attacked in a second. But she'd gotten across the camp without incident. Human, well disguised, she stood a chance.

There was a chaos of shouting and boots thumping behind her, but she ignored it. Brotherhood soldiers yelling about Gavri and Valka's escape, and bellowing orders to chase into the forest.

The unicorn's screams quieted and quieted, faded to exhausted squeals and shrieks, and the clop of hooves was near.

A large, open tent contained a mass of sage-tinted chains, all binding the unicorn so brutally it could scarcely move. Red welts, old and extensive, marred its once-immaculate coat beneath the chains, staining it bloody, and the whites of its eyes showed as it regarded her warily. It was smaller than the one she'd seen on the way to Stroppiata, with a shorter horn, and even in the dimness, dazzling green eyes.

Holy Mother's mercy, how could anyone *do* this to an innocent being? Bind it, torture it, and for what? Why even keep the Immortals? As trophies, as prizes? To study them? Just for malice's sake?

Checking the surrounding area, she found it empty, and darted to the unicorn shuddering in chains. Where to even begin?

"I'm going to help you," she whispered, and Tiny flew out of her hair again to a post behind the unicorn, where it disturbed a key ring on a hook.

Voices came from behind the tent.

She ducked inside, squeezing between the unicorn and the tent's canvas, but the voices continued—two soldiers discussing the hunt for Gavri and Valka, wondering whether they'd hidden among the tents.

No! They couldn't find her—they *couldn't*. Not when she was so close to actually succeeding in her plan. Tiny fluttered back to her, taking refuge in her curls.

She sidled in the narrow space toward the post. If they did find her, then at the very least she could free this unicorn. It quieted, too, standing utterly still as she slowly reached for the keys.

Once she had them in hand, she followed the chains until she found the lock at her side, and opened it with a barely audible click.

The voices stopped for a moment. Had they gone?

The unicorn pulled against the chains, clinking them, and the noise only worsened as it yanked into the lane between the tents, dragging the chains out with it.

An ache formed in the back of her throat, and the trembling in her limbs spread to cold fingers twisting and wringing the velvet skirt, wet with wine.

Yelling and bootsteps converged, and she huddled against the tent, hiding behind the canvas next to the entryway, shaking, reaching for the knife in her boot. But if the Brotherhood knew she was there, that knife wouldn't save her. Running wouldn't save her. Screaming wouldn't save her.

"Get them," came an order.

"Sir!"

With a swallow, she straightened, forced her arms to her sides, and raised her chin, taking deep breaths. There was only one thing that could save her now. Raising her voice.

"My name is Princess Alessandra Ermacora of Silen," she called out, firming her voice with every ounce of royal arrogance she could muster. "And I demand to speak to General Tarquin Belmonte at once."

Everything outside the tent went silent.

Holy Mother's mercy, would they charge in here, tie her up, drag her to him? Nothing and no one moved, only the sound of several men breathing indicating their presence outside.

You are a princess of Silen. Be brave.

Pulling her shoulders back, she stepped out from behind the tent canvas, into the entryway.

No less than two dozen men ringed the tent, weapons drawn.

At the center, Tarquin Belmonte's amused eyes settled on her, his thumb tucked into the belt binding his long, white officer's coat. He grinned. "The pride welcomes you home, Your Highness."

CHAPTER 24

A softness tickled against Veron's bare skin, and his eyes still closed, he reached down. They hadn't been able to find pillows, and Aless had fallen asleep with her head on his stomach, but—

The weight of her head wasn't there. Perhaps it was her hair tickling him.

But when he grasped a handful, it was fabric. A blanket.

He opened his eyes, reached next to him.

The bed was empty.

Aless was gone.

"Aless?" He sat up, looking around the bedchamber, blinking. His clothes were still on the floor, his boots in the corner, but hers—

Hers were gone.

He sprang from the bed, raked his hair back. She'd only gone to relieve herself, or perhaps for another bite to eat. Supper had ended abruptly, after all. He sank back down, his head in his hands.

It was just all of these problems with the Brotherhood. When Nozva Rozkveta had last gone to war, Ata had left. And now that war circled them anew, it dredged up old insecurities. That was all.

But as the minutes ticked by, Aless didn't return.

He swept the room with frantic eyes, and there, on the table, lay one of her books, open. He darted to it, set aside her quill, and read...

I love you.

She... Was this a—

No, she wouldn't—

But as he brushed his fingertips across the ink, across one line written in her *mother's* book, there was no other reason Aless would have done this.

Except to say goodbye.

She'd—she'd left. Without a word, she'd *left* him.

To do what? The trade? Surrender herself to the Brotherhood, who would do who-knew-what to her? The Brotherhood despised the Immortals, and the dark-elves among them, so what would they do to a human married to one?

They won't kill me, she'd said. *I'm certain of it.*

She's staked her life on it, on Tarquin, a man who'd unleashed harpies on her, ordered a witch to collapse tunnels in a queendom she'd been in. A man who might rather make an example of her than protect her.

He grabbed his clothes off the floor and hastily threw them on, dragged on his leathers and his boots, strapped his vjernost blades onto his belt.

She'd *gone* to that man, turned herself over, *trusted* Tarquin Belmonte.

Tonight, she'd been all smiles, affectionate, seductive. They'd spent the past couple of hours loving each other, together, *one*, no more fears or restraints between them. He'd fallen asleep wrapped up with her, tangled with the woman he loved, and despite the war at the gates, despite everything, he'd never felt so whole. He would have trusted her with anything, with his life, with his family, with his homeland.

And she hadn't even trusted him with her plan. Had shoved aside the trust they'd built together, their bond, and had left without a word. She wanted to trade herself to the Brotherhood, which might not even release Gavri or Valka, if they were even still alive. And then Tarquin Belmonte would shackle her, take her away, use her to achieve his hateful ends.

Holy Ulsinael, *he'd* been the one to tell her she didn't truly *see* people, see the consequences of her actions. Ever since he'd mentioned it in Stroppiata, she'd made genuine efforts to look beyond herself and what she cared to see, and to look at how she affected those around her and the larger consequences. She'd worked time and again to change that, sometimes to the point of recklessness, like in the ring in Dun Mozg.

Had she thought of the impending war tonight and decided she couldn't bear the consequences of inaction?

Mati had told her she'd had no say, to remain in their quarters, but… when someone told Aless there was no way out, she made her own.

And she'd expected him to agree with Mati and obey instead of helping her with her plan… And if that's what she'd thought, she hadn't been wrong.

Disobedient, reckless, rebellious, selfless, brave, heartrending Aless.

Please be safe. Please.

On his way out, he grabbed his bow and quiver, then burst into the hallway.

Mati would—

No, Mati would order him to stay here. As much as she liked Aless, she wouldn't allow him to interfere with negotiations or risk being captured for leverage.

But once the Brotherhood had Aless, there might not be any more negotiations. Tarquin could launch the assault, or—or take Aless and leave. Or Aless could be killed, sacrificed to spark the war irretrievably.

Mati had ordered him to stay in his quarters, but orders or no orders, the Brotherhood would not be taking Aless anywhere. Not while he drew breath. He'd let Ata leave once and he hadn't followed—as a child, wouldn't have been able to follow—but he would *not* let Aless go. Mati could rearrange his face later and he'd accept it, as long as he could bring back Aless.

He strode down the hall, headed for Heraza Gate. Already some of the palace's residents were emerging from their quarters, and there wouldn't be much time before all of Nozva Rozkveta awoke to the whitening glow of the Bloom.

Passersby greeted him as he traversed Central Cavern, and he offered pleasant replies—perhaps he'd seem less suspicious, even jogging down the walkways.

Near the entrance to Heraza's tunnel, a group of people huddled tightly, Yelena and—and—

"Gavri," he called out, and she raised her head, her face marred with bruises, blood, and a black eye.

"Veron!" She ran to him, with Yelena and Valka following. "Aless is still out there—"

He grabbed her shoulders. "Is she safe?"

She blinked, shaking her head. "I-I don't know. Last we saw, the Brotherhood was coming after us, and she went in the opposite direction—"

He released her and passed—

"Veron," she said from behind him, "when Valka and I were scouting, when we got caught... two other armies were en route. Human armies."

Looking over his shoulder, he stopped. Two human armies? "Whose? Brotherhood reinforcements?"

"We were apprehended before we could investigate further, Your Highness," Valka answered.

Had Aless's father arrived after all? But what about the second army?

A loud series of thuds echoed through Central Cavern from the earthmover tunnels—a hammer knock. Dun Mozg's.

Yelena grinned. "My mother has arrived."

"Your mother?"

That grin widened. "If it is a fight the humans want, then Dun Mozg stands with Nozva Rozkveta, to the Darkness and beyond."

Then Nendra had come with troops and weapons. And the entire queendom would soon be awake and bustling with battle preparations—all while the Brotherhood held Aless. Even *if* her assessment of Tarquin was correct, would his army refrain from harming her if their backs were pressed to the wall?

Armies had arrived, with some hungry for war. If nothing changed, there would be unthinkable loss of life.

"We have to stop this," he bit out. "Someone has to find out the identity of these two armies. Open negotiations with them." Someone like *him*. If it was indeed King Macario, then perhaps he could sway the Brotherhood to release Aless and to surrender, before any of this came to battle and deaths.

He strode through the tunnel to Heraza Gate.

"Veron," Yelena shouted, "you have orders. You can't just—"

But he did anyway.

CHAPTER 25

*I*n the lavish officer's tent, Aless sat still in the chair, following Tarquin's every movement as he poured tea service for two next to the massive map of the area sprawling over the table. A marker sat below Nozva Rozkveta—the Brotherhood, surely—and two others, one far to the south and one to the west. What did they represent?

A tall, lanky young man with long, straight black hair stood at attention at the tent entrance in a white officer's coat, watching her with a hard, hazel gaze.

"Don't mind Siriano, Your Highness. Neither he, nor anyone here, will hurt you." Tarquin put a spoonful of honey in one of the cups and stirred it without a sound. "He's a mage captain from the Belmonte Company and loyal to a fault."

Loyal to whom? To Tarquin? To the Brotherhood? Certainly not to the Crown, if he was allowing anyone to keep a princess of Silen captive.

Also, Tarquin had said *mage captain*. Was this the geomancer who'd attacked Dun Mozg?

Tarquin slid the cup toward her before bringing his own up to his nose and inhaling deeply.

"The best Kamerish black tea comes from just outside of Ren," he drawled. "Wouldn't you agree?"

The only quality of this tea that interested her right now was how badly it would scald Tarquin Belmonte if she threw it in his face.

Beneath Siriano's watchful eyes, her fingers curled around the cup, but—

scalding the only person keeping her alive was ill advised, even for the Beast Princess. "You didn't bring me here to talk about tea."

Tarquin laughed under his breath. "I didn't bring you here."

Mincing words?

"*Fine.*" She grimaced. "You aren't *keeping* me here to talk about tea."

He took a sip and then sighed lengthily through his nose. "Your Highness, I am the *only* person in this kingdom who has cared enough to save you from this forced arrangement. His Majesty manipulated you into this against your will, and that is a wrong that must be righted."

Pretty words. But if he thought she'd believe he'd mobilized an army and come all the way here just out of *care* for her, then he was about to wake from his little daydream. "And how would you right it?"

"First, by exchanging those two beasts for you. Then, by pretending to threaten your life if His Majesty doesn't annul your marriage—"

Only an unconsummated marriage could be annulled in Silen, but she'd keep that tidbit to herself.

"—and once he does, encouraging you to wed the man of your choice."

Veron. Veron. Forever and always Veron.

"And I assume by that you mean yourself?"

His mouth curled in a seductive smile. "The notion didn't seem to displease you the evening of the masquerade."

"I assure you, I was contemplating a far cruder notion."

"And found me to be a pleasing option."

Until he'd opened his mouth. A single word of hatred spoken could turn even a handsome face ugly. And Tarquin had spoken many.

Despite the idiocy of his assertion, she didn't dare laugh at him. Not while he held her captive here, thinking he'd win his path to princedom if only he just persevered. Shredding his daydream to tatters could mean he'd be holding a captive he didn't need anymore.

And imagining the outcomes flowing from that was an exercise in terror.

"Well, here I am," she said, holding his dark-brown gaze steadily. "If this is between you and me, you don't need an army. Or maybe we should be marching on Bellanzole." If she could get him moving the Brotherhood away from Nozva Rozkveta toward the capital, Papà would be forced to intervene.

"The people adore you. I have both the Belmonte Company and the Brotherhood at my command. Together, we could turn this nation on the right path, eliminate the Immortali that prey on us." Across the table from her, he lazily crossed one leg over the other. "You are a large portion of this puzzle, Your Highness, but other pieces remain."

"What other pieces?"

"Restoring the kingdom to its former glory. Before the Immortali invaded and ruined it."

"The Immortali are not some monolithic entity. They vary from person to person just like we do." Stating a belief to the contrary was just smoke. "You're a smart man, Tarquin, so I know you understand this."

His brow furrowed. "And in their shadow, danger follows. Life has never been more violent, more dangerous, than now."

"We're working to change that. The dark-elves can help us keep the dangerous among the Immortali at bay. Those who attack us first, who do nothing but murder and harm. Those are only a small fraction, but by working together, we can stand against them."

That furrow deepened. "We don't need to work together. We have mages." He nodded toward Siriano, whose hard expression didn't waver.

"But the dark-elves are just like us, Tarquin. They have marriages and families and babies. They want peace. They want love. They just want to survive."

"Spoken like a tender-hearted woman." He scoffed. "Do they need to be *stockpiling weapons* to survive? Our intelligence tells us that is exactly what the queendom of Dunmarrow is doing."

"Can you blame them? Humans have been attacking their people since they awoke. Wouldn't you prepare to defend yourself? Yet they want peace. They haven't taken a single human life."

He knocked the table with his knuckles. "Oh, but they did. Three of my scouts went missing near Dunmarrow."

"They attacked me," she blurted. That wasn't the dark-elves' fault. "I had to defend myself and killed one of them, and the other two were killed to protect me."

He shook his head vehemently. "Those men were sent to *find* you, and rescue you if the opportunity arose."

"They tried to drag me away kicking and screaming!" Her hands trembled, so she folded them in her lap. "Would you call that a rescue?"

He tilted his head, scrutinizing her. "You didn't want to be saved?"

This conversation was taking a wrong turn. "My father wanted to build a peace. That peace falls apart without me."

He stood from the chair, pacing the tent. "He built that peace on *your* sacrifice. You were a victim, just like Arabella. It wasn't right to begin with."

He wanted to talk about *right*?

"Tarquin, I saw what's been done to that unicorn. That wasn't right either."

"Unicorn? You mean that Immortali horse-beast?"

"It's not a beast. They are peaceful beings—"

He turned on her, his face contorted. "My sister, Arabella, was fond of your so-called *'peaceful being.'* She was an innocent—she loved singing and picking wildflowers and admiring beauty of all kinds. She saw one of those Immortali horses and couldn't stop looking at it, searching it out. One day, she disappeared, and not three days later, that beast trespassed onto our lands and started attacking our doors, breaking windows, terrifying everyone, destroying everything."

"So you *tortured* it?"

He leaned in. "It kept coming back, wreaking havoc, so my men caught it. Due to its size and strength, they've been trying to tame it, but it's been a waste of time. They're of half a mind to just kill it."

"So you'll just let them kill anything that won't obey?" That was what all the unicorn's injuries were from? "Tarquin, that is an intelligent *being*. It has thoughts and feelings and may be vastly older and wiser than you and me. You can't just lock it up and abuse it like that."

"*It* is the reason Arabella is gone. If not for that... *thing*, she would have been safe at home."

"It's not a *thing*! It's a—"

A shapeshifter.

She paused, and Tarquin's frown faded slightly. "It's a what?"

Veron had told her all about them. She sat up. "Tarquin, unicorns have a territory they stay in. They abhor all violence. They're pacifistic by nature."

"Not *this* one."

She nodded. That was the problem. Something didn't fit. "You said it showed up three days *after* Arabella disappeared?"

A line formed between his eyebrows as he lifted a shoulder. "What of it?"

Holy Mother's mercy, if she was wrong about this—

"You said Arabella loved unicorns, that she'd go off in search of them, just to look at them." When he nodded, she continued, "Unicorns are shapeshifters, like werewolves. They can turn people, Tarquin. And you said this unicorn showed up a couple days after Arabella disappeared? And unlike their peaceful reputation, it was destroying things? If she wanted to become a unicorn—"

"You're saying that *thing* is Arabella?" he shouted at her, his eyes wide and blazing.

She flinched. Perhaps not her greatest move ever.

"If that's true—and it's too ridiculous to be—then why hasn't she changed back? If she's a shapeshifter?"

She swallowed. "You kept her bound in arcanir chains. It can interfere with the Immortali."

He scrubbed a hand over his face. "If this is true... If that thing was Arabella..."

"Then you've been torturing the very person you set out to defend."

He froze, standing still in the dim lamplight of the tent. So many evil deeds he'd done in the name of his sister, and there was a chance she was not only alive but had been in his custody all this time, harmed by his very own men, desperate to show her brother in any way she could who she was... to no avail.

"General," someone called from outside the tent, and at Tarquin's permission, Siriano pulled the tent flap aside and let in a young officer, who eyed her, gawking at her clothes—her *disguise*.

With a glower, Tarquin motioned the officer to continue.

"Sir, scouts say King Macario's forces have made camp south of us, on the hills abutting the river to the east. The duchessa's army has taken up position to the west and is building makeshift fortifications."

Her heart pounded.

Papà had come for her.

And the duchessa had joined him.

Tarquin moved the two map markers accordingly, his face a veneer of calm. "Send a message to King Macario. Tell him he shall annul the princess's marriage to the beast—"

How *dare* he call Veron a beast?

"—and that he shall contact the duchessa and order her forces to withdraw along with his own, before dusk tomorrow. If he does not comply, Her Highness will be executed the dawn after."

No, he couldn't—with her life on the line, Papà would comply. But if Papà and the duchessa did withdraw, then there would be no one to stop the Brotherhood from starving out Nozva Rozkveta—causing tens of thousands to suffer.

No, he couldn't even be allowed to extend this offer to Papà.

She'd come this far. Papà's forces couldn't be allowed to abandon Nozva Rozkveta. And Tarquin wouldn't hurt her, not unless he wanted his entire family reduced to a pool of blood.

Tarquin's purpose would have to be frustrated to stop this now.

She swallowed. "My father can't annul the marriage, Tarquin."

His head snapped to face her, and his eyebrows drew together.

"It's been consummated."

CHAPTER 26

"*I* am Prince Veron of Nightbloom!" Veron shouted, holding his arms out to his sides as he cleared the forest. He slowly headed toward the sea of purple-and-white-striped tents through the tall grass, finding his footing in stiff boots. "Don't shoot! I seek an audience with King Macario of Silen!"

Had someone told him a couple of months ago that he'd disobey orders, betray Mati's trust, leave Nozva Rozkveta on the eve of battle, and would now be turning himself over to the mercy of humans, he never would have believed it.

This wasn't about trust. This was about protecting the ones he loved.

He'd disobeyed Mati, betrayed her, but people were more than their mistakes, and not every hurtful action was *about* inflicting hurt. Sometimes hurt, as grave as it could be, had to be a secondary concern to trying to save many lives. Or even just one.

The sun was just beginning to rise in the sky of pinks, golds, and blues as archers shuffled along the top of a hill, yelling to one another and to him.

"Stop right there!" one bellowed, and he did as bidden.

Their bows drawn, the archers descended the hill and surrounded him, demanding he surrender his weapons before they escorted him up and to the center of camp.

Officers in dark-purple coats surveyed him, and the king's page, Alvaro, confirmed his identity before he was admitted to the yurta at the heart of the royal encampment.

As soon as he entered, long arms pulled him into an embrace—Lorenzo's.

Wearing a dark-purple gambeson, Aless's brother met him with those dark eyes so like hers, and a broad grin, his shoulder-length dark hair tied back. A dozen knives were sheathed in a bandolier about his chest.

"It's good to see you." Lorenzo clapped him on the shoulder.

"I wish it were under better circumstances."

"We are about to crush the Brotherhood," King Macario said from behind Lorenzo, eyeing a map as he stroked his close-cropped salt-and-pepper beard. "The circumstances are favorable." He stepped away from the map and gestured to a nearby chair. "How is my daughter? You both did well in Stroppiata and Dunmarrow, as expected. You must have made quite the impression on Duchessa Claudia, as she is here with her forces as well."

So *that* was the second army. "Your Majesty, Aless is in the Brotherhood camp."

Both King Macario and Lorenzo paused, exchanging looks, and Lorenzo closed his eyes and heaved a sigh, rubbing his face as he turned away.

"You were supposed to keep her safe." The king stepped up to him, but soon deflated. "Only... I know my Aless. Always making a scene of some sort. Relentless, reckless, wild, *foolish*—"

"Your Majesty," Veron interrupted, a growl lacing his voice. "We didn't know whether you were coming, or whether anyone was. Aless traded herself to save two lives, which if they had been taken, would have set us on a course of no return. She didn't have complete information, but she's trying to save countless more." He held the king's gaze.

Perhaps the king's words might have once been true, but *his* Aless was brave, stood up for what she believed was right, and always with forethought. If she was wild, she was like the Bloom in her protectiveness, her boldness, her power.

Alvaro came in with a message that he handed to King Macario, whose face darkened as he read. He crumpled the message and waved off Alvaro, carefully lowering into a chair.

"Is it Aless?" Veron asked, taking a step forward, but the king didn't react.

Lorenzo pried the message from his hand and read. "To His Majesty, King Macario: You shall annul the princess's marriage to the beast, and shall contact the duchessa and order her forces to withdraw along with your own, before dusk tomorrow. If you do not comply, Her Highness will be executed the following dawn. General Tarquin Belmonte."

"Executed?" he demanded, and Lorenzo handed him the message. He read and reread the words, but they were the same.

"That's it," the king murmured. "The end of our strategy. He has Aless and isn't afraid to kill her."

Lorenzo slapped his hands on the table. "You *saw* the way Tarquin looked at her, Papà. He's bluffing."

"I will *not* risk her life," the king shot back, rising. "We have to get her back safely, whatever the cost."

On that, they agreed.

The king would accept Tarquin's terms, quit the area along with the duchess, and Aless would be all right...

And the Brotherhood would continue its siege of Nozva Rozkveta. If Tarquin did order his witch to collapse the tunnels, it was only a matter of time before Mati and Nendra would lead their forces to the sky realm and attack, annihilating the Brotherhood—

And putting Aless in danger once again.

At a threat to his daughter's life, King Macario was ready to surrender completely. Not something any dark-elf queen would ever do for a son—not even Mati.

If it were him—

If it were—

He shook his head, trying to clear it. If it were him in Tarquin's custody, Aless would be freed, sent back with King Macario, who'd then have no incentive to retreat. Both the royal army and the duchess's could stay and help Nozva Rozkveta.

And Mati would never sacrifice her people for his sake.

Aless would be safe... Nozva Rozkveta would have its allies...

And Tarquin would have *him*.

"Tell him to take me instead."

～

ALESS STARED at the paper as Tarquin finished his last bit of writing, but the letters were too small, too blurry, for her to make out the words. Under Siriano's watchful eyes in the corner of the tent, Tarquin folded the paper, sealed it, and handed it to one of his men.

There had to be some way to talk him out of this. There *had* to be.

He leaned back in his chair, his hands folded together as he regarded her evenly, some epiphany playing out behind that deep-brown gaze.

"You really did fall in love with that beast," he said expressionlessly.

"He's not a beast!" she shot back, and Tiny chattered in her hair, but she ignored it. "Veron's loving, kind, gentle—"

"Sorcery," Tarquin bit out. "He's bewitched you somehow. Those beasts have fangs, claws—"

"Dark-elves don't have magic! All they have is sangremancy, which anyone with blood, knowledge, and skill can use. You'd know that if you tried learning about them instead of just hating them from a position of ignorance."

He scoffed. "If they had a way to control your mind, do you think they'd tell you?"

"You're impossible. If they could control minds, you wouldn't be able to be here, hating them and waging war." She crossed her arms, which renewed the scent of cheap wine soaked into her disguise. "You're an educated man, Tarquin, and a general. Surely you understand the value of facts. You're acting from an emotional place, and worse, it's unfounded. Your sister wasn't killed by the Immortali. She elected to become one."

"You don't know that!" he snapped, pounding the table with a palm. "And you have no proof, just some tales you heard from beasts."

"Well, *you* don't have any proof she died, or that the Immortali killed her, yet you believe it!" she shot back. "If there's even a *chance* Arabella is alive, even as a unicorn, don't you at least want to find out if it's true?"

"You made sure I couldn't verify your tale when you released the Immortali horse." His voice dropped to a low, bitter rasp.

"I released the unicorn," she said, meeting his low voice with her own, "but I didn't make it run away. Your men did that with their abuse. *You* did that." When he only bowed his head, she added, "If that really is Arabella, then out of fear for her *life*, she had to flee her brother."

A long quiet settled in. "That's. Not. Her." He looked up, eyes fiery. "You knew you'd get caught, so you released that Immortali horse and made up a story. One you hoped would distract me from my purpose."

She shook her head. "Tarquin, *you* told me, right here, about Arabella's love of unicorns. *You* told me she disappeared in search of one. *You* told me that unicorn showed up a couple days later. *You* told me it was destroying things, attacking. That is what I based my conclusion on—what *you* told me— and I knew none of that before you sat me down in this tent." She leaned forward and added gently, "Set aside your battle plans and your hatred and everything else you've believed, and just think about these facts for a second, rationally. You know I couldn't have made it up before releasing that unicorn. You know it."

He took a deep breath and then sighed, meeting her eyes with a soft look. "Your Highness, if any of that is true, then all I've done is make one terrible mistake after another, mistakes I can never take back. If any of that is true, how can I live with myself?"

"By not making any more terrible mistakes," she replied. "You have the chance to find Arabella and tell her that you love her and that you're sorry. You have the chance to stop all of this before it gets any worse, Tarquin."

He lowered his gaze a moment, then glanced at Siriano before turning back to her. "I don't, Your Highness. Even if Arabella is still alive, even as one of the Immortali, the only people here who *would* stop this are Siriano and me. But there is an *army* outside who won't back down until a river of blood flows. And the two of us can't stop them." Before she could reply, he cut in, "So you see, Your Highness, what you're saying *can't* be true, and I have to believe that it isn't."

Heaving a breath, he rose and headed for the tent flap.

"Not just you and Siriano, Tarquin," she said, twisting around toward him. "I would stop this, too, with both of you. With everything in me."

He looked over his shoulder. "It doesn't matter anymore. The Brotherhood wants blood. King Macario offered to trade Veron of Nightbloom for you, and I just accepted."

CHAPTER 27

*T*he glowing red sun was faltering through the cloudy titian sky, and as Aless stood at the front of a company of Brotherhood soldiers, that dusky sky looked to her like a fire amid clouds of ash, billowing and graying as far as the eye could see.

The forested horizon was darkening. When she'd told Veron that Tarquin wouldn't hurt her, he might have believed that, trusted it, but Papà? Papà had never listened to her before, and he wouldn't have started now. If he'd believed Tarquin would kill her, if he'd agreed to retreat in exchange for her, that would have left Nozva Rozkveta exposed to the Brotherhood. Vulnerable.

And that, Veron wouldn't allow. He wouldn't allow his people to be abandoned by their allies, to starve, to do battle out of desperation, not if he could stop it. He'd sacrificed himself in marriage for them before. And if he arrived tonight, he would be sacrificing his life for them now.

Tarquin wouldn't hurt her, and not even the Brotherhood army would. But there was no such certainty for Veron.

Don't show up. Don't show up, Veron. Please. Don't show up.

Maybe Tarquin was wrong. Maybe Papà wouldn't agree to trading Veron. Maybe this was all part of a maneuver and an attack was imminent instead, while Veron would be kept safe, and the shifting feeling in her chest would dissipate.

In the darkness, the full moon rose in the sky, golden, enormous.

Tiny peeked out of her hair over her shoulder.

"Stay hidden, Tiny," she whispered, just barely audible. If any of the Brotherhood caught one of the Immortali—albeit a minuscule one—things could go badly.

Tiny flitted back into her locks and climbed up by her ear, chiming softly in her little bell voice.

Tarquin stood stiff as a rod next to her, his eyes searching the horizon, Siriano next to him, and a company of rigid men behind them. They were hard men, with hard eyes and hard faces, a sort of darkness emanating from them, a coldness, and it made her shiver. These were not men looking to make peace, no matter what the offer would be. That was not what they had come for.

She might have been able to turn Tarquin from this course, but the hundreds here, the thousands with him? Some had their own Arabella, and a truth behind her, and others believed things that were completely false, and yet others were so afraid of sharing the world that they cloaked that fear with aggression. They hated from a place of bitter ignorance, one they preferred to take out on the Immortali instead of taking responsibility for.

This world needed a library like the one she and Veron dreamed of building. This world needed a hundred libraries. A thousand.

She looked away from them to the dim horizon, where a small group of silhouetted figures approached.

No, Holy Mother, please...

Yet she'd know the shape of him anywhere, his gait, from a mile away, in the dark—she'd know him.

Her feet were moving before she could think, but Tarquin grabbed her forearm and pulled her back.

"Not yet," he said sternly, and yanked her into place. "One hundred yards."

Holy Mother's mercy, she'd wanted to stop a war, had wanted to *protect* Veron, had never dreamed he'd disobey Queen Zara and come after her. She loved him for it, but now what had seemed like her best course of action had become her gravest miscalculation.

Papà had to have a contingency plan. This couldn't be it. He couldn't just be turning over Veron. He couldn't.

Her heart thudded in her chest as she stared into the distance, at the broadness of his shoulders, his long hair tousled by the wind, and as he approached, the shape of his face cleared, his sculpted jaw, his straight nose, his pale eyebrows, his jutting chin... and those intense golden eyes she had looked into countless times, had seen in kindness, in anger, in frustration, in pleasure, in love...

"Veron," she whispered, and every part of her trembled, willed her to go to him, to wrap herself around him and never let go.

Next to him was Lorenzo, in a violet brigandine over a darker gambeson, with a bandolier of knives around his chest and a small squad of Royal Guard. His face was slack, eyes downcast. So Papà had sent him.

"Aless," Veron said, his voice breaking, and a pain formed in her throat.

"Veron," she whispered, leaning forward, pulling at her arm in Tarquin's hold.

Finally, Tarquin moved forward with her in his grasp, Siriano at his side, and a squad of soldiers with him. She struggled in his hold, trying to break free, until at last he released her, and she ran to Veron, into his waiting arms. His embrace closed around her, and held her close, kissed the top of her head, and when she looked up at him, brushed her lips with his.

Holy Mother's mercy, after hurting him as she had, she had no right to this, to him, and he should push her away, shun her, *hate* her, but even knowing all of that, in this one moment, she couldn't fathom not holding him with everything she had.

"Veron, I'm so sorry," she said softly, her eyes aching as they watered. "I thought if they took me instead, they wouldn't kill me, and Papà would have to intervene... and that he could stop the war. I'm so sorry—"

"Shhh," he whispered in her ear, stroking her hair softly. "No more of that. Not now. You meant well—I know that. It hurt, deeply, but I know you meant well." He raised her chin gently, rubbing it with the callused pad of his thumb, taking her in with a soft gaze.

"Are Gavri and Valka—"

"They're safe. Worried about you," he said with a soft huff, "but safe." He was so calm, so incredibly, impossibly calm.

"I'm sorry I didn't tell you," she blurted. "I knew about your father, and I—"

"I know why he did it now, Aless." His voice was even, serene, as he searched her eyes. "My father. He left without a word because he couldn't let anybody stop him. He was determined to give up his life... because he loved us. It hurt me then, but I understand now. What he did wasn't a betrayal. It was the ultimate act of love."

There was something different about him, something settled and peaceful, something so unbelievably calm, and yet it tore her up inside, raged, so much that she wanted to scream and beg and cry, do anything and everything to chase that resigned expression away, and everything and everyone but Veron.

A pair of hands closed around her upper arms—a Royal Guard's.

"No," she said, and swung her head from side to side as Tarquin's men apprehended Veron, pulled him away from her, dragged him. "Please. Wait—"

She twisted to keep her eyes on him over her shoulder, where his eyes were still on her, too. A hardness rose in them, a restraint that turned his whole body taut as they bound his wrists.

"Veron," she cried, as Lorenzo took hold of her and whispered words of comfort.

"Live, Aless," Veron called out, his voice hoarse. "I love you."

One of his captors kicked at the back of his knee, forcing him to the grass, while another grabbed a fistful of his hair and pulled his head back.

She cried out, a shrill sound she didn't recognize, as Veron kept his jaw clenched, stayed soundless, rigid, and as a blade hissed free of a scabbard, she begged, pleaded, a string of words whimpering from her lips—

"*Please,*" she cried, her pulse hammering in her chest, wild, violent. "*Don't! Veron!*" Her shriek cut the air, following by the thudding staccato of clopping hooves.

A streak of pure white burst from the trees—the unicorn—racing toward Tarquin, directly for him.

Men shouted, drew swords and bows, and the soldiers keeping Veron gawked.

"*Hold fire!*" Tarquin yelled, the unicorn closing in on a hundred yards, over a ton of muscle and power tearing up the grass.

"Shoot it!" someone shouted.

"Hold!" Tarquin faced it head on. "Arabella!"

The unicorn charged him—fifty yards, thirty—

Holy Mother's mercy, maybe it *wasn't* her—

Fifteen yards—

Four legs Changed to two, a shock of sable hair blooming from her head, and beautiful and lithe, she ran, weeping, stumbling over her own legs to trip at Tarquin's feet.

Murmurs of "unnatural" and "kill it" rippled through the Brotherhood forces as Tarquin raced to her, throwing off his officer's coat to wrap her in it. He fell to his knees before her.

"Arabella," he said, his voice breaking, and took her in his arms, where she sobbed into his chest. "I'm so sorry, Arabella. I'm so sorry." He rocked her gently, patted her back.

"Stop this, brother," she croaked, her green eyes big and dazzling as she looked up into his face. "No more violence on my account. *No more violence.* Please."

Veron's captors didn't move, and neither did he, frozen on his knees, his head pulled back—but the hand holding it had loosened its grip.

Veron—please, be safe... Veron... She moved, but Lorenzo held her back with a shake of his head. He patted one of the knives sheathed in his bandolier.

The company of Brotherhood soldiers stood, some with bows drawn, others staring. A couple neared with readied crossbows.

"Stand down," Tarquin ordered.

The crossbowmen didn't waver.

"I said *stand down!*" He glared at the crossbowmen.

"You heard the general," Siriano bellowed, stepping up with his right hand glowing a faint green.

A crossbow fired.

Tarquin lunged in front of Arabella.

The bolt lodged in his shoulder.

Veron headbutted the captor fisting his hair.

Another raised his sword.

Lorenzo threw a knife into the man's neck.

Complete chaos broke out among the Brotherhood ranks, infighting and arrows loosed as Siriano raised an earthen wall between the company of men and their forward party. Lorenzo ordered his Royal Guards to attack, and they sprang into action, swarming Veron's captors as he fought them.

One of them charged her and Lorenzo, but she ducked, covering her head as Tiny flew out and attacked the man's face. He swatted at her but missed, and Lorenzo threw a salvo of knives into the man's leather-clad chest. He spluttered and fell.

"Tiny!" she shouted, and the pixie flew back to land on her shoulder, chiming angrily.

A Royal Guard cut Veron's bonds, and he grabbed a blade from the ground, fighting until every last Brotherhood soldier on this side of the wall lay dead.

She ran to him, and he turned, catching her in his arms, breathing her in, and already they were moving back toward Lorenzo along with his Royal Guards.

"Veron, for a second, I thought—" Her voice broke.

His eyes fixed on the earthen wall, he held the blade out at the ready, but his gaze darted toward hers a moment. "So did I." He shot her an uneasy grin.

Tarquin lumbered backward toward them with Arabella and Siriano and, facing the wall, drew his sword.

Lorenzo drew his own. "Stay back, Belmonte! Or I'll have your head!"

Tarquin's eyes darted to his just a moment while he pulled Arabella in protectively. "I surrender. Please, I mean none of you any harm. I just want to make sure Arabella's safe."

The loud din of battle rose beyond the wall, chaotic, deafening, and men began to break through at the end of its length.

Siriano raised another perpendicular to it. "General, we need to *move*."

"Just wait," Lorenzo said.

"For what?" Tarquin hissed, and Arabella sobbed, trembling against him like a leaf in a storm.

The ground shook as she whirled around.

Heavy Sileni cavalry charged toward them—hundreds—thousands—with a glowing veil above them, lighting the way—pixies.

Tiny shot out and raced to join them.

"Move in!" Siriano yelled, and with a gesture, raised a triangular wall between them and the charging cavalry.

His first spell collapsed, and the Brotherhood's fighting broke through. With a nod from Tarquin, Siriano dispelled the second wall, and they all stood with the triangle's protection, huddled, as an earthquake of thundering horse-flesh pounded past them and into the infighting Brotherhood forces.

Screams and shrieks tore the air, and the sounds of horns and shouted orders.

The Brotherhood was utterly decimated, broken bodies and blood—

Veron pulled her in, tucked her face against his chest, and she shook, squeezing her eyes shut. The battle, the violence, was horrific, but Veron was here, safe, his warmth soothing into her, his breath soft on her head, his hands stroking her back, *alive*.

"Papà planned to strong-arm the Brotherhood into returning Veron once you were safe," Lorenzo said quietly. "You didn't think we'd *just* hand him over, did you?"

CHAPTER 28

On his knees in Mati's antechamber, Veron watched as she paced before him, Yelena, and Aless. There was a violence in her stride, in the contortion of her face, and he knew better than to speak until she spoke. Especially after all he'd done.

"Your Majesty," Yelena blurted, "I just want to say this was all the human's idea, and I didn't have anything to do with it. In fact, I wasn't even part of it until she asked me to be, and as a guest here, I didn't feel I could turn down a princess of—"

Mati stalked to Yelena, eyes wild, met her face to face, and *roared*. Yelena squeezed her eyes shut at the deafening sound, as he and Aless leaned away.

"*You*," Mati said with a sneer. "After your weak-willed, cowardly scheming to depose *me*, now lack the *honor* to take responsibility for your actions? Queen Nendra has given you to me as a *gift*. To do with as I see fit. And your days as kuvara are *over*." Mati stayed in Yelena's face, her stare relentless, but still Yelena didn't open her eyes. The moment lingered long past comfortable. "You will henceforth be a *sluha* and serve the kuvari and volodari in any way they desire."

A sluha. She'd have to serve as a page.

Yelena winced but did not speak.

Mati moved to Aless. "And *you*. I give you my *son*, my *blood*, and welcome you to my queendom, only for you to betray me at the first opportunity. What were you thinking?"

Aless shook, her fingers trembling at her sides. "I-I-I thought if I f-failed and was c-c-captured, my father would have to g-get involved and help. And if I succeeded, the B-brotherhood would have n-no l-leverage."

Mati narrowed her eyes, but there was a glimmer. "Be that as it may, that decision was *not* yours to make. Flout my orders *again*, I will have you harvesting cave lichen until you forget what civilization looks like."

Aless nodded hastily. "Y-yes, Your Majesty."

"It is your dark luck that King Macario and I have chosen to declare this as a joint operation, in which we both *agreed* to trade you for my two kuvari as part of a larger strategy. I don't have to tell you what it would look like if the world believed I *sacrificed* my human ally's daughter or, worse, couldn't contain a single human barely out of her childhood years."

Aless swallowed audibly.

Mati glared at each of them in turn. "*Any* of you speak of this to *anyone*, and I shall claw out your tongues with my bare hands. Do you understand?"

"Yes, Your Majesty," they said in unison.

At last, she strode to him and crouched. "And you, Veron, who have ever been a credit to this queendom and to me, have disappointed me gravely with your disobedience." Her eyes softened a moment as her eyebrows pulled together. "For that, you are dismissed from the volodari for the foreseeable future—"

Dismissed from the volodari? It was the one thing he had any considerable skill in doing. But even as his body rebelled, he knew he deserved any punishment Mati had to give, and this—by all rights—was lenient.

"—and you will be placed with the stavbali to build whatever Nozva Rozkveta requires."

The stavbali did backbreaking work assisting the inzenyri and the Stone Singers, but he'd do whatever was required to make amends.

"With that said," she added, a faint smile curving her lips, "you did everything in your power to protect the one you love." Her face went slack a moment. "I am proud that you did, that you loved fiercely and forgave, even if your actions were reckless."

She was... proud? He didn't regret what he'd done, not even a little bit, because although Mati was angry and he'd disobeyed, Aless was still here. He was still here. All of Nozva Rozkveta was still here. What they'd done hadn't been right, but it had led them to this moment, where they were all still alive and had a future ahead of them.

Mati was angry... but sometimes there were more important concerns than not angering loved ones. Like saving the love of his life and trying to stop a war. And for that, he'd take this punishment, a hundred punishments, a thousand—as long as Aless still lived and breathed.

He glanced at Aless, who was still trembling, but if Mati was fortifying the stavbali, that could only mean one thing: Aless's dream was about to come true. *Their* dream.

Sighing, Mati rose. "Despite all of your actions, we managed to avoid all-out war, reaffirm an alliance, and build a new one. Now get up and join me in the grand hall, where King Macario, Queen Nendra, Duchess Claudia, and all of Nozva Rozkveta await."

~

VERON STOOD in the grand hall's periphery, Aless on his arm, as Mati shook hands with King Macario and then with Duchess Claudia. Lorenzo was at Aless's side, along with Bianca and Luciano, who'd come to change Tarquin's mind—albeit too late. The kuvari already had him in their custody at Heraza Gate.

"What do you think was the final agreement?" Aless whispered, leaning in.

That much he'd overheard. "A reaffirmation of the Sileni–Nozva Rozkvetan alliance. A more concrete agreement between Stroppiata and the allied queen-doms. Roccalano to compensate Queen Nendra for the loss of her murdered volodari, with vast quantities of food and other supplies. The Brotherhood to be rooted out and ended by the coalition. And Tarquin Belmonte to be exiled."

It had been a kindness to Bianca and Luciano, and to Arabella. But also, as an exile, Tarquin couldn't be used as a martyr to further stoke the malcon-tents; he'd simply disappear and be forgotten.

Aless lightly rested her head against his arm, and there was something about her in Nozva Rozkvetan robes that pleased him as he looked her over. Her human clothes had always suited her—and he'd say or do just about anything to see her in that sheer red thing from their wedding night—but in these plain robes, she was saying something to him, to his family, to all of Nozva Rozkveta, without even a single word. That message mattered to him, a lot, even if his Aless could never fade into the background, never blend in—and he didn't want her to. That wouldn't be the woman he'd married... and was marrying again today at the Offering.

"What about Arabella?" she asked.

Arabella moved about Nozva Rozkveta freely, even now, although she seemed to spend most of her time with Noc, who could answer most of her questions about her new nature.

"She wants to learn control of her Change," he answered. "And my mother has agreed to help her." Unicorns had always been a benevolent force in the world, and Arabella herself had saved him from imminent death and prevented a war.

Soon, Mati would send out a team of the volodari to track other unicorns

—who generally didn't want to be found—in an effort to find Arabella's maker, who could help her control her Change by lifebonding with her.

"And in exchange, Tarquin goes quietly." Aless took a deep breath.

"Something like that."

She gave him a faint smile, although it soon faded. This entire situation had hit her hard—they'd nearly lost one another, a war had almost been instigated, people had *died*, and not all of them hateful Brotherhood members. And all of it born of ignorance.

It was by Holy Ulsinael's dark grace that a peace had survived.

Mati turned to the assembly of humans and dark-elves and raised her hands. "Today, we reaffirm a friendship between the kingdom of Silen and Nozva Rozkveta, between humans and dark-elves, built on a shared land, a shared purpose, and the marriage of our children." Smiling, Mati gestured to them both, and Aless curtseyed as he bowed. "That friendship was forged with a wedding, and today we renew it with a wedding once more. I invite you all to join us at Baraza Gate in one hour for the Offering between my son, Veron, and his wife, Alessandra."

Everyone turned to them and applauded, and he couldn't help a jittery hum coursing through his veins. If Aless would but have him, today would change their lives forever.

He was a dark-elf, Immortal, and the love of his life was a human.

Today, he had come so dangerously close to losing Aless, and he never wanted to feel that way again. Ever.

"We have also chosen to share our knowledge with the sky realm, to forge a partnership going forward that will help protect both our peoples against those who would mean to do us harm, while welcoming the people of the sky realm to know us," Mati said.

Next to him, Aless's breath caught.

"A *library*," Mati declared, with applause filling the silence she left.

Aless held his hand tightly, practically brimming.

"We will invite knowledge from around the world that we could use to learn about our new circumstances, all the while sharing with the world *our* culture, *our* knowledge, *our* language, teaching any who wish to learn. To that end, the Order of Terra, a monastic order devoted to serving the goddess Terra, has agreed to be our partner." Mati gestured to the Paladin Grand Cordon next to Duchess Claudia, who inclined his head to the applause.

"My daughter-in-law will oversee the project and ensure it meets everyone's needs." Mati smiled at Aless, who gasped, scarcely able to catch her breath.

Despite everything—or maybe even because of it—it was safe to say Mati had a fondness for his wife.

After another round of applause, Mati held out her hands. "Now, let's all get ready for a wedding."

"The library," Aless whispered, her cheeks reddening. "*Our* library... and the second ceremony. All in one day. Veron, I..."

"I know." He grinned. "Come on, let's prepare."

He was ready. Today, with all his heart, he would offer her everything he had and everything he was. And pray she'd say yes.

～

ALESS GRIPPED the ancient stone balustrade in the ruins behind Baraza Gate, where the Bloom curled around crumbling stone pillars and every bit of stone in the courtyard, a lovely weave of verdant vines and glittering red roses that only glowed brighter as the world darkened.

It would soon be dusk, and she'd be making the Offering to Veron.

They'd stopped a war, still had each other, and he didn't hate her after she'd abandoned him. *And* Queen Zara had announced the library.

It was happening. It was all happening.

She took three deep breaths.

"Alessandra," Papà's voice came from the steps. He ascended with a peaceful sigh. "You should be happy. You finally got your wish."

Did he mean the library or Veron? "Papà, this is the best day of my life."

He stroked her cheek, his gaze soft. "Your mother's wish came true, and she is gone. I wish you'd see the danger in this."

She shook her head. "Mamma died doing what she loved. It was important to her, and she—and her purpose—are important to me, too. I want to keep that alive."

"Alessandra, I have tried all your life to protect you. This—getting involved in something so risky, putting yourself out there and accessible to any lowlife..." He shook his head sadly. "You are still here, and your mother is *gone*. You should just live safely."

It was not in her to hide and live a *safe* life. Not while she still had two hands, and there were people who thirsted for knowledge but didn't have the tools to acquire it. Mamma had tried to shine a light on the world, to fight the ignorance that begat fear, and that was a worthy cause, one she'd continue the fight for.

"Mamma is gone," she whispered to him, "but she doesn't have to be forgotten. We did that, by disregarding her wishes, her life's work, everything that mattered to her. I understand that you mean well, but I choose a different path, Papà."

A heavy sigh left him, but he kissed her cheek. "Congratulations, daughter."

I may not agree with you, but I know your mother would be proud. Both of your library and you."

She couldn't help but smile, and with a final nod, he descended the steps and headed to the front of the ruins.

Bianca crept up next to her with a beaming Gabriella. "Well, *that* was unexpected."

She couldn't help a laugh as Bianca looked her over.

"Are you sure this is the right dress?" Bianca asked.

Aless brushed her fingers over the rose-red tulle netting of her wedding gown from Bellanzole. It fit her perfectly, and the skirts flared out gently, a ten-foot train behind her.

Veron had asked her to wear this gown, this same gown, and she hadn't brought another for the second ceremony, so she'd reluctantly agreed. Besides, when everyone in Bellanzole had seen it as shocking, he hadn't—at all. It meant something different to him.

"I'm sure."

"You look beautiful," Gabriella said, sweeping a stray lock of her sable hair off her face. She and Danika had returned with Papà and Lorenzo safely, thank the Mother.

She took Gabriella's hand. "Thank you. For taking the messages to Bellanzole. You did a very brave thing that saved lives."

Gabriella blushed, then inclined her head. "It was my honor."

Bianca's eyes widened, and Aless spun to see Veron approaching, in his best leathers, astride Noc. She blinked, and suddenly she was in L'Abbazia Reale again, watching a dark-elf prince on a massive black horse trotting down the hall, decked out for battle, regal and intimidating, well built and hale like the heroes of old, hewn from Carrerra marble.

She blinked again, and Veron was the same man, but so much more. The man she loved, who loved her. The man who listened to her. The man who wanted to live her dreams with her. The only one she could ever imagine wanting to spend the rest of her life with.

A smile on his face, he drank her in with his exploring gaze, and her cheeks warmed.

"I think he *does* like the dress," Bianca whispered in her ear with a giggle.

She shushed Bianca and approached the balustrade. "Is it time?"

"It is." He extended a hand to her, here, in this blooming courtyard of daydreams. "Will you do me the honor?"

She took his hand, descended the steps, and let him help her into the saddle. He gave a nod to Bianca and Gabriella, thick as thieves, who watched them leave. Bianca even gave her a wink. The troublemaker.

Their teasing made her heart flutter, and here, enshrined in Veron's arms, she had all the reason in the world to be giddy.

Her eyes closed, she tucked her head under Veron's chin, settled into his embrace, breathed in his pure forest-stream scent. "You're sure you like the dress?"

A soft breath. "I am. It suits you, my love." A light, playful tone danced in his deep voice. "But I do have something to ask you," he added, and that playful tone faded.

"Hmm?" She opened her eyes, straightened a little.

He let the silence stay a while. "Are you sure you want to do this?"

She looked up at him, but there was no room to see his face. Now, minutes before their Offering, he doubted her?

"I once told you I couldn't release you," he said softly. "But now, Aless, if you tell me this isn't what you want, I will help you, whatever it takes."

That's what this was about? He'd told her in Stroppiata that he couldn't release her, but she didn't *want* to be released. She wanted this—*him*—with every fiber of her being.

But he... he wanted her to *choose* this, not just accept it. He supported her decision, whether it was to do what he wanted or not.

If they weren't in the saddle, and about to stand in front of hundreds of people, she'd tackle him right now. "Veron, I want a life with you. I choose this. I choose *you*."

He let out a heavy breath. "That's a relief." A few deep breaths. "But I needed—I wanted—to ask."

"And I love that you did." She nuzzled his chest as Noc took them to the front of Baraza Gate, where no less than three hundred guests surrounded the vine-wrapped ruins. The Bloom shimmered all around them, glittered, and the gentle glow like stars all around was the pixies in attendance.

One raced from the rest, a little glowing star, and landed on her shoulder with a happy chime in greeting. A little pink-haired and leaf-wrapped pixie.

"Tiny," she breathed, and smiled. "You came."

"Tiny?" Veron asked, bending to look. "Hello," he whispered brightly.

Tiny fluffed her hair and crossed her legs, fluttering her wings as if to demonstrate their shimmering beauty.

"Did you do something new to your hair?" Aless asked, receiving a lively wing-fluttering in reply.

Xira, the mystic from the lifespring, stood at the top of the ruins' steps in her violet robes, her white hair ruffled by the breeze. While Queen Zara—Mati—seemed to preside over nearly all events in Nozva Rozkveta, Offerings were the mystics' preserve.

Veron dismounted and helped her down from Noc's saddle. "Thank you, old friend," he said softly, patting his neck.

Noc swished his tail and sprightly headed off to the side, where Arabella took in the whole assembly with interest, turning her horned head this way and that. Dhuro and Gavri stood with her, occasionally whispering things.

Veron took her hand, and together, they ascended the steps to stand before Xira. When her eyes met his, he was smiling, and she couldn't help but smile, too. They were doing this. They were finally doing this.

"Nozva Rozkveta bids you welcome," Xira announced to all the guests. "Today we gather in support of Prince Veron of Nozva Rozkveta and Princess Alessandra Ermacora of Silen as they make the Offering to each other, before Deep, Darkness, and Holy Ulsinael, and pledge to walk their lives together. Let us take a moment to welcome Holy Ulsinael here, to bless their union with his dark grace."

Xira clasped her hands together, closed her eyes, and bowed her head, as did Veron, as did Mati, as did every dark-elf in attendance, and Aless did the same.

Holy Mother, bless our union. Holy Ulsinael, bless our union.

She prayed, willing with all her heart that her prayers be heard, and when she opened her eyes, both Veron and Xira were grinning at her. Her cheeks warmed, but she only held his gaze, even as that playful grin warmed her cheeks even more.

Xira took their hands and joined them. "Make your Offerings."

Holding her hand, Veron stroked her fingers, his grin fading to a pensiveness, intensifying those warm golden eyes as he shifted in his boots. In Bellanzole, he'd arrived with a full arsenal of weapons and made an Offering to her right there, in L'Abbazia Reale, in the hallway. It had been a stunning moment, one she'd never forget.

Today, he had no sword, no bow, no knives, no shield, nor scroll.

He stood before her, holding her hand, regarding her warmly. "Aless, when we first married in Bellanzole, I offered you power, survival, skill, defense, and wisdom. I didn't know you then," he said to her, searching her eyes as a subtle smile claimed his lips. "But I know you now, and you require none of those things from me. You're a force to be reckoned with in your own right, and it is my great fortune to be by your side."

Her breath caught in her throat, and shallow breaths were all she could muster.

"Alessandra Ermacora, princess of Silen, I, Veron of Nozva Rozkveta, offer you my love, my loyalty, and my life"—he held her hand to his chest—"to harness for your ends or ours, as we walk our lives together from this day forward for as long as the Deep allows."

His *life*?

His golden eyes stayed locked with hers, and her shallow breaths only became shallower.

His life—his *life*—

Did he mean... a lifebond?

She gasped. "Veron..."

He couldn't! Holy Mother's mercy, a *lifebond*? Offering to share his life force with hers, to strengthen her, to weaken as she weakened, to die when she died?

He nodded to Xira, who held a bright, metallic little star, shaped like a crystal cluster.

"I'm a mortal," she whispered. "You can't—"

He kissed her hand. "It won't make you Immortal. But together, we'll have something more than a mortal life, and something less than an immortal one. That much I know."

This was... She shook her head. "Veron, are you sure—"

"I want to spend our lives together, Aless. Always together. Whether that's a hundred years or a thousand, whatever the Deep, Darkness, and Holy Ulsinael allow. Please make me the happiest man alive and say yes."

Say yes? Say yes to a lifetime shared with Veron, to years and decades and centuries in love, in joy, together? His sacrifice was enormous, and she wanted to argue, but as he held her gaze, pressed his lips to her hand, he gave her his answer.

"Yes," she whispered, and when his smile broadened, so did hers. "I accept your Offering."

A beaming Xira nodded to her.

It was time for her Offering. She'd planned to Offer him her knowledge, her boldness, and her ambition... but he had been right. Those weren't the things they truly needed to Offer each other. "Veron, prince of Nightbloom, I, Alessandra Ermacora of Silen, offer you my love, my loyalty, and my life, too," she said, threading her fingers through his, "to harness for your ends or ours, as we walk our lives together from this day forward for as long as the Deep allows."

He held both her hands, and grinned. "I accept your Offering."

Xira held out the small, bright metal cluster, and placed it between their palms. As they squeezed, there was a pinprick, and Xira held their hands between hers, chanted in Elvish, and when she finished—despite the pinprick, there was no mark, no blood.

"You are now lifebonded," Xira said, "joined in life and death, able to sense each other, draw each other, call to each other."

What that meant, she'd find out in the coming days, but as long as she got to be with Veron, the lifebond was perfect.

"What Offerings made and accepted today before the Deep, Darkness, and Holy Ulsinael, let no other pursue," Xira declared to the guests. "We swear this by the Darkness."

"By the Darkness," the crowd murmured, and Veron's lips met hers.

CHAPTER 29

*A*fter an evening of feasting, games, and dancing—for the humans in attendance—Veron opened the door to their quarters with a sigh of relief.

"So you'll take me hunting tomorrow?" Aless asked, breezing past him as he shut the door. "I need more practice."

"Perhaps not tomorrow," he said with a smile. When she pursed her lips, he added, "The Stone Singers and stavbali are breaking ground on the library tomorrow. I think you'll want to be there."

"*What?*" She jumped into his arms, squealing. "*Tomorrow?* Veron, really? Tomorrow!"

"Yes, really," he answered. "Tomorrow."

Aless kissed his cheek once, then again, then his lips, then slowly claimed his mouth, her fingers raking up into his hair as she leaned into him, a soft moan humming in her throat.

"Hold that thought," he murmured, although his body had different ideas. As she smiled mischievously, he cleared his throat and led her out of the antechamber and into the bedchamber, where on his table was his copy of *A Modern History of Silen*. "I know we already gave each other Offering gifts in Bellanzole, but I wanted to share this with you." He held it out to her.

Her eyebrows rose as she took it, paging through it to get to the blank pages—only, some weren't blank anymore. He'd filled in the details of their journey, sketched in drawings of, well, mostly her. Nearly all of them—well, if he were honest, *all* of them, her.

She traced a sketch of her in the duchess's garden, surrounded by lavender and pixies, and gasped. "Veron, this is... This is stunning."

He stepped in closer to her and brushed her voluminous dark tresses over her shoulder. "My father taught me, when we used to study sky realm flora and fauna together. I hadn't drawn anything since he died."

For a long time, he hadn't wanted to do anything that had reminded him of Ata, and yet he'd become one of the volodari, just like him. The knot of pain Ata had left behind had untangled, faded, and he understood now. Understood what it meant to be ready to do anything—*anything*—for those he loved.

"It's beautiful, Veron," she whispered, and brushed his lips with hers. Smiling, she pulled away. "I'm not sure mine will mean as much..."

"You got me something?"

Her face bright, she rushed to one of her trunks, opened it, and pulled out a box. "You see, when I wrote to Bellanzole from Dun Mozg, I *might* have included a certain request to Lorenzo." She handed him the ribbon-wrapped box.

Raising an eyebrow, he pulled the ribbon undone—some days, he *did* miss the ease of his claws—and opened the lid.

Inside lay a pair of boots—perfect, supple, well-oiled leather, buttery soft, and—

"Try them on!" she urged.

"You found time in a war to ask your brother for boots?" he asked with a laugh.

She nodded happily.

He did pull them on, and—*Holy Ulsinael.*

He walked a circuit in the bedchamber, shifted on his feet, crouched, jumped, all while Aless laughed.

"By Deep and Darkness, you *laugh*, my love, but these—these boots are the most comfortable I've ever—" He leaned back into the heel, but it was just... pillowy... and...

She covered her mouth as she giggled. "Lorenzo's cobbler is born of a long line of cobblers, only he was born an enforcer, too. He uses his skills *and* his magic to make what Lorenzo calls 'the shoes of the gods.'" She smirked.

"Holy Ulsinael, he's not *wrong*, Aless. These boots are—they're—" It was unthinkable, but he almost wanted to go on a hunt right now. *Almost.* But it would be some time yet before Mati would allow him back among the volodari.

"Oh! One more thing," she said, clapping her hands together.

After making the Offering with Aless and lifebonding with her, if there was a thing in this realm that could make this day any better, he didn't know it.

"Close your eyes." Her dark gaze practically sparkled. What was she planning?

He did as she asked and then sank into the bed.

There were flitting footsteps, and the creaking of a hinge, more quick steps, rustling, and—

"All right. Open them." Her voice brimmed, and he was laughing under his breath when he opened his eyes.

By Deep and Darkness, it was the *sheer red thing*. His laughter ceased instantly.

She leaned against the wall in that ethereal red nightdress from their wedding night in Bellanzole, and its folds of thin fabric teased shadows and planes beneath a crimson veil. It hung from her frame by thin, delicate straps, its sheer fabric pooling on the floor.

Her shoulders and her long, elegant arms were bare, so much of her soft, beautiful skin bared to him, and his fingers clutched the mattress as they longed to touch her. That night in Bellanzole, he'd been prepared to do his duty as ordered, and neither of them had been ready for it, not in the least, but this image of Aless in her sheer red nightgown had lingered in his memory, more and more in the past couple of weeks.

And here she was now, as if she'd stepped out of that night into this one, his brave, intelligent, beautiful wife, his love, his Aless.

By Deep and Darkness, he wanted to see her, every part of her, commit her to memory, and know her by the tip of a finger or the curve of a collarbone.

Biting her lip, she took slow steps to him, stood between his knees, stroked through his hair, over his shoulders, along his jaw, and he closed his arms around her, pulled her in and down to him as he moved deeper into bed. His hands found the smooth skin of her back as her lips met his, as her kiss deepened, as she breathed the same air, and he rolled her over, pinned her to the bed.

Gleaming dark eyes danced as she looked up at him, a smile playing on her lips. "What will you do to me, dark-elf prince?"

He huffed a soft breath. Oh, he had plenty of things in mind, but above all one. "Love you till the end of time, Aless. Till the end of time."

THE END

ABOUT THE AUTHOR

Miranda Honfleur is a born-and-raised Chicagoan living in Indianapolis. She grew up on fantasy and science-fiction novels, spending nearly as much time in Valdemar, Pern, Tortall, Narnia, and Middle Earth as in reality. She writes speculative fiction starring fierce heroines and daring heroes who make difficult choices along their great adventures and dark intrigues, all with generous doses of romance, action, and drama.

When she's not snarking, writing, or reading her Kindle, she hangs out and watches Netflix with her English-teacher husband, and plays board games with her friends.

Reach her at:
www.mirandahonfleur.com
miri@mirandahonfleur.com

IN THE GARDEN OF GOLD AND STONE

RYAN MUREE

Proofreading by Patrycja Pakula for Holabird Editing

She is a beast by nature.

Nida, a descendant of a magical reptilian race, anxiously awaits the day her new sisters hatch in their temple sanctuary. But without a decent human male, that day will never come, their race will go extinct, and the jungle that they protect beyond their gilded walls will die.

He is a beast by duty.

Rowec, a human warrior from a local village, wants nothing more than to move on from his bloody past, to be a force for good, and a leader for his clan. But when he gets captured by Nida's people, he can only be free if he agrees to participate in their hatching ceremony.

Each made to believe the other is nothing more than a murderous animal, Nida and Rowec must untangle the jungle of lies between their worlds before it's too late and lives on both sides are lost.

Will Nida put responsibility before love? Can she pay the price to save her family, or will she choose to save the man she's grown to love?

Genre: Young-Adult Fantasy
Heat level: Sweet

CHAPTER 1

*R*owec slung his empty leather pack over one shoulder, slid his clean, curved *peicha* knife into his belt, and grabbed his leather-wrapped spear. It wasn't too long before that he was grabbing these things to prepare for a fight against another clan. A darker time. A bloodier time that he, even in his twenty-fourth year, understood wasn't best for his people.

Raz, his tiny, pink-bellied kurimolle, stretched and yawned on his shoulder.

"Better sleep in my pocket, Raz, or a bunch of fruit could end up crushing you."

The white, furry rodent with beady, black eyes stepped onto his palm and into his front vest pocket. Raz spun around in his confined space until finally settling down for the night.

Rowec turned to the curtained entrance of his straw hut and found his lanky—if not gangly—brother, Maur, leaning against the frame. His long black hair was tied back, but the thin scruff on his upper lip was still too sparse even for his twenty years. Black ash had been smeared on both of his cheeks.

Maur twirled his knife and grinned. "Ready?"

Rowec rolled his eyes. "It's not a raid. We're harvesting fruit."

"In the jungle."

"Like we have a million times."

"At night. We could run into some of the Crola clan. I'm ready."

Rowec shoved Maur aside and strolled out of his hut and toward the far side of the village.

Everyone else was winding down for the night, tying up their working animals and coming down the path from the side of the mountain where the tiered paddy fields had been worked all day.

His brother wasn't wrong about the possibility of running into a rival clan. Their chief had started sending the warriors out for harvesting certain resources, since some of the other clans had gotten restless and eager to test their tenuous treaty. A treaty his father had fought to secure before his death.

Still, it was gathering fruit. Not hard. Not complex. And if they did run into the Crola, or any of the other Yvelkian clans for that matter, the treaty dictated they politely split the resource and leave.

"Come on," Maur said, following on his heels. "You know you hate the treaty, too."

"It's smart."

"Look at you!" Maur held his hands out wide. "You *used* to be the best warrior in our village. We've trained our whole lives to fight. What happened to the good times?"

"Since when is killing good?"

"*Since when—?*" Maur's mouth gaped. "Seriously? Did my brother, the famous Yvelkian Zchi warrior, slaughterer of fifty men, just say… 'Since when is killing good?'"

Since their screams, their last breaths, echoed in my mind and told me, one day it will be me on the other end of that stick.

"I've changed, Maur." He nodded to a neighbor grinding coarse grain and continued for the village's west exit. "I've grown. Peace is good. Killing should only be when necessary, and it's not necessary when we're harvesting fruit. We're just being sent to get *in case* something happens."

"Dad killed to save us and our village hundreds of times."

"And he fought for the treaty, too. He didn't want us to follow in his foot-steps forever, Maur."

His brother sniffed and adjusted his dirty leather pants as they walked. "Eh, whatever. Animals are fair game though, right? If I find myself a slither-skin, I'll finally get new boots." He bit down on the spine of his knife and tugged his belt out a few inches for Rowec to see. "Shee? New beld."

Rowec yanked the blade from his brother's mouth and slid it into his belt loop for him. "Don't be stupid. It's too cold. They'll be asleep."

"Not true. They eat *paratils* when they're desperate. They could be hiding in the bunches. If one drops down on me — whoosh!" He made a slicing motion with his hand.

Rowec shook his head. "You're unbelievably stupid. I'm going to laugh when one bites you, and you're squirming on the ground in your final moments of death."

Maur grabbed him by the bicep. "Just promise me you won't tell the girls if I wet myself."

Rowec yanked his arm free and rolled his eyes. "You're so dumb."

Etta, the chief's daughter, had turned the corner, and his heart sunk. He had been so close to the edge of the village, so close to not having to deal with her. Now, there was no avoiding it. He shook his head.

Maur elbowed him. "Hey, hey. Here's your girl. Spirits, she looks like a damn dream this evening."

Etta's jet-black hair fluttered behind her in soft curls. Her deep-crimson skirt had neither one thread out of place or one smudge of dirt on it. Such was the luxury of being one of the Zchi ruling family.

She smiled and nodded at the villagers cooking on their porches. To them, she was perfect and precious. To him, she was nails grating down stone.

She approached with a smile and bowed with her chest dipped low. Her long black eyelashes batted over dark eyes, and her small fingers went to the fragile, pale skin at her neck.

Maur leaned on Rowec. "You're looking lovely this evening, Etta."

Rowec snorted. *More like underworked and privileged.*

"I know." She grinned, and her focus wandered to Rowec, as did her hands to his chest. "When are you two planning on digging out the foundation for my father's extra room?"

If I had a say? Never. "Can't wait to abuse some more free labor?" he cut.

She narrowed her eyes. "I just like your company, Rowec. I like watching you work. We need the extra room for—"

He huffed. "Tilly and Vin have needed a new roof since last year's rainy season. Kipper has needed her walls repacked since the fire. The training hut has needed the floor smoothed because we've created so many holes with our spears and knives that the warriors twist their ankles while sparring. But I'll get right on that *extra room* for your father."

She blinked and said... nothing.

Silence. Sweet silence. Had she finally understood—

"Well, how long does all that take?" she asked. "Like a day?"

He squinted at her, shook his head, and went to move past her.

She stepped in front of him with a softer gaze. "Are you going hunting tonight?"

"We're going out to get paratils f-for the holy day." Maur swallowed hard. "It's, uh... it's, uh, in a few weeks, so we need them to ripen—"

Rowec sighed. "She knows when the holy day is, Maur."

"Right." He licked his lips. "Right."

Etta ignored him but giggled at Rowec. A fake laugh. A lie. A ruse.

"You're so big and strong," she cooed. "One day, I'll make sure you won't have to lift a finger unless you want to." Her fingertips traced the lining of her dress, which barely contained her breasts.

Rowec, done with the lack of entertainment Etta thought she had provided, moved around her to head out for the jungle.

"Be safe, you two," she called after them. "I wouldn't want my future husband and brother-in-law to get hurt."

Rowec nearly stopped, but his orders for the evening were already taking him farther away from that parasite.

As soon as they were out of earshot at the edge of the jungle, Maur punched him in the arm. "Brother, you have got to be one of the luckiest jerks on this planet."

"Funny how you measure luck."

"Etta? As a wife? Come on. You have it made."

Rowec slid his peicha knife out and cut a path through the brush at his knees. "Not if I can help it."

Maur made his own way through the jungle a few lengths beside him. "I wouldn't be able to handle it. I'd never leave the hut. Coming home to that after every raid?" He whistled. "Not to mention she's the chief's only daughter. You'll be well taken care of forever, and eventually, chief. I mean, that's the life. She's perfect in every way."

"Until she opens her mouth."

Maur snickered. "I happen to like—"

"She knows absolutely nothing about anything." He sliced through a branch with fervor. "She doesn't do anything. She and her family leech off the village, even in droughts. If I become chief, things will be a lot different." A drooping leaf near his head bobbed as a creature slipped under it.

He just had to uphold the treaty, prove he was more than just a fighter. More than his father, and his father's father. If he proved he was more, he could petition the elders and the chief to let him out of their stupid arranged marriage. He could request travel, learn from other cultures, bring back ideas and solutions to help with crop rotation and watering systems. He could stop the clans from needing to fight for certain resources in the first place. He could do more for the people, more for himself, than being chained to that idiot.

"Can you imagine Etta doing anything?" Maur laughed. "At least she's nice to look at. And think about."

"Imagine how I feel knowing my brother would kill to spend five minutes alone with her, and yet, I'm supposed to marry her."

"I know. It's an absolute nightmare for me. Whack!" Maur liked making annoying sound effects as he chopped his way through the jungle.

They cut their way toward the patch of paratil trees they knew to be just off the village. But as they neared, it seemed each tree had already been stripped bare. Not one bud. Not one seed left over by animals. Nothing. They'd been picked clean.

Maur slid his knife into his belt and shimmied up the trunk with its hairy ridges. "They're all gone," he called down.

Rowec followed the trail of trees, using his spear to knock around the leaves above his head. They were all empty. "Did you know the patch went back this far?"

Maur jumped down from the tree he had climbed with a grunt. "Nope. And it's too dark to see past 'em. What do we do?"

Rowec checked the sliver of moon poking through the canopy. "It's not too late. We still have time. Let's follow and see where the patch of trees ends. Maybe we'll get lucky."

"You think it was the Crola? Maybe the Brevtok?" Maur punched a nearby trunk. "Oh man, if I get my hands on one of them again, I'll teach them what the Zchians do to stealing jerks like them."

Rowec scoffed and walked deeper into the darkening jungle. "Ah yes, like stare at them intently while you drop your knife in the dirt? Is that how you'll teach them a lesson? Because I distinctly remember—"

"That was one time!" Maur blurted.

They walked deeper still, past the twisted kingwood trunks and their ashy leaves dipping low with moisture. It was difficult to see, but it was surprising how far the patch of bare paratil trees actually went. They'd never needed to travel this far, this deep. It went on for miles. Or had it circled around?

They shouldn't be out this far.

He checked the sliver of moon. Had it been hours? *Damn.*

They had walked all this way into the jungle for nothing, and now the moon was too high, and they had to walk all the way back to the village. He wouldn't be getting much sleep tonight.

"I don't get it. Who would take *all* of the fruit?" Maur asked.

Rowec shrugged. "It doesn't matter. It's just for the holy day. There's still plenty of other things to eat from the farms. The chief, however, will need to pick a substitute before the celebration."

"What's over there?" Maur trotted through the jungle somewhere behind Rowec.

Rowec slapped a buzzing *gryllid* at his neck and pulled out his canteen of water. "Don't go too far. We have to head back. We've walked for too long."

His brother slashed through the brush with additional sounds for emphasis, and then there was silence.

"Maur?" Rowec called over his shoulder. "We don't have time for this. If you didn't find fruit, then we need to—"

"I found fruit!" his brother squealed from a decent distance away from him. "You're not going to believe this!"

Rowec debated joining him since his brother usually enjoyed getting overly excited about the most mundane things. Still, if he'd found paratils, he'd need help carrying them back.

"Stay there, I'll come to you," Rowec said, replacing his knife to his belt loop and his canteen in his bag, and he followed the sound of his brother's voice.

Maur burst through the brush at him. "Look! Paratils!"

Maur's arms were full of the palm-sized orange orbs; his face was positively radiant. "You are not going to believe what I found. We can take them all. There's tons!"

As much as Rowec's stomach burned and begged him to eat some, as much as his mouth salivated at the thought of sweet juicy nuggets of paratils in their rinds, he simply grabbed them and stuffed them in his pack. "No, we need to get back before it's too late. Just shove what we can in my pack and we'll come back—"

"But there's a whole field of 'em. A square place behind a wall full of them." Maur turned back for the paratils.

Rowec followed after him. "Wait, Maur. Slow down! What do you mean a wall?"

"A wall! A great big wall. I scaled it, and on the other side were as many paratils you could eat in a lifetime!"

When he caught up with his brother, Maur was already halfway up the crude stone wall. Merely two huts high, the wall wasn't *that* great, as per usual. Maur always exaggerated.

"Come on," Maur urged.

"No, I don't think it's smart. Why is there a wall in the jungle?" Rowec eyed the stonework. Yellow. Smooth. Not Crola. Not Brevtok. Not Manut or Cilta. What in the world was this?

The other Yvelkian clans wouldn't go this far into the jungle either. This was... different. He swallowed.

The elders had their stories of cannibals and evil spirits. But they were stories to keep them from wandering into the forest as children, to keep them safe from the carnivorous and poisonous creatures.

Maur was already down on the other side and chucking fistfuls of paratils over the wall at him. Rowec caught them and stuffed every last one into his pack.

A leaf moved to his left, then a bush to his right.

He slid his knife out of his pocket so that both his spear and his knife were ready for anything. Low light in the shadow of the canopy, they would be fighting blind. Whoever this wall belonged to would not take kindly to them stealing.

"Maur, let's go! We have company!"

Maur grunted as he reached the top of the wall and then slid down the outside. His mouth was sticky with paratil juice, and he held his hands outright. "Go, go," he said with a nod.

They started for the village. Rowec led back through the broken brush with Maur a few feet behind him.

"Pull out your weapon," Rowec commanded. It felt like someone— or something—was watching him, following them. He couldn't hear or see them, but the shiver up his spine told him to run faster. He picked up the pace until a sucking noise followed by a pop made him check over his shoulder. "Are you licking your fingers clean?"

Maur had fallen behind by twenty or thirty feet. "I couldn't help it. The paratils were right there. We have to go back tomorrow. We have to see—"

A shadow tackled Maur to the side; he screamed.

"Maur!" Rowec turned back, immediately following the trail of his brother's screams. He struggled with the dense foliage of the vines and tree trunks.

Maur's voice was moving. Was he being carried? Dragged? Who the hell was out here? Who could tackle a grown warrior and drag him away that easily?

"Maur!" he shouted again, following his brother's cries.

He turned again toward his brother's voice, the brush too thick, too dark, to keep up.

A figure dropped down from the trees directly in front of Rowec. A being so large, the ground shook beneath his feet when it landed. It towered over him, nearly twice as wide, too, and it held a lit torch just above its head.

Rowec could barely make out a hood, a robe, and yellow armor. But this... *thing* was not exactly human. It couldn't be. It was three heads taller than him, and he was the tallest in his village. The hand that held the torch had crimson scales— *scales!* —claws for nails, and two big round eyes glistening under its hood.

"What the—" He stumbled back and adjusted his grip on his spear. "Where's my brother?"

It hissed.

He lunged at it with his spear, but the thing knocked it away effortlessly. The spear snapped against a nearby trunk.

He twirled his peicha knife in his hand. He wouldn't let him get Maur without a fight.

The brush around him rustled. Were there more? He spun to keep his eyes on his attackers, wherever they'd emerge. He could probably take on one, but several?

"Maur?" he called out

"He is a thief," the creature before him said tightly.

"He's a—" Rowec glanced around as several other similar figures stepped out of the jungle and into the torch's light. They were just like the first, tall, gross beasts bearing down on him. "The wall is yours?"

"Drop the weapon," one snarled.

He was outnumbered, and these things... they... they had spoken. Had they been part of the treaty? He tilted his head to try to see their faces. Had this been anyone—anything—else from another clan, he would have killed them in seconds. They wouldn't have had the chance to speak or make demands. But he was supposed to be proving himself diplomatic. He was supposed to be more than just a fighter if he ever wanted out of his village.

"Drop the weapon," it repeated.

He lowered the knife. A quick glance around, he counted five giant warrior creatures with armor and claws... and scales. None of it was making sense.

"The man stole from our gardens," hissed the first. "He must pay."

They were talking about Maur.

"You steal from us, and then try to kill us?" another added.

A creature to Rowec's right dragged Maur out into the torchlight, pulled his head back, and placed a claw at his ear. His brother tried to squirm away while pleading for his life. They were going to slit his throat.

"Wait!" Rowec said, hand out. "He's my brother. My family. Don't kill him. We were just hungry, and-and-and couldn't find any paratils."

Their large eyes gleamed at him.

One curled its lip. "Stealing is not allowed—"

"I know, I know. And we're sorry. Surely, that doesn't mean he deserves to die."

The creatures glanced back at one another.

"We can give them all back. All of them." He began opening his pack and dumping the paratils onto the ground. "See? We can give them all back."

The leader, or the one in the front—he wasn't sure—leaned forward. "This one made plans to come back for more. We must take him to our queen as our prisoner. She'll decide his fate."

One of the creatures grabbed Maur's ankle and began dragging him along.

Maur screamed. "Please! Rowec! Please don't let them take me! Please!"

"Wait!" Rowec shouted. "Take me instead."

The creatures froze and slowly turned their heads.

"Take me," he repeated. "Take me in my brother's place. I'm the lead warrior. I'm more valuable. My brother is the village idiot. He's no use to you."

Maur's face soured, but he didn't say a word.

And he'd better not, the dumbass. Only Maur could find some secret clan in the jungle and steal from them.

The main creature tossed his brother away and gripped Rowec by his biceps.

"Wait! Let me at least talk to him," Rowec urged as the torchlight faded on his brother's stunned face.

Maur scrambled up. "Rowec! I'll get help! I'll get help, I promise!"

CHAPTER 2

*N*ida was sick to death of praying.

Praying for the rain. Praying for the sun. Praying for Brynn, her sister and queen, to find a mate. On her knees, Nida eyed the two statues for the millionth time.

Carved from the yellow rock native to the Tial jungle, one statue took the form of the first Tialan queen, immortalized with vibrant scales of gold and green, braided hair that fell to her waist, and a robe of leaves from paratil trees. Alongside the monument to the deceased queen was a statue of her deceased mate. He was fully human, unlike Nida or the queen. He was thick with corded muscle and carved to include his human clothes—boots, pants, a puffy shirt that exposed the rigidity of his chest musculature—and his facial hair.

Sometimes her eyes wandered to the walls and ceiling, where Tialan histories had been painted in pastel colors. But for the most part, she shut her eyes and tried to pray.

Her sister, Ascara, had been kneeling beside her with her hands clasped together. She had also been silent, and that only meant one thing—she wasn't praying either.

"You think," Ascara whispered, "all of him was that strong and big?"

Nida opened her eyes. It wasn't exactly out of place for Ascara to ask things like that. She might have been one of the prettiest of her many, many sisters, but definitely not the most mature.

"I mean, his fingers are exceptionally long. His legs, his torso, his chest, his feet..." She bent forward as if to look at the queen's mate directly in the crotch. "You think all of him was big—"

"Ascara!"

"What? I mean, you don't wonder about that?" Ascara's violet eyes and scales twinkled in the evening light pouring in from the oculus in the center of the prayer room. "Tialans haven't had males for several generations. He's human, and there's plenty more of 'em. I'm just thinking it's worth consider-ing, especially since we come here twice a day, every day. If he's so special to help bring our sisters to life, he had to be *gifted* everywhere, right?"

"Most humans are murderers, Ascara. Vicious. Cold. Bloodthirsty." She gestured at the male statue. "The last few human mates were different, sure, but he's not supposed to be questioned about his... *gifts*. His *gift* was performing the hatching ceremony with the queen."

Ascara snorted. "If they're so willing to help us, could they really be so bad?"

The villagers living outside the jungle seemed to be. Brynn had told them all about it several times—the slaughter, the starvation, the disregard for life. Humans were a blight, an affront to everything Tialans believed in.

"Come on, Nida. You should know. You're more human than any of us—"

She shivered. "Don't, please."

Though she was technically Tialan, Nida—and her sisters—never forgot that the flower bud she had been bloomed from had gone wrong somehow. Not enough sunlight. Not enough moonlight. Not enough water. Those were only guesses. Whichever sister had been in charge of the hatchery at her birth, she had failed to care for Nida properly, and Nida had been paying for it her whole life by taking on a more human physique than Tialan.

Ascara turned to her. "What do you think about when we're in here then?" She held up one hand with glittering violet scales running down the back of it and up her arms. "Don't tell me you *actually* pray."

"Of course not." Nida crossed her arms of *mostly* human skin. Her teal scales only came down as far as her elbows, and even then, they were sporadic at best. She checked over her shoulder for any other sisters who might be passing by or joining them and lowered her voice. "I mean sometimes I pray, but no."

"Then what do you think about?" Ascara whispered.

She shrugged. "Stuff. My job, the hatchery, mostly. Where the future mate might be—"

"And you don't think about that?" Ascara jabbed a finger in the direction of the statue's groin.

"No! Now, stop it!" Nida pulled her sister's arm down.

"I'm just saying—"

"That you spend your prayer time thinking about human genitals? Yes, I got that." She sighed and tried to mentally align herself for a final, tiny bit of *actual* praying for her future sisters. But Ascara's silence beside her made it nearly impossible to continue. "What now, Ascara?"

"Humans are scary, don't get me wrong, but I want one. Like a pet or something. I don't think it's fair Sister is the only one who gets one."

Nida rolled her eyes. "Only you would say that. Be happy you *don't* have to deal with one." She quickly scrunched her eyes shut and grasped her hands together, praying for everything in the universe as hard as she could.

Her sister sighed. "Do you think they're capable of falling in love?"

Never mind. "Ascara, seriously?" Nida stood, dusted her hands off, bowed her head in respect to her late sister's statue, and turned for the hatchery.

Ascara followed. "If the last few weren't so bad, maybe others aren't. Maybe falling in love with one of them wouldn't be that bad, you know?" she whispered. "The last queen actually fell in love with her human. Would you want to fall in love?"

Their bare feet padded across the yellow stone as they scurried down the hall, their path lit by sconces with fires in full bloom.

"Not with a human."

"Who else would there be to choose from?"

"Exactly." Nida stayed ahead and only turned her head to whisper her reply. "And even if there were other males to choose from, *I* don't get much choice in things around here. There are many things I'd rather have than falling in love."

"Like what?"

Our sisters born, the continuation of our species, a new ruling system. No queen. No bullying. Equality. Freedom.

It was true that on the darkest nights, when the moon couldn't be seen through the oculus in the hatchery, she dreamed of leaving the temple and traveling to other places. But that was impossible to explain to Ascara. She'd never understand.

Nida rounded the final corner to the hatchery corridor and found Drathella, another sister, waiting. She stopped, and Ascara collided into her back.

"Where have you been?" Drathella's legs were planted, her hands on her hips. She stood just before the hatchery doors.

Ugh, Drathella. Always Drathella.

"Praying. Not like you ever do." Nida straightened her spine and lifted her chin. "What are you doing near the hatchery?"

"I'm allowed to go where I please. The hatchery is a holy place for the sacred—the true Tialans—not the hybrid trash." Drathella slung her dark blue hair over her shoulder. Her bright yellow scales were nearly orange in the firelight. Her matching blue robe hung loosely on her thin frame, revealing the intricate pattern of matching scales along her chest, arms, and upper thighs.

"If she's not supposed to go there, then why did sister put her in charge of it?" Ascara came out from behind Nida and put her hands on her hips, too. Unfortunately, her "helping" would only make it worse.

"Stop, Ascara, it's fine. Go to the kitchens. I have work to do," Nida whispered.

"She's not hybrid trash." Ascara leaned toward Drathella. "She's your sister. Brynn will have your head if she heard you talking like this."

"Hah. The queen would praise me for it." Drathella flashed her teeth in a terrifying smile.

"Stop, Ascara. It's fine. Just go." But as much as Nida urged her, Ascara stayed her ground.

Drathella scoffed. "I guess it's good you have at least one Tialan on your side."

"You go, too," Nida commanded.

Drathella crossed the distance and gripped Nida by her hair, placing her face inches from Nida's ear.

Nida closed her eyes as Ascara tried to stop Drathella without success. With her eyes shut, it was easier to ignore Drathella's seething rage, easier to hide the tears, easier to stay strong.

"Watch yourself, Nida," she hissed. "Brynn only gave you this job because you'd inevitably screw it up before the hatching. Then we can banish your disgusting presence, and you can be eaten alive by the jungle." Drathella released Nida's hair and wiped her hand on the wall.

Equality. I wish for equality and freedom. I pray for equality for my future sisters so they may never live this pain, and I pray for my freedom so that no one can hurt me for what I can't help being.

When Drathella's footfalls echoed away, she opened her eyes and turned to Ascara. "Go on."

"Nid—"

"No, I'm fine. Really. Tough as scales." She forced a smile. "I have work to do. You have work to do. I'll see you tonight at dinner, all right?"

Ascara nodded and hugged her. "Don't let that slitherskin affect you."

"Ascara!"

Ascara shook her head. "I don't care. She is a slitherskin—"

"She's not the only one who treats me that way. A lot of them think that."

"I don't." Ascara pressed her forehead to Nida's and squeezed her hands before running off for the kitchens.

Nida rubbed the tears from her cheeks and turned for the hatchery doors —her sanctuary, the safest place in the temple. Her other sisters were too nervous to come visit her there. They feared they'd hurt the unborn sisters somehow.

She pushed open the polished golden doors and stepped into the lavish indoor green garden. Two hundred buds pulsing with soft white light through their opalescent petals waited for her. Two hundred unborn sisters.

She and all of her sisters weren't slitherskins, curling under rocks with fangs and forked tongues. Reptilian in origin, yes, but they were more. Believed to be graced by the gods, Nida and her sisters had been born from the buds of Tialan flowers, each one imbued with the ability to use Life Weaving. Seeds in the Tialan jungle took root because Nida and her sisters willed it. Trees and flowers grew because they made it so. The jungle prospered because they ensured it.

Nida, being more human than Tialan, looked at the buds before her as her future—her salvation. She would make sure they were a generation of sisters who wouldn't care who was queen and who was… a little different. It was why she couldn't run away. Her job was here. They took priority. They would bring change, and she couldn't run from it.

She smiled and sighed. "Hello, girls."

Of course, they didn't respond. They wouldn't hatch until Brynn—their queen—held the Life Weaving ceremony with her future mate—who had yet to be found—on the holy day. Nida's job was to care for each one until that day arrived.

She couldn't wait.

She stood before the sweetly scented garden, closed her eyes, and inhaled the soft dewy air. "Okay, let's get you all some water, then I'll open the center dome for some moonlight, and then maybe a song? I'll let you all vote which one." She giggled to herself, pretending they all would inevitably answer.

But there was an answer. A scurry, some chatter, a few giggles.

She opened her eyes.

All of the buds sat growing and waiting. Silent.

The noise had come from the hall.

She hurried to shut the doors when a man hollered, "Stop! I can't believe this is all over one piece of fruit! You are disgusting, hideous beasts! I shouldn't be treated like this—"

A man? She gasped. *A human.*

She turned to her unborn sisters. "Forgive me, girls. I'll be back soon." She closed the doors to the hatchery and followed the noise.

CHAPTER 3

*R*owec's feet skidded across the stone floor.

They had taken his weapons, and *that* he could understand. But his ruddy, no-good, harvesting boots? They couldn't even let him keep them on while walking into this place?

They. Those freakish beasts.

The light inside this... What was this place? A fortress? There were gold floors, gold walls, and beast-shaped sconces with fangs and jeweled eyes that held fire along the walls. The whole place was warm and damp and massive. The ceilings went on forever above him. There were hallways everywhere. How had the clans not found this place before? It didn't matter. Maur would remember and bring an army back to get him out.

And he better bring an army. The beasts proved they weren't like anything he had seen before. They had four limbs and walked upright and everything, but scaly. They had scales like a reptile all the way up their arms and across their chests. Up their necks and down to their clawed feet. Their eyes were huge orbs with narrow pupils. They were like walking slitherskins. Sort of human. Sort of not.

Disgusting. He shuddered.

But spirits, they were strong.

Two carried him with an arm under each of his armpits—dragged more like—while another led with a rope tied around his neck. Giggles and whispers came from behind.

He strained to look over his shoulder.

The creatures following behind him were smaller than him and giggled. Children?

Another one of them poked her head out from a side-corridor. She stuck out like a fresh paratil in a rotten bunch. Her scales looked smaller. Her eyes were big, but more like a human's. Was she captive, too?

"Hey! Hey!" he called out to her.

Another creature, blue and yellow with a curled lip, grabbed the nearly-human one and pointed at him. They were discussing him. The girl-thing was in trouble? Had she been human before?

Shoved by the blue one into the crowd of his onlookers, the girl-thing stumbled and avoided staring at him.

"Hey!" he tried again, but it only caused the smaller ones walking just behind to giggle even more.

How ridiculous. As soon as he figured a way out, he was leaving. Screw the trade. He might have agreed to taking his brother's place in the moment, but that was *in the moment* of panic. This was insane.

His vest pocket wiggled.

Raz must have woken up, missing all the excitement and drama as usual. For a nocturnal, gliding kurimolle, he seemed perfectly content only waking for feeding times. He'd have to wait.

"Stay still, friend," he whispered to his pocket.

He jerked his arms to test his freedom, but they were locked in place. Some warrior he was. Raised with a *karten* stick in his hand since he was old enough to hold things, top warrior in his village, and it meant nothing, absolutely nothing, in the face of these... these... things.

He glanced around to get his bearings. How many turns had it taken to get to this point? Had they deliberately built this like a maze? All he found was gold walls and endless corridors. It was horrendously opulent. Etta and the chief would kill for a place like this.

He grunted in their grasp. "Where are you taking me?"

"Your room," the one holding the rope said.

"My room? If I get a room, then why take my shoes? Why drag me? Why force me?"

But she didn't respond, and neither did the ones dragging him, or the ones behind him.

They turned a corner down a dark hallway, too dark to see anything, and stopped. One of the hideous creatures pulled open what sounded like a metal gate and stood aside. Beyond the opened gate was an even darker space, save for the two beams of moonlight barely streaming in through small holes in the ceiling. Their idea of a room left much to be desired.

He was tossed inside and landed on the cold, muddy ground. His palms skimmed his surroundings. The more information he had, the better off he was at finding a way out. Smooth stone bench, stone walls, stone floors. The same stupid stone everywhere, except for the gate.

He spun for the metal bars, and it was immediately slammed shut and locked.

He gripped the cold cylinders and shook with all his strength. Fairly solid. "We have wildly different definitions of *room*, beast!"

But his escort and some of their lingering entourage walked away, leaving him to his dark, not-a-room imprisonment and a gaggle of creatures staring at him.

When he got home—*if* he ever got home—Maur would pay. The spirits had better save him or he'd make sure his brother would be cleaning stalls and waste ditches for weeks. Stupid enough to steal. Stupid enough to get caught. Stupid enough to get abducted by these *things*.

He sighed and leaned against the wall. And *he* had been stupid enough to trade his imprisonment for his brother's.

"Could I get some water, at least?" he asked.

But the watching and whispering creatures didn't move.

Great. The others understood him. Why not these? "Do you understand my words?" he shouted.

Nothing.

"Hey! Can you not hear me?"

"They hear you." The owner of this new feminine voice rounded the corner and stepped into the edge of the sconce's firelight. "They're just not used to hearing the insults. They're much better at giving them."

It was another one of *them*—maybe. With this low light, it was hard to tell.

"Girls, I'll take care of it," the voice said.

"Who gave you permission?" one of the gigglers cut.

"Who do you think?"

After the small group scurried off, he pressed his forehead against the cool metal. "Who are you?"

This new one was too far from him to make her form out clearly. Maybe she was their ruler. "Are you the leader of this place? The-the queen, they called it?"

He barely caught the light reflecting off her brown-green robes as she walked to the far side of the hallway, picked up something round and empty, pumped some sort of mechanism, and then returned to the bars.

Finally close enough to see her, he peeled back.

The girl-thing from the hallway. The one that looked somewhat... human.

Even up close, she wasn't *as* revolting as the others. Her hair had a tinge of teal at the roots, but it fell to her shoulders in a normal, human auburn color. The red was accentuated in the faint moonlight. Her eyes weren't bulbous with slits for pupils, either. They were larger than humans, definitely, but she had normal shaped pupils, dark lashes, and crystalline teal irises. Her scales were barely noticeable. They were a pale teal, too, and they were small and sparse along the exposed parts of her body.

"You're not like them," he said.

She placed a bucket on the floor outside of the bars.

"Were you kidnapped, too?" he asked. "Did they turn you into one of them?"

She lifted a cup from the bucket and passed it shakily to him. Was she scared?

"Drink," she ordered.

He took it and sniffed it.

"Why would I go through all the trouble of pumping the water and lugging this bucket over just to poison you? If I wanted to kill you, I'd just eat you."

He jerked his gaze from the cup to her.

She bit her lip and dropped her gaze. "I was—W-we don't eat people. That would be crazy."

No. Scaly reptilian women in a secret fortress in the middle of a jungle was crazy. "Well, you kidnap men and imprison them for doing nothing. That's pretty close."

She raised her eyebrows. "I doubt this cell is worse than eating you, but I can suggest it, if you'd like?"

Her smirk was almost attractive. *Almost.*

He took a sip. The water was fresh, cool, clean. He gulped down mouthfuls, letting it spill down his vest. He passed the cup through the bars. "Another. And no, I'd rather not be eaten."

She inhaled deeply, refilled the cup, and passed it back. He gulped half of it down as quickly as he could and set it down on the floor.

"You're not the queen?" he asked.

Her eyes followed carefully as he pulled Raz from his pocket. "No, I'm not the queen. What is that?"

"My pet. He's a kurimolle."

She leaned in, her head practically against the bars.

A stupid mistake. He could grab her and slam her head into the metal. Take any keys if she had them. Worst case, he could use her as a hostage. The others might have been strong, but this one was clearly not a fighter. Had she been, she would have never been so foolish to get this close. Taking advantage of her would be easy.

"He's so interesting," she said. Her eyes glittered in the soft light as she watched Raz drink from the cup.

"Who are you?" he whispered. "What are you?"

She clicked her tongue. Was it forked? Or human, too? Her pale lips were human enough. Her teal gaze lifted, and she quickly leaned back. "I'm Nida, and I'm not anyone important, actually. So, if you want out of this cell, it wouldn't be a good idea to hurt me. I also don't have a key."

He almost grinned but fought the urge. "But you know the queen?"

"Yes, she's my sister. You apparently stole something from us, so she won't set you free, either."

He huffed and helped Raz climb back into his pocket.

"But I can get you out of that cell," she whispered, "if you agree to help us."

CHAPTER 4

*N*ida hadn't wanted to go to him. It was Drathella who'd forced her into it. "You're *human*," she'd said. "Get him to calm down and act civilized before he meets Brynn, and it'll save our skins."

Brynn wanted the perfect human for a mate, and it had cost them precious time. If he could just play nice, if humans were capable of that, then Brynn would accept him for the hatching ceremony. Her new sisters would be born.

She swallowed, inspecting his features in the light. It was dim, but she saw enough, and he looked nothing like she'd expected.

He should have had red eyes, fangs, blood-stained clothes. But he had none of that. He was just... dirty. Being dragged by her sisters through the jungle would do that.

He was tall. Taller than her, at least. He looked strong, too. His musculature was evident on his bare, scaleless arms. Smooth as the Tialan stone. If he wanted to kill, he could. Her sisters were right to tie him as they brought him in.

Instead of red, his eyes were green—the color of *lithera* vines. They softened when he saw her. She hadn't imagined it. He had nothing but rage for her sisters when he'd been screaming down that hallway. He had been full of fury at the sisters staring and giggling at him before she had sent them away. But when he'd looked at *her*, his eyes had changed, shifted.

His short, shiny, dark hair glowed in the moonlight from the pits carved out of the stone ceiling. His jaw, sharp and prominent, commanded her attention when he spoke.

The humans were detestable, and her sisters hated needing them, but they weren't fools. They knew a good-looking human when they found one. And Brynn, when she saw him, would not give him up. She had been obsessed with the last queen's love, and instead of using any regular human, she'd demanded a human that didn't exist—a *nice* one.

Nida took a deep breath, still admiring him through the bars. Every inch of him suggested human strength. From the thickness in his hands to the toned muscle at his shoulders. He wore pants cut just below the knee, exposing thick, calloused feet and chiseled calves.

What had Ascara said about the previous god's *gifts*?

She shook her head.

"No," he said.

She refocused. What was his response for?

That's right. She had told him she would help him if he helped them.

"I don't make deals with my captors," he snarled.

She blinked. A week in this cell might change his mind on that. Of course, telling him that probably wouldn't help him ease into the idea of being nice to Brynn.

"You've not heard the deal," she said.

He shook his head. "First, I have no reason to trust anything you say."

When the younger sisters were being particularly stubborn, it helped when she got on their level.

She picked a spot to sit on the floor slightly farther away but across from him. "That's not how this works, and we're not the distrustful criminals—"

"I'm not a criminal, either!"

"Who stole from our garden?" she asked.

"My-my brother." His palm went to his face.

"And who took his place?"

"They were going to kill him!"

They wouldn't have, but he didn't know that and had volunteered to sacrifice himself for his brother anyway. She smiled. Maybe he was a *nice* one. "We don't kill—"

"But they—"

"I think they were probably just trying to *force* you to take his place. They mentioned you were considerably more attractive than him..."

He swallowed. His eyes wandered a bit until he shrugged and cleared his throat. "Then what is my punishment for my brother stealing?"

"Imprisonment in this moldy cell and little to no chance of getting out after the ceremony."

If she could convince him to be nice, to get along with Brynn, and to willingly participate in the hatching ceremony instead of by force, Brynn would give him better living arrangements. Brynn would have a mate... *And my sisters will be born.*

He could fight for his freedom after.

He crossed his arms. "A ceremony? What is it exactly that you need help with?"

She bit her lip. "Our queen, along with her mate, uses Life Weaving to bloom our new sisters to life. If you agree to help in the ceremony, you will be given better living arrangements until then, and you can fight for your freedom after."

He blinked and shook his head. "If I agree to help, I get out of this cell and freed?"

"Out of this cell for now and freed after."

"And if I refuse?"

"You'll stay here and have a much harder time convincing her to let you go after the ceremony."

He squinted his eyes. "So, no matter what, I'll still have to be part of this, uh, ceremony?"

No human had ever been forced before, but they were running out of time. Brynn either liked him and accepted him, or she didn't, and he'd be forced.

She imagined it would require lots of rope to force him into the ceremony. Brynn would be miserable, which meant they all would be miserable. She glanced down at her fingers.

"And in order to participate in the ceremony, I have to be the queen's mate?" His voice hitched. "You mean we—me and her—?"

"No!" She waved her hands at him. "No, no. You're not *really* mates. It's done through Vigor. You know, energy? It's what gives Water Shapers the ability to pull rain and Fire Breathers the ability to ignite anything. No one but the queen knows all the details. It's a private thing they've handed down from queen to queen. But she uses Life Weaving to grow our next generation in the sacred ceremony. Do you understand Vigor?"

He lifted his chin. "I'm familiar, but I'm not able to use mine."

That didn't matter. Everyone had Vigor, even if not everyone could use it. "You don't have to. She's the greatest Life Weaver out of all of us. She can use it."

He shook his head. "This is crazy. You realize what you're saying sounds absolutely crazy, right? Why not just use one of the males of your kind?"

"We don't have any." She shrugged. "They died out ages ago when the queens and their mates were... *actual* mates. This has been the only way we've been able to continue."

He scratched his chin with the back of his thumb. "So, my punishment for sticking up for my brother and saving his life is to become some mate with a beast to make more beasts?" He snorted.

Beasts. He had screamed that down the hallway. It still stung. They were life-bringers, caregivers of the wild. They were far from beasts, but her arguing that point probably wouldn't help. "It was admirable to trade places with your brother."

"I thought I was saving his life. You're saying I just saved him from a marriage." He sighed. "Marrying Etta is just as bad."

"What's an Etta?"

"No. Never mind." He ran his hands over his face.

"If it makes you feel any better, the previous human males volunteered for the ceremony and fell in love with our beautiful, powerful queens—"

"I don't believe you, and I couldn't care less. I have my own people to worry about." His hands moved to the top of his head. "I can't believe this is happening."

Neither could she. *His* brother had committed the crime. *He* and his brother had been the savages. Her sisters could have done anything they'd wanted to him, but they didn't.

She pressed her lips together. "It's not forever. And you stole the fruit from our future generations. Their food. That's a crime—"

"We didn't know."

"Ignorance is no reason to break into someone's home and steal—"

He groaned loudly. "We've been over this! It wasn't even me, it was my brother. *He* got caught by you—you *things*."

"And you chose to take his place."

He crossed his arms and leaned back.

For a predatory species, he was very concerned about not being perceived as a common thief. He shouldn't have cared. Surely, he had bigger, more terrible things he'd done.

"I understand that we're not ideal mates to you, but Brynntial, the queen, expects, at the very least, a civilized human. She'd be willing to give you a chance."

He laughed. "Civilized human? She wants a *civilized* human? That's rich. Tell me again how much your kind needs me, and then insult me some more."

Her nostrils flared. Her ancestors had been able to breathe fire. If she could do the same... "Do you want a better room or not? You can stay here if you'd like."

He jumped up and paced the cell. "How do I know this isn't a trick? Your sisters are probably going to eat me, aren't they?" He stopped to pierce her with his gaze, his jaw clenched.

Could her ancestors roar, too? She wanted to. "We don't eat people. Who do you think I am?"

Hands on his hips, he gestured at her with his chin. "You're just as likely to be like the rest of them. Terrible, disgusting... Who do you think *you* are?"

Someone desperately trying to find a mate her sister will accept so that my new sisters will be born. "I want to get you into a nicer room."

"Sure, if I agree to help the people locking me up here." His gaze darted around his space.

"It's called making a deal! I thought you humans *might* be capable of being more diplomatic and seeing reason."

He froze. "That's not what's happening here. You want me to play nice, pretend I like being captured, pretend I enjoy being a mate to some *thing*, all for a nicer room and the *chance* to fight for my freedom after."

She closed her eyes. When he worded it like that, it sounded questionable to her, too. "The fact remains that your brother committed a crime, and you took his place. The queen hasn't been able to find her partner, and you're here."

He shook his head and went back to his spot against the wall.

She couldn't tell him that this was their last chance, that her sister had taken so long to take a mate that they only had a few weeks before the hatching. That without him, they'd... they'd... "You'd be helping my species."

"Why would I want to do that?" he growled. "You nearly kill people for stealing some food."

What had the humans been told about them? If he didn't see reason, everything could be ruined. Brynn would be much worse than she'd already become, and her sisters—*spirits willing*—would come into this world surrounded by hate and malice. She had to try another way. Relate to him, maybe? "Look, you have young ones in your tribe, right?"

He didn't say yes, but he didn't say no.

"You'd let another tribe come in and steal their food? Right from under your nose? And if you could save your young ones, you wouldn't do everything you could?"

He sat motionless and merely glared into the dark corner of the cell. His large chest rose and fell until he finally rubbed his hands together. "I need to think about this."

"What is there to think about? How hard is it for you to play nice?"

"You're asking me to help create a ton of little slitherskins. No, thank you. On top of that, your queen is using me, and you expect me to believe she'll free me after the ceremony?"

She had probably made things worse. Drathella's plan had failed. She stood. "I shouldn't have come down here."

His dark eyelashes fell as he rested his head against the stone wall behind him.

What could he possibly be thinking? He had absolutely nothing to lose helping them and everything to gain. But if he acted like this, Brynn would be humiliated by his rejection, and she wouldn't set him free after the ceremony. He'd be trapped, losing his future just for protecting his brother.

Was he thinking he could escape?

"You won't get out otherwise," Nida whispered.

He opened one green eye.

"You won't. These bars are solid *malkanite*. There's no breaking them. And the stone? A Tialan treasure. Unbreakable, too."

He glared at her. "My brother will bring an army."

She frowned. "Our temple has been here for thousands of years."

He closed his eyes and shrugged.

"Good luck, human." She reached for the cup to leave, but his hand shot through the bars, around her wrist, and stopped her.

Murderers. Cruel. Please don't hurt me.

"I want to talk to the queen," he said.

The heat from his hand. The softness of his grip, firm but not painful. He was up against the bars. Eyebrows pulled together. He should have been furious. He had *seemed* furious. But this was different. He was... desperate? Had his disinterest and stubbornness been a bluff?

"Get me a meeting with this queen of yours, and I'll agree. I want to hear what she wants directly from her."

His hand still around hers, her heart jumped. She cleared her throat, and he snapped his hand back. "I'm sure she'll want to meet with you soon."

"Now. Or tomorrow, at least."

Brynn wouldn't allow that. Not now. "She won't—"

"She'll want me to be her mate, and she won't see me?" His thick arm wrapped all the way around the bars.

She bit her lip. "She's sort of indisposed at the moment."

"She's what?"

She squeezed her eyes shut. *How do I explain it to a human?* "She's... molting. She won't let anyone see her for a few days."

"She's what?" he repeated, except this time so much louder it echoed down the hall.

She nodded slowly. He might have shuddered.

"F-fine. Soon. As soon as she'll allow it. You get me a meeting with her soon, and I'll pretend. I'll play nice." He reached out his hand, palm to the side.

She flinched and stared at it.

"It's just my hand. We need to shake on this."

"Shake?"

He waved his hand a little; she mirrored his action. He took her hand in his palm, squeezed gently, and lifted his arm up and down. She tried to emulate what he did.

"It's a promise," he said. "I, Rowec of the Zchi, promise to behave if you get me a meeting with the queen."

She would have laughed if she thought it appropriate. His confidence and stubbornness *had* been a bluff. Still...

Rowec. Rowec. It fit him. It was a strong name.

"Well, well. Are we making friends, Nida?" Drathella teased from down the hallway.

CHAPTER 5

*R*owec glanced up at Nida. Her smile had faded, and she dropped his hand.

The comment had come from the blue slitherskin who had shoved Nida into the crowd. She had been the one to order Nida to go to him.

"Well, what do we have here?" The blue-haired one had come around the corner. She wore an oversized matching robe and slinked nearer to the bars.

He measured the creature's movements, prey calculating its predator's next move. He gripped the bars firmly, posture strong and straight. He wouldn't cower to her. "Are you the queen beast?" he barked.

Nida winced. She'd done so every time he'd used that word.

"I am Drathella," the creature hissed. Her fancy golden bracelets and necklaces jingled as she moved. They glinted in the sparse light. Despite her decorations, she lacked the softness Nida had, the human qualities.

"Are those fangs you use to devour the poor men you capture?" Rowec asked.

Drathella inched closer as he puffed out his chest. "If I must," Drathella said. "Where are yours?"

"Look, Queen—"

"She's not the queen," Nida said. "She's just another one of my sisters, and we don't eat people."

"She's still a beast all the same." Rowec grinned slightly as he glowered at Drathella.

Nida sighed.

What was she so upset about? *They* were the weird ones. *They* were vile beasts hunting men in the night with claws and big eyes. If anyone should be shuddering, it should be him.

"Call us that again, and I'll chain you to the walls," Drathella snapped.

He lifted one eyebrow.

Nida pulled on her sister. "Drathella, you're not helping. Go—"

"You do not tell me what to do!" she shouted, chin turning toward Nida. "I will care for the human from now on." She wrapped her claws around the bars and refocused on him. "You'll be lucky to receive water under my watch."

"You *have* to give him water," Nida said.

Drathella's eyes lit with fury. She turned her full focus on Nida.

Nida shrank where she stood like prey. He was no longer Drathella's target—Nida was. Drathella's cold stare wasn't sitting right with him. It wasn't simple sibling rivalry. It was more than that. She wouldn't hurt her own sister, would she?

What should I care?

But he did. He couldn't help it. Even here, the thought of someone abusing their power…

Drathella gripped Nida's arm. "You gave him water?" she yelled.

"You're the one who told me to come talk—ow!"

He squeezed the bars tighter. They might all be beasts, but at least Nida didn't seem heartless. This one was just cruel, exerting her power for fun.

"You're hurting me!" Nida squeaked.

"That's the point, you filthy, disgusting little human-thing. You're just as bad as he is. You're vile to look at. You betray your sisters by helping him—"

Nida whimpered. "I wasn't helping him, I was trying to get him to—ow!"

Rowec spat in Drathella's face.

Nida's eyes bulged.

Drathella wiped her cheek and scowled at him. "How *dare* you." She tossed her sister aside. "Are you worried I might hurt her, little human?" She made a pouty face and gripped the bars, claws out.

That was it. That's all he needed.

He gripped her hand and pulled her against his cage with all the strength he could muster.

Her chest and face slammed into the bars. She yelped and screamed, but he slipped off her bracelets easily and released her.

She stumbled back. "What do you think you're doing?" she shrieked.

"You want them back. Come get them."

She slid a strand of hair from her face.

He dangled the thick wire rings in front of her.

"You're a trash species." She dug in her pocket for something. A weapon?

"Don't, Drathella!" Nida reached for her, but Drathella shoved her off.

"Shut up!" Drathella retrieved a small triangular-shaped object made of the same yellow stone from the temple. She fixed it into the slot at his door.

A key.

This was his chance. He could escape. She couldn't fight back. She couldn't stop him. He'd shove her to the side; he would be faster than both of them. Once he hit the jungle, then, well, he'd just have to do the best he could. No weapons, not even shoes, he'd be at a disadvantage. Still this might be his only chance at freedom.

Drathella swung open the gate.

Stupid. All bark and no bite, and unbelievably stupid.

"Give them back!" she ordered.

He held her bracelets out to lure her closer.

"Drathella, don't!" Nida warned.

Drathella hesitated. She was considering it. Her eyes gave her away.

Vain. Stupid. Naive. He knew these types; Etta, was one of them.

"Come get them." He dangled the jewelry out.

She shakily held out her hand. "Give me the bracelets."

"Drathella, this is stupid. They're just bracelets. Just go and tell Brynn—"

"She's smarter than you," he said to Drathella. "You might be strong, but you're stupid."

She growled and lunged for the bracelets as he drove his shoulder into her chest.

Slammed against the metal bars, she cried out.

He darted out of the cell, shoving Nida to the ground, too. "Sorry!"

Drathella screamed, scrambling to get up from the ground.

He spun and bolted for the darkness at the end of the hall. He'd have to sneak around, find a way out of the maze, but moving was better than being locked up. To hell with their punishments.

Two claws grabbed his thigh from behind. He glanced down—Drathella.

Damn. She was fast.

"Rowec! Wait!" Nida cried out, running for him.

He swung his arm, his fist on a collision course for Drathella's face. She shrieked as his knuckles hit scale and bone. He tore away, charging for the cover of darkness down the hall.

Drathella screamed on and on behind him for the guards.

He slipped into the shadows and made his way around the corner, and another corner, and another.

His cover would end soon. Gold reptilian sconces with their mouths wide and full of fire lit the rest of the temple. Pressed against the smooth golden wall, he edged up a ramp and around another corner.

"I'll kill you!" Drathella shrieked, her shrill voice echoing up the halls behind him.

There was no way she saw him now or knew which way he turned. But he needed to keep moving and stay oriented. It was the only way out of the maze.

Footsteps came from the right.

He darted left and then right again. Where was the exit? He'd better figure it out fast.

Through one room and into another, he whirled past slitherskin beasts who shouted to get him.

He panted and took another right, then two lefts. Two tall yellow doors loomed above him.

Thank the spirits.

He charged forward, using his speed and strength to ram his shoulder into the door.

It creaked open and revealed a green lush jungle on the other side. *Finally!*

He tore through the brush and into freedom.

When he got back to his village, he'd have a word with the chief about this clan—and his brother.

～

NIDA SCRAMBLED to her feet and raced down the hallway after Rowec.

Drathella grabbed her as she raced past. "Wait!"

"It was working, Drathella! You ruined it!" Nida shrugged her off and kept going.

He couldn't have gotten far, but she'd have to follow the commotion to figure out which way he'd gone. The maze-like hallways were meant to help confuse attackers if they came under siege, but it gave plenty of opportunities for attackers to hide inside rooms without being noticed.

Unfortunately, the entire temple was in chaos.

"Are you okay?" she asked a pair of little sisters, standing no more than waist-high.

They nodded with wide eyes.

"Which way did he go?"

They pointed left.

She followed, asked the next set of sisters, and charged in the direction of their pointed fingers. She followed all of their instructions until it was clear he had run in circles for a while. He had no idea where he was going, but he was moving. He had probably figured out how to get to the jungle.

A few more turns, a couple more questions, and she slid to a stop before the western doors.

"We'll go," one of her guard sisters said. The guards had been chosen because of their strength and size.

"He could be hiding and waiting until we give up," Nida panted. "I'll go look for him, and if I find him, I might be able to reason with him."

"Reason? With that animal?"

She shrugged. She had to try.

"It's the western jungle. He won't survive."

"He won't go far. I'll call for you if I need you, but I don't want to frighten him further. A group of guards would do that."

The guard nodded and took her position at the door.

Nida pulled her hood over her head and held up the skirt of her earthen-dyed robe as she descended the stairs into the western jungle.

If the temple was a maze, this side of the jungle was a labyrinth. Without a weapon or a tool, he wouldn't be able to make a dent in the plant growth. He'd get turned around, retrace steps. He'd dehydrate before he ever found his way out. Not to mention his village was somewhere far on the other side of the temple. He'd have to go through the jungle, all the way around. He'd have to worry about all the predators. And not just the ones that moved. The western side of the jungle was still wild, unkept, free to live—or kill—as it pleased. Vines that choked, pits that drowned, plants that chewed.

He had been *very* stupid.

"Please, Great Tial, let him survive the night," she muttered. He was their best shot at saving her sisters, and she wasn't about to let the jungle take him from her.

Sliding through the brush fairly easily, she rested her hand on the first large trunk of a paratil tree. A gash in the bark had been made, pointing deeper in. She ran her finger over it.

Fresh. Still wet in the wound and bark flaking.

She smiled. He had found a way to stay on track. Maybe he wasn't as stupid as she'd thought.

A crash in the distance caught her attention. *Nothing* made that much noise in the jungle. It called too much attention.

She groaned and dashed through the foliage in the noise's direction.

After a large rough patch of *sendrite* trees and their sharp edges, and then over the soggy bog, a grunt and a shout echoed in the night.

With the small claws she had, she raced toward the sound. "Rowec?" she called.

"Nida? Nida!"

She passed through a second patch of *lianju* trees and their overripe fruit, and found Rowec hanging upside down by his feet over a king drosera—an enormous animal-eating plant. Purple vines around his feet, he dangled over the gorgeous five-petal flower.

She slowly approached. If she didn't get him out, he'd be dead in seconds. "Rowec, don't move," she whispered.

He panted and crossed his arms. "If I could move, I would."

"Does your leg hurt where it has you?" she asked.

He glanced up toward his feet and shook his head. "It did, but it doesn't now."

Not good. The plant had already started the process of ingesting him. The first step was paralyzing him through the vines holding him up. "Okay, Rowec, don't freak out, but I'm going to have to get you down."

He began to struggle with the vine. "Right, I've tried, but—"

"No, no. Don't move."

"It's just these vines. If I could cut them, I'd be free."

She inched closer, watching the petals. It had disguised its maw well. To be so huge, this one was very old. "They're not vines. Those are its fingers," she whispered.

"Fingers?" He shot a glance to his feet again and bounced as he fought it.

"Stop, Rowec."

"Its fingers? It has fingers?" he shouted, straining harder and bobbing up and down.

"Rowec—"

"My leg. I can't feel my leg. Nida, get me down! Nida, kill it or something!"

"No! We don't kill like that—"

"How are you going to get me down, then? How do you walk into a jungle without something to slaughter or maim with?"

She lifted an eyebrow and took a step closer. "Really? You're going to ask me that? You have no weapons either. You don't even have shoes."

"Your sisters shouldn't be so cruel."

"I was trying to get you a better room!"

He bent up toward his feet and tried pulling at the drosera's fingers while she edged closer.

Sometimes it was possible to coax the two sepals on either side to close over the petals. The action would make the plant think it's being harmed, and in its panic, curl its fingers to its side for protection. It might break a few of Rowec's bones when it dropped him, but it was better than death. She just had to get close enough.

"Hold on, Raz. Don't move," he said to his pocket, then refocused on the drosera. "W-w-w-what's that?" he breathed.

The mouth in the center had begun to open. Any second it would drop him in, and he'd be dissolved quickly.

"Don't move," she whispered. "Don't make a sound. When I grab the sepals, and the fingers pull back, you're going to fall—"

"Nida."

"When you fall, you'll be a little hurt, but at least you won't die." She slid behind the king drosera and readied her hands. "Ready?"

The plant's mouth was wide, exposing its bowl of acid and letting the gas plume up.

A drop of Rowec's sweat fell into the mouth. It sizzled. "Nida, this thing could eat four of me at one time. Don't mess this up."

"Don't break promises and run into the wrong side of a jungle next time."

"Then don't capture people for small crimes!"

"Then don't steal!" Her eyes were as wide as his.

After a pause, he whined. "Okay, I'm sorry. We won't steal from your temple ever again. I won't break my promise again. Please, save me."

She smiled and started lifting the sepals. Of course, she'd save him, but it was good to know—

The vines let go, and he screamed as he fell. He grabbed on to a petal with both arms. Thick and strong enough to hold him, it still bent toward the mouth under his weight.

"Hurry, Nida. Get me out!" He was still trying to pull himself up the wilting petal. "Something's burning!" he screamed.

She ran for a lianju leaf and tore off its edges until the stem made a sharp point. "Take my hand!"

Just as his hand grasped hers, she pierced the stem through the petal.

The king drosera curled in on itself, writhing and hissing, and Rowec tumbled safely to the ground toward her.

She pulled him to a safer distance and rolled him to his back. "Are you okay?"

"My leg is... My knee—" He cried out and grabbed his right knee cap. His leg had been badly burned, and his foot had been nearly singed away.

She tried to pull him up. "I need to get you back to—"

He screamed again.

"You can't make that much noise. Other things in the jungle will hear us."

The vine's paralysis had made it so he wouldn't recognize when his body was being dissolved. It must have been wearing off.

He grunted and moaned instead, but there was no moving him. She didn't have the strength to carry him, and he'd never make it back like this. His little white rodent had crawled out of its pocket to nuzzle his neck.

There was only one choice.

As soon as she'd heal him, he'd leave. There would be no reason to stay. She'd be useless, and he'd be free. But he'd die in this jungle otherwise.

She placed her hand on his knee.

He winced and groaned, his facial muscles and clenched jaw giving away the struggle of his pain. The pink-bellied kurimolle licked Rowec's cheek.

"Remember, I'm a Life Weaver, Rowec. I'll fix this."

She took a deep breath, closed her eyes, and filled him with her Vigor. Letting it flow down his burnt leg, she envisioned the Vigor weaving along the burnt tissues and replacing gaps in his skin. Vigor of bright light within her slipped out and into him, removing all pain, all wounds.

Her head felt light, yet too heavy to hold up. It was already too much for her. She was too weak. Her sisters were so much better at Life Weaving than she was. Yet another failure she had adopted from their human side, and yet she was risking her life to save one.

He gasped and stopped straining.

She peeked out of one eye. The wound was almost repaired. Nearly there. She needed to give more.

Pushing as much of her Vigor into him as she could, her hands trembled. She was running out. She wouldn't be able to—

"Nida?"

Her heart slowed, and she faltered.

He sat up and reached for her. "Nida, what's wrong?"

She crumpled over onto the grass as a blinding white light radiated behind her eyelids.

CHAPTER 6

*R*owec swallowed, trying to even out his breathing.

His leg... he'd nearly lost his leg. It had practically been burned away, and she'd healed it. She...

Nida lay cradled in his arms. Long eyelashes closed, the few teal scales on her temples and by her ears sparkled in the sheen of sweat across her face. But her face was paling. Her lips were drying out.

No matter what he'd tried, she wouldn't respond. He'd pressed his head to her chest, his fingers to her neck, there was something—maybe? He couldn't tell if her heart was still beating. Did Tialans even have hearts? He shook his head. *Of course they do.*

He was running out of time. He couldn't leave her there after she had just saved him, but where would he take her?

Back to his village was an excellent option. He'd have his freedom, he'd be back with Maur, his people, but she...

Her lips fell open. She was in trouble.

Damn.

His healers wouldn't know how to fix her, and her sisters were Life Weavers, for crying out loud. They were Nida's best chance at surviving, but it would be turning himself in. He'd be a prisoner again, or worse, considering his escape attempt.

He sighed.

The choice wasn't hard.

"Let's go, Raz." The kurimolle trilled before slipping into his pocket.

He lifted her up and began hurrying back toward the temple, occasionally checking his carved marks on the trees for the right direction.

Nida had been willing to help him, and he had chosen to be reckless. There were more diplomatic ways of getting his freedom back than arguing with Nida, slamming her sister into a wall, and running away. He might not have agreed with the severity of his punishment, but his brother *had* stolen from them. And he had stupidly taken Maur's place.

He knew better. He had raided other tribes before the peace time. He'd even taken prisoners. Had they acted as he had, he would've laughed at their release request and told them to forget about getting within ten feet of the chief to discuss freedom.

A few years earlier, he would have slaughtered the thief on sight had it been his tribe's food.

He should have stayed focused on meeting the queen instead of acting out. Nida hadn't given him reason to doubt her, and he had been a fool to play into the other beast's manipulation.

Finally, an orange glow hovered just above the trees.

"Almost there, Nida," he panted. "I'll get you back."

Rather light and pliable, she was easy to carry. Her hands and arms were folded neatly against her chest, and her legs draped over his arm. A tiny part of him had been afraid she'd have a tail he'd have to worry about, but he'd felt none when he'd lifted her.

Her eyebrows had been drawn up in effort or concern, maybe, but she had saved him. Yes, she had come to retrieve their prisoner, but she didn't have to save his leg. She'd even acted like she'd known she would collapse after healing him. Perhaps she'd even known he could've run off after and left her there, and she'd done it anyway.

The golden brick of the temple reflected the torchlight in an orange haze. He sprinted into the clearing to the large gold doors and climbed the stairs.

Where were the guards? He'd expected to be swarmed by now, tackled and strung up in chains. But no one was anywhere.

He braced himself against one door and pushed as hard as he could until it slowly creaked open.

Nothing. The inside hall was empty, the corridors silent.

Where was everyone?

He adjusted Nida in his arms and headed down the hallway with no idea of where to take her. Screaming for help seemed like a really stupid idea.

But if Nida—

A gasp came from behind.

He spun to find a creature with violet scales and matching eyes and a hand to her mouth, staring at him. One of Nida's sisters. At least she wasn't the blue one—Drathella, was it?

He approached. "Can you help me? Nida healed me, and she—"

Nida's sister ran up and smoothed back Nida's hair. "This way. Come on." She tugged at his arm, leading him through the halls.

After a million turns and a couple flights of stairs, they entered a room. Robes and silks were draped over furniture or left on the floor. Mirrors with little tables holding innumerable bottles and containers were on the far wall, and two beds—one in a vibrant, royal purple, and the other a bright, soft teal—were to his right.

He rested Nida on the teal bed, her auburn hair a splash of warmth in a sea of pillows and blankets. He swallowed and took a step back as the sister immediately knelt beside Nida and began murmuring to her with a hand to her forehead.

He paced silently at the foot of the bed, trying to ignore all the articles of clothing on the ground. Etta wouldn't have ever let him see this side of her. She'd have rather died than seem anything other than perfect. He rolled his eyes.

"That was too close," the sister mumbled.

He jerked his head in her direction. "She's going to be okay?"

She nodded. "If you were any *slower* getting back, she would have died. We're Life Weavers, but we can't bring people back from the dead."

He tilted his head and took a deep breath. "I'm sorry, I didn't have any *boots*."

She squinted at him. "You're going to blame *us* for this?"

No. It was his fault for getting caught by the plant, and his fault Nida had had to heal him. It had been his brother's fault for stealing, and his fault for standing in his place. He groaned and wiped his hand over his head. "Where were the guards? Why haven't I been shackled and locked up?"

"Well, most of our sisters are turning in for bed, and the guards are gone because of Drathella. She lied and said that Nida had already come back through the eastern side. She said you escaped her. I suspected she was lying and found out she told the western side the same." There was a snarl in her tone. Her gaze drifted from Nida to a wall across the room.

Drathella wanted her own sister dead? He and Maur had rough patches, sure, but they'd never wish the other dead.

He shuddered and held out his hand. "I'm Rowec."

She stared at it. "Mind explaining what happened?"

Right. He retracted his hand and slid it into his pocket with Raz. "I got caught by some plant that tried to eat me, and Nida saved me and healed me. I don't know why she collapsed. I don't even know why she helped me."

Her violet eyes settled on him. "Because she's Nida. That's what she does." She rose. "I'm Ascara."

He nodded. "When will she wake up?"

She shrugged. "Soon, I hope. I have to get back down to the kitchens. Cleaning up after feeding hundreds of Tialans takes a bit of work. Can you stay here and watch her?"

He gulped. *Hundreds?* "You're not going to call the guards?"

She eyed him up and down and rested a hand on her hip. Was she measuring him up against her non-human strength, or something else?

"Eh. You brought her back, even though you expected everyone to jump on you." She looked at Nida and back at him with a grin. "I think you'll behave this time. I think you'll make sure she wakes up."

She was right. He wouldn't risk Nida getting hurt again, not when she had shown him the most compassion out of all of these beasts.

Ascara swept past him and exited the room, leaving him alone with Nida.

He cleared his throat and pulled over a nearby stool carved from a paratil tree trunk to sit beside her.

What was he doing? What was he thinking?

He shook his head and dropped his chin to his chest. There had barely been enough time to process what had occurred over the last few hours, but this? He'd had his freedom. No more creepy slitherskin temple with weird beasts inside. He could have been back home with Maur, worrying about dealing with Etta. He groaned and rubbed his hand over his face several times.

"Regret bringing me back?" Nida's voice was soft and airy.

His head shot up. "Nida!"

She half-grinned.

He scanned the room for some way of helping. "Do you need a blanket? Or some water? I'd offer more pillows, but—"

Her eyes shot open as pink flooded her cheeks. "Oh no. My room's a mess," she squeaked. She tried sitting up but grunted and palmed her forehead.

"Slow down. It's fine. I-I don't care about a mess. I was just in a cell, for crying out loud." He eased her back, helping her tuck some of her hair over one shoulder.

She thinned her lips and looked away. "Actually, you were just inside a king drosera about to be eaten."

He shook his head.

"You brought me back..." She shook her head, eyebrows pulled in. "I don't understand."

"I was being stupid. If one of my prisoners had acted as poorly as I had... I was an idiot. I'm sorry, Nida. I didn't mean for you to get hurt. I saw the opportunity when Drathella screwed up, and I took it. Why did you heal me?"

Her eyelashes fluttered. "I had to. I'm pretty bad at it, though. They think it's because I'm more human than Tialan. I really don't know why, but I can't do much Life Weaving."

"But you could have died? You all die doing it?"

"No, just me. Life Weavers take Vigor and turn it into material—tissue, blood, bone, bark, leaf, wings, antennae. Whatever's needed. But, I guess, I don't have much Vigor to spare. It takes a lot of my own to heal anything, even cuts and bruises. Like I said, I'm pretty bad at it, but I'm glad I could heal you enough."

"What you did was remarkable. It was a miracle. I couldn't believe it. You —" He stopped and sighed.

She needed him that badly to risk her own life? She had said they needed him to help her species. Perhaps she was just that desperate, willing to die to save him because she wanted to let her sisters have the chance to live.

Of course she did. He'd do the same for his brother. He *had* done it, several times, and he'd do it again. "You saved me because I really am the only choice you have for this ceremony with the queen, aren't I?"

Her gaze darted around the room with a lingering silence. "Yes," she said. He nodded.

Another silence between them swelled until he cleared his throat. "So what now? Do you take me back down to my cell? String me up?"

She bit her lip and slowly lifted herself to her elbows. He adjusted pillows for her to sit up easier. "Can you handle the cell one more night? I'll go talk to Brynn. I'll get her to approve moving you to a better room. A room you deserve until the ceremony."

A room he deserved. "You think your queen will still let me free after the ceremony? After I did all this?"

She shrugged. "Honestly? It's too important that she doesn't find out. I'll handle it, and I'll handle Drathella. I'm just not really sure what's involved in caring for a human other than the basics."

He snickered. "You at least thought of water. Do I get to eat anything?"

Her cheeks flushed again. "I hadn't even thought of food. We only need to eat once... a week." She swallowed, trying to hide her smile.

"Once a week?" That sounded horrible. "How long is it until the ceremony?"

"A few weeks."

His eyes bulged. "Well, yes, please. I'd like some food at some point. Preferably more often than once a week." He couldn't fight the grin reaching the corners of his mouth.

She even laughed. A light bubbly laugh that made his smile widen. "Sorry, it's just, we... never mind."

"As long as you don't eat me, I'm fine."

She groaned and tossed a pillow at his head. "We don't eat people!"

"Maybe not you, but Drathella?" He lifted an eyebrow.

She giggled again, and his heart raced a little. It felt good making her laugh.

"You are definitely different from your sisters."

Her smile slowly faded, the light dimming from her eyes. "Just promise me one thing, and actually keep it this time. I know you don't agree with our punishment for the crime, but we're not beasts. Please just…" She took a deep breath. "We're definitely not slitherskins, and we're not beasts. Not even Drathella. We're just… Tialans. Please, understand that." Her deep, aquamarine eyes were reaching out to him, willing him to truly hear her.

And he did. He understood. *Beasts* reduced them, all of them, to less than whatever they were. His brother had committed the crime, he willingly took his place, and she had risked her life to save him. He had treated pets with more respect.

"I understand."

"And I'll do the same."

He pointed to his chest. "You thought I was a bea—uh, a terrible creature?"

She bit her lip. "Well, we're told of your wars and enslavements and how you slaughter people…"

He closed his eyes and nodded.

"But I'll do the same. I won't assume the worst. You're nothing like I expected either."

Here he had been screaming about the beasts locking him up, and she'd thought he had been one all along.

He slapped his hands on his knees and stood up. "Do I get myself down there into my cell and lock myself in or…?"

She smiled and slid her legs to the edge of the bed. "I can walk, if you help me." He took her soft hand as she slowly rose. "I'm just wobbly, is all."

He held out his elbow and let her lead him back to his cell.

CHAPTER 7

*A*fter a night and a full day of much-needed rest, Nida darted through the halls for Brynn's chambers. She wouldn't make Rowec wait any longer. He was only back in that cell because he'd cared enough to get her back to her sisters for help.

He had smiled. Laughed, even. He had taken her hand, helped her with her walking, carried her all the way back to the temple. He had saved her. He was… nothing like the stories.

Maybe Ascara was right. Maybe there were more than just a few good humans.

The heat rushed up her spine. His arm was strong with taut muscle over his forearm. But it had been gentle, warm.

She picked up her pace. He'd seemed to have liked her human-ness, and he hadn't cringed when he'd touched her. That thought made the whole temple a little warmer despite the night air.

She skirted past sisters in the hallways, dipping her head in a slight greeting.

Hopefully, Ascara was back in the kitchens, still cleaning up after dinner the night before. It usually took a couple days, and she was so grateful it wasn't *her* scheduled meal to help with.

But as per usual, Ascara had brought Nida some paratil juice and a few durlo seeds to help her recover. She'd have to make sure they got together later to talk. She wanted all the details of Rowec bringing her back and what was said. She definitely wanted to get Ascara's opinion of him. They had a lot of talking to do.

She moved through the temple, past the dining hall, and up to the third floor without running into Ascara or Drathella.

She nodded to the two guards standing outside Brynn's room and dipped between the two sheer crimson curtains at the doorway.

"Brynn—"

A clank of metal on stone followed by a curse from her sister pulled her toward the back of the room. The queen's quarters had grown more disheveled these last few weeks. Lacy shawls and shimmery gowns were strewn across the floor alongside empty goblets. More than usual.

"Why do I even bother?"

"Brynn?" Nida followed the sound all the way into her sister's dressing room.

Brynn sat at her vanity, her robe half-off her shoulders and her scarlet hair unbraided and unkempt. She was fussing with small trinkets, opening and closing them in a hurry, smearing whatever lotions she had found on her shoulders and neck.

"What's wrong?"

Brynn gasped. "Nida. Did you hear? The human, he came back!"

How had she known he had left? *Drathella, of course.*

She bit her lip and nodded. "Rowec. His name is Rowec."

"But isn't it wonderful? Can you believe he had a change of heart and came back to help with the hatching of our sisters? To meet me? He apologized for everything. Not only did he take the place of his brother's misdeeds, but he escaped and came back! Hah! He's perfect!" She scattered several tiny glass bottles and cursed again.

Nida held her breath. Had they truly averted catastrophe? Was this all going to work out? "You saw him?"

"Oh, Great Tial, no. Are you kidding? Ascara told me everything."

That could have gone horribly wrong, but somehow Ascara pulled it off. Nida would have to thank her for that later. "But what's wrong? Why do you look so flustered?"

"What's wrong? Do you see me? I look hideous!" Brynn shrilled.

Some of her sisters were known to be a bit vain when it came for their time to molt, but Brynn had never minded before. A true queen, she had always handled it with grace, never batting an eye at what was inevitable.

"You look fine. You look like you just woke up, is all."

Brynn clicked her tongue. "But I didn't. I've been up for hours. Pacing and worrying—"

"About what?"

"About what?" Brynn shrieked. "What do you mean 'About what?'"

"Well—"

"I'm still molting, meanwhile my most generous mate thinks we look ghastly and horrid. And can you blame him?" Brynn cried, eying her skin and green scales in the mirror.

What did that matter? "But like you said, Rowec came back. He's willing to help. I'm not sure it matters to him, and besides, I don't see any—"

"Here and here!" Brynn pointed to two small spots nearly ready to pull off from the scales at her neck. "He's right! It is hideous!" She threw her head down to the vanity and sobbed. Her strewn makeup and jewelry jingled and bounced with her melodramatics.

"Brynn, I don't think that's what has him saying we're hideous..."

"What do you mean?" Brynn sat up immediately, tears streaming down her strong cheek bones.

She reached for a brush and began running it through Brynn's hair. "Well, to humans we're very close to... to..."

"Slitherskins." Brynn practically growled.

"Well—"

"We're nothing like that! They crawl around on their bellies in the brush. No legs, no arms, no hair. They have forked tongues!" Brynn shuddered. "What similarities could there possibly be?"

She nodded. "Right, well, the point is we're still pretty *different* to them."

"But I'm nice."

"And he doesn't know that because you've been hiding away in here since he was captured." She forced the brush through a matted piece of Brynn's hair.

Brynn whined. "I had no choice. I can't let him see me like this."

"No, but you do need to get yourself together and see him soon. I also..." She stopped working through her sister's hair.

Keep him happy and feeling less like a prisoner, and he'll behave. If he behaves, Brynn will accept him. Her sisters will be born. She took a deep breath.

Brynn tilted her head and glanced back at her in the mirror. "What is it, Nida, dear? What's wrong?"

"I just want to move him out of the cell—"

"But—"

"Like you said, he seems to want to help us, so I think he deserves better. And he showed that he's willing to come back. I don't think he'll leave again if we treat him with respect."

Brynn nodded. "You're so smart. Drathella wanted to leave him in the dungeon. I thought that was a terrible idea. You know our last queen came to love her mate. Perhaps there's still time for us. I want him to see me for the majestic creature I can be."

Nida began braiding her sister's long red strands. "He'll be hungry, too. He needs some food. I think humans eat more often than we do. He said so at least."

Brynn nodded repeatedly. "Of course. Of course. How silly of us." Her hand caught Nida's. "You've been caring for him, and I'm so happy for it. You have a kind heart, Nida. If he's at all good, like the last mate and unlike his treacherous villagers, he should be able to see that in you. And if not, then we'll find another male!"

She squeezed her eyes shut. That's what she had been afraid of. "I-I don't think you have any time left to be picky, Brynn. The hatching is just in a few weeks—"

"I'm sure he'll come to love us soon. You know, your heart is why I gave you the hatchery to look over. You're still Tialan to me." Brynn patted her hand.

She had come to expect the underhanded insults Brynn gave her. Mostly because they were always softer than Drathella's, but also because Brynn genuinely meant well. Brynn loved her, not nearly as much as Ascara, but more than Drathella. She respected her, too, which was why Nida had to be honest.

"Oh! You're in the hatchery all the time," Brynn continued. "Give him the room just off the hatchery. That should be nice enough."

One more thing. "Drathella needs to leave him alone, too. She's the reason he escaped. She taunted him, and he used it against her. I fear that if she keeps coming around him—"

"He'll hate us even more and succeed next time he tries to run," Brynn whispered to herself. "Fine, I'll let Drathella know."

She tied off the braid in Brynn's hair. "And you'll see him soon? He's been waiting to meet you. He wants assurances about the ceremony."

Brynn stood and made for her evening robes. "Yes, soon."

"Let him get to know you," she said.

Brynn paced the room, nibbling on one claw.

"I can't promise he'll fall in love with you, but at least being friends would be nice. Maybe it would improve relationships between us and humans—"

"What about a private dinner? On the terrace?" Brynn's eyes lit up.

Brynn hadn't been listening. Not really.

"Humans have private dinners, don't they?" Brynn continued. "Private meetings for romantic opportunities? What a wonderful idea!"

Wonderful? No, it was a horrible idea. He'd never go for that.

She circled Brynn and helped her dress into an emerald robe. "I don't think that's right—"

"What do you mean? It's perfect. I'll set up a time for my future human mate. It'll be glorious. On the terrace we can see the stars. Humans like stars, right?"

This would be a disaster. This wasn't what she'd meant when she'd told

Brynn to meet with him. "Brynn, I don't think he'd be interested in something like that—"

"Not interested in getting to know his future mate? How could that be? Look at me. You've got me all beautiful again. My hair is neatly braided, my robe and jewels look exquisite—"

Brynn wasn't understanding, and if she walked into this "private dinner" with the wrong expectations of Rowec and what he wanted to discuss, then it could end up worse.

"Brynn, he *wants* to help. Don't you think it's a little soon to push him—"

"All right, fine!" Brynn waved one hand at her. "Don't worry. I won't do it yet. I'll think about it." Brynn smiled, and Nida forced a grin in return.

"Sister!" Drathella burst into the room, chest heaving in deep breaths. Her murderous glare immediately fell on Nida.

Nida's stomach turned. No matter what Drathella would say, she'd stand her ground. His escape had been Drathella's fault, not hers.

"Drathella, what is wrong with you?" Brynn's clawed fingers went to her chest. "You nearly startled the hair off my scalp."

"Forgive me, queen—"

Queen? Nida snorted. What happened to 'sister'?

"—But Nida is working with the human." Drathella licked her lips.

Nida's heart sank. Her insides twisted into knots. What angle was Drathella playing? She swallowed. "What are you talking about?"

"He struck me!" Drathella shouted. "And she just stood there. She helped him run into the jungle and escape. He's long gone!"

"I didn't just stand there!" Nida yelled back. "He only got out because you were the stupid one to go inside. Anyone can tell in two seconds that he's a fighter."

"So, you've been looking at him closely, huh? You were even touching skin when I walked in on you."

Brynn gasped.

This looks bad. She wasn't working with Rowec, and she wasn't stealing her sister's mate, or whatever else Brynn was imagining.

"It was a handshake. He called it a handshake. It was me promising that if he at least met the queen to discuss helping us, I'd try to get him a better room, I—"

"Nida, stop," Brynn scolded, more like an older sister than a queen. "Drathella, why are you bringing this to me now? He's already returned."

The color drained from Drathella's face. If the blue had drained from her scales, too, Nida would've laughed.

"He has?"

"Yes, he returned of his own free will. He wants to help."

"He does?" Drathella squeaked.

"Yes, but I can't have you taunting him. Don't go near him again, or you'll have kitchen duty for the next six months, understand?"

Drathella crossed her arms and pouted. "You're just going to ignore that our mutant sister is getting close to the criminal?"

"He's not a criminal!" Nida shouted.

A sneer spread across Drathella's face.

"That's enough." Brynn folded her hands in front of her. "I will think on what we discussed earlier, Nida—"

Drathella roared.

"And, Drathella, mind your own business. I've changed my mind. Get to work in the kitchens, now. You'll have it for the rest of the month."

"But, Brynn!" Drathella pouted, her eyebrows stitched together.

"Kitchens, now. Nida, move him to where we discussed. I'll send food to the human's new room immediately." Brynn turned toward her guard and began giving orders.

The human? Brynn wanted to pretend she'd have a romantic meeting with Rowec and possibly fall in love with him, but he was just *the human?* What did that make her? Brynn hadn't corrected Drathella when she'd called her *mutant,* either.

And he had a name. Brynn didn't even use it. She didn't even care.

Nida headed for Rowec's cell.

Why was she so upset? It didn't matter. It wasn't as though he'd fall in love with Brynn. There wasn't enough time, and those things took time, right? He wouldn't fall in love with any of them, so her sister had better get that silly thought out of her head.

But he *would* be happy she'd gotten him a new room, real food, and some sort of meeting with the queen. Probably not what he had been expecting, but at least he had the chance to meet Brynn and discuss helping her sisters.

She darted through the halls, down the stairs, and toward the dungeon.

The best she could hope for was that he was pleased enough that he wouldn't try to run away again. Drathella just had to stay very far away, and she'd do that now that Brynn had ordered her, wouldn't she?

CHAPTER 8

*G*entle. Soft. Her hand had been soft...

"Nida. Nida." It rolled off his tongue.

I'll be back as soon as I can, she had said.

He had told her she wasn't like her sisters. He had meant it. She had warmth, for one. Eyes that didn't make him feel like a meal, for another.

He shook his head.

Whatever he felt about her, he had to focus on his possible negotiation with the queen. Nida was right. If he could meet this queen, he could possibly reason with her. He'd agree to stay for the ceremony, and then she'd have to release him because she didn't need him anymore. None of them would.

He sighed. *It might work.*

But after taking him back to his cell, Nida hadn't returned. It had been over a day since he'd seen her. She had mentioned needing to recover, and he'd encouraged it. But he'd also be lying to himself if he didn't admit he was getting nervous. Sleeping that long? Recovering that long? Maybe, but maybe not.

Images of her hair and shimmering scales lingered in his memory.

A guard twice Nida's height with crimson scales had been delivering him water. More like she threw it at him through the metal, leaving him and Raz to lap up the remains with their hands.

Apparently, word had gotten out about Drathella getting too close. He smirked.

The crimson guard had also slid a plate of dripping wet slugs through the bars. Most were belly up. Some were obviously not slugs because they had legs that twitched.

His stomach ached for food. *Real* food. Not this mush for birds. He ate what they gave him—tried to anyway—between gags and heaves. Anything to stifle the ache in his gut.

When the sunlight burned orange and fell out of view from the holes in his ceiling, he scratched a second line into the floor with a pebble he'd found.

The plate of slug parts had crusted over.

He closed his eyes and hummed an old song from his village. One the elders sang to the children about a spirit who'd drifted over the mountains, blowing the clouds into shape.

"You fight, you escape, you sing. You're proving to be quite the mate for Brynn."

Nida.

He jerked his head and jumped up, hands around the bars. "Where have you been?"

She stepped from the shadows under a dark brown cloak. "Dealing with my sisters. I'm sorry I took so long. I slept most of the time and met with my sister as soon as I could."

"And do you have good news or bad news?"

She handed him a dark brown cloak through the bars. "Good, I think?"

"Will the queen still meet with me?"

"Eh, yes. But she still is a little nervous about coming out. She has some ideas for meeting you." She crossed her arms and lifted her chin. The few scales at her temples glistened in the retreating sunlight.

"Ideas?"

"Some good, some not so good." She waved him off. "Nothing terrible, I promise. But I did steer her toward the better choice of just meeting and talking with you."

What else had the queen wanted to do that Nida felt it important enough to divert her? "Will it work?"

She lifted both eyebrows. "Maybe."

He held the brown cloak she'd given him to his chest and measured it against himself. It was wide enough, and long, too. It'd cover him completely. "What is this for?"

"We're going to look like we're going to pray."

"Is there a reason I need to hide?"

"It's so we're not hounded as we walk through the halls. You've become *quite* famous."

He slid his arms through the cloak, adjusting it on his shoulders a few times. "I doubt it. Have you seen what they've been feeding me?"

She wrinkled her nose. "Sorry about that. Brynn is sending more food, and today, I officially took over as your caretaker. So, if there's anything you require or need, I am the one to make sure you're happy."

He lifted both eyebrows and thinned his lips, the corners turning up in a grin. "Anything?"

Her cheeks flushed.

He swallowed with a dry tongue and placed the hood over his head. Raz stirred in his pocket, and he patted it gently. "Stay clear, Raz. We're changing scenery."

Nida removed a triangular-shaped stone from a pocket in her robe and pressed it against the door. The mechanism clicked, the door creaked open, and she stepped aside.

He poked his head out and glanced down the dark hall.

"If you run, I'll let the drosera eat you this time," she said. "You're not worth the trouble."

He snickered and stepped out. "Well, am I disguised?"

She stood back and glanced at him head to toe as he lifted his arms and spun a little for her. "You'll do. Let's set some rules just in case. My sisters are everywhere. This really is the worst time to take you to your new room, but I've kept you waiting long enough. It's just better safe than sorry."

He'd do whatever he needed to get a better place than the muddy cell. Ideally, he wanted out, but he'd promised to do this diplomatically.

"So, keep your head down. If you have to say anything, don't. Just stay silent."

He nodded.

"Stay right behind me, and don't make me regret this."

"Why would I make you regret this?"

"I know we're joking, but seriously, if you try to run, your life will be infinitely harder, and they'll pull me from caring for you."

He understood, and he didn't want that. "I'll behave."

She led him down the dark hallway and through yellow corridor after yellow corridor, checking around corners first.

"I was meaning to tell you that you guys have really limited decor," he whispered. "There are more colors than gold, you know."

She shushed him with a hand up for him to stop while she peered around yet another corner.

Some of Nida's sisters passed by in neighboring halls, but their heads were down as well. None of them made an effort to speak to her—

"Nida! Oh, thank goodness, there you are."

Every muscle in his body froze. He kept his head down, eyes trained to the bottom of Nida's cloak in front of him, and hunched a little to appear shorter than he was. He hoped, between the hood and Nida's body, he wasn't that obvious.

"Ascara, get out of here right now," Nida hissed.

"Okay, okay. But we need to talk. You've been out cold since that human brought you back. Which we need to talk about—"

"Ascara, seriously—"

"No, I know, but he *brought you back*. That's textbook—"

"Whatever you're about to say, *don't*. I don't have time for make-believe or the things you imagine in your head when you should be praying."

Ascara snorted. "Oh, sweetheart, fairytales are not what I'm thinking about when I should be praying. You should know that."

"Ascara, really, this isn't the time—"

"Okay, fine. Fine. But I should let you know, I heard a rumor. He's being moved... from his cell... to the room near the hatchery! You'll get to see him a lot more often!"

He nearly lifted his head but caught himself. It wasn't the fact that she'd said *hatchery* that sparked him, though it probably should have. He'd have to consider that later.

What caught his attention was the tone. Nida's sister said it teasing, light, like it was good news for Nida. Like her sister thought that maybe Nida *wanted* to see him more often.

"I hear you're going to get to take care of him," Ascara whispered. "If you bring him new clothes, tell me what his—Ow! Ow! Okay! You don't have to pinch me."

He gasp-coughed. Had she just suggested...?

"Who's that?"

"Ascara, go. Walk away, please," Nida whispered.

"Wait. Is that—"

"Ascara, please!" Nida's pitch lifted when she begged. "Don't draw any more attention."

The whispering from the neighboring halls had stopped. Had Ascara been heard and noticed by the others? What happens when a group of... Tialans... realize the only male in their entire complex is out walking around?

He itched to get to his new room.

"Okay, okay. I get it," Ascara said.

There was a long pause, and he got the sense they were mouthing to one another.

"Bye, Nida. See you later."

It was forced, over-dramatized. He nearly laughed.

Nida sighed and whispered, "All right. Let's go. We're nearly there."

He smiled and followed the tail of her cloak.

Eventually, she slowed, and rested a hand on his shoulder. "Okay, you can look up."

The yellow stone was still present, of course, but his new room was clean with vibrant, barely-used furniture. The entire space was bathed in a gold glow of firelight from Tialan sconces. Lounge chairs, pillows, and blankets in every color of every silken fabric—some extremely rare.

"Is this...?" He approached a deep violet-colored pillow, stamped with its design instead of sewed. "This is from Black Harbor. You trade with the ports there?"

She raised her eyebrows. "Trade? Not really. Sometimes sailors get lost in the jungle... Sometimes they leave really nice stuff behind."

He shook his head and cocked an eyebrow at her. "Because some *thing* scares them off?"

She giggled and shrugged. "Maybe? Is this better than the cell?"

He wandered through the center, running his fingers over several pieces of fabrics. "A little."

"A little?"

"You really like yellow." He looked up and found the ceiling had been arranged into an intricate geometric pattern.

"It's plentiful here." She removed her cloak and rested it on a nearby chaise.

He did the same and sunk into one of the great long benches with a fur covering. "So, this room is near the hatchery?"

Her color faded, her eyes widened. Her fingers ran over the fabric of a chair near her. "Yeah, uh, yes. It's right around the corner..."

He didn't catch that last part. "The hatchery is where your new sisters are, or will be, right?"

She nodded, the lines in her forehead deepening. But why?

"Can I see it sometime? The hatchery? I mean before the ceremony or whatever."

She scratched her forehead, moved a lock of hair behind her ear. "Um, maybe. It's pretty sacred. Probably shouldn't test Brynn by going in there."

No hatchery. Got it.

She crossed her arms and tucked her chin into her shoulder, withdrawing into herself.

What was wrong with her? Had he made her uncomfortable? Was she not feeling safe? Before, the bars had separated them. Now, nothing did.

He tilted his head and leaned forward on his chair. "What's wrong? If you'd rather me go back to the cell or—"

"No!" she blurted, hands out toward him. She was all the way across the room, but she had retracted them quickly as if she'd touched him.

"That conversation with Ascara—"

"Hah! It's just Ascara. She has no idea what she's talking about. She's sort of immature and thinks human men should be pets..." Her eyes bulged wider after she'd said it. "Sorry, that came out wrong."

He chuckled.

"I-I don't think you're a pet or anything. I mean, I wouldn't... treat you like that. Brynn... Brynn wouldn't treat you like that."

He stood, and she took another step back. "I never thanked you for getting my sorry backside out of that plant."

She bit her bottom lip. "You-you sorta did."

"I mean, sure, I carried you through the jungle, practically at a sprint, raced back into a temple of Tialans just to get you help..."

Her hand drew up to her neck as she smiled. Her neck was pink, like her cheeks. He was teasing, but maybe it was too far.

Silence permeated the room.

She tapped the wall beside her and gazed anywhere but at him. "Drathella claimed I'm working with you. Helping you, somehow, more than I should."

That's rich. Had Drathella been captured in his village, she'd get a taste of her own medicine. "Yes, but she hates humans and me... so anything not torturous would be helping me."

She half-laughed. "You're probably right."

The crimson guard from earlier entered the room with a gold platter. "Your food," she said, placing a tray on a table near the door with a clank. The food on it bounced.

"Thank you, Crilla," Nida said.

After Crilla left, they headed for the platter together.

"Well, what do you think?" Nida asked.

The tray was covered in the same slugs he had been served in his cell, some rotting fruit pieces, and the legs of *something* spindly and... furry. He put his hands on his hips. "Well, if your queen is trying to kill me, then it looks great."

She groaned.

Raz crawled out of his pocket, sniffing the air. But as soon as he got near enough to the "food," he jerked back and slid deeper into his pocket.

"Yup, it's official. She's trying to kill me. Raz knows." He chuckled.

She waved her hands and placed a palm on his shoulder. "No, I promise. She just doesn't understand humans. I'm sorry. How can I fix this?"

His stomach growled loudly, and they both laughed.

She straightened. "What do you want to eat?"

Several things floated in his head—*fresh cheese, roasted bird, ripe paratils, salted river fish.* "Fruits. Vegetables. Meat from large game?"

"Large game?"

"Red meat."

"We don't hunt like that."

He shook his head and bit back a laugh. "The irony in that."

"The irony in what?"

"I thought you ate people. I thought you ate whatever you could kill, and you don't even eat red meat."

"Oh." She smiled, probably out of courtesy. "I have an idea." She floated past him to stand below the three small holes in the ceiling showing the night sky. "Want to head to the kitchens?"

He drew up his eyebrows. "Are the kitchens outside on your roof?"

She laughed. "No, but everyone should be back in their rooms by now. We could hurry and sneak you down there. You can have whatever we have in there." She headed for the door.

"Will you get in trouble for taking me, though?"

She shrugged one shoulder and smirked. "Only if Drathella catches us."

"What about your other sisters?"

She poked her head out. "*If* any are still walking around, we'll just sneak. If this isn't food you can eat, I *have* to get you real food. Brynn will have to understand." She grabbed his arm and pulled him into the hallway.

Her claws were just like long, human nails, and her palms were very warm on his skin.

"This way." Nida pulled him around two corners, and then down a long hallway and a flight of stairs.

Two of her sisters rounded a corner, chatting about something, and getting closer.

They needed an escape. A place to hide. His eyes scanned the halls around them for a place to go.

Nida gasped and pushed him around another side and pressed him against the wall for cover.

CHAPTER 9

$\mathcal{N}$ ida held her breath.

With her full body against him and her hands on his chest, she was both stunned and humiliated.

This wasn't necessary. She just needed to shove him back, and instead, she'd basically accosted him in the hallway. What in the Great Tial's name had she done?

The whispers came nearer; it was too late to move. His chest heaved under her palms. He was rigid and strong like the stone built up around her. The warmth burning through her hands melted her. Was it her heat or his? She couldn't tell.

But he waited, patiently and silently. His focus dropped to her hands, as hers did, too.

He didn't move them. He didn't move. He let her hands linger against him.

He's letting me... touch... him.

As soon as the whispers were gone, she took a step back and breathed. If scales could change colors, hers would be as red as her face felt. "I think it's clear."

He nodded.

Her hands needed a better place to be. She tucked them under her crossed arms and led him through the halls.

She took the back way through some of the lecture rooms for studying. They passed the wall fountains and the textile rooms until they entered the back side of the kitchens. Clean, golden pots glistened on the stove. The long stone counters for prepping food had their golden shine. The utensils and food had all been stored away.

"Here." She pulled out a stool and slid it up to the wide island counter.

He sat carefully and leaned against the counter. His eyes roamed over everything. "This place is huge. Half of our warriors could fit in here alone."

She headed for the water basin in the corner. After turning a knob for fresh water to come pouring out of the spigot, she filled a large carafe. She grabbed a golden goblet from the shelf and placed both on the counter in front of him.

Before her hands had even left the goblet and carafe, he took them up, poured a glass, and started guzzling it.

She swung the two doors to the food pantry open and eyed the shelves. The shelves had some food, but it hadn't been restocked yet.

"That's enough to feed all of you?" he asked between gulps.

She shook her head. "It only holds what we've had most recently. Most of it is grown or farmed in other portions of the temple. Anything look appetizing?"

He pointed to the melons, berries, and some ripe paratils. She grabbed as much as she could hold, including a ripe red melon, and carried them to the counter.

"I thought we had some durlo fruit, but—"

"Durlo?" His mouth dropped open. "You have durlo?"

She cringed. "The stinky, sticky, messy fruit—

"—that gushes with sweet and sour juice when you bite into them? Yes, that durlo fruit."

She giggled. He loved durlo that much? But it sort of made sense. She and her sisters could eat it from time to time, but the younglings preferred mostly durlo a year or so after their hatching. Maybe it was the human in them.

Rowec shook his head. "We haven't found any in the jungle for some time, and we can't seem to grow it."

Raz had climbed out of Rowec's pocket and was lapping up some water. His beady gaze darted between Nida and his water. He even took some in his tiny white paws and rubbed it over his narrow snout.

"Do you need a knife?" she asked. "For the paratil—"

He'd already begun peeling the rind on the paratil with his bare hands. "Never mind."

He laid one chunk out for Raz, and then swallowed several pieces whole.

He tore through seven of them in less than five minutes, and she'd felt terrible for it. She'd known he'd needed better care, but he'd waited for her and endured this. And Drathella.

"So, the queen's agreed to meet me?" He snorted and wiped his chin with the back of his hand.

She closed her eyes. "If I tell you the truth, you promise not to freak out?"

"Promise."

She groaned. He wouldn't like it. "Brynn is considering a *private* dinner with you... under the stars..."

He coughed and covered his mouth. "A *romantic* private dinner?"

"I'm going to try to convince her that it's a diplomatic meeting, but she's not easily convinced when she has her mind set on something."

He nodded and swallowed another piece. "And her mind is set on me?"

"Well, no. Not you, specifically. It would have been your brother if he had been captured instead. She just has this idea that she should be in love with her mate because our late sister was."

"Well, if she decides on a romantic meeting, I'll play along. You got me real food, a real room. Surely I can play into her and use that to my advantage." He smirked and tossed another rind onto the pile in the center of the island.

Brynn was proving to be more difficult the closer they got to the hatching. Hiding for an entire molting, expecting a willing romantic dinner out of her captive human, the fermented drinks, the more frequent insults about Nida being human-like...

She glanced down at Rowec's hands. His fingers, so much like hers, worked another piece of fruit. It was nice to have contact with someone who looked similar to her. It felt almost normal.

"Do you really think humans are bad?" he asked.

"That's what I've been told. But now..."

"Now?"

She didn't know what to believe. He was challenging everything she'd thought about humans. "Are they mostly like you? Or..."

"Mostly terrible?" He sighed and shrugged. "I think most are like me. We tend to take care of the ones that are terrible."

"How?"

He winced. "It depends on what they do, but we're not all bad, even if it looks it."

She nodded. "Sometimes, and I'd never admit it to anyone else, but sometimes I... actually... sort of like being more human than Tialan. Less claw issues, my scales are subtler. I'm not as large or as tall, sure, but I like my size. I also like being a Tialan. I like having scales even if they're small and few. I like being a Life Weaver, even if I'm terrible at it."

He smirked. "I don't think you're terrible at it."

She smiled, grateful she was able to do enough to save him.

He watched her, munching on a new piece.

"Most of my sisters hate that we need you, but they're also scared we won't find anyone in time and our sisters will die."

"It makes sense, actually. I'd hate to rely on another clan for our survival." He stood and motioned to the basin. "I need to clean up a bit."

He twisted the knob and dipped his hands in to rinse the sugary juice off. He let the water slide all the way up to his elbows before he rubbed some over his face.

He returned to his seat, his cheeks clean and bright, and their eyes met. The jungle green had softened again.

She cleared her throat. "So, are you a leader in your village? Like my sister?"

He shrugged and helped a bloated little Raz back into his pocket. "Not really. We have a chief, but I am the lead warrior. My family was chosen to lead the warriors since we're the strongest and my father was a great fighter. He brought peace to the clans."

"Oh." So humans did fight like the stories, but his family had also brought peace.

"It's a big deal to us."

She nodded. "But you must like fighting, right? You must be good at it if your family was chosen?"

He filled his goblet with more water. The carafe was nearly empty. "It's a lot of responsibility. A lot of stress. A lot of choices I don't like to make."

She'd heard that plenty of times from Brynn. Sometimes Brynn had muttered about her responsibilities under her breath. Sometimes she sat silent at dinner, staring off at nothing. "What kind of choices?"

He lifted an eyebrow and took a sip.

"What kind of choices do you have to make that you don't like?"

He sighed and stretched back. The length of him extended into a gloriously strong torso.

She sucked in a breath to refocus.

"I have to train boys as young as four to start learning how to fight. I wish we didn't have to, but the minute we become vulnerable, we'll lose all we love."

Her mouth fell open. "What?"

"Nothing."

She furled her eyebrows. Her sisters only mentioned slaughter, cruelty; they never mentioned necessity. "No, what will you lose if you don't learn to fight?"

"Everything."

She wasn't okay with killing, but killing to protect *everything* wasn't what her sisters had described all these years. "You fight to protect? You don't kill... for sport?"

"We try to only fight to protect, but sometimes that means fighting for space or food. Some do kill for sport, but like I said, we try to stop those."

How had her sisters gotten this so wrong? How much more did she not know? "By everything, you mean family, friends...?"

He nodded.

More? Did he have a woman he loved back in his village?

Oh, how stupid could she have been. Of course, he had a *real* human back at his home.

"You have a partner," she said. *Ugh.* Had she sounded as pathetic as she thought she had? "Not that I... I mean I was just curious how humans... you know."

He shook his head slightly and set the goblet onto the stone counter. "I don't have a partner yet. Assuming I make it out of here, I have a marriage with Etta to cancel."

"Marriage? I don't understand."

"We promise to only take care of each other."

She pulled her head back. "Only take care of each other? But what about the rest of your family? Your brother? Your other brothers?"

"No, no." He waved his hand. "We take care of them, too. And I just have one brother. Humans don't have hundreds of siblings."

She nodded slowly.

"Marrying is more like saying you'll make each other your first priority. You have children together. You live together..."

Oh. "You fall in love."

"No, well, no." He snorted. "Not in my case. In most cases, yes, you fall in love and *choose* to marry the other person, like your sister wants, but not me."

"Why?"

He inhaled deep and slumped over the counter. "Because I'm the best warrior, I have to follow what's best for the village. The chief's daughter, Etta, has pushed for us to be together since we were kids, and it was arranged by our parents. I'm not sure she cares about me. I think she probably cares more for what I represent to our clan."

She nodded. "I'm sure she cares about you."

"I don't think forcing me into a marriage is showing how much she cares..." His voice fell along with his gaze to her hand resting on the table. His index finger stretched out a tiny bit more than his other fingers, a mere fingertip from hers. "What about you? You'll find other human men after your sisters are born, right?"

She shook her head. "No, we don't have mates."

"Ever?" His eyebrows lifted.

"It's not for us. It's for Brynn, and I don't see many human men lining up to be with us, all things considered." She glanced up and found him staring intently at her. Was he confused? Was he waiting for an explanation?

Her eyes roved over his body. Human eyes. Human arms.

So much like hers. And with him, she felt connected to something. She wasn't an outsider looking in. Through him, she was looking out into a world she hadn't even glimpsed before.

She bit her lip, trying to ignore the pounding of her heart. "You're trapped like Brynn," she mumbled. "Forced to do what's best for your people."

His fingertip barely touched hers. It was merely a few centimeters of skin, but she had become acutely aware of it. An odd feeling, an awkward and daring fascination, touching fingertips felt like so much more.

Her heart skipped a beat as it settled into the warm pulse of his.

"I'm trapped... like you." His low tone, barely above a whisper, slowed her heart to a lull and pulled it to him.

His finger slid slowly over hers, nearly down to the knuckle.

She caught her breath.

"Maybe being imprisoned here won't be so bad." His eyes lifted to hers. "What happens when the ceremony is over?"

She blinked and found her voice. "Uh, well, once the sisters are born, I help raise them."

He squinted a little. "And that's it? Nothing else for yourself? You get nothing you want? You can't leave?"

"I want to," she said a little too loud. "I mean, I've thought about it, but it's just like you said. My staying is what's best for the group." She dipped her head.

"But it's not what's best for you."

No, it wasn't.

He sighed through his nose. "We should make a pact. If you help me negotiate my release for after the ceremony, you come with me. I'll help sneak you out. You can escape, go wherever you want."

She blinked. But Ascara... and the others... His words hung in the air. *Wherever I want?*

"You have plenty of sisters who can help with the new ones after the ceremony, right?"

She nodded slowly. She had dreamed, she had wondered. Could it be a reality?

The solid edge of the counter stabbed her side. She had been leaning over and toward him. How did he do that? How did he lure her in so easily?

His finger slowly pulled away.

She'd hate to think how close she'd have been if there wasn't an island counter between them. It was better this way. Let him complete the ceremony, get his freedom, and then maybe she could be free, too.

A clatter of metal echoed somewhere in the halls behind them.

She jumped up, practically leaping from the table.

He jerked back and crossed his arms.

"We need to go." She urged him toward the back door. "They shouldn't be awake, but we can't risk them walking in here."

He nodded, and they skirted back the long way to his room undetected.

His gaze lingered in the doorway to his room. At one point she thought he'd reach for her, but he didn't.

She wanted to do something for him, give him something.

"I'll be back tomorrow," she said. "I'll have a surprise for you."

He grinned. "A surprise?"

His smile was nice. Genuine. It made her smile. "Just be good and don't make anyone angry enough that they throw you into a cell again."

"I'll try."

She turned to leave.

"Nida."

She stopped and glanced over her shoulder.

His hands were behind his head, stretching his chest and stomach, even under his dirty shirt. "Come back soon?"

She nodded. *Not soon enough.*

CHAPTER 10

*N*ida hurried through the halls. She had waited all day to see Rowec and had been distracted by a million and one things she had to do in the garden to prepare for the hatching.

And my possible escape?

She cringed. Was she really wanting to escape? That sounded so negative. She just wanted to leave, to learn the stories of the outside world for herself.

First things first, she would see Rowec, and better yet, tonight she'd surprise him. An entire durlo garden just for him. This was going to be good. Great, even. He was going to love it.

She rounded the corner to the hallway with his room and found two of her sisters, Veridran and Crilla, standing guard outside.

"What's wrong? What happened?" she asked.

Veridran dipped her head at her. "Brynn is afraid he'll try to escape again. She ordered it."

Was he not able to leave, then? Could she not give him her gift? She wrung her hands. "But... Brynn told me to take him to the gardens for some food. I have her permission," she lied.

Crilla nodded to Veridran.

Please work. Please work.

"Fine," Veridran said. "You'll get one hour."

She bit back her smile. "I understand."

Waiting until they'd walked down the hall and turned the corner, she rushed inside.

Rowec was pacing and rubbing his head. His face was flushed. Some of his furniture had been rearranged.

"Rowec?"

He stopped and glanced up. "Nida!"

"Are you okay?"

"I, uh, was bored."

His green eyes eased on her as he approached, bringing the scent of... yes... the night. It was silly, but she'd finally placed what he smelled like, and he smelled just like the night air when she opened the oculus in the hatchery. A fresh, night breeze brought in from the jungle in one of her favorite places.

She cleared her throat in the silence. He did the same.

"I thought I'd get the chance to come sooner, but the hatchery, and then Ascara..."

He smiled. "It's fine. I was worried my... closeness... last night bothered you."

"Bothered me?" She half-laughed. "No, no."

Was he kidding? She'd wanted more. For learning purposes, purely, and not in any way breaking ancient Tialan traditions for her sister. If she kept telling herself that, the knot in her stomach might ease.

His stomach growled.

"Speaking of which..."

"Sorry, I'm starving." He took a step back.

"Are you ready for my surprise?"

He smiled, revealing his perfect smile. "Yes."

"It's a much shorter walk than to the kitchens."

"I'm in, but what about the guards?"

"They'll be back in about an hour. Plenty of time to stretch your legs and get something to eat."

He held out his elbow. She loved that, and how it brought them closer. Maybe that's why he did it? When she hooked her arm through his, he closed his eyes.

"What are you doing?" she asked.

"You said it's a surprise. I want to be fully surprised. I'll keep my eyes closed and everything. Just lead the way."

She grinned. "You *want* it to be a surprise?"

He nodded. "If it ends with you, some place out of this room, and something to eat... then, yes."

She bit her lip and led him through the golden hallways with the sconces lit and blazing. In a few weeks' time, the sconces would be snuffed. The temple would go dark for the hatching as every ceiling in the temple that could be opened would be to honor the new sisters.

"Oh!" *The festival.* How had she forgotten?

"*Oh?*" he asked, eyes still closed and letting her lead him.

"In a few days, we'll be holding the festival."

"A festival?"

"Yeah. It's to celebrate the hatching coming up. Life gets crazy after the sisters arrive, so we hold a festival and eat and dance before they bloom. We get dressed up and everything."

He grinned, eyes still closed. "Will I get to sneak out and see it?"

She sucked in air between her teeth. "Actually, you're the honored guest."

They continued through the winding corridors of the temple.

"Your people built this like a maze, didn't they?" he asked. "It's intentional."

"Yes. It was built a long time ago. We had an entire city. Time pushed us back into this one temple."

They silently made their way toward the northern section of the building.

"The air is moist here." He tilted his nose up.

"Yeah, we're nearly there."

Good thing he had closed his eyes, or he'd see the sweat on her forehead. To have him this close again…

His shoulder bumped into hers. His arm was stiff and stable. She swallowed.

The two grand doors carved from golden stone loomed above her. "Stick out your hand and help me push this open."

True to his word, he kept his eyes squeezed shut and stuck his arm out until he reached the door. Together they pushed, and the two doors swung apart revealing a lush durlo garden.

"Okay, open your eyes."

He blinked. "Holy—"

"You can have as much as you want. Well, as much as you can eat in an hour."

～

ROWEC FOUGHT the urge to run at full speed into the garden and gobble up as much as he could hold.

A garden, at least as wide as the temple, was covered in durlo trees. Their bright yellow orbs dangled from the branches— some so heavy, so sweet and filled with juices, that their branches dipped low from the weight of them. A pebbled walkway wound through the trees, dotted with fallen leaves. Under the moonlight, the dew on every single one of them glistened.

"May I?"

She giggled. "Absolutely. Go for it."

His stomach burned, his chest ached, and his mouth watered. He hadn't eaten a durlo since he'd been six. Hoisting himself up the nearest tree, he shook an entire branch as hard as he could. Two, three, four fruits fell down onto the path.

The smell was horrendous, already seeping out their foul-smelling odor. But if he pushed past the smell, which he had no problem doing, the reward was worth it.

He dug his nails into the rind and peeled it back. Sixteen sections of sticky, juicy white fruit waited.

"Oh man," he mumbled, chewing each piece as quickly as possible. "Why habn't oo eetn awny?"

She laughed and crossed her arms. "I'm not hungry."

He shrugged. "So, more for me?"

She nodded. "There's more than enough for the new sisters *and* you."

He swallowed and wiped the juice running down his chin. His pocket rustled. "Raz!" He nudged him out with sticky fingers. "Look, Raz! Durlos!"

Raz yawned and crawled out to his shoulder.

Rowec broke off little pieces for him, and the creature smacked on them loudly. "It'll take him all night to eat one piece."

Nida glanced down at her feet. "There's a fountain in the center if you'd like to wash up."

He glanced down at himself. Fruit splatters had already stained his shirt. His fingers and hands were covered in fibers and juice. He could only imagine what his face looked like. "Are you saying I'm not fresh and clean?"

She laughed and bit her lip. "I meant no insult, but…"

"But I'm covered in fruit juices like a child?"

She glanced away and shrugged, obviously fighting a smile.

"Are you laughing at me?" He grinned.

When she smiled, it warmed him. He loved making her happy.

"Then lead the way to the fountain. I wouldn't want to insult my kidnappers."

"Hah hah." She rolled her eyes but led him toward a fountain in the center.

Shaped like a flower bud, the fountain sprayed crystal-clear water into the air and collected in a wide base underneath it.

He dipped his hands in. Nice. Cool. Clean.

He scrubbed his hands and arms.

"You missed a spot." She pointed to his shirt.

He glanced down but was soon splashed with freezing water. "Gah!"

She giggled and darted around the side. "I'm sorry, but you had a stain right there, and you were ignoring it."

Raz ducked back inside his pocket with his fluffy white tail slinking in behind him.

Rowec grinned and cupped his hands in the water. If she wanted to play, he would play, but he'd win.

"I wasn't ignoring it. I was saving it for last!" He shoved an enormous wave of water in her direction, drenching her brown robes from shoulders to waist.

She gasped and stumbled back, dripping from her robes.

"I'm sorry. Did I get some on you?" he teased.

He shouldn't be making jokes. He shouldn't be playing like a child in the garden of his captors. But the moment was too perfect to pass up.

After both were successfully drenched, head to toe, he reached for a fruit and peeled back the rind. He dangled the fleshy fruit, teasing like he was going to throw it at her.

"Don't you dare." She lifted a shaky finger and backed away.

"Come on. The smell isn't *that* bad."

"Don't!"

"And if you eat it, it tastes really good..."

"Yes, I know, but it still smells terrible, it'll get all over everything—"

"It washes out."

She wrinkled her nose and reached for her own ammo of smelly durlo. Her teal eyes were alight. Her skin was smooth and damp. Her hair fell in soft tendrils around her face, dripping wet. The need to hold her and make sure she was warm came over him. It tugged his chest. He wanted to hold her, wrap her up, protect her.

He straightened and lowered his arm. He cleared his throat. Was he going crazy?

"I'm sorry," she said. "Did we take it too far?"

He barely shook his head. "Don't be sorry. It was fun. I was just... I was just lost in thought."

She lowered her arm, too, and tossed the fruit for him to catch. "About Etta? Your brother? Your home?"

No. He hadn't been thinking of any of that, and he should have been. "No."

She wrapped her skirt tighter around her legs, sat on the edge of the fountain, and crossed her arms.

He sat beside her, shoulder to shoulder. The air was merely cool, but she was shaking. He slipped out of his filthy top shirt and unbuttoned his dryer, cleaner undershirt.

She turned her eyes away.

Was she embarrassed he was undressing? Maybe living in a temple with only women had that effect? He clenched his jaw and fought a smile.

"Here." He put his undershirt around her and replaced his drenched one on himself.

"Thanks."

The gryllids chirped across the jungle just beyond the wall encasing the durlo garden. The fires crackled in their sconces.

"I'm glad you like the garden," she said.

He ran his hands through his damp hair, shaking out some of the droplets. "I love it. It's perfect. If I wasn't here against my will, you know—"

"Naturally."

"It'd be perfect."

She grinned and focused on her feet, digging the toe of her teal flats into the pebbles. "Are you..." She took a deep breath. "Were you *really* serious about helping me leave after the hatching?"

"Of course." Was she afraid he would back out? "I wanted to say..."

She met his gaze. Soft eyes the color of cascading pools in the Zchian tiered farms. Lips like... He cleared his throat. "You should come and live with me."

Her eyes widened, as did his.

It had just tumbled out. "In my village, I mean. Of course. I mean... you could just visit. Among other places, but if you needed a place to live, my village would be decent to visit."

"I don't think your villagers would like me."

"Too bad. Nida, if this whole ordeal has taught me anything, it's that my life can change in the blink of an eye. There's no use waiting for something to happen. There's no use worrying about what everyone else wants. They get to live their lives how they want, when they want, but we're supposed to do the honorable thing?"

She nodded. "I understand what you're saying, but we both care very much for our people. I *do* care what happens to my sisters, and if they'll be hurt if I leave. And what would I be leaving to? What would I be running toward? Freedom is good, but it's scary, too. I need something more than that."

More?

"Nida, I..." What was he going to say? How was it going to sound? "Nida, I care about you-r... your well-being. I want you to be happy. You deserve to be happy. And whatever it is you need to figure out, you can do it safely in my village." He swallowed. "Stay as long as you like."

She shrugged a shoulder against her cheek. "Somehow I don't think Etta would like that very much."

"I'm not marrying Etta."

She jerked her head in his direction.

"She might think so. The chief and some of the elders might think so, but I get a say in my life. I won't be trapped into something I don't care about or don't want. I was already planning on ending it, but our conversation the other night convinced me. I deserve to be happy, and so do you." He had never been surer of something. Being with Nida had given him that confidence.

She shook her head and stood. "I don't know. At one point, I believe someone referred to us as beasts." She grinned.

He squeezed some water from his shirt. "I was wrong. I was very wrong.

You're far from it. If it helps, *Etta* is a beast. Anyone who uses and manipulates others, hurts others, or makes them feel bad for who they are is a beast."

She dipped down and picked up a chalky pebble from the path. "I haven't met her, so maybe *you* just think she's a beast."

"No. No, I swear! Do you want proof?" He scratched the stubble on his jaw. It was hard to just pick one story. How could he sum up a lifetime of terrible deeds? "When we were kids, she stole one of our classmate's lunches because she just felt like it. It was during a drought. No one had much to eat that year."

She tilted her head side to side and nibbled on her lip. "That is pretty bad. But you were children, and sometimes children can be cruel. They're learning. That doesn't count."

"Okay." He held up a finger. "Just last year, we had some flooding. Her place, which we all nearly broke our backs building to her exact specifications, was plenty out of the way from the flooding. Some of the homes lower in the valley, however, were being swept away."

She stopped and glanced up at him.

"Etta demanded that my brother and I stop helping them and help her with a tiny leak in her roof before it ruined her dresses."

She sucked in. "That's... not good."

"I told you."

"But I don't think anyone is inherently good or bad," she said. "I think we make bad choices, either because we're misguided, or misinformed, or misunderstood. I think we can become terrible if we don't focus on what's good."

He twisted the ends of his shirt to get the last bit of water out. "That sounds like Etta."

"Etta is making a terrible choice to force you into a marriage she wants," she said. "Maybe she's doing it because she genuinely believes you'll be happy. One day."

He grumbled. "What about Drathella? She abuses you. She hates you."

She took a deep breath, twirling the pebble over and over in her hand.

He stood and joined her.

"Drathella is a tough one," she said. "She's scared. Scared of things being different, of more sisters like me and unlike her. Scared of being alone. Scared of us going extinct."

"And that's an excuse?" He pointed to her palm. "You're wearing down that pebble to nothing."

She smirked and dropped it, dusting her hands off on her earthen robes. "Drathella is misguided. She makes *beastly* decisions. It's whether or not she learns from them."

"Nida, I..." Her words, her faith in others, stabbed him. He'd never treated his captives or enemies with that much... humanity.

"We should get back before we get in trouble." She turned away, but he reached for her shoulder. She slowly turned back to him.

She was so close. Just right there. Her lips parted.

How had he missed it? She was beautiful. All of her. "Thank you. Thank you for bringing me here, talking to the queen, and caring for me. I never would have treated my captives with the same grace."

He wanted to do whatever she needed. Help her sisters, have some silly private dinner with Brynntial, help Nida escape, chase away anyone who looked her way with disgust. She deserved so much more.

"You're—" Her eyelids dropped. "You're welcome."

"Will I see you tomorrow?" He hadn't meant for it to come out so desperate.

She smiled as she slowly backed away. Had she wanted to linger there longer with him? Closer? "Tomorrow. Yes, of course, I'll come see you tomorrow."

CHAPTER 11

*R*owec had been lounging on a bright purple chaise, tossing some sort of round, red egg in the air and catching it, for at least an hour.

There were only a couple weeks left until the ceremony, and his stupid brother still hadn't made his way back to even *try* to rescue him.

But the more he thought about it, the more thankful he was that his brother hadn't arrived yet. He wasn't sure he wanted to go.

No. I want to go home, but...

Not yet.

He wanted Nida to leave, too, but she wouldn't want to leave before the ceremony. If his brothers showed up before the hatching, he couldn't tell them to wait a few weeks at the temple, and it wasn't exactly the best idea to tell them to turn around and come all the way back in a few weeks, either. Then again, having an army of Zchi warriors arriving at Brynntial's temple would probably help him convince her of his release after the ceremony.

He groaned and put the egg down before he crushed it out of frustration.

Checking the moon through the holes in the ceiling, it was clear it had gotten late. Much later than any other time Nida had visited. Where could she be? Maybe Drathella had stopped her, or that other one that seemed nicer —Ascara?

Etta had surrounded herself with plenty of other women to keep her occupied, but that was mostly to let them obsess over how she looked. Maybe even Tialans fell prey to the same worries. He chuckled thinking about them fretting over their scales.

Still no Nida. Not even the footsteps or the little chatter of the younger

Tialans running off to do chores. Even the hall seemed more silent than normal.

He made for the exit and poked his head out.

His guards weren't there. In fact, the halls were entirely empty. Not one sound echoed up the corridor. Where had they gone? Maybe they assumed Nida would be there?

Ascara had mentioned that his room was near the hatchery, hadn't she?

He could go look and not take *too* many turns. He'd have to memorize the path he made, but he should be able to manage, considering he wasn't running for his life this time.

He inched out of his room toward the right side. The golden hall went on for about thirty feet and turned a sharp left. No other options, he poked his head around the corner.

All clear. Not a spirit around.

He considered calling out, but that would be dumb. The last thing he needed was some screaming Tialans when they realized he was snooping around. He'd be locked back down in the cell for sure.

He stepped carefully down the only hall to the left, ears tuned to the sound of anyone coming, until he was presented with a choice to turn right or keep going straight.

Straight ahead was the same old corridor as all the others. To his right, two large golden doors carved with swirls of reptiles with long tails and wings intertwined with flowers waited. If he had just happened on the temple, he'd assume there was treasure behind those doors. No one builds something that fancy to block a regular old room with boring stuff inside.

He scanned the halls one last time for anyone who might be coming and headed for the decorated doors. Hands against the cool, shiny rock, he pressed until a mechanism clicked and the bottom of the door swung open.

A new scent hit him immediately. Sweet and aromatic like the scented oils the village women traded with one another. He stepped inside, inhaling the smell of fresh flowers, but had to watch his feet around vines and leaves.

The door clicked behind him.

He glanced up and found himself in an indoor garden with hundreds of white, luminescent bulbs sprawled along the floor. Each one was pulsing in the moonlight pouring in from the small opening in the center. A Tialan, happily talking to herself as she bent over the flowers, popped up and faced him.

"Nida?"

"Rowec! What are you doing here?" She hopped around the vines and buds to close the distance between them. "You shouldn't be here. You need to leave!"

"I thought you were coming to visit me."

She acted as if she might push him out. Instead, she stopped and stared up at him with big teal eyes.

"I was, but I got tied up with Ascara. I was hurrying to do this before I came to you."

"I'm sorry—"

"How did you get here? What happened to the guards?" She was panting, her voice barely registering above a whisper, so he lowered his.

"They were gone. No one was there." He glanced around again, the large white buds pulling his attention. "Is this the hatchery? These are your sisters?"

She looked around the room and then back at him with a palm smoothing back the hair near her eyes. "Yes, but—"

"They're beautiful." He slowly stepped around the foliage to the nearest bud and knelt. He placed his ear against one, feeling the warmth against his cheek and hearing the pulse of something inside. Twice the width and height of his hand, he placed his palm against the closed petals.

Something knocked from inside.

"What? What was that?"

She sighed and knelt beside him. "Rowec, my unborn sisters. Sisters, this is Rowec."

How was this possible? "But you're not flowers. You're rep—" His eyes met hers. Maybe it was better not to finish that sentence.

"We might be Tialans, but we're descendants of the first Life Weavers. Before us, were... well, plants. Plants were the first Life Weavers, taking energy and materializing things from the sun."

He had heard of this before, but it was in ancient texts and supposed myths. Lousha had all the Conductors at one time. It had been the birthplace of all Conducting. His people never bothered to learn how or why since they couldn't do it themselves. Today, only Fire Breathers lived in Lousha, though there were rumors of Wind Speakers and Water Shapers in other lands. But Life Weavers as plants?

"That's not... that's not—"

"Possible? But it is, and I'm their keeper."

He shook his head and reached for the bud again. "There's life in every one of these? A—"

"Tialan-human heiress? Yes, in every one." She slowly circled the garden, caressing buds as she passed. "Our queens used to find a Tialan mate, then courted him, all things you'd expect. But the males died out. All the buds have come out female for several generations. We've been forced to seek out a mate for the queen every hatching, and humans are plentiful."

He lifted his gaze to meet hers from across the garden.

She shrugged a shoulder. "Honestly, Brynn should have found someone suitable a long time ago. Someone understanding and willing. But she didn't.

We're running out of time because Brynn was hard-headed and didn't want to gain any favor with humans."

He ran his palms around another bud, cradling the weight. It thrummed with heat, with light, with a— "Is that a heartbeat?"

She nodded.

It was... incredible. Remarkable. Life literally blossoming in his hands. A living, breathing, magical creature waiting to be born.

"Want to help?" She moved to a mechanical arm protruding from the wall.

"What does that do?"

"Come find out."

He stepped over the vines and even more carefully around the buds, opposite her at the lever. "Lift it?"

"Yes."

It took a little effort to push it up with both hands, but it slid into place several inches higher with a click.

The ceiling rumbled and slid apart into several pieces, expanding the opening to allow all of the moonlight to beam down onto the indoor garden.

Okay, some of her sisters needed to work on their bedside manner, but this place was a miracle. Even he couldn't dispute that.

"It's beautiful," he murmured.

"It's officially called *The Sanctuary*, but most of us just call it the hatchery."

"Which one will be a queen? Or is that something you won't know until after they grow up?"

She half-laughed. "Actually, it was decided by first budding."

First budding? She says that like it's normal. "So, which one?"

She paced around the edge, eyes roving over the hundreds of buds. "Well, see, that's the thing—"

He squinted at her, but she wouldn't look him in the eye.

"Right now, the queen is that one." She pointed to the bud in the very center soaking up the most moonlight. "Last night, it was that one." She pointed across the room to one in a darkened corner.

"I don't get it."

"So, the more moonlight, sunlight, and water, you get while budding makes you a better Tialan."

He stared at her.

"Makes you *more* Tialan."

Oh.

"Ensures you are *less*... human... after the human helps with the ceremony."

He nodded once. "I see. But you're moving them?"

She nodded, finally meeting his gaze. "I'm not supposed to. But I didn't think it was fair that the queen should get the most of everything while others sat in the dark, waiting to feel different once they're born." She crossed her arms. "I just keep moving them around so they all get an equal chance. The day they hatch, it'll be completely random. They can decide who will be queen when they're older." She stood beside him, solid, sure. "If Brynn had been a little more realistic, we could have had better relations with humans. Our species may have never been in danger. But because of where she grew, she makes all the decisions and could have doomed us all. And..."

"And?"

"And this is why I can't leave until they're born. I want to see that they make it, that we won't die out, and that they get a real chance at equality."

She had seen the flaws in the system, her own sister leeching off power and control from a society that needed balance and love, as well as connections with the outside world to survive. And here, she had scavenged power her sisters didn't even know she had. She was playing with the outcome of the next generation right beneath their noses. And he respected it.

"Which one was originally the queen?" he asked.

She bit her lip, peered around, and pointed to one bud among a cluster receiving very little moonlight. "I'm not sure. I've done it every night. Maybe that one."

He stepped through the garden to the one bud currently in the center. He put his hands around its waxy petals. She joined him.

"And if I don't..."

She flattened her lips. "They die," she whispered. "No other sisters will ever bud again. We'll become extinct."

He swallowed. An entire species would die? "How often do you get... new sisters?"

"I've only been alive for one hatching, but I was little. The queen and her mate were so in love, they left to explore Lousha together after."

His gaze lifted to hers.

"Brynn was the next queen in line. Since you're not in love with each other, I imagine Brynn will stay queen until one of these is old enough to take over."

"And the last queen and her mate made these buds?"

She giggled. "No. The jungle did."

The what?

"We nourish and help the jungle, and it provides the buds for us. The queen and her mate just bloom them."

He swallowed. "How often does the jungle... give you... the, uh, buds?"

"The jungle decides. These took several years after the last hatching to show up."

"And how long have you been caring for them?"

Her eyes roamed lovingly over the closed petals, petting and soothing them. "Seven years. I was only fifteen when Brynn gave me this job."

His jaw dropped. "Seven? Seven years? And they all hatch in about a week?"

Her fingers grazed over his hands, still pressed against the bud. "With your help."

His heart thudded. His palms itched to smooth her soft hair, radiant in the blue glow.

Even if his brother showed up tomorrow, there'd be no way he could just leave Nida's future sisters behind. He'd have to go through with the ceremony —he *wanted* to go through with it.

No wonder they'd caged him. They *were* desperate. No wonder Nida had saved him in the jungle during his escape.

But it wasn't just the future Tialans he worried about. He worried for Nida. She needed this, too. She wanted to give them equality, and she deserved to see her plan through. Her cause was just, thoughtful. She deserved to be happy. She deserved everything.

His fingers smoothed over hers. "Nida, I want you to know that no matter what, I'll stay for the ceremony."

She threaded her fingers through his. Though they had the bud between them, their hands were together. They were holding hands, and spirits, did he want to hold *her*.

"Why do you say it like that?"

He took a deep breath. "I'm worried. My brother swore he'd come back for me. I thought he'd be back by now, but if they come, I'm not leaving until the ceremony. I want to help you. Not Brynntial. Not Drathella. I want to help *you*."

She smiled. "Rowec, I don't know what to say."

He bent forward, focused on the light pink of her lips. The taste of her right there.

She cleared her throat and pulled back. "I'm sorry, I have to... I want to... We need to get you back to your room."

So close. She had been so close.

She had to feel the same way, didn't she? She had threaded her fingers through his hands and had leaned in, as well. She... needed to know how he felt.

There was that festival she'd mentioned coming soon. She'd said he was the guest of honor. Maybe he could tell her then.

"Help me," she said, calling his attention from his daydream. She had begun to slide the vines and buds around the room. "Move them. Just be careful and move them around."

"But—"

"Be quick. I'm already behind."

He glanced around the room. Where should he start?

"Get moving!"

He grabbed the most center bud and moved her out of the moonlight. "Sorry."

No matter how many he shuffled around, he feared they'd tip over or tear. But they moved fairly easily without any mishaps.

He reached around a smallish bud, a runt compared to the others, and gently pushed her to the very center. "There you go, little one. Grow big and strong."

The door slammed open.

"What in the world are you doing?" Drathella's voice boomed into the chamber.

CHAPTER 12

*N*ida jerked upright. Her stomach turned over. *Oh no.*

"What were you doing? You wretched little slitherskin!" Drathella glided across the floor at record speed with a hand lifted to smack her across the face.

Nida curled away and squeezed her eyes shut. She heard a slap but felt nothing.

She dared to open one eye. Drathella's hand hovered inches from her face.

Rowec had caught Drathella by the wrist, his body tall and strong before her. His fingers had wrapped all the way around her sister's wrist and froze her in place.

Without a word he'd stepped between them, commanding Drathella's full attention. Nida had to peer around him to see her sister's reaction. If it wasn't the most awkward moment already, it would have been hilarious. A full-blooded human touching Drathella. Her bulging eyes, her dropping jaw. Even if Nida paid for it later, this made it worth it.

"Let go of me, you filth!" Drathella squawked.

Rowec didn't move.

"Get out of my way, human. This doesn't concern you," she snarled.

"On the contrary, I believe this room has everything to do with me." His tone was dark, deep, and laced with warning. "Isn't that why I'm here?"

Drathella tried to wrench her hand free.

He didn't loosen his grip.

Drathella's dark blue gaze slid to her. "Brynn will lose her mind when I tell her—"

"Tell her what, exactly?" He leaned over in an attempt to block Drathella's view. "Tell her how you stormed in where you weren't wanted and threatened to hit the queen's sister?"

"You touched the buds. Both of you. You" — she eyed Nida — "are a traitor to this temple."

"What's wrong with touching the flowers?" Rowec asked, his hand still holding Drathella's wrist but higher. Every inch he lifted, she had to stretch higher on her toes, losing some of her control, her strength.

Drathella's gaze jumped back and forth between them. "They cannot be disturbed. They—"

"They will be my family, too, I believe," Rowec said.

If Drathella could crawl out of her skin, she would have. Even Nida recoiled at Rowec's response. There was no way Drathella would accept that answer.

"How dare you!" Drathella's nostrils flared as she lifted her free hand, claws out.

Rowec caught the second hand and twisted her around until both were behind her back. She was completely under his control.

Nida swallowed. She didn't *truly* fear what he could do to Drathella. He would have killed her before if he'd wanted to. But his strength. His sense of control over it. A calming nature oozed out of him. He resonated power, real power, not fistfuls of it like her sister tended to grab.

He was in his element. This was something he had done several times. Fighting? War? He had said he was his village's lead warrior. Maybe Drathella wasn't exactly an equal, but his composure and confidence matched his claim.

And it was all to protect her. Her heart skipped a beat.

"They are *my* sisters!" she shrieked. "They are Tialan. Not human—"

"Oh, we both know that's not true. Now, I don't know about your culture and customs, but in mine, the young are cherished. We talk to them, we sing to them, we hold them. What you saw when you walked in here was me understanding what your queen is asking of me—"

"You expect me to believe that—ah!"

He jerked his hands and squeezed her tighter. His knuckles had gone white. "I snuck in here, I demanded she tell me what's going on, and I suggested we hold the flowers."

He was lying for her.

Drathella growled. "You worthless skin-bag of—"

"Considering the fact you need my worthless skin-bag to save these sisters you pretend to care and worry about so much, I'm going to ignore your insults and tell you what you're going to do instead." He leaned in close, lips near her temple. "You're going to leave and never come into this room again unless Nida gives you permission—"

"You don't make the rules in *our* temple!"

"If you break this rule," he continued as if she hadn't said a word, "I'll tell Brynntial how much you like to mistreat your sisters and me, and I will walk out and leave them all to die."

Nida's heart plummeted. There was no way Drathella would keep that promise. And what about all the things he'd just said about "staying no matter what?"

Drathella grunted.

He squeezed her arms back tighter. "Do you understand me?"

Without a peep, she nodded furiously.

He let her go by shoving her toward the doors.

Drathella wheeled her arms as she dashed through and out of the garden, surely to tell Brynn what had just happened.

Nida took a deep breath. What he'd done for her, what he'd said... "Rowec, I—"

He spun and put his hands on her shoulders. "Are you okay?"

His grip startled her; it was firm but careful. She blinked once. Twice. "Y-yes, I'm fine. You stopped her before she—"

"Don't ever let her try to hurt you again, please."

She shook her head. "I don't really get a choice."

"You do. Don't take that from her. If she touches one... one scale on you, I'll—"

"You'll what? You told her you'd leave if she comes back—"

"I was lying, Nida." He ran a hand through his hair and took a deep breath. "First of all, I already promised you I'm staying no matter what. And let's not forget that your bigger sisters would tie me up before I even make it out the front door." He took a step closer and lifted his hand to her chin. "I just said it to scare her."

Too close. He was too close. If she let herself stay there like that with him, she'd betray Brynn. And if Brynn found out... No. Brynn wouldn't risk losing the sisters this close to the hatching. She couldn't... right?

But she wasn't supposed to have a mate or a *human pet* as Ascara had put it. She was not to fall in love... and yet, he was touching her chin, standing close enough that she could smell the fruits he had eaten earlier, mixed with a rustic note.

"She won't believe you." She swallowed. She hadn't stepped back. She hadn't pulled away, and she had better. Soon. Before she... before she...

Her arms and hands lifted to rest against his chest and stomach, as solid as the Tialan rock around them. She fought the urge to place her head against him there, to be as close as possible.

She wanted to tell him how badly she wanted to be with him. Seeing him had become the best part of her day, and he clearly enjoyed being with her.

"Doesn't matter," he whispered. "We just need the queen to believe me."

She nodded. That was true. Brynn could keep Drathella in her place.

His fingers hadn't left her face. In fact, they traveled. They caressed her cheek, her ear. He grazed the few teal scales by her temple with the back of his hand, and they sparked with a tingling that ran all the way down to her toes. There was no moving. There was no saying no. She wanted to be with him. She wanted to be in his arms...

He pulled away. "I meant what I said, Nida. No matter what, I'll help you."

The warmth of him that she hadn't noticed before was now gone. It followed him as he headed for the doors of the hatchery.

She bounded over her sisters to him, running after him. She wasn't ready for him to leave yet. "I'll get you back to your room. If anyone sees us, I'll just say I took you on a tour."

He stopped, one hand on the door. "This festival you mentioned before..."

She nodded.

"Will you... Will you be at the festival?"

She furled her eyebrows and smirked. "Of course."

He grinned. "I can't wait."

He *wanted* to see her at the festival? Were festivals in his village similar to theirs? Food, dressing up, dances? Her cheeks warmed at the idea of dancing with him.

She wouldn't be allowed. Brynn would be the one to dance with him, while all the other sisters just danced with each other.

But that would be okay. She'd see him dressed up. She'd see him smile and try to take in a Tialan world he didn't quite understand. She'd maybe even get to talk to him at the party.

Maybe after the festival, she could walk him back to his room, and they could dance where Brynn couldn't see.

Maybe after the party she could tell him how much she had come to care for him.

CHAPTER 13

*R*owec tossed and turned the entire night after his visit to the hatchery. He couldn't keep his mind from wondering about the festival, the party, Nida. He'd have his chance to tell her how he was feeling, how he truly felt.

And how did he feel? *Love?* That was ridiculous. But if it wasn't love, then it was something close. It swelled and called up to him as he laid still. It creeped into his thoughts when the morning light came. And if he didn't tell her, he'd burst.

His parents used to say love didn't just exist, it grew with time. He was pretty certain they were just trying to convince him to get over marrying Etta, but now…

This feeling consumed him the more he thought about it and grew Vigor in him. He could sow a whole tiered farm in an hour. He could climb a whole section of paratil trees for the fruit. He could train for hours until his body collapsed. Again.

He jumped up and started training for the second time in the last several hours. Unlike when he was in the cell, he had room to practice and objects to lift. Curls, squats, lunges, push-ups, peicha knife stances, stretching—anything to distract him from possibly bursting with this… this…feeling before he even had the chance to tell her.

Maybe he wouldn't wait until the festival. Maybe when she visited him in the next hour or so for their evening stroll to the kitchens or the garden, he'd tell her then.

Raz snored softly on a little green silk pillow, his limp tail curled around him.

Rowec sighed, picking at a serving platter on a nearby table. The moon's white glow reflected in the plain, flat surface of the dish. The moon had grown since he had first arrived. It was already over half-full.

"The queen will see you now for your dinner."

Startled by the sudden voice, he jumped and dropped the serving platter. It clanked against the stone floor and settled on a purple rug. A tall, bright-green Tialan stood in the entry to his room.

"Romantic dinner?"

He had nearly forgotten. The queen had agreed to meet with him, well over a week ago, and Nida had teased him that it might be something romantic.

He couldn't care less what the queen thought of their evening together, as long as he could negotiate his freedom for after the ceremony. And ultimately, Nida's.

The lime-colored Tialan nodded and turned to leave.

"I'm not having a romantic dinner with the queen, by the way. I'm interested only in diplomacy." He started after her, but she ignored him.

When he exited the room, she hooked her arm and claw under his armpit and pulled him down the hall.

"Wait. I can walk!" He strained against her hold but it was futile.

"I will help you escort him, sister." Another sky-blue Tialan guard joined her at his other arm.

Escort? More like dragged against my will.

"This is ridiculous. I don't need to be dragged like this. I've been walking with Nida. Where's Nida? She knows I can be trusted to walk. Talk to her!"

But they continued taking him through the maze, eventually leading him up a staircase and out onto a wide, open terrace.

The yellow-stone balcony was empty save for sprawling vines growing along the railing. Below was the jungle—a dense, dark-green blanket of trees with a cacophony of sounds. The Yvelkian mountains were just there in the distance, not too far. In the middle of the terrace, a dining table had a place setting for two. Goblets, metal pieces for probing food, green silk napkins with their ends lined in shimmering gold threads.

His chest fell.

A romantic dinner.

Brynntial really had intended this to be something more. Whatever delusions the queen had, he'd behave. He could be tactful, but he would get his freedom.

If he ignored the boldness of the queen's expectations, the scenery was actually perfect. The mountains on the horizon were cooler and drier than this place. The night breeze would be winding its way over his people's farms and through their homes. The men would be smothering the day's fish harvest in salt over a fire. The women would be peeling vegetables to roast. The younglings would be grinding seed for the bread while fighting over the mallets.

His stomach growled and burned, but his heart ached more.

His feather-filled bed. The ovens warming his feet. The songbirds in the brush. The sweet smell of herbs and oils.

"Good evening."

Rowec spun and met the gaze of a tall, shimmering green Tialan in a matching dress cinched high on her waist. Brynntial?

Gold jewelry dangled through her red hair and down her arms. Gold chains were looped around her waist several times. The green scales on the side of her face and arms glistened in the moonlight with gold accents. Her bright, big eyes were lined in gold and green paints.

Rowec's stomach turned and his shoulders sagged a little. How could she be serious? A romantic evening with him? Some personal, alone-time with his captor? She was clearly insane.

Nida followed shortly after and stood at her side; he smiled at her.

Nida looked like Nida. Earthen-dyed robes to match her smaller-than-Brynntial's teal eyes. Her auburn hair tossed over her part casually. Her hands—not claws—folded neatly in front of her.

She was a breath of fresh air. A reminder he wasn't crazy and imagining this place. The steady object to stare at when being spun and made dizzy.

If she had been made up for the date, would she have worried about her clothes?

I'd like to see her in anything.

The thought came from nowhere and rocked him. He gripped the back of the chair for stability.

She gave him a slight grin but went right back to stoic indifference.

"Please, sit." Brynntial motioned for the chair opposite hers.

He did as he was told and pulled his eyes away to the queen. "Brynntial, correct?"

She pulled her lips back revealing several teeth. A smile?

He shuddered.

"Yes, that's correct. And you are... Rowan? Rhode? Rydia?"

"Rowec."

She nodded and lifted her glass. "Forgive me. Of course, Rowec." She wasted no time drinking the contents. "I hope you don't mind. I brought Nida along in case we need a bit of translation."

He nodded and merely lifted the glass to his nose and sniffed. It was fermented, whatever it was, but it wasn't fruit. A vegetable, maybe? Rotting carcass? He sat the glass back on the table.

"I trust that you've been treated well?"

He cleared his throat. "Nida has treated me very well, yes."

Brynntial's pupils contracted a little. "She mentioned your previous living quarters were not suitable for you."

He glared. Previous *living* quarters? Not suitable? If that's how she wanted to play this, then to hell with playing this game of proper chit chat. "A dungeon is hardly living quarters for your non-prisoner guest," he bit.

She leaned back slightly as her clawed hand rested at her collarbone. "Forgive me. I was indisposed. I was not aware they put you in a dungeon. That's why when Nida came and told me, I approved you to be moved immediately."

"She's the only one who's treated me decent—"

"You must understand. We're not used to humans, and several of my sisters are quite bitter about their role in our survival—"

"And I don't care."

Brynntial blinked and straightened her spine. "You are a strong one, aren't you?" Her eyes shot sideways to Nida, but Nida's emotionless face remained steadfastly staring at nothing in front of her.

Brynntial wanted to play games; he needed to get to the point. "You kidnapped my brother. I took his place. I want to discuss my freedom."

"He stole."

"A piece of fruit."

Brynntial tilted her head. "And the punishment—"

"Was to kill him. Your-your guards—your sisters—held their claws to his throat. They were going to kill him. I traded places with him to save his life. Then, I'm dragged here and locked up all over a piece of fruit."

"I know punishment can be hard to deal with, but you chose to—"

"It's only thanks to Nida I'm not dead right now. Your other sister would have let me starve and die of thirst."

Brynntial took a deep breath. "I hardly believe that she would have—"

"Then I find out you want to use me as some life source for the future of your species." He wouldn't give her the satisfaction of coloring what had happened whatever way she wanted. He knew why he was kept for some measly piece of fruit, and he wouldn't let her think she had one over on him.

Brynn blinked several times and turned toward Nida.

Rowec followed her focus.

Nida's gaze faltered, dropping slightly.

Had he gotten her in trouble? Was she not supposed to tell him why the queen wanted to keep him there? Had Drathella told the queen what had happened in the hatchery?

Damn. Knowing that wretch, she probably had.

His stomach tightened, hands curling into fists. This wasn't what he had intended. He needed to get the focus back on him and his freedom. *And Nida's.*

He needed to remember that. His freedom meant her freedom, too.

Brynntial took another sip from her glass and smacked her thin lips. "I apologize for your treatment and what you've been informed of. Nida should not have discussed the ceremony with you."

His brain stopped. What had she just said? "You're apologizing to me for learning why you've kept me? You're apologizing because I found out?"

"Well—"

"You're not apologizing for using me. You're apologizing that I'm finding out about you using me." He stood, accidentally kicking the chair back behind him.

She jumped and stood in return. "Rowan, please."

"It's Rowec," he barked. "You want to use me, force me to stay however long you want, and you don't even know who I am. I am Rowec of the Zchi Village. I am a warrior. And if you kill me, my people will come for you."

Brynntial sat back down, unimpressed.

The gall. The confidence. She had manipulated his brother's small misstep into a massive boon for her family. And she looked damn near pleased with herself over it, too.

If she wanted to test what the Zchi warriors could do, then let her. They'd come for him, eventually. They were probably already on their way there.

The guards caught his eye. They had moved forward, no doubt to settle him down or remove him if necessary.

"Please," Brynntial whispered, "let's sit and have a meal. We are both capable of discussing this diplomatically."

He shook his head but sat nonetheless. He was really starting to hate that word. Maybe he wasn't meant for being *diplomatic.* Maybe his brother had been right, and fighting was all he'd be good for.

Ascara brought out their plates of food and smiled at him. He caught her nudging Nida on her way out, but Nida remained still and didn't react.

"Rowec, I'm terribly sorry. I'm just as flustered as you are. Can you blame us?"

Yes. He poked at his dinner.

The same slug parts and juices filled his stone plate. He could never eat this grub, seeing as the urge to vomit was already giving him trouble. He took the second goblet of water and guzzled it down.

"I have to be honest," Brynntial said. "For someone from the Zchi Village, I had not expected this sort of response."

He pushed his plate away an inch, more as a show of refusal than anything else. "What does that mean?"

"You're a fighting clan. Everyone knows that. Before the treaty, you kept all the Yvelkians in line with your strength—"

"You know about the treaty?"

"And yet," she continued, "you're surprised that we've kept you prisoner? You would do the same if the others crossed into your lands, let alone stole from you."

She wasn't wrong, but it wasn't the same. There was a difference. "What do you know about the treaty? Are you part of it?"

She took a tiny bite of her meal. "I know that the treaty is the only thing keeping all of you petty humans alive. Please, for just a moment, consider this situation from my perspective," Brynntial said. "We are a dying people. You know what it's like as a warrior to have your people's lives in your hands, yes?"

Yes.

"You'd do *anything* to save them, wouldn't you?"

Yes.

She rested her elbows on the table and folded her hands neatly behind her plate. "Now, imagine all you have to do is give up something—say, your life—to save them. Would you do it?"

Without question.

She closed her eyes as if understanding the meaning behind his lack of a response. "Now, imagine that was only a temporary solution. If you could sacrifice just one more life along with yours, you could save an entire genera-tion. You'd never take another life. Only yours and the one necessary to save your people. Would you do it?"

Against their will? The rules of war were different. This wasn't the same. He wasn't at war with the Tialans until they'd kidnapped his brother. He wouldn't ask another clan's member to give up their lives to save his own people. It would be cruel. "No."

Brynntial bristled. "No?"

"I would never take another life without their agreement. Our fighters get the choice."

Brynntial's nostrils widened as she inhaled. "Your kind has murdered your own a million times over. I'm trying to create life, and your kind is deter-mined to remove it until there's a winner!" Her voice had risen. Frustrated? Surprised?

"That's not what I meant—"

"I've seen what your kind is capable of!" She tossed her napkin to the table. "You kill randomly—"

He shook his head. "Not random. We kill out of necessity. Kill or be killed."

"Are you sure there's a difference?"

He dropped his hands to the table and rose. "It wasn't right, but those men volunteered for the fight—"

"All of them?"

No. He had told Nida himself. He had trained them since they were little. It was their way of life.

She smacked her lips. "Then there's no difference—"

"At least they were fighting for something they believed in."

"And I'm fighting for my family's lives!" She squinted at him. "We're not even going to slaughter you. We just need you to stay through the ceremony."

"Well, I'm not going to play along with this romantic dinner under some grand illusion that I fall in love with you and never leave!" His hands flew as he spoke, the fury had grown full strength to the edge of his patience. Soon, the guards would step in.

Brynntial's eyes widened as if she had been stabbed by the metal prong she had been gripping. "You should ask your elders about diplomacy."

He bent across the table at her. He had to stay on topic. "For the most part, I've behaved, and it's only thanks to Nida that I've not hurt your disgusting sisters or run away again. I will stay for the ceremony, but I want my freedom!"

Brynntial shot a piercing stare back and forth between Nida and him. Suddenly, she stood, slamming her hand on the table. "Diplomatically? Considering that I'm speaking with a murderous Zchi warrior, we should consider ourselves so lucky to be alive," she snarled. "How many clans have you decimated all for control?"

He swallowed. Where was this going? This wasn't the topic—

"How many?" she demanded, "Because I know, *and* I know that you and your kind *don't* handle things diplomatically."

He was never proud of what the Zchi had accomplished. The lives lost. The blood staining the fields until the next rains. And he had been responsible for some of the most heinous of crimes—slaughtering *anyone* in his path.

He closed his eyes and sighed. That was long behind him.

"But we're too *beastly*, though? Hmm?" Brynntial took a deep breath. "We bring life to this jungle, sustenance your people rely on, but we're the lowly slitherskins?" Her words slid out between clenched teeth. She hated him, or so it seemed.

Perhaps this was as much her diplomatic approach at working with him for the sake of the ceremony as it was his.

"You lie to yourselves," she continued. "Your entire species is a lie. *We're* not the beasts."

He rubbed his jaw and forehead and sought Nida's reaction, but she was fixated on her feet. Had the truth about him and his people hurt her feelings? Had he ruined his chance at helping her?

After an extended silence, Brynntial took another deep breath, more sigh than anything else, and closed her eyes. "Perhaps we are both too emotional. Rowec, I apologize for the way Drathella cared for you. I apologize for the way you learned about our hatching ceremony. Let's postpone this until after the pre-hatching festival. I believe that we can at the very least get along. We both could stand to make a little bit more of an effort."

He shook his head. He couldn't give her any more room. He had to put his pieces into play. "I want my freedom after the ceremony."

She scoffed. "That's just not—"

"I want my freedom after the ceremony." This time he said it louder, stronger. He wouldn't mention Nida. She could escape with him if she still wanted to, and she could go wherever she wanted to get away from here— even if it meant not with him.

There was a long pause, before she finally said, "Fine."

He squinted at her. "Fine?"

"Fine. After the ceremony, you can have your freedom. You may walk out of here freely."

This time she had a real smile, a genuine attempt instead of just a wide mouth with teeth. Why was she being so simple about this? Why the sudden flip?

Something was off. She was hiding something.

"You're lying," he whispered. "You're keeping something from me. What is it? As soon as the ceremony is over, you'll kill me? You'll lock me up back in the cell? What is it?" he demanded.

Brynntial's smile turned smug. "Out. Take him out now."

The guards dug their claws into his biceps and began dragging him out.

Nida lifted her chin and a finger as if to speak, but quickly dropped them as he passed. Her eyebrows were furled together. Worry had been etched in the creases around her mouth.

She probably hated him now. She probably didn't want to escape with him even if he figured out how—and he would. He had said too much, an utter failure on all counts and never focused on what was important. He had practice hiding his physical weaknesses while fighting, but mental games? He'd shown too much, gave Brynntial too much information about himself by losing his temper so easily.

Brynntial had been right. His people were murderous. That's why he had been set on not being a warrior but a more diplomatic leader, and he'd failed his first test.

And then there was Nida. A safe spot for his mind to rest, she was his anchor. His point of focus.

His guards dumped him back into his room. Raz popped his head up, evaluating the disturbance.

Rowec stumbled but recovered quickly to face them.

One purple-scaled, the other yellow.

He'd start keeping track of guard duty changes now, measuring up who was weakest or newest at their post, and after the ceremony, make for his escape.

CHAPTER 14

*N*ida took three deep breaths and followed Brynn down the narrow, golden hallway to her room.

Rowec had looked so concerned when he'd passed. It was fury when he'd looked at Brynn, but concern when the glint in his eyes had caught hers as he was being hauled off.

She groaned.

She knew the humans weren't perfect and could be cruel. But she also knew that generalizations were just that. She was part human and had none of those murderous tendencies her sisters talked about so much. And neither did Rowec.

Rowec had seemed embarrassed, defensive, and he'd had no reason to be. He'd already proven that he—that humans—were more than what Brynn had wanted to make him out to be.

The way Brynn had spoken. She didn't respect humans. She used them. They were a resource to her as much as the gold jewelry in her hair and the Tialan stones beneath her feet.

Rowec was good. There was good in his heart. She had seen it when he glanced at her in that hallway the first night. She had seen it in every lingering smile and touch. In the way he'd taken her hand after his jungle escape, in his playfulness in the durlo garden, in his tenderness for the hatchery.

After tonight, he might have changed his mind about helping them, though. Her stomach felt heavy.

She had wanted to go to him, but it had been better to stay in her sister's good graces for the moment.

"Can you believe him?" Brynn paced in her private chambers. "To talk so poorly of me."

Nida bristled. "I think it went both ways."

Brynn blinked her large green pupils at her and held her hands out. "What? What are you even saying, Nida?"

She inhaled slowly. "I'm saying that… you insulted his entire species and insinuated he's a giant murderer, but expect him to have a romantic dinner with you and be okay with helping us?"

Brynn stopped and narrowed her stare. "Why are you concerned with what I said to him?"

"Well, I'm just saying that—"

Brynn waved her off and began pacing again, mumbling to herself about how much he knew. "He seemed prepared for this. You helped him too much."

Too much.

Had she been that obvious? Had Brynn been paying more attention than she'd realized?

She couldn't risk Rowec's safety—or the future of her unborn sisters—by getting any closer. She had to lie. "Brynn, I'm sorry. He was asking a lot of questions, and as you see he's very demanding—"

Her sister waved her hand at her again, dismissing the thought. "No, you're right. I can clearly see how demanding and abrasive he is. It's a wonder you were able to tolerate him. Oh, how did our great sister love her mate so much? Was he this… this… ruthless?"

"For some reason, I don't anger him as much."

"Well, I mean, considering." Brynn looked her over, clearly insinuating her human likeness.

Brynn had never been as cruel about her *situation* as Drathella. But she was never as loving as Ascara either. Brynn treated her like family, but only Ascara treated her as an equal.

"I think," Nida said, trying to relax her jaw, "he's just a bit frustrated. They don't like the same foods we eat or the things we drink. I think he's used to being out and active, and he's been cooped up inside this temple, and he's lonely. That's probably why he lashed out at you like that."

An excuse was good. Well, that and it was probably partially true. But his behavior was not just because of his hunger or boredom. If Brynn had seen him the first day…

Brynn stopped and gripped the back of her chair. "Yes, of course." She laughed. "Of course, that makes so much more sense now. I keep forgetting they're so primitive."

Nida cringed. "You could do better to consider them as equals, Brynn."

It had come off so flippant, so casual, she only caught her tone when

Brynn froze and glared at her. The pause growing until it filled the room with total silence.

"Are you falling for him, Nida?"

Her hands went clammy, and a sweat broke out across her brow. "What?" How in the world...? The heat from her cheeks enveloped her. She swayed but kept her hand on the back of a nearby chair for balance. "No. No, that's... that's ridiculous—"

"Agreed."

She snapped her mouth shut and swallowed.

"It doesn't matter." Brynn sauntered over to her cluttered vanity. "He can't escape until the hatching anyway. I'll make sure of that. Then after, it won't matter anymore."

It was true, he'd have a difficult time escaping, but... "Wait. Why won't it matter after the ceremony? You told him he'd be free."

Brynn flopped her arms dramatically and reached for a decanter of fermented juice and a glass. "Oh, you know."

Nida tilted her head and rounded the fluffy white bench between them. "No, I don't know. What happens after the ceremony, Brynn?"

Brynn lifted her eyebrows at her as she gulped from the goblet and plopped herself down into a large green chair. Some juice sloshed out and onto the bright yellow rug at her feet. "He dies. I die. We both die!"

Nida shook her head. Brynn was losing her mind. How was she already intoxicated from the juice? Had she started before dinner?

Nida yanked the cup from her hand. "What's wrong with you? You don't die. The last queen and her mate performed the ceremony, and then they left to explore Lousha together..."

Brynn's eyes lifted in a smile as she took the cup back and drank some more.

"Brynn." Her voice trembled. "Brynn, no. You said—"

"I walked her and her ignorant mate—"

"Ignorant? He didn't know?" she blurted. "They were in love!"

"Love makes you blind, Nida." Brynn's glare iced over. "I walked with them into the sanctuary, Sister did her Life Weaving, they vanished in a beam of radiant, lovely light, the new sisters hatched, and I became queen."

Brynn had said it as if recalling an honorable moment, but all Nida could see was a human, whose kind had been painted as evil and cruel and had unknowingly followed his love to death.

"You really should have figured it out, Nida."

Her jaw dropped. "What?"

"Well, *you* can't Life Weave worth a damn and nearly die doing it. Hatching a generation, saving the species, takes too much life. Of course we die."

"Brynn!" she shouted. "You've been lying to us... to all of us. All the previous queens, too? How have we not known? Why did you hide this?"

Brynn half-laughed. "Can you imagine? The great Life Weavers, the forgiving keepers of the jungle, murdering human men? We'd be—" She hiccuped.

"We'd be as terrible as the humans," Nida whispered, tears forming in her eyes. "The stories, the lies." She ran her hands through her hair. "So many lies—"

"To keep us going!" Brynn boomed, struggling to stand back up. "Our existence is at stake. We help those petty humans by providing for the jungle. They *need* us."

"And *we* need them! Now you're telling me that we capture humans and murder them to stay alive? And they don't even know they're doing it?" She tried to gain her composure but her heart, her reality, was unraveling.

Were they even worth saving anymore? If this is what they'd become, did they deserve to survive?

"Wait a minute!" Brynn lifted a shaky claw at Nida's face. "We don't capture humans. Their leaders send them willingly. Well, until recently—the bastards. Apparently, our pact with the Zchi elders needs to be revisited."

Nida gasped and leaned back. Rowec's people were in on it, and he didn't know?

"Oh, don't give me that look." Brynn rolled her eyes. "The humans had agreed to it."

"The humans who made the pact? Or the humans who were being sacrificed?"

Brynn shrugged.

It didn't matter. Rowec wasn't given the choice. Rowec didn't know. "You captured Rowec, took him against his will—"

"It's what's best for us!" Brynn wobbled and rested her arms on Nida's shoulders. "Our previous queens, me, we're all doing what's best. This is just the way it has to be, Nida."

She tossed Brynn's hands off her shoulders. "You lied to me, and then you let *me* lie to him. Who else knows? Am I the only one?"

Brynn shook her head.

"You've selected the next queen..." All her rearranging of the buds had been for nothing. She had been working toward equality, and the whole time it'd never mattered. "Who? Who is the next queen?"

Brynn grinned and refilled her cup. "A strong Tialan. One willing and able to do what's necessary when *her* time comes." Brynn patted her on the cheek. "Your heart is too big, Nida. You're too soft."

"Drathella?"

Brynn smirked.

"Brynn, how could you?" She closed her eyes, warm tears spilling down her cheeks. Everything would be more unfair, less equal. Now, all she wanted to do was run. Run out of her sister's room, out of this temple.

Rowec had been right to question Brynn's plan. He had known Brynn was keeping something from him, and Nida had been part of it—unknowingly.

But as much as she wanted to, she couldn't run. Not before, not now, not ever. Simply because she couldn't let this happen. Her sisters had to be born. Even if Drathella would be queen, they would be more equal than any other generation if she had anything to do with it. They could be better.

But the ceremony still required Rowec, and he couldn't suffer for them.

Maybe there was another way. Maybe the ceremony didn't have to take lives.

"Look at it this way." Brynn swallowed another sip and wiped the corner of her mouth. "Once the ceremony's over, you won't have to suffer being a rejected reject anymore."

Nida's eyes shot open.

"A rejected reject." Brynn sneered and put a clawed hand on her hip. "He was never going to love you, being part slitherskin and all. In fact, I think you get the worst end of the deal, my dear sister. At least I get to be worshiped as a goddess for saving our sisters and bringing them to life. You, on the other hand, don't get love, don't get adoration, don't get to bring back the sisters, don't get anything honorable."

She narrowed her glare. "Stop it—"

Brynn raised an eyebrow. "Even if everything was absolutely perfect after the ceremony and no one died, Rowec would just run right back home to his wretched human village and marry one of their prettier girls."

Nida slapped her across the face—hard. It echoed and stung her palm. She stepped back.

Brynn brought a hand to the red spot growing on her cheek, but she didn't utter another word.

Nida backed away and ran down the hall. She had to tell someone. At the very least she had to tell Ascara first. If there was another way to perform the hatching ceremony where no one died, they'd find it together. She had to.

Hallway after hallway, she darted. The oculus was open in the main hall, and the moonlight was streaming in, but some of her sisters were lighting sconces anyway.

She blew past them.

She needed to tell Rowec, too, but if she could figure out how to change the ceremony so that it didn't result in death, then she could tell him after she learned how.

She ran so fast that her bare feet slid across the smooth Tialan stone as she turned the corner toward her and Ascara's room. She gripped the walls for balance and dashed inside. "Ascara!"

Her sister had been seated at their shared vanity, fixing her violet-tinged hair. She jumped and spun. "What in the world? What is wrong with you?"

"I need your help, right now."

Without any hesitation, Ascara hopped off the stool and ran back through the hallways with her. "Where are we going?"

She didn't know where exactly, but she had an idea for the best place to start. "The archives."

Ascara nodded. "What are we looking up?"

"The hatching ceremony." She turned two corners and nearly jogged down the long corridor to the archives.

Ascara jogged alongside her. "What for?"

Nida dashed inside the dim room filled with rows and rows of shelves from floor to ceiling, which were at least two stories high. A musty, papery smell filled every nook and cranny of scrolls and journals. The dust made her nose itch.

A couple other sisters browsing the shelves turned and stared with lifted eyebrows at their disturbance.

Nida ignored them and scanned the labeled signs above each aisle until she found the one titled *Origins*.

"What about the hatching ceremony are we looking for?" Ascara asked in a hushed tone.

Nida passed shelf after shelf as she surveyed their contents. "The beginning. The first few hatching ceremonies."

There were so many scrolls to sift through. *Origins of Humans. Origins of Fraygyns. Origins of Kwendi.*

"And why?" Ascara casually skimmed through the section about the earliest Vigor essences.

Nida swallowed.

"Nida, what is going on? Are the sisters going to die—"

"Shh. I don't know—"

"What?" Ascara's eyes bulged as she leaned in closer. "What happened? Are they wilting? Are they—"

"No, no." Nida checked around them for eavesdroppers and lowered her voice. "Brynn and Rowec die after the ceremony. They have to give their lives to hatch the sisters."

Ascara's eyebrows pulled together. "No. No way. That's not—"

"Yes, I swear." She nodded. "I don't have time to tell you everything, but Brynn just told me."

"No. We would know. We would know that." Ascara pulled back a little, looking her over, and dropped her voice even more. "Your eyes are red. You've been crying. Spirits, you're telling the truth?"

"Do I lie, Ascara? Seriously? Think about it. We've been so gullible. Life Weaving takes life from us. We know this already."

"I just feel tired and weak after. You're the one who passes out and almost dies."

"But if you needed to grow an entire generation? Hundreds of Tialans?"

Ascara's face drained of color. The violet scales along her cheeks and jawline lost some of their sheen.

"Brynn witnessed it," she continued. "She lied about the last queen and her mate leaving to explore Lousha."

Ascara's eyes glossed over. "Rowec doesn't know yet, does he?"

"None of the humans have known. Well, I guess some did. It sounds like Rowec's elders have been providing mates for our queens. But the victims— they don't know until it's too late."

Ascara's mouth dropped open. "That's... terrible. That's so wrong. How could she lie? How could they..." She shook her head.

"I'm not going to let him die, but I can't let our sisters die, either. That's why I need your help. We have to find another way to do the ceremony." Her hands went back to the scrolls, sliding and pushing them out of the way.

Origins of Vulkypsy. Origins of Fallen Gates. Origins of Eien.

"We would already know if there was another way," Ascara said.

"We didn't know our sisters die and murder humans. It was right there the whole time, and we just trusted her."

Ascara shook her head. "This is unbelievable. I mean, I believe you, but I can't—"

"Wrap your head around it?" Nida slid a few more scrolls out of the way and peered at a neighboring shelf. "I know. I still don't know if I believe it, but I'm more afraid that if I don't, it'll be too late, and Rowec will—"

Ascara's head shot up. "Do you love him?"

The air escaped her lungs. "No," she choked out. "No, no. I think he's a good example of what humans can be. I think—"

"You're blushing. You love him."

Nida shook her head. "I don't know what it is. I care about him. I don't want him to die."

But love?

Ascara focused back on the scroll in her hands.

It wasn't love. That wasn't possible. Rowec had other female humans he could be with.

But, he had asked her to stay in his village. He had touched her gently. Lovingly? He had asked about the festival and her being there. Suddenly, she wanted to ask what it all meant.

Focus on first things first. She couldn't find out what it meant if he was going to be sacrificed.

She glanced up. An entire shelf for Tialan origins loomed above her. She grabbed the nearest ladder, climbed it to the next level, and combed through the scrolls.

Origins of Tialans I, II, III, & IV. Dust plumed, and she coughed.

Origins of Life Weaving I, II, & III. Origins of the Sanctuary.

She grabbed the last one, slipped the ribbon off, and unrolled it.

"I don't get it," Ascara said below her. "Why wouldn't the queens themselves try to find another way?"

She scanned the text in her hands and stepped back down to join Ascara. "What if they did, and they just never figured it out?" She pushed one side of the thin scroll in Ascara's direction. "Take that side."

They read in silence, but it was the same old stuff about the hatching that she had known.

Ascara pointed to a paragraph. "This says that the jungle grows enough Tialan buds to sustain life, but it doesn't say anything about the ceremony. And this part... I can barely read this part, it's so messy."

Nida knew it well. "Brynn showed me this passage when I first accepted responsibility for the hatchery. It says that if the sanctuary dies, it never grows back. It talks about shattering a seed or something. It's just saying that if one generation of buds dies, that that's it. No more buds."

Ascara swallowed. "We knew that."

"Yeah, this scroll doesn't have anything we're looking for," Nida said. "It doesn't mention the switch to humans or anything. This is still just talking about when there were male Tialans. What am I going to do, Ascara?"

Ascara shrugged. "The hatching is about a week away. We don't have much time."

"Then where would it be?"

Ascara bit her lip. "The switch to needing humans was fairly recent. Well, last-hundred-years recent. Maybe it wasn't written down. The only parts that discuss humans being part of the process is in the prayer room."

The prayer room? "What are you talking about? There aren't any scrolls in the prayer room."

Ascara smirked. "Man, you really do go there to pray."

She rolled her eyes. "Fine, then. What's there?"

"The histories? On the walls and ceiling? Remember?"

Nida's mouth dropped as she recalled the odd-shaped figures stained with powders for color. "They show the humans."

"They show a human taking the hand of the Tialan queen—"

"And a beam of light radiating out."

Ascara crossed her arms.

"We need to go check the rest of the ceiling. See if there are any other hints—"

Crilla, their red-scaled sister, stepped into the library. "Attention sisters. We need you to return to your rooms immediately. Humans have been spotted near the temple. This is only for your safety. We believe they're going to request to enter the temple." Crilla quickly exited down the hall with the other archive browsers in tow.

Humans?

Nida shared a glance with Ascara. "Rowec's village? He'd threatened that his brother would bring an army."

Ascara raised her eyebrows. "This can't be good. I bet Brynn is losing her mind."

"I need to go." She turned to Ascara and held her hands. "I'm going to try to see if I can find out who's come. Maybe if Brynn is desperate enough she'll let me stay as a translator or something. Can you—"

"Ignore the request that I go to my room, go to the prayer room instead, see if I can solve some ancient mystery that saves the day for absolutely everyone, and report it back to you?" She winked. "What are sisters for?"

Nida hugged her. "Thank you, Ascara. Thank you so much."

"Don't thank me. I want to know how to fix this as badly as you do. I'm going to finish reading this first, and then I'll head down."

Nida dashed out of the archives for the hall but grabbed the side of the door frame to hang back. She had nearly forgotten. "Ascara…"

Ascara glanced up from the scroll in her hands.

"If Brynn dies, she's named Drathella as the next queen."

Ascara's eyes widened just before they narrowed. Her nostrils flared, and the edges of the scroll crinkled in her claws.

Nida smiled. "Good luck."

CHAPTER 15

*N*ida lifted her robes as she ran down the corridors to the throne room. If Brynn was going to meet with humans, she'd want to look powerful and wealthy. She'd want to look like a goddess.

She really needed to talk to Rowec as soon as possible. He needed to know the truth about the ceremony, about what she and Ascara were hoping to figure out, and that his people were here for him.

But if Rowec's elders had some sort of pact with them to send males for the ceremony, then why would Rowec's village send people to talk with Brynn now? Maybe it wasn't about Rowec at all. Maybe it was about the pact in general. Maybe they were done sending their men to be sacrifices.

She slid into the throne room, where Crilla and the other guards had begun lighting all the sconces as quickly as they could. "How many are coming?" she whispered at Crilla.

"Two."

"That's it?"

Crilla nodded.

Nida squeezed past the rest of the guards for Brynn, who was already seated at her throne atop a pyramid dais. Her claws tapped the golden arms.

"Find Nida!" she barked.

"I'm here," Nida said, though her sister's command sent shivers down her spine.

Brynn stalked Nida as she approached. "Crilla, is Rowec guarded?"

"Yes, Brynntial," Crilla said.

"Don't leave him alone for a second."

"Yes, Brynntial." Crilla immediately moved to talk with two sisters at the entry.

"Nida, stand on my right side," Brynn bit. "If they say anything that I don't understand, I'll need you to explain. She fluffed her hair and her robes out a few more times. "Where's Drathella?"

"Here, My Queen," Drathella said, sliding in from the side of the room.

It took everything for Nida not to roll her eyes.

"Listen, learn. Don't speak," Brynn snapped.

Drathella nodded once and took her place on the other side of Brynn.

Nida couldn't get distracted. She was doing this for Rowec and her sisters. Any information she could glean from his people, she would relay to him. She straightened herself with her hands folded neatly in front of her.

"Send them in," Brynn commanded.

After the guards opened the two golden doors to the throne room, two humans entered the wide hall.

One was male, tall, toned but more gangly. He had dark hair and green eyes—Rowec's brother. It had to be Rowec's brother. She recognized him, but would Brynn?

The other beside him was female and considerably smaller. She had dainty hands and tiny feet. Her jet-black hair was braided and tied into an elegant knot at the back of her head. She had alabaster skin in a beautiful sky-blue gown. Was she a sister? Rowec hadn't mentioned a sister.

They both tipped their heads at Brynn.

Brynn nodded back and spread her arms wide. "I am Brynntial, Queen of the Tial Jungle. What brings you to my temple?"

Curious how the sudden requirement of needing to act like a queen sobered her up.

"We-we—" The male cleared his throat and took a deep breath. "We've come to barter for my brother's life."

Brynn let one clawed finger tap against her knee. "You are the one who stole from us."

The man swallowed and nodded. "Maur, ma'am... Your Majesty." He tipped his head again.

Nida smiled.

No wonder Rowec had stepped in for him. His fingers fidgeted at his belt loop. He bumbled through his sentences. Maur was a mess. He would have never survived Drathella. She might have actually eaten him alive.

Nida caught the black-haired woman beside him staring at her. She had a cut about her, something vicious in her stare that pierced Nida. It was cold, calculating. Nida had recognized that same stare in Drathella.

"And who are you? His sister? Did his whole family come to beg for his life?" Brynn asked.

The girl bowed again. "No, I'm Etta, daughter to the chief of the Zchi Village. You've captured my future husband, and I'm here to ask for him back."

The blood drained from Nida's face for the millionth time that day. *Etta?* Etta was here demanding her future husband to be returned to her? And she was gorgeous. She was... flawless.

Brynn turned her head slightly toward Nida.

She didn't react—she wouldn't. This was Etta. The one Rowec hated and ignored but felt chained to. The one he wanted to escape from.

But if she couldn't figure out how to save his life in the ceremony, what would he choose? Death or Etta? It was clear what he'd pick when she simplified it.

"I'm sorry, but he's already agreed to go through with the ceremony," Brynn said, waving a hand off.

"That's unacceptable!" Etta burst, taking a step forward.

Rowec's brother tried to pull her back and quiet her, but she ignored him and yanked her arm free.

"He's my future husband. He doesn't belong to you. He's mine," Etta spat.

Brynn tilted her head. "And that lanky thing stole from us. How do you suggest he pay for his crimes?"

"Take him instead," Etta said without pause, shoving Maur forward.

Maur squirmed out of her hold. "Hey, wait, now, I was hoping we would negotiate a little—"

"Shut up, moron," Etta bit.

"Is this it?" Brynn sighed dramatically, seeming bored with their bickering. "Is this all you have to say? You came all this way, found your way back to the temple without getting eaten in the jungle, and you say, 'He's mine?'" Brynn rose, lengthening her torso and displaying the scales along her body.

Maur swallowed; Etta stood her ground.

No wonder Rowec felt trapped. This tiny woman was unbelievable. She truly felt like she was owed Rowec. She wasn't here for his future or for his safety, but for her satisfaction—*her* husband.

But Rowec had to see reason, all things considered. If she and Ascara couldn't figure out how to change the ceremony, Etta *was* the better choice. At least he'd be alive. Maybe he wouldn't understand it immediately, but life with Etta had to be better than death.

And her sisters... Tears welled and threatened to fall. How could she choose? Her sisters over Rowec? Rowec over her sisters? It wasn't fair!

It wasn't fair, but when had that been new? Rowec would need a backup escape plan in case they didn't find the solution to the ceremony.

In a couple days, the pre-hatching festival would be held in the main hall off the southern side of the garden. It'd be dark, crowded, and Nida could sneak him into that garden. The walls were too high and sloped on the inside, so that he wouldn't be able to climb them by himself. But if she gave some rope to Etta, who then could throw it over the wall from the outside and help him climb up, he'd get out. Etta could save him if she couldn't.

She blinked tears and wiped them away as discreetly as possible.

"... And therefore, you will return to your chief and discuss the problems with the pact. I have my solution. He needs a better one for next time."

Etta was fuming. Maur was stunned, eyes wide. Brynn was smirking. She had angered them.

Brynn waved at her guards. "Escort them out."

Etta began hollering and demanding Brynn listen, while Maur begged that they be given a second chance to explain.

This was her chance. Nida stepped back behind the throne and tore down the hall. She had to get to the storage room and outside before they got too deep into the jungle.

She tore past the classrooms and the kitchens to the storage room on the far east side. The doors groaned as she pulled them open.

Stick. Stick. Stick. Rope!

She grabbed the rope and slung it over her shoulder. She had to make it to the eastern entrance into the jungle. It was the small one by the dining hall, but if she sneaked by carefully enough, no one would suspect a thing.

At least that's what she told herself repeatedly. *No one sees me. I am invisible. No one sees me. I am invisible.*

She ducked and darted across room openings when no one was looking, until finally reaching the eastern entrance. She slid the door open wide enough for only her body to slip through and let it carefully close behind her without a sound.

The gryllids chirped their songs as she edged out onto the lawn surrounding the temple. She couldn't see anyone anywhere, and if the two humans had already made it back to the brush, then she definitely wouldn't be able to see them.

"Etta, I'm really starting to wonder about your motives."

"*My* motives. I came because you asked me to. You thought I could reason with them. I tried."

Their voices carried from around the front side of the temple. They hadn't made it to the jungle yet.

Nida slipped through the shadows to cut them off as they crossed on the eastern side of the lawn.

"So you don't want your future husband back?" Maur asked.

"I do. Of course I do. But not with you standing there like an idiot. How did you even become a warrior?"

"I just want to get my brother back—"

Nida cleared her throat.

They froze and stared in her direction.

She was still in the shadow, so she doubted they could see much of her face. It was better that way, honestly.

"Who's there?" Etta demanded.

"I-I am." Nida closed her eyes, took a deep breath, and came forward.

Etta leaned back.

"What do you want?" Maur asked.

She offered the rope. "In two nights, we'll be in the garden."

Maur just stared.

Nida urged him to take the rope from her hands. "I'm going to try to find a way to save Rowec. But if I can't, he'll need you to throw this over the garden walls, so he can climb out."

"How do you know him?" Maur asked. "How can we trust you?"

"I've been caring for him." That came out wrong. "I mean, I'm giving him food and water."

Maur swallowed and nodded, tears forming in his eyes. "He's okay, then? Really? He's alive?"

He'd feared Brynn had been lying to him? He truly cared for his brother.

She nodded and smiled. "Yes, I promise. And I want to get him out."

Etta, however, wore a grimace and shoved past him. "Why would he need a rope? Have you tortured him? Is he unable to climb? He's the best there is."

Nida inhaled deeply and decided it was best to focus on Maur. "The wall where you climbed to steal the paratils was only part of the garden. If you can get inside that garden again, without getting caught, there's another wall farther in."

He nodded. "Okay."

"That's the one you can't climb out of from the inside. It's sloped. He'll need someone on the outside to help hoist him to the top." She placed the rope in his hands. "In two nights, when the moon is right there." She pointed just over the horizon.

Etta squinted. "What are you things? Slitherskins?"

Maur shoved her toward the jungle but kept his eyes on Nida. "I'll be here, I promise. Thank you."

"Hey, don't shove me aside!" Etta whined.

They ran for the jungle's edge, Maur telling Etta that maybe his brother was right about her, which just sent her squealing and fighting even more.

Nida ducked back inside. *Now to tell Rowec and fix the ceremony.*

~

ROWEC PACED THE ROOM, did some squats and lunges, then jogged in place for a few minutes. He'd screwed up bad with Nida. He could feel it.

Raz lounged back and licked his belly.

"You need to get up and move, Raz. You've been eating too many durlos."

Raz yawned in response.

Nida probably wouldn't come to see him tonight, and he deserved that. He had yelled at her sister, lost his temper, and, thanks to Brynn, she'd gotten a generous reminder of how terrible his people could be.

He groaned and punched the stone wall. His knuckles ached, but he shook it off.

Some diplomat he was. Maybe fighting was all there would ever be for him. Maybe the elders and the chief were right in thinking he couldn't be more.

"I'm allowed to walk down the hall." Nida's voice carried into his room.

He dashed for the entrance, but the purple and yellow guards blocked the way.

"Nida!" he called.

She stepped in front of his entrance, but he could only see her between her sisters' shoulders when she stood on her tiptoes.

"Rowec, I'm here. Can I please pass?"

Her sisters didn't budge.

"We're under strict orders," the purple one said. "He no longer leaves, and no one comes in."

"I just need to talk to him," she said. "I can't even talk to him now?"

Her mouth, her eyes, were twisted. With what though? Fear? Sadness?

"It's okay, Nida. Just tell me."

She shook her head. "I can't."

The guards still didn't budge. Leaders didn't ramp up security unless they were afraid or furious. "I guess I made Brynn too angry," he said.

"No, it's me. She doesn't want me to see you."

The yellow-scaled guard gestured at her. "Go on, Nida. You can't stay."

His mind reeled. What had happened between Brynn and Nida after he'd left?

Brynn had wanted a romantic dinner. She had wanted him to accept whatever she said as truth. She was angry at Nida for telling him information about the hatching ceremony. Was she jealous?

He leaned forward, and the purple-scaled guard spun and shoved him. His backside hit the ground hard and sparked pain through his torso. He grunted and jumped back up.

"Don't!" Nida cried out. "Stop, Lavyra! Rowec, don't get in trouble. It's okay."

Lavyra lifted her scaled chin at him.

"I'll be back," Nida said.

No. She couldn't go yet. She had something to tell him. She looked distraught. He needed to hear it. He wanted to make her feel better. He wanted to fix it. "Wait, just tell me, Nida. Who cares if they hear?"

"Go, Nida." The yellow-scaled guard stepped toward her.

"I can't, Rowec. I'll talk to you as soon as possible."

Tears. She had tears. Something was very wrong.

"I'll be back soon," she croaked, and she took off in the direction of the hatchery. "I promise."

He ran his hands through his hair and squeezed them into fists. What had Brynn done? Was the hatchery in trouble?

He grimaced at Lavyra, and she smirked.

"I guess I'll just wait," he called back, hoping Nida could still hear him.

Lavyra turned back around and faced the hall.

CHAPTER 16

*N*ida finished caring for her sisters in the hatchery and raced for the prayer room for answers about the ceremony.

Her backup plan had only given them two days—*two days*—to save their sisters.

Ascara was inside, crouched in a corner, while two other sisters, Hollina and Prythi, knelt at the base of the statues of their late queen and her mate. The human mate had been carved with a smile on his face.

She jerked her head away. "Ascara?"

Ascara spun and stood. "I think I found something."

The two sisters kneeling shushed them.

Nida lifted her eyebrows and crouched beside her.

"See this?" Ascara pointed to the molding in the corner.

Embossed in the corner was a geometric pattern. Two triangles with their top points aimed at one another, a circle, and then two parallel lines.

"It's just a decoration."

Ascara shrugged. "Maybe, but it's weird. It goes all the way up in every corner."

The two sisters shushed them again.

Nida dropped her voice. "So?"

"They stretch to the ceiling. Look up there?" She pointed with a manicured claw where the molding met the ceiling.

The pattern started in the corner but continued on with the same geometric shape, only ten times larger.

"Doesn't it look like something?" Ascara asked.

"Seriously, Ascara?" Hollina asked. "We're praying."

Ascara rolled her eyes. "Seriously, Hollina? No, you're not. You're trying to eavesdrop. Pray later." She pulled them by their robes until they scooted along out the door.

Nida glared at her. "Ascara..."

"They weren't praying. Now, what does it look like?" She pointed again to the ceiling.

Nida took a deep breath.

They hadn't even let her speak with Rowec. She wasn't even allowed to see him. That gave her no time to tell him about her plan or her backup plan...

"Nida? Are you even paying attention?"

She shook her head. "Yes. No, I'm sorry. Brynn has Rowec on constant watch. I can't even talk to him before the ceremony."

"Then you'll just have to tell him at the festival. Now, look again. What's unusual in the pattern?"

She took a deep breath and tried again. "I don't know. It's triangle, triangle, circle, and then lines."

"Wow. Okay, the bottom triangle is missing its bottom line. That makes it look like legs, right?"

Nida turned her head and stood back. "Legs? Oh! It's a person lifting their arms up."

"Yes! Thank you."

"It's several little people lifting up other people all the way to the ceiling. So?"

Ascara walked toward the center of the room with her finger up in the air, following the figures. "I thought it was just a pattern to draw your eyes to the center, but they look like *humans*."

Nida followed her, eyes trained to the ceiling where time had chipped away some of the details. The oculus was always open, and beyond it was the near full moon, a glowing reminder that she was running out of time.

"What makes you think they're human and not Tialan?" she asked.

Ascara smiled. "I knew you'd ask that. Look at the pattern around the oculus."

Nida had. "It's just the same people over and over."

"Except for one tiny detail. Look again."

She squinted at the pattern again. "The arms aren't up."

"Yes!" Ascara squealed. "They're out to the side. They're touching one another. It's one giant chain around the room."

"That doesn't mean they're Tialan or human."

"No, but it shows something, right?"

It was *something*, but it wasn't an answer to saving her sisters' lives. The pieces of the ceiling that had slid out of place for the opening in the center had the pictures of the human man reaching out for the Tialan queen.

"It still shows that a human man is needed for the ceremony. And we can't see what else is part of the painting because the oculus is always open."

"Right!" Ascara ran to the side wall where the lever of the oculus waited. She lowered the lever, gears turned in the wall, and nothing else happened.

Nida shook her head. "It's too old."

"Or maybe someone broke it on purpose."

"That's a stretch."

Ascara shrugged.

"We have nothing then."

The weight on Nida's shoulders pressed down. So many lives were counting on her figuring this out.

"Not true," Ascara said. "We know there are hints in the paintings, we know this is probably the only room in the temple that even discusses humans in the ceremony, and we know that we didn't solve it in the first few hours of the plan's creation."

She rubbed her forehead, turned her face to the moon, and closed her eyes. "I can't let him die, Ascara. I did something..."

Ascara placed her hand on her shoulder. "What happened? What did you do?"

"His brother and his future mate came to ask for him to be released. Brynn said no."

"And?"

"I snuck outside and gave them a rope."

Ascara tilted her head. "A rope?"

"So that he can escape during the festival if we don't solve this in time."

Ascara wrapped an arm around her and rested her head on Nida's shoulder. "We'll figure it out, Nida."

NIDA SIGHED and slumped in the vanity chair of her room, while Ascara did her hair.

Two days had passed, and they had spent all of their free time investigating who painted the murals in the prayer room, when the oculus in the prayer room was built, and any other mentions of a pact between humans and Tialans.

They still hadn't come up with an answer for the actual ceremony, and time was up. Their plan had failed, and her backup plan to save Rowec would happen in just a few hours.

"I'm going to start researching how to fix the lever," Ascara said.

"It doesn't matter, Ascara." She swallowed. "He has to leave tonight."

The festival night had come, and Brynn had kept Rowec locked down since that night she'd learned the truth that her species could be just as cruel as the species they railed against.

She'd had no chance to prepare him to escape or tell him that his brother and Etta had come. He'd be going to the party, expecting to dance and enjoy his evening, only to find out that her people had lied to him and that she had been part of it.

Tears formed, but she blinked rapidly to hide them.

He'd get out, no harm would come to him, and her sisters...

"Hey," Ascara said, rubbing her shoulder. "Just because Rowec is leaving doesn't mean we can't still figure out a way to save the sisters. Are you willing to give your life for them?"

"Of course."

"So am I. I'm willing to bet we're not the only ones, either. If I have to give them all my Vigor and die in the process, I'm willing to try anything."

"Me too, but without a human male..."

"We'll figure it out." Ascara jutted a finger at the mirror. "You slapped Brynn. We can do anything."

She shook her head. She couldn't see how they'd figure it out, and she couldn't just blindly believe it would be okay.

Without Rowec for the ceremony, and without a new solution to the ceremony, the sisters would wilt. She'd doomed them all to save a man she wasn't supposed to... *love*.

"Come on. If everything is coming to a terrible end, and it's *not*—yet—you might as well enjoy your last evening with Rowec. Tell me again what he said when you mentioned the festival."

Nida bit her lip and tried to keep her head straight, recalling the conversation she had originally started with Ascara. "Rowec asked if I was going to the festival."

Ascara pulled out a pin she'd been holding in her mouth and stuck it into Nida's hair. It held one auburn lock just so above her ear.

"You know what I think?" Ascara asked. "He's got it bad for you, Nida. Why else ask a stupid question like that? *Hello, there's a party coming up that you just told me about, and I was wondering if you were going.*"

Ascara's deep, mocking tone made her giggle. Among the swirling tension in Nida's chest, Ascara always had a way to make her feel better. For that moment, it felt like they were getting ready for the festival as if everything she loved wasn't about to fall apart.

She was pretty sure Rowec liked her, too, which made what she was about to do hurt all the worse. "I don't know."

"What are you afraid of?" Ascara continued piling pins into her mouth for safekeeping as she looped and gathered sections of Nida's hair into place.

"What am I afraid of?" Nida scoffed. "Uh, let's see, my sister killing me—"

"Which one?"

They both giggled.

"Drathella, mostly. But also, Brynn for ruining the ceremony." She glanced down at her fingers in her lap. "Can you believe Brynn *wants* him to be in love with her?"

Ascara pursed her lips. "Brynn can *want* all day long. And too bad. This is your last night with him. Besides, Brynn has no chance. I saw that dinner conversation. They have no chemistry."

Nida shook her head, but her sister quickly straightened it. "What do you know about human chemistry?"

"I know what it's not!" She stared back at her through the mirror. "Which dress are you wearing? The gold one?"

Nida laughed. "Eh, it's okay, but I think if I wear the gold one, Rowec will puke. Everything in this temple is gold to him. He used to mutter it under his breath."

"Oh! What about my blue one?"

Nida blinked. "The one with the—"

"Split open back, high cut on the thigh, plunging neckline. It would look amazing on you."

"I don't think so." It was too much. Overkill. "What about the lavender one?"

Ascara put the last two pins from her mouth onto the counter and dashed for the closet. Within seconds, she had retrieved a soft, shimmery lavender dress. The neckline was still low, the back still dipped, but it was an elegant shape with flowers and vines embroidered with gold thread up the neck.

"Oh," Nida said. "I forgot that it's sleeveless."

"So?"

"My shoulders are—"

"Mostly human, which is quite attractive to a *human*, I imagine."

"I don't know…"

"Yes, you do. You love it. I can see it in your eyes. You're wearing it. You'll look more like a queen than Brynn." She hung it over the back of a chaise by her bed. "Turn back around. I'm nearly done with your hair."

When Ascara had finished, she spun Nida for her to see how it pulled up neatly and loosely just behind her very human ears. Her hair had been sufficient for hiding them until now. A metal clip in the shape of the same flowers from her dress held her hair together in the back.

"Okay! Make-up!"

"Not too much. I don't want to overdo it."

Ascara took a seat across from her, pulling out tin after tin of inks and powders. "Okay, so, I'm excited for you. Are you going to dance?"

"Yes. We all are supposed to dance. Don't you remember the last one? We were little, but I remember everyone dancing."

"Of course, I remember. Tilt your head back a little." Ascara dusted some powder across her chin. "I meant: are you going to dance with *him*?"

Nida blinked. "There's no way Brynn will allow it. I think he'll be too overwhelmed by a party swarming with Tialans to want to dance. He'll be starving, probably."

"Nope, I brought in some of the fruit from the garden for him. Can't have your man starving to death." Ascara sat the powder down and picked up a tin with pale-teal powder. "Lean forward and close your eyes."

"What if they have weird festival customs?" Nida asked.

"You mean humans in general?" Ascara dusted the powder across her eyelids.

"I mean human customs in general, yes. He did these weird hand things."

The dusting stopped. "What?"

Nida opened one eye.

Ascara was grinning ear to ear and staring at her.

"No, not weird. What are you thinking? I mean just normal weird things. Like they touch hands to make a promise, and he had me hook my arm in his arm... It was weird."

"Show me."

Nida went through the motions of their hands squeezing, and then hooked her arm through Ascara's to show how they walked places.

"Oh," Ascara said. "I get it. This is close. You're really close to me like this. Oh, Nida, he likes you."

She shook her head a little and returned to her place.

"He likes you. What if he wants to kiss you?" Ascara tilted Nida's head down. "What if there are other mischievous things humans do with each other to show love? Remember the statue and the crotch?"

"Ascara!" She couldn't handle another thing to worry about. Between her sisters, Rowec's reactions, the dress, her make-up, the sabotage of the cere-mony, the escape... She couldn't possibly muster enough courage to face unknown human customs with or without using their... their... parts.

"Just a little bit of gloss on your lips, and you're done."

Nida smacked her lips together and checked herself in the mirror. She looked nothing like her sister. Ascara was a beautiful Tialan—big, bright eyes; shiny scales; thin claws. Nida was... different. So different. Was she attractive or was she just a mess? She liked all the human qualities in Rowec, but that didn't mean she had enough human in her for him to fall in love with. Not like gorgeous Etta.

Ascara smiled. "What do you think?"

"I look..."

"More human? That's what I was going for. I like it. I mean, it's probably a good thing for Rowec. For what it's worth, if he doesn't like it, well, screw him. My opinion is the only one that matters." Ascara grinned and yanked her from the chair. "We should hurry and get dressed. We need to check on Brynn."

Both of them slid into their dresses, admiring their sisters' work.

Ascara had taken the blue, jaw-dropping dress and ogled herself in the mirror. "I need my own human to impress. I look good."

"I thought you wanted one as a pet."

Ascara looked back at the mirror and twisted her hips to see herself better. "Pet. Play thing. Whatever. And you're right, the lavender one is more your style."

Nida twisted her body in the mirror. It fit against her neatly, accentuated her curves. It *was* more her style.

Ascara took her arm and pulled her out of their room, through the temple, and toward Brynn's chambers.

The bustle of all their other sisters echoed through the halls, each one eager to be ready and start the party. They all moved from room to room, giggled, twirled, begged for pins and laces. This festival was to celebrate Tialan beauty, hope in the new generation, and life.

Life that might not come. Her heart squeezed in guilt.

"Nida!"

The shrieks from her youngest sisters came from behind. She stopped and greeted them.

"Oh, Nida," said Nymfan, a younger, amber-scaled sister. "You look so beautiful."

The other little girls beside her nodded and agreed.

Nida smiled. "Thank you, sisters. I love the lace in your hair. It's a very nice touch."

They giggled.

"Will you read to us again? After the party?" Nymfan asked.

"Sure. Absolutely."

The girls ran off, and Ascara pulled her into Brynn's hall. Even the guards had dressed for the evening in full-length skirts and a little bit of make-up.

"You two look great," Nida told them at the door.

They smiled and let her and Ascara pass.

Inside, Brynn's room was full chaos. Everything in her closet had been pulled out and strewn across her bed and floor. Every tin of jewelry had been opened and dumped.

Drathella was perched on Brynn's bed wearing what she always wore. Was she not attending the festival? That would definitely improve the night.

"Ugh." Drathella groaned and headed for the door. "That's my cue to leave."

"I think you could go help clean some pots if you don't want to go tonight," Ascara snapped. "The kitchen really is a good fit for you!" But Drathella had already slinked out of the room.

They carefully stepped around twisted jewels and wadded undergarments.

"Brynn?" Ascara called out, edging her way around the colossal mess. "Nida and I wanted to check on you."

She made a face at Ascara, who shrugged and muttered quietly to her, "Really, we just want to see how crazy you are, you lying, scheming, slith—"

"Girls!" Brynn burst from the bathroom half-dressed and holding a goblet. "I'm so happy you're here. You can help me."

Nida caught the sloshing goblet from Brynn's hand and set it on the bedside table. Ascara held their sister upright and evaluated the emerald dress she had managed to halfway put on.

To make matters worse, Brynn's eyes had thickly smudged gold liner. Her cheeks were smothered in red powder. Her nearly non-existent Tialan lips were painted bright red, only higher and thicker.

"How much have you had to drink, Brynn?" Ascara waved her hand in front of her nostrils.

"Just a little. I'm so nervous. I thought I was sweating, but that's silly. So I started panting, and then I saw how unattractive that was—"

"All right, all right. Just hold still." Ascara stood her up straight while Nida adjusted the dress on her sister's shoulders and laced up the back for her so it would sit in place. "We can't have her going naked."

Nida smirked.

"How does it look?" Brynn spun and put her hands on her hips.

"Isn't that the same dress you wore for your dinner with Rowec?" Ascara asked.

Nida shook her head. "Ascara—"

"It is." Brynn smiled. "I did it on purpose."

"Why?" Ascara shook her head, palms out to the side.

"Because the last time it didn't go well, and I don't want him to have any negative memories about me in this dress. I thought I'd make new memories with it tonight." She waggled her thin eyebrows. "I look gorgeous. He'll feel something for me tonight. I'm sure of it."

Ascara just nodded. Nida did, too.

"Do *you* like how you look?" Nida asked.

Brynn shrugged. "It's a little much, I admit. I was trying for a more *human* look, I guess." Her eyes raked over Nida, as if seeing her standing there for the first time. "You look positively *not-Tialan*, Nida."

That was okay. She didn't care what Brynn thought. All she wanted was one last evening with Rowec before she helped him escape.

"Tonight," Brynn said, "when I get Rowec alone, I'm going to convince him how good we are together. I'll make sure he's focused on what matters. No distractions. No outbursts. He'll see me. He'll fall in love, and if not, he'll see reason that saving others is the right thing to do. We're both strong, born to protect our people. He and I have an understanding that others don't. We have responsibilities, and tonight, he'll see how good of a match we can be for each other."

Nida inhaled. She should've bit her tongue. She shouldn't have said a word. But Brynn was taunting her. Maybe it was losing everything at once, or maybe it was because of all the guilt—either way, she couldn't hold back. "What's the point?"

Brynn froze. "What?"

Ascara held her arm. "Nida, don't. Let it go."

"Even *if* he fell in love with you, you'd only be mates until the ceremony." She had tried not to clench her jaw when she'd said it.

Brynn smiled and fixed a loose strand of Nida's hair. "Oh, sweetie, don't be upset. Soon you'll have a temple full of new sisters to care for. Everyone will be so happy, you'll be busy, and he won't even remember you." Smile gone, she lowered her chin and whispered. "Now, behave, or I'll lock you up in his old cell."

Ascara gasped, and Nida turned so Brynn couldn't see her face. Brynn might get most of tonight with Rowec, but Nida would steal a moment. Just a moment. And Brynn wouldn't get to sacrifice him.

"Come on, girls. The party is about to start!" Brynn pushed past her, and they followed.

CHAPTER 17

*R*owec peered down at his gold... suit?

He shook his head and stood back from the long mirror, adjusting his collar and his vest.

He looked... ridiculous.

His perfect-fitting pants were pressed crisp and lined with a gold metallic trim down the sides. His white undershirt, though a bit goofy-looking with all the fabric at his arms bulging out like fluffy clouds, was light and pristine. His gold-colored vest was embroidered with gold thread into geometric patterns.

It wouldn't have been his first, second, or last choice, clearly, but then again, he had never worn anything like this before. Warriors didn't dress up unless it was armor for fighting. Not to mention the weavers in his village didn't make clothes like these.

He turned again and again. So the gold was too much, but he did look trim. His arms looked bulky and strong. His thighs looked pretty good, too. Even his neck looked thicker and stronger in this get-up.

Maybe it was the suit. Maybe it was all the training he had time for. A couple days without Nida was more than he could bear.

He rubbed his freshly shaven jaw, remembering how Lavyra and the yellow-scaled guard had held him down while a blue-scaled guard had used the sharp end of her claw to shave his face for him. He didn't struggle; he behaved. He wasn't interested in being stupid with a claw that close to his throat.

A few tins of powders and paints had been brought in and placed on his bedside table. He opened them, revealing bright greens and purples, and sniffed them.

Nope.

Unless it was black, greasy, and just before a war, he would not be wearing anything on his face.

Raz stirred in his pocket for the twentieth time.

"I'm sorry, little guy." He patted the outside of his vest pocket carefully. "I know it's not my old pocket, but it's just for the night. I'll make it up to you with paratils later. I'm sure Nida will get us some."

Nida.

His heart made a silly jump every time he thought of her at the festival. He couldn't wait to see her. He couldn't wait to ask her to dance.

If that's even a thing they do.

Festivals in his village had dancing. Didn't most celebrations? Hadn't she mentioned it? She had to have. Of course they danced. He didn't want to admit it before, but they weren't *that* different from humans.

Well, Nida isn't.

She was wholesome and genuine. She was better than most humans, even. She deserved so much more than this temple and this way of living. She deserved to be free to decide what she wanted.

And he did, too.

In a few days' time, his purple- and yellow-scaled guards would permanently switch—thanks to the information he'd overheard the previous night.

And when I get home, I'll tell the chief and the elders that I'm not marrying Etta.

Screw them and their politics. He didn't care how much Etta was admired by the other warriors or by how many favors her father had given to elders. It was his life. Here, he was fighting to get back to his life. There, he would fight to live it.

And maybe Nida will be with me. Hopefully.

The curtain at his room's entrance parted.

"It's time," Lavyra said.

He took a deep breath and followed her out.

No more dragging or forcing him places, it appeared they trusted he'd follow their commands. It was most likely due to Nida's daily visits to ensure he was eating and drinking, and not being mistreated. *Daily until recently.*

Tonight would be his first chance to see what she'd wanted to tell him those few nights before. He was almost giddy to see her.

They led him through the temple and toward the main hall.

Every sconce along the way had been lit, enveloping the temple in a bright, warm glow. Some of the ceilings had the same mechanisms to open like in the hatchery, and if they did, they were open, letting in the sweet, night air under a blanket of stars. Squealing and giggling echoed down the corridors, growing louder with each step.

Finally through the maze, his escort approached two large doors.

Nida's youngest sisters stood in the hallway in front of the doors. Their hair had been done up with ribbons; their dresses glittered in the firelight. They ogled and pointed at him as he passed.

The guards peeled back the doors and revealed a yellow staircase descending into a massive hall filled with Tialans. The ceiling had been opened, sconces flickered along the walls, banners and streamers of metallic fabrics fluttered from the exposed golden trusses, and along one side of the room glass windows peered out over the durlo garden.

Easily over a hundred Tialan eyes turned and blinked at him.

The room silenced, and his stomach dropped.

What had he been expected to do? No one warned him about needing to say or present anything. Nida hadn't mentioned it.

And what was he so worried about? How could he have been expected to know what to do?

Brynntial appeared at the bottom of the stairs. She either had a closet full of the same dress or he was losing his mind. It looked identical to the last one he saw her in on the night of their "dinner."

She stood still. Was he supposed to go to her?

Ugh. I do not want to go to her.

His eyes scanned the crowd's bulbous stare for familiar, human eyes. Where was she? Nida said she'd come. She was there, right?

"Please, join me," Brynntial called up to him.

He took a deep breath and descended the stairs. At once the bustle of the hall returned, and all of the sisters refocused on their previous conversations.

Brynntial grinned; he shuddered.

Her smile was made creepier by the overdrawn red lipstick. "I'm so glad you're here to join us." She held out her hand as if to shake his.

What the—

When she held it there clearly waiting for him to respond, he slid his hand in hers and shook it.

"Nida was telling me some of your customs. I would love to hear more about them."

Nida?

He glanced beyond Brynntial's shoulder and found her—*Nida*—giggling with Ascara.

It was as if the skies had parted in a storm, and she was the ray of light in a new dawn. Her hair was up, and her skin and teal scales along her neck were exposed. Her shape in that dress...

He caught himself and swallowed. "Yes, well, she's become quite accustomed to a few of them."

Brynntial put her hands on her hips. "I know our last meeting wasn't as productive as we had hoped. But I believe, now, you're ready to be more receptive. A dance, please?"

When music began playing from a terrace above the tables of food, most of the sisters took to the dance floor.

"Sure." He suspected he didn't have much of a choice.

Brynntial bowed her head. "Move me like you move your women. Mold me into what you need." She pressed her body against his and held his hands out to the side.

"O-okay." What was wrong with her? Was she drunk? Was she insane? Was this her attempt at getting along with him?

Is she flirting?

He held back the urge to audibly express how gross that would be. She had to have been trying to appear romantic, and if she hadn't been... well, *her*, then it'd be hilarious. Apparently, Nida thought it was hilarious anyway, because she was laughing and holding her stomach while watching him.

He grinned, put some space between their bodies, and began a slow dud of a dance. It was the first one taught to the children in his village. Stiff, boring, and not anything that Brynntial would want—it was perfect.

Meanwhile it gave him the chance to see Nida behind her.

Nida was... gorgeous.

"Aren't we supposed to spin or something?" Brynntial said.

He blinked and focused on her. "Uh, no. This is it."

"Swaying in one place?"

"Uh huh."

"Barely touching?"

"It's a sacred dance of my people," he lied.

She straightened her back as if taking it more seriously.

He would tell Nida how he felt. He would go to her as soon as the song was over, he'd ask her to dance and tell her just how she made him feel. Just a few more steps. Just a few more beats...

The song ended.

"Great! Now, we get to try one of ours." Brynntial gripped his wrists and spun him.

Several sisters around them whooped and hollered in support of their dancing. Rather, Brynntial danced, and he stood there not sure how to respond.

Nida covered her mouth and smiled from the side while Brynntial danced and slithered around him.

It wasn't particularly flirty in nature. He had seen some of the other sisters dancing with one another this way in the last song, but Brynntial... She was taking it to a different level. Sliding her body against his, running her clawed fingers through his hair and over his face.

It took every ounce of energy to not appear repulsed.

Keep it together. Keep it together.

He took a deep breath and focused on Nida.

"You are the object of my desire," Brynntial breathed, and then she spun away.

"An object?"

Brynntial returned, both hands on his chest and her face close. "Yes. You are the honored guest. The source of the life Vigor we need. I was wrong before. Wrong in how I spoke to you. We need to be looking at this like a couple. A couple soon to have the greatest legacy of their time."

"I don't know about that."

She shrugged, seemingly lost in the moment of the dance and the music. She slithered alongside him, rubbing her hands down his arms and sides.

"Okay, that's a little..." He moved away slightly and pried her hands off.

They were quick to return. "All of the previous queens and their mates fell in love. Deep love before the ceremony." Her breath stunk of fermented fruit.

"Uh... sure..." *She's absolutely delusional.*

"We can do the same. You can live in my quarters for the next week. We can spend every waking moment worshiping each other—"

He glanced over her shoulder. Nida was standing alone. When the song was over, he'd have his chance.

"Let's worship each other, Rowan."

"Rowec, and I'm going to pass on that."

When the song had finally ended, she panted and stared up at him. Her eyes almost looked sad—if that was possible. But he was done being nice and dealing with her craziness. He'd already agreed to the ceremony, and he'd already told her he wouldn't pretend to be in love with her.

Another song started, and she grabbed his hand.

He yanked it away. "Brynntial, I'm sorry, but I already told you that I'm not doing whatever *this* is. I'm not interested in you. At all. I never will be. I said I'd stay for the ceremony and nothing else."

He tore away from her and headed for Nida.

"Wait, I..." Brynntial's voice was thankfully swallowed by the din of the hall.

Nida froze where she stood, her eyes growing wider.

The room froze. The music stopped. Silent. Still. All eyes on him.

Here goes nothing. He bent forward and held out his hand to her. "Nida, will you please dance with me?"

CHAPTER 18

*N*ida held her breath.

Ascara was staring her down from the food table. If her jaw could drop any lower, it would have. All of her sisters gasped and mumbled to one another.

He shouldn't have asked. He wasn't supposed to be focused on anyone but Brynn.

But how would he know that? Nida hadn't told him what to expect. He didn't know their customs, and Brynn hadn't let her near him.

She should have told him the second he was interested in seeing her there. She should have explained how it worked. There was no escaping the judging eyes of her sisters.

"If you don't want to," Rowec mumbled, "I understand, but please don't leave me bowing like this without an answer."

She blinked and glanced up at Brynn, whose eyes drooped. She huffed and nodded, waving for her to accept.

Was it a trick? Had she conceded?

Sisters quickly ran to Brynn, fawning over her, telling her how lovely she looked on the dance floor.

"Yes, yes. I know, very generous of me," Brynn said over and over.

Brynn hadn't conceded, and she hadn't said 'yes' because it was the nice thing to do.

Nida didn't care. This was her moment. Just a moment was all she needed. She smiled. "Yes, Rowec. I'll dance with you."

She slid her hand into his, and he squeezed it in return.

Warmth. Safety. The things he made her feel with just her hand in his.

He pulled her to the dance floor and into his arms closer, much closer, than he'd held Brynn. He placed her hand at his shoulder as his arm held her waist against him. Their other hands locked together to the side. He was solid, and yet bent around her like he had been made just for her.

Every inch of her wanted to squeal and cheer and melt and... and...

And yet, none of her knew what to do or what to think or what to feel. Or where to look. His bright-green eyes under thick eyebrows were right there, soft and yet piercing. Was he comfortable this close to her? He seemed so. His lips, right there. His face so smooth. It was just... him. She looked at him—all of him.

He hated gold, but it suited him. He looked like a king, like a god. And without it all on? Heat rose up her chest and neck.

Ascara had gotten to her, apparently.

She had gotten a small peek of what had been under that suit at the fountains that night in the garden.

She had wanted to ask him about the few scars he had along his toned back. She had wanted to ask him about the black designs down his arms. She had wanted to stare at him for as long as possible, wondering if Ascara had been right about him being *gifted everywhere.*

She blinked and took a deep breath

"You're blushing," he whispered.

Whispers meant only for her.

She tore her eyes away and focused on a button near his collar. "It's just that being the center of attention like this can be unnerving."

"Don't worry. You dance well."

She didn't. She just fit with him. Moving with him made sense.

She dipped her head. "Not as well as Brynn."

He released a burst of real and very loud laughter and pulled her closer. Chest to chest, she giggled.

She wanted to be closer still. She leaned forward, her forehead at his chin. His jaw rested against her temple. She glanced up at a hundred eyes watching them, at Brynn making her way through the crowd to see them.

Oh no. As Brynn's eyes narrowed, tears formed in Nida's.

So Brynn would truly only give her a moment. Not even a full dance.

The music suddenly shifted to a lighter, faster rhythm—Brynn's orders, probably.

If Nida was going to save him, now would be the time. But no one had opened the doors to the garden yet. The party was still lively in the hall, and yet the moon was where she had said it would be. His brother would be waiting.

Brynn pushed her way around the other dancers onto the dance floor.

"Our time is already up," she whispered. How would she get him outside? He'd have to sneak around somehow... in a bright-gold suit as the only male guest. "I need to speak with you—alone."

Rowec spun her and faced Brynn. "What's wrong?"

Brynn took a deep breath and lifted her chin. "It's time for us to dance again."

He hadn't let go of Nida. They had stopped dancing, but he still held her close, protectively. So close, she felt his chest deflate under her palms. "All right. I'll dance again, but I want to talk with Nida outside for a minute."

What was he doing? *He* was making demands of *her*—the queen—in front of everyone? Brynn would send him back down to the dungeon for humiliating her.

Brynn's eyes widened. "You're getting awfully cocky, human."

"And you seem to forget that without me there's no ceremony." The muscles at his jaw tightened.

Brynn sneered.

"Give me what I want—a few minutes with Nida outside—and I'll come right back and actually look like I'm enjoying my time with you," he whispered.

Brynn's gaze roved over the crowd. Was she *that* afraid of what everyone thought? Eventually, she straightened her spine and nodded. "Fine. But the—"

"No guards."

Nida held her breath. What *was* he doing? There was no way she'd agree to that.

Brynn's eyebrows lifted. "Excuse me?"

"No guards." He lifted a finger at Brynn's face. "I'm going to be very honest with you."

Nida's stomach turned. This wouldn't end well. Brynn wouldn't give in to what he wanted because she had to stay in control, always. He'd just get himself in trouble, and the plan would be ruined. He'd be—

"I don't care anything about you," he said. "You don't care anything about me. I said I'd help because I care about Nida. Not you. You either give me space before I save your species, or I'll make your life miserable."

Music, laughter, conversations all went on somewhere far away from them. Their tiny world was still and silent.

Nida looked back and forth between them, sweat beading on the back of her neck. Rowec's hand never left the small of her back, his thumb occasionally rubbing her exposed skin. Her hand never left his rigid frame, either.

Brynn smirked. "Fine. No guards. You have ten minutes."

Brynn was that desperate for the others to believe they were getting along?

Without a word, he headed for the glass doors that led into the garden, tugging Nida with him.

She scurried behind him, lifting her dress to walk more easily and trying not to look over her shoulder. Brynn would be fuming. She'd be furious. She *should* be, at least. This wasn't normal behavior for Brynn. Maybe the upcoming hatching ceremony *was* getting to her.

He swept her out into the main square of the garden to the fountain and invited her to sit next to him on its ledge.

The moon hung dangerously low. His brother would be there any second.

"Nida." His fingers led her chin to focus on him. "Are you okay?"

She shook her head, trying to gain her composure. "It's just Brynn. I have something I've needed to tell you."

"I have to tell you something, too." He laughed at himself. "Actually, I've been wanting to say a lot of somethings."

Here goes nothing. "Rowec, you have to leave—"

"I think I'm falling in love with you—wait. What?"

Her heart burst and twisted all at once. "You're falling in love with me?"

"Why do you want me to leave? Or do you mean after the ceremony? Because I do, too. I want to leave... with you." He took her hands in his. "I meant what I said about helping your sisters, but I-I want you to come with me, to be with me, not just in my village." His cheeks pinked.

She closed her eyes unable to stop the tears forming. She was smiling. That's what she wanted, too. She wanted to be with him.

"Don't cry," he whispered, pulling her in close, his lips settled at her fore-head. "Did I just sound like the stupidest man on the planet?"

She laughed and wiped her eyes. "No, no. Not at all. I really wanted to hear you say that." She buried her cheek against his chest.

It was like a dream. A warm dream of their making, the scent of him and a calming breeze holding their private world together.

But this wasn't a dream. It was the real world. His staying had dire conse-quences, and so did his leaving. She wouldn't let him lose his life for her people. She had to tell him.

He smoothed back her hair and kissed her forehead. "I'm so glad."

She pulled away to look him in the eyes. "But I have to tell you something else."

There was a grunt from the far corner of the garden. He jerked his head in its direction.

The pieces of her bursting heart sank. Time was up.

"Rowec," she swallowed, pulling his attention back to her. "You're not staying until the ceremony. You have to leave right now."

His eyebrows furrowed. "What? Why?"

The brush shifted behind them. He jumped up. "What's going on? Did she send guards to spy on us?" He began walking toward the corner shrouded in durlo trees.

"No, wait. Stop and listen, please."

His hand in hers, she tugged him back. He stopped and faced her.

"It's not a guard. It's your brother."

"My what?" He jerked his head in the direction of the corner again. "What about your sisters? The hatchery?"

"Rowec, I'm sorry. I didn't know." The tears flowed, the guilt, the disappointment. "After your dinner with Brynn, she confessed that you and she would die in the ceremony."

"What?" He stepped nearer, his chest broadening. He dropped his hands from hers.

I'm losing him. "She said it's always been that way, but I didn't know. I swear I had no idea. I would have never let you stay if I'd known that. Please, believe me." She clasped her hands to her chest.

He blinked and took a deep breath. "How does my brother play into this?"

Bushes rustled.

He glanced in the direction of the rustling; she glanced back at the glass windows and her sisters dancing inside.

"Rowec?" a male's voice called from the wall.

Rowec inched toward it, and she followed. "Your brother and Etta visited shortly after your dinner—"

"Etta?"

"They wanted to negotiate your release. Brynn refused. I snuck out and told them to meet us here, tonight, to rescue you. I-I couldn't let her kill you." She sobbed and wiped her eyes.

He cupped her face. "You got my brother to come. You set this all up... just to save me?"

She nodded, tears spilling over. "I-I didn't know the ceremony would kill you—"

He took her again, wrapped himself around her. "Why are you crying? You're saving me. But Nida, the hatchery. Your sisters—"

"I know." She took a deep breath and sniffled against his chest. "Ascara and I are trying to find another way to save them, but I can't let you die for it."

He pulled back and tilted his head down. "Nida, I want you—"

"Let's go, already!" Etta burst through the trees, hands on her hips.

They jerked their gaze to her. *Etta? Perfect Etta? His future wife, Etta?*

His hand slid from Nida's shoulders to her hand. "Where's Maur?"

Etta headed for the wall behind her, and they followed, ducking under the branches. "He's just on the outside. He's going to pull us up."

"Where are the others? Why didn't you bring more fighters?" Rowec demanded.

He must have been furious. His hand squeezed hers as they walked, tethering her to him as they hurried for the wall.

"Only Maur and I could come."

"What?" he shouted, but quickly shook his head. "I'm sorry, Etta. I'm grateful that you and Maur came."

Etta shrugged and tossed her hair. "I can't live down my future husband being used by reptile women. Imagine the reputation."

He looked back at her.

She shrugged. "She was your only way out before the ceremony."

They reached the corner where a thin rope dangled.

"Maur?" Rowec called out.

"I'm here!" his brother shouted back on the other side. "Damn, it's good to hear your voice. Let's go! We still have another wall to scale."

Rowec pulled Nida to the rope and began wrapping it around her leg. "Here, hold onto this—"

"No, Rowec. I told you already. I can't leave my sisters—"

"They'll kill you for letting me go."

"No, they won't. They'll hate me. They'll probably lock me up forever, but Brynn won't kill me. I have to stay and try to save them, too."

"What are you doing?" Etta spat. She immediately began undoing the knot Rowec had just tied. "We're not bringing this *thing* back."

"Nida!" It was Ascara somewhere far behind them. Something was wrong.

"Etta, let go!" Rowec yanked the rope from her hand and handed it back to Nida. "I can't leave you, Nida. Please come with me. Ascara can solve it."

"Nida! They're coming!" Ascara screamed from beyond the fruit trees. She was getting closer.

She didn't know what her sisters would do to her. But if Rowec didn't get out, she knew *exactly* what they'd do to him.

"Maur, pull!" Rowec shouted.

"No." She slipped out of the rope and shoved it at Rowec. "No, you have to go first."

Etta took it and wrapped it around her own foot just before Maur began pulling.

Rowec shook his head. "Nida, please don't do this."

She stepped back a foot, but it felt too far away. "No, you have to go. I can't leave my sisters. If they capture you again, they'll use you in the ceremony." She shook her head. "I couldn't live with myself."

He reached out for her.

"Rowec!" Etta dangled in the air and pointed behind them. "They're coming with guards!"

This was it. She'd never see him again, just as she'd feared. She had been so stupid to hope that everything would work out.

Etta climbed on top of the ledge and tossed the rope back down to them.

"Nida, I want to leave *with* you."

"I know, but—"

Ascara tore through the trees. "Nida!" Her curls were falling, and a light sheen of sweat shined on her forehead. "She's coming. Brynn is coming, and she has guards."

Rowec postured in their direction.

"No, you have to go now!" Nida pleaded, pushing him to take the rope.

"Hurry, Rowec!" Etta screamed.

"Nida, I'll come back for you." He grabbed her by the waist and the back of her neck. "I promise." His lips pressed against hers.

It happened so fast, she barely registered what was happening.

His fingers wove through her hair as he cradled her to him. Pressed flat against him, his mouth was liquid fire on hers. His taste, his tongue. It filled her, head to toe, with familiar security. Like anything was possible and everything was simple at the same time. It was where she was meant to be.

Her fingers gripped his vest.

More. She needed more of him. She needed all of him.

"Rowec!" Etta shrieked.

Nida had to let him go. She held back a sob and pushed him away, severing their connection, their warmth. A universe between them. "Go! They'll kill you! Go!" she sobbed.

"I'll come back. I promise." He gripped the rope as Etta screamed for Maur to pull.

Within seconds, Rowec was dangling in the air, tears in his eyes.

Pain ripped through her arms as two guards grabbed her. She nearly toppled to the ground, but her sisters' claws dug deep into her fleshy, scaleless arms and kept her upright.

Rowec would make it. He'd survive. He'd get to live the life he deserved.

Her heart broke into pieces, and she sobbed. She had just helped their best chance for survival escape. There was no going back. She either figured out how to fix the ceremony, or she'd doomed all of her sisters and the jungle to death.

The guards turned her around just as Brynn came charging.

Ascara tried to intervene. "Take a deep breath, Brynn. It's not as—"

"Get off me!" Brynn tossed Ascara to the side. "You! You, traitor!"

Nida swallowed and focused on the claw her sister had pointed at her nose. "We're *Life* Weavers. We shouldn't have to murder and trick people to live. We'll find another way to—"

Brynn backhanded her across the face, slicing Nida's cheek with a piece of her jewelry.

Nida gasped as the force tossed her head violently to the side. She wiped her bloody cheek and tears onto her shoulder and dropped her chin to her chest. A fresh new pain thundered through her skull.

"You've killed us!" Brynn shrilled, tears spilling over her cheeks, too. "You've destroyed us—your sisters! For that *man*? For a murderous *beast?*"

Nida met her sister's glare with one of her own. She clenched her jaw and said, "He's not a beast, Brynn. *You* are."

Brynn's eyes widened as she stepped back. "Take her away," she mumbled.

Nida glanced back at the wall one last time. With no sign of Rowec, she closed her eyes. He was finally free.

"Put her in the cell where she can die alone!" Brynn screamed.

CHAPTER 19

*R*owec would go back for her. He wouldn't leave her there for her sisters to mistreat her... or worse.

He climbed over the last wall of the Tialan gardens and helped Etta over the side.

Maur nudged him and nodded at her.

He shook his head. "Not now."

He was grateful Maur and Etta had come to save him. Etta had definitely done something he'd never expected, and risked her life for it, too. He would always be grateful for that.

"Hurry!" she urged.

"Why?" Maur asked. "We're in the clear. We'll be in the village in no time."

She shrugged and scurried through the jungle for their village, Rowec and Maur on her heels. They ran around trunks and under limping fronds. Etta was lithe and nimble. She didn't even need a peicha knife to slice through the trees.

"Did they torture you?" Maur panted. "Make you work as a slave?"

Rowec's thoughts drifted. Nida's dress had fit perfectly. The small of her back had been so smooth he wanted to drag his fingertips across her skin all night. Her curves had been pressed against him and fit with him. Their time hadn't been enough. He'd wanted more and had to fight not to kiss her right there in front of all of her sisters.

He *still* wanted her. And he had left without her.

"Rowec?"

"No," Rowec replied. "Nothing like that. They just wanted me to help their species."

Maur scoffed. "Sounds like you liked them."

Every time Nida smiled, it had fueled him. And that kiss? The taste of her still lingered on his lips. He wanted to make her laugh, he wanted to listen to her tell stories, he wanted... her. He wanted a future with her.

"Rowec?"

"I liked one of 'em, yeah."

Maur ran nearer. "Was it the one you were screaming for?"

Rowec didn't answer. If he wanted a future with Nida, then he needed a plan. He'd get back to Zchi and get a group of warriors organized. He'd have to bring them up to date on what they would be fighting against, but they'd be willing to accompany him. It was why he found Maur and Etta coming for him alone so odd.

He glanced up at Etta.

It was a ridiculous sight, Etta running through the jungle in her skirts and hair pinned up. He'd have to tell her father how brave she was. "Now, tell me again why an army didn't come back for me?" he asked.

Maur dodged around a tree. "The chief stopped it—"

"Maur!" Etta snapped at him.

"What?"

"My father didn't stop it—"

Maur snorted. "Really? Because that's what I'd call it. He clearly said not to send anyone for Rowec—"

"Maur!" she repeated.

"What the hell is going on?" Rowec demanded.

Etta panted ahead. "It's nothing. It'll be safer in my home."

Safe? Her home? Why wasn't it safe? Why would he go to her home? They weren't married. He had his own place. Something wasn't adding up. She'd never invited him before, and there had been plenty of opportunities. No, the first thing he was going to do was head straight for the chief.

The glow of the torches from Zchi lit up the night sky and hid the stars. He never thought he'd be so happy to see his home. But he wouldn't be staying long; he had to get right back out there.

The square was full where all the torches blazed and the light bounced off weapons and bare chests. The warriors?

"Come on." Etta tried to urge them around the back of her house.

"Why are all the warriors lined up in the square?" Maur asked.

Good question.

Ignoring Etta, Rowec walked out to the middle of the village toward the first warrior in the line. She fussed over it every step of the way. "Why are you out here? Who's attacking?"

Easily the shortest of the group, the fighter with a small bare chest and a shiny, new peicha knife at his hip blinked twice when he realized it was Rowec speaking to him. "Uh, sir, we're not being attacked. We're doing the attacking."

"On who?"

"The Crola."

But what had they done? "Did they break the treaty while I was gone?"

"I don't know. The chief ordered us out here, sir."

The chief? Rowec turned to his brother. "Maur, I'm going to challenge the chief. Will you come with me?"

Maur had been the one who'd organized his escape with Nida, but he'd have to tell him thanks for being there and saving him later. Right now, he just wanted someone he could trust by his side.

Maur nodded. "Of course."

Rowec charged straight for the meeting house.

The chief had stopped his own fighters from rescuing him, and now he was sending them off to fight in a battle with the Crola without the warriors clearly understanding why, without a breach of the treaty. It was careless, dangerous, murderous. It would get people killed without reason.

"Wait!" Etta pulled on him to stop.

She'd have to do better. She wasn't nearly strong enough, and he wouldn't stop until the chief explained himself.

Rowec marched up the hill and burst into the wooden meeting house with its leaf-carved banisters and oiled paratil walls. The heavy doors slammed against the sides.

Chief Moddin had been sitting at the head of the table in his cream-colored robe with a bright orange hem. His arms were crossed, elbows on the table, and the small lamp illuminated his tan, bald head. Beside him was Etta's grandfather, hunched over the table and talking to his son in hushed tones.

Moddin looked his way and bolted upright. "Rowec? That is some... interesting garb. What are you doing here?"

Rowec stood squarely at the opposite end of the meeting table and crossed his arms, too. "What am I doing here? Why didn't you send warriors to rescue me? You had to send your own daughter? Do you have any idea what kind of danger your daughter was in?"

Moddin glared down Etta, who had slid beside Maur and behind Rowec's left shoulder. "I told you not to interfere."

Rowec lifted an eyebrow. "Not to interfere? She wasn't supposed to help rescue the best warrior the Zchi has? Do I mean nothing to you?"

"You are not the center of the world, Rowec. I have an entire clan to protect." Moddin smirked.

Protect? Sitting in a nicely carved and cushioned chair in this meeting house? In his oversized home? What, exactly, had he done to protect them—any of them? He hadn't risked his life. He never fought. He sat in his massive home built, not by his hands, but the hands of the people serving him, making decisions and passing judgment on *who* was worth saving?

"I am the best fighter." Rowec put a hand to his chest. "I have slaughtered more than my fair share for this clan, and I wasn't worth rescuing?"

Moddin shot a glance to his elderly father, who quickly hobbled out of the room. "We were going to rescue you... shortly. But it seems my daughter has moved up the timeline. If it's ruined, it's on her head."

"I could have died," Rowec boomed.

Moddin smiled. "You would have been fine. The hatching isn't for another week. We would have come for you before that."

Rowec's mind went blank. "You know about the hatching?"

Moddin shook his head and came around the edge of the table toward him. "Know about it? We started the pact with those *things*. They stay in the jungle far away from us; we send a man to them for their slitherskin ceremony." He clicked his tongue. "It seems there's much about the world you warriors don't understand."

Rage flooded Rowec's view. There might have been things he didn't know, but not by choice. All he saw was red, and if the chief didn't have a good explanation, there'd be no holding him back. "And you knew they were dying in the ceremony? You've been sacrificing our people to the Tialans?"

Maur stepped forward. "What?"

Rowec held his arm out to stop him.

Moddin then stopped a few feet before them with his chest puffed up as best he could. "They go blissfully unaware. We're told they pass in their sleep during the ceremony. It's the best kind of death. The only death our kind can hope for, and this pact has kept the clan safe from the Tialans."

Rowec dropped his arms and balled his fists. "You're a traitor," he spat. "How could you sacrifice our own people?"

Moddin's grin spread wide. "We didn't. We used Crola men."

Crola men. Memories of fighting and capturing Crola men in raids came flooding back. He'd assumed the ones the chief had told them not to keep were because they weren't strong enough to be Zchi warriors or they wouldn't be obedient to their way of life. What had he been part of?

Rowec's nostrils flared. "You passed judgment on them because they weren't fit to be fighters..."

"Wrong. Every time we fought or raided with the Crola, I was looking for warriors that could pass as Zchi for the Tialan ceremony."

Maur dropped his head and shook it. "This is ridiculous. You've been breaking the treaty with the Crola to keep a pact with the Tialans? I'm not the biggest fan of the Crola, but even I have the sense to know this is wrong."

But it was worse than that.

"Once the Crola find out," Rowec said, "the treaty will be broken. We'll be at war. How do they not know yet?"

Moddin huffed. "That treaty with the other clans was the dumbest thing your family has ever done. It's been a thorn in our side since its inception."

Maur bristled at the mention of their dead parents.

"The Tialans didn't care who we sent, but without raids or wars, we had no Crola to give them," Moddin continued. "We couldn't just kidnap a Crola and volunteer him to the Tialans out of nowhere. They'd find out. We were stuck."

Rowec shook his head. "So you volunteered me? Or my brother? Is that it? When the treaty didn't allow you to easily take a Crola—"

Moddin laughed in his face. "No, that was just convenient. When you were kidnapped, I seized the opportunity—"

"You took that Crola warrior!" Maur blurted. His breathing had become erratic and forceful through his nose.

Rowec looked back at his brother.

Maur nodded to him. "Shortly after you were taken, a Crola warrior showed up in a cage. We had no idea where he'd come from." He pointed at Moddin. "You said he was stealing and you caught him, but you kidnapped him, didn't you?"

Moddin lifted his chin and crossed his arms. "We were going to swap him in place for your brother—"

"And then he killed himself," Maur seethed.

Rowec's mouth dropped open. "He did what?" He whipped his head around and advanced on Moddin. Etta, whom he'd almost forgotten was still there, even tried to hold him back.

"He killed himself before we'd had the chance to swap him for you," Moddin said without shame, without guilt. He said it with the same disappointment as if he'd just dropped a piece of bread in the mud.

"So that's why the warriors are out and ready? We're fighting the Crola? They're coming here because they found out that you kidnapped a Crola and broke the treaty?" Rowec's nails drove into his palms. He'd kill Moddin. Etta had better be hiding some amazing strength, because between him and Maur, they'd kill their chief.

Moddin took a step back and narrowed his glare. "The Crola have no idea we broke the treaty. They came for him, but we had already gotten rid of his body."

Rowec roared, taking another step closer. His hands and muscles were itching for release across Moddin's smug little face.

Moddin took another step back. "Your brother made an excellent case for

you, bursting into the meeting with the Crola leaders and demanding an army
to rescue his brother taken by the Tialans."

Rowec's heart plummeted. "So the Crola think the Tialans took their
fighter?"

"And they're marching on the temple as we speak. You're too late."

Too late? Rowec spun to Etta. Her hands were clasped to her chest. Her
eyes were wide like a newborn kurimolle. She was caught in his shadow.

"You! That's why you wanted me to hide at your place. That's why you
agreed to get me out without your father knowing. You didn't want me there
for the fight when the Crola showed up! You were part of this! You worked
with your father to do this!"

"I did it for you," she squeaked, hands shaking. "I just wanted to save you.
That's all that matters. Now, we can get married—"

"You think I'm marrying you?" As if he would ever have anything else to
do with this chief and his family again.

Etta froze. "What—"

"I'm not marrying you, and I never was—"

Etta's eyes went cold as she stood a little taller. "I didn't know what my
father was doing, and *I* saved you with Maur. *I* risked my life, *I* talked to
that *thing*—"

"She's telling the truth," Moddin added, seemingly amused. "I didn't tell
her any of it. Guess I should have though. Maybe it would have prevented this
headache."

This *headache*? He had let himself get distracted. The rage had yet to evaporate, leaving his muscles numb. He was ashamed. He had been a tool, and
now the Crola would be descending on the Tialans—*on Nida*. "You can't do
this. It'll be a blood bath. I've seen—I've learned things. If you don't care about
them, think about what you're doing to us. The Tialans keep the jungle
healthy. They keep it alive, we rely on it. We need to stop the Crola, and I can
do it. I can negotiate—"

"You're not doing anything," Moddin countered. "Once the Crola storm
the Tialans, both sides will weaken from the fight, and that's when our guys
will step in and take out both. Our clan will be safe, and we'll have plenty of
farmland to keep everyone fed."

"It's wrong!"

Moddin held up a finger to Rowec's nose. "I will do *anything* to save
our clan."

Was it truly saving them if they had to murder and trick others into
losing? If this was how they were going to live, if this was who they were, was
there anything about them worth saving?

Moddin smirked. "Go home, Rowec. You've lost."

Rowec punched him square in the face. Moddin's head flew back, blood spraying from his shattered nose, as his arms wheeled before he hit the floor. Etta ran to help her father.

He had to reach their fighters first before they destroyed the Crola and the Tialans. He had to change the plan. He spun for the doors.

"You're too late, Rowec," Moddin mumbled with his hand at his nose. "Our men are already halfway to the temple by now."

He was faster than a whole group moving through dense patches of trees and foliage. He could make it.

CHAPTER 20

*N*ida rubbed her sore, damp eyes and winced at the welt growing on her cheek.

She had been locked in Rowec's old cell for only a few hours with no sign of what they'd do to her. Back against the cold wall, she sat in the mud created from moisture settling on the dusty floor. Her dress was probably a mess, too. She drew up her knees and rested her forehead on them.

Her chest was the heaviest it had ever been. Worry, fear, doubt, shame—they swirled around her heart and reminded her of all the things she'd failed to do.

How could she save her sisters while locked up? She had to talk to Ascara. They had to fix the levers in the ceiling of the prayer room so they could open, and they could maybe find a way…

She sobbed.

She had ruined everything. The only glimmer was knowing Rowec had escaped. At least she had done that part right.

She sobbed again.

Every single one of her sisters probably hated her, her new sisters might not be born, the jungle would suffer if they weren't, and Rowec…

Her mind always wandered back to him but thinking about him was selfish. Brynn had been right. She had sacrificed her sisters, her family, for one human.

She had lost everything.

Something moved across her shoulder. She reached up and pulled back a shaking Raz.

"Raz! Where have you been?"

She sat him back on her shoulder, and he curled up just enough into her hair. He must have jumped out when Rowec had kissed her.

Her fingers went to her lips, and her heart fluttered all over again. Her mouth had been crushed by his, and it wasn't enough. Her cheeks burned with heat at the thought of more of him. She wanted—needed—more of him. She needed his hands on more skin than just her back, his mouth on more of her than just her lips. The rigid strength of him cradling him in her arms...

She let out another sob.

Raz crawled out again and nuzzled her cheek.

"Thanks, Raz," she said between tears. "But I'm not sure you're safe here."

He trilled, and she scratched him underneath his chin.

"I don't think," she started, but the sobs had worked their way out again. "I don't think I'll be able to take care of you for long."

"Why would you think that?" Ascara moved into the firelight of the sconces.

"Ascara!" Nida gripped the bars and knelt closer. "Did you find something? Did you figure it out?"

"First, tell me the truth." Ascara stood several feet away from the bars, her arms crossed.

What was wrong? "The truth... about what?"

"I saw that kiss. I saw that look. You wanted to run away with him."

She shook her head. "Ascara, I couldn't. I couldn't leave the hatchery before we figured it out—"

"But you wanted to."

Nida sniffled and lowered her head. "I'm sorry—"

"Why didn't you tell me before?"

She shook her head. "I didn't want to hurt your feelings."

"For him? I would have understood." Ascara stepped closer.

"It doesn't matter. He's gone. Brynn will never let me out of here, and we need to figure out that prayer room—"

"Do you love him?"

A drop of water echoed behind her through a tiny hole in her cell's ceiling. Ascara waited silently. "I asked for the truth."

"I love him," she said. She blinked, letting a small puff of air escape her. She'd said it. She'd finally said what had been building up. "I'm sorry. I should have told you, but I love him. I wanted to be with him."

"So, when we tell Brynn how to do the *new* ceremony, will you leave with him?"

She shook her head. "He's gone, Ascara. He said he'd come back, but he won't. And Brynn won't let him—" She gasped. "Ascara, did you do it? Did you figure it out?"

Ascara smiled.

"No one has to die?" Nida jumped up. "Ascara, are you serious?"

She nodded. "It still takes human males."

Nida covered her mouth and laughed. Fresh tears formed. "How did you figure it out?"

Ascara played with a temple key in her hand. "After they locked you up, Brynn was losing her mind. Everyone sort of scattered, so I ran to the prayer room."

"How'd you fix the lever?"

"I hit it really hard…"

Nida's eyes bulged.

"With a rock." She shrugged. "It was jammed."

"And? What is it? What's the change? What did the painting show?"

"Nothing. It's just… more."

"More?"

"The Tialans and humans we saw in the patterns created a chain. Light was radiating, not from the couple, but from all of them. They're all giving their Vigor. No one has to die if everyone is willing to help a little."

Nida laughed again. "That's it?"

"That's it." Ascara twisted the key in her hand to fit the lock of Nida's cell and unlatched the gate. "I mean, we won't know for sure until the ceremony, but Brynn said the last queen and her mate went in with her alone. That's the exact opposite of what the prayer room shows. And if you think about it, it makes sense."

Nida ran around to hug her, both of them laughing on each other's shoulders.

"I can't believe it."

Ascara nodded. "I'm still thinking someone sabotaged it. Maybe someone wanted a queen out of the way so *she* could be queen, then passed on the lie? Or maybe I just really hate Drathella and don't want her to be queen. We still need male Vigor though."

But that they had time for. That they could get.

"So why set me free? Brynn will know and—"

"Screw Brynn. She lied, and she's lost her mind. You should see her in the throne room."

Nida narrowed her eyebrows. "What is she doing in the throne room?"

"First, she was ordering the guards to go hunt down Rowec, but then that changed when some of the outside guards said that there was a shadow moving in the jungle."

A shadow in the jungle?

"The whole temple is losing their minds over it." Ascara shrugged. "I came down to let you out because I was certain no one would notice. They're not sure what this shadow thing is, but Brynn is treating it like we're about to go to war or something." Ascara rolled her eyes and smoothed out her gown.

"What if Rowec's warriors are coming to retaliate?" Nida asked.

It would mean death and slaughter. None of them would be safe. It would be a massacre on both sides, and the hatchery…

"We have to go now!" She pulled Ascara along.

"What do you want me to do?"

"Hide the little sisters. Then, go to Brynn and tell her about the ceremony." Ascara stopped and made a grimace. "I don't want to go to Brynn."

"If you stay with Brynn, you'll have direct information about what's going on. They'll want to keep her informed first. You'll be safe." She was already halfway down the hall.

"Where are you going, then?" Ascara shouted.

"To protect the hatchery." Nida dashed through the halls.

ROWEC CHARGED DEEPER into the jungle, the branches slicing his shins as he ran. He didn't have time to cut the flora or wind around. Straight through. It was the fastest way to her.

Maur panted a few feet beside him. "Am I seriously going back to this place?"

Rowec smirked. "Once we catch up to our men, you're going to stay with them and take the lead. I'm going to find Nida."

"Oh, yeah, so you get the girl, and I get a bunch of sweaty men. Fun."

They came up on the mass of Zchi warriors nearly at the temple. Several stopped and turned as Rowec ran up alongside of them. The chief had ordered all of their men—nearly a hundred—to interfere and take advantage of the Tialans and the Crola. He shook his head.

At the lead, he and Maur found Lyle, the chief's second-in-command, shouting orders to each squad.

Fools.

They should have done this before leaving, but the chief had been in such a hurry to get them out of there, he could have sent the men to their deaths.

"Stop," Rowec shouted, running up beside Lyle. "Stop. First of all, you give orders before you leave. Second, we're changing orders." He wiped his forehead free from sweat.

"Like hell we are. My orders were very clear from the chief—"

Maur punched Lyle square in the jaw, knocking him out and sending him to the ground.

Everyone stared at him; Maur shrugged.

Rowec took Lyle's peicha. "All right, listen up. Maur's in charge, now. Do what he says, or I'll kill you myself." He headed for the outer wall of the garden to follow it toward the front.

Maur roared. "That's right, you stupid, no-good, brainless—"

"Maur... this isn't training camp," he shouted back. "Get them inside the walls. They need to stop the Crola."

Hopefully Maur didn't do anything too stupid.

Rowec made his way around the outside of the grounds and toward the front. Jungle debris and wood shavings had been left in the clearing. The two front doors had been swung open and smeared with dark purple handprints.

Definitely Crola.

He raced up the stairs, hoping the Tialans didn't immediately kill him or throw him back into the cell when he arrived. But as he ascended to the top level and entered the temple, screams and the clanging of metal echoed down the corridors.

Bleeding bodies were strewn everywhere—both Tialan and Crola. He carefully stepped over them and followed the noises of fighting. After a few turns, he entered a throne room. Brynntial was on the floor on her knees, blood pooling around her.

With a staff, Ascara was fending off whoever must have been Brynntial's attacker. He was as tall as she was, and though she was strong, the warrior had the experience.

The Crola thrust at her with his spear as she twisted and knocked it away.

He lifted it up to slam it down on top of her head. She would have deflected it, but Rowec was quicker.

He pulled out Lyle's peicha knife from his back pocket, jumped, and sliced the Crola through the side, nearly cutting him in two.

The warrior crumpled to the ground, and Ascara froze, eyes wide with blood spattered across her skin and scales. She blinked a few times, and then dropped the staff. It clattered across the floor. "Rowec?"

"We've come to help," he said.

She swallowed as her chest heaved. "These aren't your men?"

He shook his head. "Another clan, but we're here to help stop them."

She nodded and knelt beside Brynntial on the floor. He did the same.

Brynntial's green scales had lost their luster and were chipped, too. Her hair was matted with blood and stuck to her shoulders, and her fingers trembled.

"We failed," she forced through thin lips.

Ascara cradled her sister's head in her lap. "Not yet, Brynn."

"Where's Nida?" Rowec asked. He needed to keep moving.

Brynntial licked her dry lips and groaned, "In the cell—"

"In the hatchery," Ascara said.

They had answered together, then glanced at one another, and Brynntial smiled. "Of course, she's in the hatchery." She reached out a shaky hand to Rowec's forearm. "Hurry or she'll die trying to save them."

He nodded. "I don't know where it is."

"I can take you, but—" Ascara looked down at Brynntial in her arms.

"Go with him. I'm done," she whispered.

Rowec scratched a thumb against his forehead. "Can't you Life Weave her or something?"

Brynntial shook her head. "I don't want to be saved. I failed my sisters. I failed you. Let me go. Maybe your Life Weaving would still work on the buds, Ascara."

Ascara and Rowec looked at one another before she nodded. "I'll try."

She rested her sister's head down on some gathered fabric and stepped away from her. "Goodbye, Brynn."

Brynntial grinned and waved them off. "Hurry. Nida could be in trouble."

Rowec followed Ascara through the throne room and back into the corridors for the hatchery.

I'm coming, Nida.

CHAPTER 21

*N*ida slammed the golden doors shut and rested her forehead against the cool metal, tears bubbling up again.

The screams and shouts of her sisters fighting mixed in with the shattering of sconces and clanging of weapons against stone had echoed through the main halls as she had run. The men she had sneaked past didn't look like Rowec's. They were different. They looked like an entirely different clan.

And they were destroying everything.

A part of her yearned to be out fighting alongside her sisters, but she'd be of no use to them. Too human, too fragile, she lacked the strength and the claws to fight back. Staying with and protecting the hatchery was the smartest thing she could do.

Slowly turning and resting her back against the door, she surveyed the buds. Their bases were already turning bright and beautiful with hints of fuchsia, leaf-green, violet, and royal blue. They were as long as her torso and nearly ready to bloom.

"All right, girls," she whispered. "We're not going to make a sound. We're going to be absolutely quiet so that hopefully no one even notices we're here."

The doors shook behind her, and a man's voice demanded she open it.

It didn't sound like Rowec.

She pressed her body against the door, hoping her weight combined with the weight of the doors were enough to keep the warrior from breaking in.

She took deep breaths. Rowec had said he would come back for her, but it wasn't possible that he'd return this quickly. They'd all be dead before he could make it back in time—*if* he came back.

Her heart burned.

The man pounded and shook the doors, shouting something through it; the words were too muffled to understand.

Raz jumped out onto her shoulder, trembling.

"Raz, hide!" She helped him get to the floor and watched as he scurried and hid between some leaves in the darkened corner.

Back against the doors, she stretched her foot out to reach a staff leaning against the wall. She had used it to unstick the oculus in the ceiling sometimes. Nudging it just enough with her toe, it teetered until it fell. Able to drag it close with her foot, she picked it up and slid it through the handles of the door.

The man beat against the doors again, shaking them violently, but the staff held.

Bracing herself between the wall and a nearby wooden table with supplies, she grunted as she slid the table across the yellow stone to barricade the door.

The doors jerked violently with a thud, but the table had stopped him.

She grabbed a bucket she had used for watering and stood in the center of the garden. She couldn't kill or hurt anything with the silly thing, but maybe she could knock a man out with it.

Sure. She rolled her eyes at herself and gripped the handle of the bucket tighter in her sweaty palms.

The table jerked back as the man grunted against the door again. More voices. He had brought help.

She inched back deeper into the sanctuary, tears falling. This was it.

She'd thought she had lost everything before, but now—

The table bounced back and broke into several pieces as the doors swung open and slammed into the stone. The room shook, and dust fell from the ancient ceiling.

She yelped and pressed herself against the far wall, the bucket still clutched in her hand.

Three men walked in with their dark hair tied back and their bare chests, shoulders, and faces smeared with purple paint. Their pants were made of pale leather and were splattered with red—blood. In their hands were long spears and knife-like blades as wide as their arms. Definitely not Rowec's clan.

She swallowed and gasped for air. "Please, don't hurt me. Please—"

The one on the far right screamed as claws raked through his belly from behind. Blood spurted from his mouth and gut before he fell. The one on the far left did the same. The one in the middle spun to face—Drathella! She knocked the weapons out of his hands and raked her claws down his face and chest until he, too, dropped to his knees and then his face.

She panted in the doorway, her face wild with rage and her chest heaving with speckled blood.

Saved by the sister she had thought never cared, Nida started for her. "Sister—"

Drathella hissed, and Nida froze.

"Don't 'sister' me. We are not sisters," she snarled.

"I-I don't understand. I know you hate that I'm—"

"Human!"

Nida's stomach turned as Drathella narrowed her gaze and circled her along the edges of the room. She felt hunted, preyed upon. Drathella wouldn't—

Drathella hissed again and lifted her claws.

"I'm not human, though. I'm both, just like you. I-I couldn't help that I was born different—"

"I can." Drathella lunged, and Nida jumped out of the way across the garden and against the other wall.

If she ran out of the room, she'd be caught and killed by the humans. If she stayed, Drathella would... Drathella would... "Please, don't do this, Drathella. We're sisters; we are."

"You betrayed us!" Drathella shrieked. "You favored that stupid human before protecting your sisters' lives."

"That's not true!" she shouted, back against the wall. She scanned the room for a better weapon and found the shiny long-knife of the warriors by their bodies. Drathella was already closing in. She'd never reach the blade in time. She took a step toward the bodies anyway. "The sisters are going to live. The buds will be fine. Ascara and I—"

"You're a liar," Drathella said through clenched teeth.

Nida took another step and another. "I care about our future sisters as much as you do. I care that they *all* feel loved and appreciated and not ridiculed their whole life for something they couldn't help."

Drathella hissed and charged.

Nida ran for the weapon, but her feet were swept out from underneath her. Her chest and stomach slammed into the stone floor, all the air from her lungs gone. She coughed and gasped, her fingers still stretching for the blade.

Drathella pounced on top of her, clawing and raking her skin open. She punched and pulled at her hair.

Nida screamed and cried out, kicking and stretching for the knife right in front of her.

Drathella stood, grabbed her by her robe, and threw her across the room.

Nida's body crumpled against the stone wall and fell into the vines and leaves of the sanctuary. Pain burst through her, and she cried out. She had to stand, she had to fight back, but her arms and legs were limp. She wasn't strong enough.

The scent of iron wafted around her. Every inch of her hurt. She managed to pull herself up to her knees before Drathella approached with a sneer on her lips as she lifted one small bud.

"Don't..." Nida grunted.

"This one looks rather small, don't you think? Looks like it probably might be a hindrance to the Tialans."

"Don't...please..."

"I remember someone else's bud being quite small, too."

"Don't, Drathella—"

Drathella sliced a hole through the side of one petal and dropped it from waist-high. Water seeped out of the flower. "Whoops."

"No!" Nida slid across the floor, plugged the hole with her palm, and cradled it in her arms.

Drathella screamed and kicked her repeatedly in the ribs.

Nida cried out but wrapped herself around the flower to protect it from Drathella's wrath. With each kick, each punch, each rake of her skin, she held tighter.

The light in her vision dimmed, but there was something left inside her.

She pulled up the last bit of Vigor in her chest and pushed it into the bud in her arms. She tried to focus on the hole sealing shut and the sister inside it surviving, but just as the bud grew warmer in her arms, Drathella roared.

White-hot pain shot into her back and seared through her chest. She coughed warm blood, and her eyes drooped.

"Nida!"

Ascara.

"She's over here!"

Rowec?

Every muscle relaxed. No more pain. No more fear.

He had come back for her.

He had come back.

～

Rowec ran for Nida, as Ascara leaped on top of Drathella.

Nida was covered in blood. There were holes in her chest. Her skin and few teal scales had been scratched. Her face was bruising. What had she gone through? What had Drathella done to her?

And she had held on to save this one tiny bud?

His heart gave, and he cried. "Nida. Nida... please! Please, open your eyes. Please."

He carefully slid her arms from off the bud she had been protecting and held her.

She was lifeless. Her skin was graying and growing cold as her mouth dropped open. He pressed his ear to her chest. Her heartbeat was... faint.

Two other sisters clamored alongside Ascara to take down Drathella.

They had wrestled into the garden, Drathella looking considerably weaker than Ascara. She limped, some of her scales were missing, and her hair was out everywhere. Ascara was circling her.

A larger sister, one of the guards with red scales, jumped at Drathella, distracting her long enough for Ascara to shove a spike through Drathella's chest. It burst through the other side, and she toppled.

Ascara, taking a second to catch her breath, looked back at the entrance of the room. Rowec followed her gaze. Several other sisters, young and old, had gathered in the entrance to watch the spectacle.

A guard stood protectively in front of Ascara. "Do any of you want to attack the buds or kill a sister?"

The group shook their heads and dropped their chins.

Ascara ran to Rowec, kneeling and smoothing back Nida's hair.

"She's dying," he sobbed. "We can't let her die."

Ascara sniffled. "I can't—"

He pressed his ear against her chest again. The fainting beat was gone. "It's gone! You saved her before!"

Ascara's tears fell down her cheeks. "We can't bring her back to life, Rowec. It's not possible. None of us have enough Vigor for something like that."

"She died protecting your sisters. She didn't want any of us to die, humans or Tialans, and you're just going to let her?" he boomed. His eyes searched the large group gathering in the room.

His brother and several of their warriors broke through as well. Maur blinked and dropped his chin, as did his fellow Zchi warriors.

"Help me save her. This isn't fair!" Rowec pleaded.

"Rowec—"

"Give her mine," he said, choking back sobs. "Give her mine. Use all of it."

"I can't—"

"You can! You did before! Use mine to save Nida!"

"I don't know what will happen, Rowec. You could die—"

He glanced down and pressed his forehead against Nida's. "I already have."

Ascara's red-rimmed eyes blinked.

He glanced at Maur, whose somber expression had only deepened, and nodded slightly. Rowec reached a hand out for Ascara's. "I love her. Take my Vigor."

Ascara sniffled, shook her head, and sighed. "Okay, but, if I fail—"

"I'll give mine, too," said a small voice. It was a tiny, cerulean-scaled Tialan, merely a child with smaller eyes than her sisters and fewer scales. She wasn't as human as Nida, but she wasn't as Tialan as the others, either.

"I'll give mine, too," said another, and then another, until the whole room of Tialans had linked hands and stepped forward.

Maur cleared his throat. "We'll, uh, do what we can? Can we give some of our, uh, stuff, too?"

Rowec smiled, and Ascara gasped. "I'm not sure we need all this Vigor. I don't know what will happen."

The red-scaled guard behind Ascara sniffled. "We know, but we have to try."

Ascara nodded, took Rowec's free hand with one of hers, and rested her other hand on Nida's forehead. "Wait."

"Don't wait!" Rowec shouted.

Her eyes bulged. "The prayer room. Crilla, put your hand on my shoulder. Everyone, hold hands in a chain."

The red-scaled guard took another sister's hand until everyone in the room had connected to each other, Maur and the Zchi warriors included.

Ascara took a deep breath, closed her eyes, and Nida's body grew warm until it glowed.

Rowec blinked, the light nearly blinding him. *Please, Nida. Please come back to me.*

His head felt light. He wavered, his strength waning. *Give it all to her, Ascara. She can have mine.*

There was a rush of strength, a heady daze. Overwhelming love and light, and he remembered their hurried first kiss.

Nida glowed until the whole room burst with brilliant light.

Her sisters and the warriors flinched but held tightly to one another.

"Don't let go!" Ascara shouted, eyes squeezed shut and sweat dripping down her temples.

The room was awash in white.

Please, Nida. Please come back. We love you. I love you.

Ascara gasped, and the light faded. The warmth dissipated, and Nida's wounds were gone.

"Nida?" Rowec held her close. "Nida, can you hear me?"

Nida blinked once, twice, until her perfect teal eyes settled on him and she smiled. "You came back for me."

He crushed his lips against hers and wrapped his arms around her until she was pressed against him.

Some of her sisters giggled behind them, and they pulled away, panting and smiling, their foreheads pressed together. "I love you, Nida," he whispered.

"I love you, too."

A terrified Raz, with his white fur sticking out at funny angles, scurried to Rowec and jumped on his shoulder.

Nida smiled. "You did a great job hiding, Raz."

"Hey, look!" One of the younger sisters was squatting next to a bud and pointed to one of its petals moving.

The rest of the room watched in awe as several petals began moving.

CHAPTER 22

*N*ida's body was stiff and sleepy, but that was okay. She didn't want to leave the warmth of Rowec's arms anyway.

"The petals are moving?" she asked.

Rowec helped her to sit up, and sure enough, the petals were moving. They were...

"They're hatching!" she cried, willing herself to stand with Rowec's support. "Ascara?"

Ascara's eyes were teary, and her cheeks were bright red.

Nida wrapped her arms around her. "You did it! You figured it out, and you were right! You saved me. You saved us."

She shook her head and pulled back. "They all gave their Vigor. They all were willing to give their lives to save you."

She smiled and kissed her sister on the cheek. "Thank you, Ascara."

"There's more of 'em!" another sister squealed with a smile.

Maur and the other Zchi warriors took several cautious steps back as the youngest Tialan sisters giggled and danced around in the garden between the buds.

"Wake up, girls!" another young one said. "It's time to wake up! It's your birthday!"

One by one the petals of every bud peeled back. Nida gasped as she wiped tears from her eyes.

For years, she'd thought this day would go so differently. And just hours before, she had been convinced she had lost everything.

One by one, tiny little Tialans poked their heads out of the petals in brilliant, vibrant colors. Their damp wings unfurled as they yawned and stretched.

The youngest sisters in the room gathered a few each, hugging them in their arms and introducing themselves.

Nida checked Rowec's face. His eyes were wide, his face pale. She laughed. "They look like—"

She hooked her arm through his and patted his chest. "They'll get arms and legs eventually, and after the baby stage, they'll be more human."

He shook his head. "And they can fly?"

"They will until their wings fall off. Then they walk. Are you okay, Rowec? Your face—"

"This is incredible."

She giggled and rested her head against his chest.

The littlest sisters with their brand-new wings tried as hard as they could, flapping and straining their long necks into the air. All the sisters had joined in holding them in their palms and encouraging them to fly and hover.

Nida's robe was tugged, and she glanced down. Nymfan's eyes were red and in her cerulean arms was one tiny little bud. The one Drathella had cut open.

"Oh, Nymfan." Nida knelt.

The little one sniffled and wiped her eyes. "It's not hatching."

"I'm sorry." Nida frowned. "I tried as hard as I could to save her—"

One tiny petal bounced.

The girl gasped and looked up at Nida.

Her eyes widened. "Careful, Nymfan."

The petals slowly bounced the tiniest bit open.

"Can I help her?" Nymfan whispered.

Nida nodded, and together they helped peel back the flower's petals.

The tiniest little Tialan with even tinier wings squawked in the center, blinking big round eyes at them.

Nida sighed in relief. "She's your littlest sister. She's going to need the most help. It's a lot of responsibility. You think you can handle it?"

Nymfan smiled and nodded. "I will. I will take the *best* care of her." She leaned in and whispered, "I will call you Camprillion, and you'll be my favorite sister. I'll take care of you, I promise. I'll teach you how to fly and walk…" Nymfan walked off with Camprillion in her palms.

Rowec kissed Nida's cheek, and she smiled. "I don't know how to thank you, Rowec."

He shrugged, his large frame pressed against her. "I have an idea."

She lifted an eyebrow.

～

Nida turned her back on the early sun to face the Tial temple and all of her sisters on the front lawn. She took Rowec's hand.

The sweet, tangy scent of ripe paratils swept in with the moist heat from the jungle around them.

But they wouldn't be in the jungle for long.

They'd spent the last few days planning their trip through the Yvelkian mountains, and the coast. Maybe down to Black Harbor. Maybe they'd make their way to see the Vulkypsies in the south. She didn't care where they went. She just wanted to see it all with Rowec.

He kissed her on the top of her head and turned to hug his brother.

"Don't screw this up, Maur. If you start one war between the Tialans and Humans, I'll come back and kick you myself."

Maur had agreed to settle things between the Crola and the Tialans with Ascara's help, leaving the Zchi to fend for themselves. The other human clans would be contacted soon for peace talks.

Maur laughed. "Yeah, well, don't get lost, you big dummy." He then stepped forward and hugged Nida. "If my brother does something stupid, just leave him there. I don't care if it's on the other side of Lousha. Leave him there."

She smiled and kissed his cheek. "Thank you, Maur. Be careful and take care of Ascara."

His cheeks pinked before he returned to her sister's side.

Ascara stepped forward and rolled her eyes.

"Just a pet, right?" she teased.

Ascara shook her head and bit her lip. "He's a little weird, but a pet's fine. Maybe... *more* than a pet."

She giggled. "Have fun."

"No, you have fun, and then come right back."

She took Ascara's hands. "It won't be forever. I promise."

"If you don't come back, I'll order you to." Ascara lifted her violet-scaled chin.

She mirrored her. "Oh, really? Then I guess I have to, *my queen.*"

Ascara hugged her and sniffled. "I want you to stay, but I want you to go, too."

She smoothed her sister's hair. "I love you, too."

The giggles and shouts of the younger sisters with the newborn Tialans fluttering around their shoulders ran up to Nida and Rowec. They hugged them all as best as they could.

Rowec took her hand again. "Ready?"

She nodded. "Very."

Raz climbed out of Rowec's pocket and jumped to Nida.

Rowec scratched the top of Raz's head. "I see how it is."

Nida pulled her hair back to make room for him on her shoulder. "Keep a lookout, Raz."

He yawned and blinked.

They waved at their family one last time before turning into the jungle and ducking under drooping fronds.

"I still don't know how you walk through a jungle without cutting debris out of your way," he said.

She giggled. "It's easy. Stop and think that maybe *you're* the one in the way."

She led him around trees and vines.

"Do you think we should stop by the Zchi village first?" she asked with a smile. "Pay Etta a visit?"

He wrapped his arms around her and placed his chin on her shoulder. "Considering I punched my chief in the face, and then my brother punched his second-in-command? As much as I would love to see Etta lose her mind, I don't think that's a good idea."

She laughed, and he did, too.

"Then where to first?" she asked.

He stopped her under a ray of light that had broken through the canopy. His hands spread across her back and pulled her close enough that his lips went to her ear. "Anywhere with you."

THE END

ABOUT THE AUTHOR

Ryan Muree was a middle-school science teacher for nine years before completing her first young adult series, *The Last Elixir*. Naturally, she writes fantasy. Mostly epic. Always magical. She likes determined heroines who answer the call for wild adventures across crazy worlds. And she especially likes stories about women who face hardships and consequences with grit and smarts. When she's not inventing worlds for her characters to live in, she games with her husband and daughter, draws, paints, and sometimes says funny things. *Sometimes*.

Read more about Ryan Muree at www.ryanmuree.com.

EYE OF THE BEHOLDER

EMILY ALLEN WEST

Proofreading by Patrycja Pakula for Holabird Editing

A woman running for her life. A man hiding from his past. One island community in the path of a madman.

Rose Benoit manages bands for a living, but she can't manage to break free from her stalker ex-boyfriend, who happens to be a local cop. With nowhere else to turn, she flees to a mysterious island, hoping to find sanctuary with her cousin. Instead, she discovers Burke Masters, a rich, walled-off vigilante fighting a human-trafficking ring with enemies of his own... and fighting to be himself again after his mind and body have been ravaged by war.

When a threat arrives on the island's doorstep, Burke must protect his team and the victims caught in The Ring's net. As they work to bring down The Ring – and Rose's corrupt stalker ex closes in – Burke and Rose learn a terrible coincidence has linked their lives in more ways than they realized. But tragedy strikes the island's community, and the foundation of the love between them is threatened by the fallout. With no choice left, they must confront their enemies once and for all.

When the time to fight comes, will Burke revert to that ravaged beast within? Will Rose ever find beauty in a life beyond fear? And will they be forced to learn what it's like to live without each other?

Genre: Romantic Suspense
Heat level: Sensual

CHAPTER 1

*B*urke's place was here, where his peace of mind died among the ashes. Stuck in a flashback he couldn't fight off. Anguish. Obliteration. Fire. Death. He couldn't stop his mind from turning an image of a desert sun on his computer screen into an explosion before his very eyes. Destruction in all directions. Everything he, Burke Masters, had caused—the results of his cursed existence.

He saw nothing, heard nothing but the pounding of his heartbeat in his ears. The deafening roar erupting from his chest caught in his throat.

A sharp, clanging crash near his feet snapped him out of it. He stood as his gaze settled on his fisted hand, still outstretched, the cords of muscles in his arm flexed, veins bulging and ready to burst. The monitor bounced across the floor.

It wasn't the only thing he'd smashed. He had knocked the entire computer system over, too, along with the servers and extra external hard drives. The globe he'd been given on his tenth birthday rolled across the rug and over the hardwood floors, resting against the armchair's footrest. The entire desk was practically empty. Only the mouse and a few files remained.

He squeezed his eyes shut and tried to control his breathing. *In, out. In, out. Don't fall over.*

Just to be sure, he flexed the muscles in his leg, but the weak knee didn't collapse. Without his cane, staying upright was always a gamble when he moved suddenly. His heart threatened to race right out of his chest, but the lightheadedness had already begun to fade. He slowly opened his eyes and ran his damp, sweaty palms through his shaggy hair. The dark, mahogany-paneled bookshelves lining the walls reappeared, the red brocade curtains drawn over the massive floor-to-ceiling windows.

Quick, sharp footsteps pounded down the corridor, the telltale calling card of Lucien. Heat rose into his cheeks. *Oh, hell.*

Sure enough, the door burst open. Lucien stared agog at him, one hand on the door handle, the other reaching out to him.

"Are you okay?" Lucien glanced down at the mess.

He had no response. Nothing he said could explain these flashbacks. They filled him with rage, self-loathing, and the agonizing horror of waking up every morning to the same reality he'd caused.

He turned his back on Lucien and reached down to pick up his cane, wincing at the pain in his knee.

"What happened, B—"

"Don't," he commanded. The woman screaming his name echoed in his memory, making his eardrums feel ready to explode. He stood up straight, squared his shoulders and turned back around. "I told you. Not my name. Never again."

Lucien stilled, eyes narrowing. "Fine. What happened, *Masters?*"

Friendship let Lucien get away with too much. What was he still doing here, in this manor house? It was situated on a private island for God's sake. What were any of his people sticking around for? He'd made it clear that he wanted to be left alone. But no. They treated the gothic mansion he'd inherited like a hotel with no check-out time.

"Was it a flashback?" Lucien pressed.

He turned his back on him. Serving twelve years in the Marines together had turned them into brothers, the bond between them a lifeline that had carried him through combat and brought him back in one piece. Four years later, from this very island of West Cove in Puget Sound, the two of them had acclimated to life back home and established a new purpose together: new missions, a new team, a new way to do good in a world still at war within its own borders.

Until he'd messed it up for all of them—for the people looking to him and his crew for help.

Now, shadows and shame were the only friends he wanted.

"Get out," he managed, through gritted teeth.

"Are you going to clean that up, or do you expect Polly to when she brings your lunch?"

"Leave me alone!" he roared, whirling around, heat in his cheeks. His grip tightened hard on his cane.

The last person he wanted to see was the housekeeper who had practically raised him with such unconditional love. Even after she'd learned what a monster he really was, her eyes had only watered with sympathy while her short, rounded arms reached out for him in comfort. He couldn't take the fact she was still here. That any of them were.

Lucien crossed his lanky arms. Whereas he had only added muscle mass, Lucien had slimmed down since returning from active duty. "No. You've had too much of that lately."

Two huge steps and he was around the desk, fists clenched, aching to throw Lucien out of the room with his bare hands. Physically, his friend had never been a match for him. But Lucien had the nerve to look unbothered. Unafraid.

"Last time I checked, this is still my house. I expect my rules to be obeyed."

"You're not a sultan, or some king of a castle, you asshole," Lucien snapped back. "No matter how you try, you can't run from me and Charles. We care—"

"Just because we fought side-by-side for over a decade? Or because you think you're happy now that you've found some woman who loves you, so it gives you the right to interfere?"

Lucien paled. "You know about Paige and me?"

The corner of his lip tugged up without amusement, even as his leg screamed in protest at its overuse. "You brought her onto my island, and you think I wouldn't notice? I wanted all of you out of here, and you only added to the brood." His lips twisted into a snarl. "Another freeloader."

"Get over yourself." Lucien's hands went to his hips.

The silly, blond, hipster man bun went a long way to making Lucien seem less intimidating than he actually was, but he had seen his friend's deadly capabilities firsthand. His ability to end lives quickly had set them both apart from everyone else on the front lines and bonded them in the same sick way.

And despite the urge to rip something to shreds, he didn't want to do that to the man who'd stood by his side since their first mission together, ridiculous hair or not.

Why had he suggested Lucien come stay at the mansion when they'd returned stateside? Charles, too? He had been a fool to think they could have started up their gang, went back to being comrades in arms like the way things had been before. By having them here, plus the mansion's staff and the people they'd employed, it kept him from the one thing he wanted now —solitude.

Lucien drew in a breath. "This has nothing to do with Paige. You're killing yourself, Masters, locked away like this."

"Your point?"

"I'm not letting you die, damn it." Lucien shoved him hard.

He rocked back on his heels, absorbing the brunt of the blow. "It isn't your choice."

"The mission wasn't—"

"Don't." It came out somewhere between a plea and a growl. He couldn't bear to hear the rest of that sentence.

"You're having panic attacks. Flashbacks. Exercise alone isn't helping you control them anymore. You're not eating enough. Soon that golden-boy bronze skin of yours is going to turn sallow because you never go outside. You quit physical therapy, and you keep relying on that cane even though we both know you can use your leg much more than you let on." Lucien glanced at it and back up again. "You've broken half of the inane shit in the west wing and we can hear you pacing the corridors at three in the morning."

"I repeat: your point?" He wanted him out. He'd gone eight days without talking to a soul, and he was pissed it hadn't been longer than that.

Lucien's gaze narrowed. "I started talking to Charles about what it would take to get Power of Attorney, to prove your mental incapacities in court. If you're not going to save your life, then I will."

What the—

His hand shot out, grabbing Lucien by the front of his shirt. Cotton gathered in his fist, he towered over his friend, his bearded face inches away from Lucien's.

Everything had been taken from him. Not this, too.

For a second, Lucien's eyes went wide. Then the fear left them, and they fixated back on him. Lucien raised both of his hands and dug them into the offending arm, but he wasn't about to be deterred.

"You'd undermine me to claim my fortune?"

"No." It came out of Lucien in a rasp. "But I'd do it to save your life, you son of a bitch."

Breathe.

He let go of Lucien, pushing him back into the study's door. *Triple shit.* What had he been thinking? Of course Lucien wouldn't steal his fortune—he knew the man better than that. Give the hippie a tent in a forest, and he'd be happy. He was only here because Burke had invited him. Because they'd wanted to stay in close proximity after surviving the horrors of Ba'hir.

He had no one to blame but himself for the mess he'd created.

He rubbed his beard, his shoulders sagging. Silence stretched between them. He should let Lucien take everything and lock him away in some mental ward, where they could drug him past the point of thinking, beyond the point of remembering. But his demons would trail him there. He was as sure of it as he was sure of his own name.

He was too much of a coward to suffer his final downward spiral in front of strangers and nurses. No. He'd die within these walls first.

"What do you want from me?" he said finally.

Lucien straightened his shirt and cleared his throat. "I want you to get professional help. Let me bring a psychologist here—"

Open up to some stranger when he could hardly talk to his own friends?

"No." He cast Lucien a sideways glance and saw the concern for him in Lucien's eyes. He breathed deeply. "Not yet. Start with something smaller than the warzone of my psyche. Then... we'll see."

Lucien tapped his finger to his lips and looked around, casting a judgmental scowl on the mess he'd made. "Let's start with getting a new maid."

Another new person on the island? "Why? We have Katie—"

"She came to me and asked to work with Polly in the kitchen instead. She's sort of become the de-facto sous-chef anyway, and she loves it there, so I told her okay. She and Polly are still going to tend to the first floor, but we're officially out a maid up here."

"I don't need one." His hands balled into fists. "I can tidy up."

Lucien's gaze narrowed. "But will you? The entire second and third floors?"

"It can stay dirty."

"Great. That'll just make my case for Power of Attorney even stronger if I can show you living in shitty conditions."

Both men crossed their arms, staring each other down. Neither of them liked to lose, but in the battle of the wills, Burke knew he was going to get screwed this time. If he refused, Katie would end up coming back up here to clean just out of the goodness of her heart. And he wanted her to continue cooking, if that's what she wanted to do.

"Fine."

Lucien cracked a smile. "Great. I already have someone in mind. Paige's cousin."

The resident tech genius had family? None had turned up in the numerous background checks they'd done before Lucien brought her on the team. "Since when did she have a cousin?"

"It's a recent development." Lucien shifted his weight. "They just found each other online—"

"I don't care. I haven't met Paige and you want me to meet her cousin?"

"Whose fault is that?" Lucien threw up his hands. "You scared her away."

Frowning hard, his eyes fell to the floor. "I didn't know she was watching when I threw that chair across the room. In my defense, the anniversary of their deaths wasn't the best day for her to introduce herself." Guilt gnawed at him. Part of the reason he'd sequestered himself away since Pine Ridge was to avoid exposing everyone else to the darkest parts of him. The parts he didn't want the world to see.

Aww, hell. He owed Paige one.

"Fine," he muttered. "The cousin can stay in the first suite in the east wing." He wanted to keep the stranger under his thumb, right where he could see him or her, until he knew whether or not they could be trusted. Especially around all his people. Lucien, Charles, and Paige were still vigilantes—even if he wasn't anymore—and their entire operation was here. He had to make sure the work they did stayed secret.

Still, he hated the idea of meeting with some stranger coming into his suite to clean. It would *almost* be worse than the torture session he'd endured in Iraq, and then the different kind of torture he'd endured re-living it all on Capitol Hill.

"Okay." Lucien's eyes flashed. "But if I go through the time and effort to bring this cousin out here, you sure as shit better not scare them away."

CHAPTER 2

hat color panties are you wearing?
A familiar, sick dread sank low into Rose's stomach when she glanced at the glowing text on her phone. Not again. When would it end?

"Everything okay, lady?" The voice behind her held only faint interest, barely audible over the racket of the waves. It was so dark that she could hardly see them crashing against the pier.

She cleared her throat and turned around to face Fred, the red-eyed, hungover driver of the boat she'd hired. His hangover had been why she had hired him; he was less likely to ask questions, fearful she'd report him to the harbormaster for boating under the influence. Neither one of them wanted a paper trail to follow them tonight.

"Yes, thanks," she replied. Nestled between cliffs, the dock sat against a short beach on the shores of West Cove Island. Paige hadn't told her this place was in the middle of nowhere. It felt so much more remote than she'd imagined. All she could hear was the creaking of the boat and the water lapping against the shore.

There weren't many lights out this way, just ones illuminating the path that led inland, toward a gothic, stone mansion invisible from the shore except for the lights on inside. It was set like a fortress amongst an outcrop of buildings surrounding it. Built by Jonathan Masters, the late tech giant, on the private island he'd bought for his bride half a century earlier, she had Googled it before coming. Its sheer grandeur had amazed her from behind her computer monitor, but now, the opulence of it seemed unattractive. Foreboding. Goddamn spooky.

And now another revolting text was burning a hole through her cell phone. She felt sick. Thank God her long-lost cousin had suggested that she should come out here so they could meet. She'd had nowhere else to go to get away from Gavin.

When he'd approached her in the grocery store parking lot last week, and then she had come home to her locked apartment to find her bed... disturbed, it had been the last straw. She'd known she had to leave Portland. At least for a while, until she figured things out.

A sea bird cried out. She shuddered.

"Those pretty brown eyes aren't going to get you out of what I'm owed, lady."

"What?"

Fred's bushy white brows rose, his ruddy forehead wrinkling. "My money?"

Flustered, she ripped the agreed-upon sum out of her purse, clutching the bills as they fluttered in the wind. Fred dumped her suitcase on the dock and reached for it.

He counted the bills. With a nod, he looked up at her. "You got my card when you wanna call for a lift back?"

"Yes, you'll hear from me at some point." Her thoughts were still stuck on a repeating loop of that suggestive, disgusting text. Goddamn Gavin.

"There ain't no one out here to meet you?"

Where was Paige? She stretched her neck to peer toward the shore, but she didn't see anyone. "They know I'm coming tonight."

Fred shrugged. "You're probably right. Security on these islands is always top-notch."

He did have a point; it was safe to assume she was being watched from the moment she had disembarked. She pursed her lips, resisting the urge to look around for cameras. Always someone watched her, eyes tracking her at all times. By now she should have been used to it, but she wasn't. The thought, along with the chill of ocean spray, sent a shiver down her spine.

"Pleasure doing business with ya," Fred muttered, turning his attention back to the controls of his vessel. Just like that, she watched the boat sputter and speed away, leaving her stranded and completely out of her depth.

Several weeks ago, in early June, she'd been blindsided by her best friend Rebecca's suicide. In a flash, the world had lost a generous, brilliant person, and a cornerstone in her world had crumbled. She'd been stuck in a fog for days after. Beforehand, she had already been dealing with Gavin's harassment, thinking it couldn't get any worse than knowing her cop ex-boyfriend's eyes were always on her. Boy, she'd been wrong.

She had kept trying to pull herself together ever since, but life just wasn't the same without her best friend. Sure, she had her party crowd, her live music pals that she'd meet up with at gigs or on the weekends, but they weren't ones she'd ever confide in. Aside from Rebecca and Mom, she had never let anyone get close to her.

Then, two weeks ago, Paige had found her on a social media site and reached out. Hope had flickered to life within her again.

She blinked hard. The boat was already out of sight, but she was still staring at the horizon of the black ocean against the equally ebony sky, dotted with sparkling stars more visible out here than on the mainland.

If anyone had told her then that she'd be standing in the middle of a scrap of land in Puget Sound several days later, she would've laughed at them. She would've laughed harder if they'd told her she had a cousin, though.

But here she was.

When Paige had reached out, she'd claimed her mother had been Rose's aunt, who'd run away from home at sixteen. Mom had once mentioned an estranged sister in passing, and Paige had seemed anxious for contact, so she'd accepted her invitation to connect.

They'd been messaging back and forth ever since.

Then Paige had extended the invitation for her to visit the island where she was living, and even gone out of her way to line up a temporary job as a maid that she could fill.

Anything to get away from Gavin's stalking.

She grasped the handle on her suitcase and turned around, facing the imposing manor house. She had to protect herself from him.

Please be waiting for me at the mansion, Paige.

Head held high, she squared her shoulders and started down the stone walkway. Naturally, she'd been curious about this place, too. Limitless wealth and private islands were worlds away from digs like hers. If she had to do a little light housework as a maid and take a leave from her job as a band and tour manager, it was a small price to pay.

In the meantime, she'd get to stay beyond Gavin's reach.

THERE WAS EVEN a moat around the manor house for God's sake. The wheels of Rose's suitcase clicked against the wooden drawbridge slabs as she approached the front stoop, which consisted of twelve deep, wide, curved stairs that led up to a landing, complete with two five-foot lions perched on either side—warning visitors away from the gold inlaid mahogany double-front doors, no doubt. She clutched her tote, with her Taser inside, and went up anyway. *Christ almighty, what people choose to spend their money on.*

Even if she traded bank accounts with Old Man Masters, she'd never live this opulently.

Shaking her head, she reached over and rang the doorbell. A gentle chime sounded faintly behind the doors. Above her, a camera's dark, circular orb was situated in the filigree of the arc surrounding the huge doors. She rang the chime, and the sound of barely audible footsteps approached behind the door.

A graying woman in her sixties with laugh lines bracketing her kind hazel eyes opened the door. She was round, standing on the front of her feet like she was ready to spring into action. "Miss Benoit?"

She forced a smile. "Rose, please. I believe my cousin Paige is expecting me?"

"Yes, yes." The woman stood aside. "I'm Polly, the head housekeeper. Leave your suitcase there, and I'll get it. Right this way."

She left her suitcase on the marble foyer floor, her breath catching at the grand staircase straight ahead, which split halfway up to two separate wings of the house. *Wings.* A balcony stretched behind it, and above she could see three floors up. A crystal chandelier hung from the center, more opulent than any that could've hung in a European opera house.

Beside her, Polly chuckled. "It is grand, isn't it? We don't get many visitors, so we forget how breathtaking Mr. Masters's house is."

The words barely registered as she took in the statues. And the artwork! They were originals, not prints. Fresh flowers that would easily cost a few hundred dollars each sat on tables. How many rooms were there? What were the taxes even like on a place this huge?

"This way." Polly ushered her into the first room to the left, which looked like a formal parlor. A fireplace with a ten-foot mantel stood on the far side of the room, with stuffy, Victorian-era couches facing each other on a rug before it.

Her gaze was pulled to the man in the center of the room. Tall and lean, his long golden hair had been pulled up in a man-bun style she thought looked ridiculous on most men who attempted it. Not him, though. This guy could pull it off. He wore a basic long-sleeve gray t-shirt, a vest, and jeans. He smiled, but it didn't reach his tired eyes.

Was this Burke Masters, the man who owned the place?

He stuck his hand out to her right away. "Miss Benoit?"

She smiled, resisted the urge to curtsy, and returned the handshake. "Yes."

"Lucien Reginald Roman, Paige's boyfriend. Pleased to meet you." His grip was dry, firm and strong. "We've been looking forward to your arrival."

"Me too. I'm really grateful for the job."

Lucien glanced away. "Well, yes. We can talk more about that. Polly, could you take Miss Benoit's coat and hat? She's damp from the journey."

"Of course." Polly scurried over, practically pulling the stocking cap off of her head. Her wavy, chestnut hair tumbled down into her eyes. *Great.* She pushed it away and shrugged out of her coat quickly, before Polly tore it off her. Once Polly took both in hand, she gave them a smile and left.

Lucien's aqua eyes turned serious. "I'd like to tell you a little more about this place and, ah, the man who owns all this, if you don't mind. That's why Paige asked me to join you both."

"Speaking of Paige—"

"Rose!" an unfamiliar female voice called.

They turned to the door.

Everything inside her bubbled with nervous energy.

A slight woman in workout pants and a Mariners baseball cap came rushing into the room, her blond curls bouncing.

"I'm so sorry I'm late." She threw her arms around her, squeezing her with one of the tightest hugs she'd ever had. "I got caught up in an online chat, and it took me forever to bow out of it." She pulled back.

Rose sucked in a breath, staring straight into brown eyes flecked with gold, which mirrored her own. The woman looked just like her grandmother in her twenties, like the old photographs—with a pretty, heart-shaped face, straight nose, small mouth—but flesh and blood in front of her, waiting for a response. A reaction.

To her surprise, tears stung her eyes. This was her cousin. Her family. Any doubts of Paige's true parentage evaporated. Their connection was as plain as the nose on her face. The same shaped nose she saw in the mirror.

"You're my cousin." Her hands were trembling. "You're my family."

Well, that was an obviously dumb thing to say.

Paige grinned. "You have no idea what this means to me."

"It's true," Lucien chimed in, beaming. He moved to stand beside Paige. "She's been searching for any family relations she could find for ages. She'd almost given up."

"It means the world to me, too," Rose said sincerely. "We don't really know each other that well yet, and you've already been so kind."

"Well, we'll fix that. Why don't you come to our bungalow tomorrow night for dinner?" The corners of Paige's brown eyes crinkled. "We don't get to entertain often, and we'd love to have you over."

She was so friendly, so normal. For the first time in ages, a flare of excitement rivaled the perpetual pit in her stomach.

Her smile grew. "I'd like that, thank you."

"Awesome," Paige said enthusiastically. "We're the yellow house with white shutters."

Lucien smiled too, but it didn't quite meet his eyes. "Paige mentioned that you ran into trouble back home in Portland and wanted to leave town."

She had been expecting them to ask about her reasons for leaving Portland. It was only natural for them to wonder. She'd been vague on purpose when she and Paige had messaged back and forth.

Because Gavin was a police officer, she hadn't known who to trust, or where she could turn. Even coming out here had been a leap of faith. One she was glad she'd taken.

Paige had her arm around Lucien's waist as she waited expectantly. They were good people. She didn't want to lie to either of them.

"It's not legal trouble, I promise. I'd like to just avoid someone for a while, if I can." She shrugged.

Paige wrinkled her nose. "I'm so sorry, Rose. Can the police help you? I'm sure if you contacted them—"

"No, thanks." She forced a smile. "I just needed a break—to step out of my life for a little bit. Which is why I really appreciate this temporary job and the place to stay."

Lucien rubbed his brow. "Yeah, about that…"

"We'd invite you to stay with us at our bungalow," Paige said, "but we don't have any extra beds. All of my tech equipment takes up half the place." She and Lucien exchanged a glance.

"And we didn't think you'd mind staying in the mansion too much," Lucien added.

"I'd enjoy that, thank you." Any bed Gavin hadn't defiled would be more than fine in her book. "I can start work in the morning."

"If you'd like." Lucien shifted his weight. "We're sorry we had to ask you to help fill in as a maid at all. Burke Masters, the owner of this estate, thinks everyone should have a role here."

"That's fine. I get it."

"I just want to be up front with you first, Rose. You'll also be taking care of Masters's suite. You might discover that he has some, ah, issues. PTSD, we think. The two of us and Charles, who you'll meet tomorrow, we were deployed overseas with the Marines. We completed so many combat missions that we lost count."

Geez, that sucked. Her heart went out to him. "I'm so sorry to hear that. Is he getting help?"

He shook his head. "Not yet, no. Actually, when we first got home, Masters adjusted really well. He'd found a new job and had a purpose. But it ended badly. Since then, he's isolated himself from everyone. You'll see how he's sort of become a hermit. I just wanted to give you a heads up that he's affected by some of these issues. He has flashbacks, so if he's reacting unexpectedly to anything, you'll know why."

She looked between them. "Is he okay with me coming in to clean?"

"Oh, yes." Paige responded. They both nodded.

"We just didn't want his condition to be a surprise to you," Lucien added.

"I appreciate that," she said.

"We'll pay you whatever wages you think are fair too, Rose. We appreciate you filling in like this for us. Anything you need, just ask." Lucien beamed a smile at Paige. "You're family."

She waved him off, returning the smile—the first easy smile she'd given in ages. "Trust me, you're doing me the favor."

CHAPTER 3

*T*he next morning, when Rose had headed downstairs for coffee, she'd bumped into Lucien, who'd offered to give her a tour before she started her shift. She'd readily agreed, eager to put off her date with a dust mop.

She and Lucien wandered through a kitchen that was the size of her apartment, and the clean, cream décor was punctuated with lemon-yellow touches. Half a dozen staff finished their late-morning breakfasts. Lucien explained that Polly was both the housekeeper and head chef, a point Polly proved when she forced a chocolate croissant into Rose's palm as they continued the tour.

The dining room off the kitchen had a table that could seat two dozen people. Emerald-green brocade wallpaper with Chinese-influenced depictions of birds in flight lined the walls, and above the table hung a modern chandelier that looked like lines of candles. He showed her the downstairs study that had belonged to Jonathan Masters, but told her no one had touched the leather-bound books or sat behind the huge walnut desk since its owner had died. Then, he took her to a studio, where huge French windows let light stream in on a variety of watercolor paintings, a single easel in the center of the room. It had been untouched, Lucien said, since Karen Masters had died. Neither of Burke's parents had ever seen him return from combat—the car accident had happened while he was overseas.

She felt a familiar tugging as she thought of Mom. Thank God she'd had a chance to say goodbye to her, and that she had been there throughout Mom's illness. How horrible to have it all ripped away... The walls around her heart cracked a little. It seemed she and Burke Masters could commiserate about the lonely life of an orphan. If they ever had a conversation one day.

Lucien's cell phone rang. After an apology, he answered it. "Lucien."

She tried to listen, but the voice on the other end wasn't audible.

Lucien groaned. "Well, damn. Okay. I'll be right there." He disconnected the call and met her gaze. "My friend Charles needs me over at one of the other buildings. The, uh, headquarters, as we call it. Do you mind if we finish the official tour later?"

"Sure. I can get started on cleaning for a while." Seeing the staff members in the kitchen made her realize more people called this island home than she'd realized. There was quite a little working community here, it seemed. No wonder they needed an extra pair of hands in a place this size.

She could put on her headphones, jack up the music and let herself do mindless chores for a bit. It sounded fun. Peaceful.

He gave her an apologetic half-smile. "I'm going to stop in at home to have lunch when I'm done with Charles, but only work as long as you want. Find time to relax, too. Then we can meet up for dinner. Does that work for you?"

"Yes. Give me a call whenever," she offered.

"Great." With a smile and a nod, Lucien bounded off, disappearing through one of the two wrought-iron ornate doors on the far wall behind the mammoth staircase. Curious, she followed him and peered out beyond the doors. They opened onto a huge patio area that spanned the length of the house, with a few stairs leading down to a multi-level garden complete with a pond and fountain in the center. Maze hedges lined the garden, but no one else was in sight. To the left of those hedges were a large swimming pool and tennis court, and to the far right there was a greenhouse and some sort of outdoor garden with a thinly veiled roof. *Holy crap.*

Another set of wrought-iron doors were farther down the length of the patio. It was easy to imagine lavish parties where these doors would be flung open, wait staff carrying hors d'oeuvre trays weaving in between guests in suits and dresses, mingling in the gorgeous gardens below.

She sighed. The only time she'd wished she'd been born to money was when she'd had to pay for Mom's medical treatments. Managing local bands just hadn't paid enough—even after she'd added a fourth band. If she'd had even a tiny fraction of this wealth, she wouldn't have had to spend so much time away, and she would have had so much more time with Mom.

She looked around. Mom would've appreciated this kind of lifestyle a lot more than she did. How often had she seen Mom scrimp and save every dime as they'd bounced from place to place after Dad had left?

In the distance, small buildings and gravel pathways popped up from between hills, and someone in an ATV traveled down one of them. It was like a small town.

She went inside, to go back to her room to change into jeans and a t-shirt.

Ascending the staircase, she pictured a little boy running up the stairs, with dirt under his fingernails, skinned knees, and a smile on his face. Was that how it had been for Burke Masters? The golden child of a glamourous life?

She smiled, until she thought about the emotionally damaged man hiding somewhere within the mansion. She'd do her best to just clean fast and stay out of his way.

Once she changed clothes, she ventured out into the hallway, and started to look for the cleaning closet.

She opened the doors to four unoccupied bedrooms, ran into three locked doors, a bathroom, and an empty linen closet the size of her living room. She worked her way down the hallway and into another hallway, one room at a time on the opposite side of the stairway. Maybe there was a broom around here somewhere.

Grasping the brass handle of another door, she flung it open, reached for the light switch, and flicked it on.

There were photos everywhere. Women. No, young women. Some teenaged girls. Smiling, young, fresh. They were propped up on the walls in straight lines, red X's drawn through some of their profiles. A few photos looked like they had been taken with a long lens camera. Newspaper clippings and printed-out articles littered the dusty countertops below them. Maps of Seattle and Portland were on the far wall, red circles scratched into locations, scribbles written on them. The single lightbulb above cast everything in an ominous glow, including a coil of blue rope in the corner, near drawers under the counters. What was hidden in them?

To her left, the photos changed, depicting aerial shots of a village in a desert. Next to them were far away shots of Middle-Eastern villagers, women in hijabs, children playing soccer, men sitting in a town square. Red X's doctored those, too. Official military documents were scattered amongst them.

Everyone pictured in this room had died.

She stumbled backward, catching herself on the countertop. Yanking her hand away, she turned to flee.

A huge figure blocked the doorway.

The scream got stuck in her throat.

The sky-blue eyes rimmed with cobalt reflected in the solitary light fixated on her. The far side of his face bore puckered skin that marred part of his chiseled features, long-healed burns from the edge of his right eyebrow down past his prominent cheekbone disappearing into his too-long beard. Sandy-blond, shoulder-length hair was slicked back and dark at the roots, and he was built like a mountain. Muscles for miles bulged beneath a t-shirt too small for him. They probably didn't make shirts that large anyway. It was the cane he leaned on, clutched in his strong hand, that had her attention, though. Maybe that would slow him down and give her a chance to walk away.

Then again, one whack from that and he'd crush her skull. She could be dead where she stood.

"Burke Masters?" she squeaked.

Wary eyes traveled over her and met her gaze again. "Paige's cousin." It was said with as much warmth as an icicle.

"R-rose Benoit," she corrected. What the hell is this place?" Good. She'd regained a bit of conviction, a bit of her breath again.

His lips thinned, the smile that formed twisted and pained. "My torture chamber. Isn't it obvious?"

What could she use as a weapon? She glanced around, but there was nothing. The lightbulb? She could try swinging it, shattering it on his head. He was tall enough.

"You won't get away with it," she rushed out. "Lucien knows I'm here. People will come looking for me."

"If I wanted you dead, you would be."

The comment drew her up short. That was true enough. He could've hit her from behind in this very room, before she'd ever turned around.

Who was this man? Far more dangerous than fragile, for sure.

He snorted, his gaze scorching. "I want you off my island."

Every instinct had her wanting to push past him and bolt for the door, to give him exactly what he wanted. But there were a lot of people surrounding this man, and they all seemed to care about him. She glanced at the Middle Eastern pictures on the wall. He was a war veteran. He'd killed in war...

She glanced at him. The pain in his eyes was obvious, like a window into a world of horrors greater than any she could imagine.

This room was creepy as hell, but everything in here was a nightmare he made himself live with every day. An unhealthy, terrifying reality he wouldn't let himself escape.

She squared her shoulders. "Well, I want a backstage pass to every concert at The Roxy, but we don't all get what we want."

One eyebrow rose.

"Eventually I'll find the cleaning supplies, so I'd appreciate it if you could tell me which room is yours, so I know where to start." She lifted her chin.

"You're not staying, so it won't be an issue," he snapped.

"You're not the one paying me. Mr. Roman is."

"Mr. Roman is too trusting for his own good. You're only here to get a photo of this." Burke Masters pointed at the side of his face, lips contorted into a snarl. "A photo of me, of this room, and a few sentences will get you the media scoop of the week—the freak, the disappointing fucked-up son of a genius."

The scar had to have been physically painful once, and was still an obvious source of emotional hurt, it seemed. Too bad. He was ridiculously attractive anyway—a very masculine face, straight nose, Nordic planes and angles perfectly proportioned—the only thing stopping him from being downright gorgeous was the anger in his features.

Yet she could tell that his emotions were pure. Genuine. Not directed at her or twisted into some psychotic pleasure trip like the gleam in Gavin's eyes the night he'd—

"If you go to the media at all, Miss Benoit, I will sue you." Burke Masters looked around the horrible little room. "I will not be an object of ridicule because of this." He pointed to his face and held up the cane.

He must really be worried. She needed to find a way to reassure him that she wasn't here to hurt him.

She put her hands on her hips, but her tone was soft when she said, "My mother died of cancer. She faded away before my eyes, and developed a skin disease because of her weakened immune system. It wasn't pretty, but I was still by her side every chance I got. I've seen worse." She took a step back. "And I'm pretty sure you have, too."

His narrowed eyes widened. He exhaled slowly. She hadn't run across a man like Burke before, with his broad shoulders, sculpted muscles any football player would envy, and his six-and-a-half-foot height. He stepped back into the hallway, the only sound was her heartbeat pulsing in her ears. "Ten a.m. tomorrow, my study. *If* you decide to stay."

It seemed like it should've been a breakthrough, but instead, her chest tightened.

He turned to leave, his right leg buckling a little as he put some weight on the cane. As if sensing her eyes on him, he stopped and glared at her. "But if I see your cell phone once, I'm breaking the thing with my bare hands."

CHAPTER 4

*G*avin Graves stood in the middle of Rose's apartment, the air still as death, dust particles floating through the late-day sunlight streaming through the tall windows and falling on the useless fanciful crap and clutter she loved so much.

His bitch never came home last night.

Discarded papers lay in heaps on her desk, from which her laptop was missing. The posters of the rock and indie bands she cherished still lined the walls, half of them featuring the band's drummers. She always did have a thing for dumbass drummers, so she must've been planning on coming back. She'd have taken them with her otherwise.

He gripped the key he'd secretly made to her apartment so tight he could feel it break the skin of his palm.

The place was lifeless. Where the fuck had she gone? What was she wearing? Which part of her skin were her clothes revealing – legs? The swell of her breasts? Her arms? What were those soft brown eyes looking at right now? Was anyone else daring to get near her sweet pussy?

His heart thundered beneath the blue and brass of his police uniform.

Wherever she was, she'd better not have gone to get away from him. He was trying to woo her back, for chrissake. That's why he hadn't thrown her in his car at the grocery store last week. Why he hadn't pushed his way in here while she was home and taken her right on the floor of her own place. Or against the wall. Or on the bed, where he'd had her before.

He resisted the urge to kick her ottoman across the hardwood floor. Instead, he took deep, calming breaths.

He'd go through her trash first, to see if he could get a clue as to where she'd gone. Then he'd put out a search on her license plate. If worse came to worse, he always had people he could squeeze a favor or two out of. The great thing about being in law enforcement was access to resources, after all.

There was too much on his plate right now to get distracted. He had work to do, business to accomplish. But he'd find Rose and make it his mission to make her understand that there was nowhere on earth she could go without him. That everything she had belonged to *him*.

CHAPTER 5

$\mathcal{R}$ose descended the main staircase on her way to the dining room, where she'd agreed to meet Lucien and his friend Charles for dinner, after Lucien told her Paige had to cancel at their bungalow. She'd gotten bogged down with a project and asked to postpone. As for the landlord, Burke Masters chose to dine night and day alone in his suite, it seemed. Lucien hadn't been kidding about him.

Her knees still felt weak from their encounter a few hours earlier.

Burke was nothing like what she'd expected. He wasn't frail, wasting away in emotional turmoil. Nope: he was brimming with the ability to break anything and everything if he wanted. His shoulders were like a steel beam, not hunched. The sweatpants hadn't hidden the swell of strapping thighs, nor had the beard camouflaged the chiseled cheekbones and strong, pointed chin.

On the whole, the man looked practically invincible.

But those sky-blue eyes told of a tragedy.

She glanced at her watch as she walked across the massive foyer toward the elaborate, gold-accented dining room. Ten minutes early.

Sure enough, the room was empty. Drawing in a deep breath, she smoothed a few strands of hair back into her bun and straightened her pencil skirt. Good. She'd have a few minutes to get in the right headspace. She felt a little off, anyway. A little jittery. Maybe it was—

"What's Paige's cousin like?" an unfamiliar, jovial male voice asked, from the direction of the kitchen.

She paused before she got to the doorway that connected the two rooms, by an antique chair.

"She seems kind and clever." Lucien's deep voice. "Very capable. Talkative."

Deep, baritone laughter reverberated. "That'd be a nice change of pace for Burke." There was a pause. "Unless he's scared her off already."

The voice likely belonged to Charles Carson, the other friend of Burke's that she was supposed to meet for dinner. They probably hadn't expected her to come down early.

"What do you mean?" Lucien asked, concerned.

"Earlier today I saw a brunette running out of the west wing. She looked upset, and she was so flustered she didn't even see me. Since I know everyone else here, I figured it was her."

Lucien groaned. "Great. You know that if she ran into Burke, he probably did everything he could to scare her away, which also means he'll be in a shitty mood. Just when we wanted to talk to him about what's going on with The Ring."

She sat on the antique chair and tilted her head. It might be impolite to eavesdrop, but this place was full of secrets, and she wanted to know what it was like behind the scenes. There had to be at least a dozen bungalows near the mansion on the west side of the island, not to mention whatever staff lived in the mansion. Was everyone here needed to support Burke? Were they all employees of his family company and being on the island was an employee benefit? Was the headquarters Lucien spoke of something for the company?

What was the ring?

"We know they've been operating for a while now, Lu, so waiting a day isn't going to make a difference with Burke. Apparently, The Ring figured that a year after we almost took them down—when they destroyed their *inventory* —was a long enough grace period before bringing their op back to our city."

"All the more reason for us to pull Burke back into action." Lucien's voice was rough.

Action? Who did they take out? She rubbed her brow. Was this some sort of special government agency or military team?

"But he's not—"

"You and I are committed to this, Charles, and he still is, too. Why else does he take our latest Intel from our server and add it to his torture chamber? He's checking up on us."

"After the clusterfuck in Ba'hir, those women at Pine Ridge were the last hit Burke could take."

She committed the names to memory so she could look them up later.

Lucien sighed. "We've just got to talk him into seeing a psychologist. If we'd had his help, maybe The Ring wouldn't be operating in Seattle again. Did your S.P.D. buddy tell you anything else about the woman they busted for prostitution last night?"

"Not much. Just that she had the telltale blue line around her finger. He mentioned his captain is trying to get funding for a special task force, but there are priorities everywhere for the police."

That meant that whatever was going on here at West Cove Island was probably not sanctioned by law enforcement. She drew in a breath. They might be operating outside the law.

"Well, we could try to find out this woman's real name, track down her history, but there's no guarantee it'll lead us anywhere productive. We already know they target addicts and runaways because they don't want people looking for them, so the likelihood of us learning anything substantial is remote." Lucien paused. "We also caught an unusual variance off of websites we've hacked into. You know, the ones that have reports people have posted about our vigilante efforts and veterans websites that mentioned Ba'hir. Someone from the same IP address here in the Pacific Northwest was looking at all of those at the same time."

"Trying to tie Burke to our vigilante work?" There was definite worry in Charles's voice.

Vigilantes? She could hardly believe her ears.

But he'd confirmed it—they were a trio of discharged veterans trying to play superheroes. Her heart fluttered, and she rubbed her chest. It seemed like they were trying to do good, though. It was admirable. Foolish and dangerous, but. . . honorable.

Had Paige suggested that she go to the police last night to throw her off the trail of what they did here?

"That's my theory," Lucien replied. "We don't know where it originated yet, though."

Her phone vibrated, and she pulled it out of her pocket. It was a call. *Gavin.*

She disconnected, her hands shaking. How had he gotten this number, too?

"Burke was always adamant that he didn't want the public to find out," Charles said urgently. "After he was cleared of the charges, he'd told us how important it was to him to contribute somehow again. Make things right. To be taken down by any small detail—"

"Relax, Charles. Paige said she's on it. I'll see her later tonight. But we'd better go meet Rose."

Fumbling to put her phone away, she stood, the chair scraping on the hardwood floor.

Shit.

She spun toward the kitchen and took a step, plastering a smile on her face. Would they realize she'd been eavesdropping?

Lucien's lanky form came around the kitchen table, along with a black man with short hair and a warm, genuine smile.

"I'm sorry if I'm interrupting," she began. "I know I'm early to dinner."

They exchanged a glance.

Lucien waved her off. "Not at all. Welcome, Rose."

Charles came around Lucien and thrust his hand out to her. "Charles Carson. I was a combat medic and a friend of the guy upstairs, and this one." He jutted a thumb at Lucien. "Pleased to meet you, Miss Benoit."

It was easy to return the sincere smile. "Rose. And me too, Mr. Carson."

"Charles." He thrust his hands in his pockets. "Hope you're hungry. Polly has a feast ready for us."

She wasn't feeling particularly hungry, but she nodded anyway. "Yes. It's been a long day."

"I heard," Lucien said sympathetically. "You met Burke? Masters, I mean?"

She blew air out of her nose, her smile wavering a little. "Yes. In his little closet of horrors."

Charles nodded solemnly. "So you can see why we're concerned. Polly says he spends more and more time in that awful room of his."

"She sleeps in the main house," Lucien said. "She's told us that she sometimes hears him in the early hours of the morning, coming and going from there." He wrung his hands. "But there's a reason all that's there—"

An odd, indescribable feeling washed through her. What were they having for dinner? It smelled like a burning car engine. "He wouldn't even let himself glance at all those photos on the wall." She glanced between the men. Her breathing quickened. Oh no. A seizure couldn't be happening now.

"Masters was there the night most of the girls died," Charles said.

"I-I got that sense. Why was he there?" Her eyes started to water. She ran her hands over her hair, her wavy tresses yanked tight into the bun. Everything was wrong. Her hair. Her outfit. Why she was here on this island. But it was too late now. It was bearing down on her, closing in all around her. She had to get out of there. Find her medication. But how?

Time to move this along so she could scram.

"Listen," she said, "I realize you both don't know me well, but don't worry. Whatever happened to Burke, whatever you're all doing... I can keep it a secret." After all, she was on their island with one of her own. "Paige is the last family member I have. Trust me, I'm not going to do anything to screw that up. I have no interest in exploiting Burke Masters, or anyone else. Besides, Burke already threatened to break my phone if he saw it out."

Lucien groaned. "You're supposed to be our guest, not a potential lawsuit. He knows better."

"We've tied seventeen deaths to The Ring." Charles met her gaze. "Fourteen the night of the explosion at Pine Ridge Motel. Burke was right there when it happened. Those were some of the faces on his wall."

Pretend you weren't eavesdropping. "The ring?" Beads of sweat dotted her forehead. Had she unpacked the meds yet? Were they on the bureau, or in the pocket of her suitcase?

Lucien shot Charles a frown, but he merely shrugged. "A sex trade operation based out of Portland that's also expanded their operation up to Seattle."

"You're too trusting for your own good," Lucien muttered to Charles under his breath. He frowned.

The blood drained from her face, and her fingers and toes tingled. She was going downhill, fast. Was she swaying on her feet? What excuse could she give to leave? "Is this a military or government operation, based out here on the water?"

Both men's brows furrowed. "On the island, you mean?" Lucien rubbed his jaw, then drew in a lengthy breath. "All of us here are either involved in a vigilante group Masters formed to help the authorities apprehend criminals, or staff for the island. We ask for your discretion because, of course, we have to keep our organization covert. In this day and age, you can imagine how hard that is. The eyes of the public can pretty much peer into most corners of the world now, so we try to keep ours in the shadows."

Oh, wow. He told her their big secret, just like that. How trusting of him. How brave.

"I understand." Her voice was slurred, barely a whisper, and she began to blink. A lot. She pressed a trembling hand to her forehead. Her brain couldn't come up with an excuse to give them. Not one damn thing.

They peered at her intently.

"Rose, are you all right?" Charles took a step closer to her. "You're as white as a ghost."

Had he said he was a healer? A medic? A doctor?

"M-my medication." Her muscles tightened before their eyes, her wide-eyed expression pinching in on itself. Rigid arms came up, as her whole body shook.

"I think it's a seizure." Charles hurried up beside him.

Lucien sprang forward, fear in his eyes. "Where is it?"

She couldn't answer through her clenched teeth. Lucien knocked a chair out of her way as she collapsed to the floor, spasms wracking her body.

CHAPTER 6

The next morning, Rose stood beside the cleaning cart and knocked on the door of Burke's study at ten o'clock. A few hours ago, Polly had served her breakfast in bed, fluttering over her like a mother hen.

"Really, this has happened before," she'd assured Polly as she had tucked in the sheets around her. "All I need is my phone and Bluetooth speaker so I can play some alt-indie rock to start my day, and I'm good to go."

"I'll only be convinced when you eat half of what's on that plate," Polly had retorted, as she'd placed a soft, warm hand on her forehead.

It was sweet how Polly, Lucien, Paige, and Charles had worried. Her day had started with the four of them in her room at the break of dawn. It was a good thing she'd had trouble sleeping anyway.

The seizure had been a short one, but the damage had been done: they knew she had epilepsy. She'd practically begged them to keep it from Burke—she didn't want to give him any excuse to send her packing just yet—and each had eventually agreed. Now she knew one of their secrets and they knew one of hers... and all because she'd switched medications in the days leading up to her trip here.

In hindsight, that had been a stupid move, but the other meds hadn't been effective enough. One of her biggest triggers, stress, had been building for too long, and she'd needed something stronger. Every fiber of her being had tried so hard not to let Gavin's harassment impact her life, but it was useless. The seizures had come more often, and she'd even had yet *another* glaring, ominous text poisoning her phone since 6:57am this morning: YOU'RE NOT HOME. WHERE ARE YOU?

He'd been at her apartment again. The thought made her sick. Or maybe that was residual nausea from the seizure. Even on a remote island—a place where she'd just begun to feel freer, more invigorated—Gavin's tentacles reached for her. She had to figure out if she could file a restraining order on him through a different county, one where he wasn't a police officer.

And she had to make sure that this vigilante team didn't find out about what he was doing to her. If Paige started looking into Gavin, she might accidently put herself—or all of them—on his radar. That was the last thing she wanted.

She had to chill out so last night didn't repeat itself. She needed fresh air and a way to enjoy the day, putting everything else aside.

As she'd forced herself to swallow the last few bites of toast that morning, she had gotten Polly to tell her where Burke's study was located. It was down the same corridor as his torture chamber. Polly had explained that it was the room right next to his bedroom, and that she'd know his bedroom by the splinter that ran up the door from the floor in a jagged crack.

She had resisted the urge to ask how it had gotten that way.

Now there was only silence on the other side of the door, and she rubbed her forehead, wishing the seizure's nagging headache would just disappear.

Last night, after she'd regained consciousness to Charles checking her vitals, they'd brought her up to her room. Though she'd convinced them not to call emergency services, Charles had explained that he had a makeshift clinic in one of the outbuildings, so she was supposed to meet him there at 2 p.m. Otherwise, Paige said she'd take her back to the mainland for treatment herself.

Whatever. A doctor on the island was handy.

She knocked again.

"Come in." The deep voice from yesterday made her shudder.

A power game. Make her knock twice. She frowned, and went inside, wheeling the cart with her.

It was a smaller study than the one downstairs, but almost as opulent. Built-in mahogany bookshelves with arches were on each wall, except where a door on the left presumably opened to his bedroom. Huge French windows against the far wall were behind a large, sturdy desk with a computer and two monitors. All the photo frames had been turned upside down, save for one photo of Burke and a sandy-haired pre-teen boy, and one of him with an older couple. His parents?

Two leather wing-backed chairs sat face to face on the right side of the room, in front of the dark, unlit fireplace. Mr. Masters sat in the chair closest to the desk, suspicious sky-blue eyes focused on her, elbows on the armrests, fingers steepled by his mouth.

He eyed her with annoyance. "You're a minute late."

Hello to you, too. She nodded curtly and pulled out a feather duster.

"Have a seat first."

It sounded more like an order than an invitation, so she crossed her arms and cocked her hip.

"Please," he added.

She sat in the opposite chair. Her feet barely touched the floor, whereas his knees came up high enough to sit at a ninety-degree angle. For crying out loud, he was almost too big for his own chairs. Her five-foot-four frame made her feel like a doll in comparison.

When she glanced up, she noticed his impenetrable, narrowed gaze was fixated on her, severe and scrutinizing. It made her want to fidget.

"Is this the employee interview?" she asked cheerily, resisting the urge to tell him he wasn't going to drive her away with his crankiness.

He snorted.

"Then what can I do for you, Burke?"

"Masters," he snapped. "And you can tell me why you're really here."

This again? She shifted her weight. It was almost like he could tell she wasn't really a maid, or that she was on the run from a psycho. She tried to reign back the guilt swelling below her ribs. Geez, he'd make a great interrogator.

"I'm here because I wanted to meet my cousin Paige and get to know her." It was nice that it was the truth. Not all of it—Gavin flashed through her mind—but a big part of it.

His hands dropped. "Listen, Miss Benoit—"

"Rose."

"Fine. I'll call you whatever you want, but I don't want to hear my name."

"Because?"

He said nothing.

She shivered under his icy glare. Or maybe it was the draft in the room. She was rather chilly. She stood. "It's freaking cold in here. Why don't I light a fire, clean this place up and we can call this fun little session a day?"

He shot to his feet, leaned on his cane, and turned his back on her. "This was a mistake. Get out."

She bit her lip and glanced at the fireplace.

There wasn't any wood stacked nearby, and the fireplace looked as if it hadn't been used in some time.

"Fire is one of your triggers for flashbacks, isn't it?" she said quietly. Of course. What a stupid suggestion. The man had burn marks all down the side of his face and his neck.

He didn't acknowledge her, but the set of his shoulders sagged slightly.

"I'm sorry, Burke," she said.

"It's my problem, not yours." Slowly, he turned to face her.

"But I'll try to be more sensitive," she assured him. On second thought—
"Except for one thing. There's not a snowball's chance in hell I'm calling you,
or anyone, Masters."

Blowing out a breath, he ran a hand through his dark-blond hair. Maybe
she just imagined it, but for a split second she thought she saw the corner of
his mouth twitch.

One hobbled step later, and he sat back down in the chair, leaning the cane
against it. "Fair enough." He tapped his fingers on the armrest, his posture
slumped, dark circles under his eyes.

"You look tired," she said offhandedly. "How do you sleep at night?"

One eyebrow rose. "Alone."

Well, hell. Her cheeks warmed. Why couldn't she just clean and get out
of here?

First, she had to get her foot out of her mouth. "I meant, are you suffering
from insomnia? Sometimes I think I do." How many nights had she tossed and
turned, wondering where Gavin was and when he would try to reach out to
her again?

For a moment she thought he wasn't going to answer, until he said,
"Insomnia most nights." He paused, then added, "Lately I've noticed it helps
my sleeplessness if I get sunlight in the morning, so I've been going out on my
balcony to watch the sunrise."

"I'm glad something helps," she said.

He shrugged.

"On the bad nights, do you visit that"—she struggled for the right word
—"room where we met?"

He frowned. "The staff talks too much."

Genuine curiosity made her ask, "What do you get out of staring into the
faces of victims who have died?"

Burke's lips thinned. "I'm a killer. Killers keep trophies for when they revel
in their actions. They go over and over it again in their heads. I'm no
different."

"Except you did not kill those women, or those villagers."

"Yes, I did."

No, he didn't. He'd been acquitted of the crime committed in Ba'hir. She'd
Googled it late last night, when she'd been recovering in bed. "If you'd
murdered them and told me, you'd be the stupidest criminal in history."

His fists tightened. "Maybe I want people to fear me, cower and quake.
Maybe I'm so dead inside, so cold and calculating that I don't care who
knows it."

There was no threat in his gaze, though. Only a deeply guarded hurt he
was trying to hide from her. She was sure—she'd seen the opposite from
Gavin before. "Not true."

His lips parted. "What?"

"If you were cold and dead inside, you wouldn't let yourself be surrounded by people who genuinely care about you and look out for you. They love you. Adore you, even. Lucien and Charles told me you tried to get rid of them, and the whole staff, but they're still here, and they still get their paychecks. That tells me a lot." The visit with the two of them and Paige, after her seizure, had shed some light on a few things.

Raising a fisted hand, his thumb jutted out, pointing to his chest. "I'm not someone anyone should look up to. And *I'm* sure as hell not the one who should be on the hot seat. You're good, rookie, turning the tables like that. But this is your interview, not mine."

Huh. So, she'd been right. It was an interview.

"Okay, then." She stood up. She wanted fresh air, and he needed to get out of this room. "If it's my interview, I'd like to do it while we go for a walk." She waved her hand toward the abandoned cart. "It's not like I'm getting any cleaning done anyway."

His eyes widened.

She lifted a shoulder. "I'm serious. I know you're enjoying the life of a hermit, but this is still your island, and I want to see some of it before you possibly decide to bounce me back to Portland. That's where I'm from, by the way." She crossed her arms. "Paige has been too busy to show me around, and anyway, who better to give me a tour than the owner?"

He stayed still.

"By the time we get back, if you still want me to leave the island, I will." Holy crap, what was she saying? Why gamble like this? All she had to do was keep her mouth shut and clean, and she couldn't even manage that.

"Fine." The corner of Burke's mouth lifted, his eyes glinting. He gripped his cane and stood. "Well played."

ROSE HURRIED TO KEEP UP, continually glancing at Burke as they walked down the manor's back steps, toward a path that led into the woods.

Near the greenhouse, they passed a gardener holding a plant, dressed in dirty jeans and a ball cap, with the cutest Irish setter beside him.

He gaped at them. "H-hello, Mr. Masters," he stammered.

"Roger," Burke replied, nodding.

She reached down to pet the dog, who licked her hand. "Who's this?"

"Sadie," Roger said, beaming.

Burke shot her a sideways glance and kept on walking.

"Sadie's adorable," she said, smiling, as she hurried after him. "I don't own a dog, but I like them," she said to his back. "That's a little bit more you didn't know about me." If she could just get him to like her—even a little bit—maybe he'd just let her keep her head low, do her job and hide out here a little while longer. One could hope.

They walked along a steep, rocky incline bordered by trees as he led her across the southeastern part of the island. The hills and cliffs were sharper here, so it made sense why most of the other outer buildings had been put up on the western side of the mansion.

She should've worn better shoes than sandals. She hadn't packed enough casual clothing and outdoor wear.

"How big is this island?" she called up to him.

"Thirteen acres," came the response.

The volcanic rocks here were dark, almost black, and seemed slippery to her, but maybe that was because of the hazy air today, or moisture from the surrounding ocean. At a fork in the path, they passed an old treehouse—Burke's, she suspected—and a few signs, but the area was mostly untouched. Even this path showed signs of overgrowth.

Still, he forged ahead, moving with far more agility than she expected, over its terrain.

Maybe his cane was more for show than actual support—a way for him to have an excuse for staying withdrawn.

She spent most of the time staring at the scar that was on the right side of his neck. The burn from the side of his face continued down a bit, it seemed. The news article she'd seen about the explosion in Ba'hir mentioned the injuries Burke had sustained, but not the extent of them. He'd been unable to attend the first few hearings since he'd still been recovering in the hospital. It seemed like this man in front of her had gone through hell and had gotten lost coming out the other side.

"You're noble to go this long without asking me about it," he muttered, keeping his gaze straight ahead, hand on his cane.

She furrowed her brow. "What?"

"You've got to be wondering what happened to my leg." He spoke evenly, but she detected a hint of defensiveness.

"No," she said honestly. "I was wondering what kind of hell you suffered in Ba'hir that scarred you and kept you in the hospital during part of your trial."

Burke drew up short. Drawing in a breath, he turned to face her, and she was drowning in the black sea of his shadow.

She met his gaze. "You're walking just fine, by the way. You're hard to keep up with."

His eyes bored into hers. "You're not what I expected from a maid."

"You're not what I expected for a billionaire."

A heartbeat passed between them. "The leg doesn't hurt much anymore most days, unless I do something stupid. The doctors did their best rebuilding it. As for the scars," he scratched his beard. "Who cares? I walked away. Those people didn't."

Butterflies fluttered in her stomach.

"How does that make you feel?" she said tentatively.

He turned his back to her, forging ahead. She followed. Moments later, he pushed a low tree branch aside and motioned for her to go through while he held it. "It makes me *feel* guilty for having all this."

The branches gave way to a clearing at the top of a huge cliff. An iron bench, with only the flaking suggestions of white paint, sat in the small grassy area. A rosebush, with brilliant red blooms, grew nearby it. Far below, the ocean waves crashed against the mossy, lava-hewn cliff, and to the right of it there was a short beach, and the pier where she had first arrived.

"This is the best view on the island," he said, while she tried to catch her breath. "We call it The Overlook. This is mostly south-facing, so you can see the Olympic mountains over there on a sunnier day." One large arm came up, and he pointed to the general area of the mountain range. Then it swung over to the left a little. "If it was clearer, you could see Seattle over there, too."

She felt a little lightheaded, but it wasn't from the hike, or a precursor to a seizure. It was from the beauty, the untouched perfection of this place, something that had been here for ages before and would endure for ages to come.

She sat on the bench, feeling some of the tension in her shoulders and spine ease. The smell of the roses carried on the air.

"Beautiful is too small a word for this," she said.

Normally, fun for her was getting lost in a crowd of people dancing and singing along with musicians on a stage, but maybe she had been missing out. Beauty like this was calming, if overwhelming.

Burke looked over at her, wind blowing his jaw-length hair loose from behind his ears. It fluttered around those sculpted cheekbones, those sky-blue eyes fixed on her, and she forgot about catching her breath. He stole the rest of it. He stood like a Viking, a warrior, a conqueror, a Greek god who'd escaped from Mount Olympus. A *leader*. The sight seemed to imprint itself in her brain in an instant, and even though she'd be out of his life soon, she knew she would never forget it.

Coming over, he sat beside her, his large frame taking up two-thirds of the small bench. She didn't mind, though. He blocked the breeze, and the heat from him felt nice against the damp chill in the ocean air.

He stretched out his injured leg, gaze fixated on the bay.

"I promised someone that I was going to get her and her friends help, but I let her down." His voice was low but sharp, jarring the tranquility. Slowly, she looked up at him. His features were contorted with an anguish that seemed familiar—one she'd seen in the mirror a few times before, like when Mom had died. Lucien and Charles had said Burke had led the mission that led to the deaths of the women at a motel... women stuck in sexual slavery... It must be what he was referring to.

"She screamed my name as she burned to death behind a closed door, because I couldn't get her out in time. It is the last thing I heard from her as she died right in front of me." His voice caught. "That's why I don't want to hear my name. I hate that I failed them all. I despise what I did, what it made me." He met her gaze. "Burke Masters has never been enough for anyone."

CHAPTER 7

"*Y*ou both know better than to bother me." Burke leaned on the door of his study, staring down Lucien and Charles. They'd double-teamed him. Something must be up. *Crap.*

The last hour or so he'd sat behind his desk, computer off, a pile of books untouched, staring into the black rectangle of the monitor and thinking about Rose Benoit.

Why had he shared so much with her? More importantly, why hadn't he told her to pack her bags and go home? Instead, he'd just told her he would see her tomorrow and had taken off back down the path.

What had come over him?

Maybe it was that unwavering, bold look in her eyes when she said she wouldn't call him Masters. Or the fact that he'd had to snort to cover up the snicker he'd felt when she'd made that crack about the employee interview.

He'd done his best to try and not notice how her chocolate-brown eyes were dotted with flecks of gold. It was like they could see right through him, loosening the hold on his defenses. She moved gracefully. The gentle, sympathetic expressions on her heart-shaped face, and the pursing of the full, pink lips in concern for him were equally treacherous. He had to be careful.

Still, he couldn't shake the fact he wanted to see her smile again. Being near her created a slow-spreading warmth in his chest—one he hadn't experienced since missing his parents when he had been overseas. But he had never seen them again.

Rose left something entirely new in her wake, though: a desire within him to share. He'd *wanted* to tell her about Pine Ridge, though he didn't know why.

The longing to open up to her was more intense than any he could recall. He didn't want it.

Lucien crossed his arms. "We've got to talk to you about The Ring."

He'd failed. Why did they still involve him? Turning his back on them, he limped back into his study, allowing them to follow so they wouldn't be overheard. Pain spread up the back of his calf, behind his knee, and into his thigh. He grimaced and gripped the cane harder. He'd overdone it hiking up to The Overlook, but for some reason he'd wanted to be the one to show that spot on the island to Rose, instead of letting her find it herself or with Paige. He was paying the price now.

"My buddy from S.P.D. confirmed they're operating in Seattle again," Charles said, his tone lighter. He was always the one who tried the hardest to lift Burke's spirits. It was Charles who emailed Burke the most, keeping him informed about Masters Industries, ever since he had made him his de facto go-to guy to the Board of Directors when they had returned home from Iraq. Charles had never relinquished the duty. Instead, he'd taken on more and more responsibility not only with his company, but here on the island, too.

Charles quickly told him about the woman the police had arrested for soliciting, and her ties back to The Ring.

When he finished, Burke turned around and glanced between them. He leaned back on his desk.

"We can't ignore The Ring anymore, Masters." Lucien put his hands on his hips. "I know you said our vigilante days were behind us, that you wanted us to pack up and move on, but Charles and I want to stop them. Both of us have sisters, mothers, friends." He paused. *Probably thinking about Paige.* "We need to put a stop to it."

"The other fourteen girls needed us, too." He dug his fingertips into the desk he leaned against. His breathing came shorter, faster. He wouldn't let himself picture their faces contorted in agony. He wouldn't let himself hear their screams.

"You had no way of knowing their leader had rigged the place to blow," Lucien retorted, falling back into the same argument they'd had half a dozen times before. "We've got to find out who he is and nail that bastard. Make him suffer."

Charles's jaw set as he stared Burke down. He resisted the urge to squirm beneath it.

Damn it. He was outnumbered and too exhausted to fight them on it anymore. There was no hope The Ring had self-destructed and ended their operation—Charles had proof now. And the two of them could've gone ahead and done whatever they deemed necessary to stop The Ring without involving him, yet they had. They hadn't given up. They didn't know when to quit.

"There's something else, too," Lucien added when he remained silent. "Paige said someone is looking for you, or trying to tie you to our vigilante work. She got a hit on you for the Ba'hir mess and our vigilante work through some forum chatter that she's tracking on the dark web. It doesn't necessarily mean there's a direct threat to you, though. Not yet. It's just... interesting. She's trying to narrow down the identity and figure out who it was."

A shiver shot up his spine.

The news just went from bad to worse. Once upon a time, he would've been energized by the challenge of digging his way out of messes on multiple fronts, but now, the responsibility of it had magnified. And no matter what he did, his friends still looked to him. What if he made the wrong call—again?

Whatever Paige discovered, it didn't change the fact that The Ring was operating in his backyard again. Women were still subjected to sexual slavery. He didn't have a choice.

Repressing a sigh, he kept his features blank, unreadable. He glanced at the photo he'd taken with Polly's son Chad a decade ago, when he'd taken the kid on a fishing trip. It was one of the only photos he'd left standing. "Is Chad still interested in law enforcement?"

"He graduated this past spring and is applying for jobs, but yeah, he is," Charles said, unable to hide the enthusiasm that sprang into his dark eyes. "He's staying here with Polly in the meantime, and he's been trying to get involved more with our vigilante work."

"He said he wanted to learn coding and hacking, so Paige is showing him a few things." Lucien's flat tone spoke volumes. "He could do a little recon work for us in the city, maybe."

That was the same thought he had. Test the kid a little, get his feet wet.

"You're just offering him up because we're both busy and you don't like it that he's sniffing around your girlfriend." Charles grinned at Lucien.

"Coding my ass. He follows her around like a puppy dog." To his credit, Lucien didn't try to deny it.

"Ask Chad if he wants to go, tell him what we'd look for," Burke said. "Have him report back and make it clear that whatever he finds, he's not to engage them at all."

There was a pause as his friends stared at him, one holding his breath and the other with a flare of hope in his blue eyes.

"Would we"—Lucien cleared his throat—"will you help us nail them if we can track them down?"

A low, pained groan rumbled deep in his chest. "One thing at a time."

◈

TEN A.M. the next morning, Burke let Rose in to clean, then turned around, sat at his desk behind his computer, and avoided looking at her. After baring the truth to her about why he couldn't stand his name—one of the many wounds that had festered within—he didn't trust what he'd say next, afraid of what it would do to him. Staying behind his monitors seemed like a safer bet.

Earbuds dangled from the phone in her back pocket, but she didn't put them on. She worked in silence, though occasionally, he felt her glance his way.

Finally, as Rose put away the dust rag, she drew a breath and said, "I saw Polly on the pier waving goodbye to someone around dawn, while I was taking a walk on the beach. Who left?"

The early morning memory of Rose walking along the strand, dark hair billowing in the breeze, sprang back into the forefront of his thoughts.

He'd awoken with the first rays of sun painting the sky, shocked to discover he'd slept six hours straight. That hadn't happened since before Pine Ridge and, even then, only sparingly. He'd gone to his master bedroom balcony to see Chad off, as he'd anonymously done countless other times for his friends who called this place home. He'd seen Chad's distant speck climb aboard the skiff, Polly's slightly larger speck wave him off, and Rose wandering, watching.

"Chad." He picked at the stitches in the leather of the armrest. "Polly's son."

"The boy in the photo?" She pointed to it.

His lips pursed. "He went ashore on"—Hmm, how did he want to put it?—"business."

"Vigilante business?" His eyebrows rose, and she added, "Lucien and Charles told me."

Of course they did. "They want to keep going with the vigilante bullshit. I couldn't stop them anymore, so Chad went." That was as much as he wanted to talk about that.

Rose shifted, almost like she could sense his mood. She eyed the cart of food Polly had sent up that morning. "You're served your meals here? By whom? Polly?"

He scowled.

She tapped her fingers on her cleaning cart. "Wouldn't it be nice if—while she's distracted by Chad's absence—you give her one less chore to do and go down to get food for yourself?"

She was making too much sense. How frustrating to have every part of his life picked apart like this.

"It's my business how I eat." He took a breath. Well, he didn't have to be a jackass about it. She was right; he'd let Polly indulge him for too long already. "But I'll consider it," he added.

The corners of her lips twitched as if she were trying to suppress a smile.

"Speaking of business, are you still involved in any of your family's company, Burke?" She pointed to his computer.

He expected the sound of his name to detonate an explosion of guilt in his chest as it had since Pine Ridge, but there was nothing. Just a strange tingling starting to spread as she gazed at him expectantly.

Why did she want to know? Now his curiosity was piqued.

Pushing back his chair, he stood. "Not really. I let Charles deal with it directly. He was a medic, but he has a keen sense of business and I trust him, so he takes care of day-to-day decisions on my behalf." And kept him informed every single day. He had the emails to prove it.

"Not Lucien?"

He snorted. "Lucien's taken it upon himself to make this island entirely eco-friendly. I'm sure you saw the solar panels. That was just the start of it. He's made it his personal mission to change everything he can get his hands on and make it energy efficient. Plus, he takes care of personnel and staff issues, so I let him."

She tilted her head. "How do you know all this?"

"What do you mean?"

"I mean, you're remarkably well informed for a guy who's shut himself off from the world."

He frowned. Why the hell was he talking so much? "I may," he hesitated, "read my emails."

"Why?"

His jaw locked. Might as well tell the truth. "Sometimes it is the only thing getting me out of bed in the morning."

"At least it's something." Rose rubbed her brow. "I had a best friend who recently died, Burke. She was brilliant in every way, and I miss her." Her eyes glistened. "I can't imagine what you've been through, or how you live with it. Just, take your health seriously, please." She swallowed hard. "It's so important."

Heartbreak reflected in her tear-filled eyes, hitting him squarely in the chest. She remained still, barely breathing.

He felt his heart skip a beat, and he looked away. "I will."

∽

LATER THAT AFTERNOON, Burke walked into Rose's suite to survey the damage.

She had caught him at the top of the stairs on his way down to get a snack. So much for sneaking into the kitchen unnoticed.

"The rod is too high up for me to reach." She moved aside as he entered her suite's bathroom. Since he'd seen her earlier, she'd pulled her hair back into a ponytail, the brown tresses waving as she moved. She'd also changed into jeans, a V-neck white t-shirt, and a loose yellow sweater with a frilly edge.

Part of him wanted to reach out and touch it, to see if it—and the woman beneath it—was as soft as he imagined.

"I just brushed the curtain back, and the whole thing collapsed," she explained.

He bit the inside of his cheek. Had it really been an accident, or some cockamamie rouse to get him out of his suite again? Did it even matter?

No. Not since she'd intercepted him and turned those brown eyes on him expectantly, hopefully.

They entered her bathroom and, sure enough, the Tuscan gold shower curtain lay at a diagonal from the rod that had partially collapsed.

Rose sucked in a breath as she crossed over the curtain quickly and snatched two lacy pairs of pink undergarments—a bra? Panties?—from the towel rack. She hid them under a stack of neatly folded white towels on the counter.

He cleared his throat and looked at the problem at hand.

It was an easy fix. The end needed to be raised above the groove and reinserted. A quick glance at Rose and the edge of the tub told him she was indeed too short to raise it up high enough on her own.

He set his cane against the vanity and braced himself for the discomfort in his leg that he was about to feel.

"Your leg—" she began.

"This will just take a second." He stood on the edge of her tub, keeping his weight mostly on his dominant leg, and put the end back in the groove. Metal screeched in protest, but it slid back into place.

He hopped down, hiding his grimace with familiar, controlled practice.

Shaking her head, she smiled. "What it would be like to be born with height," she murmured. "Thank you, Burke."

"Sure."

Rose tugged the curtain back, pulling it into place. "Now when I shower, I'll think of you." Color rushed to her cheeks, and it was lovely. Like petals. "I mean, I'll have you to thank." She looked down at her toes.

For a brief moment, he let himself smile.

"My pleasure." He turned to the vanity to get his cane, and their eyes locked in the mirror. Wrong word choice. He had to fall back and regroup to where there wasn't lingerie under a towel and a beautiful woman only inches away.

He went back out into her bedroom, noting the discarded Metallica t-shirt lying on a nearby chair. She liked classic rock, it seemed.

As he passed by her desk, he noticed a PTSD header blazed across the top of a small stack of pages. He paused and looked closer.

"I, um, found a wealth of treatment information online," she said quietly from behind him.

This had taken time and research. He even recognized some of the resources as ones he'd already found. His heart thudded.

"I wanted to understand more about it, and I wondered if any of it might help you."

He didn't trust himself to look at her, because he could barely breathe. The gesture shook him to his core. What could he say to her—how thoughtful it was? How much it meant to him? That he was happy she cared, even a little?

A moment passed, then he turned back around. His gaze was fixed on the papers in his hand, but slowly, it traveled up to her face.

"Thank you," he said, though the two words didn't come close to capturing everything he felt in that moment. "Mind if I take this with me?"

She smiled. "No, not at all. And thank you for the help with the curtain."

He crossed the hallway from her room, so lost in his thoughts that he almost bumped into Polly.

"B-burke," she sputtered, her soft eyes going wide, probably shocked to see him outside of his room. It was just his luck, running into someone *yet again*.

He took her shoulders and steadied her, worried she'd topple over. "Were you coming to see me, Polly?"

"Why yes, sir. It's quite strange, actually. We have a visitor."

Instantly, his muscles tensed. "Did you get Lucien? Or Charles?"

"Lucien and Paige are... preoccupied at Headquarters, and Charles is tending to Katie in the clinic, I think."

Great. "Okay, I'll be down momentarily." He lightly squeezed her arm. "Thanks, Polly."

He turned and strode into his room and set Rose's papers beside the computer.

With a few clicks of the mouse he pulled up the interior cameras on his computer. A middle-aged man of average height and build, with brown hair, stood in front of the parlor fireplace. He peered closely, trying to distinguish facial features from the overhead viewpoint. A square face, eyes close together. Oh yeah. Tom Wagner.

Groaning, he went downstairs, glad he'd put on a nicer pair of jeans and button-down shirt that morning instead of his sweats. Rose's cleaning visits were, for better or worse, changing his choice in wardrobe.

He hadn't seen Tom since the last Board of Directors meeting of Masters Industries, right after he'd been acquitted of his involvement in what went down in Ba'hir. A chief financial analyst for Branaugh, Collom, and Menk, Tom was serving a four-year term, and was not only a shareholder, but had been a personal friend of his father's.

Burke had never given a crap for the guy either way, but then again, he had done everything he could with his life to distance himself not only from the company, but from the social circles his parents had traveled in.

He paused in the parlor doorframe. "Tom."

Tom whirled around to face him. A few more lines were etched in his forehead, a little more weight around the middle, but he still emanated the same nervous, pretentious energy he always found annoying about him.

"Burke, it is you," Tom breathed out, walking forward with his hand outstretched. "Charles told us you were fine, but how many times can a guy tell us you were voting in absentia without us wondering if you were off slumming it somewhere, or worse, pushing up daisies?"

He clenched his fists and resisted the urge to throw him out on his ass. He'd communicated his current health, in the broadest of terms, to the Board. Yet here was one of the members, speculating about him to his face.

"It's Mr. Masters," he said through gritted teeth. "Why did you come here to my home without calling or emailing first?"

To his credit, Tom's amused grin faded, giving way to a wary gaze. He stood up straighter. "Sorry, Mr. Masters. The Board of Directors convened an emergency meeting regarding one of the company's subsidiary holdings, Ishimoto Telecommunications."

His hand shot up. "Stop right there. Anything I need to know about it I'll get from Charles. You wasted a trip."

Tom began to cough. "But sir, Ishimoto's stock has been plummeting since the app fraud scandal. We need to dissolve the company as soon as possible, before it becomes an anchor around Masters Industries."

So he was supposed to put people out of jobs, just like that? "Tom—"

"Sorry, sir, but would you mind getting me some water? I have a frog in my throat."

Feeling heat rising to his face and steam practically shoot out of his ears, he turned and, emphasizing his limp, went to the wet bar in the room, hidden behind a decorative wooden panel. He pushed the panel aside, got a bottle of water out of the mini fridge, and set it down in front of him.

Tom didn't take it, though. Instead, he said, "Sir, it's my understanding that Charles, um, Mr. Carson, resides here, too. Maybe you could fetch him and the three of us could speak briefly about this? I'm afraid the Board will need an answer about Ishimoto before I leave."

A fantasy of dragging Tom Wagner over to his doorstep by the hem of his expensive sport coat replayed in his thoughts, but a nagging feeling of guilt tugged at him. Maybe there was a way for them to avoid closing the company and costing people jobs. Problem was, he didn't have a clue in hell as to what was going on, nor did he particularly care what it cost Masters Industries. But the employees deserved better.

Charles was probably done with Katie by now anyway.

First, he wanted to get as far away from Tom as he could. "Stay here," he growled.

He stalked into the kitchen, feeling like he was dragging a thunderstorm over his head with him. Polly saw him in her kitchen and dropped the spoon she'd been stirring with. Katie gasped.

"Katie, do you know where Charles is?" he asked quickly.

She took a step back, eyes wide. Did she think he'd forgotten her name or something? "R-roger, you know, the gardener, came in right after I finished seeing him. He cut himself on some wire, so C-charles is stitching him up."

Crap. There'd be no dragging Charles away from a patient. He was going to have to deal with Tom Wagner himself. He thanked her and turned back to the parlor and was halfway there when he saw Rose coming downstairs, book in hand.

She looked over the railing, smiling when she caught his eye. "Hi. You're downstairs." It was said with a hint of surprise. "I was just going to read on the beach until dinner."

If he didn't have to deal with the twerp in his parlor, he would've offered to show her the north beach on the opposite end of the island. She probably hadn't ventured there yet. But he couldn't right now.

His lips drew into a thin line and he looked away. "Have a good time, then." He turned into the parlor, but it was empty. Goddamn it. Where was Tom?

His heartrate picked up, making his blood boil. Going back the way he came, he paused, hearing Rose's footsteps behind him. Then he threw open the door to Dad's study.

Tom Wagner was huddled over his father's desk with something that looked like tape in his hand. The portrait of his mother on the wall behind the desk had been pulled out, revealing the family safe embedded in the wall behind it.

Tom knew where the family safe was? And he was lifting his fingerprints? *What the fuck?*

The edges of his peripheral vision faded as Tom bolted upright. He charged at Tom, but as he tackled the man into the safe, ready to crack his skull against it, Tom grabbed a letter opener from his father's desk and plunged it forward.

CHAPTER 8

*B*urke twisted away, the letter opener slicing through the air an inch away from his stomach. He grasped the wrist with the blade and turned his hand, hoping Tom would drop it.

Instead, Tom kicked his bum knee.

The howl erupting from his chest sounded far away, but the agony made his head spin. The whole leg felt like it had been ripped right off. He fell against his dad's desk, barely able to see because of the blinding white pain clouding his vision and landed a half-assed punch into Tom's soft middle. The man grunted but didn't collapse.

Tom sank the letter opener into his shoulder.

A small bomb detonated in his muscles, setting him on fire, but it wasn't a new feeling. He'd been stabbed before by bigger, stronger men. He'd endured torture once, for God's sake. This was unacceptable. He was letting his injuries make him incapable of defending himself.

Pain exploded in his chest. He grabbed Tom's arm and shoved him back. The letter opener, still clutched in his hand, slid out. He took Tom's head with both his hands and banged it into the safe. Tom's forehead slammed against it, and he bounced back while Burke tried to collect his breath. He swayed on his feet. *Stay upright. If you fall, you're screwed.*

Mucus and tears smeared down Tom's face as he turned back to him, eyes lit with a detached desperation he'd seen from many men before. *Not* ruthlessness. It drew him up short. How the hell would he end this without killing Tom?

Tom dipped low, trying to undercut him in the ribs, but he bounced back.

Tom grabbed a paperweight from the desk. He saw it the split second before it crashed down on his head.

He saw stars as he fell to the carpet. Blood warmed his shoulder.

Above him, Tom lunged for him, that letter opener still in his hand. There was no room for him to twist away. *Shit.*

A goddamn suit would be his angel of death. The irony.

Instead, Tom began convulsing erratically. His vision faded in and out, but he managed to see Tom collapse on the floor only feet away, crumpling like paper thrown in the trash, with wide eyes and a gaping mouth.

Huh?

Tom's twitching stopped, and he went slack.

Keep your eyes open. Don't lose consciousness.

"Burke?" Rose's face filled his vision, her dark hair spilling down and tickling his cheeks. Her eyes were as wide as saucers. "Oh my God…"She dropped something clunky next to him. "Help!"

"Did you"—he gasped—"stun him?"

Nodding vigorously, her gaze zeroed in on his shoulder. "I carry a Taser."

He couldn't help the smile that tugged at his lips. Maybe he was delirious, but that was just about the sexiest thing he'd heard in ages. *She* was sexy, soulful, strong-willed…his eyes grew heavy. "Pressure," he slurred.

She got up and returned moments later, a pillow in her hands from the stuffy leather couch in the corner.

"Hang on." She bit her bottom lip and pushed the pillow down onto his throbbing shoulder. The pain broke open again, erupting.

Thank God she's here. He passed out, falling into oblivion.

THERE WERE TOO many people in his master suite. Burke could hear them before he even opened his eyes: the bustling, the talking—at full volume, not hushed—the wheeling of his food tray over the threshold, the jostling platters and cutlery when it hit one of the double doors. He burrowed deeper into his California king mattress.

He listened for Rose's voice, but didn't hear it.

After that fiasco, she was probably back in Seattle by now, on her way to Portland. His heart thudded tiredly, and he drew in a deep breath.

"Hey, buddy, open your eyes." Charles's gentle, firm command came from beside him.

He didn't want to. He wanted to go back to sleep, wondering why fate kept denying him death over and over.

Charles pinched his arm.

He opened his eyes, looking into his recessed ceiling, the huge painting of an oak tree with light shining through it on the wall above his bed, then his friend sitting beside him.

A gleam reflected in Charles's gaze. "You'll do anything to get attention."

Despite himself, he gave a half-smile. His mouth felt dry, his shoulder a dull, aching mass. "Must be some exciting board meetings you're going to, Charles." *Speaking of. . .* "Where is that bastard?"

"Polly, he's awake." Lucien's voice came from the couch by the door to the balcony. It was tempting to imagine flinging himself out that very door, just to avoid the ruckus around him.

The two of them hurried to the bed, each wearing worried expressions. Polly had unshed tears in her eyes. Hands shaking, she brushed his long, unruly hair from his forehead in a move so maternal, he had to swallow hard over the lump in his throat. God, how he missed Mom, missed the way things had been once with Polly. With his life in general.

"Thank heavens you're all right." Polly's apple cheeks lifted as she smiled.

"You scared the shit out of us, Burke." Lucien pinched the bridge of his nose. "You didn't even leave your own home, and you still managed to almost get yourself killed."

"Seems to be a habit I can't break," he muttered. He leaned forward, looking at Charles. "How bad was it?"

Charles shrugged. "I've patched up worse. You were lucky; he missed the major arteries and tendons. I'd rather have you taken to Seattle for scans and therapy, but I know you won't want to, and I'm too glad your stubborn ass is alive to fight you on it." He took a breath. "I'm going to work with you on a bit of rehab for the affected muscle and tissues, but you'll recover full mobility. *If,*" he emphasized, "you rest and do what I tell you."

He dropped his head back to the bed, grateful they weren't trying to move him. He needed to be here in his suite where he was safe, with people he trusted. "Where's Tom?" he demanded again.

"Zip tied in the cellar," Lucien said. "We didn't want to call the cops because, you know. At least not without your approval."

He *did* know. Calling the authorities to his island would inevitably expose their vigilante efforts, landing them in legal hot water. Been there, done that. Not one part of him wanted to see a courtroom again.

"What did he want in your parents' safe?" Lucien asked.

"Probably the two million my parents kept in there." He bit the inside of his cheek. What else could it be?

"I'll talk to him about it unless you want to do it yourself."

"You can," he said, feeling physically worn but oddly energized by the conversation. "But do your best to find out. If he doesn't talk, we'll re-evaluate. Who had the zip ties?" They always used heavy duty plastic handcuffs on criminals, which held them securely until the authorities arrived.

"I did."

Everyone looked over to the couch. Rose stood, then came toward him across his polished mahogany floors that almost matched her hair color. She was pale, the freckles across the bridge of her nose and tops of her cheeks more pronounced, but she was *here*.

He tried to sit up, grimacing at the pain in his shoulder while the bedsheet dropped to his waist. His torso was bare except for the large bandage and wrapping holding him together between his arm and neck. Despite the river of lava flowing through his veins near the wound, he smiled. She hadn't left, and by God he was glad she'd been there with her Taser. He'd never met anyone spunkier. That kind of bravery and ferocity was magnetic.

"Talk about a badass maid."

Polly, Lucien, and Charles looked at him wide eyed, gaping like he'd sprouted two heads. Was it because he was smiling?

"I'm glad you're going to be okay." Rose stopped near his bedside.

"Me, too," he said, meaning it. He glanced at Lucien. "You'll talk to Tom?"

"Yep." His friend looked between them, taking the hint. "We'll give you guys a second." He nodded to Polly.

Charles stood. "Sure." He pointed over to the tray near his bookcase. "If you try to self-medicate from there when I'm away, I'll rip your stitches out, Masters. I'll be back soon."

Charles could be one hell of a badass himself, when he wanted to be. "Okay," he said.

Even after every disaster he'd inflicted, he had never turned to drugs. He hadn't wanted to let himself dull the pain he felt he so richly deserved. No, if people were dead because of him, he was going to live every agonizing moment of guilt that followed, free of drug-induced oblivion.

The three of them left. Rose watched after them, then her gaze wandered across the corners of his suite: the doors of the master bathroom and walk-in closet, the dusty bookcases, the television he'd smashed long ago, the coffee table overturned near the couch.

"Aren't you glad this room is my responsibility to clean, not yours?" he wisecracked.

Finally, she looked at him again, and slowly nodded. What was she thinking? Her thoughts a mystery to him. So much of her was. The only personal things he knew about her was what she'd shared about her mom, and that she liked music. He wanted to remedy that.

"I've never seen a fight like that," she murmured, sitting near him on the edge of the bed. A respectful distance.

"You're not part of any underground fighting circuit in Portland?"

She gave him a half-smile. "No. I prefer clubs with live music and concerts to cockfights and attempted murder." Her lips fell. "I'm not used to it."

He grimaced, felt a faint rush of heat in his cheeks. "I'm not used to losing, so I understand the feeling. I'm sorry you were caught up in it."

Looking down, she picked at something on his comforter. "I'm sorry I couldn't stun him before he stabbed you."

"Not your fault. It isn't the first time I've been knifed." He pointed to a two-inch scar on his bare ribs. "This was from a makeshift bayonet in Iraq."

Her gaze wandered down his bare chest like a quiet caress, and he sucked in his breath, his abs clenching. *Bad idea.* He readjusted the sheet around his waist. She was his employee, for God's sake.

"From Ba'hir?" she asked softly.

He shook his head. "No. My back, the side of my face, and leg are my prizes from that nightmare." If she saw his back she'd run the other way. It was bad enough the burn from the side of his face went down his neck to his collarbone.

He waited until she met his gaze again and held it. "Thanks for stopping him. You saved my life."

"It's a life worth saving, Burke."

"Depends on your perspective."

"No, it doesn't." Then she smiled at him, but it didn't reach her eyes. "I know I don't have a right to ask you for anything, since you're letting me stay here and have given me a job, but if I could, I want to ask you to get professional help. See a therapist. Don't let yourself rot away, or to allow some knife-wielding jackass to finish the job you started by shutting yourself out." Reaching down, she placed her small, soft hand on top of his. The touch jolted through him. "Then maybe you could find other ways to leave the mansion like you did yesterday, and maybe the island one day."

Other ways. Was he just a sympathy case, an outlet for her caregiving? A paycheck to her? Peering at her through lowered lashes, he said nothing. Why should he have hoped for anything different—and when the hell had *hope* become part of his vocabulary again?

"Because it's so great out there in the world," he said flatly.

She leaned back, pulling her hand away. Something—hurt? Frustration?—flashed in her eyes. "Yes, I still think it is."

His gaze fell. "I'll consider it, rookie."

She stood, wringing her hands. "Reach out to the people you need, Burke. Let yourself lean on them. Trust them, please."

She stood before him, in a t-shirt still splattered with his blood and a look of compassion on her face, making him wonder how the hell he could only let himself think of her in a professional capacity. He was teetering on a dangerous edge. If she stayed he'd have to fight to bury his instincts, his emotions, whenever she was near. He'd never want to do anything to make her or any employee feel uncomfortable... It would've been easier if she'd just gone back home. It would've left him emptier than it should have to lose her presence in his life.

Rose turned and headed for the doors.

He didn't want her to go. "You stayed for Paige or because you need the job?" he called after her.

She turned to face him, her features composed and unreadable. "I stayed because it was more important for me to be here." With a nod, she left.

For several minutes he stared after her, wondering what the hell that meant.

Then he reached for his laptop. He might as well check in on company business a bit more to see if he had anything else he wanted Charles to take care of for him.

Burke awoke in a cold sweat, his laptop still in hand, to the sound of deep, resonated thumping. It wasn't the sound of mortar shells, followed by explosions, though, as it had been in his nightmare. It wasn't the sound of engines or grenades.

He glanced at his clock. 11:45pm. Great. He still had all night to suffer.

The sound continued, so it wasn't a part of his bad dream. No. It was a throbbing base from *music*.

He sat up on his elbows, frowning at the discomfort in his shoulder. The painkillers were starting to wear off, but he had to know where the music was coming from.

Besides, he was so tired of being laid up with injuries that he wanted to break something.

Getting up, he grabbed his dressing gown, threw it on over his bare chest and—careful to avoid the injury—he picked up his cane and headed down the west wing hallway. Rose's suite door was open, the room inside dark, so he descended the main staircase, the music growing louder. He could hear the vocals and guitars.

At the bottom of the sweeping staircase, Charles turned the corner and almost bumped right into him. His friend's surprise was quickly replaced by a scowl.

"I thought I told you to stay put."

He gestured away from himself, palm up. "I did. I rested, and I'm not jostling my shoulder. But you never specifically said I couldn't move my lower half."

Charles rolled his eyes. "Smart ass."

Lucien turned the corner, too, his eyes going wide. "We were going to check on you before we went home," he said, his tone accusatory.

"I'm fine," Burke replied. Enough about his injuries. The grand foyer was empty except for the three of them, so he asked, "Did Tom Wagner tell you anything?"

"He spent the better part of our time together crying, telling me he was in trouble and needed the money," Lucien said. "He was after the $2 million and stock options in your dad's safe, as well as your mom's jewelry."

No shocker there. "How did he know what was inside?"

Lucien scratched his cheek. "He said he talked to your dad about it at a holiday party your parents hosted a few months before they died, admitting that he watched Jonathan take out your mom's ruby necklace from there, so he could give it to her after the party. That's how he knew he needed a fingerprint to open it."

Charles removed the edge of his bandage and examined the wound. "Hold still."

"He betrayed my dad." Darkness clouded his vision. "Who is Tom in trouble with?"

"He's laundering money through his company for some dirty cop's side business, but he refused to tell me anything beyond that—no names, no idea what the business is, nothing." Lucien crossed his arms and shifted his weight. "He's scared shitless of the guy to the point where I think he'd rather go to prison than go back home. I didn't even have to threaten him."

Charles met his gaze, nodded, and then replaced the bandage. He winced at the pressure.

"What are we going to do with him, then?" Charles directed the question to him, his expression grim. He always hated it when they were faced with situations where they were directly breaking the law.

Lucien crossed his arms. "We have more than enough to bring to the cops, Masters. Paige hacked Tom Wagner's company hours ago and found evidence of money laundering. We could drop him on their doorstep with the proof and let them take it from there. We don't even have to involve this assault on you. But if you want," he said while glancing at Charles, "we can call the police out here. There's no reason for them to search the other buildings on the island and find headquarters, and aside from your torture room up there, nothing in the main house that would raise suspicions. We could make it work without risking everything."

It was an option, but one that left him unsatisfied. "But we don't know who the dirty cop is," Burke finished.

"No."

He took a breath. He'd already known what he wanted to do about Tom before speaking to them, but he felt more certain now. "Okay. Send him back to Seattle."

Lucien's brow furrowed. "And?"

"And nothing. Let him go."

Both men stared at him. "You're not serious," Charles said quickly. "He tried to kill you, Burke."

Rubbing his jaw, he let the name slide. Maybe it wasn't so bad after all. No images of Pine Ridge popped into his head. He focused on Tom, detained in his wine cellar. "He also has cancer. A fourteen-month prognosis."

Hands on his hips, Lucien asked, "How do you know that?"

"There was an article on him in last month's company e-newsletter for Branaugh, Collom, and Menk. It also talked about how his mother died in February. He's having a shitty time of it. Whatever his reasons, I don't care."

"Are you crazy?" Lucien barked. "There have to be consequences for trying to skewer you."

He met Charles's gaze. "Fire him from our company, but we'll leave it at that. Oh, and I want to talk to Brent Shoemacher in the morning, too. He and the Board were supposed to take care of something for me that hasn't been done yet."

Charles nodded as Lucien demanded, "And since when are you paying attention to company business again?"

Blowing out a breath, he said, "I check my emails once in a while."

Charles grinned. "About time."

He held up his hand. "I'm doing what I can. Now, where's the music coming from?"

"Come on," Charles said, nodding his head to the side.

He trailed them to his family's ballroom, light spilling out of its doorway, the sound of voices mixing with a rock song he didn't recognize. He peered into the room.

In the center of his parents' ostentatious ballroom, stood Rose on an elevated platform next to two giant speakers, her phone in hand. She was scrolling on its screen. Over a dozen of his employees either danced or talked on the outer edge near the pillars. Between the two crystal chandeliers, someone had hung a disco ball.

The laughter… the chatter… They were echoes of a happier time, when his parents had been alive. When West Cove had been a community. A time before he'd let them all down and disappeared into himself.

"It was Rose's idea," Charles said quietly. "She thought it'd be nice to get people's minds off what happened and let them have some fun."

Paige went up to Rose, cupped her hand and said something to her. Rose threw her head back and laughed. His heart swelled, the ache inside it magnifying into something else. Something intangible, but strong.

"She asked me and I told her it was okay," Lucien said. "I figured you wouldn't mind."

He stepped back, away from the celebration and the fun. Away from her. "I don't." Rose fit in well with his people. More than he did.

Lucien held the door open a little wider, and he moved behind it, out of view. "If you're feeling well enough to get downstairs, you might as well ask our deejay to dance."

"No." She worked for him. It wouldn't be right to hold her... to be close to her. There had to be boundaries.

Turning, he retreated into the shadows.

CHAPTER 9

*B*urke heard raised voices outside of his master suite. Charles had restricted him to bed rest for the entire morning, but he wasn't tired. Time to get up and do something.

Right now, that something consisted of a video call into Masters Industries. He stared at the laptop's monitor, waiting for Brent Shoemacher to return to the call. In the meantime, he was about to have other visitors.

"He won't want me here," a light, but firm, feminine voice piped up. Paige? "It's always just been you, Charles, and Polly. I was the only staff person hired since Pine Ridge until Rose—"

"You can explain everything better than I can." Lucien. "And he smiled yesterday. If there was ever a time to rip off the Band-Aid, it's now. I'll go in first, though, if it makes you feel better."

There were two short taps on his door. He looked back at the monitor as Lucien strode in.

In that same instant, Brent Shoemacher sat back down. The sheen of sweat on his brow and his blotchy skin was obvious, even through the screen. It wasn't every day Brent got a call from the boss.

Burke sat upright, propped up on pillows against his dark, gleaming wooden headboard, with a button-down shirt left undone, and his bandage visible.

"Sir—" Brent began.

"It always amazes me how you exude authority even while convalescing," Lucien began.

"Hang on," he said with a wave. He kept his gaze on Brent. "Where are we on changing the name from Masters Industries to Techstart?" He glanced at Lucien, who stopped near the foot of his bed.

"You want to move forward with that?" There was hesitation in Brent's high-pitched voice.

"Yes."

"I urge you to reconsider, sir," the man said. "If you have a child someday—"

"They'll grow up knowing their value lies far beyond a name," he said, through gritted teeth. "Make it happen." He slammed the laptop closed and glanced up at Lucien. "Brent from the Board."

"I have no idea who that is," Lucien said.

"Have you seen Rose today?" He tried to keep his tone casual. He hadn't heard her cleaning in his study this morning.

"No."

"What's going on?"

"Charles took Wagner back to Seattle before dawn and dumped him there. He's taking care of the logistics of firing him now, but otherwise, the asshole will be free to go."

His jaw worked back and forth. "It was the right move, Lu. He doesn't have long anyway."

Lucien shook his head. "Sometimes, even after seeing your ruthlessness overseas and fighting crime here at home, I'm still surprised by your capacity for compassion." He took a deep breath. "Though you might feel differently in a few minutes. But before we get to that, Paige is outside. I think you should finally meet her. She spent a ton of time chasing leads for you."

He scratched the burn scars on the side of his face, near his trimmed beard, and nodded. "Fine, Lieutenant." He bit back the smirk at using Lucien's rank against him.

"Good, *Captain*." Lucien rolled his eyes, then pointed to his bare torso. "Make yourself presentable first."

The grin that he flashed was quick. "Afraid this six-pack will have her encouraging you to hit the gym more?"

"More afraid she'll ask me to explain all your scars."

He chuckled.

Lucien ushered Paige in, his hand on the small of her back. Her blond curls bobbed every time she moved. She was lithe, pretty, with brown eyes that—

"M-Mr. Masters, it's good to finally meet you." Paige's white knuckled hands were clutched in front of her. "Thanks for letting Lu hire me and trust me with the work you're all doing fighting crime in Seattle. It means a lot to me to contribute. I know he told you my mom died in a home invasion a couple of years ago, so I want to do my part in creating more justice for victims."

Paige at the foot of his bed reminded him of Rose being here yesterday. How he wished she was here now.

"If you ever need anything, I hope you know you can count on me," Paige continued.

He held up a hand. "I've been remiss in thanking you personally, Paige. I know I haven't been involved lately, but what you've done for us hasn't escaped my attention. I'm grateful."

Paige smiled, her entire face lighting up. "Any time."

"I do have a favor to ask."

"Yes?"

"Can you help Lucien with his wardrobe?" He raised an eyebrow, looking pointedly at the blue scarf wrapped around Lucien's neck, draped over a matching blue and white striped sweater. "It's getting more preppy than hippy."

Paige laughed as her boyfriend scowled. "You're on your own," she said lightly. "I like his scarves. They give me something to grab onto when I want to pull him in for a kiss."

Lucien blushed. Burke could've seen it from yards away, and he resisted the urge to chuckle.

Lucien cleared his throat. "Please tell him what you found out about Tom Wagner."

The twinkle in Paige's eyes faded as she looked at him and said, "I think Tom is laundering money for The Ring."

He sat forward and immediately winced. "What makes you think that?"

"I back-traced the financing of the Pine Ridge Motel, which switched ownership three times in the year before the explosion, and found out which firms moved the money. One was a subsidiary tied to Branaugh, Collom, and Menk. I also found government records that had Pine Ridge scheduled for a building inspection six months before the explosion, but—for some reason—the inspection never happened. Weird, right? So I found the name of the inspector who had been assigned to it. He received a twenty-thousand-dollar mystery sum in his checking account. Guess where it was routed through?"

"Branaugh, Collom, and Menk." The words felt like poison on his tongue. "Who the hell has my company been involved with?" He snatched his phone from the bedside table. "I want Charles to cut ties to them. Masters Industries will have nothing to do with them starting today."

"Yeah, we'll take care of that," Lucien agreed.

"Goddamn Tom Wagner." He balled his massive fists.

"Chill out, Burke. You look like a giant ready to leap from that huge-ass bed. Wagner wasn't going to cough up everything he knew."

If only they weren't above using torture... "There was never a good way to end the Tom situation," he said. "Besides, you're the one who told me he didn't know what the dirty cop's side business was. He was probably smart enough not to ask too many questions."

"I'm back tracing all his calls and still digging through surveillance videos in Tom's neighborhood, in case I can come up with anything," Paige said. "Maybe we'll get lucky."

He exhaled loudly. "Luck's never been on my side before. If you get time, too, maybe start to run checks on the guys in S.P.D., in case anything pops up right away."

"What do you want me to look for?"

"Big purchases," Lucien suggested.

He shook his head. "The opposite. Someone flying really under the radar online and in his or her accounts. Someone with something to hide. It might help us figure out who's dirty."

Paige nodded.

"One more thing," Lucien added. "Remember when I told you about the websites we monitor—the one where someone was looking into your history, our vigilante work and Ba'hir?"

His features tightened, until they felt ready to crack. "Yes." It was just one thing after another.

"It came from Salem, Oregon," Paige said. "I don't know any more than that. It's more of an FYI."

Salem. The home of his archnemesis. The man who'd pointed the finger at him for Ba'hir.

He leaned forward. "Graves." He uttered the name with such contempt there might as well be black spittle shooting from his mouth. "He was from there."

Lucien, Charles, and Burke had served in the same unit as Gavin Graves in Iraq, to the detriment of them all, particularly the innocent people of Ba'hir.

That fateful day their unit was securing the town when a teenage boy surprised Graves, who'd shot him. As Burke had raced over to the teen, his mother wailing, Graves had promptly lifted his M4 carbine and mowed down civilians with a clinical detachment even he hadn't seen before. He and Lucien had hit the ground, but the people weren't so lucky—especially when Graves went for the gas tank.

At the memory, the scent of burning flesh and smoke filled his nostrils.

He pinched his eyes shut, trying not to remember every horrible casualty. *Focus on Graves.* They'd fought in the sand like heavyweight champs in an all-out brutal clash. He remembered every second of that, until the explosion behind him... then nothing.

Lucien told him he'd been on fire, which Lucien had put out himself.

Later, while Lucien had gotten him medevacked, he had learned that Graves had run back to the convoy, spilling lies the second he got to them. Laying the blame on Burke like he'd gone berserk.

To this day, he still couldn't believe that bastard had had the gall to try and pin the mass murders on him. Was it because he'd seen through Graves's smarmy charm from the beginning? Because he'd outperformed them all and came from money? From day one, Graves's resentment toward his wealth had been a festering poison simmering below the surface in their unit.

In the end, it had been their word against Graves, and he was exonerated, even though Graves had used his weapon. But there wasn't *evidence* against Graves, and it haunted both he and Lucien.

"There's 160,000 people in Salem." Lucien shook his head, some of his hair falling free from his bun. "He doesn't live there anymore. Last time you checked on him, he was in San Francisco, right?"

"That was almost three years ago," he replied. "Paige, can you find out everything about him now? Rip his life apart? It's him." It couldn't be anyone else. No one else in this world gave a crap about him anymore, except the people on this island.

"There's no evidence tying him to The Ring, Burke. Graves isn't behind every awful thing we deal with."

He pointed at him. "No evidence *yet*."

Lucien shifted his weight and held Burke's gaze, eyes narrowing. "We've been down this road once before, after Ba'hir. You're grasping at straws. We haven't seen or heard from that shit heap since the tribunal, and we need to focus our time and attention on the real problem. We don't have time to resurrect ghosts."

"We can do both." He looked at Paige expectantly. "Right?"

Paige folded her arms and glanced between them, a small smile playing at her lips. "I can do anything, boys. I'm going to go glue myself to my computer monitors and hunt down digital leads like a tracker ready to turn prey into a carcass."

Despite his concern over Graves, he smiled. Yeah, he could see the resemblance to Rose.

CHAPTER 10

*R*ose pinched her eyes shut, trying to push away the remnants of her early morning headache, and Gavin's latest lewd text from earlier that morning. The four tequila shots last night had been a mistake. A fun mistake, but a mistake nonetheless.

But she'd been trying to ignore the guilt she felt for keeping Burke in the dark about why she was here. For not telling him that she was using his home to hide from Gavin. He was a good guy. She hated deceiving him like this. And then when she'd talked about the therapist, she'd really stepped in it.

Burke's reaction had been swift. He'd put up a wall she'd thought she was breaking through. She had seen it in his eyes.

How would he react when he found out who she *really* was? Her stomach churned.

So, she'd cleaned the second-floor salon instead this morning. It was easier to give into avoidance than it was to face him and come closer to forgetting who she was supposed to be to him.

His employee.

She rubbed her temple against the pressure there. Maybe that was the real problem—she hadn't been speaking as a maid. She'd only been herself in that moment: a haunted, damaged soul reaching out to another. The woman to the man.

She threw her head back on the worn, comfortable red sofa, which sat near the bottom of a round, wrought iron spiral staircase leading up to the library's second floor. Every wall had white shelves with rolling ladders, and the etched bronze ceiling cast everything in a glow.

This library was the coziest room in the mansion. She felt comfortable here, so she hid out, happy to find the romance section and tried to sit and read.

The problem was that in everything she picked up, all the characters reminded her of Burke.

Trying to ignore him and the fact she cared so much was getting her nowhere. As were the images of his smile, his perfectly sculpted, bronze chest, the cleft in his chin where his beard indented, his strong hands, and his soulful sky-blue eyes. They wouldn't stop turning over and over in her thoughts.

But it was more than that. The man was resilient. After everything he'd gone through, every hurt he endured, every loss, he'd still held the hand of his housekeeper and gazed at her with affection. He still listened to his friends and thought someone like her was a badass with a Taser, and not the coward hiding from the man tormenting her. He'd joked with her. He kept everyone on the island employed, and still helped her with the shower curtain when she'd asked him, even though his leg had probably hurt in the process. That kind of strength was admirable. It was striking.

Oh God, attraction was the last thing either of them needed. Since Gavin—

She closed her book decisively. No, not like Gavin. She quickly flipped through mental snapshots of her past lovers. Yeah, being around Burke was entirely different, though she didn't know exactly why. His gaze was like a magnet pulling her into a vortex that somehow made her feel safe and understood. He was sexy as hell, and made her veins turn into molten lava, while words seemed stuck on the tip of her tongue. She wanted to taste him. She wanted to see him smile again.

"You're lucky you never had this problem," she muttered to the books beside her.

It was time to turn her attention to something she *could* change. She could try, once again, to figure out why his attacker, Tom Wagner, had seemed so familiar to her.

When she'd stumbled on him attacking Burke, his face had resonated with her somehow—like she'd run across him once before, but she couldn't figure out where. It was unnerving.

From her gym? From a club in Portland? Someone who'd come to one of her band's gigs?

Ugh. For now, wracking her brain was getting her nowhere, too.

She couldn't change her reaction to Burke, she couldn't force herself to remember, but she could take her own advice and confide her baggage with Gavin to someone. After all, if she was going to preach it to Burke, she couldn't be a hypocrite.

Then maybe she could find the courage to tell him who she really was, too.

When they'd parted ways last night, Paige had mentioned she was going to spend time in the greenhouse before lunch. Maybe it was time to tell her all of it and get the vigilante team involved. They were former military and a genius hacker: maybe they were the solution she'd needed all along.

After dutifully putting back the books, she headed to the kitchen. The clanging of pots and pans, the conversations of staff, and the sound of faucets turning on and off floated down the hallway. As she entered, Polly was in the middle of setting lunch out. A platter of meat, cheese, fruits, and vegetables was sitting out on the large island, and Katie was setting out plates. A few other staff members were laughing and talking in the corner.

She exchanged greetings with them. After giving a smile and a wave, she ducked out of the kitchen and headed out to the back patio, into the bright, tranquil midday sunlight.

God, she really liked this place.

The greenhouse was situated on the east side of the patio. It was separated from the mansion by a walkway, but the main entrance opened above the garden, with a few steps leading down to the hedges and flowers. It was sunny and comfortable outside, but when she opened the greenhouse door, heat and humidity whooshed out at her. The smell of dirt and vegetation filled her nose.

"Hello?" she called out as her eyes adjusted to the shadows and steam. Small trees and beds of flowers lined the walls, with the center of the greenhouse filled with even more annuals and perennials. Everything was flourishing.

Her stomach fluttered like a bird in a cage.

"Hello," Paige's friendly voice called back. "Rose, is that you?"

"Yes." She followed the sound of the voice and went left. When she turned the corner, she bumped into Paige, who was bent over a thriving red rose bush. She regained her balance. "Oh, I'm sorry."

Paige laughed, straightening. With all the natural light filling the room, she noticed Paige had more freckles across the bridge of her nose than she did. "No problem. I've been searching this bush too long anyway. I'm looking for the perfect long-stemmed rose."

"Let me help you." She leaned over, looking at each bloom. Maybe she could work the truth into the conversation naturally, so she didn't just spring the fact that she had a stalker on Paige out of the blue. "What kind are you looking for?"

"Mostly open, I guess." Paige kept her eyes glued on the bush. "I'm leaning toward that one." She pointed to a picture-perfect rose, a deep ruby color, unfolding gently and utterly flawless.

"It's beautiful." She nodded. "I'd go with it."

"Awesome." Turning, Paige picked up a set of clippers on a bench nearby, overflowing with rhododendrons. Leaning down, she picked the rose, then held it up between them, smiling. "Lu's going to love it."

With her shallow breathing and quick movements, Paige practically radiated excitement. "Is it a special occasion?"

"I'll say." Paige's smile beamed as bright as the sun. "I'm proposing to him tonight."

She gasped. "What?"

Paige's wide brown eyes gleamed. "Well, I'm reproposing, I guess. Lu told me he wanted to get married a few months ago, but I told him I wanted to wait to get Mr. Masters's blessing. And guess what? I met him this morning, and he was a nice guy. I liked him. He *joked* with me, and Lu said he was smiling more lately, and I think things are looking better between them, so why wait, you know?" The words tumbled out, one over the other. The flower bounced in her enthusiastic grip.

"That's true," she said, her thoughts whirling around.

This changed everything.

She couldn't get the team involved in her mess on the same day her cousin was so over the moon to marry the man she loved. It would upstage her happiness. She wasn't going to rain on her parade.

Damn it.

Paige's gaze searched hers. "Is something wrong?"

She quickly shook her head, forcing a smile she didn't feel. "No, not at all. I'm so happy for you."

"Thank you." Paige's tone lowered, and she put her hands on her hips. "But something's wrong, Rose. What is it? Is it about Burke?"

Why would Paige assume it was about Burke? She bit her lip. Could Paige guess how unprofessional, how intimate, her thoughts about him had gotten? Hopefully not.

"No," she said. "Well, except for almost watching him get murdered. That was pretty upsetting." That was the understatement of the year. Her heart had practically stopped then and there in his father's study. It hadn't truly started beating until after she'd been alone with Burke. After she'd seen him smile.

Paige eyed her warily. "Are you sure?"

Geez, why didn't she have a better poker face? Mom could always see right through her, too. Maybe it was a family trait.

"I was, um, thinking about telling him who I really was," she admitted. "I don't like lying to him about being a maid, when this was only ever just a temp job."

"Okay... but seems like there's more to it than that." Paige stood up straighter. "What made you want to leave Portland and come to meet me now? What's the other reason you came here to West Cove?"

She didn't know if she should tell her anymore. Dropping the Gavin bombshell would screw up her proposal to Lucien. She knew her cousin would—

"It's an ex, isn't it?" Paige asked. "Are you going through a divorce, or a nasty breakup?"

"You could say that." Withering under Paige's scrutiny, she clasped her hands together. "My ex-boyfriend is stalking me."

Paige's delicate features paled, and her lips parted. "What?"

"It's been going on for thirteen months. He sends me text messages. He calls. He comes to my workplace, or ambushes me at the hair salon, or the grocery store. I only slept with him once." Fresh, hot tears stung her eyes, the frustration and fear of the past months hitting her like a tidal wave.

"It was such a mistake, Paige. We'd gone out for a third date. I'd had too much to drink, I guess, because I somehow ended up back at my apartment with him, but I don't remember inviting him over. But I woke up next to him naked. Used. I told him I didn't want to see him again, but he didn't take no for an answer. It's been going on ever since."

A tear escaped, and holy crap, it felt so good to get it off her chest. She hadn't told anyone before. The shame had been too real. But now, the only thing she felt was relief—which lasted only for a moment, driven away by the look of utter horror in her cousin's expression.

"Oh my God, Rose." Paige blinked hard. "Have you gone to the police?"

"Going to the authorities was complicated, and I didn't know where to turn to." *Because I don't know who's in Gavin's pocket back home. I don't know who to trust.* "Then you came along. And this place." Burke's face flashed through her mind. "You've all saved me."

"Not yet we haven't." Paige planted her hands on her hips. "Who is he?"

She shook her head. "We can talk more tomorrow."

"What?"

She lifted Paige's hand with the rose in it. "Tonight, you're going to propose to the man you love."

"No way." Blond curls bounced as Paige shook her head. "It can wait until a time when some psycho-lunatic-rapist isn't out there looking for you."

"It's been going on for over a year, Paige. One night's not going to make a difference." She ran a hand through her hair. "Both of us know that if I tell you his name you're going to go back to your bungalow and find every scrap of dirt on this guy that could possibly exist. You'll rally the troops and then this second proposal of yours sits on the backburner again."

"But—"

"I'm okay." She took her by the shoulders and looked her in the eyes, smiling. "I'm here with you on a remote island, he doesn't know where I am, and I sleep down the hall from the biggest, toughest man I've ever met. Plus, I have my Taser. I only told you because you asked, and I didn't want to mislead you. I wanted you to know the truth."

Paige didn't move. They were at a stalemate.

She let her hands drop. "Paige, you've been entirely selfless since we connected online. You've given me a family again. You handed me a temporary job and, more importantly, offered me a place to stay where I can be free. I don't have to look over my shoulder every two seconds here. You have no idea what that means to me—what you've given me. Please, let me give you just this one night in return. Let me do something for you that will make you happy."

Paige frowned. "Are you sure? I don't mind—"

"I know you don't, but I do. Go." She lifted her chin. "Ask him to be yours and enjoy your night. Trust me, I'm good for a few hours. Then we can figure out my next steps."

A heartbeat of silence passed. "*Our* next steps," Paige corrected.

She smiled. "Ours."

CHAPTER 11

*G*avin stood barefoot on the damp gravel and pavement of the Portland International Airport's long-term parking lot. He stared straight ahead, unblinking, at Rose's red Ford Taurus. Hers. The license plate and one of her band's bumper stickers confirmed it.

Where the fuck was she?

When he'd gotten the call, he'd run straight from his shower, barely throwing on pants and a shirt. Rivulets of water still trickled down his neck from his wet hair, the clothes clinging to his damp body.

Only now did he realize he didn't have shoes on.

It had taken his colleagues days to track down her goddamn car. Gavin rubbed the creases of his forehead hard with his thumbnail. What was the point of being a well-connected cop when you couldn't pull strings within your own goddamn department, not to mention Homeland Security? There were cameras everywhere in the city, for chrissake, and he wanted access to them.

It was a good thing he had dirt on the right people. Otherwise he'd never know that Rose had hopped a flight at all.

She could be *anywhere.*

He kicked the tire of her car. Now he had to resort to tracking her credit card and hacking into her phone—expensive shit that would cost him hard-earned money. More than his meager municipal salary could afford. It was a good thing he had other avenues of income. This new group of girls seemed particularly promising…

She'd abandoned him.

Darkness swelled inside of him like tar, ready to erupt.

How dare she.

He was going to catch up to her, and he was going to make her pay him back for every miserable moment she was making him suffer. He'd get her apology. He'd get her tears, her shame, until he was sure she'd never do something this thoughtless again.

Time to call in reinforcements, starting with his contact at the FAA. He'd get her flight information, and video surveillance from inside the airport. The man would cough it up if he didn't want Gavin to share a video of his own: one featuring the FAA asshole and two underage hookers.

It was just a matter of time until he'd come face-to-face with Rose again. Days. Maybe hours. His blood began to boil.

Then she wouldn't walk away from him anymore.

CHAPTER 12

*R*ose trailed Paige back to her bungalow and they shared a cup of tea and lunch. Then she helped her make an elaborate dinner of oysters, pasta primavera, steamed vegetables and triple chocolate cake, while they chatted.

Eventually, she left mid-afternoon, so Paige could prepare for her special evening with Lucien.

She walked back to the manor house slowly, her thoughts in a jumble. Most of them revolved around how she was going to tell Burke who she really was tomorrow. However she did it, she had to make sure to take responsibility for it. She didn't want her lies to affect his relationship with Paige and Lucien. Especially now.

Following the sidewalk, she went around a cone-shaped topiary and ascended the patio steps, the late day sun casting long shadows. But when she'd tell him, she had a feeling that her time on the island would end.

She entered the mansion and headed for the staircase, music from the 1970s floating from the kitchen. An off-key, gentle voice sang along. Polly. It tugged at her heartstrings. This place was a home, and the people in it—especially Burke—deserved the whole truth.

Something crunched under her foot as she stepped into her bedroom.

It was a note, slipped under her door, with Burke's monogram at the top of the page. She sucked in a breath, her heart leaping just a little too much.

He'd asked her to join him in his suite at seven for dinner.

She bit her lip.

She wanted to, but she shouldn't.

It was still a few hours away, so she'd figure it out later. Until then, she decided on an easy task first: checking her email. Relief ebbed through her— just the usual retail and spam emails in her personal account. But when she checked her work email, there it was. An email from Gavin, from a new account, with a subject line: *You left.*

Bile rose in her throat, and she swiped block and delete as quickly as her shaking fingers allowed. Her breathing quickened. She couldn't take much more of this.

Gavin knew she was gone. He'd never stop looking for her.

She slammed the laptop cover down. Burke's handwritten note fluttered to the floor, so she bent down to pick it up.

Turning the paper over in her fingers, she stared at it. She couldn't control Gavin or the fact that she had epilepsy, and she hadn't been able to stop Mom from dying. She couldn't change the fact that she'd have to return to Portland eventually. She had responsibilities there, her bands were waiting for her... It didn't matter that every fiber in her being was terrified to go back. She'd be on her own again, a target for a madman.

But no one here at West Cove was alone, and it was all because of Burke. Even though she hadn't known him long, she'd seen how constant, kind and strong he was. He was here, and he wasn't going anywhere.

Well, I don't have to be alone tonight.

She got ready for dinner with Burke, settling on a black, flowy skirt with white lace detailing and a white, V-neck shirt. She put her hair in a bun to maintain professionalism, then took it down because it felt stuffy. With a quick touch-up of her makeup and her phone in her clutch, next to her Taser, she knocked on his door at seven. Should she have shaved her legs again since her shower that morning?

Keep it casual, Benoit. It's not a date. It's a friendly meal with your employer.

Burke opened the door. His blond hair was dark, damp, and combed back, the scent of evergreen aftershave light in the air between them. Dressed in dark trousers and a blue shirt only buttoned halfway up because of the bandages still stuck on his shoulder, he filled the entire door frame. Gosh, he was tall. She dragged her gaze from those pearled buttons of his shirt in front of her up to his face.

The corner of his mouth lifted. "Prompt as usual, rookie. I'm glad you came."

She swallowed hard. "How are you feeling?"

"Good. Come in." He leaned on his cane as he moved aside for her to enter.

She walked into the room, which had been tidied since her last visit. The broken television was gone. The coffee table sat upright between the two couches, with dinner spread out on top of it.

No flowers were on the table. She let out a breath. No flowers meant it wasn't a date to him, either. The uncertainty was all in her head.

"I wasn't sure you were going to come." His voice pulled her from her thoughts.

She was alone with a man in a bedroom. That hadn't happened since Gavin. He didn't deserve to be compared to that bastard, but still... she felt her muscles tighten, the reflex to run at the ready. She turned to face him. "I wasn't sure either."

"I would've suggested dinner downstairs, but the staff uses the dining room and people are always coming and going." He shrugged awkwardly. "I thought it'd be nice to keep it quiet and casual."

She smiled. "Good idea. But it *was* a little strange getting a formal invitation to a man's bedroom."

"I can imagine." Burke shifted his weight. "I mean, it's just a professional dinner."

Her shoulders dropped, but reason cheered like a crowd at homecoming in her mind. "Right."

He opened his mouth, like he was going to say something more, then closed it.

"I've been single and on my own for a long time, though, so it was nice to get an invitation of any kind," she added, smiling. For some reason, it was important that he should know that.

Maybe it was because she was standing at the foot of his big, plush bed, and he was so— "Why am I here, Burke?" she blurted out.

The direct question seemed to catch him a little off guard, because he looked away. The knuckles on the hand that held the cane turned white. When his gaze came back to her, he said, "I can't remember the last time I wanted to be around someone, but I do with you. I've been slipping on an edge for ages, Rose, barely hanging on by a thread. I can't promise I'm good company. But I want to get to know you." He paused. "If you want."

She drew in a deep breath. "Okay." Besides, if they went over to the couches to eat, then they wouldn't be by the bed, and she wouldn't imagine him sprawled out on it, reaching for her, drawing her in. God, she felt lightheaded.

Burke smiled. "Shall we, then?"

She smiled back. "It'll give you more material for my employee interview." *Don't tell him you're not really a maid yet. Don't ruin tonight for him, Lucien, and Paige.*

He chuckled lightly as they went over to the food. "Nah. I used to be an excellent conversationalist before the war. I had to, as the only child of famous parents. Do you know how many parties I was forced to go to? I got very good at it, so I promise I won't make you feel like you're on trial. Trust me, I know what that feels like."

It was said matter-of-factly, without animosity, so she ducked a look up at him. The burned side faced her, and her fingers itched to reach up and trace the puckered skin beside his beard, touch the eyebrow shortened by it, the ear that bore similar marks. Life had given him every reason to be bitter. Yet here they were, at a dinner he'd arranged to have with her. Too bad she wasn't hungry.

He gestured to the couch and she sat. Beyond the windows, dusk was descending, the sky painted with brilliant shades of coral, indigo, and navy.

Then he sat across from her, and took the lid off one of the several platters scattered around the table. "Compliments of Polly," he explained. "When I told her I'd hoped for company at dinner, I'm afraid she overcompensated."

There had to be half a dozen dishes for each of them, mixed aromas of pork with rosemary, potatoes, and bread wafting up. "It all smells divine." It did, but for some reason, nausea tugged at her. "I've never enjoyed cooking for myself, or tried to be a foodie before, but Polly might turn me." She took the silver cover off of a platter, discovering a salad beneath it. Okay. It was safe to start with salad for now. She could probably get through that without retching.

Maybe it was just nerves over Gavin's latest message.

"It wouldn't be the first time," Burke said, smiling. "Katie started out with your job, but has become a sous-chef, I've heard."

"I can see how keeping an estate like this would take an army." She forced a bite of salad down.

"Sometimes it feels like I've employed one," he agreed. "What was your place like in Portland?"

She thought back to her apartment, which had been full of comfortable furniture, and photographs on the windowsills. She'd framed Mom's cross-stitching collections on the walls, next to artsy posters of bands. She'd have to go back there soon. The thought was disheartening.

"I had an apartment that was too small for all of the albums and books that I own." She met his gaze. "Besides going out to shows, I like to read."

He sat forward. "I have a library here. You should see it—"

"I found it." She glanced down. "Sorry. I shouldn't have been poking around."

Smiling, he shook his head. "No, I'm glad you did. I want you to make yourself at home." The word hovered between them, and he looked down, taking a bite of bread.

"I loved the library," she said, eager to brush past the "home" comment. "The sofas in it are like the one I have, all plush and comfortable. My dining room only seats four, instead of a dozen, and I have mementos from my mom on almost every flat surface." She shrugged. "It's a cozy place, I guess." And somewhere she didn't feel safe anymore. Gavin had taken that away from her.

He uncorked a bottle of wine, those impressive biceps barely flexing beneath his shirt. "What kind of music do you like?"

"Almost anything," she said quickly. Time to test the waters and see if this attraction was all in her head. She took a deep breath. "I've been on an Afro-Cuban kick lately, but I like music that has a sweeping, sensuous melody, lyrics that hit the core of what it means to be alive, with beats like a primal drive pushing and pulling toward something profound."

He set down the bottle. When his gaze traveled up to hers, the heat burning in his blue eyes was unmistakable. Inescapable. She could drown in those sky-blue depths. She couldn't breathe. *Oh my.*

He wanted her. He'd shown her what she'd secretly hoped for but couldn't let herself have. There was that lightheaded feeling again, like she was floating outside of herself.

She cleared her throat. She must be ten shades of red right now. Her cheeks felt like they were on fire. "Do you like music?" *Steer the conversation away from sex.* She stabbed salad with her fork.

Sitting back, Burke shifted on the couch. "Yes. I played drums in school and for the hell of it before the war. Not after, since my leg's been a problem."

Oh, Jesus. A drummer. She was screwed. "Why the drums?"

His gaze held hers. "I've got really great rhythm."

The fork dropped to her plate with a clatter. "I'm sorry—I forgot. I need to reply to a message from a friend back in Portland." It was a thin excuse, but she needed to regroup. Get her bearings before she embarrassed herself. She lifted her clutch. "I just need a second with my phone, but I'll step out into the hallway." She stood.

He got to his feet with her. "Rose, you don't—"

"I remember your no phones policy." She forced a smile. "Don't worry, I'll be back. The food smells fantastic." She fled the room before he could argue.

She held her clutch to her breasts, taking deep breaths and willing her heart to slow the hell down. He had to know he was hitting on her too, right? He had to know he was approaching the hazard zone at the edge of professional boundaries.

She didn't know what to do with this level of attraction. She'd never felt so drawn to someone before, or longed so deeply.

Boundaries had to be put back up. It'd be better for them in the long run. When she told him the truth of who she was tomorrow, he'd feel betrayed. He'd probably hate her.

The thought was devastating. This time she would lose whatever this was between them. This time she'd lose *him.*

Watching him get stabbed by Tom Wagner, the man who looked annoyingly familiar to her somehow, had scared the shit out of her. The look in that man's eyes. The rage. The determination. The way his voice had cracked when he yelled sounded exactly like that guy from the museum...

Hang on.

She dug out her phone, her teeth clenched, and opened her gallery. She started flipping back to the photos from over a year ago.

That second date with Gavin had been at an art museum. Gavin had seemed bored by it, so she'd thought it was a weird choice, and he had looked at his watch a lot. When they had gone outside, he'd told her he needed to speak with someone and walked away, talking to a man in a suit under the streetlight. She'd meandered only a few feet away. That was when Rebecca had texted and had asked how the date was going. She had taken a selfie of an eye roll and sent it back. Gavin and the other guy had been in the background.

There it was. The selfie. Under the lamplight, clearly arguing with Gavin, was the man who'd stabbed Burke. Tom Wagner.

What did this mean? She slumped against the door. Was it all a weird coincidence? Lucien had said the man had something to do with finances. Maybe he was Gavin's accountant? Or maybe Tom Wagner had been assisting the police on an investigation of some kind last year?

Her head started to pound. Too many questions. But she had to tell Burke.

Nausea clawed at her organs. The throbbing in her skull intensified. Not another seizure. Not now. Shit.

Tell Burke about Tom, give him the phone and leave. Get to the medication.

She poked her head back in the room. Burke still stood beside the couch, his hands in his pockets. His lips were pursed, the skin on his chiseled cheekbones pulled tight. God, she wanted to know what it would feel like to have his arms around her. But her racing heart wasn't just because of him. Neither was the lightheadedness.

"Everything okay?" he asked.

The edges of her vision began to blur, and he was the only thing that stayed in focus. This one was coming on too fast.

"Tom Wagner. I just realized where I'd seen him before."

His frown was instantaneous. Hard. "What?"

She felt herself sway, her muscles tighten, her pulse pound in her ears.

Fear sprang into his eyes. "Rose?"

He sounded worried... and far away.

"S-seizure."

She gasped as spasms wracked her. Her vision began to go black, and her body smacked onto his shiny, dark wood floor.

CHAPTER 13

*F*our hours. Four *agonizing* hours dragged by.

Burke did his deep breathing exercises to keep his PTSD in check as he sat in an armchair by Rose's bedside, his legs splayed out and his shoulder protesting with a dull throb from having carried her across the second floor from his room to hers. But he didn't care. He would've carried her to the goddamn boat himself if Charles hadn't stopped him.

She lay on top of the duvet, her hair spread out like a chocolate curtain on the pillow, a soft gold blanket draped across her legs. His mother had been quite the ostentatious decorator, but oh, how he missed her. Tonight he had thought he'd lose another person he cared about.

Watching Rose collapse had scared him to death.

He was experienced at pushing past fear in firefights, focusing while getting shot at in combat, but nothing had prepared him for seeing someone important to him crumple like a paper bag flattened under a car tire.

He'd stayed calm, fighting for control so he wouldn't trigger a flashback. Thankfully, none had come. This time.

She had been just fine one moment—a little pale, maybe, and a little nervous—but he'd thought it was because of what had been going on between them. Without a doubt she'd felt it, the shift, the sparks flying. But he'd also sensed that he made her nervous. He'd been about to ask her about it and what he could do to fix it when she had come in from the hall, then...

It had been the first time he'd actually seen someone having a seizure. He'd raced to her side, his cane crashing to the floor, but he hadn't known how to help her. He'd never seen someone so rigid. No one alive, anyway. He'd called

Charles, who had told him what to do and not to call 911. By the time Charles came bounding up the main staircase, he had her in her room, his heart pounding furiously, his own pain overshadowed by panic.

Why hadn't she told him she was epileptic? It was none of his business, really. But still, he wished he had known.

And how the hell did she know Tom Wagner? He rubbed his temple.

Charles had examined her, administered the medication, and then told him they had to wait until she woke up. In the meantime, he was going to sleep in the guest room next to Rose's so he could check on her every few hours.

They'd called Paige, too. She and Lucien had abandoned their dinner and had rushed over. They'd waited with him up until a short time ago, when he'd finally insisted that he would keep vigil and that they should turn in for the night. Paige hadn't wanted to go far, though, so they went to sleep two rooms down.

He was so anxious he wanted to crawl out of his own skin, replaying every moment of this dinner with Rose, wondering what warning signs he had missed, going over the strange, new sensations she had evoked in him: the ravenous desire, yes, but the mystery of her that drew him in, the light in her expressive eyes, her passion for music, and her love for her mom. Most of all, how huge, seismic earthquakes had rocked him to the core with just one of her smiles.

What the hell was happening to him? He was starting to want her in a way he shouldn't allow himself to want anyone. Not after what he'd done. But something about her ran deeper, reaching far into his soul, beginning to crack off shards of the darkness that had taken root there.

But she was here to do a job, for God's sake. She wasn't there to save his soul; or to tame the beast enraged by helplessness. By loss. By the deaths he'd caused.

Rose's breathing changed and became lighter. He sat forward, strands of hair falling into his face, hands clasped between his knees. When her eyelids fluttered, so did his heart. He leaned in more, holding his breath.

Brown eyes opened and focused. Tilting her chin down, she met his gaze.

He smiled, warmth bubbling up in his chest. "Welcome back."

Bracing herself on shaking elbows, she sat up against the pillows and headboard. Her porcelain cheeks turned pink. "Not again." She pressed a hand to her forehead and wouldn't look at him. "I'm so sorry."

He frowned. "Why?"

She didn't answer. Her gaze fell on the far wall, then the dresser, and then the mirror.

Maybe he was making her uncomfortable. He stood, trying hard to quell his curiosity about Wagner. "Charles should know you're awake. I'll go get him."

Her head snapped back around. "Please don't go. Not just yet."

He stopped in his tracks. Drawing in a breath, he said, "Paige said this happened before, right after you came here."

"She was here?" she asked, upset.

"Yes. She and Lucien rushed over when they heard."

"I ruined their night. Everyone's night."

"You did no such thing," he said. "But why didn't you want them to tell me, Rose?"

Picking at a thread on the duvet, she mumbled, "I was already the rookie. I didn't want to be Charles's new patient, too." The thread snapped off between her fingers.

Ah, he understood. She was embarrassed by her vulnerability. "If we compared the number of times each of us has been a patient, I still think I'd beat you."

Her smile was quick, tired, but grateful. "I shouldn't have changed medications before coming here." Her nose inched up, her gaze catching his. "I'm sorry for putting you and your staff out."

"Don't." It sounded sterner than he intended, so he added, "Thank Charles when you see him. He was the one who convinced me not to call an EVAC chopper out here, or take you back on one of the boats. He gave you your meds." He jutted his chin toward the bottles on her nightstand. "I would've had you down at the helipad in a heartbeat if it was up to me."

"I didn't want that."

"He said that." He leaned on her bedpost and crossed his arms. "Can Paige, Charles, or anyone else get trained on how to help you handle these, now that you live here? I did a little of online research when Charles was tending to you, and everything I read said it helps to have people around who know how to manage seizures with you." But she could still live a long life. That had been his first question. The relief he'd felt reading it in black and white had been staggering.

Her shoulders slumped. "Mom used to help..." Her voice trailed. "My best friend Rebecca knew how to manage my medications, too, but she died last month. Maybe in the future Paige can, but for now, no one manages these with me."

The level of loss, of isolation that she lived with was amazing. She seemed so outgoing, so easy to talk to, loved life so much—why was she so alone in it all?

"What are your triggers?"

"Stress. Other things, sometimes, but mostly that." Her wavy brown hair swayed when she shook her head. "My doctor will want me to have more testing if I don't adjust to this medication pronto."

Guilt gnawed at him. He was probably putting all kinds of strain on her by grilling her in those interviews. Plus, she was in a new place with people she didn't know and had been trying to remember who Tom Wagner was to her up until last night. No wonder she had anxiety.

"I don't know about you, but I think the manor house has never looked cleaner." And he'd never felt more in control of his PTSD than he had these past few days. Ever since he'd started talking to her. Against his better judgment, he said, "We can hold your job for you so you can go back to the mainland to take care of this, if you want."

"I'll go back when I have to." She bit her bottom lip. "If that's okay with you."

It was more than *okay* with him. He didn't want her to step one foot off the island. He nodded. "Sure." Good. He hadn't sounded too eager.

"I'll be better in the morning." She glanced at his shoulder and back up again. "I hope you keep feeling better, too."

What she did to him with one small glance, one simple endearment... It went straight to his heart. Just having her nearby calmed the storms that usually raged inside of him, soothing a part of his soul he thought he'd lost.

"I wish you had told me."

The words came out before he could stop them. They hovered in the air between them, suggested an intimacy overshadowing the façade of ignorance they were both clinging to. He could see it in her expression, how her chest rose with an intake of air, the softening of her gaze.

"I don't tell anyone."

But she *had* wanted to tell him about Tom Wagner. "Can you tell me how you know Tom Wagner?" He couldn't help it. He had to know. "You said you remembered where you'd seen him before."

She nodded slowly, and some of the color in her cheeks drained. "I think he knew my ex-boyfriend. I have this photo of him." She reached over to her nightstand, grabbed her phone, turned it on and handed it out to him.

Taking it from her, he zoomed in on the photo. "When was this taken?"

"Just over a year ago."

"Where?" It was hard to tell. There was a sidewalk and road, some trees, the figure of Tom Wagner visible in the lamplight over Rose's shoulder as she rolled her eyes for the camera. Another figure, dark and shadowy, was barely visible opposite of Tom. All he could tell was the other man had his hands on his hips.

"Outside of the Art Institute in Portland."

There was a knock on the door. Charles peeked his head in. "Time to check on my patient." He smiled. "I'm glad you're awake, Rose."

"Hi, Charles." Her voice was thin, but warm. She looked back at him. "I just realized I had this photo, and that's where I'd seen him. Sorry. I would've told you sooner."

"That's okay," he responded as Charles brushed past him and sat next to Rose. "Thanks for this." He waved the phone. "Can I message the photo to Paige?"

"Sure."

"Do you know what he was doing with your ex-boyfriend?"

Charles waved his hand at him. "Can you pick this interrogation up later, buddy? I'd love to check her vitals." He paused. "In private."

"Of course." He turned to leave. Paige would figure out—

"The answer is nothing good, Burke." She said behind him. "My ex wasn't a good man."

His muscles tensed as he looked back at her, but he forced his face to stay smooth. "I'm sorry to hear that, Rose." He came forward, stopped by her bedside and handed the phone back to her, smiling. "We can talk more later. Feel better soon."

With a nod, he headed for the door.

It wasn't his place to feel anger toward her ex. Rose had her own life. No matter how she made him feel, the reality was that she was his employee. He was only her boss, and she deserved his professionalism. This was combat of reason versus sentimental nonsense, and in every conflict, his rationality had always triumphed. It made him one hell of a soldier. And a soldier also knew when to fall back and regroup.

He sensed her eyes on his back.

"Burke?" She called after him.

He turned back around. "Yeah?"

She smiled. "Thank you. Don't be a stranger."

He'd never suffered for female companionship before. It hadn't been hard to find. But no past relationships had prepared him for Rose, the woman looking at him with such sincerity, such openness that even if he wanted to speak, he couldn't.

Something profound was between them. Something exponentially special. He could feel it.

But he was her employer.

Swallowing over the lump in his throat, he gave a brief nod, then went out into the hall. He shut the door behind him to her room, letting his hand linger on the handle. Maybe, for the first time in his life, this was what it felt like to fall in love.

CHAPTER 14

*B*urke tapped his phone on the armrest of his chair the following morning, wishing a text from Paige would magically appear and tell him Rose's photo of Tom Wagner had given them a lead. Wishing she'd used some sort of recognition program to identify Rose's ex in the photo, just so he had the bastard's name.

And had any other lead popped up on The Ring's operation? On its mysterious leader? On whatever loser was looking into his life from Salem? From Chad in the field? Had Paige uncovered what Graves was up to nowadays? Curiosity made it hard to sit still.

He closed the medical app on his phone, letting the names of renowned psychologists from Seattle go dark.

Last night had been so chaotic that he hadn't done his deep breathing exercises before bed, and he'd paid the price with sleeplessness. But today was a new day. He unrolled his mat and moved to the floor to begin stretching. If he was even considering getting back into the field, he had to take steps to manage his condition.

After a few minutes, a knock on the door interrupted him. He got up and answered it.

"Good morning," Rose said, standing behind her cart. She glanced from him to the floor, her long eyelashes fluttering.

"Uh, morning," he returned. "I didn't expect you today. Don't you need time to recover?" He turned and pushed his exercise mat out of the way.

"I feel all right, thanks." She gave him a small smile. "I haven't swept in here yet, so I thought I'd just do that and be out of your way."

He stood aside to let her in. "You're not in the way. But you don't have to do this. Not after yesterday."

She met his gaze, and her cheeks turned the prettiest shade of pink he'd ever seen. Was she still embarrassed about the seizure? About the rising attraction he'd sensed between them before she'd collapsed yesterday?

He'd been able to think about little else. He hadn't been able to control how his heart swelled every time she came to mind. How his every impulse was to find himself at her side, to hear what she'd say next, to hope that whatever he said or did brought a smile to her face.

He didn't want her to clean for him. He just wanted to spend time with her.

She swept quickly while he pretended to be engrossed in something on his computer. In truth, he just stared at his inbox.

"Okay, that's it," she said eventually, putting the broom back on the cart. "Unless there's anything else?"

Huh? His brows rose. "Oh. There is, actually."

He stood and came around to her. "I'm in the process of finding a therapist to help me manage my PTSD." He cleared his throat.

Her face lit up. "That's wonderful, Burke. Truly."

His breath caught. "I thought you'd want to know."

"I'm glad."

"And, um, I was wondering if we could try dinner again tonight, maybe somewhere else, since the last one ended before we could eat. Only if you want to." He clutched his cane, wishing he could break it in half. He was being ridiculous. Hadn't dinner with him caused her so much anxiety last time she'd had a seizure? "And only if you feel up to it. There's no pressure. It doesn't need to be stressful." Maybe it was crossing the line to ask her, but she was worth the risk. He just wanted to talk to her outside of times like this, when she was here doing a job.

Rose ran a hand through her hair, pulling strands free from the half-updo. "My seizure wasn't your fault, Burke. I'm sorry if I made you think otherwise. My triggers are more complex than—it wasn't because"—she paused—"it's because of the meds. Honestly."

Then she smiled, and it was like rays of sun shining through parting clouds.

"You should see your face." She laughed lightly. "You're so sweet to be concerned. I really would like to have dinner with you again. It would be nice to talk when I don't have a broom in my hand or smell like cleaning solution."

He blew out a breath. "Great." He grinned back. She thought he was sweet. She wanted to talk outside of the session. Outside... "Let's have dinner in ballroom number two, then."

She cocked her head to the side. "You have *two* ballrooms in this place? How many does a castle need, anyway?"

He chuckled. "Hey, I didn't build the place."

"Where is it?"

A smile teased his lips. He stood, ready to walk her out. "Ask anyone and they'll tell you."

Her smile fell. "Are you going somewhere?"

"Just to Headquarters," he said. "I was going to check in with Paige about that photo you gave us, in case she got any leads off it. And to see if Lucien has any more info about The Ring. Why?" Hope bubbled up. She wanted to talk?

She walked around him to the door. "Can I come with you? We didn't finish our talk late last night when Charles checked on me."

"Sure. You didn't have to wait to talk to me, Rose." He held the door open for her, smiling.

She hesitated for the briefest moment, then went through, ducking up a glance at him.

They walked in silence, while he waited for her to talk. When they reached the top of the stairs, she linked her arm in his, while his other arm flexed as he leaned against the cane.

His heart skipped a beat. The simple gesture, so unassuming, so gentle and steady, made him swallow hard over the lump that formed in his throat. It wasn't an act of pity—he'd be on the receiving end of that enough to know the difference. It was a moment of camaraderie, her to him.

No, *employee* to *employer*.

He couldn't ask her out for a date unless he fired her, and he couldn't do that. She'd done nothing to warrant it. This was all on him. Whatever these feelings were, they weren't going anywhere, but that didn't mean he could use them as an excuse to make her life more complicated.

"I wanted to tell you more about my ex in the photo," she said finally, as they descended. "If Tom Wagner was caught up with him, I guarantee you they were up to some sort of scheme."

"What kind of scheme?"

"I'm not sure. But knowing Gavin, it would've been a bad one." She wrinkled her nose.

The hair on the back of his neck stood up. His heart thundered. "Gavin?"

"Yeah. He had such a bad temper, Burke. Very violent." She shuddered, then bit her lip again. "But he's a cop, and I got the sense he thought he was untouchable. Maybe he was hiding confiscated funds he'd seized on the job with Tom Wagner. I'm not sure."

Alarms raged in his ears, and warning lights blinked behind his vision. A dirty cop. Gavin. It had to be Gavin Graves.

They reached the bottom of the stairs not a moment too soon. He whirled to face her. "What was his name, Rose?"

Her eyes went wide. "G-Gavin Graves."

She'd dated his sworn enemy. Graves, with Rose. *Rose.* All he could see was a red haze of fury. *Stay calm. Take deep breaths. Stay in control.*

He blinked hard and tried to focus on her. "How do you know Gavin Graves?" She couldn't be his contact. She couldn't be a mole, sent to spy on him. She couldn't—she'd dropped Graves's name.

Furrowing her brow, she shook her head. "Wh-what do you mean? How do *you* know him?"

His fingers dug into his cane. "He's the one from my unit who killed everyone in Ba'hir," he ground out. "He's the reason my back looks like the lunar surface. I served with that son of a bitch. He betrayed us, murdered them, and tried to frame me for it."

She gasped. "Oh my God."

"Tell me you're not working for *him.*" The word held too much rage. Too much disgust. He took a deep breath. "Tell me he's not blackmailing you, and that this is all some sort of misunderstanding. Tell me he has nothing to do with why you're here." The online searches about him, originating from Salem, had coincided with her arrival on the island. He felt sick.

The confusion in her gaze was replaced by hurt. "How can you think that?"

"Then how would you explain it?" He latched onto the wounded look on her face, desperate to believe her. "Am I supposed to believe this is some sort of coincidence?"

Her chin lifted, and she squared her shoulders, her defiant brown eyes meeting his. What surprised him, though, were the unshed tears glimmering there. The sight of them were like a shot to the heart. "I didn't know, I swear. I'm not with him."

He wanted to believe her. He was desperate to. "Do you know what this looks like to me? Like you came to spy—"

"I came here to get away from him!"

Her voice reverberated throughout the great hall, her chest rising and falling with deep breaths.

He took a step back, the words hitting him like a punch to the gut.

"I went on three dates with him last year, Burke. *Three.* I didn't like him all that much to begin with, but he was a cop and my friends thought he was a catch, so I tried to make it work. That's what single people do, right?" She glanced away. "On the last date, I don't remember the details, but somehow I ended up sleeping with him. When I woke up, I was sick with regret and didn't want him there, so I told him to leave." She bit her bottom lip. "He didn't take it well. I learned that rejection wasn't acceptable to him the hard way, through the bruised jaw he gave me that night... and the past thirteen months that he's stalked me. He's followed me, harassed me." She pointed a furious finger at her chest. "Ruining *my* life."

Graves was stalking her. That fucker was tormenting her.

Holy shit. His gaze traveled over her as she trembled, chin raised, poised, composed, yet utterly exposed. It was the truth. He could see it in her eyes, unflinching and haunted. It was a look he had seen in the mirror before, and he felt like crap.

He reached for her. "Rose, I'm sorry—"

She flinched and blinked hard.

His hand dropped, pieces of him cracking into shards. Bad idea.

But then her shoulders sagged, and a single tear trailed down her flushed cheek. "I didn't mean—I'm not afraid of you. I'm just heartbroken—"

His phone rang. Of all the crappy timing! He yanked it out of his pocket, gripping it so hard he almost crushed it. "What?" he barked.

"Hello to you, too," Lucien responded.

"Not now." He kept his eyes fixed on Rose, his heart doing somersaults in his chest.

"We need you to come down to HQ pronto, your majesty. We've got news." Lucien disconnected.

"I heard," she said softly. "I need to see Paige anyway, so let's go." She moved past him.

He risked reaching out and laid a gentle hand on her arm.

She paused, looking at the floor. "I didn't know he was your nemesis, I swear." She looked up at him. "I need you to believe me. Gavin's fucked us *both* over."

"I do." He replied quickly and unequivocally. "I'm so sorry, Rose. More than you could know." He let his hand drop.

"Whatever he's up to, it's about more than just me." She walked to the door that led to the portico. "If Tom Wagner's laundering money, Gavin's got to be operating some sort of business."

It took more strength than he expected to stop himself from reaching out to her again, to stop and keep her there so he could face her for this conversation.

He held the door open for her instead, and she went through.

"Whatever he's up to might be ruining more lives than just mine," she said quietly, squinting up at him in the sunlight.

"You're the one I'm worried about. Why didn't you tell me?" He searched her gaze, alarmed at the vulnerability and uncertainty behind her eyes. "You know what we do here. We would help you so you never had to live this way again." *Helped her by tearing Graves apart a piece at a time.*

"I didn't want my problems to be yours, Burke," she said softly as they descended to the garden. "You've had more than your fair share already. How could I demand more from you? I never expected to feel..."

Feel? She had feelings for him? He wanted to leap for joy off the stairs. Then he wanted to run down to the dock, race to Portland and choke Graves to death.

His pulse pounded in his ears as he kept a steady pace beside her. They headed through the garden. "Rose—"

She sniffled and brushed another tear away. "I don't want to take advantage of you. Of this." She moved her hand back and forth in the air between them as they went around a topiary.

He pursed his lips as they went down the next path toward Headquarters. "You aren't taking advantage. Let me help you. You have to be safe—" The thought of Graves anywhere near her made his blood go cold. He was going to *kill* that bastard. Rip him apart limb by limb.

"I want him to be taken down legally—for him to be held accountable. That's the only way this will work for me. I can't afford any mistakes."

He clenched his fists. He'd been a vigilante for years, and he was good at not getting caught. But he couldn't force her to trust or rely on him. They reached the sidewalk that led up to Paige's bungalow.

"I don't want to be—" he put his hand on the gate to open it, then paused and waited until she looked him in the eye. "I mean, I don't want you to think of coming here as a mistake."

Shaking her head, tears refreshed in her dark eyes. "It could never be that. But I also can't just let you take care of my problems for me. If you got hurt—" Her voice broke. She pushed through the gate and walked up to the door.

He stared after her. Could it be...? Was she falling for him, too? He rocked on his feet, but inside he was flying high. He wanted to contradict her. Convince her he could take care of himself and that he could help her. But she'd left him tongue-tied.

Hopeful.

Slowly, he went over and joined her. She scooted aside.

His hands ached to take her in his arms. Instead, he knocked. "Lucien," he called, "this had better be important."

CHAPTER 15

$\mathcal{T}$he door to Headquarters jerked open so fast Burke stepped back, bumping into Rose behind him. Lucien stood on the other side in a polo shirt, his man bun particularly messy. Paige was behind him at her wall of computer monitors, her blond, curly hair equally tussled.

"Shady Tree Motel," Lucien said quickly. "We think The Ring is operating from there."

Burke raised his hand and leaned against the doorframe, frowning.

Lucien's eyes widened.

From behind him, Rose stepped around, peeking out under his raised arm.

"I was wondering if Paige was at home," she said, hands clutched in front of her.

He let go of the doorframe and rubbed his forehead. Rose had known a little about The Ring already, knew they were vigilantes, but he'd still wanted to keep details of the operation quiet, unless she asked him about it specifically.

Then he'd tell her, because he trusted her. After she'd told him about Graves, he trusted her now more than ever.

"Uh, yeah." Lucien stepped aside, but she stayed beside him.

Paige, sitting only a few feet away, jumped up from her chair and came over. "Hey, Rose!"

He moved out of the way so Paige could hug her. "I'm glad you're both here. Look." Paige lifted her ring finger.

Beside her, Lucien puffed up his chest as he moved behind his fiancé. His *fiancé*.

Rose's pressed lips turned into a grin and grabbed Paige's hand. "Oh, how wonderful!"

His best friend was getting married.

Slowly, the hatred for Graves that was burning a hole in his stomach morphed into a gradual warmth. He felt himself smile until he was grinning so hard he was sure his dimple beneath his beard would be permanently indented. Grabbing Lucien, he pulled him in for a hug.

The tension in Lucien's shoulders eased as he hugged him back.

Burke pulled back, clapped his arm. "I'm happy for you."

His friend beamed back at him. "Thanks, best man."

Best man. Speeches. Attention. Bachelor parties. Crowds. *It'll be okay. I'll prep for it. I won't miss out on this.*

He chuckled. "You move fast."

"Well, you get to share it with Charles, so don't get too excited."

He turned to Paige and took her hand in his. "I knew you were special to him from the beginning. I'm so glad you applied for our tech job, and even happier you can put up with this one." He elbowed Lucien. "West Cove Island and anything else I have is yours for whatever kind of wedding you want."

She beamed. "Thanks, Mr. Masters. This place is home, so I think we'll take you up on it."

Home. His, theirs, and now Rose's. He glanced over at her, but her eyes were downcast. When they flipped back up, he looked back at Paige.

"Burke," he corrected Paige, hoping she didn't hear how his voice croaked. He'd gotten used to Rose saying his name. He'd have to learn how to not hear the echoes of it screamed in agony when everyone else said it. He'd have to learn how to let go.

Out of the corner of his eye, he noticed how Rose tilted her head, felt her eyes trained on him. She'd probably caught that, too.

"Awesome." Paige leaned into Lucien, who smiled warmly at her. "We're so excited. I just couldn't wait to tell you both."

"Both." Lucien repeated. "Rose, did you need Paige and me for something, too?"

She stepped forward, angling next to him on the small porch. His heart picked up its pace when the light scent of her—strawberries and roses?—reached his nose.

"I just tagged along with Burke because I'd promised you we would talk more today, and I didn't want you to think I forgot." She smiled at her cousin. "But why don't we catch up a little later, before dinner?" Rose glanced at him and a hint of blush tinted her cheeks, below her freckles.

Was she still going to have dinner with him? It was hard to tell.

Lucien peered at him with a knowing look that told him exactly what his best friend was thinking: a lot more was happening between them than there should be between a boss and employee—Burke would bet every dollar in his primary checking account on it.

"For sure," Paige replied, her curls bouncing as she nodded. "I can come over later."

"That would be great," she replied enthusiastically. She gave them all a small smile, her gaze lingering on him. "See you later, Paige. Congratulations again." With a wave, Rose darted down the pathway from their bungalow, back to the main road, brown hair waving in the ocean breeze.

Lucien directed a glare at him, but he didn't want to hear whatever criticism lay on the tip of his tongue. Even if it would come from a place of love and concern, he didn't need it now. Especially when he didn't know where things were going with Rose, and *especially* when he had an enemy to track down. But first things first.

"How do you and Lucien know it's the Shady Tree Motel?" he asked Paige.

Lucien rolled his eyes.

"We have a few new leads. Come on." Paige led him and Lucien back to her computers. "The police reported that a body washed up on shore near SeaTac overnight. Maintenance workers found it. I, uh, got ahold of the crime scene photos, and look at this." She pulled up gruesome images of the bloated, destroyed corpse, but it was one that hadn't been in the water long. Still, he had to swallow the bile that rose in his throat, and he took a deep breath. Then another, trying to stay focused and fight off any risk of a flashback. They had to stop The Ring. They just had to.

He set his cane against her desk and leaned over, peering at the yellow box sticking out of the victim's pocket. "That looks like a carton of cigarettes."

"Yep. But not just any one. Look." She zoomed in on the photo, the pixels spotty, but a logo appeared. "It's for unfiltered Black and Gold Ultra Menthols. Only two places in the Seattle metro area sell them, and one is in the SoDo district, south of SeaTac, at a convenience store across from—wait for it—a motel. The Shady Tree."

"Chad is still in town," Lucien said. "He'd been snooping around the International district, but I asked him to go over there and to see what he could find out." He opened his mouth to protest, so Lucien added, "I told him to make sure he wasn't made, and not to engage in any way. Chad called back a few minutes ago."

"And?" He leaned forward.

"It was booked by a private group last weekend, Friday through Sunday morning, and it is again tomorrow through Sunday night." Lucien blew out a breath. "Chad went in, posing as a customer who wanted a room on a Friday night, but they turned him away with that explanation."

Gripping the edges of the desk, he said, "That's it."

"Yeah."

He pushed off and stood, without his cane. Soreness spread in his knee. "Let's go."

Lucien held up a hand in caution. "I'm glad to see you're anxious to leave the island for once, buddy, but it's not until tomorrow night. If we went now, we're only exposing ourselves and the operation. For once, we know where they're going to be and when."

He frowned, but nodded. "We strike tomorrow." He turned to Paige. "In the meantime, can you look for information that ties Graves to The Ring?"

Lucien sighed. "We've been through this, Burke—"

"Graves is Rose's ex. He's been stalking her for over a year and he's the one in that photo I sent Paige of Tom Wagner, from her cell phone."

They looked at him incredulously. Paige went ashen and Lucien gaped like a fish.

"She just told me," he muttered. He hated betraying her trust. . . He pulled his shoulders back. It was time to finish their fight, once and for all.

"I'm only telling you because it could pertain to the case. We know Tom's crooked, and that Graves worked with him. The photo is evidence. Tom was working with a dirty cop, we know he's on the force in Portland, and Rose suspects he's doing something illegal. It isn't a leap to assume he could be the one behind sex trafficking in Portland and Seattle."

"That psychopath is running a sex trade operation in two different cities..." Lucien murmured.

"And we're going to get that son of a bitch. Where is he now?" he asked Paige.

She leaned back in her chair. "About an hour ago he bought concert tickets for a show in Portland this Saturday night."

"So he'll be in Portland at a show while his lackeys are at the Shady Tree in Seattle. We'll have to be at two places at once." Lucien eyed him.

He crossed his arms, every nerve on edge. "I'm going after him with you."

"You're still recovering, Burke, and if we're pulling off a double-header tomorrow night to stop The Ring and Graves all at once, we need you in top form. You can't half-ass it."

He shook his head, hair falling free from behind his ears. "I can go to Portland tonight and stop him."

"You can't. If he gets wind of you coming, or if he's taken out of the picture, it'll tip our hand. His operation will disappear with those girls, and we have to save them. Until then, we can't let anything else, like vendettas or possibilities, stop us from focusing our energy on that."

A growl rumbled in his chest. Damn Lucien for being right. "There has to be a way. I can at least do recon, make sure he's there."

"And Paige can't?"

Silence stretched as Paige looked between them.

"Fine." He raised a finger and pointed at Lucien. "But if Graves so much as sneezes in Washington state I want to know about it."

"Fair enough." Lucien blew out a breath. "Now why don't you scram after Rose and let us enjoy our engagement day?"

At the mention of Rose's name, his posture loosened. "Speaking of which…" His voice trailed, and he cleared his throat. "I want to do something for her. Before I go, can you help me out with an idea I had?"

~

WHEN SHE ENTERED HER BEDROOM, Rose shut the door behind her and leaned against it. Tilting her head back, she willed her heart to slow down.

She'd done the right thing.

Telling Burke about Gavin's stalking hadn't been her intention—she'd just wanted to tell him about her suspicion that her ex was shady—but the look on his face when she'd said Gavin's name had said it all. He'd been stunned, enraged, but intent and focused. Intimidating as hell. When he had told her Gavin was the man who'd tried to kill him, then pin him for Ba'hir…

She shuddered, and the door rattled. Poor Burke. Finding out their enemies were one in the same had sent shockwaves through her, too. He'd suffered so much, and was still living with such trauma, all because of Gavin.

It had been unbearable to let him think she'd had any part to play in Gavin's evil operations. In that moment, having him know the truth was all that had mattered.

Now all she had to do was tell him about her real job.

Oddly, the moment the words had left her mouth about her past with Gavin, she'd felt a switch flip inside of her. Relief. More tangible than any she'd known since her mother was alive. And seeing the instant concern in Burke's gaze, the compassion behind it, the trust… Somehow, just by being who he was, he'd managed to reassure her.

He made it easy to need him, in every possible way. So easy she'd almost told him she had feelings for him.

She opened her eyes and put her hands on her heart, almost like she could feel how he had taken root there. It wasn't fair for her to rely on him this way, but she did. His sheer presence, his strength, pulled her in like a magnet. Seeing his deadly glare when he spoke of Gavin had left her little doubt that the justice he would exact would be swift and final. It was so tempting to just set him loose on Gavin and let him destroy her stalker, for them both. For all the lives he'd ruined.

But Gavin was dangerous, and Burke was injured. The disadvantage to him would be too great.

And no matter how much Gavin deserved to die, she didn't want to risk

Burke getting arrested for it. And could he bear to live with another life on his conscience, even Gavin's? She wasn't sure.

Maybe she could comb through the files on her laptop to see if she could find anything else they could use against Gavin. But before that... She went to her suitcase and pulled out the flask she tucked in there for emergencies.

She needed a drink first.

～

THE KNOCK on the door pulled Rose's attention away from her computer screen. Late day sunlight streamed through the windows, and she glanced at the clock. Wow. Time had flown by. Too bad it had all been unsuccessful.

She crossed the room and went for the door.

Paige stood on the other side, arms crossed, and a garment bag slung over one of them. "Gavin Graves is the jackass you've been dealing with?" Those arms widened, and she drew her into an embrace. "I'm so sorry, Rose."

She pulled back. "Well, *I'm* sorry my seizure screwed up your proposal."

Paige lifted a shoulder, smiling. "It just delayed it for a few hours. The important thing was that you were all right. Trust me, for me and Lucien, third time was the charm." She waggled her eyebrows, and she laughed.

"Burke said the two of you might be having dinner tonight." Paige tossed the garment bag on her bed. "After the Graves shocker, I bet you could both use a little breather."

It wouldn't feel like a breather when she laid all her cards on the table to him.

"I want to tell him why I took the job, Paige." She shook her head. "I don't want there to be anymore secrets between us. I'm sorry that you and Lucien are caught up in my lie—"

Paige waved her off. "Nonsense. If he's upset with us, Lu and I can handle it. I wanted you here, you wanted to find a safe place to be and Burke told Lucien he didn't want any freeloaders on his island, so we did what we had to do."

She made it sound so easy to explain.

But for Rose, those sea-blue eyes of his drew her in and made her feel safe, respected, and wanted, shaking her to her core. The rest of her reasoning— the entire world, in fact—fell away when she was with him. It was unbearable trying to hide how he made her feel.

She liked who she was when she was with him. She'd never felt happy with anyone else, so free, or so sure of what the right course of action was. She wanted to be the person he seemed to think she was.

More than anything, she wanted to gain his trust because he deserved it. He was worth it.

"Ready for tonight?" Paige's voice snapped her back to reality.

"I, um, I guess." Right. She had to get ready for dinner.

Paige cocked her hip. "Well then, it's a good thing I brought this." She waved at the bag on the bed. "I think your ripped jeans could be quite a mood-killer."

"I don't know what I'm doing," she mumbled. Truer words were never spoken. The last time she'd gone on a date was with *Gavin*. "Dinner like this… It's leading into dating territory."

"I sincerely hope so," Paige retorted. "There's something deeper, more personal going on between the two of you. It's easy to tell. He looks at you like he wants to devour you. It's *so* sexy."

Her stomach clenched.

"So," Paige turned back to the bed and unzipped the bag, "I have a dress that will knock his socks off." She held up the dress, and her eyes bulged.

Crimson red with a halter top, it cut down into a deep V in the front, then flared out at the hips, where the color gave way to a deep pink ombré. A slit came up the right side, high enough to show off a great deal of leg, and a white ruffled hem jutted out from below the shades of pink, like petals.

"Oh my," she breathed. "It's gorgeous, Paige. I love it." It was too much, though. Too revealing, too racy, in its own classy way. "But I can't. It's yours."

Paige shook her head, blond curls bouncing. "I've never worn it. I mean, look at it. How often do I go flamenco dancing? It looks like it was made for it. Besides, while we're about the same height, your chest will fill this out much better than mine."

It was a dress that screamed *special occasion*, a beautiful piece of clothing she was unworthy to try on. "Paige—"

She waved her off. "Rose, for the next few months I'll be the one buying the dress and veil, making the decisions, being the center of attention. You're my family. I want you to wear it."

Tears sprang to her eyes before she could stop them. She nodded, swallowing over the lump in her throat. "Thank you."

"Of course," Paige replied, smiling. "It just sets a high bar for whatever your maid of honor dress will be."

～

THE TWO OF them spent so much time talking that it was, in the end, a race to get Rose ready for the dinner. Within twenty minutes, she threw the dress on, decided to leave her hair down, touched up her makeup, grabbed her clutch with her phone inside, and bid her cousin goodbye with the strongest hug she could remember.

Now all that was left was telling Burke everything. It would not go well—of that, she was certain.

The thought created a knot under her ribs.

"Oh my, Rose, aren't you beautiful?" Polly—not the person she was expecting—stood at the bottom of the stairs. Her warm eyes washing over her as she clasped her hands to her chest.

"Thank you." She bounded down the stairs and pointed to the location of the ballroom where she'd held the party for the staff. "Is the other ballroom this way, too?"

Polly shook her head. "Mr. Masters is waiting for you in the outdoor ballroom."

Her brows rose. "Outdoor ballroom?"

"The white tent behind the greenhouse," Polly explained. "The one backed by the wall of flowers. I think you've seen it before."

She had, though she'd never walked that way. "Okay. Thank you." She touched Polly's soft arm. "And thank you for dinner in advance."

Polly's eyes gleamed. "It's my pleasure, Rose. Burke is special to me. I've loved him since he was a little boy, and I want him to be happy. I'm so glad he is with you."

Her heart sank. This community, this family had been nothing but welcoming—except for Burke in the very beginning—and she would never be a part of it. Her real life hadn't gone anywhere.

Forcing a smile that faltered, she turned and headed out to the back of the house. When she went back to work on Monday, all of this would feel like a dream.

CHAPTER 16

The glow of soft white lights illuminated the gauzy tent, a crystal chandelier visible through it at its center. Rose walked toward it. The pillars were columns of white lights intermixed with climbing yellow roses. A wooden dance floor stretched from the greenhouse to a matching, raised stage, a backdrop of yellow roses on trellises. Lights shone down on instruments on the stage.

In the center, a round table was draped in a white tablecloth, prepared food adorning it.

Burke stood. He wore a deep blue shirt and a dark pinstripe vest, with solid charcoal trousers that matched his sport coat. The top few buttons of his shirt were undone, giving a tantalizing glimpse of the solid, golden skin of his chest. But it was the look in his wide eyes as he gazed at her that shot right to her heart and filled her with awe.

He was magnificent.

Red roses sat in the center of the table. *Unquestionably* a date. Her stomach fluttered.

"Rose." He said her name on a breath as she approached. "You look," he paused. "There aren't words."

She felt herself blush. "Thank you. You, too."

Burke shifted his weight, standing without the cane. It leaned against the table. "I wasn't sure you'd come. Things got a little… tense earlier."

Yeah, because she'd almost shared how she felt about him. She'd almost let herself need him. She swallowed hard.

He put his hand out, palm down. "I've done a lot of things I'm not proud of, and my PTSD might make me a little unpredictable, but I don't want to give you any reason to be wary of me. I want to prove to you that you can trust me."

That's what this was about? She shook her head. "I do. Burke, you're nothing like Gavin." That was such an understatement. "You're not even"—she blew out a breath—"the two of you are worlds apart."

She and Burke were, too. Forget the fact that their bank accounts were polar opposites, that their social tendencies were as different as night and day. He had morals, and because she'd been lonely and afraid, she'd thrown hers out the window. He was the one worrying about *her* trusting *him*, when she was the one who'd lied to him about being a maid all along. Her shoulders sank, along with her heart. He was too wonderful. He deserved better than her.

The tightness of his features eased, and he smiled. "I'm glad."

"Burke, I think there's something we should talk about—"

"I know this *looks* like a date but just for now, let's enjoy our dinner, forget everything else, and just be you and me. Okay?" Turning, he gestured to someone nearby. She tried to peer around him. "In the meantime, I have a surprise."

They hadn't made it through dinner last time, and it'd be a shame to waste this wonderful meal.

He pulled the chair out for her.

Maybe the truth could wait just a bit. She sat, then he took a seat across from her. She set her clutch on the edge of the table.

"What is it?" She leaned forward eagerly, returning the smile.

He chuckled. "We'll have some music while we eat." Looking over his shoulder, he waved his hand. A band walked on stage. Each took their spot near their instruments: bongo drums, a trumpet, a trombone, a guitar, a string bass, and a keyboard. The singer, a black woman in her forties, carrying maracas, took center stage behind the microphone. A beat started, and warm tones of music began.

Afro-Cuban music.

Emotion caught in her throat. Her heart pounded. She kept her gaze on the performance as the woman started to sing, because she couldn't look at him. If she did, she was afraid he would see it written all over her face.

She was falling in love with him. Inescapably spiraling into an emotion deeper than any she'd ever known.

"This is"—she took a deep breath—"amazing. Thank you."

The rumble of a chuckle was his first response. "You're welcome. I finally found a good use for some of the cash in my bank accounts."

She brought her gaze back to him, a smirk playing at her lips. "I'm sure I'm not the first woman you've wooed this way." She'd said it playfully, but felt how loaded it was.

He scratched his short beard. "You're the first since I tried to impress Marcy Zwellinger by getting her a car for her sixteenth birthday party, and my dad found out."

She laughed. "I bet the shit really hit the fan."

He grinned. "You have no idea."

While the music played, they ate seven courses, including pastries with chicken and mushrooms in white sauce, marinated roast tenderloin with port wine demi-glace, tortellini primavera, stewed okra and tomatoes, and lemon crème pie. Conversation flowed as easily as the music.

She sipped her cabernet as he told her about his parents, their over-whelming loss while he was overseas, memories of happier times together, and their personalities. She talked about Mom, Dad walking out on them, and how music made her happy. She told him stories about times she'd shared with Rebecca before her death, and tales from parties and clubs she'd gone to. He told her about adventures and mistakes from college, trips he had taken, and even a few missions from his time in the Middle East.

"I can't eat another bite," she eventually declared, pushing the last half of her pie away. A haze of satisfaction hung around her, from the food, from the man on the other side of the table. "If I do, you're going to have to buy your-self a forklift, ship it out here, and have it hoist me up to the second-floor window."

Burke snickered, and she quivered inside. How she loved seeing him happy. "I can think of worse ways to spend money. But nah—I lifted you once. It'd be my pleasure to do it again."

"Let's hope we're both conscious for it next time," she cracked. Oh my— what was wrong with her? It must be the wine talking.

He sat up straighter and his lips parted. What would they taste like?

"I'm sorry," she said quickly. "I don't know what's come over me." She wanted *him* all over her. She pressed a hand to her mouth, scared those words would follow.

Burke glanced toward the stage. He was so still she wasn't sure if he was breathing.

"As tempting as that is," he said, his voice low and rough, "would you care to start with a dance instead?" He stood and held a hand out to her.

She rose and let the gesture and the music pull her toward him. The singer's voice thrummed with emotion, vibration, the beat of the bongo drums pulsating. The sounds were so rich, so sensual, and so evocative. Tentatively, she reached for him.

He filled one of her hands with his, as the other rested on the small of her back, where her bare skin met her skirt. The air left her lungs. It felt so right, his hand in hers, the warmth he emanated. Tears pricked her eyes.

When he started to move, she felt his leg buckle. A flash of anxiety sparked across his features as his grip tightened on her. She stood firm and supported them.

"Sorry," he rushed out.

Shaking her head, her dark hair swayed. "Don't be. I'll steady you."

They took a tentative step, then another, and another. The song changed, and a slower, deeper rhythm began, so she angled closer to him. His scent of evergreen was comforting and erotic all at once. How she longed to rest against the solid wall of his chest, letting the defined muscles confined in the tailored suit cradle her head. If only she embodied half of the determination, kindness, strength, and the quiet courage he gave to her.

He was the best man she'd ever known.

Bringing their joint hands to his chest, he pulled her in until their bodies aligned. A sound between a sigh and a growl rumbled in his chest.

She tilted her head up, her gaze fixed on his mouth. An inferno raged under her skin.

His gaze, which had been on her lips, too, came up to meet hers. They locked eyes.

Tell him the truth, before it's too late.

"Burke," she whispered, "I need to tell you... We need to talk." Part of her was amazed she'd managed to speak at all. She blinked hard, trying to make the rosy glow fade from her vision.

The strong arm that had held her tight at the small of her back fell away, leaving little lightning bolts of sensation trailing across her skin.

He cleared his throat. "We do." He breathed deeply. "Tomorrow night the team is going to the Shady Tree Motel to take down The Ring," he said. "We're sure it's Graves's operation, and I'm going with them."

No. Her eyes went wide, her own confession caught on the tip of her tongue. Her chest felt like it caved in. What about his PTSD? His injuries? How could he?

Burke looked over at the band and waved to them. "Thanks for everything." One by one, they shuffled from the stage as he faced her again.

He could be killed trying to stop The Ring. Even if he wasn't, he was the most focused, determined man she'd ever met. He'd never come back home without exacting justice on Gavin, once and for all. The operation could get him killed. A lump formed in her throat.

"I can't—" She laid a hand on his chest, searching his soft eyes. She should've told him the truth first. She should've ruined their moment with her lie before he spoke because now, all she could do was imagine awful ways he could be hurt.

"What's wrong?"

"I don't want you to go."

His head fell back.

"I don't want to either," he said softly. "You have no idea how much I'd rather stay with you. But it's time to put it out of business for good. We'll do it together, as a team." He clasped her hands in his, his tone earnest.

"But—"

His frown was quick. "There's a threat in the world we can eliminate. We must try, Rose. I can't live with myself any other way."

"And I can't live with myself unless I can finally tell you this. I've wanted to all along. You deserve the truth, no matter what it costs me."

His hands released hers, his gaze locked on hers. "What are you talking about?"

"I'm not a maid, Burke. I never was."

CHAPTER 17

*R*ose put a hand on her forehead. She'd done it now.

His brows furrowed. "What do you mean?"

Time to shoot it all to hell. "I'm not really a maid. I took it as a temp job because I was scared and looking for somewhere to hide." She had to forge ahead. Tell him all of it, despite the look in his eyes.

"I told you Gavin was stalking me, but what I didn't tell you was how it had escalated recently. He approached me in a parking lot a week before I came here, then I went home to my locked apartment a week before I came here to find my bedsheets rumpled. That was the last straw. I messaged Paige, who'd already invited me to meet. She encouraged me to come out here and take the job. I'm actually a band manager. I'm sorry. I didn't realize. . ." *How wonderful you are. How strong and resilient you are.* "I made a huge mistake."

His eyes pinched shut. Taking a step back, he ran a hand through his hair, shaking it loose. His breathing was fast and heavy.

When his eyes opened, they were trained on the floor.

"Is Rose really your name?" His voice low and deadly, laced with anger.

"Yes." She rested a hand on her chest, maybe to try and convince herself she still had a beating heart. "I'm so sorry. So desperately sorry, Burke. Please look at me," she begged, tears burning her eyes. How enraged was he? It was hard to tell.

He shook his head. "No." He spoke to the floor. "I don't want to. If I do, I'm afraid I'll only see a person who's lied to me since the moment we met instead of the person I felt I'd grown close to." A heartbeat passed. "If I look at you, then I'll have lost her for good."

A tear fell down her cheek, humiliation hot on her face.

"She never was worthy of you anyway. She wanted to be, but she wasn't."

Slowly, his sky-blue eyes climbed up, the ruins of his good opinion of her churning in their depths. When his shattered expression finally settled on her, the overwhelming disappointment directed at her made her suck in a breath.

"Every day. You lied to me every day."

"I did. But I've been desperate and terrified to tell you, mostly because I've never met anyone who values the truth as much as you do. You honor it in your memories, and for better or worse, you cling to it all. You use it in the pursuit of justice to take care of people." She swallowed hard. "You're the most honorable man I've ever known."

"Then the *truth* is, I don't even know you." His voice rumbled like thunder in the distance.

"You do."

He shook his head and turned his back on her.

"You do know me, better than anyone ever has," she insisted. "You know all about me, from my quirky humor and triggers for seizures to my drummer attraction. But you also know what really matters. How I look when my smile is entirely sincere. How losing my loved ones left me feeling exposed and alone. You're the only one who's ever seen my expression when I'm longing for everything I could've ever wanted."

He stayed entirely still, except for the faintest tilt of his head.

She took a deep breath. "And I know you. I know how you like to make a point in every conversation, and how your eyes sparkle like the sunlight on Puget Sound when you're happy. How you don't need your cane quite as much as you pretend to, and how your willpower is utterly relentless. I know the subtle inflections in your voice when you're talking to only me." Her voice broke. "I know how you take on responsibility for other people's actions and blame yourself for anything that goes wrong, but most importantly, I know how your greatest strength is your affection for the people in your life."

He looked back at her, his features drawn but his expression unreadable.

She let it all go. "They're just some of the reasons why I've fallen in love with you."

In the faint glow of the ballroom lights, his eyes glistened.

It wasn't enough.

Taking a ragged breath, she started to back up. "So whatever you decide now, I'm going to cling to the one thing I've been given again since coming here to West Cove: hope. Hope that you'll find a way to forgive me, and that you might be able to let me in again one day."

The gaze that met hers came back blazing, but not with fury. With desperation. Desire. "Then I hope you're ready now."

He closed the distance and swept her up in his arms. His lips met hers. Demanding and gentle all at once. Perfect. Made for her. Her world tilted and spun and with a vice grip on his vest, she pulled him even closer. She wanted his warmth to be her own, to touch his golden skin.

She moaned.

Taking her head in his hands, he moved her back, kept her head tilted up until she looked him in the eye.

"Please forgive me, too."

"For what?" She couldn't think straight.

"For not making you feel like you could tell me the truth from the very beginning."

He fit his lips to hers again, moving stronger, deeper, drawing the air from her lungs. Sending her senses into overdrive.

He broke away first.

"I was losing my mind trying to keep my hands off you." His voice rumbled like waves cresting, crashing. "Do you have any idea how much I've wanted to be the one to make you smile? How many times I've wanted to touch you, to know you saw me as more than my problems, as someone *you* wanted to be with? You've brought out a part of me that I never knew I had." A heartbeat passed between them. "Rose, whatever lie brought you to the island is the best thing that ever happened to me."

Oh. Tears sprang to her eyes. Warmth radiated from her chest.

For the first time in her life, she felt ready. For him. For love. For everything they could have together.

"Please take me inside, Burke," she said quietly.

Planting a firm, hard kiss on her lips, he gave her a quick, tense smile and turned back to the table. He took his cane as she grabbed her clutch, and then the two of them rushed to the patio. Within minutes they were inside, his cane thumping with each deliberate, hurried step.

He led her up the grand staircase, her hand in his, but paused at the top of the landing. She was a little winded, but he wasn't.

His expression was serious, and his posture stoic. "Are you sure this is what you want?"

Her heart pounded. Was she? She hesitated. Once she'd been with Gavin, she'd never been able to get rid of him. Geez, she didn't want to let that asshole in her head now. Burke wouldn't steal her freedom, though. He wouldn't claim her, or try to possess her. He wouldn't try to make her love him, even though she already did.

Tilting his head, he eyed her carefully. "It's okay if you want to wait.

Nothing has to happen now." The corner of his mouth lifted. "What's between us won't change for me."

Yep. She wanted him *now*. "Your room. My bed is too small for you."

He let out a low growl.

She took his hand in hers, leading him. They strode down the hallway together, and he kicked open the door to his master suite. When they were inside, he snapped an arm around her waist, crowded her against it and kissed her.

Then he pulled back. His perfect sky-blue eyes darkened as they traveled down her.

Vest off. She unbuttoned it and it would've gone faster if her fingers weren't trembling. Helping her, he took over and threw it on the ground as she attacked his shirt next. It hit the floor beside the vest. Her eyes dropped from his face. He stood before her in his pants, riding low on his hips. The wound on his shoulder, scars here and there from a lifetime of battle did nothing to diminish each flawlessly sculpted muscle. He was so strong. So good.

He moved her, right down to her soul. It was the most powerful feeling she'd ever known.

She pushed against him, and he allowed her to flip them until his back was against the door.

One shoe slipped from her foot, then the other. His broad, perfect chest was hers for the touching. On her tiptoes, she pressed her lips against his skin, trailing kisses across his collarbone. His hands flexed at her shoulders and his groan filled her ears, and it was the best sound she'd ever heard. Her lips dropped to his uninjured shoulder, then slid down his chest to his tight abdominal muscles, wanting to explore every part of him.

Kissing her way down until she was on her knees, she glanced up at him. Breathing heavily, his head was thrown back against the door. Her throat tightened. *What a beautiful sight.*

With a smile, she teased the edge of his pants, and felt every muscle in his stomach jump as his hips bucked forward involuntarily. She tugged his zipper down while her other hand helped her cause by pushing his pants and boxers down over his perfect ass.

Finally naked before her, his erection jutted out, long, and thick. *Oh my.* Her mouth went dry in an instant.

His chest heaved, like he was trying to keep control of himself. So sexy. Just how far could she push him? She couldn't wait to find out.

"Rose." His voice was low, deep, and desperate. Reaching down, he wound her dark tresses in his fingers and tugged her upwards.

Okay. It'd been too long since she'd tasted his mouth anyway.

She brought her hands to his hair, threaded them through, and brought his lips to hers, then gasped when his tongue sought hers. *Yes.* She drew him into her mouth, drew him flush against her until the only air between them was shared in their kiss.

His hand landed on the knot of fabric on her neck. She broke off their kiss, took a step back and pushed him away with a finger on his chest and a shake of her head. Oh-so-slowly, she untied the knot at the top of the halter dress, behind her neck, and let it slide down. His sharp intake of breath filled the room as she stood, revealed to him for the first time.

Her pulse raced.

Why didn't he grab her? Take back control even as he lost control? She'd expected him to drag her to the floor, to the bed, burying himself in her. But he waited, that intense, soulful gaze fixed on her, allowing her to lead. Her arousal climbed even higher.

She took his hand in hers and brought it to her chest, so he could feel her thundering heart.

His fingers grazed her skin in a quiet caress, and her breath caught. She loved his touch.

She led him over to the bed. Kissing him lightly, she pushed him down until he sat. Keeping hold of her hand, he pulled her down with him, and she went, straddling him on the mattress.

He held her waist, but made no move to pull her on top of him. The tenderness, the yearning and desire in his eyes went right through her. Why was he looking at her like that?

"I love you, too. With all my heart."

She inhaled sharply. He loved her. *Her.* It was everything. All that mattered. Smiling, tears of joy brimming, she slowly lowered herself onto him, every sensation bursting with pleasure.

Fingers winding in his hair, she brought his head forward to her chest, a silent plea to be touched. He closed his lips over one hard nipple. She squeaked. Each breast was lavished by his tongue in a continuous, torturous cycle of teasing and soothing. She threw her head back, incomprehensible whimpers spilling from her lips.

Encircled in his massive arms, his hands trailed light patterns on her back. Everywhere he touched, he left a fire in its wake.

Now. She needed him now.

She guided him into her. He looked up, so they were face to face. The pressure built. Unrelenting. Overwhelming. Delicious. Complete. Her mouth fell open in a silent exclamation.

His fingers pressed deeper into the soft swell of her hips as the pressure grew inside.

He knocked the wind right out of her. Her eyes squeezed shut. *Oh.*

"Move, Burke. Please. Oh, God."

He began their rhythm, pulling back and coming in, the friction unbearably pleasurable. Again and again. This is what it felt like to combust. She brought her arms around him, nails pressed to his shoulder blades.

The skin of his back was pitted, ruddy, uneven. Her eyes flew open. Chunks of him were missing. He'd said it was scarred, but as she moved her hands around, she realized it was everywhere, ending only at the small of his back. Such burns. Such pain he'd endured. Her heart cracked open.

Burke stared into them, the sheer combination of agony and ecstasy in his gaze giving way to a flash of sympathy. "I've never been more whole in my life, Rose, than in this moment."

Her thoughts exactly.

Over and over they moved, her hands grasping and sliding across his smooth, sweaty pecs. Everything was too tight. Too much. She was going to split in two.

His mouth found hers, claimed it, tongues dueling even as they both struggled to find their breath. He drove harder. Faster. She dug her nails into his thighs, pushing onto him head on. He thrust once, hard and utterly overwhelming, and her whole world splintered apart. Millions of pieces and perfectly whole all at once. Light filled her vision as she came, the sound of their lovemaking drowned out by the ringing in her ears.

This. Him. Together. Perfect happiness.

Another earth-shattering thrust, another, then another brought her higher once more. When he found release he shouted her name. She crested again, riding the aftershocks out with him. As a part of him.

They spiraled down together. Breathing hot in her ear, she felt his beard move as he smiled against her cheek. Then he pulled back.

She opened her eyes, saw herself shining through his sky-blue gaze. She touched the side of his face, the burns... He overwhelmed her. Her heart belonged with his. Together. In a love more profound than she'd ever known.

No matter what tomorrow would bring, coming here had not only saved her life, but it had helped her find it.

CHAPTER 18

*B*urke breathed raggedly. Rose was draped over him, warming him to his soul. He felt her head tilt up, so he glanced down at her. A smile played at her lips. Her beautiful face was flushed and glowing. Her hands trembled as they rested against his sides, mirroring the fluttering in his heart.

As the years had passed, with every life he'd taken and then every life he'd tried to save, he had felt himself moving farther and farther away from this kind of happiness. He hadn't done anything to deserve her, the way she looked at him, this unquenchable passion for her. It was almost... transcendental.

Her thumb stroked his side, and the light in her brown eyes turned serious. "I'm sorry I misled and lied to you, Burke. I saw this as a chance to leave my problems behind, but I never imagined meeting someone like you. I never meant to hurt you. Please believe me."

A small twinge of hurt flared in his chest, but it was quickly quelled by the thudding of his heart—a heart that had come to life the first time he'd spoken with her.

"I wish you'd come to me with the truth from the start, but I know I wasn't an easy man to deal with. I'm sure I'm still not." He traced a lazy pattern on her back. "Leaving Portland and coming here was smart. Protecting yourself was the right thing to do." She should never have had to in the first place. He shook his head. "You never need to apologize to me again. My love is unconditional. There's just here and now between us."

She expelled the breath she'd been holding. She pressed a kiss above his heart, then said, "But what happens when we *do* leave this room?"

Instantly, images flashed through his mind: Rose in pajamas on the opposite side of his kitchen table in the morning. Cheeks flushed, a white veil in her hair, love in her eyes. Cradling their child in a nursery rocking chair. Streaks of gray in those brown locks, blowing in the breeze of their sailboat. Everything he absolutely, unequivocally, wanted the future to look like.

But he couldn't tell her. Not one part of him was willing to risk what he had right now. Her, in his arms, where she belonged.

He could never ask her to leave her job, her life in Portland behind. It was her call to make. He wouldn't be the guy to impose his hopes on her.

"Well," he said hesitantly, "I won't be able to keep up this vigilante justice forever." There. A small truth he could admit without scaring her off. "You already know I'm having issues resolving the, uh"—he swallowed hard—"collateral damage of my actions."

A small pause from her, then, "What will you do after?"

They both knew he never needed to work another day in his life. Still, there was no way he could sit by, idle, any longer.

"I don't know," he said honestly. "All I know is that I want it to be worthwhile. Maybe a foundation, dedicated to victim advocacy. Maybe law school. I've been useless too long already."

A small smile played at her lips. "Such a military mindset you have, my dear. Mend, fix, solve, make right. I noticed that with Lucien and Charles, too. A hero mentality."

My dear. Hero. He breathed deeply, chest swelling at the thought of her, thinking him some sort of superman. He wanted to be, for her. The corner of his mouth lifted.

"I suppose so. There's a certain... bond, between men and women who serve. An understanding that's hard to put into words."

Leaning down, she pressed a gentle kiss to his chest. "Will you tell me more, some day, when you can?"

One simple, tender kiss from her and his heart skipped a beat, threatening to burst right out of his chest. "Yes." He nodded. "You're the only one I've ever found myself wanting to share it with. The shit that happened, the good times, too. The things we did..." There was so much history behind him, many parts of it gruesome and grotesque.

She breathed slowly, deeply. "I can take it all. It won't change how I feel." Her gaze captured his, certainty and unwavering courage in her expression. "Please don't keep yourself from me."

"Done." He responded without thinking, instinct taking over. He'd share anything with her. She encouraged him to imagine a life free from the prison he'd created for himself. No one had ever made him smile so easily, stretched his boundaries, and pushed his ideas of happiness for himself to the breaking point.

She'd broken him open.

"The burns are from an explosion in Ba'hir," he said softly. "The side of my face and down my neck were the small ones. But I should've told you about my back. Sorry. I know how repulsive it must look."

She tilted her head, her delicate, arched brows furrowing. Bracing herself up on her arms, she held his gaze. "I know what I want, and I know what I need. You protecting me from what you've suffered isn't one of those things." Her eyes gleamed. "Besides, you know what they say about beauty."

It's in the eye of the beholder. She thought him beautiful?

"But it's more than this, Burke." Her fingertips ghosted over his abs, running over his nipple. "More than how irresistible you are."

He gasped, small stars bursting behind his eyes.

On their way to his jaw, her fingers danced in his short beard. "It's everything I see here." She came up and he closed his eyes. She pressed kisses to their lids.

Shuddering, he flipped them over, settling her beneath him.

A short laugh escaped her mouth, until he covered it with his own.

WITH ROSE'S head tucked under his chin, her hair tickling his chest, Burke stared at the recessed ceiling above his bed. His breathing was slow, but his pulse kept a steady, elevated pace. Moonlight poured through the windows. Arms wrapped protectively around her, he felt a new, sudden chord strike deep inside. He'd do anything to keep her safe. Absolutely anything.

She sighed contentedly, her breath caressing his skin. Her breathing was even and peaceful. She wasn't in a deep sleep, but dozing.

She'd trusted him. Let him in, left him feeling worthy, invincible... special. Everything between them had been rooted in what really mattered, so he ultimately didn't give a crap that she'd lied about being a maid. She wasn't getting a prize with him anyway. He still had nightmares, panic attacks, flashbacks. He had a laundry list of regrets that stretched a mile wide.

No. Overall, he was getting the better end of what was going on between them, by far. And maybe having a cousin on this island would make her want to stay, or at the very least, provide additional incentive for her to come back often. She'd already brought up the topic of the future, so that was a good sign—

A knock on the door startled them both.

"It's me." Lucien. "Get decent and open up. Now."

Of all the bad timing. . . Suppressing a roar, he slipped from the bed, grabbed his pants and threw them on. What could Lu possibly need in the middle of the night?

"Hmm?" She sat up in bed, waves of tousled brown hair in different directions, her body relaxed and draped across his mattress. It was that satiated smile, though, that moved him to his core. She was magnificent.

"We have company," he rumbled, hands fisting at his sides. "You might want to, uh..." He wiggled his finger at the bedsheets.

"Oh, yeah." Her eyes widened, becoming alert. She scrambled to pull the sheets around her.

When she was covered, he whirled around and yanked open the door. "What?"

Lucien's once-over of him and sideways glance at Rose was instantaneous.

"Now's not the time, Lu," he growled.

"I have bad news, and an update on Graves."

He didn't risk a glance back at Rose. Rose—another one of Graves's victims. Just the thought of Graves made him feel ready to explode. He wanted to find him and choke the life out of him with his bare hands.

Lucien locked his jaw. "I mean it, Burke. We need to talk. The shit just hit the fan."

Everything was going to turn upside down. He could feel it in his bones.

His eyes narrowed, but he stepped aside and let Lucien in. Rose got up, the bedsheet trailing around her, and grabbed her dress. She went into his walk-in closet with it.

Lucien entered the massive room as he grabbed a t-shirt, then threw it on. The room was too quiet. Too calm. Lucien had that guarded expression he often got right before a dangerous mission. This wasn't going to just be something bad—it was going to be disastrous.

He ran a hand over his bearded jaw. "What's up?"

A second later, she emerged in her dress.

"Chad was killed."

The blow was swift and went straight through his chest, creating a chasm. He swayed, his jaw slack. "No."

"Yes."

"Oh my God," Rose breathed.

He couldn't look at her. He couldn't. They'd been... While Chad had been lying dead somewhere... He put up a hand. "Tell me it's a mistake. Tell me I didn't send that kid off to his death. Tell me anything but this."

Lucien's features hardened. "A single shot to the head, execution-style. It was bold. The Ring isn't dicking around anymore. They sent a message loud and clear. I'm sorry."

Words he'd heard from Lucien too many times before.

He had to breathe. He had to keep his head straight. "He was like a little brother to me. I remember when he was born, when Polly brought him home. It must be someone else. It can't be Chad."

"Paige has the photos on her computer. Trust me, you don't want to see them."

He slumped down, sitting on the edge of his bed. Bending forward, hands clasped, he lowered his head to his legs. "I did it again." He spoke to the floor. "I got another person killed. A friend."

A small, soft hand rested on his shoulder, but even Rose's touch couldn't soften the anguish making him collapse from the inside out.

"Burke," she murmured, "this isn't your fault."

"She's right," Lucien said. "You didn't kill him, and you didn't blow up a motel full of girls. I can't watch you blame yourself again."

Breathe in. Out. In again.

Yes. The true enemy was still out there.

He lifted his head, his features tightening. "Graves." Only then did he dare glance up at her. She was completely ashen, and her lips were parted. Was she afraid she'd be next on that bastard's list?

"Yeah." Lucien nodded.

Raising a brow, he asked, "You know that for sure?"

"They dumped him at Masters Industries headquarters in Bellevue with a picture of a hand flipping the bird taped to his chest."

His vision went red and he sprang to his feet. "I'm going to *destroy* him. I'm going to tear his limbs off and make him suffer."

Rose stepped away from him.

Lucien scratched his forehead. "Graves was never stupid. Fucking around with his business put a target on our backs, so it was only a matter of time until he figured out who we were."

"And he probably kept tabs on me anyway," he said. "He was fixated on me overseas and being back from service didn't change it. But I'm not his only obsession." He glanced at Rose, who was wringing her hands. "We're going to get him tonight, Rose. I promise. You'll be safe."

"Burke, we have to have a plan," she said softly.

He nodded, turning back to Lucien. "Graves has those concert tickets for the show in Portland, and we know his operation is running at the Shady Tree tonight. We'll go down to Oregon and intercept him during the day, before the concert. Once we get him, we'll fly back and go to the Shady Tree, so we can take down Graves's operation together. If we can't get Graves before the concert, the three of us will split up to cover our bases."

Rose.

Taking a breath, he turned to her. "I'll be back as soon as this is all over."

"You want me to stay here." She crossed her arms.

He had to tread carefully. "Well, we're the vigilantes. We're former military. We have experience—"

"This is happening too fast." She looked between the men. "There's only three of you, and you're hurt."

His jaw locked.

"What about the police—" she started.

"We can't involve the cops," Lucien said quickly. "They're after us, too. It's not like vigilante work is sanctioned. Besides, can you imagine the media circus it would be if they nabbed us, or were able to pin our activities on Burke?"

She bit her lip.

"Too many things could go wrong or fall through the cracks if it isn't us," Burke added. "For the first time we've been able to pin Graves as their leader, and we know where he is and where his operation is going to be. We have to free those women and stop him. I can't let him get away."

"I want them saved, too, but I can't watch a personal vendetta get you killed." Her voice broke as her spine bowed a little, deflating her like a balloon.

He touched her arm lightly. "This isn't just for me. I'm doing this for you, too. You could've ended up in his trafficking ring. Thank God you didn't, but that doesn't mean it couldn't still happen." A shudder shot down his spine. "After what he did to you—"

"I know." Her voice was low, calm... almost detached. "I was there. I suffered through it and the doctor's appointments and daily reminders that followed. That's why I want him behind bars, Burke. I want him on trial, exposed and humiliated, for all the world to see him for the pig he is."

Forget a trial and a stint in prison. He wanted to shove Graves's face through a concrete wall instead. Hell, a thousand concrete walls still wouldn't be enough to satisfy him.

"We can try to take him in alive—"

"But will you?"

The three words struck him like a blow. They'd left every other criminal apprehended until the police found them. They'd never dealt out lethal punishment as a team before. But he'd also never considered letting Graves walk away, either. Not this time. Not after she had told him what Graves had done to her. The asshole was beyond redemption, but what she wanted mattered to him, too.

He couldn't promise her one way or another. He just didn't know how tomorrow would play out.

Words were stuck on his tongue.

She glanced between the men, nodded, and moved to the door. "We can talk more tomorrow."

He reached for her. "Rose—"

"Ending his life isn't worth risking your own." She walked out, head held high.

CHAPTER 19

*B*urke climbed the stairs up to the second floor, his combat boots thumping against the inlaid stone, his joints aching beyond his years. A cannonball of emotion was lodged in his chest. After he'd dressed in his combat gear that morning—the first time since Pine Ridge—he'd told Polly about Chad, and then spent the last few hours with her. Holding her. Softly speaking words that could never truly help her. Sharing in her devastation.

Nothing had ever prepared him for losing someone. Every time had been a shock. Fellow soldiers, his parents, now Chad. He knew better than anyone how the whole world could just change in a minute.

Isolating himself since Pine Ridge hadn't changed the fact that he still had so much to lose. Instead, it had shown him the ferocity of his friends' loyalty and love. He'd give them no less in return. Reaching the landing at the top of the stairs, he paused, gripping his cane tighter.

Graves's reign of terror was up tonight.

The people of Ba'hir. Fourteen women at Pine Ridge. Chad. He'd make Graves pay for every one of them. The countless hours he'd personally spent in rehab, working through his injuries. And Rose... His skin tingled. Graves had violated her on every level. No words could ever describe the fury he felt for her sake. She had to be safe. He'd stop at nothing to guarantee it.

The pommel of the cane cracked under his squeezed fist.

He frowned.

Soon he'd meet Charles, Lucien and Paige at Headquarters to discuss the logistics of the mission tonight, but right now there was only one person he wanted to see.

Going over to Rose's door, he knocked.

The door swung open, her arms outspread. He wrapped his around her and clung to her as if his life depended on it.

Eventually, he released her enough to look at her. She looked up at him, put her hand in his hair and drew his lips to hers.

Yes.

He took the back of her head in his hand, tangling in her brown waves, and deepened their kiss. Hours of heightened emotion collided with overwhelming, barely restrained desire for her, for her every touch. She was so sweet. So natural and free.

She was his dream come true.

Her breath escaped against his lips and she melted, angling into him.

He pulled her into him, close enough to feel the rise and fall of her breasts against his chest, the memory and feel of them fueling the passion simmering under the surface of his skin. His tongue coaxed hers and she met it with her own. She felt so good. So right, so familiar, so mind-blowing. Like coming home.

She broke away, clutching his shoulder holster like a lifeline, her breathing deep and uneven. Then she rested her head against his chest, right below his thundering heart.

The overwhelming emotion made him choke up.

He squeezed his eyes shut and locked his hands around her lower back.

"I'm sorry. I know how hard this morning has been for you," she said against his t-shirt. She released her hold on him and leaned back.

He forced his eyes open in time to see her waver on her feet, breathless and flushed.

Then a slow, bittersweet smile spread across her face. "But I'm glad you're here."

The five little words detonated a grenade of relief and happiness in his chest all at once. "Me, too." He touched her arm, his thumb skimming across her skin. "I'm sorry about upsetting you last night."

Her smile fell, along with her shoulders.

"I wish I could change your mind about going after Gavin. More than you could know." Running a hand through her hair, she added, "but I decided my desperation to keep you safe is your fault. You made me love you too much."

He barked out a half-laugh, half-groan, then kissed the top of her head, inhaling her scent of strawberries and roses.

"I'll happily take responsibility for that." He pulled away, meeting her gaze. "It's the same for me with you, Rose."

"I figured out a way I could help you before you plan the mission, though." She took his hand and led him over to the desk, near her bed. "I've been busy while you were gone." Leaning down, she opened her laptop and nodded toward it.

He peered at a list of names, email addresses and phone numbers. A contact list, but he didn't recognize any of the names.

"I switched phones after Gavin started contacting me." She looked away, a slight blush staining her porcelain cheeks. "Naturally, I lost a lot of the contacts I'd had at that time. The more I switched phones, the more people fell through the cracks. But one of those contacts is Gavin's partner." She bit her lip. "Then this morning it occurred to me that I might be able to go to my old cell phone service provider and find that guy's number. This is him." She pointed to the name. Bruno Jones. "So I called him."

He took in her straight spine, the why-the-hell-not expression on her face, the shrug she just gave him... *Damn.* He grinned. What was sexier—her with a Taser in her hand or her mad Intel gathering skills? It was hard to decide.

"He remembered me," she continued, "from when we'd met at a precinct party that I went to with Gavin on our second date. I told him Gavin and I recently got back together" —she furrowed her brows—"and that I wanted to plan a surprise for him tonight. Bruno said Gavin bailed on his shift this morning. Bruno dropped him off at the airport so he could fly to Seattle." The corner of her mouth lifted. "Those concert tickets weren't for him. I think he'll be at the Shady Tree. You guys don't have to be in two places at once, or split up."

She never ceased to amaze him. What had he ever done to get this lucky? "Inspector Benoit, you are one outstanding sleuth." He beamed at her. "Care to join the team?"

Glancing away, she rubbed her forehead. "I might consider it if you let me come with you tonight."

Just like that, his smile fell.

"Just hear me out, Burke. If I stay behind I'll lose my mind not knowing what's going on."

"You can listen in on the comms with Paige—"

"But if I'm nearby at the Shady Tree, maybe I can run and get help if someone gets hurt. I know you don't want the police there because they're after you, too, but if something goes wrong I can be there to call them, meet them and try to help." Her tone became more high-pitched with each word.

"Rose—"

"I just..." She blew out a breath. "Let me come with. Let me stay with you."

The sentiment, her earnestness, made him want to agree at the top of his lungs. But all his training told him the risk was too great. They both knew it.

"I don't want to leave here without you," he said quietly. "But I won't be. You're here." He touched his chest. "Always."

Tilting her head, her gaze filled with sudden, unshed tears. She brought her hand to her throat, then slowly nodded.

"I know it was a crazy idea. I just"—she dropped her hand— "I don't want to know what it's like to mourn you."

He swallowed hard. "You won't. If anyone's going to be able to stop Graves, it's me. We've fought each other before. I know his physical capabilities and his limits. I can get under his skin more than anyone else." Except her, probably. He blew out a breath.

"What if something triggers a flashback?" Worry filled her gaze.

He lifted his good shoulder. "It could happen. Lucien, Charles, and I will work out how to handle the possibility before we go, but"—*How could he explain it?* —"in those moments when everything goes down, in that darkness, I know myself. I can hold on, until *I* decide to let go." He brushed a strand of her chestnut locks away from her face. "And you have given me more to live for than I ever thought possible."

To his surprise, her eyes started to glisten. She put her hand on her chest. "I love you, Burke. I truly do. I never, ever thought I'd finally fall in love with anyone, but I knew you were special from the beginning. Someone I could cherish." She smiled. "You're my light in the darkness. I love you so deeply I glow."

His heart stopped beating because it burst right out of his chest. In the middle of this nightmare, he'd been handed the universe, the greatest of all gifts.

Leaning down, his lips brushed hers, then he rested his forehead on hers. "Stay here with Paige, Rose, please," he said quietly. "This home and the people on it are the most important thing to me. Please protect our family on this island."

She leaned back, meeting his gaze. "I promise."

Her sincerity was overwhelming and humbling all at once.

He held her close. "And I promise that nothing is going to stop me from coming back."

~

IT TURNED out there was more than one pier on the island. When Rose had arrived at West Cove, she'd come by the main one on the south side in front of the mansion. Now she followed Burke, Lucien, Charles, and Paige from Headquarters to the pier on the island's west side instead.

The shorter dock had two boat lifts on either side of it, with a wooden shelter built over the edge of the water.

"We have three skiffs," Burke told her, gesturing at the boat bobbing in the water, attached by a rope. "We dock them here. The other side of the island has the helipad."

Wow. "I thought you were kidding about that," she mumbled.

He chuckled. "To get there you hang a left at that old treehouse, instead of going right and up to The Overlook."

"Ah. Okay." She forced a smile for his sake and shielded her eyes from the sun.

Charles and Burke went down the dock with the supplies they'd carried from Headquarters, and began to load them on the boat. The skiff. *Ugh, nautical terms.*

Burke's demeanor had taken on an air of resolve and readiness since the five of them had met and gone over the mission. It'd been nice to be included, but as they talked about weapons they were going to use, pressure points, sightlines, possible placements of henchmen and so on, she'd worried herself into a frenzy. She didn't want to trigger a seizure, but she couldn't manage to quell the overwhelming stress. If only she had half of his focus.

A dull and persistent ache formed in her chest.

Next to her, Lucien and Paige were locked in an embrace. A part of her wished she and Burke were at that stage—that all the awkwardness of a new relationship was gone and there would be no inhibitions between them.

Burke straightened, a duffle bag slung over his shoulder, and said something to Charles. His dark blond hair swayed in the breeze, and his long eyelashes blinked over that intense stare of his. A black shirt clinging to every beautifully sculpted muscle. Every inch of him screamed toughness. Invincibility. Like Rambo, but way hotter.

If only lives weren't the balance. If only Gavin were already in jail.

He tossed the final duffle bag aboard, then turned to her and gave her a small smile. The light in his eyes when he looked at her... It meant everything. She walked toward him.

"Come on, Lu," he called, even though he kept looking at her.

She hated that he was going without her. She absolutely hated it.

"I, uh, I've been thinking about it, and you're right," Burke said, when she stopped in front of him. Behind him, Charles jumped aboard. "We'll try to take him alive, if that's what you want. I mean, I can't guarantee it, but he should stand trial." The muscle in his jaw ticked. "It's what we've always believed. As long as he's apprehended, that's what counts."

Launching herself at him, she held onto him for dear life. His enormous arms wrapped around her, locking her to him. He was so solid. So strong. So confident in what he needed to do and who he was. It was inspiring.

"I don't care if he's dead or alive as long as you're okay." Pulling back, she said, "Don't do anything heroic, Burke. Stay safe. I can't go back to Portland without knowing you're all right."

A shadow passed over his gaze. "You'd go back to Portland?"

Well, um... She bit her lip. "I mean, my job is there." She shrugged and forced herself to smile. "I think my bands might be counting on me to come back."

He sucked in a breath. Looking down, he pulled something—black fabric? —out of his pocket and clutched it in a death grip.

Stupid big mouth of hers. "Just focus on rescuing those women, getting Gavin and staying alive while we protect everything you've built here. We'll worry about the rest later." Time to distract him from worrying about their future. She looked at the thing in his hand. "What's that?"

He held up the ski mask for her, his lips thin.

Wearing a mask made him seem more like a criminal. She tried to hide her frown under an expression of indifference. "Oh, so no one can identify the three of you."

"He's the only one who needs it, because he's a celebrity in Seattle." Lucien said over his shoulder as he got on the boat. "We don't want anyone to recognize him."

Burke lifted a shoulder. "The price I pay for my birthright."

Right. Because he was famous. She shifted her weight. It was so easy to forget because he was such a down-to-earth guy.

"If Burke was recognized or arrested, he could go to prison," Paige said softly, looking at her. "His companies' stocks would tumble and people in every division would be laid off. The people he employed here would be out of a job."

"It shouldn't be all about me—" Burke began.

"She's right, but it's more than that." Rose shook her head and took a step closer to him. He looked at her, his laser-like gaze going right through her. "People look up to you. Your public, your friends. You're the heart and soul of this place, its anchor."

Tears stung her eyes, and her throat was tight. She placed a hand on his chest, felt him lightly shudder. His skin was scorching beneath the shirt.

"No one could ever replace you," she whispered.

He placed his large hand over hers, keeping her against him. His heartbeat was steady and strong beneath her touch, but when he smiled, it didn't reach his eyes.

"And no one could ever mean more to me than you." Leaning down, he kissed her lightly.

Just like that he let her go, strode toward the boat and jumped aboard. Her stomach was twisted into knots and her heart was stuck in her throat as he cast off the rope. She wouldn't—she *couldn't*—look away from him as the boat jetted away.

She linked her arm with Paige's. They stayed that way, until the men disappeared into the edge of the horizon.

CHAPTER 20

The whimpers by Gavin's feet were goddamn pathetic. He bent down, grabbing Tom Wagner by the top of his graying hair, wrenching his head back. Terrified eyes stared up at him, mucus trailing down the businessman's face, over the duct tape across his mouth.

The sun was setting over the water, but there were no boats. Nobody was within screaming distance except his men surrounding them. Maybe now Gavin's scalp would stop burning, too. The close-cropped hair wasn't protecting it enough from the sun's rays. Frowning, he ripped the tape off Tom's mouth.

He whimpered.

"I gave you one job, Tom. *One*," Gavin hissed. When he'd taken Tom on as his money launderer a couple years back, he'd chosen Tom because he had offered the one thing no one else could: access to Masters Industries. When Gavin had learned the man had been a friend of Jonathan Masters, he'd retained him then and there. What better way to keep tabs on his nemesis, the asshole who had everything?

He'd hated Burke Masters the moment he had met the cocky bastard. Handsome, more physically fit than the rest of them, friendly even in the middle of a shitty desert war, money coming out of his ass... Everyone had clamored to be his best friend. Everyone except Gavin. It wasn't fair. Masters had been popular without even trying. A golden boy just because of his parents. No, it wasn't fair at all.

Too bad pinning Ba'hir on him hadn't worked.

But Tom had reported back that Masters had remained on his estate, never showing up to the office or to the Board meetings, sending an emissary in his place instead. While Gavin had established his operation in Portland, it hadn't bothered him all that much—as long as the world kept thinking of Burke Masters as the miserable piece of shit he was, he hadn't cared that much. And, as a bonus, it seemed the man had gone nuts, isolating himself on his island and living in seclusion.

All the easier to find him and end him when the time came.

"I – I'm sorry," Tom muttered, his face red and splotchy.

"Whatever was in that safe was supposed to be mine." He put his hands on his hips. "When you couldn't pay me back what you owed me, who gave you a second chance to redeem yourself?" He jutted a thumb to his chest. "Me. I didn't have to, but you swore to me you knew how to get into Masters's goddamn safe."

"I did. I do." Tears streamed down his face. Pitiful.

There was only one reason the nitwit was still alive, and she had a curvy ass, wavy brown hair, and nipples that hardened in the slightest breeze.

"Tell me again why Rose Benoit was there," he snarled.

Tom shook his head. "I don't know, I swear. I didn't know who she was."

When Tom had first blurted out the mysterious woman who'd Tased him on Masters's island, while his henchman Ray had poured acid on Tom's hand, Gavin had thought it was just Tom's pathetic attempt to distract him. But his description of her—the hair, the freckles, her physical features—had seemed like too strong a resemblance to the woman who'd haunted his very existence since the moment he'd set eyes on her. Showing Tom one of his many photos of Rose had only confirmed it: she was on Burke Masters's island. Probably in his bed.

His fists tightened, the vein in his temple throbbing. No one laid a hand on what was his. And how the fuck had she ended up with his sworn enemy, the man who rubbed his nose in everything he didn't have?

Well, Masters couldn't have Rose.

He lifted Tom up by the front of his torn, filthy shirt. "Did it look like they were together?"

"Together?" Tom quaked.

"Are. They. Fucking." Spit flew from his mouth, landing on his captive. If he said yes, he was going to rip Tom's windpipe out.

"N-no. I don't know. I don't think so."

He let him go with a shove against the railing, Tom's skull smacking against it with a thud.

Rose Benoit was the single biggest blemish in Gavin Graves's history. She was the most gorgeous woman he'd ever convinced to go out with him. She'd been the ideal, but she was too headstrong. She'd screwed everything up by telling him to leave after he'd had his way with her. But he'd been embarrassed. It wasn't like he'd ever had to resort to drugging a woman before to fuck her, but he hadn't been able to help himself. She was too beautiful, and he had been able to tell she wasn't going to put out, even on their third date.

How could she blame him? She should've thanked him for not ripping her clothes off her the first night they had gone out. She'd worn a delicate gold necklace against her pale skin that had stretched down to the cleavage she'd hid in a blue silk blouse. See? He had been a gentleman. He still remembered.

But hitting her had been his mistake, he could see that now. He'd overreacted when she'd been upset, trying to push him out the door. If he could just tell her that, she would forgive him, and they could move on.

Then, he could try to forgive her for whatever had brought her to Burke Masters's island. If she hadn't fucked him.

Finally, it was dark out over Puget Sound. A picture-perfect end of a summer day for the rest of civilization, the start of the pleasure he sold at night. About time. This rebooted venture in Seattle had to work, to set him up for the future. The market in Portland had been scarce lately. The women were always plentiful, but P.P.D. was starting to sniff around his business a little too much. He was a cop, and he had the inside edge. For this latest payday, he had to lay low in his own backyard and pillage someone else's.

So he was back in Seattle, ready to stick it to Burke Masters in his own hometown.

But he should've had the extra millions in Masters's safe to go with it. He kicked Tom hard, and the man grunted, doubling over to the deck.

Burke Masters—washed up vigilante. Broken son of a bitch who had choked on the golden spoon in his mouth. He guffawed.

He had big plans for that motherfucker, every one of which ended in finishing what he'd started in Ba'hir—burning that shithead alive. But not before he showed Masters just how much he'd underestimated him.

Speaking of which. He turned to Ray, the pale, fifty-something former gym-teacher-turned-opioid-addict-and-pimp. "Is everything set at Shady Tree? Does Farlan have everything he needs? Does he know what's expected of him?" Farlan and Ray had proved to be his biggest earners, and they'd worked the girls the hardest, and remained the most loyal. He went over the earnings personally to make sure they weren't skimping on him.

"Yes, sir," Ray said, over the sound of the engine.

"He'd better have his shit together when I show up later."

"I'm sure he will, boss. It was smart to leave half the guys with Farlan and take the other half with us tonight."

He jutted his chin up. "We only need those eight to watch the girls, and keep 'em in line. The customers, too. Did you leave enough Molly? Coke? Heroin?" Sometimes the girls needed a hit to do their jobs.

"Yeah. There's plenty for tonight, and for us when we get back to Shady

Tree." A dull hopefulness widened Ray's tired gray eyes. "So where are we headed to, boss?"

"We're going to get my woman back." He scratched his chin, remembering Rose's silky hair between his fingertips. She'd smelled so goddamn good. Like a department store. "Did I ever tell you about her, Ray? Tom?" He looked down at the man near his feet, crying.

Ray tilted his head. "I don't think so, sir. Is she one of the girls you, uh, were with these past weeks?"

"She's no whore," he shot back over the sound of the engine, biting the inside of his cheek. *Asshole.* "No, Rose has class. Tight and curvy in all the right places. Breasts almost as big as my palms, skin soft like butter, a mouth made for sinful things." He was getting hard at the memory, as he had a thousand times before. "She had a real job. Probably too clever for her own good, but she was the type you marry, not just the kind you screw. I had big plans for her." Those involved having kids at some point. Someone to leave his empire to. Boy, girl, didn't matter, as long as they were molded to his likeness and image, merciless and driven.

"I had kids," Ray muttered.

He frowned. "This op should set us up with enough cash for me to have the life I deserve. We'll see if Rose is worthy of that life, too." He'd been thinking of somewhere in South America. He could nab a couple of tourists, college girls, start a business somewhere small, and still lounge on sandy beaches to his heart's content. A house on the beach, a woman to come home to, ready for him when he was horny. She'd cook his dinner, raise their kids—how was that too much to ask for?

Why had Rose gone and fucked up all his plans? Not once, thirteen months ago, but *twice.* And this time, it was almost too much to forgive. Heat spread up into his face as his fists clenched. He'd show her. Teach her a lesson she'd never forget.

"So we're meeting her somewhere?" Ray asked.

Meeting her. Yeah, right. He smiled. Rose had no idea what was going to hit her, just like she hadn't last year, when he'd fucked her. And he was going to again. Soon. Shit, he was hard again, his pulse starting to throb.

He rubbed his hands together. "You could say that. We're going to West Cove Island to get my girlfriend back and put an end to a meddlesome motherfucker at the same time." He grinned at Ray. "Two birds with one stone. Now, shut up and steer the goddamn boat." He glanced down at the pile of garbage at his feet. "Now, put a hole in that and throw him overboard."

CHAPTER 21

*B*urke ducked into the open second floor motel room as the bullet whizzed by. There was only one guy who hadn't surrendered yet. Even though it was dark out, he'd been easy to spot under the fluorescent catwalk lights. The last of eight, he was skinny, with beady eyes and sunken cheeks, hiding behind an ice machine one room down. An ice machine on *this* side of that room's door.

The guy took another shot. Then another.

Now he was just wasting ammo.

"You got him?" Lucien called from a room away, through the motel's thin walls. He was rounding up the women and herding them into a room down the walkway, where they could stay until the police arrived. Charles was cuffing the other henchmen.

He checked his clip. All good. "Yep."

Beady-eyed guy took another shot. A few yards away, a woman shrieked.

He lifted the crowbar at his feet and went over to the interior room wall. He tapped the wallpaper near a print of some beige modern art, listening. Ah, there it was. No studs. He swung the crowbar at the wall like a batter blasting a baseball into right field.

A huge hole broke open.

He swung again just as the guy began to shoot into the room. Just the opening he needed. He sprinted out and around the corner. The guy was still shooting at the hole he'd created when he came up behind him. *Whack.* He cracked the crowbar across his back.

The guy let out a grunt and fell face-first onto the floor in the doorway. But he didn't lose consciousness.

He kicked the guy's gun away, out of reach.

Kneeling on his back, Burke expertly grabbed his wrists, wrenched them behind him and cuffed him.

"Where's Gavin Graves?" He searched the guy, then knelt harder as he lifted a pocket knife from the back of his jeans. Then he took his phone. Nope. No more weapons.

Spit spewed from the guy's mouth.

"We counted eight of you, but not him. He wasn't one of the johns that ran out of here, either. We didn't miss him. Where is he?"

They'd been meticulous, scoping every face, every location as the operation began. It had unfolded like clockwork, except the man of the hour was nowhere to be seen.

"N-not here." The guy could barely form words against the carpet.

He hauled him up. "This is his operation." He whirled the guy around to face him.

Those beady eyes narrowed. "Fuck you."

Ah, so the guy felt like he had some confidence back. *Keep him talking.* "If you tell me where he is, you get to meet the police in one piece."

"Eat shit." A cruel smile twisted his lips.

He lifted the crowbar and swung at the guy's head. Screaming, the guy ducked. The metal rod missed his head by an inch and destroyed the side of the ice machine.

"Okay!" The guy raised his hands, his eyebrows halfway up his forehead. "Fuck. Okay!"

He grabbed him by his dirty t-shirt and slammed him into the battered ice machine. The whole thing rocked, almost toppling. The guy gasped.

"He ain't here!" he exclaimed. "He left me in charge."

He believed him. The other henchmen had gone to this guy for instructions, and they hadn't set sights on Graves at all.

"Where is he?" Burke hauled him forward, slamming him again.

"Ow! I dunno. He told the guys they were driving to some pier. He'd ordered a boat. That's all I know."

The pier. Boats. Home. No. Not the island. He froze, a black hole of fear enveloping him. Every coherent thought vanished, but he had to focus. He couldn't give into the dread and terror that gripped him.

"How many men?"

The henchman's shoulders sagged as he whimpered.

They were too far away. Rose... Paige... Polly... Everyone was there. They were sitting ducks. While he, Lucien and Charles were here. Too far away.

He landed a punch in his stomach. The henchman doubled over, grunting.

"Burke!" Lucien called from down the walkway. "Get him to Charles!"

An army could be headed toward the woman he loved. He might never see her again. Graves couldn't get his hands on her. He couldn't.

"How many?" he shouted at the top of his lungs.

"'Nuther eight," the guy muttered.

They'd been concerned that returning to the island by chopper would have been too visible and would've only drawn police suspicion. There hadn't been a need to race back, so they'd just planned on using the skiff.

He had no way to get there fast. No way to stop Graves from getting to Rose. His worst nightmare was unfolding right before him.

Breathe. "When was this?"

When the guy didn't answer right away, he lifted him and dangled the top half of his body over the railing. The guy started to flail.

"When will he get to the island?" he yelled. It took two hours to get back to West Cove, and he had the fastest skiff, with the most horsepower, on the market. It would take Graves a little longer. He knew the longitude and latitude by heart, while Graves wouldn't know a belay from a bulwark. He had no clue what to do on the water.

But the skiff wasn't an option anymore.

"They left right before dark." The guy's voice was laced with pure panic. "That's all I know."

That was almost two hours ago. He had to get there *now*.

He set the guy on his feet, pushing him in front of him. "Guys, we gotta go," he called.

Lucien poked his head out of one of the rooms, presumably the one with the women inside. "Sirens?"

"Not yet." Eager to be rid of the dead weight, he pushed the henchman at him as he whipped out his cell phone. "We have to get back to the island right away." His fingers shook as he dialed Rose's number.

Alarm sprang into Lucien's eyes. "What's going on?"

"Graves."

Just then, Charles exited a room and strode toward them. "Is he here?"

Ring. "No," Burke said. "He's going to the island."

All the color drained from Lucien's face.

"What?" Charles exclaimed. He pointed his gun at the simpering henchman. "He told you this?"

"Yes." *Ring.*

Come on Rose, pick up.

"Paige." Lucien took a step back. "We have to warn them."

He was trying! *Ring.* Shit. His muscles were coiled tightly, his heart in his throat. They'd left them alone. Unprotected.

"I'll reactivate the comms." Charles fiddled with his earpiece. "Paige, can you hear me?" There was a pause.

"I'm not getting her either," Lucien said, his voice up an octave.

Ring. Click. "Hi. This is Rose. Sorry I missed you. Please leave me a message and I'll get back to you. If it's for a band I represent, please call—"

Son of a bitch.

The first echoes of sirens sounded in the distance.

He took off for the stairs. "Let's go," he said over his shoulder. "We have to grab our shit and then we can try again in the car."

"The skiff—" Lucien began.

"I know." He bounded down the steps three at a time, any discomfort in his knee forgotten. "You're going to call the island. I'm going to call one of our helicopter pilots and dangle enough cash in front of him that he'll beat us to the airport. We're flying in."

CHAPTER 22

"Rose, are you there yet?" Paige's flustered voice cackled through the two-way radio.

"No," she breathed, sprinting up the manor house's grand stairway. Only minutes ago she and Paige had been online shopping for bridal dresses—a thin attempt to distract themselves from worrying about the men—as they waited for them to reactivate their comms to tell them the mission had gone down as planned. Then Paige's proximity alert had flashed on the monitor.

Rose reached the top of the landing and dashed down the dimly-lit hall to Burke's study.

A boat was headed this way. Eight men on board. The satellite image was grainy, but she'd recognized one of the figures immediately.

Gavin.

Her blood had gone cold, fear paralyzing her where she stood. How? Why? How had he found her? Or was he here to hurt Burke and clueless that she was here? Burke—he was so far away! She didn't even know if he was all right, or hurt, or arrested, and even if he wasn't, he couldn't help them. At least *he* was beyond Gavin's reach. But they were too isolated. No one could help them in time.

Within moments, Paige had activated an evacuation notice, and a siren had begun to wail outside. Rose had offered to get people to the boat, but Paige had said she needed her in Burke's study instead, and while she'd furiously typed code onto her computer, Rose had raced out of the bungalow, running into a few bewildered staff members who'd come out of their homes.

One of them had been Katie.

She had tasked Katie with getting everyone to the boats. Many of them had gone to sleep already, but Katie knew where they all lived. She'd promised to get them to the west pier and to have some woman named Ellen prep the boats. Rose had thanked her, told her she'd be in Burke's study, then she'd raced inside to hear Paige's instructions and get the radio.

The island's network had a self-destruct, but the fail-safe linked it to two computers: the one in Headquarters, and the other in Burke's study.

She flung open the door and landed in Burke's chair, bringing his computer and monitors to life. She set her Taser beside it.

"I'm here," she said into the radio. "What do I do?"

Paige rattled off programs for her to open.

"Can you call the guys?" Rose breathed, while she did what she was told. Where had she left her cell phone? In the pocket of her sweater at Paige's. "The police?"

Her gaze darted to the other computer monitor, where multiple video feeds blinked back at her, showing various parts of the island and manor house. A few people ran. One was Katie. Good. She was getting them to the boats.

"I can't," Paige said. "When I activated our Evacuation signal it cut us off. It's one of those glitches I just hadn't figured out how to fix yet." Something slammed on her end—her fist on the desk? "We keep electricity and our defense network, but we don't have phones or Internet."

Crap, crap, crap. No way to reach Burke!

"This must be the defense network." Her eyes scanned the program she'd pulled up.

"Do you see the grid, and blue lines that run below the topography map?"

"Yes."

"Good. Time to blow it up. They're here."

A quick glance at the bottom-right video feed confirmed it. Gavin's boat docked on the south pier, where she'd landed when she first arrived on West Cove. It felt like a lifetime ago.

He'd be at the mansion in minutes.

"What about our people? If we detonate stuff could they get hurt?" she asked Paige.

"Everyone here knows the places to avoid. They've been drilled. They know to go to the west pier, where the weapons are, and where we placed traps. You're the only novice. And you get to set off the first charge. Get rid of that pier!"

There was a little circle with an "X" over the base of the south pier, where it met the topography. She glanced at the video feed into Headquarters, looking at Paige at her desk, even though Paige couldn't see her. "What do I do?"

"Does it say armed on the upper corner of your screen, too?"

She checked. "Yes."

"Good. You have control of the three explosives by the mansion. Just click on the grayed-out circle at the top of the south pier. That's it."

She clicked on it.

Boom! An explosion rocked the otherwise quiet night, the windowpanes behind her rattled. She glanced over her shoulder. Flames shot up in the distance, down the walkway.

She glanced at the south pier's video feed, but she'd lost that signal. That camera only showed digital snow. Her heart pounded. Had she killed someone? Hopefully not.

"It went off," she told Paige.

"I heard. We have to do this fast, Rose. I can see them climbing onto the shore. They'll probably send most to the mansion and fan out the rest. I've already started the process of wiping any traces of our digital footprints, but I'll need your help to activate the final self-destruct sequence."

Sequences, explosions, the worst villain imaginable—but one that was all too real—headed this way... This was like something out of an action movie. One that would become horrific all too soon.

"Who the hell sets up bombs and a defense network anyway?" Rose exclaimed.

"Lucien and Charles wanted this for Burke after the trial when they were afraid Graves would retaliate, but it didn't happen. Then I came, but I haven't had a chance to do more yet." The explanation came out in a breathless flurry of words. "Focus, Rose. Detonate the ones on the boardwalk leading up to the mansion and the drawbridge over the moat. That's the last one we have, but if it's gone, it'll take them a little longer to get in. They'll have to go around to the back. It only buys us a couple of minutes."

She clicked on the last two, and two subsequent explosions burst behind her. The study went bright, as if a firework were right outside the window, then went dark. The walls shook, the lights flickered and breakable objects shuddered.

"Good job."

Half of the video feeds went snowy.

"Paige, I lost the cameras to the entire mansion. I can't see them. I don't know where Gavin is." The thought felt paralyzing. At least she could still see her cousin in Headquarters.

"I lost them too. All the southeast cameras are gone. Just the northwest ones are okay. Pull up the program on Burke's computer labeled *Semper Fi.* That's the self-destruct sequence. I'll walk you through it."

Pop, pop, pop. Someone was shooting outside! Where was it coming from? She couldn't tell. Was anyone hurt?

"G-gunfire," she stammered into the two-way radio. "Hurry, Paige. Tell me."

Paige started to tell her, and she followed every instruction. The gunfire stopped, but every two seconds she glanced at the remaining monitors. She saw two men with handguns raised, pointing, headed toward the west.

She and Paige completed steps one and two of the sequence, and started in on the final one.

Katie raced in. Oh, no. She was still on the island?

"Rose," she said breathlessly, cheeks flushed. "The first skiff is gone. Everyone except you and Paige are on the second one. We've got to go. Some guy almost saw me. He's searching the bungalows, and other ones are coming in around back here. I came up the service stairs. I think they're searching room by room."

"Go." She shooed Katie away with a wave. "Sneak out. By the time—"

"Rose!" Paige cackled through the radio. "It'll still take another fifteen seconds for the system to dissolve once we enter the final sequence. Find the icon with the padlock and open it."

"Katie, go," she implored while she did what she was told. "Get the last boat off. Bring Paige if you can. We're almost done destroying the evidence so you can get her on the way to the pier. Go!"

"But—"

"Go," she practically screamed.

Katie turned and fled, her long ponytail waving goodbye. Hopefully she'd get to the boat safely. Hopefully she knew the right places to hide. Hopefully everyone else could get off this island before they were caught.

But any hope at all couldn't change the fact that she was now stranded, up shit creek without a paddle, left at Gavin's mercy.

She'd have to hide. But where?

"After that last line of code type in *destruct, destruct, destruct* now!"

She did. And nothing happened. Paige had said there'd be a delay, though.

Rose jumped to her feet, grabbed her Taser, and looked onscreen at Paige behind her computer. "We need to run," she said into the radio.

The black and white image showed the door behind Paige swinging open. Gavin rushed into Headquarters. Her blood turned to ice. She opened her mouth, but no sound came out. Paige whirled around, and—

The monitor went dark and the electricity shut off. The siren stopped. So did her heart.

CHAPTER 23

"We're coming up on West Cove Island," Al, the pilot, shouted back to Burke, over the chopping of the helicopter blades and the air racing past the cabin doors.

It wasn't quick enough. Every agonizing moment seemed suspended in time, his thoughts churning one disaster after another on a continuous loop in his mind. He had to get back. They all did. Charles sat beside him, Lucien across from them, each of them armed and ready for combat. Like a thousand times before.

But this time, everyone and everything they loved was at stake.

A white dot in the black water beneath them caught his eye. "There!" he shouted. "Al, take us down so we get a better look. I think it's our skiff!"

Lucien and Charles leaned over.

"Got it," Al said.

They couldn't get too close and risk capsizing it, so he grabbed the pair of night vision binoculars they always carried on missions. The chopper dipped and circled, bringing them closer.

"Seven of ours." He expelled a breath. Over half of them were safe. "I see Polly. Felix. Todd." He scanned as many faces as he could, recognizing each of them, his heart sinking lower. Where was she? "Five are missing. Rose and Paige aren't onboard."

Maybe she still managed to get off in the other skiff. Maybe she was even closer to the mainland than Polly's group.

Charles put a hand on Burke's shoulder. "Do you see Katie?"

"No, sorry." It wasn't the news he wanted to tell his friend, either. He knew Charles was carrying a torch for the sweet sous-chef.

Stray hair fell from Lucien's man bun as he shook his head. "Maybe—"

"Another boat starboard," Al called back.

Oh, thank God. The three of them leaned over to the other door.

"Bring us closer, Al," Charles called.

Two people. He only saw two people. No. The body types were wrong. He peered closer. Ellen was steering... and Roger.

Rose, where are you?

"They're not there." His mouth was bone-dry. "It's Ellen and Roger. The three of them didn't get off the island." He leaned forward, shouting, "Take us there!"

The chopper banked hard and Burke turned his attention out the front. There was his island... with three small puffs of smoke curling up from the south side, by the manor house.

"The bombs." He turned to Lucien and Charles, pointing out the window. "They must have set off the explosives."

There weren't signs of any other blasts, though. No raging fires. At least it wasn't worse. That he knew of.

If... if Gavin hadn't killed her yet... she had to be positively terrified, in a place he'd wanted her to feel safe.

"Land this thing now!" he told Al.

"There's no electricity," Lucien pointed out. "The island's dark, which means Paige and probably Rose managed to self-destruct the network."

"Good." That meant she'd been alive long enough to do that. That reminded him— "Al, drop us on the helipad then lift off right away. We've got the EVAC chopper coming in behind us." While he'd arranged for Al's services in the car, Charles had contacted the authorities. They were only minutes behind them.

Al began his descent.

He didn't give a damn if their vigilante operation was discovered. It didn't matter what became of him if he could only get to Rose in time.

But he had to stay on point. Keep to the mission. Try to push all his fear for her deep down so he could stay objective.

An image of her lovely face blazed across his thoughts.

Easier said than done.

Focus.

"That asshole at Shady Tree said there were eight of them," he reminded them. "When we land, we split up. Charles, go around the front of the manor house and come in that way. I'll circle around back, through the garden. Lu, get to Headquarters." He held radios out to them. "If you find any or all of them, send clicks through the radios. When Charles and I clear the manor house, we'll come your way, Lucien."

The ping of gunfire hit the side of the chopper. A shooter. The three men exchanged glances. Charles peered out his door, Burke the other, their guns raised.

"Get it down," Lucien said, leaning forward toward Al, his hands gripping the pilot's seat.

There, at ten o'clock, the top of the henchman was visible between a few trees along the edge of the helipad. Right by the path that led to the manor house and The Overlook. He took his shot.

The man fell the same instant the chopper touched down.

"Show off," Charles said, as they jumped out. Wind whipped their clothes and hair in every direction. He took off toward the fallen henchman with Lucien.

Burke went around and waved the pilot up. "Get out of here."

Al nodded and lifted off.

He sprinted after them. They'd already reached the man and disarmed him.

Lucien had the man's torso hauled up and pushed against a tree, and even though Burke had shot him in the collarbone, he was still conscious. Good. Drool fell into his wispy blond beard, his face contorted in agony.

"Where is she?" Lucien looked ready to rip Blond-beard's head right off his shoulders. He knew the feeling well. "Where are our people?"

"Graves—" Burke began.

"I only know the boss got one girl," Blond-beard wheezed. His fist opened, a radio dropping from his limp arm. "We missed lots of people 'cause there were boats on the other side of the island, we think, but Boss has a woman in one of the small houses. Said there was a lot of tech shit there."

Headquarters. Shit. Where was Rose? With the self-destruct, someone had to be at the computer in his study… She'd probably gone there and Paige had probably stayed at HQ. Right? He had to get to her.

Charles was busy looking at the wound as Lucien cuffed him. The guy winced.

"A blond or a brunette? What did she look like?" Lucien demanded.

"Dunno," the man whined. "He sent me here."

Pchew! Pchew! Shots flew.

"Fuck!" Lucien exclaimed as the three of them ducked. Bark on a nearby tree splintered and shattered. Burke took cover behind a tree, Charles behind a boulder.

Damn it. Eight men and Graves. Despite the explosions, all they knew for sure was that one was down, possibly the rest to go. With that noisy entrance they just made, all of them could be descended on them here at the helipad.

More shots were fired. Dirt flew up. The three of them returned fire.

Every fiber of his being wanted to ignore the shots—just run and find Rose. Every moment away from her brought her one step closer to suffering at Graves's hands.

A bullet embedded itself in the tree only inches from his head. Too close for comfort.

He was going to kill him. Right after they managed to advance their position and secure the helipad for the EVAC chopper.

Right after he eliminated every threat that kept him from finding Rose.

CHAPTER 24

*R*ose flattened herself against the wall, Taser pressed to her chest, and waited for the heavy boot steps to retreat down the hall. She'd made it down the main staircase, but then she had heard him coming, so she'd dashed into the alcove below the stairs and hidden between it and a massive bureau full of antiques.

There was no way to know how many of them could be in the manor house, but one thing was certain: she had to get to Headquarters. If she didn't get caught, maybe she could trade herself for Paige. She was sure Gavin would go for it.

Don't think about it.

All she had to do was go through the kitchen and out the back door, down the portico, through the gardens—where she could hide in shrubs if she had to—down the boardwalk and over to Headquarters.

This was a terrible idea. She swallowed over the lump in her throat. But there was no turning back now. This was her last chance to make everything right.

Somewhere upstairs, doors were being opened and slammed with force. But the henchman's footsteps disappeared down the main foyer to the opposite side of the building, toward the ballroom. Now was her chance.

She made a run for the kitchen, her heart skipping a beat when she realized it was empty. Thank God. Making a beeline for the backdoor, she heard the racket coming from outside. Was that a helicopter? And—she pressed her ear to the door—gunfire?

Hope flared in her chest. Had someone managed to call for help?

She smiled. She still had to get to Paige, though. Taking a breath, she tried to steel herself for the next part of this cockamamie scheme.

"What the fuck?" Gavin. Gavin's voice. Right on the other side of the door.

She stilled, her hand almost on the handle. Her heart stopped.

"Isn't this the lady you're looking for, boss?" Another sniveling male voice replied.

"No, you moron. I had to get Phil to guard that other bitch for *this?*"

Paige.

Move. She made herself tiptoe over to the nearby window. She ducked down low, then peeked out between the plantation shutters. A man stood directly in front of her. He was wiry, thin, and holding a gun against Katie's temple. *Katie.* Oh, no.

Just over the man's shoulder, she made out part of Gavin's profile. Then she looked down at her Taser. It wouldn't be enough to take on two men. And if she tried anyway, what would happen to Katie?

"You grabbed the wrong one," Gavin said. "How many women are on this goddamn island?"

"She's the only one I found so far—"

Gavin decked the man. She squeaked, covering her mouth. The gun didn't go off, though. The henchman still had Katie, who'd cried out. She was trembling.

Somewhere on this island, a battle was still going on.

She had to do something. Moving away from the window, she stood beside the backdoor, trying to push her nerves aside. *Focus, like Burke.*

"Our time is running out," Gavin barked. "Bring my woman to me in the next five minutes or I'm letting those assholes at the helipad have you."

"Yes, sir," The henchman mumbled. "What about her?"

"Take her inside."

The backdoor swung open, and she was face to face with Gavin's henchman. Their wide-eyed gazes fixed on each other.

Thinning brown hair. Ruddy skin. Bloodshot eyes. Rose lifted the Taser.

The man let go of Katie and wrenched it out of her grasp. *Shit.*

Her mind raced. Acting. That was the only thing that could save her and Katie now.

From over the man's shoulder, Gavin's square face and dark, evil expression filled her vision. Her spine turned to jelly even though all her muscles clenched. But with a willpower she hadn't known she had, she filled her expression with as much joy as she could muster.

"Gavin!" She raced past the man and threw her arms around him. He was a foot shorter than Burke and wider, his skin dry and hot. Putting her arms around him felt like embracing a dragon. Any second she'd be scorched. "What're you doing here? What's going on?"

She could tell she'd shocked him, because he went totally rigid.

Please, Katie, stay quiet. I'm trying to help.

When he pulled back from her, the tears in her eyes were real. Hopefully, he thought they were from relief, not the utter terror gripping her heart.

"You have to get me off this island," she rushed out. *Play the fool. Play the girlfriend, or this was it.* "These people are some kind of vigilantes. We're under attack!"

Gavin's thick lips pursed. "What the fuck are you doing here, Rose?"

She furrowed her brows. "They wanted to hire one of my bands to play in that outdoor ballroom there"—she nodded toward it—"so they flew me out here to look at the venue. But I think they're doing something illegal on this island, Gavin, because there are men with guns all over the place!"

Delay, delay, delay, until the authorities can make their way here.

"I *knew* you were on this goddamn island." Spittle flew from his twisted mouth. One hand grasped her upper arm, his fingers digging in so hard she wanted to wince.

"She had this, boss." The henchman handed him her Taser.

"Where'd you get this?"

"O-one of the people who works here handed it to me. What's going on, Gavin?"

He waved her Taser dismissively at his henchman. "Bring that bitch down to the dock, Hank. We're leaving."

She didn't dare glance at Katie, but she heard her whimpering as Hank walked her away, down the portico. Her heart sank. How would she save Katie now, when she was left alone with her worst nightmare?

"Why've you been avoiding me all this time?" Gavin demanded. "When I saw you at the grocery store, you got in your car and took off. You don't answer my calls, texts, emails. And you're happy to see me?"

She nodded vehemently. "Well, to be honest, you scared me for a while, Gavin. No one had hit me before. I mean, maybe I deserved it, but it still freaked me out, you know?" If she kept him talking, maybe he wouldn't drag her to the dock right away, too. How was she going to get her Taser back?

His dark eyes narrowed, and his hands dropped. But he was still crowding her. She wasn't going anywhere.

Taking a deep breath, he muttered, "I've been trying to apologize to you 'bout that."

He could take his apology and shove it up his ass. But it was an opportunity.

She gave a small smile. "I appreciate that. But these past months I found that I've been thinking about you. Missing your presence. You're so. . ."

Brutish. Disgusting. Evil. "Manly." For crying out loud. "When I saw you last at the grocery store, at first I thought, maybe? But then I got scared, because what I felt for you wasn't fear, Gavin. It was strong. Overpowering. I've never been in love before, but..." She tried to fill her gaze with as much feigned adoration as she could. "I wanted time to think about how to tell you what I feel. But I'm so glad you're here." She risked touching his hand, rubbed her thumb across it.

The sound of another engine caught her ears. Another helicopter was coming. Was Burke on one of them? Oh God, was he still alive? Was he here?

Gavin's gaze was scrutinizing, boring into her as if he were trying to read her mind.

"Are you here for me?" she asked. Whoever was coming on those helicopters could be getting closer, though. The shooting had subsided to only a few shots, which meant that either the rescuers were dead, or they were on their way to her. She had to let them know about Paige and Katie.

"Can you get me to safety?" she asked. "I don't know what's going on. We're all so scared." Could playing the dumb bimbo work?

"I *am* here for you, Rose." Gavin gestured away from his chest, her Taser in his hand. "I'll get you out of here, like you want, but first you tell me something." His features hardened. "What'd you know about the guy who runs this place?"

Her knees wobbled, but she couldn't look stunned. She couldn't think about Burke, so she plastered an innocent expression on her face. "The owner is a guy named Mr. Masters. He's a recluse who doesn't leave his master suite. A man named Lucien Roman hired me, and I think he works for Mr. Masters. Mr. Roman's the one who's been supervising my work." Where was Lucien? Charles? Were they even alive? She needed to move this along. "Can we talk about this later? Please? There's a lot of shooting going on."

He took her by the arm again. "We'll go when I say I'm ready," he hissed.

Damn. Overplayed it too much.

"Okay. You're right, I'm sorry." *Sorry I didn't get to stun your ass before you caught me.* "I'm just scared, Gavin. I'm glad you're here." That was partially true. If he was with her, he wasn't anywhere else, hurting anyone else.

His eyes flickered with that same unpredictable, maniacal glow. "Have you fucked anyone since me?"

She shook her head. "No. No, I swear, Gavin." This time, her fear was entirely genuine and it made acting effortless.

Help was on its way—if she lived beyond the next few seconds. She spared a glance at the Taser. She'd taken the safety off. It was armed and ready.

"There's only you, Gavin. Being with you has ruined me for anyone else." Maybe that was true, but all she needed to do was convince this asshole that it was a good thing, instead of the opposite that it truly was.

Gavin grasped her by the upper arm, his grip like an iron vice. He pulled her alongside of him. "Good. Time to get out of here."

No, time to go.

She grabbed his free hand and shoved the Taser into his crotch. A strangled scream burst from his mouth as his body jerked. He let her go, but topped over, right on top of her.

CHAPTER 25

"*T*hat was the last one," Burke told Lucien as he checked his gun and put a new clip in. Their exposed position by the helipad had been a disadvantage, but they'd finally taken out four of the henchmen. A minute ago, Charles had been able to go ahead of them, flanking the final shooter and running for the mansion via the beach. Now it was their turn.

"Go." He looked at Lucien. "Get to Headquarters and stay safe."

Lucien gave a quick nod and headed off through the trees, taking a shortcut.

Burke sprinted down the path leading to the manor house just as the other chopper began its descent to his island.

There was no pain in his leg. There was no throbbing ache in his shoulder. There was only Rose. Only his people that needed help. He would get them all off this island alive.

He rounded a bend in the trail. Thankfully there was enough moonlight to see where he was going.

A woman dressed in a blue buttoned-down shirt, embroidered jeans, dark hair fanning behind her— Rose appeared out of the dark forest far down the path, like a vision.

He gasped. Alive. She was alive, and right at the junction of The Overlook and helipad paths.

He opened his mouth, ready to call out to her.

She was tackled from behind, the two figures crashing to the ground. Graves. Even from here, he'd know that bastard's coloring and body type anywhere.

He ran faster. If he called out to her now, it would give away his position and Graves was close enough to use her as a human shield. They might lose the upper hand.

She somehow managed to roll away. What was in her hand?

Look up! He willed her. *See me!*

She stumbled to her feet and ran up the path to The Overlook.

He took aim at Graves and fired.

The bullet ricocheted off the stone wall a few inches behind his head. *Damn it.*

Rose had vanished, but Graves expertly got up, like the trained soldier he was, and chased after her.

He fired at him again, but it missed. Graves was too far away, and they'd disappeared. He had to gain ground on them before it was too late.

He bolted across the uneven ground, fueled by adrenaline and desperation.

Finally! He reached the pathway, sprinting up the rocky incline. He could hear them up ahead, their footsteps. Someone screamed. *Rose.* The sound twisted the invisible knife in his heart.

Moving as lightly over the black rock as possible and pushing through the overgrowth, he ran higher and higher. He was closing the gap. Any second now—

Their figures were up ahead, barely visible between the last few trees. Graves had her by the hair, then shoved her forward roughly.

"How can you fucking hurt me like this?" Graves raged at her, waving the gun in his hand.

He burst through the trees onto the small landing, his weapon pointed straight at Graves.

Rose's terror-filled eyes met his, and she ran for him. A shot rang out and she stopped, right in between them.

Scanning her body, he braced himself to see a blossom of blood from a bullet wound. But there was nothing. The asshole hadn't shot her. Nope, he was pointing the weapon at Burke instead.

They were locked in a standoff, neither of them with a clean shot because she was caught in the middle. The three of them were so close they were almost within arm's reach of each other.

He fixed a deadly glare at his enemy, fighting the overwhelming urge to open his arms to Rose and draw her away from him.

"Drop it," Graves barked, his fist tightening on the gun. His stance seemed a little off-centered, almost like he was injured, but it was hard to tell by looking around Rose. "Now!"

Quickly, he glanced at what Rose was holding. Her Taser.

"Don't, Graves. Let her go." Well, he sounded calmer than he felt, which was good, because his heart was racing at a damaging pace.

"She's coming with me. Throw it on the ground over there." Gavin jerked his chin to the area near the bench he'd sat on with Rose a week ago, near the rose bush. "Do it."

He didn't have a choice. His jaw clenched, but he did as Gavin said, leaving his hands up.

"Rose, get behind me," he said evenly. The other chopper was landing, sending gusts rushing at them like a gale. They were only medics on this one. Stalling would only prolong the danger to them, too.

He wanted his gun back, but even if he put every bullet in Graves, it wouldn't be nearly enough to satisfy the rage behind each shot.

"If you take a step in any direction but back to me, I'll kill him. Got it?" Graves shouted over the noise of the engine. But then he gave a bone-chilling grin. "I've been wanting to for years anyway. Don't tempt me. It's been too long coming, Masters."

Despite the wind whipping their clothes and hair, she didn't move, her wide-eyes holding onto his like a lifeline.

"The only thing we'll ever agree on, Graves." He inclined his head toward Rose. "Let her off this island and you can have me."

"No." She shook her head and went to take a step, but Graves's finger flinched. She halted.

Graves waved the gun. "I have both of you already. But Rose is *my* woman." His free hand went to his chest, his eyes glinting. "Did you fuck her, you deformed shithead? She told me she hasn't been with anyone, but then she stunned me with that thing, so I don't think I believe her anymore." He laughed, the sound malevolent and vile. "But she'll just have more to pay for when she makes it up to me. The only question is whether or not I let you live so you can watch us leave together."

In the moonlight, Rose's eyes filled with tears. "Gavin," she called, "please. If you let him leave, I'll go with you. I'll do anything."

No, no, no... "Rose—"

"Please."

Everything was spiraling out of control. Her body began to shake. She was pale, her eyes wide. *Shit.* Was this the start of a seizure, or sheer terror?

"It's me you want, and I'm here," he snarled. Hands in the air, every inch of his body was tensed to the breaking point. "Let's finish this, you and me."

She glanced at him, her hair flying like a halo around her. Her beautiful brown eyes held all the warmth, tenderness, and love he'd ever known, but they also reflected something else. Something inevitable.

A tear fell down her cheek.

"Finish this, you motherfucker." Graves aimed the gun at him.

Rose lunged in front of him, arms outstretched, her scream caught in her throat.

She fell into the rosebush. She'd taken the bullet.

"Rose!"

Shot. She'd been shot.

His heart stopped. His vision blacked out everywhere except her bloody abdomen, red like the roses around her. Near the ribs. She was gasping.

Petals flew up, surreally hanging in the air from the chopper's downdraft, before sailing over the edge of the cliff.

He looked up. Graves's unhinged eyes were wide as he lunged at him. They crashed onto the grass, struggling for the gun. His iron grip clamped around the bastard's wrist, locking the gun in his hand against the ground, only feet from the cliff's edge. Graves squeezed off another shot.

The medics. He had to get Rose to them.

Graves tried to knee him in the groin, but he evaded, landing a blow to his shoulder. The man howled. His own shoulder screamed in protest, but he twisted the gun away. Graves squeezed off another shot. It hit the dirt.

Roaring, Graves suddenly released the gun and head-butted him.

Stars burst behind his eyes. His skull felt like it'd cracked in two.

His abdomen caved as Graves landed another blow, throwing him off. They staggered to their feet, inches from the edge of the cliff, but he got a good angle on Graves's knee, so he kicked it. He followed it up with a punch, then a left cross.

Graves doubled over, so he widened his stance and lifted the asshole back up, wrapping his hands around his throat. Graves's hands dug into his arms as he flailed, his feet slipping on the wet grass as he started to sag.

"Gavin." Rose's voice was nearby. What? His head whipped around as his jaw dropped. She was standing right beside him, white as a ghost, her lips a dangerous shade of red, matching the hole in her stomach. How was she even upright?

Graves suddenly howled, his entire body jerking.

Rose had shoved her Taser into his chest. Her hand fell away limply. Graves's body jerked in his chokehold and he let him go, over the edge of the cliff. A scream followed him down. Gone, just like that.

Finally.

"I'm free," Rose whispered, collapsing.

He whirled around, throwing himself between her and the ground, catching her. He cradled her in his lap, his hand in her wound.

No. She couldn't die. Her face was contorted in agony, and his heart collapsed in on itself.

She gasped. Her wide eyes met his terrified ones.

"Rose. Oh, shit. Rose, stay with me," he pleaded, unzipping her jacket. She had to be okay. She had to live.

Voices drifted up from the path. The chopper had landed.

"Help!" he called, looking over his shoulder.

"B-bur—" Her voice failed.

He felt her neck for her pulse. It was slow, like her last ounces of energy were flowing from her with the blood. Her skin was damp and chilled.

"Is someone there? Does someone need medical attention?" an unfamiliar voice called from the path.

"Up here! Hurry!" he yelled back, never tearing his gaze from her. "Please, Rose. Hang on." He looked at her wound, frantically applying pressure, and felt the hot tears trail down his cheek.

"I love you." As the words died on his tongue, he was afraid she had, too.

CHAPTER 26

*B*urke stared out at the perfect blue waters of Puget Sound almost two months later, the afternoon sunlight creating a sea of sparkles around his island. He was waiting for the skiff with his heart in his throat.

Reaching down, he petted the head of the golden retriever sitting patiently at his feet, quiet except for his soft panting. The midday sun was bright, the temperature climbing steadily.

The serene setting was a complete contrast to his memories, stuck in those last chaotic moments of when he'd last seen Rose as she'd been wheeled down the hall of University of Washington Medical Center. She had been as white as the sheet covering her, completely unresponsive since the island. They hadn't been able to wake her on the EVAC chopper, her vital signs hanging by a thread the entire flight.

Besides a gash in Charles's leg, she'd been the only casualty.

If only the police officers hadn't been there when they had landed. It had taken three of them to tackle him to the ground… If only they hadn't stopped him from going with her.

But he'd resisted arrest. Of course they'd locked him up.

While Rose had been in a coma for twenty-eight agonizing days, he'd been behind bars. When the police realized they couldn't technically charge him for anything, they'd let him go, straight into "protective custody", where he got to answer never-ending questions from the FBI and ATF.

They'd only released him late last week, when Polly had a breakdown.

When Charles had first told him how Polly had collapsed, gone catatonic, his gut had hit the floor. Charles had begged him to do something. And he did.

He'd marched out of the hotel room, one of the agents pulling at his arm. Then he'd whirled around and threatened the biggest lawsuit against the United States Government in the modern era, and went to Polly.

The way he'd wanted to go to Rose, but couldn't.

They'd talked on the phone since she'd woken up, but he hadn't gotten to see her face-to-face yet. It was eating him alive. But she'd been in a special physical therapy facility in Olympia, watched over dutifully by Paige, and he'd had to wrap up the government inquiries and the legal fallout from the ambush. The one night he'd managed to get free, he'd even driven down to Olympia to see her, only to find out she and Paige were out. He'd had to return to the island the following day to oversee renovations.

West Cove had needed to be ready for today—for the wedding that was about to take place.

But knowing he hadn't been there when she had awoken had been like a knife to the heart. It still was.

Today would be a happy day, though. Lucien and Paige were getting married, and Rose was finally returning home.

Nope. Just... finally returning. He couldn't get ahead of himself.

Beside him, the dog looked in the same direction, letting out a light *yip*. He was a cute, happy fellow. They'd really bonded this past week. He pet him again.

There she was.

A boat made its way straight to his island.

His heart hit the floor. He swallowed hard over the lump in his throat, grateful Paige had let him meet her alone.

He'd known Rose was coming, but until this moment, maybe he hadn't really believed it to be true. Too many things had kept them apart since she'd taken a bullet for him and watched Graves die.

Beside him, the dog stood up, his tail wagging eagerly and his ears lifting as she approached.

The skiff came closer, and he saw her clearly for the first time in months. She stood, her back straight but her shoulders pulled forward, wringing her hands. Her long brown hair was loose around her shoulders, and she wore a slender, floor-length gold dress with single straps, nipped in slightly at the waist, embroidered but simple white roses on one side of the deep V-neckline.

She was an absolute vision.

He blinked hard. The stinging in his eyes was from the salty sea air, though.

When she came even closer, he saw her biting her lip. She must have seen him notice her mouth, though, because she stopped, and her wide eyes met his.

And his heart ripped right out of his chest and flew over to her.

The driver cut the engine as the boat sidled up to the pier. Breathing deeply, he held his hand out to her to help her disembark.

She hesitated a moment, then put her hand in his.

"Hello." His voice was raspy and strained, but hell, he was just happy he was coherent at this point.

"Hello," she said softly. Her gaze traveled over him, head to toe, and he felt almost giddy when he saw her draw in a breath.

He was already in his tux.

"You look... well, Burke."

"You look—" *Perfect. Like my dream come true.* "Ready for a wedding," he finished.

"It's so silly that I'm nervous."

About being Paige's maid of honor, or being with him again?

She looked down at the golden retriever pushing his wet nose into her hand. Smiling, she rubbed the top of his head. "Who's this?"

Right now, he was envious of a *dog*. "Maurice."

The smile turned into a grin. "You got a dog?"

Boy, he hoped this went well. "He's for you, actually."

Her eyes went wide.

He shifted his weight. "I read about dogs that can be trained to help predict seizure activity. He's from an organization that specializes in placing dogs with people who suffer from them."

A strong breeze blew over them, and she shivered, pulling Maurice closer to her. By the way she kept touching him, he could tell she liked him.

Those beautiful, chocolate brown eyes filled with tears. Well, that wasn't good.

"Are you all right?" Was there a complication with her epilepsy? With the bullet wound?

"Burke." His name came out as a whisper, but then she smiled, like the sun breaking through clouds. "I love him, thank you."

He took her cold, clammy hands in his. Touching her again sent lightning bolts racing through his veins. "You're welcome. More than welcome. There isn't anything I wouldn't do for you."

"I know," she said quietly. "I feel the same for you."

Yeah, he remembered. She took a bullet for him. Frowning hard, he let go of her and leaned down to the boat to grab her suitcase—and to get rid of their audience.

"Well, I can start by getting your bags for you," he told her.

The burley middle-aged man held it up for him, and he took it, setting it on the dock. That was it. She wasn't planning on staying, then.

"Thanks, Fred." She waved to him. "I'm good to go."

Fred nodded, jetted the engine and took off.

He waited until she met his gaze. "One bag?" He'd tried not to sound judgmental or disappointed. He really tried.

Shifting her weight, she glanced down at Maurice again. "I, ah, wasn't sure. I didn't want to assume anything." Her gaze came up to his. "You didn't mention anything about me staying after the wedding the last time we talked, so I just didn't know. I'd hoped—"

"You know I want you with me." He hadn't said it because he hadn't thought he'd have to. How could she have doubted it? "I want you to have everything and anything I am. You make me the happiest man on earth, and all I want is for you to feel the same."

A single tear fell from one of her glistening eyes. Her shoulders eased.

"I do. You have no idea how much I do." She breathed rapidly, lightly, a blush staining her cheeks. "Are you sure? We've only spent a week together. After everything that happened with Gavin—"

"I won't ask for you to change your life for me, Rose." He shook his head. "If you need to recover from what that bastard did, or to let yourself love again, I'll wait." He lifted his chin. "My feelings won't change." He was as sure of it as the sun rising in the east.

"'Love again'?" She tilted her head. "I've thought about you every minute of every day. You have no idea how much I love you." She placed a hand on her heart, her gaze falling. "My God, Burke, I feel like I can't breathe without you. One look from you makes me shiver all the way down to my toes. Within a matter of days coming here, I suddenly couldn't picture a future for myself without you in it." She paused.

Maybe she heard his heart exploding with joy? For the first time in ages, he felt hopeful, because he could see that hope in her eyes. It lit him up.

"I can't live without you." Her voice broke. "You're the only one who kept me going. The reason I woke up."

She loved him, she wanted to be with him, she loved him.

It was all that mattered.

He smiled. "I feel the same, Rose. You have no idea how much."

She grabbed the lapel of his suit and tugged. He went willingly, her mouth meeting his.

Christ, he'd almost, *almost* forgotten how perfect she tasted. Like strawberries and sunshine. She deepened their kiss.

A helpless groan rumbled in his chest as he kissed her back more intently, every ounce of passion, the anguish of the past weeks and desperation driving his need. His hands went around her back as he bent himself into her, her breasts against the wall of his chest, her hips angled into him.

Beside them, Maurice let out a cheerful bark.

They needed to stop. Now. Before he discarded her of her gorgeous gold dress here on the pier.

She pulled back. He opened his eyes to see so much love and devotion pouring forth from her gaze that it left him breathless.

"I'm yours, too. Always." She laughed and ruffled the dog's ears. "I mean, who else would be thoughtful enough to get me my new baby boy?"

He threw his arms around her, holding her to him with bone-crushing strength, and she held him back with equal measure.

Staying like this all day would be just fine with him, but duty was calling.

"I missed how I feel when I'm with you," he murmured, pulling back.

She smiled up at him. "How's that?"

He grinned. "Like the superhero I think I was secretly trying to be." He touched the side of her face. "But it's been you all along. Thank you for saving me."

What would it be like to stand in front of an altar with her and vow to love each other and give their lives to the other? To know that he would be by her side every day, sitting next to her on the couch, waking up with her in his arms, to know her every touch, every smile, read her every reaction, bring her joy, peace, happiness? He wanted it, always.

He wanted to marry her.

She shook her head and touched the side of his face. "It's mutual, trust me." She sighed and looked back at the mansion, a contentedness in her expression.

Another time soon. When it wasn't Lucien and Paige's day, he would ask her for the honor to have their own.

She took his hand in hers, pulling him close as they walked down the pier. "Time to celebrate the love of our favorite happy couple."

Bringing their joined hands to his lips, he kissed her knuckles, relishing the feel of her body pressed against his. He grinned. "Tale as old as time, my love."

THE END

ABOUT THE AUTHOR

Emily Allen West writes romantic suspense and heart-pounding thrillers with a love story. She can usually be found in an office of some kind during the weekday and packing everything else that still needs to happen into a weekend. She copes by listening to music, coming up with ways to put her characters through the ringer and delivering high emotional stakes for you and me to read. She enjoys the company of family and friends, an occasional glass of wine, and lives with her puppy in the land of 10,000 lakes.

Find out more about Emily Allen West at www.emilyallenwest.com.

EXCALIBUR

EMERALD DODGE

Proofreading by Patrycja Pakula for Holabird Editing

What is freedom without love?

Heather Harris, a San Diego superhero known as the mighty Excalibur, has a problem: she's been ordered to return home to face punishment for someone else's failures. If she doesn't, her entire team--known locally as The Beasts-- will be targeted by a strike team, so she's determined to make the sacrifice for their sake. But her leader, Eleazar, refuses to let her go. The race is on to find an alternative that both saves Heather and allows the team to escape unscathed.

With the clock ticking down to an uncertain fate, Heather and her teammate Courtney strike a desperate deal with Alejandro, leader of a gang known as Las Bellas. Alejandro agrees to help the team fake their deaths and flee to Mexico in exchange for the credit of supposedly killing the team. Little does she know that Las Bellas have secrets and an agenda of their own--and a man determined to win her love.

When swords are crossed and guns drawn, Heather realizes that leaving San Diego behind means leaving behind the man who has captured her heart. Forced to choose between freedom and love, will Heather choose her heart or her team's life--and her own?

Genre: Superhero Fantasy
Heat level: Sweet

CHAPTER 1

03AUG – 1994 – That lame time of day when soap operas are off, but prime time hasn't started yet, so it's mostly just kids' shows.

The chalk outline of the corpse was still visible on the sidewalk. Talk about a mood killer.

There was never enough rain in San Diego to wash away the evidence of recent violence—not the chalk, not the bloodstains on the faded gray blacktop roads, not the occasional bullet casing in the gutter. No, the August sun beat down relentlessly on us, fading everything its rays touched: the grass, the stains, the torn shingles on our roof, and even the blue USPS uniform our mailman, Jorge, wore as he walked up and down the cracked and uneven sidewalks of the barrio we all called home.

I waved to Jorge as he approached. "Hey, there!"

He readjusted his enormous letter sack and reached into it. "Warm afternoon, isn't it, Miss Excalibur? Shouldn't you be inside doing...superhero things?" He produced a thick wad of mail for me. "There's two sacks down at the post office, by the way. We scanned them. No bombs or powder."

"Aw, not even ricin?" I murmured as I flipped through the junk mail, or what I figured was junk mail. "It's like the criminals around here don't even care. The Atlanta team gets it all the time."

Jorge looked pointedly at the chalk outline by the mailbox. "He cared."

"That was actually a drive-by," I said, leaning on the mailbox and then immediately jumping back, my arm stinging from where it had touched the metal. "The police don't think it had anything to do with us, though you'd laugh to see how we all hit the ground the second we heard shots. Some of us were watching television, and we didn't even turn down the volume." I reached the end of the pile and frowned. "Oh. It's...not here."

"It?" Jorge asked, fighting a smile. "Are you waiting for something special?"

"Um, no," I said, blushing. "Don't worry. Thanks, Jorge."

"Actually, let me check my sack again." He smiled so wide that his laugh lines appeared. He reached into his sack and pulled out a small white envelope. "Silly me."

"You're mean!"

"Let an old man have his fun." He handed me the letter with a flourish. "Happy reading, Miss Excalibur," he said, pointing to the same words on the envelope.

I pressed the letter to my chest, unable to keep my sappy smile off my face. "How's Leticia? Juanmi? Is he all better from the flu?"

"Leticia is doing well. Juanmi is recovered and back running around with his silly friends. I'll tell them you said hello."

"Do that, please. Thanks for everything, Jorge."

Jorge continued to stroll down the street, whistling without a care in the world as he delivered his mail. I envied his carefree job. While walking for hours every day in the summer sun couldn't have been the easiest career, it beat my life: a superhero caught in a losing war with the gangs of south San Diego. Woohoo. We'd even earned ourselves a dumb local moniker: Las Bestias.

Well, it wasn't entirely hellish. The flowers were nice.

I idly stroked the velvety petals of one of the roses on the bush by the front steps. My teammate Courtney had planted it in her bid to make our house prettier, and in the soft embrace of the California climate, it had flourished. A butterfly flitted past my face as it jumped around each soft red bloom alongside fat bumblebees. The sweet perfume from the bush filled our entire yard; I'd have to open the window when I returned to the house. Having grown up in central Georgia, I still marveled at the concept of enjoying the summer air during the day.

A glassy glimmer amongst the thick leaves made me blink, then mutter darkly to myself. Not *again*. I plucked out the little glass jar that had been placed in the bush and held it up to get a better look. A tiny figurine of a hooded and cloaked skeleton swam in—oh, yuck—human waste. Urine-soaked bits of paper inside bore scratched curses. There must've been something toxic on the jar, too; every leaf that it had touched was already browning.

I chucked the jarred "curse" into the metal trash can by the side of the house. "Nice try, lady," I muttered to the witch who'd undoubtedly created the macabre present. A nearby bodega was run by an ancient woman known only as Ágata—unless you needed a good hex or curse. In that case, she was La Bruja, a practitioner of *brujería*, or witchcraft.

I recognized the skeletal figure as Santa Muerte, the disgusting patroness of criminals, thieves, gangsters, and other denizens of the underworld. According to our informants, she was frequently invoked against us. I kicked the trash can and spit into it for good measure, and if Santa Muerte ever showed up in person to throw down, I mentally promised to kick her ass, too.

At the violent thought, energy swirled in my arm, aching for release. I took a deep breath and summoned it back. *Calm. Peace. Don't get worked up. Calm. Peace.*

When I was back in the house, I hurried into the living room. "Minnie, can you—"

Morris banged the side of the television, his black curls bouncing from the effort. "Work, dang it!"

The screen wavered, the suggestion of a picture appearing for a fraction of a second before the entire screen went dark with a *beeoop* sound. There was a pause, and then the rabbit ears fell off.

I crossed my arms. "I'm going to borrow Minnie for a minute. If that television isn't fixed when we get back, I am going to *kill* you. That TV is the only thing around here keeping me sane."

Morris turned his unimpressed icy blue eyes onto me. "Aw, no love for me?"

"Morris, if I had to choose between you and a Fanta, I'd choose the soda."

We glared at each other, but then I winked. He grinned and went back to fixing the television.

Minnie put her feet up on the coffee table and looked over the top of her newspaper as she said, "What's up, girlfriend?"

"My letter came!" I held up the envelope. "Can you...?"

"Oh, yeah," she said, immediately folding her paper and tossing it on the table before jumping to her feet. The headline was written in unusually large, bold letters. I pointed to them, and she leaned in and whispered, "The headline says 'budget cuts loom.' The article talks about how the city is in financial crisis."

I shrugged. That was unfortunate, but superhero teams were necessary to the wellbeing of the city. We were okay.

When we were in the kitchen, I perched on the table and tore open my fan letter with shaking fingers. Every month *he* wrote to me, and every month his letter was the highlight of that week. If only I could write back, though; my admirer had never identified himself beyond signing his letters "Your Faithful Servant," as if he were a hero in one of the books everyone seemed addicted to. And of course, there was the *other* reason I couldn't write back.

Minnie held out her hand. "Here," she said kindly. "Let me."

She began to read the letter aloud. The contents were much the same as the others, a long page of praises for my beauty and charms, appreciative things people had said about my team and me, and thanks for defending people from criminals.

"I'm sure you must be wondering who I am—"

"Uh, yeah," I grumbled to myself.

"—but please understand that I know superheroes and civilians can never date, so it's best if I admire you from afar—though what I feel for you is more than admiration. I'll never forget the day that you saved my best friend from being hit by a car. That was when I saw you up close for the first time. You spoke so gently to him, and I could see how beautiful your brown eyes are. You remind me of the warrior goddesses in Greek myths, both strong and lovely. I've talked to my friends about you, and they say that you can be really tough and fierce when you fight the gangs. But I think that's a façade. I think the real Excalibur is the woman who held my friend and told him that he was safe."

I had to blink several times. I'd saved so many people from getting hit by cars in the last year that I couldn't recall which particular incident he was referring to.

"Aw, your fan even got your buck teeth right," Minnie said. "Talk about dedication to details."

"What?"

"Check out the back." She handed the letter to me.

I flipped over the notebook paper and startled. The sender had meticulously sketched my likeness, taking care to replicate the way my bangs curled slightly, the slightly-squished shape of my face, my perma-pouty lips, and oh yes, my crooked front teeth. Even the noticeable darn in my cloth mask was there.

As I traced a finger over the pencil lines, imagining a sketching pencil in my hand, I couldn't help but feel that the artist had drawn those features with utmost tenderness. He'd recalled my features with love, no doubt wishing he were drawing from life instead of memory, imagining that I could speak to him and tell him about my many adventures.

But then again, if I were there to speak with him, he'd quickly find out some of my unsavory attributes. He'd find out I was raised in a cult. That I was just nineteen. That I was a truly terrible hand-to-hand combatant.

That I was unable to read his letters myself.

I slipped the paper back into its envelope, then walked back into the living room and threw myself back into my chair, staring up at the cracked ceiling. Though Morris had indeed gotten the television back in working order—*Full House* was playing now—I couldn't enjoy the show.

I was so trapped. We could not leave this broken-down house in the heart of a shot-up slum. We could not apply for better lodgings; this is what the city gave us, so this is what we had. We could not leave San Diego. We could not drive to Coronado and hang out on the pier. I couldn't even disappear into a book for hours at a time like Courtney and the others so often did. On top of it all, now that I'd dumped Eleazar, the team leader, I couldn't even spend time with a special someone to distract myself.

My Faithful Servant was the only sunny spot on my horizon, and he never bothered to put a return address.

While I stewed in my unhappiness, the shadow cast by the living room sofa wavered, then darkened, taking on the appearance of an oil spill. A liquidy black figure of a man rose and shimmered as his proper features appeared, the jet-blackness lightening to freckled pale skin, nondescript brown hair, and an unshaven jaw. My teammate Armando stepped out of the shadow, which went back to just being a dark spot on the carpet.

"If you couldn't take the time to walk down the stairs, this must be important," Minnie said. "What's up?"

Armando glanced at Morris and Minnie, then turned his deep brown eyes to me. "Eleazar needs you," he said quietly. "Right now. Try to talk some sense into him, will you?"

I was halfway up the stairs before anyone could ask. Eleazar had been in a low mood for months, what with all that was happening in the city government and the budget difficulties, but what could've happened now? And why did he want to talk to *me* specifically? At least, why me before the rest of the team? We'd broken up two weeks ago.

Before I visited Eleazar, I dashed into my room and stowed the letter with the others in my bedside drawer. I couldn't read them, but I loved to hold each letter and breathe in the pencil smell.

A minute later, I sucked in a nervous breath and entered the office. My emotions made my secondary power prickle, and foreknowledge swept through my brain: shouting, unhappiness. I'd have to navigate these waters carefully. We'd agreed that our breakup wouldn't affect our professionalism, but...still...

Eleazar stood at the open window, his hands in his pockets. He didn't turn to greet me, nor even acknowledge that I was there. I could see his face reflected in the windowpane: pale, lined, despondent, but always handsome.

I shut the door. "El," I said. "What's wrong?" Eleazar turned, and I gasped. His red eyes betrayed recent tears. "Talk to me," I whispered.

"I just got off the phone with the mayor's office," he said, his voice a broken echo of its former strength. "The council has decided that the team is too large and a drain on the city budget. I have to send one member of the team back to the camps. I have until the end of the month to get affairs in order."

There was a hard silence. "Oh," I finally breathed.

Back to the camps—more like back to prison. The elders would not look kindly on the person who had to return to the camps in disgrace, since if that person had served as they were supposed to, San Diego wouldn't ever vote to get rid of them. Or so the logic went. The elders, we'd all come to understand, had a tenuous grip on reality, if any.

But the elders also held the means to punish, and there *would* be punishments. They'd be public and memorable, a warning to all future superheroes of what would happen if they were ever sent back to the camps in similar circumstances.

Calm. Peace. Keep calm.

Eleazar closed his eyes. "I can't do it. I...I can't do it, Heather. I never wanted this responsibility and now someone will be flogged. I'm the leader, our team's failure to serve the city adequately is on me, and I..."

I pushed away and raised my hand to his cheek, then thought better of it, opting instead for his shoulder. "That's garbage, and you know it." My voice was a lot more even than I felt. "We're the best thing to ever happen to San Diego. Crime has gone down. Half the gangs have broken up. Hell, even teen pregnancy is on the wane." I tried for a coy smile. "I bet all the civilian girls broke up with their boyfriends when you came to town," I said. "Once they saw what a real man was."

Eleazar gazed into my eyes for several seconds. "You're too kind."

The intimacy of the eye contact was uncomfortable. "I'll help you work through this. Maybe you don't have to decide. We can draw straws, and then that way fate is the bad guy, not you."

A shadow passed behind his eyes. "It's not that simple. I still have some thinking to do, but already I'm clearer-headed. Seeing you was what I needed."

Hidden meaning lurked in his words, but my premonitions didn't activate to tell me what it might be. "What do you mean? Armando told me to 'talk some sense' into you a few minutes ago. What are you thinking about?"

He turned away again, looking back at the window. "I *was* thinking about turning myself into the elders and confessing to dereliction of duty. If the elders believe that I'd consciously and deliberately misled the team, it would let you off the hook."

"They'll kill you for that!" Was he out of his mind?

He pinched the bridge of his nose. "Yes, I know. Armando ripped that to shreds, and besides, I'd have no guarantee that you'd end up safe. When teams fail, they're sometimes broken up and distributed around the country to *better* leaders," he said with a sneer. "You could easily be assigned to serve under some brainwashed, power-hungry sicko...or...or sent to retirement in

Virginia...or..." He began to breathe heavily. "No. I can't leave it up to chance."

"Then you send home one of us," I said, swallowing. "Our lives aren't easy, nor are they fair. I would've thought that that was abundantly clear by now."

He turned around again, stricken. "You don't understand. I *can't.*"

"Then we run. We pack bags and we run. It's a big country. They can't—"

"Have you ever seen a strike team in action?" His words were cold and sharp. "No, you're just nineteen, of course you haven't. But I have. My aunt is on one, Heather. They're unstoppable. We're trained to fight muggers and rapists. They're trained to fight us. There is nowhere we could go where they won't follow."

"I've seen a strike team," I said, quivering. "Don't treat me like an idiot. My niece, Ember, is being evaluated for eligibility this year, in fact." I took a breath. "I'm prepared for that. I can fight." I held out my hand and summoned my main, more spectacular power. Emotion converged, taking shape. Yellow and white sparkles appeared in my palm, solidifying...

He shoved my hand down and the sparkles disappeared. "Your niece could very well be the one that eventually finds us. She's a telepath, right? I'd be shocked if she doesn't end up on a strike team."

"She's two, El."

"She won't be two forever, and when she's old enough to be on the strike team, she'll have had years of listening to stories about her evil aunt who needs to be destroyed."

"You don't even know if—"

"If not her, then someone else! An entire team! Two teams, three teams! We can't run!"

Knowing the shouting was coming didn't make it less unpleasant.

He stormed out of the office, leaving me standing by the window. I knew better than to follow; the shouting was new, but he'd always been prone to shutting down under the stress of his position.

It was why we'd broken up. He'd been Mr. Leader 100% of the time...and Mr. Boyfriend 0% of the time. On top of that, being around a hulking mood monster wasn't good for my power continence. Even right now, I was already perilously close to failing. I'd had two near-accidents in the last half hour—a full-blown episode was probably around the corner, and there was little I could do to prevent it except continue my breathing exercises and try not to get worked up about anything.

Good luck to me. Someone was going back to the camps to be flogged, then probably sent to another team.

I breathed in through my nose and out through my mouth, then walked out of the office and down the hall to Courtney and Minnie's room. I raised my fist to knock on the door.

"Come in, Heather," Courtney said in her distinctive New York accent before my knuckles touched the door. No doubt she'd heard me.

My whole team, sans Eleazar, were in the small bedroom. Courtney and Minnie were laid out on one of the beds, while Morris and Armando sat on the other.

I took my place on the edge of the designated lady bed and clasped my hands in front of me. "I take it we're all waiting for El, now." Their expressions told me that they'd heard the news. Courtney was nervously unbraiding and rebraiding her long, black hair.

"Any luck?" Armando asked. "Or is he still stuck on the martyr plan?"

"No, he's moved past that," I said, blowing out a breath. "And there's no hope of us running, either."

Minnie cracked her knuckles. "Okay, real talk. Which one of us is going home? If it comes to it, I'll volunteer. My mom was born into St. James, and that's an elder line. I'll probably get a light lashing, if any at all."

"Good God," Morris said, jumping up from his chair. "Can you hear yourself? Why are any of us acting like the elders are a legitimate authority anymore?" Minnie opened her mouth to argue, but Morris shook his head. "Can it, Min. You might be the most sarcastic bastard I've ever met, but over my dead body are you getting flogged."

Minnie turned pink. "Well, if you feel that strongly about it. Keep your shirt on."

Morris scowled. "We all feel that strongly," he said. "Nobody is allowed to discuss self-sacrifice in front of me. It's not an option. Armando, you're SIC. Back me up."

Armando massaged his temples. "Okay, fine, you're all ordered to be positive. But I do think we need to start making contingency plans. There's a real possibility that this is just the beginning for us. First one person, then another, and then suddenly the whole team will be dismantled. We need to prepare to, uh, *unlearn* a few things. No television, no books, no music."

"Books aren't an issue for me," I muttered. "But yeah. No pretty civilian clothes, no equality." I'd taken to life outside the camps' control like a fish to water. I couldn't imagine suffocating again.

Courtney let out a delicate sigh. "I can't return to pretending that my mind hasn't been permanently altered by what I've experienced here. Pretending that the principles are the source of heroism will be impossible when I've read about Eowyn and Meg Murry—and seen Princess Leia! Sometimes I have to pretend I'm a member of the Rohirrim just to get excited about patrol." She threw herself on her back. "Life without fantasy was so meaningless. I could just die."

There was a long silence while we all stared at her.

I turned to the others. "*Anyway.*"

"I can't go back to life without grunge," Minnie said, wringing her hands. She pointed to her elbow-length box braids, which she'd roped together to make one large thick braid. "Do you know that some leaders make their female teammates curl their hair to be more beautiful? My sister says that she has to wear a Wonderbra because it makes civilians like her more. Nobody gives a crap what *she* thinks is pretty, or that we wear sports bras for a reason."

Beneath Minnie's seemingly vain complaint was a thread of truth: if we went to different teams, all of our progress would be wiped clean and we'd be mindless peons of the camps again, in behavior and appearance. Moreover, we'd have to empty our brains of everything we'd ever learned about the civilian world, including the idea of young women having any degree of free agency.

Armando nodded along, sober. "Minnie raises a very material point. If we go back to the camps, or to other teams, several of us may face compromising situations. I myself confess that I struggle with our appearance standards even now. I can't imagine going to another team." He touched his attractive, highly-forbidden scruff. "And frankly, it goes against my personal ethics to knowingly let my friends go to other teams where someone might dictate what underwear they don, especially my female friends. That's beyond inappropriate."

A premonition surged over my brain: *Guns. Fear. "Pendejo!"*

I mentally swept it aside. If someone was getting called a *pendejo*, the forewarning didn't concern me, only someone near me who was arguing with a Spanish-speaker. Since we lived in a neighborhood that was almost entirely Mexican, that could've been anybody.

Courtney sat up. "We're about to have company." She turned her sensitive ears towards the door.

"On your feet," Armando said.

We all obeyed, jumping to loose attention as Eleazar entered the room.

"Please don't do that," he said, exhausted. "How many times do I have to ask?"

"Always just one more," Morris said, his face uncharacteristically kind. "What's the verdict, fearless leader? Who's going home?"

Eleazar took a deep breath and then said, "Heather."

All eyes turned to me.

My back prickled as if a ghostly lash was already tearing the skin off. "I see," I said, covering my mouth. Of course it was me; I'd broken up with him. Who else would he have chosen?

Minnie and Morris stood at the same time, their faces identical masks of hard judgment.

"Why Heather?" Morris asked, his tone laced with suspicion. "She's got two powers. Simple math says it should be someone else."

"You're not stupid," Minnie added. "You know how this looks. You guys break up two weeks ago and suddenly she's on the way home to the pillory?"

Eleazar looked at me, stricken. "It's procedure. I'm so sorry. The rule is that when something like this happens, the newest member of the team goes back. It's not personal, Heather, I swear. I..." He held out his arms for me. "Please."

But Minnie pulled me into her embrace, hiding my face in her neck. "Save your sorry and *fix this*, El."

The strike team plan was sounding better and better—at least our deaths would be quick. *No, stop that.* I chided myself for my cowardice. *Whatever comes, you will face it with courage and calm.* A few seconds passed, but I didn't experience a power surge. The danger zone had passed. I let go of Minnie and took my place again, this time determined to stay strong.

Eleazar sat on the bed, defeated. "So, yeah. I have to send home my Heather to be whipped for my failures." His eyes took on the glazed, lifeless appearance I knew so well; he was shutting down again under the stress.

However, a breeze ruffled my hair, despite us being in a sealed room. I grabbed Eleazar's hand. "Take it easy," I hissed. "Keep it under control. If I can, you can, too."

"Okay, you know what?" Morris said, his scowl deepening. "There are two godforsaken teams in this city. Let's get the north San Diego gang on the horn and figure something out. Joey Nussbaum and Sapphire Calhoun joined their crew only, what, two months ago? Let *them* go back to the freaking camps."

Eleazar cleared his throat with sarcastic delicacy. "It is the...*feeling* in the city council that the north San Diego team is more necessary to the city's operation and tourism industry than the south San Diego team, since we're confined to the barrio and they're zoned in the more developed areas."

"So, basically, screw the Mexicans in the slums and the superheroes who protect them," Minnie said flatly.

Eleazar nodded. "And their little dog, too." Some emotion flooded back into his face. "Yeah, that's...that was, uh, the *gist* of that phone call. If Heather doesn't report home by the end of the month, we're all going. Damned if we do, damned if we don't."

Minnie sank onto the bed, blinking repeatedly. "Well. That's...well, that's just..."

I'd never thought I'd see the great Dreadnought robbed of speech.

Morris sat down next to Minnie, paused, and then put his arm around her shoulders. She didn't even acknowledge that she knew he was there. As usual, her line about being in an elder line had been hot air, like most of what she said.

Morris looked up at Eleazar, his eyes bright with grief. "What are our options?"

Minnie raised her hand a little. "I, um, I have a suggestion. It's not a great one, but..."

Eleazar held out a hand. "Anything can go on the table at this point."

Minnie bit her lip and unsheathed her combat knife, which gleamed ominously in the light from the window. "If Heather is definitely staying, and we are definitely not going back to the camps, then we're going to have to fight a strike team, right? That's not a nice death. But...I can put you all in a trance. You wouldn't feel a thing."

Beneath the caked-on black lipstick and kohl, the real Minnie shone through: scared and small, lost in fear of the unknown.

"Put that away," Eleazar said, though not unkindly. "It hasn't quite come to that, yet."

Minnie looked relieved.

Courtney sprinted to the window. "Guys! Code three! Diablos!"

Code three—an altercation with a gun. All of us bolted for the door at the same time.

Two guns shots pierced the air.

Courtney bowed her head, shaking it in disappointment. "End mission. Fight's over. I've never seen an altercation go south that quick."

The world tilted, shouts of alarm and bright colors of Courtney's Tiger Beat posters swirling down a mental drain. Far in the recesses of my mind, the pain from falling to the floor collided with the sensation of warm arms around me.

An arid and threatening desert spread out underneath my feet like a shaken rug, flies and buzzards swarming around me. Fanning out on both sides of me stood four of my teammates. I sensed another one behind me. Ahead of us, a coyote led the way. The scent of decay and despair filled my nostrils, making me cover my nose. The blazing sun high above divided, then divided again, and then again, repeating the division until fourteen suns burned. I turned to look behind me, but my fifth teammate had been replaced by a figure in black, hooded, their face in shadow. The figure stood on the other side of a great river. They could not follow.

Beneath it all, a word: *south.*

"Heather! Heather, can you hear me?"

My eyes were already open. Faces swam in my normal vision until they sharpened. My team had lifted me onto a bed. Eleazar patted my cheek with one hand while his other produced a cool breeze for my face. "I swear to God, I can never tell if you're having a vision or a seizure."

I sat up, fighting the urge to vomit.

"What did you see?" Courtney asked, kneeling next to me. "Did you see something about the fight? The gangs?"

"South," I croaked, still able to smell the scent of rotting corpse. Why was that still present? "Go south."

"What do you mean?" Eleazar asked, cocking his head.

I let out a long breath. "I mean I saw a vision of how we'd escape the strike team." I pointed out the window. Beyond the edges of the barrio, the shanties and tenements of Tijuana, Mexico beckoned. "We have to go south."

CHAPTER 2

03AUG – **Dinnertime because I didn't like anything in the television lineup.**

I stirred my glass of Nesquik, determined to get rid of the chalky little lumps. *C'mon...one more...die, you powdery little booger...*

"Let me make sure I've got this," Morris said as he took a bite of his Hot Pocket. "We were all running south from a member of a strike team, and there were dead people everywhere?" He leaned against the kitchen counter and chewed thoughtfully. "That's not exactly promising."

"I never said dead people," I replied, trying to keep the annoyance out of my tone. We'd been over the vision only a million times in the last few hours. Even Eleazar had stopped asking me questions. "Just the scent of death. You know, with flies and stuff. And fourteen suns, for fourteen days. We'll skip town before the seventeenth."

"I'm on board with the fourteen days thing, since that's obvious. But how did you know the scent of death was from a real person? Maybe it was a dead dog or something."

"Morris, how do I have visions of crap that's going to happen in the future? I just do, okay? Stop deconstructing them and just be happy that you've got a Magic Eight Ball for a teammate."

He rolled his eyes. "Quit buggin' and see the bigger picture."

"I did see the big picture. In a vision."

"What I mean is, see the bigger problem. Which teammate was behind you? Why were they behind you? And how are we going to get away from Mr.

Big Bad Strike Team Guy? You know, the one across the," he set down his snack and made air quotes, "'freaking huge river.'"

"I'm *working on it!*"

I hadn't meant to shout, but my words rang around the room. Thankfully, only Courtney was home, upstairs reading on her bed.

Morris winced. "There's no need to—"

"Obviously there is! I've been telling you for hours everything that I saw, and that I don't really know what it means, and yes, there's death and decay and the strike team—"

Morris sighed, waving away my words. "I'm sorry," he said. "I just want to know what's coming. It makes me feel like I'm more in control. Speaking of which, you're sparkling."

I threw up my hands in disgust, one of which was indeed producing little bits of light. I turned my back to him and began to count to ten in Spanish as a distraction.

"Pardon me for interrupting," Courtney said from the doorway, "But it's time for us to go out. Also, Morris, don't lie to her." She put some dirty dishes in the sink. "That's not what you told me."

Morris shot Courtney a furious look. "What are you...that was a private conversation."

She put her hands on her hips and turned to me. "Morris keeps pumping you for information because he wants to go out in a blaze of glory with the strike team. He's hoping he'll be the dead person from your vision."

Morris's mouth dropped open. "I didn't say that!"

Courtney pointed to the clock. "You're overdue for patrol."

Morris stormed out without another word.

Courtney began to fill up our plastic water bottles. I rudely grabbed mine from her hand, hoping the aggravation came through. "That wasn't nice."

"Lying to you isn't nice, either, especially when he's planning a suicide mission."

"Why on earth would he—"

"Because he's a *Monroe*. You know, the cursed family? Morris's dad was on Battlecry's team, the one that got murdered years ago. Then his sister Lisette got killed by the Westerners. Every Monroe has either been killed in service, or at least died young. He's determined to, shall we say, live up to his family legacy." She waggled her eyebrows at me. "He thinks that if he's cursed to die, then at least he'll control how it happens."

I crossed my arms. "Cursed? You sound like La Bruja."

She shrugged and took a sip of her water. "Hey, I'm not the only one. He told me a few months ago that before he was put into service, he was courting this one chick, Gemma. Turns out that Gemma's parents believe in the curse, and her dad said she couldn't marry him because of it. Gemma ended up marrying one of Minnie's cousins, some dickbag named Toby. Now she's pregnant with their, like, third kid or something."

The mundane conclusion to her thrilling tale made the pieces click together. Eleazar had warned me about her theatrical streak on the day I'd arrived to the team, and with good reason.

"And now Morris is nursing a broken heart," I finished. "Courtney, I love you, but you're doing it again. Did Morris actually say that he wants to die? Did he say those *exact* words? Or did you remember that he was sad about the woman that got away and decided to elaborate?"

She faltered, as I knew she would. "Well, I mean, that's what he was implying. He said his father had died bravely and he wanted to...make him proud..." she said, trailing off. She turned red. "I may have gotten carried away."

"No, that's just pulling stuff out of your ass. *Why* do you do this? Is our superhero life not interesting enough? Are my visions not dramatic enough for you?" I grabbed her mask from the little basket next to the door and chucked it at her. "Maybe it's a good thing I can't read, if this is what books do to a person. Get in the real world. And you should apologize to Morris." When I'd tugged on my mask, I opened the side door. "Real world," I reminded her.

"Books did not *do* anything to me," she growled. "I've always been like this."

"A liar?"

She sputtered. "So I've got an imagination. Bite me."

"I think I'd rather wait for reality to bite you."

She scowled and stormed past me. "Pardon me for wanting more than this stupid life," she said over her shoulder.

~

UNFRIENDLY EYES FOLLOWED us as we walked under broken streetlights and glowing neon signs towards the rendezvous point. My Spanish was passable, if somewhat formal, so I frequently met with informants. Courtney was backup in case the meeting went badly, which was likely.

Even though she was nearly twenty-two, Courtney twirled down the cracked and pitted sidewalk as if she were a peasant girl on a grassy knoll, our recent spat forgotten.

"This is nice," she said as we passed a strip joint with an actual naked woman in the window. "We haven't hung out in forever."

"That's true," I said with a sigh. "You can't blame me for wanting to patrol with El—Laser when we were courting."

"Dating. You two were dating. Cut the camp talk."

"Right. Sorry."

She ceased twirling and elegantly leaned up against a lamppost. "So what's it been, six months? That's how long you two were going out, right? You never did tell me why you guys broke up."

I rested against the side of a building, tilting my head back as memories washed over me. "For someone who says he hates being a superhero, he sure takes it damn seriously. I mean, don't get me wrong, I'm all about protecting civilians from Los Diablos and stuff, but never once in those six months did he take me anywhere. I asked him to take us to the movies, but he always said that would take too much time. Can you blame me for dumping him? I just want a guy who will spend *time* with me."

Even as the words were still in the air, my heart ached for the kind of attention that television heroes lavished on their leading ladies.

She smirked. "Well, your choices are Armando or Morris. Take your pick."

"Oh, gee, lucky me. The guy who thinks dancing is evil or the guy who's, you know..." I leaned in close.

She raised an eyebrow. "What? What is he?"

I grinned. "Cursed."

She smacked my shoulder. "It's true! That family *is* cursed!"

I stifled a laugh as I rubbed where she'd hit me. "You should've seen your face."

Courtney's sheepish grin faded, and she frowned. "Wait a minute. *You* dumped *him*, right? He didn't end things?"

"Well, yeah. What's wrong?"

"How did he take it?"

"About as well as can be expected, I guess. He didn't want to break up, but I said it wasn't working out and I wasn't happy. He was moodier than usual for a week, but he hasn't asked to get back together. Why do you ask?"

She chewed on her fingernail. "Okay. What I have to say, I'm saying as a concerned friend."

I straightened. "What's up?"

Courtney's eyes were big behind her mask. "Haven't you ever heard why we're called Las Bestias?"

I paused. "No."

"It's because of how hard he fought against the gangs when he first arrived. Los Diablos used to be way worse than they are now. Whatever he's like when he's angry, it was enough to evoke fear in the civilians and the gangs around here. We're beasts, and he's the *big* beast. You're already talking about seeing other guys, and you just said that he didn't want to break up. Maybe...maybe you should act a little more like you're bummed out." She lowered her voice. "Heather, he's the one keeping you from going back to the camps."

She spoke with such gravity. Perhaps I needed to give her words more consideration than usual.

"I've never seen Eleazar show any capacity for personal revenge," I said slowly. "Do you have a concrete reason to think he'd turn me in? Not something in a novel. Nothing something you've guessed. Something you've *seen*."

"Well, there's this book I got from the library—"

"*Not* something in a book."

"This was nonfiction. It's true stuff. The library has an entire shelf with books about relationships. There's this one book, and it's full of stories about women who were married, and after the divorce their ex-husband went crazy and chopped them up and threw them into a river, or burned down the house. There's this long list in the back about signs of a predatory partner, and oftentimes you don't know they're going to go nuts until it's too late. It really happens. I can show you the book at the library."

I sighed. "Listen. He wasn't happy, but I trust him. He's a good guy."

"You trust him, but Minnie and Morris don't."

I faltered. How did they play into this? "What?"

"Remember after he said that it was you who had to go home? They instantly knew that there was more going on than 'procedure.' I mean, since when does Eleazar Lloyd care about procedure? He was going to send you home right up until they both called him out."

I wanted to deny her claim. I wanted to say that she was making it up as she'd always made stuff up.

But...but it was true. I'd been there myself.

A shiver shot down my spine. "Listen. We're going to go see my contact and hammer out a place and time to meet her ex-boyfriend. I think she said his name is Alejandro. He's a former *coyote*. After that, we'll go home and talk a little more about all of this."

We resumed walking, and Courtney tapped her chin as she thought. "Does Eleazar know that you're going to set up a meeting with a former *coyote*?"

"Yes, of course."

"That seems pretty dangerous."

"We *are* superheroes."

"What's he doing tonight?"

"Um...I don't know."

What *was* he doing? I'd told him I knew Maria, and he'd waved me off and told me to investigate the lead.

"Maybe he wants you to get hurt," she said quietly.

I opened my mouth to reply, though I hadn't picked my words yet. However, her head jerked and she looked up at a high window of a nearby building. A curtain moved, and she pulled me into a dark alleyway that led to a back road.

"Stay low," she hissed. "I heard someone on the phone up there. They were reporting our descriptions and movements." She pulled off her mask and gestured for me to do the same. "They'll be looking for these. Let your hair down."

I didn't question her—her tone held no room for it. I shook my bun loose and stuffed my mask into my pocket. We took off our uniform tops and tied them around our waists, then doffed our bulletproof vests and hid them in a damp cardboard box next to a dead cat.

In our baggy cargo pants, tank tops, and long hair that cascaded to our waists, we were somewhat fashionable again. More importantly, we looked like civilians...though, in this neighborhood, a leggy half-Asian New Yorker and a short, funny-looking Georgia girl didn't blend in much better than two women in masks.

We popped out onto a shadowy section of the back road and hurried down towards the dilapidated apartment building where we were going to meet our informant.

When we arrived at the building, Courtney put her hand on my shoulder. "I know it's a little late, but are you *sure* this is safe? There was a murder here last week."

"I know Maria well," I assured her. "She won't betray us."

I'd saved Maria from being the victim of a horrible code ten—her against four drunk Diablos wouldn't have ended well—and she'd been a trusted informant since then.

Courtney glanced around us, then leaned in and whispered, "I don't actually know what a *coyote* is. I assume you mean something other than the animal that kills chickens."

I suppressed a laugh. "A *coyote* is someone who smuggles people across the border, usually south to north."

We began to climb the grimy stairwell to the fourth floor. Now that she was mollified, she let out a Courtney-ish sigh. "A *coyote*," she said, giving the word a dramatic flair. "It sounds so wild and—"

"*Coyotes* commonly fleece their victims and leave them alone to die in the wilderness. Shut up."

"Oh, take a chill pill, Heather."

"Me? You're the one who's being all..." I trailed off as we reached the third floor.

We'd turned on the landing to go to the fourth floor, passing a ridiculously handsome young man about my age who was leaning on the railing, observing the nightly comings and goings on the street below. We made eye contact, allowing me to fully appreciate his black curls, five o'clock shadow, and large eyes framed by thick eyelashes. He had a novel in his hand, which he flipped shut as we walked by.

"Hi, there," he said, giving me a dazzling grin.

I ducked my head in greeting, beaming from ear to ear, but didn't break stride. As cute as he was, I was not here to flirt.

I was still warm-faced when we arrived at apartment 4C, with its steel door covered in peeling brown paint. I banged on the door, waited a few seconds, then banged again. A woman at 4B poked her head out, then shut the door.

Someone on the other side of 4C's door unhooked the chain, and then the deadbolt turned.

A handsome, muscular man in his early twenties stood in the doorway, his affected boredom battling his obvious raging curiosity. He'd styled his glossy dark brown hair nicely, and he wore a black button-down that brought out the rich onyx color of his eyes. He'd rolled up his sleeves to his elbows, allowing us to see elaborate tattoos on his light brown forearms, most of which depicted curvy women in various stages of undress. The others were of stylized bumblebees, of all things. He looked vaguely familiar, but I couldn't place him.

He leaned against the doorframe. *"Güeras? Son putas? O están pérdidas? Si son putas, pago bien."*

So Inky McGee thought we were hookers. Fabulous.

Courtney's face lit up. "You're going to have to translate," she said, never taking her eyes off him. "Man, I wish I spoke Spanish."

I crossed my arms over my cleavage and continued with the conversation. *"Somos amigos de Maria Sánchez. La conoces?"* I identified us as Maria's friends, but glossed over who we actually were or what we wanted. If he thought we were *putas*, well, fine.

He straightened as comprehension hit him. "You're the superheroes," he said in accented, but clear, English. "Maria said you were coming. I thought I'd be meeting with Laser or Wraith." He rolled the *r* in Eleazar's and Armando's codenames, and Courtney nearly choked.

"Oh, you speak English?" she said, bouncing on her feet.

"Yeah, I speak English," he said, returning Courtney's appreciative look. He offered a hand. "Alejandro. And you are...?"

"Not going to stand in the hallway all night," I said, raising my voice.

He extended his arm behind him, inviting us in. "Come in to my humble home," he said. "Well, actually, it's Maria's home. But she's letting me stay here while she's out of town. And yes, I'm armed. No need to ask," he said with a touch of smugness.

"Cool! I am, too," I said, smugger. I sincerely hoped I'd get to show off my weapon for this pretty boy.

His smile flickered, then returned when Courtney sat down on the plastic-covered sofa. He opened a mini fridge by the couch and tossed her a glass bottle of Coca-Cola, which she caught with her usual quick reflexes. He opened one for himself and walked past me, smirking. When he'd settled next to Courtney, he casually rested his arm on the back of the sofa and pointed to her. "So, Maria said you had some questions for me," he said. "Ask away, Miss...?"

"Frenzy," she cooed. "And my teammate is Excalibur. She's the one who arranged the meeting."

Alejandro tore his eyes away from Courtney and glared at me. "Yes?"

I dragged a kitchen chair into the living room and sat, then leaned forward. "Maria said you used to be a *coyote*. Is that true?"

There was a quiet knock on the door, followed by a young man's voice. "Alejandro, open up!"

Alejandro sighed and got up. "That's my friend Miguel. I'll send him away. Don't worry." Alejandro opened the door to reveal his friend, and I rose to my feet despite myself. Miguel was the man I'd seen a few minutes earlier.

Alejandro ordered Miguel in Spanish to go away, sticking his hand on the jam to bar his way. Miguel merely peered over Alejandro's shoulder, caught my eye, and waved.

"No, that's quite alright," I said, charmed. "Let him in."

Miguel didn't even wait for Alejandro to move aside. He ducked underneath Alejandro's arm and walked up to me, his hand held out. "I'm Miguel Alvear. I'm such a fan, Miss Excalibur. Such a fan." He grasped my hand with both of his, his eyes shining. "How can I help you?"

Oh, he had *freckles*. I was such a softie for men with freckles.

"That's usually my line," I said, blushing. "You're a civilian. How can *I* help *you*, Mr. Alvear?" I bit my lip. "*También hablo español, si lo prefieres.*" I hoped he didn't prefer to converse in Spanish, as I'd just offered—I was much cleverer in English.

Alejandro scoffed. "Miguel is a *pocho*. American as you two. Never set foot in Mexico. Toothy speaks better Spanish than he does."

I put my hands on my hips. "Hey! It's Excalibur or nothing, *cabrón*." Calling him that was an insult to male goats, honestly.

Miguel glared at Alejandro. "I am not a *pocho*, and you should show more respect to the people who've sent Los Diablos running with their tails between their legs. They're helping us. If this is some machismo thing—"

Alejandro rolled his eyes. "*I'm* helping *them*. If you're going to hang around, cut the back talk and go heat up the food in the fridge."

They made faces at each other, but Miguel dropped my hand and tipped his head at me before disappearing in the kitchen.

I fell back into my seat, resisting the urge to pout.

"Sorry. Now, where were we?" Alejandro purred, turning back to Courtney.

"Tell me about being a *coyote*," Courtney replied, obviously relishing this.

He said something. I saw his mouth move. Courtney laughed. Behind my eyes, though, played a fractured reel of images and noise that made no sense: a red sports car, lines of ink-drawn beauties, the nigh-demonic eyes of a man whose glare chilled me to the core. Roars of car engines mixed with frantic shouts in English and Spanish. And it was all so vivid, so close that I could almost smell it. The clawing sense of imminent danger scraped my insides.

I slammed back to reality. They hadn't noticed.

"—but my compass had broken, so I followed the stars to the border, and when we saw *la migra* we knew that—"

I stood up. "Frenzy."

"Hmm?"

"We need to go. We'll come back later. Alejandro, thank you for your time."

Courtney glanced at her watch. "Already? We've been here for five minutes."

"I *saw* something," I said, glaring at her. "If you catch my drift."

"Oh." She jumped up. "Yeah, we gotta go."

Alejandro glanced confusedly between us. "What? Why? What did you see?"

Courtney held out her hands, staying both of us, her brow furrowed in concentration. "A man is coming up the stairwell," she murmured. "Not a cop. He's on the phone and speaking Spanish." She gasped. *"Dos mujeres blancas,"* she said slowly, butchering her pronunciation. "That's 'two white women', right?" She wrinkled her nose. "I'm *half* white."

I could hear boots now.

Alejandro jumped to his feet and let out a string of colorful Spanish curses. "Someone must've seen you." He ran a hand through his hair and cursed again. "I hope you really do have a weapon in there," he said, looking at my pants. "If that's who I think it is, you're going to need it."

"Who is it?" I asked. "In case you forgot, we're trained fighters. I can handle it."

A loud male voice shouted in Spanish from outside the door for "Awl-eh" to open up. It took me a second to realize that the speaker meant "Ale," a short form of Alejandro. A diminutive nickname from an enemy? Odd.

Miguel bolted out of the kitchen, his eyes wide. "Why the hell is he here? Did you call him?"

"Hide," Alejandro hissed, shoving us towards the bedroom. "I can make him leave. Miguel, act casual."

I grabbed Courtney and dove into the bedroom, which was sparsely furnished. There was nowhere to hide, nor was the tiny window conducive to a thrilling escape. I pulled open the closet door. It was too small to hide both of us—but the tiny, sparkly clothes hanging on the rail gave me an idea.

"Follow my lead," I said to Courtney as I yanked two tube tops and miniskirts off their hangers and tossed them to the floor.

A minute later, Alejandro began to protest loudly for his guests to not go into the bedroom. He was obviously warning us that someone was coming, but he needn't have bothered. We were prepared.

A huge man burst through the door, gun drawn. Alejandro and Miguel followed him, all but biting their nails.

The man's cold stare, depthless and hostile, seemed to bore right through me where I sat on the bed. I'd seen it minutes before in a vision. His hair was cropped prison-style, and indeed, Avenal State Prison tattoos covered his arms and shoulders, visible beneath his thin white t-shirt.

I pulled the sheet up to cover my nakedness. "H...hola," I stammered, purposely screwing up my accent to embarrassing levels, complete with a spoken H sound. I looked at Alejandro with big Bambi eyes. "Ale, you said it would just be you and Miguel tonight," I whined. "Your friend is going to have to pay for the whole hour even though he's late and we didn't bring a third girl. That's the rule."

If Alejandro's eyes had been any bigger, they would've fallen out of his head. Miguel, on the other hand, had turned the color of tomato sauce.

Courtney batted her eyes at the new man. "He's cute, though," she said, her accent suddenly Japanese. "Such *muscles*. Maybe we can give him a discount or something?" I suspected she was only half making up her admiration. She turned to me. "Let's call Pavel and ask if we can do that."

The man sighed and holstered his weapon, then turned to Alejandro. He castigated him in Spanish for not being honest about having *putas* over, and Alejandro had the sense to look ashamed as he said that he was sorry for lying, but that he didn't want to scare "Karen" and "Sakura." The man punched Alejandro's shoulder, then walked out. A few seconds later, the front door shut.

Alejandro hurried back into the room, flushed. He shut the door and locked it, sinking down and breathing hard. "I'm sorry," he said, pressing the heels of his hands to his temples. "I didn't think he'd show up. Word got out that two lady superheroes are around here and one of my neighbors saw you earlier. She dropped the dime on you."

"Who was that?" I demanded.

Miguel scooped up our clothes and handed them back to us. "That was Roberto Guerrero. He's the leader of Los Diablos. Maybe you've heard of them?"

Courtney and I exchanged a significant look. Of course we'd heard of them. Los Diablos were a growing local gang, bent on the destruction of law enforcement in the barrio: cops, feds, and most importantly, "Las Bestias." The Beasts.

Us.

"Well, he's a stupid gangbanger if he looked us in the eyes and thought we were hookers," Courtney said with a sniff. "No wonder they can't get a decent hit on us."

Miguel's face darkened. "I'll go heat up dinner. Join me when you're dressed and we can talk about it."

He left, and I turned my attention to Alejandro. "He knew you."

"Yeah, he knows me. And they can get a hit on you," Alejandro said, dropping his head. "They're choosing not to. Killing a superhero would ignite a war with Las Bestias that they wouldn't win with their current numbers. They're trying to recruit as many of the smaller gangs as they can before they do anything."

He absentmindedly rubbed his forearms, reminiscent of a nervous tic. His action drew my eye to his tattoos, one of which was a naked woman whose goodies were covered by a scrolling ribbon bearing text. The second word looked like the phone company's name, a word I saw all the time in commercials.

"Las Bellas," I said slowly. "That's what your tattoo says. The Beauties."

He turned his head, allowing me to see his face against the white of the door and jogging my memory. Oh yes, I'd seen him before—in a police file of local troublemakers.

My lips curled up into a sly smile. "Alejandro Cipriano, founder of Las Bellas." I was struggling to contain my laughter as I elbowed Courtney. "We're in the company of barrio royalty."

Alejandro blushed. "That's not our name," he said. "When I founded the gang, we were—"

"But isn't that what your police files say?" I asked, pretending to think hard. "Yes, I think it is. You've done time for petty larceny, your gang is roughly five guys strong, and you're known for smack talk more than anything."

There was an unhappy silence. Finally, he said, "Does it actually say that in my file? That we're all talk?"

"Yes. What did you steal?"

He looked away. "A VCR." He dropped his head and sighed. "What do you want, superhero? You come to laugh at Las Bellas?"

After hastily pulling on my clothes, I walked over to him and held out a hand to help him up. "Go get me a Coke and we'll talk."

CHAPTER 3

03AUG – Around the time that some stations go to a test pattern.

*A*lejandro blew a little breath over the mouth of the Coke bottle while he thought, making a low hum. "Nobody's ever asked me to take them *into* Mexico. It's always the other way around."

The four of us had been at the table for fifteen minutes. He hadn't spoken much while I explained that we were looking to hire a *coyote* to take us south to escape the camps.

I finished shredding the corn tortilla Miguel had given me along with my refried beans. "I bet nobody's ever been on the run from a superhero cult, either. Get ready for a lot of strangeness, *muchacho.*"

He scoffed. "Who says I'm helping you? I got out of the *coyote* business because it's dangerous as hell."

Miguel started to argue, but I held up my hand. "We can pay you."

Instead of replying, he walked over to the freezer and opened it, then pulled two boxes of popsicles, which he turned upside down. Stacks of cash rained out of them onto the floor. "As you can see," he said flatly, "I have money."

"What do you want, then?"

He scowled. "There's nothing you can offer me that I can't already buy if I wanted. I have cash. I have gold. I have guns. I have drugs. If I want women, I can call real *putas* and have them here in twenty minutes. So you might as well just go and stop risking my life by hanging around in my kitchen."

"You can't buy love," Courtney said. She was leaning on her elbow, tracing little circles around the mouth of her Coke bottle. "You can't buy respect and admiration. What's a hooker when you could have someone who goes to bed with you because they *want* to be with you? Your life is so devoid of love. Can't you see that?"

Miguel nodded emphatically. "She's got a point, you know."

Alejandro blinked. "Wha—what?"

I told him in Spanish to ignore my *loca* teammate.

"I know what *loca* means," Courtney said, still playing with her bottle. "I'm not crazy. He has a need and we can fill it, if you'd just dream a little bigger than money and hookers."

Alejandro shook his head as if getting rid of a strange thought, then turned back to me. "You have your answer. Go now."

Miguel jumped to his feet. "They need help!"

I folded my arms across my chest. "We don't need this guy, Frenzy. Let's just go. Have fun with your disease-ridden *putas*, Cipriano."

"No," Courtney said sharply. "We're not done. Alejandro, you said that Los Diablos want to absorb every gang in the barrio into theirs. Why haven't you joined?"

She spoke with such intent that I sat back down. What was she getting at?

"I don't like Roberto," he said flatly. "He runs his gang like a...like a..."

"Like a cult?" I offered, unable to help a smile.

"Yes!" Alejandro threw his hands up. "Roberto is the god of the barrio, as far as he's concerned. His soldiers are practically slaves." True anger flashed across his face. "He used to be a *coyote*, too, before infecting this place. He says he serves our people," he spat. "*Los cojones!* He preys on *our people*. Ask the people who hired him to be their *coyote*."

"How so?" I said quietly. I hadn't expected righteous anger from someone like Alejandro. *Coyotes were* nasty—that wasn't prejudice on my part. If Alejandro were one of their number, I had many reasons to distrust him. This was a...*strange* turn of events.

"My rates were fair," Alejandro growled. "Half of the money before, and half later. We reviewed routes and I took them all the way to San Diego, or wherever they wanted to go as long as it was on the way. *He'd* let them die half the time. Sometimes he'd demand sex from the pretty girls. Sometimes he'd stuff them into a truck and leave it locked in the sun and run with the money. He's a sociopath."

"He really is," Miguel said, his voice heavy with emotion. "He sends his soldiers into the local schools to recruit. Kids go in, Diablos come out. He finds out information about you and hits you where you're weak. A lot of people around here come from nothing and he promises them everything. Then he covers them in that skull woman and sticks a gun in their hands."

"And how do you serve the barrio, Ale?" Courtney asked. While I would've injected as much sarcasm into the question as humanly possible, her words contained the genuine sweetness of a fairy tale princess. She probably thought she was one, and Alejandro was a knight in tarnished armor.

Alejandro sighed. "We run the nasty people out. Muggers, rapists. Well, I'm trying to. It's a lost war, honestly. There's a lot of broken families around here. Kids need a sense of belonging and importance. I can offer them that, if nothing else."

"Is it blood in, blood out?" I asked, tilting my chair back cool-as-you-please. "I've heard about gang initiations."

"No," he said. He pointed to his arms. "Ink in. Nobody's tried to leave, so I don't have an exit, um, ceremony. Maybe I'll make them cover it up. Ink in, ink out."

"The whole 'hot chica' theme kinda backfired on you, didn't it? Gotta say, a gang of pretty ladies doesn't exactly inspire fear. But you know that."

"*Anda a cagar*," he muttered. Loose translation: get lost.

Courtney leaned forward. "Would you like to inspire fear and awe in Roberto? In the whole barrio? The whole country? If you do, then we can give it to you...if you help us."

My eyebrows flew up. *What on earth...?*

The corners of Alejandro's lips lifted in a curious little smile. "How can you promise that?"

She smiled beatifically. "Easy. We need to disappear in such a way that the strike team won't follow. You need to do something bold and memorable to establish your dominance. Have you considered killing a superhero team?"

So that's what she was getting at.

Courtney's macabre suggestion had merit. Few criminals could boast of successfully murdering an entire team. In fact, I could think of just one instance, and that had been nearly thirty years prior, when Philadelphia's team had been kidnapped and murdered, including Morris's dad, and my great-uncle. Their leader, Battlecry, was known as either a pathetic failure or a martyr, depending on who you asked. Moreover, though hundreds of super-heroes had served since then, people still talked about Battlecry's team.

Alejandro's little gang would become notorious overnight. Other gangs would fear them. The whole world—and every superhero for the rest of time —would know their names.

Alejandro appeared to do some calculations, his eyes darting back and forth. "You want to fake your deaths...get across the border...two weeks from now..." He stood up, still thinking and talking to himself. "Do I have enough people? Is that enough time?"

He strode to the counter and opened a cutlery drawer, from which he removed a handgun.

A day's worth of pent-up stress and frustration propelled me out of my seat. Alejandro was on his back on the kitchen floor in less than a second, his gun skittering across the room.

Miguel shouted in alarm. "No! Don't hurt him!"

"So that's why you're called Excalibur," Alejandro breathed. "*Madre de Dios.* You really are armed."

Pure energy coursed through my arm and out of my palm, forming a glowing white sword that pulsed with the beat of my heart. Tendrils of light and sparkles soared in gentle arcs around my hand and arm like vines, slowly snaking back and forth. Experience had taught me that the blade could cut through steel, stone, flesh, and earth. It had even deflected a bullet once. And best of all, I could alter its appearance at will. I turned the hilt to show off the engraved blade that bore the word EXCALIBUR.

As bombastic as the name was, nobody had ever questioned my choice. I always figured that if they could produce a glowing magic sword from the power of thought, they'd pick that name, too.

"Why'd you pull the gun?" I stepped on his chest and pushed the tip of my sword even closer towards his Adam's apple. Even Courtney was somber, poised to strike if he made one wrong move.

He held up his hands. "I took out the gun without thinking. I wasn't going to shoot you, I swear. I was going to suggest that we fake a war for the two weeks you saw in your vision, so the conclusion seems natural. I'm not known for drive-bys and shoot-outs, so I doubt anyone would believe that Las Bellas had taken out a six-man team."

"Right," I said, narrowing my eyes. "Las Bellas are just an after-school club for the disadvantaged kids of south San Diego. Don't try to feed me that *mierda, coyote.* I know your kind. You used to traffick people across the border and now you prey on vulnerable boys in a slum. For twenty dollars and a soda I'd turn you over to INS myself for being the scum of the earth."

"My gang is just myself, my friends, and their younger brothers," he said, not taking his eyes off the blade. "Maybe we get into scrapes once in a while. Maybe I've been in jail. But we're not Los Diablos. My hand to God, Excalibur, I was a *coyote* because my older brother made me do it. I was sixteen when I started and twenty when I stopped. I'm not a terrible human being. I swear, I never hurt the people I led into the country and I would never hurt Las Bellas."

I snorted. "You're a crappy gang leader, aren't you?"

He stared up at me, a great sadness in his eyes, and I let out a disgusted sigh.

Yes, he was a crappy gang leader—and we all knew it. Las Bellas weren't even a gang, they were a group of friends terrified of the devils of the barrio. Alejandro himself had been preyed on by family, and now he was just doing his best to keep a handful of teenagers safe from Roberto Guerrero.

We stared at each other for a few seconds before I removed my foot from his chest. My sword disintegrated into nothing with a silent puff of sparkles.

He clambered to his feet and scrambled backwards. "Where'd it go?"

"I put it away, next to my six knives, staff, and laser cannon."

His eyes grew round. "Are you joking?"

I grabbed another can of Coke from the fridge and popped the cap off by banging it against the counter's lip. "Wanna risk finding out?"

Miguel was watching all of this from the table, his mouth open. His previous exuberance had disappeared, replaced by a shocked wariness. *Well, there goes any future with him.*

Courtney stepped between us. "Alejandro, we have to go home and speak to our leader. If he agrees to the plan, we'll be in touch to work out the terms. Are you okay with that?" She placed a gentle hand on his arm. "We'll all find a way to make everyone happy. We can disappear and you'll get the respect you want. Roberto will never boss you around again." She smiled shyly. "I'll feel better knowing that someone like you is running the barrio when we're gone. I think we both care a lot about its residents."

I was going to get cavities from these two.

Alejandro gulped. "Of course," he said, his voice suddenly higher. "Are you going to be safe getting home?"

I merely pointed to my hand.

"Understood," he said with a little nod.

I crossed my arms. "Though, quick question: Roberto called you 'Ale.' That's a cutesy little nickname, right? Are you his former best friend or something?"

Alejandro made a face. "He does that to make me feel small. Why?"

"Because it's one thing to go up against Roberto when he's just a gang lord," Courtney said. "It's a whole other thing if it's personal for him. Is he your friend? Your brother?"

Miguel snorted. "They're not brothers. Man, that would be a nightmare." He sighed and shook his head. "I promise. We were never friends."

Satisfied, I waved to Miguel. "It was nice to meet you."

"You too," he said softly.

Alejandro guided us to the door and closed it behind us with one last parting look at Courtney.

When we were alone, I turned on Courtney. "Are you *seriously*—"

"I think he's genuine," she said, still smiling at the door.

"Genuinely scuzzy, you mean."

She leveled a cool glare at me. "Laugh all you want, *chica*," she said in a low voice, "But I just set up a meeting between the team and his gang, and more importantly, I made him think that we need him more than he needs us. He's so desperate for recognition and affection that he's making a deal with a team of superheroes, risking everything by doing so. Didn't it strike you as odd that he invited us in even though he knew who we were? That he told us all of that the second I gave him some attention?" At my expression, she had a dark little chuckle. "I'm not the only one who wishes I had a different life. Come on, let's get home. Eleazar will want to hear about your *puta* charade."

She headed down the stairwell, leaving me to wonder if I really knew her.

CHAPTER 4

04AUG – So early in the morning, only infomercials were on TV.

ind on my face. Shouting. Danger.
The warning swept over me when I touched the doorknob
to go into Eleazar's office.

Courtney's warning surfaced, and I pulled my hand back. Shouting?
Eleazar was going to shout? About what? Why? And danger? What additional
danger was I in?

Who was really on the other side of the door? My colleague and leader—
or my enemy?

I quietly opened the door and shut it behind me, working my face into a
pleasant smile. "Hello."

Eleazar was at his desk, his head in his hands. Around him lay papers and
folders, beneath which peeked a map of Mexico. Crumpled newspapers
littered the floor around his desk. He looked up when I spoke, the gray eyes
red-rimmed from exhaustion.

"Hey, you." He pushed away from his desk and began to tidy up his work-
space. "What did Maria say?"

"Now, there's a tale," I said lightly. I sat across from him. "First off, Maria
wasn't there, but the *coyote* was. Also, someone spotted two white women,
correctly guessed who we were, and called the leader of our favorite local
hoodlums, Los Diablos."

"Roberto...Roberto...darn, what's his name..." He snapped his fingers as he tried to recall the name. "Roberto Guerrero...Guerrero Ober...Obra... something," he finally said. "Long rap sheet. What happened?"

"I'll cut to the chase. Mr. Cipriano will take us across the border. That's Alejandro Cipriano, by the way. Leader of Las Bellas."

Eleazar exhaled heavily. "Oh, we're just up to our elbows in class acts, aren't we?"

"It gets better. He'll be our guide *if* we fake our deaths and let him take the credit for killing us beasts."

Eleazar pondered that. "He sounds charming. Is that all he wanted?"

"I'm pretty sure he wouldn't say no to some private time with Courtney. You should've seen them. It was gross. Oh, that reminds me," I said, straightening up. "I wanted you to hear it from me, and not Courtney's lewd reimagining—there was an incident. That's where Roberto comes in."

He raised an eyebrow. "I've got to hear this."

"Okay, so, Roberto got the drop on us and we had maybe sixty seconds to prepare. I didn't want a gun battle, so Courtney and I pretended to be hookers. It worked, and Roberto left."

"How'd you pretend to be hookers?"

"How do you think? We got naked and under the covers. Threw some lady's clothes on the floor. Talked the talk. Stuff like that."

A hint of anger passed over Eleazar's face, and a breeze picked up, stirring the papers on his desk.

I braced myself—I knew what was coming, and now I had to ride it out. There was no point in telling him to not get angry; that just made things worse. His moods were odd that way—he never got angry about the things that angered me, but when he did blow his stack, things got nasty. I'd always chalked it up to the stress of his job, but now, after Courtney's warning...

He jumped up and paced back and forth, then turned on me. "That was your best plan? You could've been killed."

"It was far more likely that we would've been killed in the probable shootout," I said evenly.

He sputtered. "You can make a sword come out of your hand!"

"Which, last I checked, was not a ranged weapon."

"Don't be glib about this, Heather. You were in the company of a violent felon. You were undressed, right? You didn't have your vest on."

I folded my hands in my lap. "El, I need you to trust that I made the best decision I could in the circumstances." *Breathe in. Breathe out.* Already my hand ached from the energy swirling in my palm.

"But why on *earth* did you risk your life like that? I'm trying to get us out of here. Don't...don't just throw it all away, okay?"

Why *was* he mad? Concern I could understand. But I'd never been able to put my finger on the pulse of his moods, and once again I was floundering to keep up with him.

"I'm confused," I said slowly. "Are you angry because I was doing my job?"

"*Your job* does not require..." He exhaled. "Never mind. Just...just never mind. I've got a lot on my plate right now."

"Get to the point," I spat. "We arranged the meeting, we got our angle, and now you need to make a decision. Sorry for risking our lives like, I dunno, superheroes. What's your call?"

He slouched in his chair, his eyes taking on a flinty note. "Lose the attitude, Heather. Just keep it going and update me as needed."

I'd seen that dark tiredness in him before—two weeks ago. He'd gotten cold and stony when I'd ended our relationship, and now he was in that mental place again. Courtney had warned me to tiptoe around him lest he change his mind, but I was no coward. I wasn't going to let an ex-boyfriend's caprice ruin my life.

I narrowed my eyes. "Why don't *you* deal with Alejandro?"

He made a face. "Why should I? You've already got the rapport with him."

Because you're the freaking leader. Because he's obviously dangerous and you should lead from the front. Because I don't believe you really care about my safety.

The last reason drew me up short. Had it really come to that for us? There was only one way to test.

"What if I said he makes me feel unsafe?"

Dark amusement flickered in his eyes. "I'd say that you're, I dunno, a superhero. Risking your life is what you do best, right?"

There was an ugly silence.

"You absolute prick," I growled.

"Excuse me?" He sat up. "Is that what we're doing now? We agreed to keep things professional."

"Professional, El? You want to talk about professional? I was following a lead with a *coyote* tonight while you were doing god-knows-what back here. You're the leader! You should've been the one to go meet this guy, not me and Courtney! How is it professional to sit on your ass while your two teammates risk their lives?"

"I was chasing gangbangers!" he shouted. The breeze picked up more. "How can you stand there and say that to me? You're talking lunacy."

"Lunacy? You want lunacy? You were the one who told us to go meet Cipriano but got angry when I did!"

"I got angry because I'm frustrated!" he roared. "We've got the cult on one hand, the strike team on the other, gangs in front of us, and now you and Courtney jump into bed, butt naked, with a known murderer in the room! You could've been shot to all hell!"

"If you'd died," he continued, "In the stupidest way possible, I should add, then all of this would be for nothing. I'm sorry for getting upset. I know it was the only thing you could've done, given the circumstances. But God, you just come in here and laughingly tell me about how you were almost gunned down with no thought of how that would've left the rest of us exposed. There would've been an inquiry. The north team would've gotten involved. So much investigation! There can't be any casualties until we're fully ready to disappear."

So that's how it was: he blamed me for risking my life in the moment, possibly jeopardizing the team.

"You're mad because I made the only call there was to make, even if it risked my life and the team's safety. But it *was* the only call. You can't blame me for that," I said, trembling.

He threw up his hands. "Heather, what the hell do you want from me?"

"Nothing... anymore." I gulped heavily. At least there was one person who respected what I did, who trusted me. "Did you know that someone has been writing me fan letters?" I said, struggling to keep calm. "He says I'm an asset to the city. He says I'm incredibly brave. He says..." My voice died as I recalled my favorite sentence of all the letters he'd written. "He says he wishes he could spend all his spare time with me."

I envisioned my faceless, nameless friend standing next to me, his hand on my shoulder. *He* believed in me.

Eleazar fell into his chair. "What are you...I don't have the energy for this. How would you know what he's writing you, anyway?"

"*Shut up!*" My scream almost knocked him out of the chair. Furious tears streaming down my cheeks. My hand throbbed.

His eyes flared light blue—and the tempest began.

Wind coursed the room, knocking papers everywhere and destroying any semblance of order. The small lamp on the desk fell and we were plunged into darkness. Eleazar covered his eyes and turned his back to me.

I grabbed his shoulder and spun him around. "You're going to destroy half of the house, idiot!" I yelled over the roar of the contained gales.

"I can't stop it!" As the words left his mouth, the wind grew stronger, pushing me sideways into the wall. All of my strength turned to containing the sword that begged to come out. A gigantic blade wouldn't help this fight.

Minnie burst through the door at the same moment Morris appeared in the middle of the room with a popping noise. I looked away from Minnie, but it was too late—I'd already made eye contact.

The world receded and fell into shadow, narrowing to just her and me, as if we were standing in a spotlight on a vast and lonely stage. My limbs were loose, like jelly, and already the memory of the argument was far away...

"Heather," Minnie said, holding out her hands to me. Her hair was in its natural loose curls, and her pretty face was devoid of the stark mask of makeup she always wore. "You're so tired. It's time to go to bed. Walk to your bedroom, get into your pajamas, and go to sleep." I took her hands, my troubles floating away like feathers in the breeze.

I *was* tired. I was bone tired. Why hadn't I noticed before? I could feel, somewhere out there, my cheek touch my pillow.

Sleep. Minnie's voice was as soft and tender as my mother's.

And then I did.

CHAPTER 5

04AUG – During *My So-Called Life*'s broadcast time, unfortunately.

I did not like mind control.

Minnie had held her ground, though, when I'd confronted her the next morning about using her power on me. Despite my protests that it was an enormous violation, she'd asked me if I'd preferred that Eleazar and I had come to blows.

"It wouldn't have come to that," I'd said, disgusted.

"Your eyes were glowing."

"That was an accident!" It was. It really was. For all my flaws, I'd never purposely pull my sword on a teammate. However, I'd skulked off before she could start reciting a list of those flaws. I wasn't ready to speak to Eleazar yet, so after completing every conceivable chore around the house, I put on civilian clothes and knocked on Courtney's door.

"Come in," she called, sing-song. I opened the door. Courtney was spread out on her bed, laying on her stomach with her legs crossed girlishly behind her, munching on the contents of a brightly-colored bag of Mexican snacks and reading yet another thick novel. She tucked a bookmark into her stopping place and tossed the book onto her bedside table, where three more were stacked. I swallowed down the throb of jealousy that rose in my throat.

Television was better, anyway.

I sat on the bed. "Wanna go out? I gotta get out of here."

She offered me the bag. "Sure. Here, have one. The gray ones are hella good." To illustrate the fact, she put one in her mouth and hummed in pleasure.

Intrigued, I obediently popped a gray candy into my mouth, then choked. "Ew, black licorice. You like this?"

She giggled and spat out the nasty candy into the little trash can next to her bed. "Gotcha. Yeah, they're gross."

I considered my hairy-fairy teammate. My experience with Courtney in Alejandro's apartment forced me to interpret her differently. What might've been a mildly childish prank was now a clever deception, and moreover, she'd eaten the candy to trick me into going along—an action that struck me as significant, though I couldn't say why. Why had I never seen this before? What else about her was not what it seemed? Had I been taking her at face value?

"Hey, Courtney?"

"Yeah?" She hopped off the bed and rooted in her bedside drawer for a second, then pulled out a blue scrunchy and put her hair up into a long pony-tail. "What's up?" she asked as she perused her closet. She selected a blue jumper and white blouse to wear under it, then ducked behind the modesty screen to change.

"Did you *really* like Alejandro?"

Her head appeared from behind the screen so she could shoot me a surprised look. "Why do you ask?"

"I dunno," I grumbled. "Yesterday was weird. You acted like you wanted to date him. He just seemed…a little below your league, I guess." She'd never mentioned a boyfriend or suitor from back at the camps, but if one existed, he certainly wouldn't have been a criminal. She could do better. Was Alejandro another piece of black licorice, so to speak?

She nodded in agreement. "He'd have to shape up first. I could never go with someone who uses that much hair gel. I mean, honestly. He wears more of it than Mario Lopez." She disappeared behind the screen again to finish.

Talking to Courtney was the conversational equivalent of having a stroke.

"I was referring to the fact that he's done time in the slammer, used to be a human trafficker and, hello, has a *gang*."

Courtney reappeared fully dressed. "No, that doesn't bother me. He was forced into being a trafficker and got out of the business as soon as he could. And if you think about it, we're kind of a gang, too. I suppose we're not crimi-nals or anything, but we're big and scary and rule the streets through intimi-dation. In a slum without much police presence, the biggest bully in the schoolyard is the boss. That's us."

It was hard to argue with that. "And the jail time?"

"He stole a VCR."

"Which is bad!"

"You waved those letters in front of him. Whatever your reason, you were trying to make him jealous. Since you dumped him two weeks ago, that was kind of low."

"Oh—what are you now, Oprah?"

Courtney hooked a sexy little choker necklace around her neck, completing her civilian ensemble. She surveyed me placidly before she said, "Am I wrong? Did my superpowered ears deceive me?"

"No," I grumbled. "I guess I...I was just scared about what you'd said, and I lashed out. It's not an excuse, but it's the truth."

"Are you going to be more careful like we talked about?"

"Yeah," I said softly. "I won't make him mad."

The weight of last night's argument finally hit home. In my fear, I'd lashed out against Eleazar and risked angering the one person I couldn't afford to anger. And now that I'd identified a new, deeper side to Courtney, I needed to acknowledge that perhaps Eleazar had a deeper side, too: a dangerous one. So many surprises to take in so little time. The camps and strike team were only weeks away if we did not run, but now I had to contend with the threat posed by my ex-boyfriend. Peer pressure had forced him into finding an escape for me, but I could not rely on that forever.

"Hey." Courtney placed her hand on my shoulder and gave me a reassuring squeeze. "It's going to be okay. We're heroes, and heroes always win."

I bit my lip and nodded.

A minute later, we walked downstairs and headed out through the front door. On the porch, Courtney paused, then bounded down the steps and around the railing to her rose bush. She plunged her hand into the dying leaves and removed another glass jar, hurling it with all her might into the potholed road.

"What did the roses ever do to you?" she said to the sky, in lieu of the actual culprit. She rounded on me. "We're going to see La Bruja. I want to know who's cursing us."

"That's probably a whole lot of people."

She exhaled sharply, thinking. "No. La Bruja makes curses to order, and the curse always takes the same shape, with Santa Muerte in the middle and our names around her. It's the same person. I want to know who and why, and I want to know what the curse is. It's killing my flowers." She began to storm down the sidewalk and I hurried to keep up with her long strides.

The sun was setting, casting long shadows over the barrio and beckoning the nocturnal activities to begin. The afternoon siesta period was long over, and now the bustle began anew. We passed busy little *tiendas*, their wares oftentimes hanging from the ceiling, crammed onto shelves, and spilling out of bins. Street food vendors stood behind shabby stalls and carts, frying up whatever bits of animal they could scrape off the bones and wrapping them in fresh tortillas.

Though we were technically in the United States, our surroundings spoke only of cities south of the border. This was where the immigrants lived and worked, and it was where the city had decreed we live. I'd never gotten to know them as much as I'd wanted, but some of the locals greeted us as we passed.

"*Hola!*" a woman called from a small stall.

"*Hola! Que pasa?*" another called.

"*Hola!*"

"*Buenas tardes!*"

A man selling fresh-baked bread passed by, waves of delicious steam tickling my nose. Men chattered happily in a small barbershop, outside of which gossiping teenage girls braided each other's hair. A few children ran back and forth across the road, risking life and limb in a ball game.

Courtney stopped at a fruit vendor's cart that was piled high with fruits in every color of the rainbow. She selected a juicy-looking mango and handed the old woman fifty cents. Without a word, the fruit seller peeled and chopped the mango with an ancient knife, placed the pieces into a plastic cup, then doused them all with various powders and sauces. She plunked a stick of candy into it and gave the completed snack to Courtney, who smiled sweetly.

"*Muchas gracias, señora,*" she said slowly, her horrendous accent grating on my ears.

"*De nada, cariño,*" the woman replied with equal sweetness. She gave no indication that Courtney had all but murdered her language. The old woman pointed to me. "She...want?"

"*No gracias,*" I said, but I immediately regretted my refusal when Courtney ate a piece of dripping mango and sighed in indecent pleasure.

I hurried her along into a shady spot underneath a large tree. "What is that?" I asked.

"*Mango con chamoy,*" she said in her hideous accent. "Hell if I know what chamoy is, but it's good."

"Can, uh, can I have some?"

"Be my guest."

We munched on the sweet, spicy, sour treat for several silent minutes. Halfway through her last piece of mango, Courtney said, "The fruit lady's grandson was almost hit by a bike messenger a few months ago. I jumped into the road and grabbed him. I can't talk to her, but I always make sure to buy something when I see her. The guy who sells that chalky hot cocoa down the road gives me free cocoa when I see him since I stopped a guy from stealing his money once."

"They know your face?" Now that I thought about it, the fruit lady shouldn't have known Courtney on sight, since we always patrolled with a mask.

"Heather, I'm five foot ten and half white, half Japanese."

"Right. Sorry."

The masks were stupid, anyway. If this "internet" thing was as big as the talking heads on the news said it was going to be, one day everyone in the world would know our faces. We'd have to find some other way to obscure our identities. I privately doubted that would be in my lifetime, though.

Courtney tossed the cup into a nearby trashcan and pointed across the street to La Bruja's bodega. "C'mon, I need to have a word with a witch."

"I don't think she speaks English, Courtney."

"If I start yelling, she'll get the point."

Over my dead body was I going to let Courtney get into a fist fight with an old lady in a bodega.

"Okay, you know what? I'll talk to her. Go pick up some dinner for us," I said, massaging my stomach. Eleazar had been in the kitchen whenever I'd tried to get some food all day, so I hadn't had a square meal yet. The mangos had only whet my appetite. "Can you get some tacos from the guy down the street?"

Courtney scowled. "Fine, but how do I say I don't want, like, cow eyeballs in them?"

"*Sin ojos,*" I said, laughing, then pushed open the heavily-reinforced door of the creepiest bodega in recorded history.

Half convenience store, half witchcraft superstore, La Bruja's corner bodega stood in the dead center of the barrio, a wart on an otherwise quiet street. Every manner of *brujería* ingredient was filed away in dirty little boxes, floor to ceiling: dried parts of mummified animals, graveyard dirt, candles in all colors, slips of paper with words written on them, blood from who-knew-what, foul and sweet incense alike, twists of hair, tiny dolls depicting all nature of people, and, oh yes, the loathed rictus of Santa Muerte. She was everywhere—in dolls, on cards, and even on little medals meant to be worn around the neck.

Nausea curled in my stomach. I hardly believed in such superstitions, but I believed in hate and ill will, and Santa Muerte was the personification of both. In fact, this whole shop was making me sick. Cold perspiration beaded on my forehead as I wove through the dark aisles towards the back, where La Bruja would be.

She was waiting for me behind the counter, her wrinkled face tightening when I made eye contact with her.

"No English," she said sharply.

"*Yo hablo español,*" I replied with equal sharpness. She startled. *Yeah, that's right, you can't hide behind the language barrier.*

She squinted at me. "What do you want?" she asked—in English.

I pulled myself up to my fullest height and put my hands on my hips. "Who's been buying curses for my team?"

"I don't curse and tell."

Very clever. "Well, what do you have against my team?" I continued, refusing to be thwarted. "We protect people around here. If your bodega was robbed—not that anyone wants to steal dirt—we'd catch them. So what's with the little jars, lady?"

From the backroom, a man called, "Ágata!" There was a pause, then he asked where the duct tape was. His voice sounded familiar.

She sighed in annoyance, then shouted for the speaker to go have a cigarette.

The man replied that he didn't smoke, and what the hell was going on?

I crossed my arms and tapped my foot, fighting a smile. Her mystique was quickly waning, and she knew it. Indeed, she waved me away with an embarrassed scowl and disappeared behind the curtain that cut off the store from the backroom, shushing whomever had spoken. I caught snatches of words, including "*gringa*" and "*una bestia.*"

Alejandro's friend Miguel poked his head out from behind the curtain, his curls falling into his eyes. He locked eyes with me.

It was as if he were seeing a sunrise for the first time. Awed wonder softened his facial features, turning his rather rugged, scruffy face into a beautiful one. He pushed aside the curtain, the corner of his lip trying to lift into a smile, but hesitation making it go back down.

"Hi, there," I said, waving a little as I returned his oh-so-suave opening line from the night before.

He rubbed the back of his neck and looked down, blushing furiously. "I can't believe you're here."

Ágata balked. "You two know each other?"

Miguel gave her a sly smile. "Why don't you go have a smoke?"

Ágata practically rolled her eyes into the next county, but she disappeared behind the curtain.

Miguel raised the jointed counter and crossed into the customer side of the store. "How can I help you, Miss Excalibur?"

I raised an eyebrow, fighting a smile. "I thought we'd established that I help you."

"You said that, but I never agreed."

"Yes, I think Alejandro stepped in and decided to be a pill."

"He *is* a pill, isn't he?"

Real laughter bubbled out of me, and I extended my hand, which he took. "It's good to see you again, Miguel. I'm sorry you had to see my uglier said last night. I hope you believe me when I say that I'm actually quite pleasant."

He shrugged. "Consider it forgotten. I really am happy you're here, since it seems like you'll be spending more time with Ale now. I never dreamed you'd come into the bodega, though. You must need something if you're here. What can I help you with?" He gestured all around. "We've got drinks, snacks, toiletries, some makeup over there, and of course, every bit of *brujería* claptrap you can imagine, but I don't suppose you're here for that."

"Actually, that's exactly why I'm here. Ágata has been selling curses to someone and I've come to put a stop to it."

Horror flashed across his face. "Excuse me," he said before striding back behind the counter and beyond the curtain.

Um, okay. I didn't know what was about to happen back there, but I was glad I wasn't Ágata.

While he was gone, I walked around the little aisles, taking in the unfamiliar brands and wrappers, unbothered by the hissed, furious whispers drifting from the backroom. As I wandered, I couldn't help but notice that someone had stowed little paperback novels here and there behind merchandise. I didn't need visions to know that this was Miguel's doing, though I couldn't begin to guess his purpose.

When I found each one, I carefully sounded out the title. The large, blocky letters helped. Free from distractions and my teammates' teasing giggles, I was able to remember the half a dozen or so phonics lessons I'd had, plus a few bits of letters I'd picked up since moving to San Diego.

"The...Ree...turn...Return of the...King," was underneath a bag of bread. Who was the king? Where had he gone?

The smaller book guarding the snack cakes had a tricky word in the title, "Phantom," but I knew it by sight since that was Morris's codename. "The... Phantom...Toll...booth." Whatever a phantom tollbooth was, it sounded interesting. Did it appear at toll plazas at midnight and charge an arm and a leg?

A thick book by "Joo-les Ver-nee" had been surreptitiously tucked underneath a similarly-colored box of votive candles. It was bound in leather and embossed with gold, so I carefully replaced it. Who knew what valuable information it contained?

On the last aisle, I knelt down in front of the cooler and opened it, then reached behind the tamarind soda.

"Cass...ee...no Roy...alleee," I read aloud as I removed the battered book from the fridge. Casino Royally? No, that couldn't have been right. The cover picture, a tuxedo-wearing man with a revolver, didn't offer any more clues. I flipped through the tanning pages, letting the papery perfume waft across my face. Once again, my chest throbbed, and this time my eyes began to itch.

I would've given anything to be able to read.

Reading and writing weren't mandatory at Oconee camp, my childhood home, and I'd been shunted into the Spanish class at the same age most others had been sent to reading and writing lessons. It hadn't bothered me until I'd arrived in San Diego, where everyone seemed to derive such fun from their books, lost in fantasy and romance. How happy I'd been when I'd discovered television—but even then, Courtney had told me that television couldn't compare to books. But had she helped me learn how to read? No. Worse yet, even people *in television shows* made fun of people who preferred television to books.

What a weird creature I was, a superhero who could speak two languages and read or write neither.

"Miss Excalibur?"

"Over here!"

Miguel hurried around an endcap and up to me. "Did you want a soda? You drank a lot of Coke last night. Is that your favorite?" He zeroed in on the novel in my hand, his brilliant red blush returning. "Oh. You found my book."

"This is yours? Do you like it?"

He took the book from me and hastily stuck it on a shelf of office supplies. "James Bond is my favorite. But, uh, I'm not supposed to read on my shift. Don't tell Ágata, okay?"

"Tell her about what?" I said with a little shrug. "What were you guys talking about back there?"

"We had a word about the curses." His tone ended the subject. "But tell me, what do you like to read?"

And here we go.

"Are you a big reader?" I hedged.

"I love reading." He beckoned me to follow him around the aisles. "I have a shelf in the back where I keep my books for my breaks. Like I said, I'm not supposed to read on my shift, but sometimes I can restock with one hand and hold a book with the other. All the books on the shelves are from when Ágata called me and I had to stash them quick." He removed a book from the lipstick display. "Check out what I've got. Autographed and everything. Cool, huh?"

The title was in cursive, entirely hiding the word from me.

"Uh, wow," I said, handing it back. "That's awesome. What do you like to read?"

"Everything! I've recently gotten into high fantasy. Tolkien and Lewis, but a few lesser-known authors, too. Spy thrillers are the best. There's also some legal thrillers that I'm looking to get with my next paycheck. I read *The Firm* last month and couldn't put it down.

"My mom has been trying to push me towards Shakespeare, but I confess that I'm really not into classic literature, but I liked *A Tale of Two Cities*. Science fiction tends to get too technical these days, though I've been reading some official *Star Trek* novels, and I really like how they mix philosophy, action, and drama. It makes for a lighter read that still stimulates the mind, you know?"

"I know *Star Trek*!" I burst out. "They make *Star Trek* books, too? Wow!" Books about television shows. What would they think of next?

He gave me a playful smile. "Kirk or Spock?"

"Uh, secret third option, pal: Picard. *The Next Generation* was such a better show than the original."

He covered his heart. "Was not."

"Was too. But I'll concede that the movies are pretty good."

He tilted his head, his eyes sparkling with delight. "A fair compromise. I never imagined you to be a Trekkie, but now that I know it, it makes sense. Do you like *Star Wars*?"

I sighed. "Unfortunately, I've never seen them. We don't have a VCR and I can never catch them on TV. I've heard they're really good, though."

"Miguel!" Ágata called from the back. "Stop talking and get back to work! And bring that box I told you to unpack three hours ago!"

He scowled over his shoulder, then turned back to me. "Meet me after you're done talking to her, okay?"

"Only on one condition."

He looked surprised. "Name it."

"You have to call me Heather," I said quietly.

The soft radiance of happiness lit up his face again, transforming his features into that of the loveliest person I'd ever seen.

"I'll see you after work, Heather." He gestured to a large cardboard box on top of a high shelf. "But back to the old salt mines." He removed a stepping stool from beneath the shelf and rolled up his sleeves, revealing intricate artwork on his light brown forearms. I took a step back.

Miguel was a member of Las Bellas. He'd soon be taking credit for killing me.

"I'll just take this back to Ágata," he said as he stepped off the stool with the box, oblivious to my dismay. "Don't take too long." He winked and hurried off.

I stood in the empty aisle for a few seconds, then grabbed one of his hidden books and chucked it at the wall with all my might.

CHAPTER 6

04AUG – It's very strange when the real world becomes more dramatic than
My So-Called Life.

*W*hen I returned to the front counter, Ágata was at the register, a sheepish expression on her face. "I think we got off on the wrong foot."

"Maybe," I said, placing my hands on the counter and drumming my fingers. "Is Miguel your grandson?"

"My neighbor's son," she said with a sigh. "They're a good family, one of many around here. But that's not important. Why are you really here?"

"I told you. I want you to stop cursing us."

Ágata took her spectacles off and rubbed her eyelids. "The people who come to me for curses aren't…they aren't…they won't like it if I stop offering this service. The only way I could stop serving them without arousing their anger is if I stopped serving everyone, and this is most of my income." Her English was rapid and only lightly accented, hinting that she had a different past than most residents of the barrio. Where was she from? And how had she ended up here?

"Are you afraid of these people?"

Her eyes darted away. "It doesn't matter."

"I'll take that as a yes. How much do you charge per curse, or spell, or whatever?"

"Twenty-five. American."

I pulled out my wallet and removed fifty dollars, my entire week's allowance, and held it out. "I can do better than that."

She slowly accepted the cash, looking at it as though she wasn't certain it was real money. "Why?" she asked. "What do you want from me?"

"I want to know who's cursing us."

She shook her head and held out the money for me to take back. "Please understand, it's not personal. But I will not cross them."

I shoved her hand back. "Then how about this—mess up the curses. The next two, anyway. I'll be back in a few days with more money. Just mess them up and don't tell anyone, okay?"

Ágata studied me. "White women don't normally believe in *brujería*. Do you?"

I paused. No, I didn't believe in all the stupid hoodoo around me. Why *was* I doing this? I took a long breath. "I think the people who buy your curses believe in it, and I want to stick it to them as much as I can. If it's really not personal..."

She put the money in the till, then reached under the counter and removed three small dolls, each no more than six inches long. One of them bore the crude likeness of a man, with little bits of black hair on his head. The other two were clearly women, curvy and sporting hair made of brown or black thread. Ágata held them up to me. "These are for the latest spell," she explained, reaching for a red marker by the till. "I will not say what dark purpose it was supposed to have, but I will do this." She started drawing little red x's over the doll man's eyes. "I'm...altering the spell. It serves him right for ordering it."

I took the male doll from her. "It's Roberto, isn't it?"

Her expression said everything.

"Never mind," I said, frowning at the little dolls. "And like I said, I'll be back."

I turned to go and deflated at once.

In the doorway, almost shoulder to shoulder, stood a gaggle of older teenage boys led by Miguel. Behind them, Courtney and—oh, heck— Alejandro were eating tacos. Where the flying fart had he come from?

The group, which were obviously some if not all of Las Bellas, tittered as I approached. Nothing about them said "hardened gang members." If their appearance and demeanors said anything, it was more like that they had to be home by curfew and had Selena fan club membership cards in their wallets.

Miguel held his hands behind his back. "Guess what I have," he teased.

I was disarmed by his rakish grin. "What?"

"May I present...your dinner," he said, holding up a steaming pastry that smelled strongly of spiced meat. "It's better than Aarón's tacos, believe me."

I accepted the delicious-looking food, my mouth already watering. My fingers brushed his and we both blushed. "Thank you," I said, my too-cool-for-school pretense evaporating with the steam. "This smells delicious."

Alejandro pointed to a nearby apartment building. "Let's get off the street so we can talk," he said. His friends obediently hurried into the building, and Courtney and I followed, exchanging an amused look.

Alejandro unlocked a door on the first floor, leading us into a small, plain apartment. The only decoration was a large wall hanging of Our Lady of Guadalupe above a tiny altar bearing a lone votive candle and a grainy picture of a pretty woman, two small boys on each side of her. They both looked familiar.

He locked and bolted the door, then spun around. "Courtney, tell her what we were discussing."

I stopped chewing. She was "Courtney" to him now? Great. Miguel was harmless. Alejandro was an operator.

Courtney rubbed the back of her head, not meeting my judgmental gaze. "We were discussing how we could make it seem like Las Bellas and Las Bestias are at war, since Alejandro and his crew aren't known for being belligerent. We thought that if everyone believed that we'd impounded him and wouldn't release him, the gang would have a material reason to suppos-edly attack our house," she explained. "We'll make it look like we died in the attack, but in reality we'll be halfway to Oaxaca by then."

"We think the south of Mexico is better," Alejandro said quickly. "In case this strike team learns the truth. That's a long way to go."

"Miguel and the boys can stage some trouble," Courtney continued. "Graf-fiti, a fight in a parking lot somewhere, and perhaps even a fake drive-by shooting. Everyone will catch wind of the war, and then bam! It's over. Nothing will have to get out of hand."

"The boys" all looked at each other in mild surprise, then at Courtney and me.

"And then what?" the shortest of them asked. He couldn't have been out of high school.

"And then you're infamous," I said. "You'll have killed a superhero team. Only bona fide supervillains can claim that. Nobody will ever challenge Las Bellas again."

"No, you've got it wrong. *Everyone* will challenge Las Bellas," Miguel said quietly. "Ale, please forgive me for disagreeing with you, but if killing a super-hero team is what it takes to be in charge, imagine what it would mean to take down a gang that actually did it. We're not exactly set up for a war."

"I don't really want to," the short one mumbled. He inched away from Alejandro. "Can I go? I told my mom I'd take my little sisters to the library."

How badass.

I sat on the arm of the couch. "If you guys don't want to fight us, pretend to fight us, or even get famous, then why the hell are you in a gang at all? Just start a band or something. You're cute enough to sell a few records. I mean it."

They giggled and blushed like the innocent cutie-boys they were. Alejandro sighed and ordered them in Spanish to go into the kitchen, reminding them to not eat all of his food. The four youngest disappeared into the next room and headed immediately for the fridge, but Miguel hung around and asked if he could stay. Alejandro paused, then nodded.

We all huddled in the room, our heads together.

"Let's get down to brass tacks," I said in a low voice, a heat in my chest. I could smell Miguel's cologne. "Ale, I'm beginning to think that this is a mistake. No offense, but I don't want to get into a fake war with your gang. Nobody will believe it, and—" My eyes traveled to Miguel, who shyly looked away. "—I think even pretending to murder someone isn't really your thing. You all should be in school or working for your dads or something. Not striking this type of deal. It's wrong."

Alejandro's face was more serious than I'd ever seen it. He sighed before he said, "Excalibur—"

"Heather," I said. "My name is Heather Harris. I grew up in Georgia. I have parents, five siblings, six nieces and nephews, and I love to watch television more than anything in the world." If he and his gang were going to go down this path, then they'd do so knowing full well who they were going to get involved with: real human beings.

He winced. "Heather," he said. "It may be hard to believe, but I do care about my boys. I want them in school. I want them in jobs. I want them to succeed—*but they can't succeed with Los Diablos in the barrio.* If I let them go, Roberto will take them. The only reason Roberto hasn't already claimed them is because he wants a peaceful takeover. He doesn't want a pile of bodies, he wants control over the living."

"And killing us..." Courtney said as she covered Alejandro's hand with her own.

Alejandro looked at her sadly. "It might just give us enough respect to live on our terms."

"Might," I bit out. "You'll risk everything for a 'maybe.'"

He looked down. "Yes."

I pursed my lips. "If we do this, people are going to think you're nasty. All of you are going to turn into Roberto in the eyes of your neighbors. They won't see your long eyelashes and pretty smiles. You'll be hardened criminals to them. They'll think you're unafraid of federal prison. Those girls on your arms? You probably killed them. Say goodbye to good marriage prospects." I stared Alejandro square in the eye and pointed to Courtney. "After this war, you're going to be known as the kind of guy who'd rape and kill her if you had the chance, and you'd brag about it to your friends over a beer later."

Alejandro and Miguel reflexively covered their forearms, doubt on both their faces. After a few seconds, Alejandro's face hardened into a mask of determination and he looked at Miguel. "I'd rather us pretend we are like that then work for someone who actually is," he said. "We're doing this."

"Fine," I said, rocking back on my heels. "Then we're taking you home tonight. Miguel, tell everyone that we've...kidnapped him, I guess. That we're torturing him for information. I don't know. Be creative."

Miguel's eyes unfocused. "I suppose, to make it more realistic, it should look like there was a fight. You could...Heather, punch me."

"What? No!"

"No, I'm serious. I'm going to have to miss work, so if you punch me, then I can report to Ágata that our conversation went bad and that we're enemies now. It'll be the first rumbles of war, plus I won't get fired."

"Miguel, I'm not punching you."

"I want to do what I can to protect you. Ágata knows we were talking. People saw you and Courtney with Las Bellas. We can make this work. After Ágata finds out that we're enemies now, I'll disappear along with Alejandro. I'm willing to take a punch for you."

There was so much more in his words than what he'd just said, but I couldn't deduce his meaning. However, I took a large step back and produced my sword, its glow lighting up the room. "A scratch. That's it. And for the record, I'm not enjoying this. Hold up your arm."

Miguel held up his arm, and I sliced a shallow scratch across one of his naked women. His jaw tightened, but he made no sound.

"That's it," I said, making my sword evaporate. "I'm not hurting you anymore. Go to Ágata and tell her there's a war on, and maybe grab some books on the sly. There won't be a lot to do at our house."

"I think it'll be suspicious if I look like I'm packing for a trip. I'll just read whatever you have around."

Courtney snorted. "You're barking up the wrong tree. The rest of us have plenty of books, though. Don't worry."

The blood drained from my face. She had to know how cruel she was being. She had to. Nobody was that freaking dense.

"Barking up the wrong tree?" Miguel asked. "What do you mean?"

"It means I can't read or write," I said, my own voice barely audible above the rushing sound in my ears.

Disappointment flashed across his face. "Oh."

"Yeah. So there you go."

And that was it for me and Miguel. Courtney had outed me—I was a dunce, devoid of the one quality that Miguel clearly valued above all others. He was better off flirting with Courtney or Minnie, and one day he'd have kids who would be better readers than I was by the time they were five. I needed to make my peace with that fast, or else—

Miguel took my hand in his. "Ágata sells little workbooks for early readers. If you don't mind, I'd like to pick some up for you. We're going to have a lot of time together. I can't think of a better way to use it."

Courtney blanched. "You're going to teach her to read? She's—"

Miguel glared at Courtney. "The only member of your team, I believe, who speaks Spanish. She's also the one who came up with a plan to save you two from Roberto on the spot, and then she didn't break composure while staring down the barrel of a gun. And now she just offered to call off the deal with us to spare our futures. It would be my privilege to tutor her. What were you going to say, Miss Frenzy? What is she?"

Alejandro stepped between them. "That's enough. Miguel, go get whatever you need at Ágata's and start spreading that alibi. I'm going to tell the boys what we're doing. Heather, Courtney, wait here for half an hour before leaving. We're going to be down by the elementary school; it's a known gang hangout. We'll be tagging the fence."

Miguel nodded and let go of my hand, our gazes lingering on each other.

～

AT NINE O'CLOCK, Alejandro and Miguel slipped out of his apartment with cans of spray paint in hand. Courtney and I were going to "catch" them in the act of spray painting anti-superhero messages and haul them back to the house. Accordingly, we waited a little while before we left.

Courtney wandered around the living room and gazed blithely at Alejandro's photographs and artwork, lost in thoughts of whatever it was she thought about. Meanwhile, the shortest member of Las Bellas plucked up the courage to talk to me, introducing himself as Juan Carlos.

"Juancho Pancho," corrected the pimply teenager on the couch with a snicker. "That's his street name."

It turned out that the speaker was Diego, and the boy sitting next to him was "Paco the Taco," whose nickname stretched back to time immemorial, apparently. The fourth and final member, Gabriel, was so enraptured by Courtney's beauty that he asked her for permission to tattoo her likeness on his arm. When she said yes, he nearly fainted.

When thirty minutes had passed, I unlocked the door and turned to Las Bellas, who were as shy and unsure as ever. "Remember," I said, looking each one in the face as I spoke. "Be bad. I promise you that Miguel and Alejandro will be safe."

They all nodded, and Courtney and I slipped out into the darkness.

Roberto was waiting.

He'd parked his cherry red Mercedes on the street in front of Alejandro's building and was leaning up against the door. When Courtney and I walked out, he stood, then burst out laughing. "Well, well, well. Ale's obviously got a crush on you two."

I was too taken aback to come up with a plan. If he'd seen us casually exit Alejandro's, there was no point in pretending there was a war. We definitely didn't look like hookers now, and lightning didn't strike twice. There was no way he wouldn't recognize who and what we were.

"Ladies," he said, stepping aside and opening the passenger door. "Need a ride?"

The yellow glow of the street light illuminated the intricate tattoos on his arms: spider webs, gothic lettering, and the ubiquitous figure of Santa Muerte.

"No, thank you," Courtney said calmly. "We have another appointment nearby."

How was she so nonplussed?

And why hadn't he pulled a gun on us yet?

He tutted in disapproval but closed the door. "Another night, then," he said, his eyes traveling over our figures. "Soon."

"Look at the time," I squeaked.

We ran until we were blocks away and out of breath. Courtney leaned against a brick wall and wiped her forehead. "Can you believe he didn't figure it out? How stupid is he?"

I leaned forward, my hands on my knees. "Yeah," I said, breathing hard. "He's…"

Memories surfaced of Ágata crossing out the eyes of a Roberto doll, but I didn't feel protected. On the contrary, I wanted to get away from Ágata, the dolls, Roberto, everything. The faster we got out of the barrio, the better.

"Let's go," I said. "We have some gangbangers to apprehend."

We ran under the cover of darkness down the dark streets towards the elementary school. At the last intersection, Courtney slowed.

"I see them."

I followed her line of sight, and sure enough, the shape of two men took form—one bulky, the other comparatively rangy—by a large wooden fence on one side of the schoolyard. Miguel reached into a backpack and pulled out a spray can.

"Evening, gentlemen," I called, my words filled with as much malice as I could muster.

Courtney and I deftly leaped over the low chain-link fence. Alejandro and Miguel stood side-by-side, ever tall and sure.

"My, my, what a pleasure," Alejandro said as we walked up, casually shaking his can. "Two of the pretty *bestias*. Oye, Miguel, you think they'll go on a date with us?"

I pointed to the words they'd painted, which were too stylized to be legible. "That says Las Bellas, right? Sorry, I don't swing that way."

Courtney cleared her throat. "Actually, it says 'kill all superheroes,'" she whispered.

"But more importantly," I plunged on, my face growing hot, "Are you threatening us?"

Miguel tossed his can back and forth, bouncing on his feet. "We're tired of your team. If you don't get out of the barrio in the next two weeks, we'll make you leave."

I stepped forward. "How are you going to do that?" I got into Miguel's space. "What can *you* do?" I lowered my voice. "*Soy una bestia*. I'm a beast. I fight anyone who challenges me, Las Bellas or Los Diablos. Your pretty face won't stop me, Miguel."

I had *not* intended for his name to come out so huskily.

He leaned in closer, our faces inches apart. "I'm not afraid of beasts *or* devils," he said, his breath brushing my lips. "You don't want to fight me."

"I think I do," I breathed. "I want to see what you're like when you're bad."

Alejandro cleared his throat and we both startled and looked over. Courtney and Alejandro were staring at us, their mouths open.

I had forgotten they were there.

Miguel stepped back, his face hardening. "Like I was saying, if you and your team don't leave us alone, you'll regret it. I've killed a lot of people."

Courtney jabbed her thumb over her shoulder. "Um, there are three Diablos coming up the street. Let's hurry this up."

I grabbed Miguel by the collar and spun him around, shoving him up against the fence with his arm in a submission hold. "You think you can threaten my team and get away with it?" I shouted. "Think again, you *pinche* gangbanger!"

Alejandro hit the wood in the same way. When he tried to protest, Courtney bent his arm higher. He let out a slew of curses.

"Yeah, well, same to you," Courtney shot back.

"Ooh, Excalibur said '*pinche*' to me," Miguel mocked, his voice slightly muffled. "Nice accent, *gringa*."

"You're not one to talk about accents, *amigo*," Alejandro murmured.

Courtney thumped his back. "Shut up, both of you. We're taking you back to the house and you are going to answer our questions."

"The hell we are!" Miguel exclaimed, though he did not struggle. "Let me go, you nasty *coño!*"

Male voices floated our way. The three Diablos rushed across the street.

Alejandro stilled. "Heather, pull out your sword and threaten me by name. I'll explain later."

Courtney and I hastily traded hostages, and I whipped out my sword with a cascade of golden sparkles. I grabbed Alejandro's hair and lifted my sword to his throat as the three Diablos approached.

"If you take one step closer, I'll slice Cipriano's head off," I barked. "Try me."

One of the Diablos extended his arms to keep the other, younger, men at bay. "Okay, we're not moving. What do you want, *bestia?*"

He sounded almost placating. In all my many dealings with Los Diablos, I'd never heard this tone from any of them.

I mentally sent a surge of light to the sword, making it gleam. "Ale, tell them what I was telling you." *Because heck if I know what's going on.*

Alejandro grimaced as if I were hurting him. "Las Bestias want you all to know that they're cleaning up this place," he said through gritted teeth. "And that if you all challenge them, you're next."

Courtney wrapped her long fingers around Miguel's neck. "These two are going to answer some questions we have. We'll release them when we're satisfied that they've told us everything we know."

The lead Diablo gasped. "You can't do that!"

"I'm going to count to ten," I growled. "And when I'm done, you'd better be on your way."

"Or what?" the Diablo shot back.

I kicked Alejandro to his knees. "One...two...*eight*..." I placed the sword at the back of his neck. "*Nine*..."

"Go, you idiots!" Alejandro shouted.

They ran.

When they had disappeared, I helped Alejandro to his feet while Courtney let go of Miguel. The men switched places again at once, and Courtney gently stroked Alejandro's throat, inspecting it. "No sword wound. You're going to be okay."

I made my sword disappear. "Oh, please. I was never going to hurt him. Guys, get your stuff. The message is out now, so we should go home and get some sleep before the war really begins. Now that Roberto knows about it, word will get around the barrio quick. I'd say we could skip town even earlier, but the vision had fourteen suns, so we'll stretch this out for two weeks."

I swung Miguel's backpack over my shoulder and grabbed his wrists. "You're coming with me," I whispered in his ear. "Scared to enter the lair of the beasts?"

"I'm trembling," he whispered back.

I leaned in closer. "Are you really going to teach me to read?"

His lips turned up. "Y-e-s."

Context clues helped me figure that one out. I gave his wrists a reassuring squeeze and unsheathed my sword again as a message to all who saw us: Las Bestias had taken Las Bellas as prisoners.

CHAPTER 7

05AUG – **The infomercial hours again, because my stupid job keeps me away from the really good shows.**

*A*lejandro and Miguel tumbled face-first into our foyer. I shut the door behind the four of us.

"Guys!" I shouted to my team, wherever they were. "We've got company!"

Eleazar came down the stairs, the rest of the team behind him, caution written on their faces. "What is this?" Eleazar asked, his voice like steel. "Who are these men?"

Alejandro sprang up. "Alejandro Cipriano," he said. "Well, Cipriano Obrador, but I never use my mother's name. Leader of—"

"Las Bellas," Eleazar snapped. "Yes, I know. And you are?" he said, glaring at Miguel.

"Juan Miguel Alvear Ortiz. Call me Miguel."

Eleazar smiled without humor, then turned to me. "Heather. A word." He jabbed his thumb towards the adjacent workout room. I backed into it, already feeling my power swirling in my arm.

"There wasn't time to consult you," I said, heading him off. "They were right there, and you *did* give me decision-making power."

"It's contingent on you making sensible decisions!"

"No, it's not!"

"Then what the hell are two scumbags doing in my house?"

"We're starting the war, moron!" The insult left my mouth before I could stop it. I'd have to be more careful.

Eleazar's anger morphed into shock and hurt. "They could be freaks or perverts or sociopaths! And now they're in our home!"

Oh, my death in Alejandro's apartment would've been an inconvenience, but this he cared about. I lifted my nose in the air. "What is this really about, Lloyd?"

My use of his last name must've sideswiped him, because he held out his hands, then dropped them loosely at his sides. "Heather, there were five people in your vision."

That brought me up short. "What?"

He was trembling. "There were five people in your vision. Obviously one of us is going to die, and your friends Alejandro and Miguel could be the people that kill one of us."

I resisted the urge to roll my eyes. They'd discussed the identity of my missing teammate ad nauseum after the vision, completely ignoring my insistence that my visions were an eclectic, unpredictable mix of symbolism and literality. For instance, the fourteen suns in my vision were obviously fourteen days. On the other hand, Alejandro, the *coyote* that would lead us to freedom, was very clearly not an actual wild dog.

The door to the workout room opened. Morris and Minnie strode in, their eyes sparking. Minnie faced me, while Morris went toe-to-toe with Eleazar.

"Last night you told me to stop you if you started shouting again," Morris said. He narrowed his eyes. "Well, now I am. Stand down or take me on. I dare you."

"She started it!"

I peered around Minnie. "I did not!"

Minnie pushed me into the now-empty hallway. "Heather. Shut up. Get the gang guys situated or go to bed. Good *grief*."

Furious shouts were coming from the workout room now, so Minnie shoved the door open again and jumped into the fray.

I stomped up the stairs, regretting the day I'd ever met Eleazar. His head was so far up his butt that he hadn't even come up with one good plan to get away from the camps and the strike team, but I'd already secured a connection with a gang, come up with a decent cover story, gotten the guys to our house, and now we just had to wait it all out.

Okay, Courtney had helped.

Well, Courtney had done most of it.

But I'd been in the room. That counted.

Courtney was practically dancing on her tiptoes outside of Armando's bedroom, her ears pressed to the door. She beckoned me close and pressed a finger to her lips. "Armando's talking to them," she whispered. "Come listen with me."

"Move," I snarled. She sprang away from the door, blinking in surprise.

I didn't bother knocking, instead barging right in. "I'm here," I said flatly.

Alejandro and Miguel were sitting politely on Armando's bed, looking up at the stern SIC, who was in the middle of a lecture. "—stay in here, and not leave without the expressed permission of a team member, nor leave their presence—"

"Heather!" Miguel exclaimed, rising partially to his feet when he saw me. Alejandro pulled him back down with a curt shake of his head.

"Armando, you're needed downstairs," I said by way of greeting. "There was a, um, incident in the gym."

Armando let out a world-weary sigh. "I'm kinda busy right now. And *why* do they know your name?" he said, a groan in each and every word.

"Because they're our allies, like it or not. If we're going to be living together, it's the least we can do. Alejandro, Miguel, this is Armando de la Cruz. He's the second-in-command."

Alejandro and Miguel's faces lit up. "Oh, a Hispanic superhero!" Alejandro said, jumping to his feet. "That's so cool. I didn't know there was one." He rubbed his chin thoughtfully. "I wonder if this could affect your popularity at all. I bet it would. People don't like that you're outsiders. This could change everything. If we move fast, we could probably start a petition or something to keep the team here. If all the Hispanic people in San Diego got behind it..."

Miguel nodded fervently and asked in Spanish where his family was from.

Armando blinked, unimpressed. "I grew up in the Idaho panhandle, as did the previous three generations of my family. I don't speak a word of Spanish. Don't ever mistake me for being anything like you, punk."

He walked out, leaving me with the stunned men.

"Looks like we found a bigger *pocho* than you, Miguel," Alejandro muttered after a moment.

"I'm sorry I'm not as exciting as Armando," I said, fighting a smile. "But I'm here to help you guys get settled in. What did he tell you so far?"

"Ale and I are going to be confined to this room," Miguel said with a sad little pout. "No books, no movies, no contact with the outside world."

"Gee, that's rough, pal," I said, nodding. "I was going to take you downstairs for dinner and tell you more about why we're leaving, but I guess I'll just leave you in your dungeon to starve."

They both laughed. Miguel slipped his hand into mine, and before I could stop myself, I gave his fingers a little squeeze and was leading them down the hall to the kitchen. When we passed the gym's open door, I couldn't help but see Eleazar.

His eyes darted to my hand in Miguel's.

CHAPTER 8

05AUG – Yet more test patterns and infomercials because Eleazar was too cheap to spring for cable.

$\mathcal{E}$leazar and Armando were so angry about the situation for a multitude of reasons that they boycotted the ground floor and, accidentally, left us in peace while Courtney and I cooked dinner. The rest of the team were either in bed or "watching television"—also known as eavesdropping from the living room.

Miguel stood next to me while I browned the ground beef in the skillet, shaking little bits of spices and herbs on the meat, and soon a warm aroma bloomed from the skillet. I wordlessly drained it and poured it into a bowl, where Miguel added cooked beans and rice. As meals went, it wasn't terribly exciting, but at least it wasn't frozen food.

The four of us sat down at one end of the large dining table and began to eat. Courtney speared a pinto bean and held it up. "What's the Spanish word for 'bean'?"

"*Frijole*," the other three of us said in unison.

Alejandro chewed thoughtfully. "Heather, why do you know Spanish but not Courtney?"

"A few of us are selected for foreign language education when we're kids," I explained. "I studied along with a few other trainees."

"What's a trainee?" Miguel asked.

"Future superheroes."

"What else do you study?" Alejandro had stopped eating and was looking at us in open curiosity. "How does your schooling work? Courtney can't speak Spanish but she can read. You can speak pretty good Spanish, actually, but you say you can't read or write English," he said, gesturing to me with his fork.

"We studied fighting, mostly," Courtney answered. "The principles, which are the big list of, like, ideals we try to aspire to. What civilian life is like. It's all bullcrap, though. That was the hardest part of being a superhero, back when I arrived on the team."

"What do you mean?" Alejandro and Miguel asked.

I put down my fork. "I explained a little bit about the strike team and the elders, but I never really told you guys why we are so desperate to leave. Do you guys know what a cult is?"

There was a beat.

"Santa Muerte," Alejandro grunted.

"Sort of. That kind of destructive, dogmatic, blind zeal is what I'm talking about. Superheroes have been around for, what, seventy years now? For the last thirty years, though, we've been under the total control of the elders, the male line descendants of the people who founded the camps where we live."

"We learned a little bit about the camps in American history class," Miguel said. "And how you all live by yourselves to keep civilians safe. But nobody ever said anything about...*any* of this."

"Propaganda," I spat. "All of it. Whatever you think you know about the camps, forget right now."

Courtney cut in. "We couldn't watch television, movies, read books, or anything. We didn't even have an education. Hell, we didn't have electricity and plumbing. It's superhero-themed stuff or nothing. The elders don't know we have a television or library cards. We work very hard to keep it that way. We even have a drill for if a camp representative drops by—hide the TV and our books, stuff like that."

"But *why*?" Miguel asked, his eyebrows drawn together in confusion.

"Control," I said. "Every aspect of our life is mandated, even our appearances. Women have to have long hair, the men have to be trimmed and shaved. Women can't lead teams. None of us can date civilians. We can't drink caffeine. We can't eat sweets or desserts. We can't get jobs."

She rolled up her sleeve and showed off an ugly scar. "We can't even go to civilian hospitals. There's stupid reasoning for all these rules—for example, if we went to a hospital, supposedly we'd endanger civilians." She rolled down her sleeve and wrinkled her nose. "As a result, we have to take care of nearly everything ourselves. If it's *really* bad, we can call the police, who call a nearby hospital, who get in touch with the one official Super hospital in freaking Virginia. We'll be leapfrogged across the country to get there. I'm not even kidding."

I cut in. "We strongly suspect we're forbidden from hospital access as a motivator to perform better. Believe me, if you don't have guaranteed medical care, you'll take better care of yourself."

Courtney nodded along. "And the individual camps have their own dumb rules, too. Eleazar and Armando are from the Idaho camp, which apparently is the strictest. They can't dance, and women can't wear red. Though you'd never guess it, from Eleazar. He's on a one-man crusade to be the worst elder's son in history."

"What do you mean?" Alejandro asked curiously.

She smiled fondly. "He hates the camps so much that the second I arrived on the team, he sat me down in a chair and explained that I'd been brainwashed, and that life was going to be different. All the rules were out the window. The only rules we still live by are that we have to protect civilians, and that we can't attract undue attention."

"He's kind of hung up on not letting the camps interfere with our affairs," I grumbled. I stirred my food around my plate, the veracity of my words still stinging. He'd been so hung up, in fact, that when we'd dated he'd been too afraid to take me out on a date...or ever sit down with me and ask how I was doing...or consider that I'd made the best call I could in Alejandro's apartment. For him, it was all mission, all the time.

My mind wandered upstairs to my bedside drawer, but my gaze drifted over to Miguel.

He was staring at me.

"How did you all get out of the cult?" he asked, blushing. "Obviously you're not part of it now."

"Education and experience are the biggest threats to the cult," I said, brushing past the fact that I'd caught him staring. "Which is probably why we're raised behind steel walls and aren't allowed to get real educations or take in civilian media. When I got to San Diego, the whole team had already mentally defected. It took a month or two to get a handle on what they were telling me, and I'm still struggling with some aspects. For one thing, we were always told that criminals are pure evil, completely beyond redemption. This goes double for gangs."

Miguel and Alejandro exchanged a wary glance.

"But don't worry," Courtney said. "I sure don't feel that way."

"Courtney is our free spirit," I said, tongue set firmly in my cheek. "You Yankees up in the New York camp are always weird."

"You said you're from Georgia, right?" Miguel asked. "And Eleazar and Armando are from Idaho?"

"Yeah," I said. "There's six camps—one in New York, two in Georgia, one in Idaho, one in Arkansas, and one in Virginia, but the Virginia one is a retirement camp. Nobody comes from there. That's where we all end up when we're too old to fight or are forcibly retired for misbehavior. Oh, and speaking of misbehavior, I face flogging when I return for supposedly failing the city."

Alejandro leaned back and crossed his arms. "And all your families live in these camps?"

"Yes," I said.

"And you'll leave them behind?"

It was Courtney's and my turn to exchange a glance.

"Yeah," Courtney said sadly. "We don't have any good option. We're leaving a lot behind. Eleazar is Elder Lloyd's only child—he would've been the new Elder Lloyd one day. The rest of us have parents, siblings, cousins, all of that. Take a moment to think about how bad it must be if we want to hide in Mexico and have them all believe we're dead."

"It must be really bad," Alejandro agreed, sober. "And I'll take you all. But since there are no superheroes in Mexico, you'll have to live quietly. People with powers in Mexico are extraordinarily rare. Word would get around."

"You speak from experience?" I asked.

"I knew a guy," he said with a shrug. "You see a lot when you're a *coyote*."

"Speaking of which," Courtney said. "How will that work?"

"It really depends on the route. If we went due south, we'd be crossing into Baja California, which is a heavily populated area. Now, more Americans go back and forth between Tijuana and San Diego than at other crossings, so you'd blend in, to a degree. However, I'm more familiar with the Texas route. There's lots of wilderness we can go through. I'm not going to risk a road crossing with this many people."

"What about you?" Courtney said. "Will you get back safely?"

Alejandro gave her a dashing grin. "Don't worry about me. I'm a wily *coyote*."

Courtney laughed while Miguel and I groaned.

Loud boots on the stairwell interrupted our banter and I twisted around in my chair. I knew those footfalls.

Eleazar walked into the kitchen, Morris on his heels. Alejandro and Miguel stood, but I just draped my arm over the back of my chair and narrowed my eyes. What now?

Eleazar oozed exhaustion as he said, "Since it's nearly zero one, I have to insist that you all go to bed, so we can all be fully rested for the gang war, which starts later today. I've spoken with Armando and we agreed that as long as you stay in the house, you're free to move around freely. No closed doors, though, except in the bathroom. Stay away from the windows."

"Thank you," Alejandro said lightly. "Ay, Eleazar, any ideas on what you'd like to do first? For the war, I mean."

Eleazar blinked, probably thrown off that Alejandro knew his name. "Uh, well, whatever you want. I don't really care, as long as it works."

Alejandro shrugged. "Anyone have any ideas?"

Morris glanced back and forth between Courtney and me. "Since Heather and Courtney are the main players, I think they should be at the center of it. Maybe a messy fight between them? It's a common enough scenario—some guys catcall two women, and then the women go get reinforcements."

"I'll stop you right there," Miguel said, an eyebrow raised. "Every man for miles around knows not to catcall any woman who lives in this house."

"Because you'll get your ass beat by said women," I pointed out. "So it follows that the guys who do it must have pretty big *cojones*...like Las Bellas. That's the point of this whole thing, remember?"

"So how's this going to work?" Miguel asked. "We need it to be memorable."

"Oh, it will be," Courtney said, her lips curling in a catlike smile. "I have some ideas."

CHAPTER 9

06AUG – Tragically, during *Days of Our Lives* airtime.

"*Y*ou're addicted to that crap," Courtney said. She leaned against the dented street sign and shook her head.

"Am not," I said right before I knocked back my third orange Fanta of the day. The sharp flavor and palpable sugar hit my system like a shot of heroin. *Ah, that's the stuff.*

We were down the street from our house, in eyesight of the front porch but not so near that someone would automatically snap to good behavior. In civilian clothes and loitering, we appeared to be standard catcalling targets—if we weren't obviously "beasts." As Miguel had predicted, nobody had dared even honk at us, much less attempted to do what a bunch of teenagers were about to.

"You going to use the bottle in the rumble?" She mimed breaking a bottle against the pitted brick wall next to us and brandishing it like a weapon. "That would mess someone up."

"We're not messing anyone up. Shouting, a light scuffle, maybe someone gets shoved. Nothing serious."

Courtney snorted. "Can you imagine getting into a real fight with someone named Paco the Taco?"

"No...or Juancho Pancho. Did you know that Juancho Pancho is the Spanish Old MacDonald?" I began to sing. "*Jauncho Pancho tiene un rancho...*"

"E, I, E, I...oh, we're about to have company," Courtney said, her song trailing off as she straightened. "It's show time."

I turned and spied what had cut off her little tune. Down the block and across the street, Las Bellas were coming towards us. When they spotted us, Diego pointed and said something to the others, and they automatically pulled their shoulders back and puffed out their chests. Instead of their usual t-shirts, they'd changed into wife-beaters. I was reminded of trainees back home trying on their masks for the first time; no matter how much they'd prepared for that moment, the mask always hung a little oddly on their face.

Courtney and I exchanged an amused glance, then settled into our roles. She twirled her hair around her finger with a coquettish simper while I began to prattle on about a hot actor on a show I'd seen the day before.

Foreknowledge prickled through my mind: *buzzing*.

What? Buzzing. Freaking *buzzing*. Why couldn't my visions and premonitions ever be *useful*?

Las Bellas crossed the street. "Ay, *mamacitas!*" Diego shouted.

His compatriots made those annoying kissing noises I'd heard from other local men whenever a fly honey passed by.

Courtney spun around. "Piss off!"

Las Bellas were just down the sidewalk now. As I'd hoped, I could see a few neighbors peeking out of their windows at the confrontation. Down the street, my teammates were almost certainly watching, too.

"Aw, don't be like that," Paco said as they drew up to us. "How about a kiss, sexy?"

I had to hand it to him—his acting was better than Gabriel's, who had already dropped his macho swagger and was biting his lip.

I put my hands on my hips. "If you even try to kiss us, I'll pound your face in."

Diego raised an eyebrow. "I think we can take a couple of *chiquitas.*" As rehearsed, he made a grab for my butt.

I shouted and roughly shoved him backwards into Paco, and the scuffle began.

Diego swung for my nose. I ducked and kicked his shin. He winced. Courtney slapped Juan Carlos, and he called her a choice slur in return. A shouting match exploded, the two of us balling our fists and screaming obscenities at Las Bellas, who shouted back in English interspersed with Spanish.

"Hey! What's going on?"

Morris's shout from down the street made me internally sigh with relief.

He teleported with a little puff right next to us, making Las Bellas gasp in obvious admiration. I shook my head quickly, and they assumed their scowling facades.

Minnie sprinted down the block towards us. She pointed a finger gun at us and—

Thwip. The metal bolt she'd shot out of her hand thudded next to Paco's head, embedded deeply into the brick. Las Bellas yelled and ducked, though she shot no more.

She skidded to a halt at the edge of the fray. "What's going on here?"

A male voice down the intersecting side street repeated her question, but in Spanish.

We all turned and tensed at the same time. Half a dozen rough-looking young men approached. Courtney squinted, her sharp eyes no doubt reading their tattoos, because she inhaled and said, "Los Lobos. A few San Quentin tattoos. No guns that I can see, but they don't look friendly."

Morris rolled up his sleeves. "Los Lobos? What are they doing here? They're from the north end."

"One of them has a fresh Santa Muerte tattoo," Courtney murmured. "Los Lobos belong to Los Diablos now. Alejandro was saying that Roberto is absorbing the smaller gangs."

"Las Bellas, leave," I ordered.

They obeyed, skedaddling at top speed back the way they'd come.

As the Lobos neared, we four remaining superheroes stood our ground. Their wolf-themed tattoos and prison markings didn't scare me; at least Santa Muerte's hideous skeletal grin wasn't leering back at me for once. Compared to Los Diablos, this petty gang from the north end of the barrio looked like rogue zookeepers, all covered in faded, badly-rendered wolves.

"What do you want?" Morris's voice was deeper than usual.

"We want you gone," the largest man said in English. "And we want you dead."

Minnie breathed a laughed. "Dude, pick one."

They traded insults for a few seconds, but I wasn't paying attention. There were six of them versus four of us. Not impossible odds, but not the best. However, if they'd been packing heat, they would've pulled it out by now. Though the power swirled in my hand, demanding release, I held steady. Not everything had to end with a fight.

I stepped forward and told them in Spanish that they were in our neighborhood now, and we made the rules.

The largest one shoved me into the jagged brick wall. There was a bright burst of pain on the back of my scalp, then a warm wetness that flowed down my neck and under my collar. I fell to the ground, stars circling above me.

Shouts and the sound of fists colliding with flesh brought me back to earth. The six wolves were locked in a dead heat with my three teammates. Morris popped in and out of space, surprising his opponents and throwing them off guard.

A foot met my stomach. I grabbed the kicker—a huge guy with tear drop tattoos—and pulled him to the ground, raising my fist to break his nose. The stupid man reached for a fistful of my hair, making me yell in pain as my laceration was pulled open. Power surged through my hand, taking form.

Wait. What was that noise?

Somewhere above, beyond the dizziness from the pain, an insect-like buzzing was drawing near. Everyone stopped and looked up, confused. A dark cloud, but far too near and fast-moving to be rain, converged over the sun, casting us into premature gloom.

I realized what it was the second one of them shouted, *"Mierda! Son avispas!"*

"Crap, they're wasps," I repeated faintly, my mouth dropping open.

And oh yes, they were wasps—and more. Wasps, bees, hornets, and every other type of horrid stinging monstrosity descended on the little corner battle, surrounding us in untold numbers. It was as if every hive insect in Southern California had converged on us at once. I curled up in a ball, only barely able to hear the terrified shouts of Los Lobos. The insects landed on me and crawled everywhere...

But they did not sting me.

I slowly opened my eyes and peered around at the Biblical-level horde. My teammates were similarly unscathed. Los Lobos, however, were on the run, large welts already appearing where they'd been stung. They sprinted down the sidewalk, shouting curses and pleas to God for relief.

When our enemies were out of sight, the insects lifted away from us and flew up and away, disappearing over the rooftops of the barrio.

There was a long silence.

"What the hell just happened?" Minnie flicked off a dead bee from her shoulder.

I struggled to my feet, wincing the whole way and then swaying.

Morris caught me. "C'mon, let's get home. That cut looks nasty."

It did? My teeth began to chatter—I was losing a lot of blood. Was I going to need to go to the clinic? Get stitches? A blood transfusion? A shot?

Minnie patted my hand. "Aw, naw, it's not that bad. I've seen way worse."

Courtney grimaced. "I dunno, that's a buttload of bl—"

Morris and Minnie's glares shut her up quick. We limped down the street, Morris never letting me walk on my own, until we were in spitting distance of the house.

The front door burst open and Eleazar bounded down the steps. "Heather!"

"I'm okay." I grinned crookedly. "I lost a fight with the brick wall. You will not believe what happened."

Armando stood in the doorway. "What was up with that dust cloud?"

Morris handed me off to him and he guided me toward the living room. Eleazar ran into the kitchen to get the first aid kit, a large chest of every conceivable medical supply ever made. Armando pushed me down on the chintz sofa and made me lay my head on a throw pillow.

"That's what you won't believe," Morris said. "It was bees and wasps and stuff."

They were all fretting over me now, wiping the blood off my neck and shoulders, dabbing at my scalp—I yelped once—and speaking over each other. Their voices began to mix together with the pain in my head. Miguel appeared in the corner with Alejandro, watching me with large brown eyes filled with concern. Alejandro patted his shoulder and directed him out of the room. I weakly extended my hand, but it dropped a second later.

Minnie kneeled down in front of me. "Heather, you need stitches. I'm going to distract you while Courtney sews up your wound, okay?"

I grumbled something, my eyes still on the corner where Miguel had been. Alejandro inclined his head and mouthed something: *Later.* I frowned and dragged my gaze onto Minnie.

The black pupils of her eyes seemed to widen, then pull me in, becoming like a train tunnel through a mountain. I fell into the inky depths, landing in an invisible pool of warm water. I plodded around in the darkness, each step making a wet, echoing sound. "Hello?"

Minnie appeared with a peaceful whisper of sound, once again bare-faced and sporting loose curls instead of box braids. "You're going to be in a lot of pain after the stitches, so Armando is getting ready to inject you with some morphine," she said kindly. "I'm going to guide you into a...well, not a dream, exactly. Something between a trance and a vision. Any requests?"

Why did her voice echo like that?

"I don't know," she said, answering my unspoken question. "And I can hear your thoughts because we're both in your head. You're making my voice sound like that." She sounded amused. "Now, think of the happiest place you know."

A breeze—and then I was back home in Oconee, Georgia, surrounded by gently waving grass and my laughing siblings.

I sat down in the velveteen grass, inhaling the perfumed air. Spring blossoms on trees floated around me like snow while birds called to each other, their song mixing together to create a tune of carefree joy.

Soft hands covered my eyes. "Guess who," Miguel teased.

"My reading tutor?"

"That's right." He uncovered my eyes and sat next to me. "I'll read aloud and you follow along, okay?"

Somewhere, far away, a needle was sewing up the back of my head—but I didn't care. Miguel's honey-sweet voice led me through the letters and words of a fairy tale I knew from my childhood, and for once, I was happy.

CHAPTER 10

06AUG – During *Cops* and *America's Most Wanted*, which was totally fine because when you're a superhero, those shows aren't really that interesting. It would be like a professional chef tuning into a cooking show—he's not going to see anything he doesn't deal with every day. Although if a chef wants to watch *Cops*, that's fine. I'm not here to judge.

I cracked an eye open and groaned. It had all been too good to last.

Was there an egg on the back of my head? That's what it felt like. I reached up to touch my scalp, but a warm hand caught mine and guided it back down to the mattress. "Armando said to make sure that you didn't touch it."

"M-gel?" I mumbled into my pillow. My lips felt like cardboard, and the inside of my mouth was about as dry, too. "Zat you?" My eyes were closed again already. What on earth had they injected me with? Morphine was powerful, but I felt like a sack of rocks.

"It's me," Miguel said from near my head, a smile in his words. "Courtney and Alejandro are in the corner, just so you know."

"*Hola,*" they both chimed at the same time from the other end of the room.

Before I could reply, Alejandro corrected Courtney's pronunciation in a low voice, patiently explaining the correct way to stress the syllables. She repeated it, plus a bit of garbled Spanish that was probably meant to be "*buenas tardes.*"

He laughed and said it again, slower.

The astringent smell of mentholated chest rub brought me closer to full wakefulness. I scratched under my nose, my finger sliding through a large goopy swipe of it.

"What? Who put this stuff here?"

"It's, um, to help you wake up," Miguel said. "If you want, I can also sing the frog song." He cleared his throat. *"Sana, sana, colita de rana..."*

Clearly, I was tripping balls on whatever they'd given me for the pain. Some bozo who sounded like Miguel was singing about frog tails. I opened my eyes. He'd carried the ottoman from upstairs into my bedroom and was sitting next to me with a hesitant little smile on his face.

"Hi." He slid gentle hands under my neck and waist and helped me sit up. Rarely had someone touched me so kindly, and when he pulled away, I felt cold.

"You've been out for a few hours," Alejandro said. "Your boyfriend and the *pocho* are speaking with the rest of the boys back at my apartment about the next step in the war. Everyone else is canvassing the locals and asking about my gang's whereabouts to make it seem like you're hunting them."

I rubbed my forehead and eyes, trying to catch up with what he was saying. "And Eleazar left you two alone with Courtney and me?"

"I saw Courtney roundhouse kick a man today. I wouldn't try anything on her if you paid me." He shot her a bright smile. "Please teach me how to do that. You're like Chuck Norris, but prettier."

Courtney hopped to her feet and held out both hands, pulling him to his feet and towards the door. "Sure, but I gotta tell you now that I'm a mean teacher and perfectionist. I was the best hand-to-hand pupil..."

They disappeared down the hall, leaving me alone with Miguel. I picked at my faded patchwork quilt while I searched for something to say. I was startlingly aware that I was about as interesting as drywall.

Miguel sat next to me and leaned forward on his knees. "Morris and Minnie reported that you were saved from Los Lobos by a massive swarm of bees. Courtney said it was probably magic. What do you remember?"

That was the sixty-four-thousand-dollar question, wasn't it? What had happened out there on the sidewalk? I couldn't explain it as anything but bug telepathy, though I knew of only one bug telepath, and he was a little boy I'd met when I'd visited the big superhero camp up in the north end of Georgia for a funeral—and he was an ant telepath, to boot.

"I don't know," I admitted. "One second someone was kicking my stomach, and the next it was bee city. I guess someone out there is looking out for us. I don't know about magic, though. The only magic I know of is from La Bruja."

"Ágata isn't in the bee business," Miguel said, holding back a laugh. "She's more into...well, not bees. If the way she reacts when a fly gets into the *conchas* case is any indication, I don't think she likes bugs."

If Miguel said it, I believed it.

I made to stand and stretch, but he placed his hand on my thigh, shooting an electric tingle straight to my lower back. "Heather?"

"Hmm?"

"Why don't you fight as well as Courtney?"

I gulped down the sudden self-consciousness and embarrassment. Behind the image of a badass with a sword was a short, round, sunburned girl—and he'd seen her.

I tucked a lock of hair behind my ear. "Courtney has lightning-quick reflexes and senses. I've got weird visions and a sword that comes out of my hand. All the training in the world won't make me as good as her."

He looked away. "You were all covered in blood when they brought you in, and Ale said you'd been kicked in the stomach. I'd always assumed that super-heroes never really get hurt in fights like that—just from guns and things. It was...hard..."

I placed my hand in his; it felt as though it was meant to be there. "I won't be in fights like that much longer." I made to stand, but swayed from the drug that still lingered in my system.

Miguel helped me back down and pulled the blanket up around me. "You should stay in bed," he said. "Can I get you anything? Water? Food?"

"Can you get a scrunchie from my bedside drawer, please?" I'd put my hair up, prop up my pillows, and dig into the copy of *Soap Opera Digest* that lay on my bedside table. I loved to look at the pictures, a quirk that gave my teammates endless amusement.

Miguel opened the drawer and paused, then slowly removed the thick pile of envelopes from my sketch artist admirer. "Oh," he breathed. He unfolded the picture of me, then turned over the paper to read the letter.

"Those are nothing," I said quickly. "Just—just fan mail."

"Do you save all your fan mail? Even though you can't read it?"

Why was my face so hot? "No, I don't get any other letters. Those are very special, and I just like having...um, can you put those back, please?"

As much as I liked Miguel, my fan letters were far too precious to show him at this point in our relationship. My faithful servant had stood next to me in spirit when I'd faced Eleazar. He'd believed in me when nobody else did. He'd extended kindness to a public servant whose true name he did not know. I'd never meet him, but right now...Miguel wasn't allowed to read those letters.

Miguel carefully folded up the paper and slipped it back into the envelope, which he placed in the drawer before handing me my scrunchie. "That was a very romantic note. You never mentioned him before. What's his name?"

I swept my thick hair into a ponytail. "I don't know. He never identifies himself. And it's not romantic."

"He says he feels more than admiration for you. That's a shy boy's way of saying he loves you."

I gulped. "He could ask me to marry him and it wouldn't mean anything, since we don't even know each other's names. And I doubt he'd really like me, if he got to know me."

"Why?" Miguel's tone was suddenly hard.

"Because of everything." I gestured all around us, as if my walls represented my life. "The cult, the strike team, my appalling lack of education. He writes so well—even Minnie has commented on it. He's a words person, just like you. How could I keep up with that? It would disappoint him."

Miguel appeared to ponder that. "I never thought I'd have competition from a man in a letter. This is an interesting turn of events." He took my hand in his again. "But I don't think you give yourself enough credit. Maybe you can't read or write, but that's fixable. And you can make a sword come out of your hand. You're very pretty, and I'm sure you can tell me anything there ever was to know about current television shows. And just between you and me, watching you intimidate Alejandro in his kitchen was maybe the funniest thing I've ever seen. Once I got over the shock."

"I'll give you the Alejandro thing, but nobody really cares about television, Miguel."

He smirked. "You sound like my mom when I talk about going to college and traveling the world. Nobody wants a boy like me, apparently. Not one who is always reading and pretending I'm somewhere else."

Well, that was just silly. "You want to go to college? What would you study?"

A small smile played around his lips. "Art."

"Art? Really? That's...wow, I would've thought that you'd want to study literature or something."

"Don't get me wrong—I love books. But my true talent lay in art. I even won a contest at school when I was a senior."

"What type of art?" This was so cool. Miguel was ever more interesting, and I loved a man who could work with his hands and produce something.

The playfulness increased. "I'm a rather talented portrait artist. I drew a picture of my parents that was so good, it was displayed at the big shopping mall downtown. My name was on it and everything."

I could see my shocked eyes reflected in his own, which were shining with humor. My blush returned as his meaning sunk in. If he was saying what I think he was saying...

"*You* wrote that letter with the picture? All of those letters?"

It was his turn to blush crimson. "I wasn't originally going to send the picture. My mom caught me drawing it and said I had to send it to you. I actually wrote the letter second."

I shook my head to clear my jumbled thoughts, then fished a notebook and pen out of the drawer. "Can you draw another? I want to see this in action."

I didn't want to say that I didn't believe him, but talk was cheap.

Miguel merely crossed his legs and tapped the pen against the notepad while he studied me. He lifted his hand to make a little frame, presumably to capture my face in a mental portrait, then hummed to himself while he thought.

After a few seconds, he said, "I don't suppose you had a *quinceañera* party when you turned fifteen."

"Me? No. We don't do anything like that in the camps."

"That's a shame. You'd look very lovely in a *quinceañera* dress."

I was about to ask what on earth he was on, but then he put the pen to the paper and began to draw.

His hand soared over the notepad like a conductor's hand moved for his orchestra, a mix of long sweeps and darting little touches. My face took shape, ever squished and pouty, yet lovely in a way I'd never seen myself. He drew my hair in an elegant partial updo, with some of it tumbling around my shoulders. I wore an elegant ball gown with a skirt that resembled a frilly cupcake, and even elbow-length gloves. A few flourishing strokes of the pen— and I was descending a grand staircase.

He signed the bottom corner and handed it to me. "It's based on the *quinceañera* dress in the window of Juancho's parents' store."

I brushed away the fat tear that was rolling down my cheek. "I'm sorry, it's the drugs," I mumbled.

He really had been writing me for months. Letter after letter after letter of well-wishes were tucked in my bedside drawer, filled with expressions of gratitude and even jokes to cheer me up—all without a return address. He'd wanted to take me to his prom. He wanted me to be happy without worrying about a reply. He thought I deserved to wear a ball gown.

He cared about me, personally, in a way no guy ever had.

He'd said he loved me.

"Hey, hey." He scooched towards me. "Please don't cry. I didn't mean to upset you. Is your head hurting?"

"Why are you so *sweet?*" I squeaked, the tears coming faster. "You're a terrible gangbanger, Miguel. Just the worst. Nobody will believe that you killed us."

"Why do you keep my letters?" he asked brightly.

"Because they're the nicest thing anyone's ever done for me," I said, finally drying up a little. "You're the only person who's ever sent me fan mail. Why do you send me fan mail, anyway?"

Miguel sighed and stretched back and looked up at the ceiling—I could see the line of dark hair on his lower stomach. I swallowed and glanced at the wall.

"You always have this vivaciousness about you. I can see it at a distance. And your accent! You're so obviously not from around here. You're just self-evidently exciting and different and...and exotic." There was a touch of longing in his voice.

"Alejandro's lived an amazing and exciting life, too. He always tells me about his adventures as a *coyote* and life in Juárez. Even my parents are from La Paz, and they flew in a plane to come here. Me? I've never been anywhere. I've never even left the barrio. I told my parents that I wanted to go to college, and you know what they did? They got me the job with Ágata. Sometimes they'll say, '*Hijo*, we know a lovely girl back home for you. Stop drawing your silly pictures and save up some money and we'll bring her here.'"

He closed his eyes. "I want...*more* than what they've got planned for me. I want to see the rest of the country. I want to start a band, meet movie stars, climb Mt. Rainier." He bolted upright. "You're from the south, right? I have an encyclopedia and I saw pictures of Spanish moss once. Does it really look like green mist in the trees? And have you ever been to Little Havana in Miami? I'd love to go there. And do people really eat pickled pig's feet? Is it gross? It sounds gross."

"You sound like Courtney." I stroked my ponytail. "Dreamers and schemers, that's what you two are."

His earnestness softened. "Books are an escape. James Bond novels are the best." He mimed shooting my poster of Mark-Paul Gosselaar. "Some of Las Bellas make fun of me, but Alejandro says whatever keeps us off the streets and out of trouble is a worthwhile pastime. I, uh, also like my Super Nintendo. I bought it with my first paycheck. But books are my favorite."

My respect for Alejandro skyrocketed, even if he was probably playing tonsil tennis with Courtney in the gym at that moment.

I shook my head. "Why do you guys call yourself a gang? You're just friends, and he's the head friend."

He laughed. "Why does anyone call you beasts? You're all so normal. You like television. I saw Armando fussing over his face fuzz in the mirror yesterday. Minnie's into grunge, and Morris is clearly into Minnie. Eleazar naps at his desk."

"And Courtney? Is she normal?"

He scoffed. "Courtney is just like every other starry-eyed girl I went to high school with who read *Romeo and Juliet* and thought it was a relationship manual. Why, she's probably down there with Alejandro right now, trying to convince him to run away with her and make sweet love all night long."

The thought elicited a delicious tingle in my lower belly. Here was Miguel in my room, happy...eager...

I inched closer to him. "I can't run away with you, but would you like me to tell you about Georgia?" I asked quietly. "My home's really beautiful, especially in the summer. The grass is so green, and we're always running around with flowers in our hair. It gets so hot there at times that we girls dress in little tank tops and skirts. We probably look like fairies with our long hair and flowers."

Miguel gulped. "I'd like to hear more about that."

I took the notepad from him without breaking eye contact, setting it to the side. "Chattahoochee's up in the mountains, all forested and green. My home, Oconee, has the most beautiful river running through it. It sparkles in the sunshine. I once saw Elder Campbell's little boy, Patrick, make drops of water move with his mind. In the setting sun, they looked like little rubies floating in the air."

Miguel's face was inches from mine. "What else?" he whispered.

"Georgia has the most beautiful coastline in the country." My voice was soft. "Savannah has ancient lowlands filled with fishing boats, and the air smells like sleep and salt. Saint Catherine has golden sand where women with golden skin lie, soaking up the sun while wearing little bikinis."

His hand cupped my cheek. "I'd like to see that."

I leaned toward him, so close I could smell his sweet scent as it swirled in the air between us. I closed my eyes.

"Will you come with me?" he whispered.

I broke away and turned my face from him.

Man, I was *stupid*. What was I doing? Flirting with this poor boy so I could...what? Seduce him and distract myself for ten seconds?

Shame on me. I was going to be leaving in a matter of weeks. I had no business using Miguel.

"What's wrong?" Miguel asked. "Was I coming on too strong? I'm so sorry." He scooted back. "In fact, I'll go. Please rest."

"No! No, I—no, wait," I said, catching his hand in mine. "It's just that I'm *leaving*, Miguel. For good. It's not fair of me to do this to you. Not when you're going to be known for killing me."

"Oh, yeah," he grumbled. "I forgot. And of course, there's Eleazar." He side-eyed me. "Courtney said you two had a huge fight the other day and he tried to blow the house down."

I scowled. "Courtney needs to shut the hell up."

"Is it true, though? If it is, I don't think you should trust someone who uses his powers on you like that. Dad always says that a man who has to use his fists to make a point isn't a man at all. I think he'd include superpowers in there, too."

I squirmed. "No, it's not like that. Honest. I wasn't harmed. In fact, I was trying to get him all riled up. Obviously, it worked."

If Eleazar had ever actually tried to deliberately hurt me with his powers, he wouldn't have lived long enough for Morris and Armando to swoop in and beat the tar out of him.

Miguel's confusion increased, and he rubbed his forehead. "You wanted to make him mad? Why?"

I crossed my arms and swallowed the sudden lump in my throat.

"Listen. We...well, we dated for six months and I dumped him two weeks ago. He never spent any time with me, and during our conversation he was just so upset about how I almost jeopardized the escape plan in Alejandro's apartment that I kinda needled him about how, um, *you* said that you want to spend time with me, in your letters. He got sarcastic and teased me about being illiterate. I started shouting, and then things devolved from there. I'm not a jerk, I promise. But if he'd been a better leader, I wouldn't have been a nutcase."

Miguel studied me. "No, you need to learn how to control your temper. Eleazar may have been unkind, but he's not responsible for your actions. You are."

"Hey!" I complained. "Were you and Courtney discussing this while I was out?"

Miguel lifted my hand to his lips and pecked my fingers, then gave me a small smile. "Good night, Heather."

"Night," I grumbled.

Miguel slipped out of my room, leaving me to fume in the bed.

However, as soon as I heard his bedroom door close down the hall, loneliness gripped me. I laid down again and stared at the wall, then flipped over, trying to get comfortable on my lumpy mattress.

"Heather."

I bolted upright. A woman had spoken my name from somewhere in the house, but she wasn't Courtney or Minnie. I threw back the covers and whipped my arm, my hand clenching around the hilt that appeared there. This person knew my name—that was the most suspicious part. A strike team member? Someone from the north San Diego team? My mom?

Instead of announcing myself by thudding down the stairs, I slid down the bannister.

In the hallway, I took in my surroundings. Low murmurs and masculine chuckles were coming from the gym. The living room lacked the comforting glow of the television. The kitchen was empty except for our resident mouse, who was squeaking in the pantry.

"Heather."

I spun around and faced the backdoor. She was in the backyard, maybe even on the deck. How did Courtney not hear her?

I ran through the front door and opened it as quietly as I could, then slipped out into the hot night.

I stopped mid-step on the doormat.

The hooded figure from my vision was standing by Courtney's rose bush.

Her outfit blended in with the night so well that I could not see its details, just that it covered all of her. She bowed her head as she stroked the mummified leaves. "Heather," she repeated. "They're dying."

"Who are you? What do you want?"

She didn't look up. "They're dying."

Her accent.

I paused. "Say that again."

"They're dying."

She pronounced it like I did: *dyin'.* She was a southerner. How...completely bizarre. Of course, people could be southerners. *I* was a southerner. But for a spooky, faceless symbol of impending doom, that was a weird detail for my mind to conjure up.

Unless she *wasn't* a symbol. It was very possible she was a real person: a member of a strike team. Plenty of them came from the camps located in the south. Maybe she had a message for me about her team's plans.

I put my sword away. "What do you want?"

"They're dying, Heather."

A dog barked down the street. A man holding its leash shushed him and continued to walk towards us.

I lowered my voice. "Yeah, you only said that a million times. *Who* is dying? The flowers? Thank you, Captain Obvious."

"I'm not a captain," she murmured, still stroking the flowers with her gloved hand.

"Then what are you? Tell me or *anda a cagar.*"

Somehow, perhaps because she was literally a figment of my own mind, I knew she was smiling beneath that freaky hood of hers. "True heroines always speak joyfully, Heather. Didn't you know?"

"Oh, fu—"

She grabbed a knife from a sheath on her thigh.

I brandished my sword, throwing sparks everywhere.

The bullet hit the blade with a marvelous twang and flew off into the stratosphere. The man walking the dog was standing in shooting stance at the end of the walk.

"Die, *bestia!*"

I leaped down the steps and zigzagged toward him while shots rang out. Behind me, Courtney burst through the door with her own little war cry.

I grabbed the man's wrist and pointed his gun high, then slammed my fist into his solar plexus. He dropped the gun, which I caught and tossed to

Courtney. While she unloaded it, I kicked the man and rolled him onto his stomach, bending his arms behind him.

"Frenzy, anybody else nearby?"

"No."

"Let me go!"

"Yeah, right," I said with a humorless laugh. "Who are you?"

"I'm not saying—"

I ground his face into the pavement. "Who are you?" I shouted.

"I'm with Los Diablos! Roberto told me to kill one of you as punishment for kidnapping Ale!"

"Punishment," I repeated. "He wants to punish us."

"Yes!"

Courtney squatted down and grabbed a fistful of the man's hair. "What else did he say?" Her voice had lost all of its usual dreamy sweetness.

Blood streamed down his face from where I'd rubbed his skin into the sidewalk. "He's ordered hits on all of you. He's even getting *brujería* involved. You've got death curses on you. He wants to make you all suffer for taking Ale. He talks about torturing all of you, making examples of you. It'll be slow."

The tip of my blade missed his face by a quarter of an inch. I slowly pushed the fiery, crackling sword into the earth, the heat causing bits of the sidewalk to begin to glow. I stopped when the hilt was halfway to the ground.

"You see that word?" I said quietly. "What does my blade say?"

"Excalibur," he whispered.

"You go back to Roberto and tell him that if he ever threatens me or my team again, that word engraved on my sword will be the last thing he ever sees."

"I can't go back a failure. He'll kill me."

"That's your problem, *cabrón*. Not mine." I stood up and kicked him. "Go before I change my mind."

He sprang to his feet and sprinted down the sidewalk, his yappy little dog hot on his heels. Courtney and I exchanged a dark look, then turned and headed back towards the house, where Alejandro and Miguel were waiting at the door. My hooded visitor was nowhere to be seen.

Inside, Alejandro gathered Courtney into a fierce hug, but I just tipped my head towards Miguel.

"*That's* why we're called beasts."

CHAPTER 11

08AUG – You know what I don't like about *60 Minutes*? They never talk about things that matter to me. I was SO excited to find an in-depth news discussion show when I moved here, but they never talked about the camps, the city politics that led to the barrio falling apart so spectacularly, the rise of Los Diablos, or anything like that. No mention of how completely we were dicked over by San Diego. Nothing like that. No, it's just murders and stuff going on in Europe. But you know what's worse? The local evening news barely covers the barrio, too. We have on average three murders a week around here, all gang-related, all REALLY violent, and that's actually less than when my team started, apparently. Do the citizens not know? Or do they not care? Is this why I'm being sent home? Because the city is out of money and nobody cares about us?

The musical jingle of the over-the-door bell was the only sound that could be heard when I walked into Ágata's bodega a few days after the first "battle." Though Santa Muerte continued to leer at me from every direction, I couldn't help but feel a warm sense of nostalgia. This was where I'd met Miguel, though my head knew that he would not be behind the counter today.

I passed the coolers filled with delicious-looking sodas and walked up to the counter. Another exciting telenovela was on the screen of the small television, and this time a man in a tuxedo and an eyepatch was brandishing a knife and shouting at a crying woman who was sporting gravity-defying hair.

Another man ran into the scene and drew a rapier from a scabbard and challenged the tuxedo man to a duel.

Wherever we ended up in Mexico, I hoped it had television. Nothing on American television could hope to match Telemundo's daytime lineup.

Ágata poked her head out of the curtain. "Oh, it's you."

"I told you I'll be back," I said in my best Terminator accent. She raised an eyebrow. "It's from...oh, never mind. I brought more money."

She removed a stool from behind the counter and gestured for me to pull up the stool on my side. "There's been no new orders, so I'll keep the money for the future. My neighbors tell me that your team is having trouble with the gangs, though," she said, as mild as milk.

I handed her fifty dollars. "Las Bellas have been tagging local fences and walls. Los Lobos tried to throw down near our house, but we stopped them. We're worried about Las Bellas, though," I said in an undertone. "We've heard reports. It sounds like they might be trying to start a war."

She snorted. "You mean Alejandro's boys? Please. They couldn't fight their way out of a churro shop."

I laughed so hard I almost fell off the stool. When I'd calmed down, I wiped my eyes. "Maybe," I said, another spasm of amusement fighting its way out of my chest. I had to salvage this plan somehow, so I plunged on, "But Alejandro seems like bad news."

Ágata tutted. "Are we talking about the same man?"

"Well, sure. He did time for larceny. He has tattoos and everything. He's trouble."

She gave me an odd look somewhere between disbelief and pity, then got off the stool and went back to the hot plates, which were steaming away. Using tongs, she removed a foil-wrapped item and brought it back to me.

"Juanmi was complaining the other day that he was worried about pursuing a crush of his. I'll tell you what I told him. Do you know what this is?"

"Sure," I said, eyeing the item. "That's a tamal, right? Also, do you mean Juanmi, Jorge the mailman's son?" It didn't surprise me that we knew the same people. The barrio was a close-knit community. If I ever met little Juanmi, I'd give him advice on how to woo his schoolyard crush. Cookies were a good start.

She nodded and unwrapped the tamal, allowing savory, meaty steam to rise from it. "The very same. I told him that some people are like tamales." She pointed to the corn husk wrapper. "Sometimes, people develop rough exteriors to protect themselves, to keep themselves together in the intense steam and heat. For some people, that steam is a family member," she said darkly. "For others, the requirements of their job cause them to become hard and tough. Juanmi was worried that his cariño was mean and standoffish because of how she acts when she's under pressure. But if we only judge the tamal from its outside, never take the time to open it..."

"...You'll never enjoy the contents," I finished for her, biting my lip.

She pulled open the corn husk and revealed the perfect tamal, then reached under the counter and produced a plastic spoon, which she handed to me.

While I ate, I thought about what she said. "You really trust Alejandro?"

"With my life. I've been in the barrio for a long time. The gangs are an infection in this place, a virus in the streets. Alejandro does what he can to protect his boys from Roberto's influence. You can sneer at him starting his own counter-gang, but life is no fairy tale. And it's not like they do anything bad. If I need my stockroom organized, I call them and they're here the next day."

"What about Miguel?"

She scoffed. "That boy always has his head up on some cloud. I can't depend on him at all. He used to rearrange my shelves while reading until I got after him because he put the bread in the cooler and the candles for the *santos* with Santa Muerte's candles. Believe me, my customers did *not* like that." She shook her head. "If it weren't for how much his mother looked after me when I broke my ankle, I'd fire him."

"Well, thank you for keeping him on board," I said as I dug into my tamal. "He's so sweet, he probably shouldn't stand out in the rain."

For all her derision of Miguel, she smiled affectionately. "I'm glad you think so. He's very fond of you."

I choked on a bite of tamal. "He talks about me? What does he say?"

"I haven't seen him since the other day, but did you know that he's been writing you letters?"

"I, uh, just found out about those," I said, blushing so furiously I could see it in my reflection on the glass counter.

"You'd better be nice to him." She whisked away my wrapper. "He might be a useless employee, but he's a good useless employee."

"I'll be very nice to him, I promise."

The bell rang as another customer came in. I turned around on the stool, then jumped down when I saw who it was.

"Excalibur!" Jorge said, waving. "I didn't know you knew Ágata."

"Oh, we go way back," I said with a shrug. "Also, since I'm in public and not wearing a mask, please just call me Heather." It belatedly occurred to me that I didn't care about people knowing my name or face anymore. I was going to be "dead" soon anyway. Might as well humanize myself as much as possible.

Jorge smiled pleasantly at me, then pointed to the cigarettes behind Ágata. "I'm just here for my usual."

While Ágata rang up the cigarettes, I leveled an expression of stern disapproval at Jorge. "You shouldn't smoke, you know."

"You sound just like Juanmi," Jorge said, shaking his head. "Leticia already has me drinking those weight loss shakes for lunch. Let an old man have his comforts."

"Your little boy and your wife love you. Don't you want to see Juanmi grow up and get married? His little *hijos* and *hijas* run around with their friends?" It was a bald emotional manipulation, to be sure, but whatever got him off the coffin nails.

Jorge sighed. "I'll think about it. Speaking of running around with friends…Ágata, if you see Juanmi, please tell him that his parents' home isn't a hotel. He's been spending these last few nights sleeping over at his friend Francisco's house, or so he said on the phone. But when I went there, Francisco was there, but not Juanmi."

"Do you want my team to look for him? Frenzy can probably track his scent if you get me some of his clothes. I'm sure he's not in trouble. You know how kids are."

It wasn't technically my team's area, but for Jorge we could probably put up a little search for Juanmi. Jorge didn't seem concerned, so I wasn't, either—we both knew his son was undoubtedly up to boyhood shenanigans.

Indeed, Jorge shook his head. "No, please. He's done this before. It's summer, so if I really need him, I know where I can find him." He chuckled. "Anna's *heladaría*, the movies, the library, chasing the elote cart, or drooling over the new Nintendo games over at the Hernandez's apartment."

"Your boy needs to grow up," Ágata said, her hands on her hips. "He needs to get serious. You and Leticia spoil him."

"He shouldn't grow up too fast, though," I said. "Childhood is short."

Ágata gave me a funny look, but before she could speak, the phone on the wall rang. She answered it, her face darkening immediately. "*Sí*," she said, before asking him in Spanish what the caller wanted. Her eyes widened, and she looked me directly in the eye, an expression of deep significance there.

I gestured for Jorge to leave before turning my ear back to the conversation.

Ágata made notes on a small notepad next to the till, asking a few questions about "who" and "how." After a minute more, she told the caller to come by in an hour, then hung up. She closed her eyes and held onto the phone for several seconds, then pinched the bridge of her nose.

"Roberto?" I asked.

"May God strike that man where he stands," she said quietly.

"What did he want?"

Instead of answering, she bent down and retrieved a small glass jar from beneath the counter, as well as a tiny figurine of Santa Muerte, a sheet of red paper, and tiny bits of animal claws and fur. On the paper, she wrote my team's codenames. After a second, I realized I could tell that they were spelled incorrectly: Exkaliber, Raith, Phrenzy, Drednot, Lazer, and Fantom.

"That's not—" I began.

"I know," she said. "My policy is that if someone orders a spell like this, they'd better be ready to do the footwork themselves. Even if you weren't paying me, I'd mess it up. Lucky for me, he never checks the details."

"Ugh. What did he want?"

"Death," she said simply. "He wants you all dead."

"So I've gathered. I also know this isn't the first spell of this kind you've made."

"Indeed. As he's gathering the gangs to him, he's also summoning the forces of darkness to his side. Screw your courage to the sticking place, Heather. This man means business."

"So do we. We're already moving the pieces across the board."

She looked up from her work, startled. "Is that why you were saying all that ridiculousness about Las Bellas? Are they involved with you all and Los Diablos?"

"I'm not at liberty to share the full plan, but I can say that they're involved, and I promise you that they're not in danger. But you can't share that with anyone, least of all Roberto or his goons. In fact, just stay as far away from him as possible, okay? Stuff's going to go down around here."

Ágata's eyes sparkled with an old lady's wicked amusement. "I'll make this spell for Roberto because he doesn't know about the other spells I've made."

Though all the talk of spells and magic were turning my stomach, I leaned forward. "What other spells?"

She reached underneath the counter and removed a wooden bowl filled with items. "Protection for you and your team."

I pulled the bowl toward me, unsure of what to think. The rough-hewn wooden bowl contained a picture of Roberto with words written on it in black pen, feathers, a green and white candle, a bundle of herbs wrapped in black thread, and a Mexican peso.

"Oh," I murmured. "Well, thank you. What does it do?"

"He wanted you all to die in battle. This negates it."

"And the dolls? What did you do to his spell?"

"I wasn't certain that he was speaking of you, but he described meeting two white women in Alejandro's apartment. He hoped that his spell would make you pay special attention to him. I changed it and—"

"—now he can't see who we really are," I finished, nodding along. "You crossed out his eyes." Holy crap, this *brujería* stuff was dark.

"But don't tell him. It's *brujería*, not a disguise. If you tell him who you are, the spell will break." She put the bowl away under the counter and pinched the bridge of her nose. "Madre de Dios, I regret the day my mother began to teach me the craft."

"Then why do you do it?" I pointed all around us, at the uncountable bits and bobs for spells and magic, ending at the grotesque shrine to Santa Muerte, where several burning candles and small bits of paper were littered. "Nothing about all of this says you *dislike* it."

"It's good money," she said flatly. "I save every dollar I can, so I can return home to my family..." Her eyes took on a faraway stare. "Though I'd be lying if I said that leaving would be easy. We may be living in one of the biggest cities in the country, but this barrio is its own little town, full of little people. It's not hard to love them."

Guilt made me look away. She had no idea how true her words were.

"I have to get going," I said. "Thanks for the tamal and advice, Ágata. And, well, the other thing." I glared at the jar.

She waved me off and I left the bodega, reviewing the list of errands I had to make next: buy some groceries, pick up some hair oil for Minnie, submit a report to the local precinct, see if the used bookstore had any new fantasy novels in stock for Courtney—she'd given me a list of titles to ask for—and then go to the library and do some research on our exit. Courtney was already at the library with Alejandro and Miguel, who were incognito.

As I passed a small boutique, a mannequin out front caught my eye. The mannequin bore a beautiful dress made up of a roomy royal blue skirt and blue-and-white peasant blouse bodice, the latter embroidered with delicate gold flowers and leaves. I risked an indulgent peek at the tag, then sighed. I knew enough of numbers to see that the price was beyond my means, and besides, when would I wear it?

A man's arm snaked around my shoulder. "Is Ale not giving you enough money? I know that look on a woman's face."

Roberto Guerrero was touching me.

I stood stock still, not daring to breathe lest he figure out that he was cuddling up to a beast. What was I supposed to do in this situation? Eighteen years of training hadn't covered how I was supposed to react when a local gang lord repeatedly mistook me for a hooker because of an old lady's Mexican black magic.

And why couldn't my powers activate over *this*? Buzzing? Sure, yeah, let me know the bees are coming, even though nothing bee-related actually happened to me. But Roberto sneaking up behind me and touching me? Nah, go screw yourself, Heather.

"Let's go see about that dress." He guided me into the store.

"I'm, uh, not working right now," I stammered. "I really can't—"

But he'd already taken out his wallet and pointed to the dress out front, ordering the flustered saleswoman to bag the dress for me. The lady almost tripped over herself as she retrieved an identical dress from the backroom, wrapped it in tissue paper, then placed it in a paperboard box, which itself went into a bag. She handed it to Roberto and backed away.

Roberto gave me the bag. "My dear."

I was going to burn the dress, everything I was wearing, and possibly my own skin when I got home.

I let out a shaking breath and smiled. "Thank you. You're very generous."

He guided me out of the shop and towards his scarlet car. I pulled away, trying not to hyperventilate. "I really, really, really can't go with you," I said. "Please don't take it personally. You're so kind to buy the dress for me."

Was I able to kill Roberto in one strike? Of course. But now was not the time. We needed to leave without raising a fuss, and me killing the leader of the biggest, baddest gang around wasn't conducive to that.

On the other hand...he *had* sent a man to kill me...that could count as a reason to strike back...

Instant knowledge flooded through me: *extreme danger.*

So that was a no, then.

Roberto leaned back against the passenger side door. "Are you afraid of me, Karen?"

I swallowed. What would "Karen la Puta" say?

"I, uh, well, the last time I saw you, you were going to shoot me and Sakura. That was pretty scary." Man, my Midwest accent was awesome.

He tutted. "I really wasn't. I thought you were someone else. Just forget that, hmm?"

I ducked my head. "I can forget that," I said, nodding. "But I'm a little confused why you seem to like me so much. I'm nothing special." Maybe if I convinced him of this, he'd stop this...whatever it was he had for me.

But he crossed his arms and tilted his head, an amused little quirk in his eyebrow. "Who told you that?"

"Everyone."

"But not Alejandro," he said thoughtfully. "He likes you a lot, and therefore I like you a lot. If you're pretty to him, you're pretty to me."

"Why?" The word came out without thinking.

Roberto straightened and dropped his arms. "Because I want everything he has."

Was this normal gang leader behavior?

I rubbed my forehead. "I think I need to go. I'm on a tight schedule before work tonight."

"Who's your pimp? Some guy named Pavel, right?" Roberto appeared to do some quick thinking. "I haven't moved into prostitution yet. One of these days, though...soon enough you'll be my employee, not this Pavel's. Tell your coworker that you and she won't have to deal with Pavel soon. I know how to handle competition." He gestured to his pocket—and it had nothing to do with how he felt about seeing me.

I backed up. "I have to go, please."

He opened the passenger door. "Let me take you where you need to go. I insist."

And...premonition. And...one premonition. Just one. Please tell me what'll happen if I get in that car. Now. Now, dammit!

The lazy vision goblin that lived in my head woke up and showed me the future: myself, walking into the library.

"I need to go to the library, please," I said, sliding into the air-conditioned sports car. Had it been anybody else's car, I would've enjoyed the experience.

"Ugh, libraries," he grumbled as he sat down in the driver's seat and put the car in drive, not bothering with a seat belt. "Books fill your head with silly ideas. If you read too many, you'll start thinking too much."

I was offended for both Courtney and Miguel's sake.

"Oh, don't worry." I placed my hand on his. "I read books just to learn how to talk to the fancy-pants guys from downtown. Sometimes they like it when I sound like I went to college. For example, Mr. Roberto, you could say that malefactors like you keep me and my coworkers in business." I'd learned that word from a spelling bee on PBS.

He grinned. "Aw, thanks."

Antediluvian. I should've called him antediluvian.

Less than five minutes later, we came to a screeching stop in front of the library, a large white-brick building covered in colorful murals. I stepped out of the car, bag in hand, and went to close the door. Roberto leaned towards me. "I'll be in touch," he promised. "I want to see you in that dress."

A vapid smile spread across my face. "Thanks for the ride."

I slammed the door and rushed into the library, stopping when I was at the circulation desk, where I leaned against a pillar and took deep breaths, tilting my head back so I could look up at the ceiling.

Mexican food, magic, and murderers. That's what my life was now. The barrio, once a quiet place to call home, had become a spider's web the moment we'd decided to leave—all of our actions to escape had merely turned the predator's eyes towards us, and now he was moving in for the feast. I just wanted to run. I wanted to forget Los Diablos, *brujería*, being a superhero, everything. I'd never asked for any of this.

I counted to ten in Spanish, tightened my ponytail, then stood up straight. In a matter of days I'd be gone. Now was not the time for a freak out. First things first—where the heck were the others?

I peered around. Alejandro and Courtney were in a forgotten corner near the employee's lounge, entangled around each other and kissing with mindless indecency. They weren't going to be much help today.

Ahead of me, however, stood Miguel. He stood at a small table by the nonfiction section, stacks of books and atlases surrounding him where he took notes. He looked up and smiled, his face suddenly brighter than the recessed fluorescent lights above us. Even with his thick fake glasses he was wearing as a loose disguise, he was the most beautiful man I'd ever seen.

I floated to his side. "You've been busy," I said quietly.

His smile turned playful. "Go get the love birds and I'll tell you how you're going to escape the strike team."

CHAPTER 12

08AUG – For some reason all I can think of is the scene from *Saved by the Bell*
where Jessie was trying to say how excited she was, but then burst into tears
and admitted that she was scared. Of course, I think my life is a little scarier
than her raging caffeine pill addiction, but I don't think they were allowed
to use real drugs on that show.

The four of us crowded around the table while Miguel pointed to a
terrain map of the Arizona-Mexico border. "Here," he said, pushing
his glasses back up his nose. "This small canyon right here will be how you get
into Mexico. See those marks? That means it's the bed of an intermittent
stream. I'll bet my next paycheck that it's a seasonal stream, and since it'll be
high August when you escape, that stream bed will be as dry as a bone. After
nightfall, you'll follow the stream bed into Mexico."

"Any chances of flash floods?" I said, frowning at the map. "Besides
wildlife, that would probably be the next concern, especially if we'll be on low
ground."

He pursed his lips. "I thought about that, but short of checking Yuma
County weather, I can't say if rain will be in the forecast."

"What's wrong with my Texas route?" Alejandro asked. "I could do it in
my sleep."

"Your route involved crawling through a sewer and, at one point, being
within sight of an Immigration and Naturalization Service station." Miguel
snapping the atlas shut. "I think we can do better than that. Also, your route

ends in Juárez. That's a huge city. Heather and the team can't be seen by *anyone*."

"Yuma County is a lot closer to San Diego, too," Courtney pointed out. "And by, what, five hundred miles? That's less time on the road in the US."

Alejandro sighed. "Fine. I can still get you across the border, but I'm warning you now, there might be surprises. For one thing, I want to know the weather. Like you said, flash floods happen. I've seen them, and you don't have any warning. If we're going to be running in a stream bed, I want to know if rain is in the forecast in that entire area."

I squirmed. "Well, what can we do? Our weather is only local, unless someone has cable and gets weather for the whole country."

"We could search the internet," Courtney said. "I heard that the internet has all the information you could ever want. You just have to know how to access it."

All of us turned and stared at the lone computer terminal by the circulation desk. Enormous and utterly technological, the machine seemed to both beckon us to it and hold up a sign of caution, warning of untold dangers.

"The internet," Alejandro said in a low tone that bordered on reverence. "I hadn't thought about that."

"This escape is going to be...high-tech," I said to Miguel. "Something out of *Star Trek*."

"Let's do it," Miguel said, biting his lip with excitement. "Let's get on the internet."

～

"OKAY, the book says to click the icon to go onto the browser. When you're in the browser, you can search the World Wide Web." Miguel turned the page, then flipped back, frowning in concentration. "It doesn't say what the icon looks like."

"Maybe the little globe?" Courtney suggested, pointing to the blue-and-green ball in the corner of the screen.

I carefully pushed the rectangular mouse and directed the arrow onto the globe, then clicked the large mouse button. We all held our breath.

Nothing happened.

"Miguel," I whispered. "What does the book say to do now?"

Miguel rapidly flipped through the thick volume we'd found on a nearby shelf marked Technology, entitled *How to Use the Internet*.

Alejandro peered over his shoulder and pointed to a paragraph. "There. Heather, it says to double-click. Not too fast, not too slow."

I double-clicked, and a white page filled the screen: the City of San Diego's official "page." It was seriously advanced, with menus and bars on the top and side, a search bar, and articles.

"Whoa," we said in unison.

"Look, there's us!" Courtney exclaimed. She jabbed her finger repeatedly on the screen over a bar. "San Diego's Super Teams! Oh, that's so cool! Alejandro, we're on the internet!"

Alejandro pecked her on the lips. "That makes you famous, doesn't it? I've never been with a famous lady before."

"Focus, you two," I muttered. "Okay, Miguel, what next?"

Miguel didn't answer right away, instead turning to Alejandro and Courtney and saying, "You two are crowding Heather and me. We'll take care of it from here."

They didn't need to be told twice. Alejandro grabbed Courtney's hand and pulled her back into their dark corner. Female giggles and deeper male murmurs picked up almost immediately.

Miguel pulled up the second chair and sat down next to me, far closer than was necessary. The wispy hair on his arms tickled my own, sending shivers up into my neck.

"Are you cold?" he murmured in my ear, his hot breath causing yet more shivers. "Here, let me." He wrapped his arm around my waist.

"You're fresh as paint," I whispered back, a hysterical little giggle escaping me.

"The book says to go to NOAA's website to check the weather," he said, trailing a finger along a page and tapping a section about weather. "And from there, you can enter your location in the search bar." He nudged my finger across the keys to N. "There…and then O…and A twice. NOAA stands for the National Oceanic and Atmospheric Administration." He blew against my ear. "They monitor the winds and weather with satellites and all kinds of instrumentation."

His fingers were playing with a lock of my hair, curling it around his fingers and stroking it. I had to double my concentration as I pecked out the "address" supplied by the book, checking each letter as I typed it in.

Bit by bit, NOAA's splash page loaded, complete with the somber seal of the organization in the corner. Best of all, the search bar was front and center. Miguel repeated each digit of the zip code from the atlas so I could type them out.

A premonition replaced the screen in my vision: my hands, covered in blood.

I jerked back to reality and swore.

"What?" Miguel asked, removing his arm. "It's two weeks of sunny days. See the little graphics? Fourteen suns."

There was a long silence between us as a slimy feeling curdled in my stomach. "Repeat that?"

Miguel looked confused. "Two weeks of sunny days. Fourteen suns."

I'd seen fourteen suns before—in my vision. I'd interpreted them to mean that we had fourteen days, and our entire plan hinged on the seventeenth of August being our run date. It was long enough to plan the fake war, but also a few weeks out from when I had to report to the camps.

What if the fourteen suns *didn't* mean fourteen days? What if they were just a representation of this moment? And if they didn't mean fourteen days, what did any of the rest of it mean? The hooded woman? The missing teammate? The coyote? The overbearing smell of death and decay?

I stood up, trying to control my breathing.

Miguel rose and placed his hands on my shoulders. "Heather? What's wrong? Talk to me."

"We need to go back to the house. I think I messed up. I think I might've interpreted a vision wrong and I may have endangered us all."

He gathered me into a hug, rubbing my back and shushing me. "We'll go home right now and figure it out. Get your bag and I'll go pry apart those two."

I obeyed and picked up my dress bag, walking on shaking legs towards the library entrance. *Calm. Peace. Keep calm.* My old mantra to control my sword flooded through me but didn't help much. I changed tack. *You don't know if the suns mean anything. You are making this to be bigger than it probably is. Besides, the camps gave you until the end of the month to go back, right? No matter what, you've got time.*

I leaned heavily against a pillar. I did *not* trust the camps. They were self-evidently evil, and though Eleazar was reticent to speak about the elders, I'd gathered that he would've faked his death to avoid being counted among their number no matter what had happened to our team. I suspected that they were corrupt in ways I could only guess at, but Eleazar wasn't talking.

The perfume of flowers and salty seawater wrapped around me when I stepped out into the warm night air. The north star glittered above me, one of the few stars visible. I stared up at it, trying to imagine Alejandro following it through the desert. Was there a south star? I didn't think so, and that fact alone seemed ominous. There was no way to go south.

"You're buggin', aren't you?"

Courtney's sympathetic voice pulled me out of my pessimism. She walked up to me and took my bag.

"Miguel said you saw something that freaked you out. He and Ale are cleaning up and then they'll come out. Talk to me."

"I don't think the fourteen suns meant two weeks," I said, squeezing my eyes shut. "And now that I'm so unsure about even that, I don't know if my vision meant that we should go south. I don't know anything anymore. I'm so...I just doubt everything now."

Courtney turned thoughtful. "What if we just run anyway, and to hell with visions? If your power is that unreliable, then don't rely on it."

What a weird concept. If I didn't act on my visions, then I was basically tripping without the acid all the time.

"Do I have to make that choice now?" My voice was pathetically small.

"No," Courtney said, smiling. She bowed her head toward me, and I copied her. "But I should say that those men over on the far side of the parking lot are Diablos. I can hear them."

I turned, ostensibly to look down the street as if waiting for a ride. Two men were loitering in the corner of the parking lot, partially hidden by a car. I made a face and sighed. "Great. Are we going to drive them off or...?"

"Forget about it," Courtney said with a shrug. "They're not discussing a future crime. I'd rather not get more involved with that crew than we already are."

"Speaking of which," I said, "Roberto wanted you to know that he's planning on taking over local prostitution rings. He's looking forward to being Karen and Sakura's boss."

Courtney's eyebrows drew together, and she opened her mouth, then closed it again. Finally, she said, "Wow. I...have literally never wanted to run away to Mexico more than I do at this moment."

A car with heavily-tinted windows drove up to the men. Courtney and I watched out of the corners of our eyes until—

"Oh, no!" she exclaimed.

Rapid gunfire was immediately followed by the screeching of tires. The tinted car peeled away, disappearing around a corner in seconds. The two men were no longer standing, but I could see a pair of legs sticking out from behind the car.

We ran to the scene, and I slowed when I saw the carnage: two dead men, no older than Miguel, lying in a growing pool of blood. Medallions bearing Santa Muerte's image had tumbled out of their shirts and into the blood. She smiled at me from their arms, her skull face shrouded by a hood. I knelt down, the wind knocked out of me. I'd deduced that the hooded figure in my vision had been a strike team member—or maybe she even represented an entire strike team. But now...

"Heather! Courtney! Are you okay?" Miguel called from the library entrance.

Alejandro and Miguel dashed up to us and gasped. In the distance, wailing sirens grew louder. A crowd of onlookers began to gather, everyone keeping a safe distance.

"Alejandro, take Miguel and go. Stay low," I ordered.

They nodded once and left, slipping into the crowd unnoticed.

Everything happened in a blur after that. The police cars and ambulance arrived, and the paramedics loaded up the corpses with a speed that spoke of practice. While the scene was cordoned off, Courtney and I identified ourselves to the police officers, giving our identifying information.

Since the officer we spoke to, Officer Gutierrez, was a member of the barrio's precinct, he knew us; taking our names was just a formality. After he'd ascertained that we didn't need medical attention ourselves, he directed us to a bench and pulled out a little notepad.

"I just need the usual, ladies." He uncapped his pen with his teeth. "Who, what, when, all that."

"We were just hanging out over by the library entrance," I said. "We saw the two men, but they were all the way at the other end of the parking lot, and we didn't pay them much mind. No reason to."

"Right, right," he murmured.

"A car came up for a minute, and then the shooting happened," Courtney said with a delicate shrug. "It was over as soon as it started."

Officer Gutierrez nodded along as he wrote. "That's usually how these things go. This looks pretty simple. The tattoos indicate that they were with Los Diablos. Any idea who the shooters were?"

Courtney looked at me, and though I was no telepath, I knew exactly what she was thinking: this was our chance to establish Las Bellas' notoriety. If two superheroes swore that they'd seen Alejandro's boys gun down two of Roberto's boys in cold blood, nobody would question it. In such matters, our word was as good as fact.

Officer Gutierrez waited for me with a polite expression on his face.

"No," I said. "I didn't see who it was."

He asked a few more questions, then shut his notepad and bade us goodnight, promising that we'd soon be in touch with Captain West, the official superhero liaison at headquarters in downtown.

When everyone had finally dispersed, and Courtney and I were alone, she handed me my dress bag, her lips forming a grim line. "Why didn't you say it was Las Bellas?"

I hugged myself and averted my eyes. "Do you really want this life for them? Shootouts and dying on the pavement? Now that...now that I don't know what my vision meant, I can't do it, Courtney. I can't. I wouldn't be able to enjoy freedom knowing that we'd left them to this kind of life."

She let out a shaking breath. "Let's go home and talk to the team."

I bit my lip, but inside, my resolve hardened into steel. Yes, I'd go home and have the conversation that we should've had days ago. I'd tell Eleazar and Alejandro that there was no way we could continue on this path. Where there was a will, there was a way—and we *would* find a way out of California and away from the strike team.

CHAPTER 13

09AUG – Does it matter? The remote is broken.

*T*he conversation had not gone as planned.

More than twenty-four hours after the library shooting, I scraped the spackle over the dent in the wall with the little palette knife. The spackle wouldn't erase the dull embarrassment I felt, but at least I wouldn't have to be reminded anymore of *last night* every time I walked through the living room.

But, first things first. Now that I'd had a full day to think about my failings, I needed to admit where I'd gone wrong before chewing over everyone else's flaws. Miguel had been right—I needed to learn to control my temper. I was responsible for how I'd reacted. In fact, it was my fault for not taking the temperature of the house when I'd come home with Courtney.

I'd walked into the house, intent on speaking with Eleazar. However, he and Alejandro were deep in conversation in the living room, both grave.

Eleazar had jumped to his feet when I'd walked in. "Heather. Is that your blood?"

"No," I'd replied. "It's Diablo blood. Can we talk? Alone? There's not a lot of time."

"Miguel said you think the time table is wrong," Alejandro interjected. "I think we should all talk about this together."

And that's where things had fallen apart. Alejandro had beaten me to the punch and told Eleazar about the shooting, but instead of citing it as a reason to call it off, they'd both come to the ludicrous decision to increase the "war effort."

I reacted badly, to say the least. I'd have to apologize to Alejandro if I ever calmed down enough to speak to him again. I'd start with an apology for ordering him to get out of my house and "go die."

And then I'd apologize for shouting, though I couldn't remember half of what I'd said.

I vaguely recalled screaming that he was *"un pinche cabrón"* at the point in the evening when I'd lost the ability to speak English. I'd have to apologize for that, too.

I would also have to apologize for replying to his answer to *that* with *"chinga tu madre!"* while hurling the remote at him so hard that it had made a hole in the wall and fell, smashed, to the floor. If I ever met his mother, I'd also apologize to her for bringing her into it. She was probably very nice.

I smoothed out the edges of the spackle patch and closed the little container, then set everything down on the living room table. Now that Minnie, Morris, and Armando were out on patrol, I could probably get in some screen time. Forget everything. Ignore that everyone was going to die.

I slumped forward, my face in my hands. I'd done what I could, and it hadn't been enough. Sobs began to wrack my body yet again, just one more crying jag in a long line of them. It wasn't often that I felt this helpless.

A comforting arm pulled me into a man's chest, but it wasn't Miguel.

"I'm sorry," Eleazar whispered. "I'm so sorry."

"Can't you stop them?" I wailed. "You're the leader! Make them go home and be safe!"

Eleazar stroked my hair. "I could make them go home, but I can't make them be safe. Alejandro made a very good case that the shooting last night was part of a bigger war in the barrio. Las Bellas are so small, and so young, that they need a strong leader at the helm—or the veneer of one. It might give them longer to save up and get out of here. The benefits of this arrangement outweigh the drawbacks."

My crying slowed. I gulped and sniffled, then said, "The drawbacks are awful, though."

Eleazar was quiet for a few moments, then stood and walked into the kitchen. I heard the fridge open and shut, and then he reappeared with two cans of orange soda, one of which he handed to me. He sat down again, a vague sadness on his face.

"In the beginning of the team, back in '92," he began slowly, "It was just Armando, Minnie, and me." I opened my mouth to say that I knew the team history, but he held his hand up. "Please let me finish. The city had had gang issues in the barrio for years, but only when they began to spread into the wealthier areas did they decide that things had gotten unacceptable. So, we were called in. At first, I thought that a three-man team was sufficient for such a small area. The general guideline is one team member per fifty thousand people. Easy peasy, or so I thought."

He opened his soda and took a long swig, clearly thinking.

After a second, he continued, "The week we arrived, the three of us toured the barrio on foot while dressed as civilians. We saw playgrounds without children, parks without people, café areas where nobody ate. People walked around with their heads down."

"What was going on?" I asked, surprised. I'd never heard this story.

"We asked ourselves that, then went to the precinct and asked them. They told us to look for the letters SM on buildings, or LD."

"Santa Muerte and Los Diablos."

"Exactly. Wherever those tags were, the locals knew that the gangs were in charge. They'd turned a thriving neighborhood into a concentration camp." His eyes softened. "That's what gangs do, Heather. Real gangs. As soon as I heard that, I requested more team members. They sent me Courtney and Morris. You came last, after I was able to show that we were driving out the gangs."

"Courtney said something like that. That's why we're Las Bestias, right? Because of how you fought the gangs?"

He shrugged. "For once, she's not making it up. We cracked down hard. We had to."

"Why are you telling me this?"

He took a deep breath. "You've never seen a time when Los Diablos ruled this barrio. Alejandro and I *have*. I was angry when you dragged those two into our house, but I can see now why Alejandro is so desperate. Los Diablos are spreading their cancer again, and he can't stand by and watch people like Miguel and the rest of those boys get consumed.

"There's no denying that Alejandro has broken the law, but he's paid his debt by doing time. Now that I've calmed down, I can see that he's a lot like me. He doesn't care if he's viewed forevermore as a scumbag. He just wants his friends to be safe. I don't care at all about my being assumed dead, nor the camps and the world we're leaving behind. *I* just want *you* to be safe. We can help him achieve notoriety. He can help us escape."

I bit my lip. After that speech, I felt even more like a piece of *mierda* for shouting and calling Alejandro every obscene name under the Spanish sun.

"El?"

"What's up?"

I swallowed heavily. "You really do care about getting me away from the camps, right?"

"Of course," he said, setting down his drink and taking my hands in his.

"Why do you doubt it? This isn't the first time one of you have questioned my motivations."

My lips twisted as I plucked up the courage to ask what I'd been afraid to ask since the beginning of this drama. "Were you ever going to..."

"To?" he prompted.

"...to send me back to the camps? I mean, if Morris and Minnie hadn't sort of forced you that afternoon?"

Shock appeared on his face, swiftly replaced by shame. "You're wondering whether I'm still upset about the break up."

"Yeah. And then there was that argument, and what you said about me not being able to read Miguel's letters, and how you reacted when I told you about what happened in the apartment. Courtney said—"

He put a finger to my lips. "Forgive me, but I have to know: were you scared before or after Courtney said whatever she said?"

I sniffed. "Um..."

He let out a massive sigh. "Oh boy. What was her dire warning? What was I going to do to you?"

I shifted uncomfortably. "She said she'd read a book about women who were killed by their exes and that I'd better not make you angry, and that you were so scary in the beginning of the team that *you* are the reason we're called beasts."

Eleazar blinked, then cracked up.

"I'm serious!"

"That's so *stupid*, Heather. Don't you see how stupid it is?" He shook his head, still chuckling. "I'll admit that I was unkind to say what I did about his letters, and I am sorry. Please forgive me. But goodness, I lose my cool for ten seconds and suddenly I'm murderer material? What have I done to deserve that?"

"You were going to send me home."

He took my hands in his. "Heather Harris, I was never going to send you home. For a while I couldn't see a way out for us, but on my honor, you'll never go back to the camps as long as I'm alive to stop it. To answer your main question...yes, I would go to this trouble even if those two hadn't said anything. They just gave me the mental kick in the pants I needed at that very second. I may be the worst son of an elder there ever was, but I really do care about this team, and I care about the barrio. If I ever came off as brooding or a jerk...well, I'm only human, and it's embarrassing being dumped because I was a terrible boyfriend."

"So your frustration isn't because of me? It's just...normal moodiness?"

"Yeah. It really is. I'm so sorry for what I said that night, I really am. It was alarming to hear about how close you came to Roberto, but I was still reeling from the shock of hearing that we're being downsized. I didn't handle it well. It's not an excuse, but it's the truth."

I'd said those exact words to Courtney about my part of the fight.

His face darkened. "Bringing this all back to what happened last night...we're waging a losing war. Los Diablos are getting more aggressive. Roberto is growing bolder by the hour. Los Lobos are just one gang of many that work for him now. He sent someone to kill any one of us just because we have apparently threatened Las Bellas. The city will not help us—that was made crystal clear when they ordered you to leave. Call me callous, but I don't see the benefit of staying here to die in gang warfare. But I do see the benefit of looking like we died in gang warfare, because it might just piss off the citizens enough that they'll demand real action."

The clock chimed the hour, and he stood up. "Where are you going?" I asked.

"On patrol. There's a gang initiation planned across the barrio," he said wryly. "You and Courtney can stay here and watch the evil VCR thief and the shop boy."

He was halfway to the stairs when I said, "El?"

"Hmm?"

"Would you be upset if I started spending more time with the shop boy?"

He looked confused for a second, then his face softened. "Didn't you say he's been writing you the letters?"

I scratched the back of my head, suddenly shy. "Yeah."

"Then what are you waiting for?" He checked his watch. "Tomorrow is the next, and last, battle. Whatever you have to say, say it quick."

I could do that. But first, I had to ask Courtney for some help.

CHAPTER 14

09AUG – I once heard that cable plays racy movies this late. Not that I'm interested, or anything. I just heard that once.

*C*ourtney held up the hand mirror so I could see the back of my hair. "I do good work, if I do say so myself."

I turned my head from side to side, admiring her handiwork. She *was* rather talented with a brush and hairspray, having turned my frizzy long hair into a poofy, voluminous 'do. "I look like Jennifer Aniston," I said, smiling.

"Who?"

"Madeline from *Muddling Through?*"

"From what?"

"Never mind," I said, waving her off. "I look nice."

She touched up my lipstick, then stood back. "There. What are you wearing?"

I stared down at my tank top and stonewashed denim shorts. "...This?"

Courtney slow-blinked. "Try again. What's in that dress bag?"

"Ugh, Roberto bought it for me because he thought I was Alejandro's hooker friend and wanted to butter me up."

"A tale as old as time," Courtney said, suppressing a laugh. "But I don't think Miguel needs to know that. Put it on."

I sighed dramatically, but quickly jumped behind the modesty screen and put on the light cotton dress. It fit well, and the blue-and-white fabric contrasted nicely with my suntanned skin. When I stepped out from behind the screen, I twirled a little, enjoying the attention.

Courtney fretted over my stubborn curly bangs until I shook her hand off and smiled. "Thank you for all your help. What will you do while I'm out on the deck?"

"Alejandro said he'd make us some food. We'll probably just be up here chatting."

"No coming out on the back deck, right?"

"Right."

"What did you tell Miguel earlier? You know, about my plan?"

She clasped her hands behind her back. "Oh, just that you wanted some alone time to talk to him later. Meet him on the back deck at eleven, it's nothing serious, all that." There was a playful, almost secretive note in her tone, but I already knew she'd never tell me what she was thinking.

I glanced at my watch. "Well, since we're done, I might as well go downstairs now."

I went to the door, pausing when I saw my reflection in the vanity mirror. My light brown hair had been teased, sprayed, and coiffed into a beautiful, majestic mane. The hair of a bold woman. A daring woman. A woman who was ready to be Miguel's girlfriend—if he wanted.

That's what I'd confessed to Courtney after Eleazar had left for patrol. After shoving Alejandro out of her room, I'd told her that she was a freaking lunatic for worrying about Eleazar, and could she please make me look somewhat pretty?

She'd suggested a "romantic fairy tale fantasy night"—yeah, whatever, Courtney—but a plan had slowly emerged as we talked. I'd take Miguel on the back deck and tell him how I felt, then ask if he'd like to be my boyfriend. I wasn't worried about seeming too forward, since this *was* the 90's. Superheroine, standing up to the man, and asking out Miguel? I was practically a Riot Grrrl.

I hurried out of the room and traipsed down the stairs, my skirt swishing around my legs. However, when my foot touched the bottom of the steps, I paused.

There was music coming from the back deck. As I approached the curtained sliding glass door, the music grew louder.

I slowly slid the glass door open and stood there, lost for words.

Miguel was standing by the railing, gazing up at the stars. Around him, spread out on the edge of the railing, were Courtney's floral candles. Their fragrance mixed in the warm night air, and the little flames danced along to the music coming from Courtney's boombox in the corner. A crooning R&B singer I recognized from Top 40 sang about falling in love. It was all so magical.

But nothing beat Miguel.

He'd put on a sharp white button-down shirt and black slacks, and he'd rolled up his sleeves to the elbow, just how I liked it. In his hand was a single rose, obviously snipped from Courtney's rose bush out front.

"You look beautiful."

Miguel's soft voice brought me down to earth, but I still floated over to his side, unsure of how to reply for a second. "So do you. I mean, you look handsome. Very handsome."

He handed me the rose. "I hope you're not upset. Courtney told me a little of what to expect."

"I'm not," I said, shaking my head and laughing a little. "No. This is...I should've known. This is *classic* Courtney. She thinks we're in a fairy tale, doesn't she?"

"Hmm. I think Courtney thinks she's in a fairy tale. Ale certainly thinks they are. He was talking to me while I was getting ready." He lowered his voice and thickened his accent in an uncanny mimic of Alejandro. "'Miguel, it's like I've been asleep under a witch's curse and she came along and kissed me awake. I'm free now.'"

"Oh, so *he's* Sleeping Beauty?"

"Or Snow White. There are a lot of sleeping women in these stories, now that I think about it."

I twiddled my rose. "Did she tell you why I wanted to talk to you?"

"No, actually," he said, crossing his arms and leaning against the railing. "I hope it's as exciting as I've made it to be in my head."

I stepped closer to him. "Did you know that you were the first person to ever offer to teach me to read?"

"No," he said, frowning. "And I don't understand why that is."

"Well, you were. Are. And throughout these last few months, your letters were the only source of genuine appreciation and admiration that I ever received. And when I got that last picture with your drawing, I realized that even though I wore a mask, you saw *me*. You have me in your mind's eye." I swallowed the emotion that had solidified in my throat. "You like me. Not Excalibur. Not some pretty lady superhero in your neighborhood. I think you like Heather Harris."

He stepped closer and took my hands in his. "Can't I like Heather Harris *and* the pretty lady superhero? One of the first things I ever noticed about you is how lovely your lips are. They were the only thing I could see, after all."

"Really? You like my mouth? I always thought it was too pouty."

He smiled and shook his head. "You have no idea. Every time I see your lips, I want to do this."

He closed the distance between us and kissed me.

My arms wrapped around his shoulders of their own volition, drawing him closer. His lips, soft and warm, moved against mine like they were meant to be there. I melted into his arms, falling into his embrace—the embrace of a man who *desired* me. Who wanted this. Who had time to give me, attention to lavish on me, and the kindness to offer to tutor me. He thought I was worth teaching. Nobody ever had.

He surfaced for air. "Be my girlfriend?"

"I thought you'd never ask." We fell into another kiss.

The song on the radio ended, and the next song began. A popular power ballad began to loop around us, easing the palpable, though enjoyable, romantic energy. Miguel held out a hand. "Dance with me?"

I took his hand and he led me a few feet into the center of the deck, where he placed his hand on my hip. We began to sway back and forth to the music, making a little circle as we danced. I rested my head on his shoulder, and he hummed with pleasure.

The song ended, as all songs must do, but we didn't part. Instead, we kept dancing, our heartbeats in tune with each other.

"Miguel?"

"Hmm?"

"Will you still write me when I go to Mexico?"

I felt him gulp. "Yes," he said quietly. "Of course I will. I suppose I'll have to keep in mind that your letters will have to be read to you, since I haven't had time to teach you to read. So much for that plan."

I pulled away and we stopped dancing. "Please don't be upset."

He walked back to the railing and leaned on it, his head bowed. "How can I not be upset? Everything is so messed up. You're going to the wilds of Mexico, I'm going to be known as a psychotic thug for the rest of my life, my parents will be ashamed to know me, and I may never see you again. I want more time," he whispered, covering his face with his hand. "More time with you. More time to be me. I'm not a criminal. I can't even jaywalk without feeling bad." I moved to put my hand on his shoulder, but he faced me. "Make no mistake, Heather. Even Alejandro feels the pinch of this plan. If we had more time, we could come up with something better. But now...after what happened at the library..."

Everyone needed more time, the one thing that nobody was in a position to offer.

Except...

Except me.

Taking him by the hands, I guided us to the little bench on the side of the deck. I didn't speak for a minute, carefully choosing what I'd say so that I didn't have to explain myself.

"Miguel, if you had more time to come up with a way to get out of the barrio and away from Roberto, what would you do?"

He answered immediately. "I meant it when I said that I want to go to art school. There are huge ones up in Northern California. Some of them feed into the big animations studios, and if I could—"

I held up a hand. "What's *really* stopping you from doing it now? It's not your parents, is it?"

"No, it's money. I couldn't afford to apply to the schools. I have the job at the bodega, but it's not much. I really need to get a second job. I've actually been looking around, but getting a job is easier said than done."

"What would Alejandro do, do you think? You know him better than me."

"Alejandro's talked about being a car mechanic a few times. Apparently, his father owned a garage in Juárez and he'd give him and his brother car parts to play with when they were kids. His brother's a car aficionado now, or so I'm told, but Alejandro is more into the grease and tools."

Art school. Cars. Brothers and fathers. These were the stuff of life—the things worth living for.

I had to leave.

But Miguel studied me for several seconds. "You have a weird look on your face. What are you thinking about? Are you planning something?"

"No!" I cleared my throat. "No, I'm not planning anything."

He narrowed his eyes. "You're lying."

"No, I'm not. I'm not planning anything." Dang, he was quick. He really had been watching me.

"Yes, you are." He gasped and stood. "You're going to leave, aren't you? That's why you asked about my plans! You're psyching yourself up! Oh my *God*, Heather!"

"Miguel, please calm down. If I do this, I can ensure that you have enough time to make that money. I can ensure that Alejandro can lead my team into Mexico without having to smear your names."

"How?" he spat. "How on *earth*—"

"I was ordered to return home within a month. All of this was a slapped-together plan to help me avoid punishment, and to keep the strike team off our trail when we ran. If I just *go* and take one for the team, you could say, everyone will be better off."

"And you? What about *you*?"

"I will be just one of many superheroes sent home for team failures. Or, in this case, budget cuts."

"Oh, so, you'll get whipped because the city is cheap and doesn't care about us slum rats?"

"Our lives aren't fair." My voice broke. "I've always known that."

He began to pace like a caged lion. "No. Absolutely not. Hell, I'll take you into Mexico myself if I have to. This is completely unacceptable. I can't believe you'll just—"

I ran up to him and kissed him, tears slipping down my cheeks. He kissed me back, but with such bittersweetness that I cried harder.

"Believe that I love you," I said. "Believe that you have made me happy before I ever met you. Believe that I want you to have a *life*."

"But what about you?" he said. "What about your life?"

We stood in the darkness for a long time, clinging to each other like we were life preservers in the ocean.

~

I DRAGGED my feet as I walked up the stairs, my eyes itching with fatigue. I needed to get into bed before the rest of the team returned from patrol, lest they start asking questions that I didn't want to answer.

Miguel had gone ahead of me, and when I reached the top of the stairs, he poked his head out of his room. "Alejandro's not in here. Where'd he get to?"

"He's probably still with Courtney," I said, eyeing the low light that glowed from underneath Courtney's door. "I'll tell them to get to bed. Good night, Miguel."

I knocked on Courtney's door, but there was no answer. I gently turned the knob and opened the door a crack, then let it swing open, my jaw dropping.

Courtney and Alejandro were sound asleep in her bed, a tangle of arms and naked torsos. She was tucked next to his side, her black hair messy and wild where she'd laid her head on his chest. He had his arms around her, his face displaying more peace than I'd ever seen it show in the waking hours.

As much as I wanted to let them sleep, I didn't think Minnie would be so understanding of the two nudies, since her bed was six feet away. I shut the door with unnecessary force, and they startled awake.

"Heather!" Courtney said, pulling the blanket up to her shoulders. Alejandro schooled his face into his usual coolness, though his cheeks were red.

"I trust you two had a nice little chitchat." They both giggled like children. I tossed him his pants. "Don't let anyone else catch you like this, okay?"

Shaking my head, I left them to get dressed and went into my own room. I was in the middle of taking off my makeup when Courtney came in, still blushing. "Please don't tell Eleazar."

I snorted. "Like he'd care."

"Well...he's never had to deal with this kind of thing before. Let's not push him, since he's already under a lot of pressure."

I smiled at her in the mirror. "Fair point. But take it easy. You're both moving kind of fast."

Her face fell. "We don't have time to go slowly."

I froze, my makeup wipe hovering over my cheek. "No, I guess you don't," I said softly. I resumed removing my makeup.

There was a knock on the door, followed by Miguel's voice. "Can I come in for just a second?"

"Sure," we both said.

Miguel popped his head in. "Courtney, Heather is thinking about running away to the camps to save the rest of us. Pass it on."

He wisely closed the door before I could chuck something at him.

Courtney rounded on me. "What. The. Hell."

I set my jaw, refusing to blink this time. "Do you think I can actually enjoy freedom knowing it cost you your relationship with your...your prince? Miguel his happy life? Las Bellas their futures? All of this was caused by us not having any time because of the deadline to send me back. If I go home, you all could mount a better plan, one that would necessarily take time to plan and execute."

Courtney's eyes filled with tears, but her face was a mask of fury. "Don't you dare," she hissed.

"Or you'll what?" I said, springing to my feet. "Fight me?"

"No, I'll tell everyone that you're planning something that stupid. I'm staying up and telling them all what you just told me. Go to bed."

She stormed out, leaving me to stare at the door, the weight of defeat and hopelessness settling on my shoulders. So much for that plan. Knowing Courtney, she was going to tell them that I'd already bought a bus ticket or had called the camp allies and arranged for a ride.

I sat back down on the stool, took a deep breath, then spun around to finish my routine.

Something in the mirror moved.

I slowly lifted my head and took in what I was seeing. My heart skipped a beat.

In the reflection, the hooded woman I'd been seeing stood several feet behind me. In the light, I could see her features clearly for the first time. Clad in black tactical gear, wearing camp-issued combat gloves and bearing multiple knives on her arms and thighs, she watched me intently from behind a superhero's mask. Black eyes glittered through her mask, and matted black hair spilled out from beneath her hood, cascading down her front. Whoever she was—whatever she was—she was no stranger to violence and death. I knew for a fact I'd never met her in person.

"Are you Santa Muerte?" I whispered, touching her reflection in the mirror. "Does Santa Muerte look like a strike team member to superheroes? What *are* you?"

She merely tilted her head.

"What do you want?" I demanded. "Tell me!"

"Soon, Heather." Her twangy voice was a dusty whisper in my head. "Don't worry. I'm coming for you all soon."

I gasped and whirled around.

My room was as empty as it had ever been.

I ran to my bed and dove under the covers, pulling them up over my head, letting the tears return. My visions had never spoken to me before I'd come to San Diego, and they'd never integrated into real life like that. Maybe it was the stress. Maybe it was magic. Maybe I was just going insane. All were viable possibilities now.

My door open and shut, and then Miguel slid into bed with me. "Courtney said I can't let you be alone."

I didn't answer. Instead, I curled up in his arms and closed my eyes. If I could not leave, and I could not stay, then what else was there to do but lay there with the man I loved while I still could?

CHAPTER 15

11AUG – Eleazar calls the evening news the "daily body count." He's not wrong.

I caught Gabriel's eye from across the street. He nodded almost imperceptibly, then turned away to apparently study a poster advertising an upcoming street fair. I also turned my back, taking a few seconds to admire a frilly purple *quinceañera* dress in a store window.

Darn, was my shoe untied? I knelt down, slipping my purse off my shoulder and placing it next to me. Behind me, heavy footsteps came closer, but I was slowly double-knotting my shoes. I was about to need those double knots.

Gabriel nabbed my purse and bolted.

I spun around. "*Oye! Pinche ladrón!*" When the locals heard me say "*pinche,*" they'd know I meant business.

I roughly shoved past vendors and residents, shouting in furious English and Spanish for Gabriel to stop. He darted in and out of the people, expertly navigating the barrio as if he snatched purses every day. Though it appeared as though this was between him and me, familiar faces watched: Eleazar from a dark corner, Courtney from a park bench, Minnie in a parked car, Armando —half man, half shadow—from the gloom of an alley. Today wouldn't end with stitches, but it also wouldn't end with me making a break for the camps.

On the corner in front of the only bodega that mattered, Gabriel whirled around and raised his unloaded Glock to eye level, aiming it at me with a flinty note in his eyes. The squawking bystanders disappeared into the nearest building.

I slowed and raised my hands. "This doesn't need to come to violence."

"Back off, *gringa*," he growled. "This street belongs to Las Bellas, and everything in it." He held up the purse. "Including this. Now, if you'll excuse me, I have a cash register to rob."

No criminal in the history of time would say something like that, but whatever.

"Alright, I'm leaving." I took several large steps backwards. "Put the gun away, kid."

Gabriel ran into Ágata's bodega. I counted the predetermined ten seconds, crept up to the doorway, then peered through the bars.

One second was all I needed to know that going through the front door would get me killed.

I dashed around to the tiny, damp alleyway between the buildings, turning sideways to slide at one point, and maneuvered through the reeking trash bags. There was no time to get the others, as much as I wanted to. I needed to get in there *now*. Thankfully, Ágata had propped open the back door of her shop with a brick, allowing me to silently enter the backroom. The curtain had been pulled across the doorway to the front of the store, but I could hear the voices of the people beyond it. They were speaking Spanish, and they were pissed. One of them was horribly familiar.

Roberto asked Ágata why her spell hadn't worked. He'd ordered it almost a week before and nothing had happened.

Ágata pleaded that sometimes spells don't work, and nobody knew why.

The unmistakable sound of a slap was followed by Roberto demanding his money back and then, a few seconds later, the whish-clang of the register opening. Roberto said he was taking everything as repayment for the failed spell.

A whimper—Gabriel.

An unfamiliar male voice told him to shut up, or he'd paint the wall with Gabriel's brains.

This had gone on long enough. My gaze darted around the backroom, searching for anything I could use. Sure enough, a roll of duct tape lay on the metal shelf by the far back door. I grabbed it and silently jumped into the back alley, where I pulled off a long strip as quietly as I could. When I had a five-foot long strip in hand, I tore it off and hastily taped it across the doorway to the front of the shop, at about shin height.

I pressed my back against the wall, partially hidden behind a cabinet, and unsheathed my sword. A deep breath, then called out:

"*Esta es la policía! Sal con las manos en alto!*"

Lies, lies, lies. I wasn't the police—and that was their misfortune, especially if they didn't come out with their hands up as ordered.

Two henchmen charged through the doorway...and fell face-first onto the cement floor. I kicked them in the head, jumped over their still forms gymnast-style and into the shop.

Bullets rang around me, shot by a wild-eyed man who'd just shoved Gabriel into a shelf. The shelf couldn't handle his weight, and a domino chain began. Shelves fell backwards one by one, causing magic ingredients and cheap snacks to rain down.

I ducked, then darted to the left.

A jar exploded above me.

I sprinted behind one of the few standing shelves—nope, dead end. Another volley of bullets. Bottles of soda burst, flinging glass and liquid everywhere.

I swung my sword, slicing neatly through the metal and creating a wonderful shield. I tossed it at the shooter, who bent back ninety degrees like some kind of gun-toting Latino ninja.

Gabriel and Ágata were shouting in the background, behind the blood pounding in my ears. I ducked again, then re-merged behind a lower shelf... and eye to eye with the shooter, who had his gun trained on me.

With a wet crunch, I ran him through.

He dropped his gun. Blood trickled out of his mouth.

I slowly stepped back, my chest heaving as I withdrew my sword from his abdomen. My glowing blade was at waist level, easily cutting through the thin metal shelving and into my assailant. As soon as I'd pulled away, the shooter dropped out of sight with a soft thud—my third kill in the line of duty.

A broken groan made me crash-land back on earth.

Ágata was lying on the ground behind the counter, a pool of blood slowly inching out from under her. I sank to my knees beside her, my teeth chattering. "Hey, hey, I'm here." I picked up her ice-cold hand. Where was Gabriel? Roberto? Anyone? It had all happened so fast. I needed to get to the ph—

The phone had been destroyed by an errant bullet. There was no time to go find another.

I gazed down at her pale, lined face. Scared eyes met mine and stared, unblinking, for an eternity. She was trying to tell me something, but I couldn't understand. "I'm sorry," I whispered.

Her eyes unfocused, and her hand went limp.

A light flickered and buzzed, then went out. I glanced over, an instinctual reaction. Only one item had fully survived the gun battle and carnage: a statue of *pinche* Santa Muerte, surrounded by black votive candles and grinning at me, the offerings filling the air with the putrid odor of hatred and blood. Los Diablos wore her on their flesh; what they did, they did in her name. Bile rose in my throat. I brushed my fingers over Ágata's eyes, closing them forever, then laid her hand down and rose to my feet.

I'd asked her to cancel those spells. Her blood was on my hands.

I screamed and sliced through the statue, the cheap plaster shattering upon contact with my blade.

The front door of the bodega burst open and my "backup" flooded in: Eleazar, Courtney, Morris, and Armando.

"Heather!" Eleazar exclaimed. "What happened? We heard shots and saw Roberto—"

"Where the *hell* were you all?" I resisted the urge to throw something at him. "I've been in here *forever!*"

"We ran as soon as we'd heard gunshots." Eleazar's eyes darted all around. "That was only thirty or forty seconds ago."

Of course. Life or death in the space of a minute. That was how these things usually went down, just like at the library.

"Where did he go?" I said through gritted teeth. "Which way?"

Eleazar frowned. "He went towards the school. Why—"

I shoved past them all and bolted, making a sharp right turn on the sidewalk and running towards the local elementary school two blocks distant. I didn't know what the hell I was going to do, but damn it if Roberto wasn't going to pay for Ágata's death with his own. Behind me, my teammates shouted at me to stop. There wasn't time, and they were all useless, anyway.

"Heather?" Alejandro's call made me finally halt in the middle of a road. He was wearing a hoodie, and his posture was off—he was uncharacteristically slouchy, clearly disguising himself. He walked up to me, frowning. "What's wrong? Why are you covered in blood?"

I pointed towards the school with a shaking finger. "That—that murderer held up Ágata's bodega. She died in the shootout. I'm going to kill him. I swear to God, I'm going to bring back his head. Don't even try to stop me."

He gasped and ran a hand over his face. "*Madre de Dios.* Where's Gabriel? Is he okay?"

"He left when the bullets started flying. I don't know where he is. Go look for him while I—"

"No." Alejandro's voice was cold. "*We* will go deal with Roberto." He pulled back his hood, his jaw hard. "I came to speak to the boys, but they weren't at my apartment even though we agreed they would be. My gut tells me they're in trouble."

"Fine." I peered into the darkness of the quiet street that led towards the school. "Let's go."

We hurried down the sidewalk until we came to the chest-high chain-link fence that rimmed the perimeter of the playground. The gate was already open. In the distance, by the broken swing set, a handful of men were huddled together.

"Los Diablos leadership," Alejandro murmured. "Roberto and his main underlings."

We were still entirely shrouded in the shadows of trees; Roberto hadn't noticed us yet. How could we surprise them? Surely, they were all armed. I twisted my lips.

An idea formed. I put a hand on Alejandro's arm and a finger to my lips, then beckoned him to join me behind a large tree trunk. "Go tell Roberto you want to join Los Diablos because of the war with my team." I brushed some of Ágata's damp blood on his fingers and face. "You fought your way out of the house, see?"

Alejandro nodded once, then darted out from behind the tree. "*Berto! Soy yo! Necesito hablar contigo!*"

Berto?

Roberto and his lieutenants turned and drew their weapons. Alejandro put his hands up and again said, in Spanish, that he needed to talk *ahora. Now.* As he drew near, some of the men gestured to his face, presumably noticing the blood smears.

Roberto ordered his lieutenants to leave. That was…weird. Alejandro was demonstrably not Roberto's ally, so why was Roberto speaking to him in private like this? I didn't know the first thing about being a gang lord, but the situation seemed off. Still, it was small ball. I needed to focus.

The other men holstered their weapons—or more accurately, tucked them into their pockets—and walked towards me. As they approached, a premonition prickled: *danger.* I rolled my eyes at my stupid power. *No, really? I wouldn't have guessed.* I pressed my forehead into the scratchy bark and held my breath.

The four men didn't notice me. They walked right by, speaking quietly about "the plan." When they were gone, I looked back at the park. Alejandro had taken a seat on the lone working swing. To an outsider, that might've come off as an odd, even submissive gesture, but to me it merely underlined his cleverness—because now Roberto had his back to me.

I crouched on the ground and slunk forward like a cat, itching for more blood. Maybe Las Bestias were preparing to run to Mexico with our tails between our legs, but goodness, I knew I was a real superhero. Taking out someone like Roberto was what I was paid to do.

As I crept closer, however, I paused. I could see them a little more clearly, and their relaxed body language communicated a familiarity between them I hadn't expected. Roberto had put his gun away and was listening to Alejandro talk with his arms crossed and his head tilted, very much like Eleazar when we were giving him the rundown of a patrol.

Alejandro and Roberto weren't friends, but they weren't enemies in the strictest sense, either. Alejandro had some explaining to do after this was all over.

Slipping through the open gate was easy enough, and I walked as quietly on the pitted asphalt as I could. I could hear Roberto now; he was asking Alejandro if he'd killed any of my teammates.

"No," Alejandro said, shaking his head. He explained that he'd overpowered *el pocho*—I had to stifle a laugh—and run as fast as he could, adding that he'd injured Armando, but wasn't sure if he was dead.

Roberto asked if we'd tortured him for information.

Alejandro paused, and for the smallest fraction of a second, I thought I saw him look at me. He dropped his gaze before he replied that Excalibur had threatened to run him through with her sword.

Hint taken. If I could just get close enough to Roberto, I could stab him straight through the heart. I'd have to time it just right...get close enough so that my sword would impale him at the same moment it appeared—

Roberto kicked Alejandro backwards off the swing in the same movement that he drew his revolver and pointed it at me.

"Good evening," he said calmly.

Well...*mierda*. I put my hands up. I wasn't in stabbing distance, but I was certainly in shooting distance.

"Roberto, don't!" Alejandro scrambled to his feet.

Roberto cocked his gun. "You were at Ale's apartment a little while ago. You and your friend. Interesting."

Ágata's spell had died with her. *Steady your breath. Don't panic. Don't panic. Don't panic.*

Alejandro gulped. "I...I can explain this. She—"

"—is *una bestia* and you're screwing her. That's simple enough, Ale. You're both traitors. Do you know what I do to traitors?"

"It's not like that," Alejandro insisted. "Please, let me explain."

Anger and fear gave birth to tears, which started to flow down my face. What a way to go out.

Roberto grinned. "Crying for your life?"

I'd acted my way out of trouble once—could I do it again?

I wiped my eyes and stomped my foot. "Armando's dead!" I screamed, recalling Alejandro's wild tale. "I tracked down this *hijo de puta* so I could kill him with my bare hands!" The hysterics sounded real to *me*.

Alejandro recovered quickly, taking a step forward and making fists. "He had it coming," he spat. "I wish I'd killed more of you."

"Shut up, Ale," Roberto ordered, never taking his eyes off me. "I know she's your girlfriend."

"Girlfriend? Please. I traded sex for information," I mumbled. I wasn't about to let my pride get in the way of saving my own life, and probably Alejandro's. "I wanted to know more about the goings-on of the barrio."

"She got lies, and I got laid," Alejandro said, bouncing on his feet. "It was too good of a deal to pass up, even if *she's* ugly as sin. Her teammate is hot."

I swallowed the lump in my throat. "Bastard."

Roberto studied me for another few seconds, then withdrew yet another revolver from his pocket and stepped to the side. "Ale, this is your initiation into Los Diablos." He handed Alejandro the weapon and retreated a few more feet, swinging his arm so that Alejandro was his target now. "Kill her. A head shot. I know they wear vests."

I'd been very, very stupid to come here by myself. I couldn't even be mad— I'd sown impulsiveness, and now I was reaping the profits. My heart beat wildly against my useless bulletproof vest as Alejandro walked towards me, slowly but surely. Maybe he had a plan? Maybe…maybe…

No. There was no way out of this that included both of us. Sometimes that's just how it was. Alejandro had to choose between himself and me, and I could not fault him for this. My team would, though. I hoped he was ready for that.

"Excalibur," Alejandro said quietly. "Please get on your knees."

My knees crumpled, and I crashed to the ground, hyperventilating. What was my last thought going to be? *I love my family. I wish my life had been longer. I wish I'd had more time with Miguel.*

Miguel. Oh, sweet Miguel. Just to have one more kiss.

Alejandro, still out of stabbing reach, turned to Roberto. "Just one thing."

"What?" Roberto snapped. "Make it quick."

"She's religious. I saw her praying at the house. She should have a minute to say her final prayers."

Roberto rolled his eyes. "You're such a girl. Thirty seconds, *puta*. Starting now."

My mind raced. I'd never prayed in my life. In fact, until I'd come to San Diego, I'd been told that God was for civilians only. What was he playing at? Still, I clasped my hands together as I'd seen civilians do before and whispered, "What are you doing?"

"*Estoy salvando tu vida,*" he whispered back.

I'm saving your life? I risked a confused glance at him.

Alejandro's eyes were black. *Flat* black. Iris, pupil, sclera—gone, replaced with a ghoulish stony blackness that glittered in the light of the moon, stars, and streetlights. He stared down at me with an inscrutable expression —how could I discern meaning from howling blackness? What the hell *was* he?

And then he smiled. It was somehow even scarier.

I recoiled.

"Don't look so shocked, Heather," he murmured. "After all, your eyes glow silver when you draw your sword."

Before I could answer, a familiar sound made all three of us look to the night sky: buzzing. The bees were back, and this time there were even more. Three hellacious swarms converged above us and descended like fog. An evil fog. Roberto bellowed and started to run in circles around the playground like a goose, waving his hands in the air and cursing.

Alejandro merely pulled me to my feet and held me close, inching us towards the brick wall of the school, his black eyes staring without blinking at Roberto. The stinging insects flew around us, but none of them touched either me or him. It was if they didn't know we were there…or as if they were being controlled.

I looked up at him. "*You're* the bug telepath!"

He just continued to stare at Roberto, lost in thought, his jaw hard. Eyes narrowed in pure hate, he lifted the revolver Roberto had given him and took aim, his hand steady as steel.

"Alejandro! Heather!"

The shout came from the edge of the playground. Courtney was standing on the far side of the fence, her arms up in a loose protective gesture in case the bees came her way. "Are you okay? I'm coming to get you!" She jumped over the fence and raced towards us.

Roberto took aim at Courtney.

"*Berto*! *No*!"

Alejandro's shout and multiple gunshots cut through the buzzing at the same time with horrible clarity.

Courtney collapsed, the sound of her body hitting the ground lost in the din. Roberto sprinted past her totally unharmed, tossing his gun aside in his haste to get away from the insects.

The roaring drones fell away into the background as I dashed to Courtney's side. The swarm, angry, began to race in chaotic fury. Individual bugs bounced off of me as I sank down by her still body, and all I could hear was the rushing in my ears as I picked up her hand to feel her wrist. "Please," I breathed. "Please."

Alejandro collapsed at her side too, and brushed her hair out of her face with trembling fingers. "*Mi sol*," he whispered. He began to whisper actual prayers.

Mi sol—my sun. His source of light and warmth. Of life.

Her pulse beat steadily in her veins. As I watched, her eyelids fluttered but did not fully open.

"She'll live." I cradled her hand to my face. "She'll be bruised and sore for a while, but her vest saved her. I'm sure she'll want you there when she wakes up."

Alejandro's stricken expression didn't relax as he picked her up and held her to his chest, but the bees and wasps finally lifted from us and dispersed. He let out a long breath and said, "I'm taking her back to your house. We have a lot we need to talk about."

"You don't say?"

"I know you have, er, questions."

"Yeah, mostly about how you know..." I trailed off, turning to look behind me. I'd heard something in the distance.

More gunshots.

CHAPTER 16

11AUG – Don't know, don't care.

*A*lejandro ran off towards the house with Courtney in his arms, but I produced my sword and rushed toward the distant fray. Multiple pop-pop-pops were bouncing around the buildings—there were several shooters.

As soon as I turned the corner where the bodega was, Armando sprung out of the ground and pulled me into an alleyway.

"What is—?" I began.

He put his hand over my mouth. "Stay low," he said, glancing around the corner. "Los Diablos are everywhere. Where's C—Frenzy?"

"She got shot in the vest," I hissed, crouching down. "Alejandro is running her home. Where's everyone else?"

"Holed up in the dress shop and across the street. They're trying to pick us off one by one. I'm going back in."

Intermittent gunfire interrupted us. Orange flashes from an upper window a few buildings down alerted me to a shooter there. I needed him gone before I could go deeper into the firefight. I signaled for Armando to take out the sniper, and then signed my next moves. He nodded once, then melted into the ground. After a few seconds, there were rapid gunshots from inside the upstairs apartment where the sniper was. Armando's hand poked out of the window and flashed me the thumbs-up.

I hurtled down the sidewalk towards the dress shop. If I could just get close enough to a shooter—

The terrified screams of a woman made me dive into the stairwell of an apartment block and race down the corridor towards the open door from which it had come. Sword drawn, I kicked the door open with a bang.

A bullet tore through my pant leg and grazed my thigh, eliciting a hiss from me. I hadn't even seen my assailant.

The man jumped behind a plastic-covered sofa, then reappeared with his gun up. I fell behind a small table and flipped it up as a barricade shield, then sliced through it and tossed the piece as I had done in the bodega.

He somersaulted away and raised his gun again. It clicked. I prepared my sword for a charge.

A petite woman in a frilly floral apron sprang from the kitchen, wielding a meat hammer and screaming her head off with a ferocity that terrified even me.

The shooter gasped and tried to jump up, but it was too late—Meat Hammer Lady was obviously determined to play Los Diablos whack-a-mole to the bitter end. She swung her hammer over and over again on the man's face and head until, finally, I stepped forward and held out my sword to keep her back.

"*Señora. Eso es suficiente. Él está muerto.*" I didn't know the Spanish word for "overkill."

And he was obviously dead. Dents marred his face and head, obscuring his features. Blood oozed everywhere, staining her otherwise-immaculate carpet. I wasn't sure, but the man couldn't have been much older than me. Yet again, Santa Muerte's face, ingrained forever on the dead man's arms, leered up at me. She'd claimed another victim.

Tears immediately replaced rage on the small woman's face, which was buck toothed and slightly squished, just like mine.

"He came for Juanmi," she said, dropping her hammer and falling to her knees. "He came and said that if I did not tell him where my son was, he'd cut off my fingers with my paring knife."

Juanmi...Jorge the mailman's son, the boy who'd had the flu a few weeks earlier. He ran around with his friends and had a little crush he'd wanted to woo. I'd never met him, but I imagined him to have puppy fat and messy hair. Why the *hell* did a Diablo want a young boy? Why threaten his mother with dismemberment? What was so important? Ransom? No, these people had no money.

First questions first. "Are you Leticia? Jorge's wife?"

"Yes!" she gasped. "You're Heather, aren't you? Jorge and Juanmi have told me all about you. You look exactly like they described you."

They? This mystery wasn't getting any shallower.

"Ma'am, I'm sorry, but I'm confused. I know your husband, but I've never met Juanmi." I wracked my brain to recall every Juan-anything I'd ever met in my time at the barrio. I'd met a Juan Carlos, a Juan Pablo, a Juan Roberto, a Juan Diego, a Juan Luis, a Juan Alvaro, and even a Juan Vicente... but never a Juanmi. "Did I assist him during a crime? I just can't think of a Juanmi."

She shook her head and stood on shaking legs. "I suppose he thinks he's too *cool* now to go by Juanmi. That's a nickname, short for Juan Miguel. His hoodlum friends call him Miguel."

My sword disappeared with a puff of sparkles, sucked back into me at the same time the air left my lungs.

"He came for Miguel?" I whispered.

"Yes!" she repeated, wringing her hands. "Do you know why? Heather? What's going on?"

I was already backing out of the apartment, my gaze darting back and forth while I was trying to make sense of what she was saying. One of Los Diablos had broken into Miguel's home for Miguel. He'd been prepared to maim Miguel's mother to learn his whereabouts. Why? *Why?* What did Roberto want with Miguel? Las Bellas weren't even a real gang! They were a silly group of friends who raided Alejandro's fridge and had matching tattoos. They didn't belong in wars, real or fake, with anybody. All of this was so wrong.

I stumbled out of the corridor onto the sidewalk. I had no idea where my team was, but the bullets had stopped, allowing me a little headspace to think. If Los Diablos were looking for Miguel, they were probably looking for all of Las Bellas. They were supposed to be at Alejandro's, but...

They hadn't been there when Alejandro had gone to meet them.

"Oh, *mierda*," I breathed. "Oh no. Oh, God, no."

I leaned against a tree, my chest heaving. Something terrible was happening, something that I could only grasp at. The pain in my leg flared, and I winced, wobbling slightly. Great. Las Bellas were probably dead in a ditch somewhere and I was injured. Could this night get any worse?

A cherry red sports car drove up next to me, answering my question.

Roberto stepped out of the driver's seat, his face its own evil spell. Never breaking eye contact with me, he opened the trunk and pulled out Gabriel, who was bound and gagged with duct tape. Bruises and cuts marred his youthful face, and he was clearly terrified. Roberto held Gabriel by his collar in one hand, and yet another gun in the other.

I stood my ground. "If you kill either him or me, my team will hunt you to the ends of the earth, Guerrero. That's a promise."

Roberto looked back and forth between Gabriel and me, a cold smile on his face. "Kill? No. I just want you to send a message. Tell my *pinche* baby brother that if he doesn't return home to me in forty-eight hours, I will send his friends to him in pieces, starting with little Gabriel."

Gabriel whimpered, and I gave him a soft look before turning back to Roberto. "Excuse me? Your *brother?*"

Roberto's smile turned into thin-lipped annoyance. "Ale."

I paused. He had to be making this up. "Um, you guys have different last names," I said slowly, like I was reminding him of his lines. "He's Cipriano. You're Guerrero."

Roberto sighed and shoved Gabriel into the truck, slamming down the lid and then turning to me and crossing his arms. "So he claims. My stupid brother is always pretending we didn't grow up together. He's Cipriano Obrador. I'm Guerrero Obrador. Same mother. That's how Latino names work, dumbass."

The cute little nickname, the overly-familiar body language and conversation, the Diablo who'd been sent to punish us...it all made sense now. The sheer fact that Roberto had *repeatedly* asked Alejandro to join his gang instead of, maybe, shooting him in the head when he'd first refused implied at least some regard between them. Roberto was talking sense, as much as I hated to admit it.

I gripped the hilt of my sword, studying him. "Forty-eight hours. Got it."

He narrowed his eyes, then shouted, *"Vamonos, muchachos!"*

A few hidden men dashed away from various places around the street, disappearing like rats down alleyways and side streets. Talk about a power move—they could've shot me at any time.

Roberto backed into his car, never breaking eye contact until he'd slammed his door and floored it, tires screeching.

My leg collapsed, and I fell to the ground. A dark red stain was blooming near my knee. Gritting my teeth, I pushed myself up and limped down the sidewalk towards the dress shop.

The street was deserted, the residents wisely staying inside while beasts and devils tore themselves apart. I'd be gone from this place soon. All of us would, and we'd never look back.

But first I had to mount a rescue, and possibly decapitate Alejandro Cipriano Obrador for not disclosing the oh-so-minor detail of being our local gang lord's half-brother.

My hands were balled so tightly that my knuckles were white. He hadn't even lied by omission—he'd just plain lied. I'd asked him if he had a past with Roberto the night we'd struck a deal with him. I'd explained the importance of his answer; if we'd known of a familial connection, we never would've taken him in—Roberto's involvement was far too personal. Personal motivations were the strongest, the most lethal. Alejandro was going to get people killed.

I stepped through the halo of broken glass that had used to be the door of the dress shop. "Hello?"

The shop was in disarray. Rack upon rack of colorful frills had been pushed over and destroyed, blown to shreds by bullets. Two dead Diablos lay prone on the floor in pools of blood. Posters of smiling Latina women in large wedding dresses hung off the walls in long strips. A blue plastic water cooler had been shot by a single bullet and had leaked its contents all over the industrial carpet; my boots made little wet plopping noises as I walked through the carnage.

Above me, on the second floor, someone moved. I quickly hurried through the shop towards the back. At the bottom of the dark, narrow stairwell, I cupped my hands. "Is anyone there?"

The unmistakable sound of hurrying feet carried through the ceiling, and then Minnie opened the door at the top of the stairs. "Heather! Thank God. Come quick."

I limped up the stairs as quickly as I could. The door led to a small apartment, in which lay a scene of different devastation. My leg threatened to collapse again, and Minnie had to hold me.

Eleazar was spread out on a cot in the middle of the living room, unconscious and barely breathing. He was bare-chested, with nothing but strips of blood-soaked white sheets covering his torso. Next to him, a battered Armando was holding Eleazar's wrist and studying his watch. On the couch, Morris sat next to a middle-aged couple holding each other and weeping silently.

Minnie swallowed and made me turn away. "They came for Juan Carlos's family. Eleazar gave his vest to Mrs. Hernández early on. When Los Diablos turned their guns on the girls, Eleazar jumped in between them. It all happened so fast, we didn't know what happened until..."

"And the girls?" I asked faintly. "Are they safe?"

"They're fine. They're in their room."

Morris swore. "Heather, you're bleeding. Minnie, get some bandages, please." I'd never heard him sound so tired.

I sank to my knees by Eleazar's side and stroked his face. "What's going to happen?" My voice broke on the last word.

Armando gently placed Eleazar's hand on his chest. "His pulse is slowing," he whispered. "He's got minutes. If you've got anything to say, s...s-s-say it..." He jumped to his feet and retreated into the kitchen.

"*Llama una ambulancia. Él necesita ir al hospital*," pleaded Mrs. Hernandez through her tears. Her husband nodded along.

Everyone looked at me. I took a shaking breath and quickly explained that superheroes weren't allowed to go to civilian hospitals.

Forget control. The camps hated us and wanted us dead. That was the only explanation I could think of now.

I trailed my fingertips over Eleazar's jaw and cheeks, tears sliding down my face. He'd been so afraid for me when we'd received the terrible news that I'd have to return home for punishment. He'd served the barrio at the expense of his relationship with me. He'd claimed to be a poor son of the camps, but truly, he'd been one of the best.

His breathing began to slow.

No. *No.* He was going to live. He was going to get up, walk off the minor bullet wound, and lead us to victory. We'd all run away, he'd meet a beautiful woman in Mexico, and they'd get married. He'd die an old, old man, surrounded by grandchildren who adored him.

Mrs. Hernandez crossed herself and pulled a rosary from her pocket, her trembling fingers sliding over the beads as she began to pray.

"Team," I said, my voice small.

Armando reappeared from the kitchen, and we all huddled by Eleazar's side in the quiet. I held his hand, alternating between stroking his fingers and kissing his knuckles.

There was no gust of wind, no prophetic thunderclap, when Eleazar Lloyd passed away a few minutes after midnight on that hot August evening. He was just twenty-three years old. Armando draped a sheet over his oldest childhood friend and whispered the traditional words of honor reserved for those who died in the line of duty. Minnie and Morris held each other, crying unashamedly. I stood there, numb, utterly at a loss for what to do next.

We'd had a death on the team, and moreover, it was an elder's son. Most of Las Bellas were in the clutches of Los Diablos. We'd gone so far off the rails that I couldn't even begin to formulate a contingency plan.

"We have two days to surrender Alejandro," I blurted. "Otherwise Roberto will kill Las Bellas and send them to us in pieces."

Armando, the default new leader, didn't respond. Instead, he gently picked up Eleazar's body and arranged the sheet so nothing could be seen. After gulping heavily, he turned to me, never betraying how heavy the corpse must've been. "Who told you that?" He sounded a bit strangled.

"Roberto himself." I blinked back tears. "A Diablo came for Miguel, too, but his mother killed him. As far as I know, Miguel is still at our house." The one small mercy of this whole grotesque night.

Armando gazed down at the covered face for many painful seconds, then looked up at me, his face hardening. "We're going home."

CHAPTER 17

12AUG – The screens are just darkness and snow this time of night.

I'd been kneeling next to Eleazar's body for an untold amount of time, but still I did not return to my room to try to sleep as the rest of my team had. No, I had far too much on my mind to even think of sleep, such as the logistics of his funeral.

I wasn't thinking about Mexico. After all, we weren't going anymore. Eleazar himself had warned me that a death on the team would throw our escape plans into chaos—and I'd blown him off, because I'd been stupid and childish. I hadn't been able to take that mature step back and see the bigger picture.

Well, I could see it now.

I closed my eyes and laid my forehead against Eleazar's cold, pale hand—the only part of him that was visible. The rest of his body lay under a sheet on his bed, waiting for his funeral pyre. Normally we would've immediately notified the camps and arranged for transport to his home in Coeur d'Alene, but we'd agreed immediately that he wouldn't have wanted that. He'd be burned here, surrounded by those who'd served with him.

A silent sob shook my body.

This was Alejandro's fault.

Oh, this was *completely* Alejandro's fault. The Diablo had shot him, but Alejandro had unwittingly enabled the chain of events that had led to this. We would *never* have shaken hands with him if we'd known he was Roberto's brother. My shock and aggravation at the lie had given way to a thirst for vengeance. I wanted to simultaneously beat him, stab him, and throw every-thing I owned at his lying face. Courtney hadn't yet regained consciousness when we'd returned following the firefight, so I hadn't had a chance to confront him. His good luck.

A soft knock on the door partially lifted me from my murderous thoughts.

"Heather?" Miguel said from the other side of the door. "I'm coming in."

I didn't answer.

Miguel slipped into the room, his face gaunt. "Armando woke me up and told me what happened. "I'm sorry. I'm so, so sorry."

He kneeled down next to me and gathered me into his warm embrace. The exquisite tenderness rubbed away some of the roughness around my heart, and I began to cry into his shirt. He didn't shush me or whisper trite plati-tudes. Instead, he massaged my back and let me release the load of guilt and grief.

Finally, after several long minutes, I sniffed and cleared my throat. "Did Armando also tell you what happened at the bodega?"

"The bodega? No." Worry clouded his features. "What happened?"

I cupped his cheek. "I'm sorry, Miguel, but Ágata was shot during a battle with Los Diablos. She died a few hours ago. Later, one of Roberto's men broke into your apartment and threatened your mother. She killed him, but I'm certain your parents are still in danger."

"Mamá?" he whispered. "Ágata?"

"Your mom is safe," I assured him. "I'm so sorry about Ágata."

"What about Papá? Is he safe? You know, he's always walking around for his job, anybody could jump him, is he safe? We need to—"

"It's the middle of the night," I said quietly. "He won't be on his route. We will check on them as soon as we can."

"Why is this all happening?" He fell backwards and leaned against the bed. "Why my parents? Why did they attack Juancho's family? They're all the nicest, most boring people on the planet."

I settled on my knees across from Miguel. "I know why it's happening. Have you ever met Alejandro's brother?"

As I thought, Miguel shook his head. "No," he said dully. "Why?"

I pursed my lips. "Go get Alejandro. He has something he needs to tell you."

Miguel looked confused, but obeyed. He disappeared out the door, then returned a minute later with Alejandro and Courtney. Courtney's new bruise stood out dark and disgusting on her collarbone, plainly visible in her tank top. Alejandro looked exhausted, his face shadowed and lined.

Courtney saw Eleazar's body and covered her mouth, squeezing her eyes against the tears.

Alejandro hugged her tight and crossed himself. "He was a good man. I had hoped to get to know him more."

I stood, a strange heat spreading through my face. It was time.

"Alejandro Cipriano Obrador," I said slowly.

Alejandro blinked, and Courtney's tears slowed. "Yes, that's my name," he said, confused. "What about it?"

"Roberto—"

Alejandro gasped. "Heather—"

"—Guerrero Obrador."

Miguel took a quick step back. "Roberto is your half-brother?"

I turned to Courtney. "He's been lying to you."

Though Alejandro's eyes were as round as saucers, Courtney looked down, her face pink.

Oh, hell no.

Miguel continued to stare at Alejandro. "You're his half-*brother*?" he repeated. "Why didn't you *tell* me? Ale, he's so pissed about the war with Las Bestias that he sent—"

"Miguel," Alejandro said quietly, "I have a feeling that I'm about to hear a complete description of my shortcomings. I will speak to you after I'm done with Heather."

I closed my eyes, then opened them, hoping they communicated the level of anger I felt.

"Heather," he began. "Please, understand that—"

"People are dead, Cipriano."

"I know! I didn't—"

"I asked you directly if you had a history with Roberto. You looked me square in the eye and lied despite me telling you that we would be in greater danger if you did have a history. Later, a man came to our house and almost gunned me down on the front porch as punishment for supposedly threatening you. It is pure dumb luck that *I* am not under a sheet.

"Tonight, a man broke into Miguel's home on Roberto's orders and was going to cut off Leticia's fingers. Another one was going to shoot two little girls. Eleazar took those bullets. Your friends are in the clutches of a monster. *I* am injured." I gestured to my still-painful leg. "None of this would've happened if you'd just told us the truth. Maybe we would've worked with you, maybe not, but we never would've chosen to appear as your enemy in a neighborhood ruled by your brother. Your lie killed people."

He hung his head. "I'm sorry. I didn't want to be associated with him."

It wasn't enough. Nothing he said would, or could, ever be enough.

"Get out. Leave this house and don't come back. I don't care where you go. Go to Roberto and save your boys, or go to Juárez, or go jump off the pier at

Coronado and get eaten by sharks. I really, truly, literally *do not care* what happens to you as long as I never see you again."

Courtney stepped forward. "Heather, please—"

My sword at his collarbone made her freeze. "That wasn't a request, *Ale.*"

Alejandro put his hands up and backed up. "Okay, I'm gone," he said softly. They shared a desperate last look, then he left the room.

Courtney whirled around. "Heather!"

I lowered my sword, but did not make it evaporate. "How long have you known?"

Her eyes widened. "What do you mean?"

"Do not play stupid with me, Courtney Mukai. How long have you known?"

She bowed her head. "Since I saw the photograph of him and Roberto at his apartment. I asked him about it later and he told me not to tell."

"And you didn't think that was pertinent information?"

Courtney twisted her fingers. "I love him, Heather. I knew you'd all send him away. Besides, you didn't do due..." She caught herself.

I didn't do due diligence.

She was blaming me for trusting her to tell me the truth. For not picking apart Alejandro's past. For being in such a hurry because of our pathetically small window of time that I bullheadedly charged ahead at the first lead I'd had.

Had I not served alongside Courtney for a year, I would've killed her on the spot. She was not foisting this on me. I would acknowledge my own failures and shortcomings one day, but right now she was going to answer for her own part in what had happened tonight.

"Let me get this straight. You flew off the handle when I said I was going to make a sacrifice to keep everyone safe, including Las Bellas, but all the while you weren't willing to share extremely material information with your team, thereby ensuring that Eleazar had to make the *ultimate* sacrifice. Is that right? Have I got the measure of your thought process?"

A tear dripped onto her bare foot. "Yeah."

"You got so caught up in the drama that you lied. And now people are dead. I warned you about doing this. I swear to God, Courtney, if any more of us die because of this mess, it's on you." My teeth began to chatter. "I'm going back to the camps. That *is* on you. You sent me back. Not Roberto. Not the elders." A tear slipped out. "You. My friend."

She finally faced me, tears flowing down her cheeks. "I'm so sorry, Heather. I didn't intend—"

"If you finish that sentence, you're going to personally find out what the road to hell is paved with."

She gulped and wiped her eyes with the heel of her hand. "Is there anything I can do to fix this? Anything at all?"

I jutted my chin at the door. "Get out and get lost."

"Heather—"

"*Get out!*"

She let out a wail and fled, following Alejandro down the stairs and out into the night. From the window I could see her run into his arms on the sidewalk and sob into his chest. He stroked her hair, then led her away into the darkness.

I turned away.

"I swear I didn't know," Miguel said from the corner. "Please believe me. Please don't send me away."

"I believe you," I whispered, gathering him into my arms again.

"What now? What will we do? I don't know the way into Mexico, and Eleazar needs to be buried. It's only right."

I inhaled the natural, masculine aroma of Miguel. *Please let me see a future with him. Please let me see that we win.*

My power failed me, but my imagination filled in the holes. His voice fell away as flashes of a life with him played in my mind like a television screen flipping between channels: Miguel leading me by the hand along the beach, his skin aglow with sun. Him lifting a gauzy veil from my face, beaming with excitement. Small children around us, filling our home with laughter. Sitting on a porch swing somewhere, old and lined and gray, our legacy around us.

It was the life his parents wanted for him, their *hijo*, their precious Juanmi.

But it was never meant to be my life. My life was over.

I cupped his cheek again, stroking his fine features and memorizing his face. I'd never noticed a light scar on his forehead, nor his faint widow's peak. One of his lips was slightly fuller than the other. His nose was ever so slightly crooked. His eyes had the barest flecks of gold—gold!—in them. Beautiful. So utterly, heartrendingly beautiful.

Our lips met, and we kissed, sad and slow. He held me close, letting go long after I had.

He knew.

"You need to go now." My lips brushed his.

"I can't. I can't go." He kissed me again. "I'll stay. I'll tell your elders everything. They'll understand. They have to."

He really was a dreamer.

I stroked his cheek. "Go home and tell your *parents* everything. No more lies. Tell them what happened here and how much I love you. Live that life you told me about. Live it for me."

He laid my head on his chest. "What'll happen to you?"

"I'll go back to the camps. After that, maybe I'll be punished, maybe not. I'll probably be sent to another team."

"You'll go back into the cult and die, you mean. If not physically, then in your heart."

"Plants need sun to live," I whispered. "And you're my sun, Miguel."

Miguel and I held each other's gazes for an eternity until, at last, he turned and ran from the room. Down the stairs, out the door—and unlike the other two, he did not stop to cry. He sprinted away from the house, disappearing into the shroud of the night.

I fell to my knees and screamed.

CHAPTER 18

13AUG – Minnie destroyed the television with an ax because I'm a huge baby.

I sliced through Courtney's largest bookshelf, neatly turning it into kindling. Morris had once helped build a funeral pyre back home, and he'd told us that it took an unimaginable amount of fuel to burn a human body. Hence, we were breaking down every spare bit of furniture while he was purchasing gasoline from a nearby gas station. The first things to go were any bit of "contraband": bookshelves and all books, the television, magazines, posters, and anything else that a camp representative would look askance at.

We weren't sure when they'd come, but we knew it would be a "when," not an "if." Eleazar was dead, and an elder's son's death would not stay hidden long. Courtney was technically AWOL. I had to make travelling arrangements to go back to Georgia. It was a wonder that the north San Diego team hadn't stepped out of their white tower to come visit the war zone in the south end of town and ask what was going on.

I stacked the last bits of the former bookshelf and moved onto the smaller one. Goodness, had Courtney spent her entire allowance each week on books? To save time, I just tipped the shelf and let the books rain down.

I kneeled to gather them up, but stopped.

The brightly illustrated covers hinted at worlds and universes beyond my imagining, places of romance and adventure. Beautiful women in ball gowns twirled around rooms. A man on a horse commanded an army, a look of fierce determination on his face. A witch stirred a bubbling cauldron. But it was the most battered volume, a slim book depicting two kissing teenagers, that caught my eye. She'd dogeared nearly every page, and a bookmark stuck out from the middle.

"Ro…me..o," I murmured, tracing the title. I already knew the next words. "And Juliet."

I'd seen the story in a PBS production: two houses, both alike in dignity, forever at war in a fair city. Two young lovers torn apart by circumstance. A secret marriage. Death everywhere. A ticking clock threatening to destroy everyone and everything.

Miguel had joked that Courtney viewed the play as a relationship manual. How could she *not?*

I gently closed the book and slipped it into my roomy pocket as a premonition of flickering flames lit up my brain.

Maybe I didn't have the power to see the future. Maybe I just had the power to see the obvious.

ARMANDO, Minnie, and I industriously cleaned out Eleazar's room, putting his personal effects in a small box and throwing out anything that his father wouldn't want, which was most of them. My ability to cry had shut down around the time that Minnie had chopped the television in half, so it wasn't hard to sort through his clothes—they still smelled like him—and small items like his action novels. Some of his official documents had doodles in the corners.

"Yeah, he was always like that," Armando said when I pointed them out. "His mind elsewhere, never…never paying much…excuse me." His voice cracked, and he melted into Minnie's shadow.

"Don't tell anyone," Minnie muttered as she worked through a pile of cassette tapes, "but I have a few bottles of beer under my bed. I have half a mind to make him drink some. You on board with that?"

"No," I murmured. "I don't think that would really help anything."

Minnie grumbled but said no more.

The front door burst open with a bang, and then Morris poofed into existence in the hallway. "Guys! Code black! Not a drill!"

We were on our feet before he'd said "drill."

Code black. An assault on the house.

In less than three minutes, all windows were bolted shut. The back and side door were blockaded with tables and chairs, then the fridge was pushed in front of it all. Bulletproof vests were donned, boots tied, and weapons placed in hands. In the living room, my sword burst into life as I tuned my ears to anything I could hear outside in the twilight of the evening.

"Morris, report," I said breathlessly.

Morris raised the ax Minnie had used to destroy the television as he stared at the front door. "I don't know what happened, but Roberto must've gained whatever control he didn't have over the barrio. He's got a crowd of the nastiest-looking guys marching down the street, and they're armed. They're coming for us."

"Did you see Las Bellas?" I asked, my chest throbbing.

"No. I don't know where they are."

Pounding on the front door made us all jump.

"Open up!" Courtney cried. "Please! Hurry!"

I shoved aside the couch and unbolted the door. Courtney and Alejandro tumbled in. Alejandro was carrying a black duffel bag, which he immediately unzipped. It was full of every weapon imaginable: handguns, a shotgun, aluminum bats, cans of pepper spray, and even a taser.

"What—?"

Alejandro kicked the door shut, then tossed Minnie the taser. "Sweetheart, you can stand there and ask obvious questions, or you can clear out this room so there's more room to fight. They're going to come through the door one way or another. I saw a battering ram."

There was no need to tell me twice. I grabbed the cans of gasoline and the box of matches Morris had brought and stowed them in Eleazar's room, then pushed the chairs and coffee table into the kitchen.

When I came back, my team was manning the windows.

"I see them," Courtney said. "Minnie, give me a bat."

Alejandro loaded his shotgun, then pumped it. "I hope none of you object to a little gang violence."

The shouts of countless men were finally audible.

"We're allowed to make a last stand." I looked him square in the eye. "I sent Miguel home. Is he safe?"

Alejandro faltered. "I haven't seen him since last night."

"They're five houses down in both directions," Courtney said. "Ale, now!"

Alejandro's warm eyes were absorbed by the same howling blackness I'd seen at the playground. "I really am so sorry." He placed his hand on my shoulder. "I shouldn't have lied. I'm with your team until the end."

Behind him, Courtney glanced at me, her face saying it all: they'd come back to die with us.

The buzzing of his obedient insects mixed with the shouts of the men advancing on our house. I could hear Roberto now; he was screaming directions at the mob like the lunatic he was.

Courtney squinted. "They're setting something on fire...tires? Why are they burning tires?"

Alejandro swore colorfully. "For my bees. Friends, it's about to get ugly."

"Back!" Courtney cried out, moving away from the window. "They've got bricks!"

A brick crashed through the window. Alejandro ran to the spiking opening and fired his shotgun with a tremendous bang. Return fire rang out, piercing the windows and walls with bullets.

Alejandro's swarm funneled in through the broken window, quickly filling the room in a cloud of stinging insects. "Get to another room!" he shouted above the din. "They're at the door!"

The front door bowed slightly as men on the other side began to batter it.

I leaped up onto the couch and shoved my sword through the door at chest height. There was a strangled yell from the other side and a general commotion.

The door splintered where the ram hit it, allowing me to see the frenzied mob beyond. Bees and wasps surged through the hole, but the men weren't pushed back.

Alejandro shot more through the hole in the window.

The back door crashed open elsewhere in the house. Armando and Minnie ran off, weapons up.

I backed up into the center of the room, my sword at the ready. The door bowed again. Courtney stood by my side, her aluminum bat held up. "This is it, Heather."

"Let them come," I whispered.

The door crashed down, flipping partially over the couch. Men in masks and hoods climbed over each other, some waving guns, others knives, all of them bent on our deaths.

Courtney and I swung wildly. I didn't care what I was hitting, so long as it wasn't her. Alejandro's swarm, cut down because of the choking smoke that blew in from outside, made the ground slippery, and I lost my purchase several times.

Bodies began to fall near the door, and I moved back into the living room. Nobody wanted to get too close to the chick with the glowing sword, but Courtney was having trouble.

A man grabbed her long hair—only to be blasted in the face with pepper spray by Alejandro.

"Upstairs!" he shouted. "I'll follow you!"

I grabbed Courtney and fled up the stairwell, where the mob had not yet infiltrated. In desperation, I jumped into Eleazar's room, where his body was still lying in gentle repose. Alejandro sprinted in, then slammed the door shut. He still had his shotgun and the pepper spray, but nothing else.

"The other three are fighting outside," he said, wheezing. "There are at least a dozen in the house. The bees scared away a lot of them, and we killed a bunch. Help me bar the door."

We began to push Eleazar's bed in front of the door.

Spanish shouts and heavy footfalls downstairs gave way to the sounds of breaking furniture, shattering glass, and unidentifiable heavy thuds—had they knocked over the refrigerator?

The power went out.

They began to climb up the stairwell, the whole house shuddering as they moved. We were stuck, trapped in a tiny room with nowhere to go. None of our powers could take out people en masse, nor did we have an advantageous position. Alejandro and Courtney embraced, sharing one last passionate kiss.

The ghost of Miguel's first kiss tickled my lips.

My eye twitched. I'd reached my tragedy quota for the week, and *I was going to live.*

I grabbed the gasoline and began to douse Eleazar's body, the door, and even got down on my knees and tipped it under the bed so it would spill into the hallway.

Alejandro gasped. "What are you doing?"

I held up the box of matches. "Sweetheart, you can stand there and ask obvious questions, or you can open the damned window so we don't immolate."

Even now, in the heat of battle, I ached to give Eleazar his hero's funeral. This would be my last gift to him.

Alejandro and Courtney unbolted the window and pushed it up together, then punched out the screen. Alejandro helped Courtney onto the roof, then turned to me, his hand out. "I'm not leaving until you're on the roof, Heather."

I made a little trail with the last of the gasoline, then lit the match and dropped it.

Orange and yellow flame coursed through the room, up the bed, onto Eleazar's body, and up the walls and door. Men cried out in alarm and terror as the ignited fluid burned in the hallway.

Alejandro helped me onto the roof, and then stepped out after me. "*Madre de Dios!*"

The yard and street were a battlefield of dead, dying, and injured Diablos, all of whom were coming in and out of visibility because of the choking, oily smoke from the three dozen burning tires scattered here and there.

Courtney waved to get our attention on another part of the roof. "There's a drain pipe over here, guys! Let's get down!"

We clambered across the faded shingles to where she was. There were no men in the side yard at the bottom of the drain pipe, so we climbed down carefully, landing with little thuds on the crunchy grass.

"I tossed my bat in the rosebush," Courtney said. "I'm getting it." She disappeared into the smoke.

Crackling above us made us jump. Flames were leaping out of Eleazar's window, licking their way up the siding.

"Just a few minutes left," I said. "Ale, go get Courtney and find the others. I'm going to search the perimeter of the house for Diablos."

He nodded and ran after Courtney. I produced my sword and stayed low, searching through the smoke for anybody who wasn't my teammate or Alejandro. The backyard had a few dead bodies, but nobody I knew.

The code black was over, and I returned to the front of the house. Much of the mob had retreated, if the number of dead men around were any indication, and hopefully Roberto was one of the corpses. High above, invisible because of the drifting smoke from the tires and our house, the thuds of a helicopter rotor repeated endlessly. Surely reinforcements were on their way.

But where were Courtney and Alejandro? And everyone else?

I stepped onto the cracked and potholed street, searching with my sword in hand. All I could hear was the raging infernos around me and the groans of the injured. A slight breeze blew some of the smoke back.

Several feet away, Roberto Guerrero was holding Courtney in a chokehold with one arm, and a handgun in the other. Alejandro was in front of him, clearly pleading for her life.

I rushed at him head-on.

Shots rang out, deafening me but not stopping me. Something grazed my arm. I swung my sword at Roberto, but he tossed Courtney at me and I had to jump back with a cry.

I leaped over her and swung again, not caring what part of him I hit as long as I struck him.

His fist collided with my temple, and I fell, dazed. He stomped on my sword hand, eliciting a scream of pain. My sword disappeared, and Alejandro let out a strangled shout. "Get away from her!"

I grabbed a fistful of Roberto's pant leg and pulled him down with me. Grappling with all of my might, I head-butted him, then kneed him in the stomach. I could fight as well as Courtney. I'd fight *better*—for Miguel.

I rolled on top of him and aimed as many left-handed punches as I could for his face, but he blocked most of them.

"Get Courtney!" I ordered Alejandro, who was behind me. "I'll kill this freak myself!"

He wriggled under me, but I stayed on him through the sheer weight of my fury. He'd destroyed the barrio. He'd destroyed the lives of countless people. He'd killed Ágata. He'd told his goons to go after Miguel. Eleazar was dead.

I'd kill him if it was the last thing I'd do. I'd—

"Heather? Heather!"

I knew that beautiful voice, masculine and sweet. The sunshine through the storm.

I looked up. "Miguel?"

Far in the distance, barely visible through the smoke, was Miguel. He was running towards me on the sidewalk, disappearing in and out of the smoke as he went, making strange motions with his arms, like he was trying to push something out of the way. What was he—

I never saw Roberto's hands. One second, I was on him, the next, he had my head in an unmistakable snapping hold. "*Adios, puta*," he growled.

Alejandro threw his entire body against Roberto, freeing me. My vision cleared, and I saw what Miguel had been trying to tell me through his gestures.

I grabbed Alejandro's collar and pulled him away from his brother mere seconds before the dim lights of a large speeding mail truck cut through the smoke and hit Roberto.

Roberto bounced up onto the mail truck's hood, then flew off onto the road, rolled several feet, then lay prone on the cement.

Jorge, still in his uniform, poked his head out of the truck and spat, then beckoned to us. "Get in the back! Minnie, now!"

The back door of the truck slid open with a bang. Minnie, Armando, and Morris—bloodied and bruised, but very much alive—were huddled in the back of the truck among boxes and enormous canvas mail sacks.

Minnie beckoned and hissed, "Get in!"

Alejandro helped a limping Courtney into the truck while Miguel ran up and literally pushed me inside without any further ado.

Before I'd even gotten situated, he banged on the inside.

"Dad, go!"

Jorge floored it, roaring down the road so fast that all of us were thrown around a bit. However, whenever we shouted in alarm, Miguel shushed us.

After the tensest half hour of my life, I felt the truck slow and then stop.

Jorge got out of his seat and stepped into the mail area, where we were. "Everyone, get in a sack. Minnie, the plan. Just as we rehearsed."

Miguel tossed each of us an enormous canvas bag, which we slipped into while shooting each other confused looks. Minnie, however, hovered by Jorge's seat, squinting ahead of her. What on earth was going on?

I opened my mouth to ask Miguel for an explanation, but he put a finger to his lips and gently pushed me into the bag. "Soon, I promise. Soon."

I obediently bowed my head and curled up in the mail bag, which Miguel pulled shut with the draw string.

After a few minutes of silence, a man spoke from outside the truck in accented English. "Your papers, please."

"Of course," Jorge said. "Here."

"I'm assuming your purpose for visiting Mexico is mail delivery?"

"Yes. I'm headed for Oaxaca."

"I'm going to need to check your cargo," the man said. "Please step out while I..." His voice became dreamy and vague. "That checks out," he said airily. "Welcome to Mexico. Enjoy your stay."

~

SEVERAL MINUTES LATER, long after the engine had roared to life again and we'd begun tootling down the road at a steady pace, Miguel opened up my bag and helped me to my feet while Minnie freed the others.

The tan, scrubby countryside on the outskirts of Tijuana, Mexico, visible through the truck's windshield, was the most beautiful landscape I'd ever seen. Miguel beamed while I stared at it as we drove down the highway.

"Are we really going to Oaxaca?" I asked faintly. "Are we free?"

"No, and yes," he said. "We're going to La Paz and paying a visit to my relatives."

Tears borne of an unnamable emotion fell down my face. "You came back."

He ducked his head. "When I returned home, I told my parents everything. Mom and Dad agreed that they had to help however they could...so here we are. The police are raiding Roberto's hideout right now and rescuing the others. Dad called his brother. We've got a place to stay and everything. Tío Rico owns a rental north of Cabo San Lucas. The Oaxaca thing was to throw off anyone in case they followed us. I doubt they will, though. They're going to be combing through bodies for weeks."

"We've got a place to stay?" My fingers interlaced with his.

"Well, yeah. Tío Rico said—"

"No," I said quietly. "*We* have a place? Not just my team?"

He paused, bashfulness appearing on his face. "Yeah, we do. If you'd like. We won't be in the rental forever, but I thought you'd pick new names and we could maybe get jobs or something. Start a new life. I could probably make money drawing tourists—Baja California Sur has a lot of those."

"You'd leave it all behind for me? Your adventures?"

He smiled from ear to ear. "Heather, from the second I first saw you, you were my adventure."

He pulled me into my first kiss as a free woman.

EPILOGUE

20AUG – I've gotten them all addicted to Telemundo. I have no regrets.

"*N*ews is on!" Minnie shouted from the small living room. "Get in here!"

We all gravitated from our various places around the house: Courtney and Alejandro from the tiny walled patio with its many flowers, Minnie and Morris from where they were pouring over a book about learning Spanish, Armando from the deck chair where he was reading the English newspaper, and myself and Miguel from the kitchen, where he was drawing my portrait instead of helping me do the dishes.

Minnie turned up the volume on the tiny television. By some miracle, we picked up the San Diego station.

The familiar blonde anchor stared soberly at the camera.

"Federal investigators announced this afternoon that the superhero team of south San Diego have been officially declared dead after last week's unprecedented attack on their home. City officials were able to recover what are believed to be the remains of the team's leader, who apparently died in the assault. A postal worker has stated that he saw members of San Diego gang Los Diablos removing the bodies of the rest of the team from the scene. The investigation is ongoing.

"In the meantime, San Diego citizens have already begun to petition for a permanent memorial to be installed at City Hall. Our correspondent downtown…"

The screen fizzled, then went to snow. Morris banged on the screen while we all shouted "aw, come on!" and "stupid television!" but our anger couldn't make it come back on.

We eventually wandered back to where we'd come from. Miguel resumed writing a reading primer for me at the kitchen table; we'd officially begin my lessons tonight. I picked up the sponge and returned to washing the dinner dishes, humming a quiet tune along with the small transistor radio on the windowsill.

I couldn't help a smile as I mulled over the broadcast; the same city that had thrown us away was now going to build a memorial for us. There was no probably about it—an entire team had apparently died in the line of duty. We were going to be in the same ranks as the infamous Philadelphia team lead by the late, great Battlecry.

I didn't know how I felt about that.

But at least Los Diablos were gone. Jorge had promised us when he'd dropped us off to say that he'd seen our bodies, and he'd kept that promise. No strike team would ever search for us.

After a few minutes, Miguel grunted and stood up. "I need to go get my pencil sharpener."

"Sí, mi amo," I murmured, taking the chance to practice my Spanish. As soon as we were in our permanent residence—in about a month's time—I was going to begin living under my assumed name: Josefina Ágata. I might as well start talking the part.

Something outside the window, far in the distance, caught my eye. My eyes flickered up, and I stilled for a moment before putting down the sponge and drying my hands on my skirt.

I slipped through the back door, the sea breeze filling my nose with salt and freedom.

The white sand was still warm from the late August sun as I walked across the dunes towards the Pacific Ocean. The turquoise water lapped gently against the beach—"la playa," we called it now—and the melancholy call of seabirds mixed with the hissing of the water as it receded, making a natural song that already comforted me greatly. I came out here often with Miguel, sometimes to talk, sometimes to do *other* things.

But at sunset, when the fiery sun was sliding west and out of sight, I came here to be alone.

That's probably why the hooded woman was waiting for me. She knew.

"Why are you here?" I asked the lone figure on the beach. Curiously, she too was watching the sun set, an almost wistful expression on her face. She didn't turn to face me until I was right next to her, close enough to see that for the first time, she wore no mask. The breeze did not ruffle her hair, nor did the sun reflect in her eyes.

And she was crying.

"You're not Santa Muerte, are you? What's wrong? Are you someone who needs my help?"

"No. They need *my* help. They need *your* help." She reached into her pocket and produced a scrap of cloth: a worn, bloodstained mask. "Help me help them. The cult is killing them."

She was a superhero.

I backed up. "No," I said firmly. "Absolutely not."

"They need your help, Heather."

"I made my choice. I have a choice. Do you hear me? I have a choice, and I've made it. I'm never going back. I'm staying with Miguel, and that's final. I'm not a superhero anymore. Excalibur died last week. You look like you're capable of taking on a strike team. You do it. What's your codename, anyway?"

As annoyed as I was, I was curious to know who had the ability to contact me across the void like this.

"Please help me. Please."

Her voice, so heavy with emotion, pricked at my heart. Maybe she wasn't one superhero. Maybe she was all of them.

"I fought my fight," I said quietly. "I was forced into this life, and there's no dishonor in leaving. I'm not the one meant to free them. I'm going to stay here with my friends and we're going to *live*. Pass the torch to someone else, because I refuse to carry it. That is my choice."

Slowly, she raised her hand and stroked my cheek. As she did so, the sound of a newborn baby's cry lit up the recesses of my mind.

I brushed her hand off. "Take it easy, lady. Miguel and I are just trying to catch our breath right now. Kids later."

She nodded, then put her mask on and pulled up her hood, casting her face into shadow as I'd first seen it. She walked away across the sand towards the east, leaving no footprints. Finally, at the crest of a dune, she faded into the night.

I turned my back to face the west, which was already dark and showed the first stars of the evening. The north star glittered brightest, but I would never follow it back to the United States.

"Heather!" Miguel's voice cut through my quiet thoughts. "What are you doing?" He ran up to me, his curly hair that much livelier from the beachy air. "I'm almost done with your portrait. Can you come back inside?"

"In a minute." I entwined my fingers in his. "I'm watching the sun set."

"Watching the sun set?" he repeated, rubbing his chin. "That means the temperature will drop soon... It could be cold out here in the sea breeze. You need someone to warm you up."

I fell into his embrace and tucked my nose by his neck, inhaling the wonderful smell of his skin. "Oh? And how will you do that?"

We fell onto the warm sand, giggling like the careless young lovers we were. A shooting star flitted across the sky, but I ignored it.

All of my wishes had come true.

THE END

ABOUT THE AUTHOR

Emerald Dodge is a writer, mommy, and general daydreamer. All her life she's loved a dramatic story–and that's what she writes. Whether it's a saga of superheroes escaping from the cult in which they were raised, or the more homegrown tale of two lifelong friends trying to work out their place in the world, her novels will resonate with their readers long after they've closed the book. Her work examines the heights and depths of the human condition, yet always retains an irresistible sense of fun that makes it excellent reading for any occasion.

Find out more about Emerald Dodge at www.emeralddodge.com.

THE BLOOMING

KATHERINE BENNET

Proofreading by Patrycja Pakula for Holabird Editing

Beneath the safe confines of a peace treaty exists a shadow war most people know nothing about...

As a new graduate of the Academy, Sophia will do whatever it takes to defend Nios--except lose her father. When he's assigned to a new role on the mysterious and dangerous black ops team, she volunteers to take his place.
The team's new leader, Niko, knows what it takes to succeed in black ops, and it isn't Sophia's powerful contacts or the awards and recognitions on her spotless record. Test after test, he's determined to prove she doesn't belong. Little does he know she has no intention of quitting.

When the team is ambushed on a mission, the consequences of the shadow war hit too close to home. Niko finds himself at the center of a whole new battle, a political one where his commanders don't need real blades to take him down. Determined to prove his innocence, Sophia sets out to expose the truth--and when it comes to Niko, she finds so much more than she bargained for.

Can Niko and Sophia work together to find who betrayed them? With enemies closing in on both sides, will love bloom between them, or will their hidden enemy kill them both?

Genre: Romantic Science Fiction
Heat level: Sweet

CHAPTER 1

"Come on. You can do better than that."

Sophia thrust her left fist into a strong uppercut.

Dad smiled, faint wrinkles growing along his eyes. "Okay. Now faster. Right-left combination."

She gritted her teeth and punched again, faster and harder.

"Not bad," he said, the corners of his mouth stretching farther as he lowered the pads.

The sun had just peeked over the horizon, casting long shadows behind the planters that lined the sprawling white marble patio of their home. The lush green vines framing the back door and windows rustled in the cool breeze. The facets of the protective shield overhead gleamed with golden sunlight, sending silvery threads shooting across the cerulean sky, and alongside their home, the white cobblestones of Nios's main square reflected the early morning light, almost shimmering like the sea.

She tucked a thick, dark curl behind her ear. In an hour, it would be bustling with people. The farmers would be teleporting their produce to the markets. The bakers would be delivering bread. There would be a million things to do. But for right now, all was peaceful. It was just her and Dad. He wrapped an arm around her shoulder.

"I love the view out here in the mornings," she said, smiling.

He nodded. "I'm not sure the founders could have ever imagined a place like this. It's a pity we have to hide it from the rest of the world." He took a step back and held up the pads. "Okay. One last time before we have to go inside. You're graduating from the Academy today with honors. Show me what you can do!" He grinned playfully, but she knew that look. He was serious.

Smirking, she sank into her stance and sprang forward. She landed one punch on the pad, then a second before following through with a rear round-house kick. He had worked with her for hours to perfect the combination, and she couldn't help but feel pride in the execution as her momentum carried her leg toward him.

But he didn't move out of the way.

The kick landed with devastating force, and he fell backward. "Dad!"

He wiped a drop of blood from his mouth with a weak smile. "It's fine. I told you to show me what you could do, and you certainly did."

"Let's get you to medical." She grabbed his arms to pull him up. How had he missed it? He'd taught her the move himself. They had spent hours working on it.

"No. I'm okay." He rose and faced her, rubbing his jaw and then running a hand through his jet-black hair. For a senior officer, he still looked quite young. "And I wouldn't miss your graduation ceremony for the world." He brushed another curl from her face. "You look so much like your mother. I wish she could have been here to see you become a Niotian Guard."

Mom...

A familiar wound ached in her heart. She had been killed in the war eleven years ago. Sophia had only been ten. Dad's emerald eyes glazed with a distant look, but a moment later they blinked back to life.

"The sun's almost up," he said with a faint smile. "We should head inside and get ready. Are you really taking all those boxes with you to the barracks?"

She rolled her eyes. "Yes. All of them."

She couldn't wait to move into the barracks, but she would be taking some of her things to remind her of home—especially her books.

Inside, he stared at the boxes stacked by the front door with drooped shoulders. "You know, we can still apply for a waiver. You don't have to move."

She sighed. They'd been through this. "Level-1s are usually required to live in the barracks. I don't want special treatment just because you're a senior officer. Besides, you can come and visit me any time you want, and I can be home in as little as five minutes." She hugged him, knowing the waiver would have been more for him than for her, but he had spent his life teaching her to stand on her own merits and skill versus his title.

He squeezed her tight. "If I can't convince you, then we should get ready to go so we're not late. It's going to take forever to get all these boxes over there."

He didn't have to remind her. She bounded up the stairs and rushed through her routine. An hour later, she smoothed her charcoal-gray tactical uniform in the mirror. She tightened her ponytail and retwisted a curl; her hair wasn't cooperating, but it was one thing she had gotten from Mom, so she wasn't about to complain. After a couple more attempts to smooth the unruly strand, she gave up and emerged from her room.

"Come on, kiddo!" he yelled from the patio. "People are already starting to show up at headquarters."

"Coming!" She rushed to meet him. He was holding two boxes.

"You don't have to do that right now. We can teleport with them later," she said.

He raised an eyebrow. "If we're headed over there anyway, why not bring a load now?"

He'd always been the efficiency expert. She grabbed a third and followed him down the staircase to the main square to begin the half-mile trek across it to headquarters. Sweat beaded along his forehead even though it wasn't overly hot.

"Do you want me to hold another box?" she asked.

"Huh?" He panted and shifted the boxes in his arms. "Of course not. I can handle it—"

"Captain Anuva!" a male voice shouted.

They stopped and turned around. Dad set his boxes down to greet the man with sandy-blond hair running toward them, trailed by a smaller man with dark hair. Both wore the gray uniform of the Niotian Guard, but a shiny new commander's eagle gleamed from the blond-haired man's chest.

Anton Cipriani. He had assisted with a number of her classes and had just recently been given his own division. He grinned brightly as he approached, pointing to the boxes. "You should have sent for someone to help with those. Gideon, give them a hand."

The smaller man scurried forward, but Dad stopped him. "No thanks, Gideon. We can handle it."

She dropped her chin to hide her grin; she hadn't even bothered to extend her box forward for Gideon. From coffee runs to cleaning, Dad never asked anything of a junior guard that he could do himself.

He tilted his head to her. "This is—"

"Sophia." Anton's gaze fixed on her. "I know. Her academic record precedes her."

Dad put his arm around her shoulder. "Yes, she's graduating with honors, just like you did."

Her cheeks flushed. While proud of her record, she preferred quiet success over open recognition and accolades. It felt more genuine.

Anton's blue eyes never left her. "I'll be excited to see where her career takes her."

She hid a cringe and turned her focus to the light playing off the Niotian marble pillars lining headquarters while Anton and Dad continued to talk. Iridescent swirls gleamed in the morning rays like constellations from outer space.

The main entrance doors behind them opened and people started to file in. Her shoulders sank. Where was Emma? Her friend since childhood, Emma had always run late, but she should have been here by now. Bouncing up on her toes, she searched the crowd. A woman lurched nearby, catching her eye.

A man—no, a giant—muscled his way through the crowd without any visible acknowledgment that he had bumped into the woman. He wore a gray guard's uniform, as did the three others who followed him, but she had never seen any of them before. The pointed tips of black tattoos jutted out from the neckline of his shirt as he walked, and as if he needed another way to stick out, he scowled as he surveyed the happy crowd.

As he neared, his gaze darted from Dad, to Anton, and finally to her. The intensity of his cold brown eyes looking her over sent a shiver down her spine, and she looked away. "Who is that?"

"Who?" Anton asked loudly, inclining his head to see over the crowd.

Subtlety must not be his strong suit. She paused as the giant passed, then nodded to him as he moved away.

"Niko Kalos," Dad replied in a low tone. His eyes remained on him with a gravity Sophia rarely saw.

She stole a sidelong glance. "Is he new?"

"New?" Anton's laugh had a hint of condescension. "No. He's an L-5 like me, but he's black ops so he's not around very much… probably for the best."

Black ops? She raised her eyebrows. Of course she'd heard of the black ops unit before. Everyone had. Their missions had been legendary, but the war with Octavius had been over for five years.

The terms of the truce were clear, and every guard graduating today could recite the peace treaty, from beginning to end—especially the rules of engagement. A unit dedicated to fighting it out behind the scenes violated just about every rule she could think of, so they couldn't have been that busy anymore.

"I should run. I have a million things to do before all you L-1s report tomorrow morning, but hopefully I'll see you soon, Sophia." Anton held out his hand, and she shook it, his grasp gentle, almost intimate.

She tried not to jerk her hand away too fast as he turned to Dad.

"Sir, it's always a pleasure," he said before stepping away with Gideon in tow.

Dad nodded his goodbye, and Sophia folded her arms.

"Black ops?" she asked.

"Yes. Kalos is..." He paused as if considering his words carefully. "He's built for that world, but where's McCade, their captain? Normally, he'd be with them if the unit is together. Hopefully nothing's wrong."

She shook her head. "I'm sure it's fine. Everyone would know if they'd been in combat; the treaty bans that."

Dad raised an eyebrow, his gaze still following the unit, and he muttered so only she could hear, "For such an ironclad treaty, it left a lot of holes."

She folded her arms. "I've taken three years of military history and another two years of policy. I think active black ops missions would have come up."

"And I'm Captain of Personnel Command. It's my job to approve every assignment and review every disciplinary issue, so I know a thing or two." He stepped closer and whispered in her ear. "I don't care what your courses told you. We've had more deaths in black ops in the last five years than all other units combined."

"Deaths?" she whispered back. Guards killed in battle were given full honors and a state funeral, which Academy students were required to attend. "We haven't had a military funeral in years."

He shot her a fleeting glance with a heavy expression. "Not every dead guard has the luxury of a funeral."

The starchy feel of the flag they'd presented her at Mom's funeral came rushing back, and her hands splayed to get rid of the sensation. She expected some level of this from someone like Anton, but her own father? "That's not funny."

He glanced around to make sure nobody was listening. "It's *not* funny. Beneath the clean terms of the treaty is a whole shadow war that most people know nothing about, and most of the Niotians fighting it never come home." He craned his neck to see over the crowd. "I'm just not sure why they're here. They normally don't come to these kind of functions—not as a unit, anyway. McCade's a friend of mine. I wish he were here. I'd ask him."

"Julian. I've been looking everywhere for you." A tall, slender woman approached. The Head of the Guard.

Sophia's eyes widened. Commander Mendoza's dark, silvering hair was parted in the middle and pulled back in a bun, and the medal rack on the left side of her chest was so full it looked like a joke. An entourage followed, all of them sporting the commander's gold eagle on their chests. Every single one of them was staring at Dad.

"Commander Mendoza." Dad greeted the Head of the Guard with a salute. "How can I help you, ma'am?"

Sophia saluted, and Commander Mendoza returned it before her gaze returned to Dad.

"Actually, I was hoping to have a word with you." Commander Mendoza inclined her head away from the group. Sophia bit her lip as they passed. What could be so important right now?

Out of hearing range, Dad nodded once, then again, a thoughtful frown clouding his face. He froze and glanced at the main entrance to headquarters. His color drained, but he nodded. Moments later, Commander Mendoza excused herself and hurried away. Dad returned to Sophia, but his eyes had that distant look again.

"What did she want?"

He smoothed a curl on her head. "Let's just say I figured out where the black ops commander is. Let's get you inside for the ceremony." He held out a hand to guide her, but she planted her feet.

"What's going on?" she asked.

He smiled at someone as they passed by. "We can talk about it later." He nudged her and bent down to lift up his boxes.

"No. Dad. Please. I'll worry the entire ceremony. Just tell me now. Is he okay?"

He sighed, staring at the ground. "No."

She dug in her heels. "Is he...Is he *dead?*" Never during her entire Academy career had she heard about any casualties. Sure, being a guard had been dangerous during the war, but now?

He lifted the boxes. "He'll live, but black ops will need a new commander."

"Well, that's a relief." She lifted her box, but it wasn't until several paces later that it hit her.

New commander...

"Dad..."

"Not here," he muttered. "We can talk about it later."

She froze. "You? Tell me you said no!"

He couldn't accept the position. She had already lost one parent, and with an assignment in Personnel Command, his days in the field were behind him.

"I go where I'm needed."

The memory of him falling to the ground after her kick replayed in her mind. How long would it be before he missed something on a mission? What if he got hurt? Or worse?

"No," she said, her voice quivering. "You could die."

"We're guards, Sophia. This is what we do, and I'm intimately aware of the risks, having lost your mother. Now *let's go.*" He emphasized the last words in a low tone that ended the conversation.

She took a step toward headquarters, the pillars still gleaming in the sunlight as if nothing had happened.

We.

She was a guard now, too, called to protect Nios from its enemies. She had been well trained and was confident in her abilities.

The happy crowd flowed inside, past the green vines creeping up the side of the white brick and stucco walls. They'd soon bear the beautiful red magnolias Nios was known for. Her hands trembled, but it wasn't from the weight of the box. If there was a need for a black ops unit, that meant all this —everything she loved—was threatened. As a guard, she would dedicate her life to protecting it.

But she would not lose Dad.

CHAPTER 2

The next morning, Sophia filled a small paper cup with green tea, hoping it would soothe her stomach from being up all night. Yellow sunlight shone in through the floor-to-ceiling windows of the headquarters cafeteria. Spring was definitely here, but it was hard to care when she had Dad's news hanging over her head.

Checking the time on her implant, she strode for the door. She'd need to be back for in-processing in two hours, and if she knew Dad, she would need every second.

The teleportation zone wasn't overly crowded this early in the morning. She stepped over the steel lip, pulled up the coordinates on her implant, and blinked. Static crept up her arms and legs just before the blue flash. She blinked away the spinning sensation as she arrived at the zone just outside Dad's home.

Before the ceremony, he'd tried to convince her to live here, but after his reassignment, he'd insisted she stay in the barracks overnight. She had complied, but if he had thought that would end the conversation, he was mistaken. Placing her palm under the blue-lit sensor to unlock the door, she let herself in.

"Sophia, what are you doing here?" Dad asked, approaching her from the kitchen.

"I think you know." She kept her voice steady even though the cup shook in her hand.

He rolled his eyes. "This is not up for discussion."

"I want you to apply for a waiver."

"It doesn't work that way."

Sophia folded her arms. "You're the Captain of Personnel Command. Sending you out in the field would be seen as a demotion."

"There's no one else!" His angry voice filled the living room. "Guards in black ops can't be paired to have children."

Her head jerked back. What did that have to do with anything? Yes. Pairing to have children was a basic tenet of their society—control evolution by controlling the outcomes—and it had played a large role in what had set their society apart from the rest of the world. But what was he saying? He was being sent to black ops because he wasn't going to have any more children? "That's what this is about?"

"That's what it's always been about. It's what the Enlightened Society set out to do. Create better, smarter, healthier—"

"*Stronger humans.* Yes, I know, but you're really willing to die so someone else can have children?"

His green eyes iced over, and she bit her tongue. She'd gone too far.

"I don't want to die," he said in a low, raspy tone. "But the war changed things. For our society to continue, for the Enlightened's body of research to be preserved, and to protect those discoveries from those who want to use it for personal gain, we need to replenish our ranks. Children are a big part of that." He took a step closer. "And being a father myself, I wouldn't fault anyone for wanting to be paired."

She searched the floor. He loved being a father and wanted to give others the same opportunity. How could she argue against that? But he was *her* father. There had to be someone, anyone, who could take this assignment. "Maybe someone younger who isn't looking to be paired yet? What about that big guy we saw yesterday? Kalos?" He looked like he hated anything joyous.

Dad nodded. His eyes looked as tired as she felt. "I'm sure Kalos would take the role if I don't, but..."

"But what? You said he was built for that world! It sounds perfect!"

"He's a strong fighter, but he's also a loose cannon. He's got a record of disciplinary action longer than anyone else's I've seen. Even with his record, I think Commander Mendoza would promote him if she felt like she had strong recruits, but she doesn't. If she moved him up, there would still be an open spot in the unit, so it doesn't solve the problem."

He had good reasons—really good reasons. Her chances of convincing him were dwindling by the second. "There has to be another way."

Dad kissed her forehead. "I wish there were, kiddo, but I'm not going to ask someone else to take that position so I don't have to do it myself. I'm not going to ask for a waiver."

She shut her eyes, as tears overflowed, and laid her head on his chest. She'd never hesitated when it came to dedicating her own life to service, but this was different. His life was too high of a price to pay. She scrambled for any semblance of a convincing argument, but none came. After almost a minute of silence, Dad ushered her toward the door. "You should head back. You don't want to be late on your first day."

∽

Sophia stood with Emma in a line of their fellow Level-1s, a long day of in-processing ahead. The line had wrapped all the way around the main corridor of headquarters. Big enough to be used for certain ceremonies and events, no expense had been spared there. Large windows overlooking the main square lined one side. The domed ceiling was painted with a mural of the world's greatest art masterpieces. The commander's offices lined the other side. Shy smiles and nervous energy surrounded her, but she couldn't bring herself to care. She used the alternating Niotian marble pillars and busts of famous guards and scientists to mark the line's progress.

Emma bounced up on her toes and craned her neck to see the table at the front. "What are you requesting?" she asked.

Her deep-brown eyes had that over-alert look to them again, like she was ready for anything—and she probably was. She'd known her since the first day of school when they were five.

"The Protocol Office might be good." Emma shrugged. "That would be a clear pathway to the Head of the Guard's executive team."

She drew in a breath through flared nostrils. Did it really matter? If Dad's decades of service didn't mean anything, her first assignment certainly wouldn't.

Emma tilted her head. "Then again, drone combat guards seem to get a lot of commendations, which we'll need if we're going to promote to anything impressive." Her pale skin and blond ponytail made her look like a porcelain doll, but she was far from dainty and fragile. If the commanders didn't judge her on appearances, she'd probably prove she could do any job she wanted.

"Why so glum? You've barely started." Anton's voice was full of playful humor.

Silence followed. Was he speaking to her? She started. "Anton—I mean Captain Cipriani—"

He held up a hand. "I appreciate the courtesy, but please call me Anton."

Her gaze fell to the ground. He outranked her by four levels. She shouldn't even know his first name.

He slid a hand over her shoulder. "Why don't you come with me. We can discuss whatever's got you down."

She glanced at Emma but didn't find any help there. Her wide-eyed expression all but physically pushed her in his direction. "Um, no. That's okay. I really don't want to lose my place in line."

Anton shook his head. "Don't worry about that. Gideon's working the table at the front. I'll walk you up myself if you need it."

Emma nodded next to her, but Sophia bit her lip. She didn't want his help—

Wait.

Maybe she did. She didn't know enough about the inner workings of the Guard to stop Dad's assignment, but Anton might. She followed him to the side of the wide corridor.

"If someone were to get an assignment..." Her heart fluttered. She needed to phrase this just right. "But it wasn't a good fit—"

"Is that what this is about?" He chuckled. "You're worried about your assignment?"

"No. I mean—"

"How about this, I have a friend in Personnel Command. He's handling the L-1 assignments. You tell me where you want to go, and I'll make it happen."

She nearly choked on her tongue. Emma may applaud a move like that, but Dad would kill her if she used a back channel to get an assignment. "No. It's not me."

He frowned, but a moment later his shrewd blue eyes lit up. "Your father."

Her mouth dropped open. "I... How did you know?" She could already picture the livid look on Dad's face if he figured out she had been asking about a reassignment for him.

"It pays to know what's going on around here." He glanced up the corridor, smirking. "I wish I could help, but his orders came directly from the Head of the Guard. No one can change them."

"Okay." Her shoulders sank. She'd known the answer; she just didn't want to accept it. "I should get back to the line."

"For what it's worth, rumor has it that Commander Mendoza didn't want to move your dad. Black ops jobs are notoriously hard to fill, and they need at least five guards to be operational. Junior guards can't be assigned—they have to apply—but captains like your dad and me are a different story." He puffed out his chest a little more, and she wanted to roll her eyes.

She knew all about life as a senior officer, having lived with Dad.

"Captains have to go wherever the Guard needs leadership, and trust me when I say that unit needs some strong leadership. Everyone agrees your father is good at what he does, but there weren't any other captains who could move. Either they're like me and aren't up for reassignment yet, they're paired, or they're looking to be paired."

She pressed her lips together in a tight smile. He made it sound so rational.

Was she the only one who wasn't thinking about future children with a yet-to-be-named partner?

She hadn't had many casual relationships, but they were commonplace—even encouraged, in some cases. Pairing was for children, so everything about it had to benefit the child. The application process was extensive. They reviewed everything before a pairing was approved: whether you had the means to provide for a child, a compatible genetic profile with your partner, a job that would allow you the time to care for children, and much more. Frankly, she couldn't understand why half the people went through the trouble. "It seems people are a lot more concerned about being paired than I had realized."

"It's certainly something I've thought about." His gaze pierced her as she sat speechless. Why did she get the feeling she'd played right into his hands? He stepped a little closer, giving her the urge to step back. "I've got a lot of goals for my career, and to achieve them, it's going to require a lot of careful planning. I can't be paired with just anyone."

"Well, you're certainly ambitious enough." She laughed nervously, unable to look him in the eye. Yes. Pairing could also be a stepping stone on your career path, but that wasn't something she'd even begun to think about. Why had she ever left the line? This was a huge mistake. "Thank you so much for listening. I should be going."

"If you ever need someone to talk to, I'm here for you. My office is just down the corridor." He pointed as she backed away.

She couldn't get back fast enough.

"Is he gone?" she murmured to Emma as she returned, too afraid to look herself.

"He's walking away. What did he want?" Emma whispered, staring in his direction.

"He was trying to make me feel better about assignments."

Emma was a lifelong friend, but they were polar opposites. She wasn't about to tell her the truth.

"He's a captain now—not just a unit leader, Sophia. He's a *division* leader. Did he offer you a spot on his staff?" Emma asked, still staring.

"No. It's nothing like that—"

Emma arched an eyebrow, a smirk playing on her lips. She lowered her voice so only Sophia could hear. "Oh, I *saw* what it was."

Sophia's cheeks burned. She knew Anton had been flirting—anyone would have seen that—but she wasn't going to get ahead that way. "Emma Riles. You know I'm not like that."

"Yeah... the question is why?" Even with her voice so quiet, the words packed a punch.

Sophia drew in another sharp breath through her nose. Why? Because she was a good enough guard to succeed on her own abilities. She didn't need favors to get ahead. "I'm not okay with getting ahead that way. He's..."

Emma planted a hand on her hip. "Everyone knows who he is. He's rumored to be on the fast track to Head of the Guard. He's the only L-5 to be selected for division command this year. He's a powerful *friend* to have."

Emma didn't mean *friend*, and they both knew it.

"I'm not interested in him that way."

"Why not?" Emma raised her voice.

"Shh!" Sophia looked around to make sure no one was listening. "It doesn't matter if he was flirting with me or what he may be in the future. He's probably just looking for something casual."

Emma tilted her head back and forth. Her eyes, still fixed down the corridor, slowly descended and bounced back up. "I'm still not seeing the problem." She lowered her voice. "Plus, if there's any chance he'd be Head of the Guard, that would be good enough for me."

Sophia glared. She wasn't going to sleep around to get ahead, and she might have been crazy, but she wasn't attracted to Anton. All the subtle things about him were building up and nagging at her. The way he treated the guards under him, the way he'd offered to walk her to the front of the line despite the fact that everyone in front of her had been waiting for just as long as she had. Then she thought of Dad. Mom had been dead for eleven years, and he still couldn't bring himself to be paired again.

Emma groaned. "You're thinking of your fairytales again, aren't you?"

"What?" Sophia's voice shot up two octaves.

"You are. How many of those books did you bring with you to the barracks?"

Sophia folded her arms. "They were a gift from my dad after my mom died. They're very special to me."

"You brought all of them, didn't you?"

"So what if I did? They're great stories!"

"I'm sure they are, but they *are* stories. You can't be paired based on shooting stars, magic spells, or wilting flowers. You have a similar background to Anton. You both graduated with honors. Your father is a senior officer. You'd make quite the power couple!"

"I don't want to be part of a power couple," Sophia said through tight lips. "I know I'll be paired one day, but I am hoping to actually love the person I'm paired with."

Emma rolled her eyes. "How very worldly of you. Why would you pair yourself with someone because of the way they make you feel? Feelings change. The rest of the world marries for love, and look where that got them. Almost half of marriages end in divorce. I can't understand why anyone does it."

Sophia understood it. It might be foolish, but she wanted the fairytale: the prince who would do just about anything to be with her, someone who could fight a monster yet still bring her flowers.

Someone to love her the way Dad loved Mom.

But once again, she wasn't about to tell Emma the truth. "I don't want to pair with someone like Anton just to be their prop. Who wants to be paired with the Head of the Guard? You'd never be known for what you've done; everything would be about your partner."

"Whatever assignments I want? All those formal dinners? Summits in Aspen, Paris, and the Bahamas?" Emma rose her hand. "Me! I want that."

Sophia shook her head. It was impossible to argue with her, but thankfully they had reached the head of the line.

Gideon didn't even bother looking at them as he thrust the forms in their direction. "Fill out these forms, then walk through that door. Someone will assist you after that."

Combat, Logistics, Maintenance, Mobility…these were assignment requests. She narrowed her eyes at Emma, who immediately and diligently started filling out her form. Sophia hadn't had time to think about it yet. "Gideon, what should we do if we're not sure what to request?"

His gaze darted up from the table. "I'm an L-3. Address me as *sir*. And it doesn't matter what you put on those forms. Personnel Command will assign you based on the needs of the Guard."

Sophia was speechless. Yes. She should have addressed him as *sir*, but why would they make new guards go through all the trouble of filling out these forms if it didn't matter?

It didn't matter for Dad.

Right. She checked boxes without bothering to think about what she had selected and barged through the doors.

CHAPTER 3

*S*ophia tossed in her bed. Emma had been asleep for hours, and the sun would be up soon. She took a deep breath. Another night of sleeplessness and futile calculations. There was nothing more she could do to stop Dad's assignment—even Anton had said so. Yet every time she closed her eyes, fear would take over. Dad could be in trouble. Even McCade, the black ops commander, had gotten hurt. It could happen to anyone.

I have to save him.

She sighed. Would she really have to go through all the arguments again? Anton had been clear. He said there were no other captains who could take the assignment. She flipped over to stare at the white ceiling. Emma had done her best to decorate the walls with paintings of magnolias and pictures of them together, but the room still felt empty, foreign.

The embossed ink from one of her books stacked in the corner glistened in the moonlight, a call to escape from reality just as she had so many times after her mother had died. But there was no escaping this. She could feel herself already bracing for the worst, never knowing, always fearing, going to bed each night hoping to see him again soon. The only glimmer of hope she'd received was that Kalos would have gotten the job if they'd had more recruits to fill the ranks—

More recruits.

She sat up, ramrod straight, in bed. Recruits. Could it be that easy? She flew from her bed to get dressed in her guard's uniform. Anton had said they needed the black ops unit to stay at five members, and junior guards could apply.

That was just what she would do.

She didn't need special favors or back-door access. She would save Dad, and not even he could argue with the way she was going to do it.

She crept from her room, careful to not wake Emma, and headed for the cafeteria. It was like coming out of a cloud. Her anxiety melted away, her hunger returned, and a peaceful sense of purpose rooted inside her. Outside the window, the first rays of sunlight were just starting to show over the white rows of buildings on the rolling hills. The scene would never get old. This was her home, and she'd fight to protect it.

When enough time had passed, she tossed her plate in the trash and strode for Anton's office. Like most of the commander's offices, the white marble tile floors matched those in the main corridor. Simple dark-wood desks lined the back wall for junior staff and an arched doorway sat behind a much larger desk with ornate woodworking across the front. Gideon sat at that desk, sipping a coffee.

"Good morning, Lieutenant Ravella," she said in her most cheerful voice. "I'm not sure if you remember me from yesterday, but I was wondering how I could change my assignment request."

Gideon stared at her over his steaming mug, his gaze settling on the one bar of rank on her shoulder. "Are you serious?"

Sophia shifted on her feet, her pants rustling. "Yes. I wasn't fully aware of my options yesterday. I'd like to apply for black ops."

"I don't care."

Sophia paused. He was making the point that she was wasting his time. "I know exactly what I want now. It'll only take me a second."

He raised a thick, black eyebrow. "You should have thought about this yesterday. I can't make amendments for every L-1 who didn't come prepared with their choices."

She hadn't come this far to be rejected. This plan had to work; there was nothing else. "This is for the good of the Guard, sir. I wasn't aware there was such a great need in black ops—"

He rolled his eyes. "Spare me. I'm not amending your form—"

"Good morning, Sophia." The smooth notes of Anton's voice hit her like sandpaper. "To what do we owe the pleasure?"

"I was here to amend my assignment requests," she replied with a tight smile.

"That's an easy fix, isn't it, Gideon?"

"Yes, of course, sir. I was just going to find her form now." He spun in his chair and sifted through the pile of papers behind him. Sophia clenched her fists at her sides. It was his job. It had been that easy all along, but he wouldn't help her because she wasn't important enough.

Anton beamed. "Fantastic." He stepped closer and placed a hand on her shoulder blade. "I'll keep my promise. What assignment do you want? I'll make it happen."

She didn't want favors, but it wasn't like she'd be able to keep her assignment a secret. "I'd like to apply for black ops."

Anton blinked. The warm smile dropped from his face. "Black ops..." He hesitated. "It's a very demanding career path. Are you sure that's—"

"Very sure, sir," she replied as Gideon spun back to them in his chair, paper in hand. He looked to Anton for direction. "You said they had trouble finding recruits. I think my record speaks for itself, and I'll go where I'm needed." If Dad was allowed to have that prerogative, so was she.

"Sophia, I didn't mean *you* should join black ops. Although..." He smiled, tilting his head. "It will certainly fill out your resume, I suppose, but there are easier ways to earn recognition."

She didn't care about recognition, and she had never opted for the easy way. She met his gaze, sure of her decision. This was about saving her father and protecting Nios, plain and simple.

After a few moments, he nodded. "Sounds like I'm not the only ambitious one around here. I'll make it happen, but this doesn't have to be a long-term thing. Do a tour, check a lot of boxes, and then get out and compete for higher assignments, okay?" He flashed a grin. "You trying to beat my record of making it to division leader?"

"Not at all, sir." She smiled even though she felt like grimacing. He had proven he could be very perceptive when he wanted to be, but he had completely misjudged her—not that she would correct him. "Thank you. I should be going."

"I'll walk you out and head over to Personnel Command right now." He guided her to the door.

She had to report to a commander's call in the same direction as he was headed, but she went the other way, a bounce in her step. She'd done it. When everyone had told her it couldn't be done, she'd found a way. Circling back, she found Emma, and they sat through hours of policy and procedure reviews —as if they hadn't just graduated from the Academy.

"Hey, where'd you go this morning?" Emma asked as they filed out of the auditorium and into the main square. "I woke up, and you were gone."

"Sophia!" Dad's voice echoed above the milling crowd. He was closing the distance between them fast, and judging from his tight expression, he wasn't happy.

She smiled at Emma. "I'd better go talk to him."

It would probably be less like talking and more like defusing a bomb.

He reached her within seconds. "My office, now."

She had to scramble to keep up, and he stared straight ahead for the whole walk. This wasn't going to be pleasant, but he wouldn't change her mind. She walked through the arched doorway to Dad's office, and he slammed the door behind her.

"Black ops?" he asked. "What *were* you thinking? I'm still Captain of Personnel Command! You really didn't think I'd figure it out?"

Leaning on the large, mahogany desk in the center of the room, she lifted her chin. "Actually, it's *because* you're still in Personnel Command that I did it. This way, you can keep your command job."

"You think this is a game?" He pointed to the outer office beyond his closed door. "They put your paperwork through! I can't cancel that!"

She narrowed her eyes. "I never asked for you to cancel it, and you know me better than to think I'd be playing games."

"You seem so confident now, but you have no idea what you've just done." His shoulders sank, and he searched his office as if he'd find the words somewhere between his shelf full of books and the files on his desk. "I've had a lifetime of experience. I've been in combat. You're fresh out of school."

She launched herself from the desk. "I'm not a child anymore. I am qualified for this job."

"I don't want this for you. It's not an easy life." He glanced at her, starting to pace.

"You raised me to never opt for the easy path!"

"This is different."

"No. It isn't. I'm taking the assignment, and you get to stay here."

Mission accomplished.

He laughed bitterly. "You think you have it all figured out, don't you? Did Anton give you this idea?"

"What?" The mere mention of him made her skin crawl, and she hated that she couldn't deny his involvement.

He raised his eyebrows. "Did he mention that Commander Mendoza approved your orders at the same time as she announced a reorganization plan that brings the black ops unit under his division? You just handed him another leadership accolade!"

Her mouth hung open. *Say something.* She couldn't. None of this had been for or about Anton, but he'd somehow weaseled his way in to capitalize on it.

Dad turned and paced the full length of his office, waiting for her to respond.

"I applied for this assignment—me," she said, thrusting her finger at her chest. "It was my choice, and I followed procedure to amend my form. I did this the right way. It shouldn't matter what Anton did with my request. It should be given fair consideration."

He shook his head. "Don't be naïve. You think Anton fast-tracks every L-1 assignment request?"

Her face burned. "It shouldn't matter if he fast-tracked it or not. I'm qualified. My application would have been considered eventually, and I can do this."

He walked the length of the room. "Forgive me for having my doubts after everything I've seen today. You had absolutely no interest in combat before I got reassigned, and if you were really looking to do this the right way, I would have seen your application, but your *friend* saw to it I didn't."

Not him too.

It was the same word Emma had used to describe Anton—and just like Emma, his tone seemed to hint at a misnomer.

"I don't care how it looks; I've never asked for special treatment!" She strode for the door. "I *am* taking this assignment, and I won't fail. Do you have anything else to say, or am I free to go?"

He stared at her, eyes glinting. "No, that's all."

She opened the door and stormed out. What had she done to make everyone doubt her so much? She rubbed her arm, but it didn't stop her skin from crawling.

She'd done the right thing, but Anton had seen to it that it didn't feel that way. She glanced around the corridor, hoping she might see him and tell him exactly what she thought of his *help*. Even though she deserved this assignment, everyone would think otherwise because of him.

She drew in a deep breath and headed for the main entrance. Screaming at Anton would be satisfying, but it wouldn't get her anywhere. She needed fresh air. She thrust at the handle, and the doors flew open to the wide-eyed surprise of those around her. Storming to the middle of the square, she took slow, deep breaths.

They wanted to doubt her? Fine. She'd handled a full course load and interned in the Head of the Guard's office at the same time. She'd qualified as expert in small arms and hand-to-hand combat. Black ops certainly wouldn't be easy, but she could handle it—she would handle it, and she'd prove all of them wrong.

CHAPTER 4

*N*iko inhaled the sharp aroma of black coffee and chicory as a staffer escorted him into the Head of the Guard's office. Papers were arranged neatly on the desk, with an engraved fountain pen to the side. Frames holding embossed certificates crowded the walls. He sank into one of the chairs and took another gulp of his steaming coffee. He'd take a full Tavian assault any day over this nightmare.

He rose as Commander Mendoza walked past him and around the desk, giving him an unnecessarily large berth. She shuffled the papers on her desk before sitting down. Deep frown lines stretched across her face. Niko smirked. She didn't like him very much.

"I think you've been made aware of the current set of circumstances in your unit?" she asked, still busying herself with the papers.

Made aware? He could still feel the weight of McCade's body as he'd dragged him to cover with pulse gunfire whizzing past his ears. "Yeah, I think I'm up to speed."

Her dark gaze darted to him. "Yeah?"

He sat up straight. "I mean, yes, ma'am. My apologies."

"You're lax on your customs and courtesies. Your hair is too long, and your tattoos are showing above your neckline. How many regulations are you going to break in front of me?"

None of that mattered in combat. He adjusted his shirt, but he couldn't wait to get out of this office and back to real work.

She leaned back in her chair and stared at him with a hardened expression. "It sounds like McCade has you to thank for keeping him alive."

He shrugged. When his unit had stumbled upon two Tavian units trying to covertly move supplies, they'd all known they were outmanned and outgunned. McCade had done what he needed to do to protect his unit. Niko had simply made sure he hadn't died on the battlefield. "I'm happy to hear he's going to make it."

"As am I, but I'll be reassigning him." She read over a paper as if she'd just mentioned the sunny weather.

He leaned forward in his chair. McCade was his unit leader. He'd been in charge for years. Not just anyone could fill that spot. "Ma'am, the nature of our work. It's very... McCade is a great leader. I'm sure he'd ask you to reconsider."

She raised an eyebrow. "He won't."

He wouldn't because he didn't want to... or because she wouldn't let him?

"Seems his little brush with death has led to a shift in his priorities. He's requested to be paired, and I've granted the reassignment so the paperwork can move forward."

Niko forced his face to stay relaxed. McCade had been spending a lot of time with his supposedly casual girlfriend lately, but he was going to leave the unit? He had nearly lost his leg, but his life had never really been in danger.

"That leaves you and me with a problem." She planted her elbows on her desk, looking him over. "We both know you're probably the best fit for the leadership role, but your disciplinary record is a mile long."

He stopped himself from rolling his head back. It was easy for the brass to sit in comfy chairs in their pristine offices and wag their finger about what had happened in the heat of battle. He'd done what he'd needed to do.

"So here's what will happen. I'm moving you up to unit leader, but the black ops unit will need some close oversight for a while. Captain Cipriani has volunteered for that position, so I'm moving the black ops unit into his division."

Niko kept still. Cipriani was an awful choice, but he was a division leader. It wasn't like he'd go on missions with them. How bad could he be? And Niko would be the unit leader? It was a better solution than bringing someone in from the outside, but the responsibility weighed heavily on his shoulders.

McCade had done everything he could to protect his guards. Of course Niko would do the same, but he knew the nature of their work better than most people. Sometimes his protection wasn't enough. "I'll do my best, ma'am."

"I'm counting on it." Her gaze was just as hard as it had been when they'd begun their conversation. She must have really hated promoting him. She flipped through a few more sheets of paper in the stack. "You need to meet with McCade as soon as he's able to discuss the leadership role and duties. You'll be expected to brief your commanders on any and all missions." She stopped shuffling and glared at him. "Other than that, keep doing what you're doing."

He rose and saluted her before leaving with his coffee cup in hand. The front office was much more crowded than it had been when he came in, but people tended to move out of his way, allowing him to move quickly. The sooner he could get out of there, the better.

Unit Leader.

Extra responsibility, extra paperwork, extra headaches, but if that's what it took to keep some outsider from telling him how to do his job, he'd do it.

"Niko, hold on a minute," Anton called from behind him.

The hairs on the back of Niko's neck stood up, and he looked at his near-empty cup. He hadn't drunk enough coffee to deal with Anton yet. "What do you want, Cipriani?" He kept walking, forcing Anton to run to catch up.

"I was over here discussing the new reorganization plan. It sounds like you and I will be working together more closely from now on."

Niko curled his lips and looked him over. Clean, pressed uniform. Styled hair. Bright, shiny new eagle denoting a leadership position—division leader in Combat Command. Had he ever even seen combat?

"We should get together soon to discuss my vision for the black ops unit."

Niko lurched to a halt. "Vision?" he sneered. "Run along, Anton. I've got real work to do. If you're smart, you'll stay out of the way."

Anton grabbed his arm with surprising strength for a man with manicured hands, and Niko tried not to laugh out loud. He could flatten Anton—and he would enjoy doing it.

"I wasn't asking," Anton said in a low voice.

Niko jerked his arm away. "Are you trying to pull rank and boss me around? I'm an L-5, same as you."

Anton's features tightened. "I'm your commander now."

"Are you hoping I'll kiss your ring?" He leaned forward, using his size to tower over Anton. "It'll never happen. You haven't earned it."

Anton chuckled, but it had an impatient edge. "Man, you just never change. You're lucky I need a favor."

Niko sucked in the last gulp of coffee. He should have known. "What do you want?"

"Your unit needs a fifth member to stay operational. I'm sending a new recruit your way. Sophia Anuva. Keep an eye out for her, will you? She's got a promising career ahead of her."

Anyone sent by Anton already had a strike against them. "I'm not your babysitter, Anton. Don't send me recruits who can't handle the risks."

"Anuva's approval came from the top, and her father is a senior officer—"

Niko's shoulders tensed. "Does that make her bulletproof?"

Anton shifted. "I'm not sure I understand—"

"Is she able to take on Tavians twice her size?" His voice inched up. He hadn't been the leader of his unit for more than five minutes, and already Anton was trying to tell him what to do. "I don't care if her father's the Minister, and neither will the Tavians. If she isn't qualified to be in black ops, don't send her."

Anton smiled, but his eyes were electrified. "I'm your commander, and I say she's coming."

Niko met his glare. It wouldn't be good if his first act as unit leader was to deck his commander, but it would certainly make him feel better.

"I don't even know why you're mad. You should be thanking me. If it wasn't her coming to your unit, it would have been her father—a captain. You wouldn't have been in charge of black ops, Sophia would be going elsewhere…" Anton peered down the hall as he stepped closer. "And I wouldn't have been able to acquire another unit for my division. See? Everyone wins. I'll make you a deal. I'm grooming Sophia for higher things. Give her some opportunities, let her get some time in the assignment, and I'll promote her quickly."

Niko flexed his jaw. This was about politics and pairings—two things that had no business in black ops. "Do you think we just sit around and play with toy guns? I don't care what you want to do with your girlfriend, but do it somewhere else."

Anton's face reddened. "Your unit needs a recruit. This is who I'm sending. Keep quiet, or one of my first acts as division leader will be to reassign you." He strode away before Niko could respond.

Niko crushed his paper cup. Anton's pretentious smile had already returned when he greeted someone halfway down the corridor, but Niko was far from calm.

Unbelievable.

He cracked his neck. Anton wanted him to accept a subpar candidate, and he actually thought Niko would be happy about it? He descended the three flights of stairs to the underground offices. The white-florescent light of the barren hallway welcomed him. No sunlight down here. No Niotian marble or painted masterpieces. This was the engine of the ivory tower upstairs—critical to their survival but shoved out of sight.

And that's just the way he liked it.

He rounded the corner in the maze of hallways. Normally the top brass was more concerned with looking the other way than they were eager to delve into his business. Normally, that is, until Anton had showed up with his well-connected girlfriend. His lips tightened.

Layla sat with her feet up on the large beat-up table in the center of the black ops office, watching a giant screen she'd projected from her implant. Her face brightened, and she sprang forward when she saw him, her thick black ponytail bouncing around her shoulders. "Hey, *unit leader*. I got the message on my implant just a second ago."

Niko snickered. "Just be glad it's me. You wouldn't believe who they're promoting these days. Where is everyone?"

She scanned the sealed concrete walls with a subtle gleam to her dark eyes. "Let's see, Horacio went to get a status update on McCade, and Guthrie was with a new girl last night so…"

He raised his eyebrows. It wasn't an excuse, but he counted in his head. "Isn't that the third time this month he's been late because of a girl?"

Layla crinkled her nose. "Fourth, I think."

He shook his head. Guthrie had certainly gotten a lot of mileage out of the *only casual relationships clause* of the black ops job. He rounded the table to the unit leader's office—his office now. Opening the door, he peered inside. Everything, from the poster-sized photo of the beach to the messy stacks of maps and documents, was exactly as McCade had left it. It didn't feel right intruding like this. He'd have to visit him at the medical facility as soon as possible.

"Hey, boss," Layla said, following him. "We gotta talk about the new recruit."

Tension wound through his shoulders. "You heard about that too, huh?"

"Personnel Command sent her package down. She seems okay."

"I'm not so sure about that." Any friend of Anton's was not *okay*.

"She graduated with honors."

"The Tavians won't care about that." His voice got sharper. Why would Layla press this?

"She sounds better than some of the muscleheads they send us. I'm not sure the unit could handle another Guthrie."

"Guthrie can hit a target from 350 yards away on a windy day. I'd take ten more like him."

"All I'm saying is that we should give her a chance. Bring her in tomorrow, we'll see what she's got in the workout room. If she's not up to it, we'll turn her back to Personnel Command."

It might have been a great idea for a normal recruit, but Anton had made it clear he couldn't fire this one, even if she was a doe-eyed piece of dead weight who would probably get herself or someone else killed.

But if she quits…

He smirked.

"They want to know where she should report tomorrow," Layla said.

His smirk turned to a full grin. "Tell Personnel Command that I'll pick her up from her room in the barracks tomorrow."

CHAPTER 5

The blaring noise of a horn reverberated off every surface in Sophia's dark room, and she nearly launched herself out of bed. Emma screamed in the bed next to her. The silhouette of a large man stood in the doorway. "Good morning, sunshines! Which one of you is Sophia?"

Kalos. She pushed the warm blanket aside, scowling. "That would be me, sir."

"Welcome to your first day of training. Let's go." He stepped to the side of the door.

"Yes, sir. I…" Sophia glanced down at her pajamas. He couldn't mean like this—her gaze returned to his hulking shadow—could he?

"Five minutes." He stormed out and slammed the door behind him.

"What the…" Emma clutched her blankets to her chest. "Who is that?"

Sophia leaped out of bed. "He's my new commander."

"It's 4:15 in the morning!"

She nodded. It was only a couple of days ago that she'd first laid eyes on him, but it already seemed like something he would do. She threw on her uniform, wrestled her curls into a ponytail, and was out the door in three minutes.

Kalos stood outside, twirling an air-horn canister. "Let's go!" he yelled without any regard to the time or other sleeping L-1s on the floor. Instead of heading to the unit offices, he headed outside, where the streets were still shrouded in darkness. Her pace slowed for the slightest of moments, but somehow he caught it. "What's the problem, L-1?"

She squinted in the shadows. "I thought—"

"I didn't ask you to think right now," he replied without turning around. "We're going on a run."

She bored holes through the back of his head, but she could handle a run no matter what time of day—or night—it was. They reached the dirt path that the Academy students often used for physical training. If she had to run in the dark, at least she knew the trail.

"We're running three miles. Try to keep up."

She hid a smirk. Three miles was easy. "Yes, sir."

He took off at a steady pace, and she followed. They passed the three-mile marker somewhere around thirty minutes in, but he didn't stop for another two and a half hours. Her lungs burned, and her legs felt like jelly. They had run at least nine miles, but she'd made it.

He glanced at her more than once, looking her over, searching for something. She did her best to flop one foot in front of the other without showing how tired she was.

Back at headquarters, he led her through a stuffy maze of stark halls several floors below ground. The air seemed thicker, and the low ceiling and white brick walls felt like they were closing in on her. "Here we are. Home sweet home!"

The two men and one woman who had been chatting at a table fell silent. A large muscle-bound man with jet-black hair, which contrasted with his fair skin and blue eyes, grinned brightly at her. A second, leaner man with dark skin and his hair buzzed stared at Kalos. Rubbing his fist against his chin, he shook his head. And the woman with a beautifully intricate braid wrapped around her head stared at both of them like she was about to watch an explosion.

Sophia smiled, but Kalos kept moving. "Let's keep the workout going in that room." He pointed past an office to a room full of pads, weights, and a punching bag, which she would have normally welcomed—but not after running nine miles.

Hours and countless repetitions later, her muscles were beyond the point of sore. Stretched out and numb, she yearned to collapse into a heap on the ground.

Kalos circled. "You tired, L-1?"

"No, sir," she lied, barely able to make eye contact.

"Great. Let's do some bench presses." He loaded the bar with enough weight for a full-grown man and gestured for her to take her spot on the bench.

He can't keep this up forever. All I have to do is prove myself, and then this will end. Her body was so tired, she couldn't remember if she was really here to save Dad or prove him wrong about her capabilities. Either way, she couldn't quit. "How many repetitions?"

He shrugged. "I'll let you know."

I can't quit. I can't quit. I cannot quit. She trudged to the bench and scooted under the bar. Arms trembling, she lowered the bar to her chest.

"Let's see what you know about the current conflict. How did it start?"

Her whole chest was tensed to push the bar back up to its resting position, and he wanted to have a conversation? His gaze was heavy on her. "You mean the war?" *The one that ended five years ago?*

"No, I mean my ongoing feud with Guthrie about which of us can hit a target from farther away. Of course, I mean the war."

She held her breath as she tried to lower the bar again. She could retell the story with the best of them, so she started from the beginning. "We started as one society of scientists and engineers who called themselves the Enlightened. They discovered how to control and manipulate matter like the rest of the world manipulates electricity in the 1930's..."

Speaking of electricity, it felt like white-hot currents were shooting through her chest and arms. She pushed the bar up. "Octavius Renaud and the Tavians argued we should use the ability to defeat Hitler and establish ourselves as a ruling class over all of humanity. The Niotian faction stopped him, and we make sure they don't use the discoveries of the Enlightened for their own gain."

Her arms wavered and he grabbed it with one hand, placing it back on its rests. "And now?"

She panted as sweet relief spread through her arms. Had he asked another question?

He cleared his throat. "What about now?"

"Now that the war is over—"

He laughed so hard he doubled over. "Good one. Okay, get up and give me twenty pull ups."

Her gaze darted to him. He couldn't be serious. Despite the remnants of laughter in his expression, he watched her with raised eyebrows. She wasn't sure she could lift herself off the bench let alone complete a single pull up.

Kalos clapped. "Come on, L-1. It's almost dinner time, and I'm hungry."

Bile rose in her throat at the mere mention of food. She used momentum to roll herself onto her feet. Her arms barely moved when she tried to lift them. *This has to end, right?*

"Twenty pull ups," he yelled. "Go!"

She hopped up, swinging and kicking her way into a single pull up.

"What are the rules of engagement with the Tavians now?"

She tried to control her descent from the bar, but her arms gave out.

He stepped forward. "Rules of Engagement."

She panted. What were they again? "Um..." She knew them by heart, but her brain wasn't processing anything but pain at the moment. She'd talk forever if it meant she didn't have to do another pull up. "Neither side—the Niotians or the Tavians—is allowed to interfere in world affairs. We're not allowed to share our discoveries, and we're not allowed to use them for personal gain if it's at the expense of the rest of humankind. If we violate these terms or if we're caught operating outside our districts, a grievance is filed through official channels, a summit is called, and reparations will have to be made."

He roared with laughter once again. "That's just about the cutest storybook version I've ever heard. You should have gone into education."

She scowled. "What's that supposed to mean?"

His laughter stopped, and his eyes darkened. "It means that those answers may have earned you a gold star in school, but they're far from the truth. We are still at war, and while the manipulation of matter may have been the original cause, the only thing the Tavians care about now is expanding their empire. They won't stop until Nios is gone because Niotians are the only ones who can stop them from enslaving the rest of the world. They will not hesitate to kill you in the field, and if you think you'll have time to file a *grievance* or that a political summit will actually solve anything, you're already dead."

He took another step toward her, his sheer size blocking every thought. "You want to be part of this unit, you check those fantasies at the door. You come ready to fire your weapon, and you better not miss because you might not get another chance. If you can't do that, quit."

Quit. The word hit her like a punch, but it reminded her she couldn't—she wouldn't. She lifted her chin.

Someone cleared her throat from behind him. "Um, boss?"

He kept his gaze squarely on Sophia. "Not now, Layla."

"It's dinner time, and Guthrie might start eating the punching bag if we don't get him some food," she continued. "You coming?"

He took a step back, but his gaze didn't soften. "In a minute. Do you have any questions, L-1?"

Sophia cleared her throat, and broke eye contact. "No, sir."

A smile—that same cocky smile from before—spread across his face. "You don't like me, do you?"

Nope. Not at all. Why had she broken eye contact? He was playing games. "You're my commander, sir. What I think isn't—"

"But you don't." He was beaming now, but he'd never get an admission from her. "Good. I think we're finally beginning to understand each other."

The triumph in his expression made her feel like she could do another fifty pull ups.

"Go home and rest up, L-1," he said over his shoulder as he walked away. "We have another big day tomorrow."

She listened to her breath rush out her nose. He would not win. She'd get through this.

"Hey." The woman with the braid slipped into the workout room. "I'm Layla Ahmadi." She shrugged. "Didn't really get a chance to introduce myself back there."

"Sophia Anuva," she replied, trying to smile.

Layla pointed over her shoulder with her thumb. "We're about to grab something to eat. You wanna come?"

She'd rather gnaw her own hand off than eat a meal with Kalos. "No, thank you. I'm going to go... take a shower." Take a shower, seethe, and seethe some more. At least she wouldn't have trouble sleeping tonight.

"Okay. Can't blame you," Layla said, backing away. "Hopefully we can get to know each other soon."

"That would be nice." She stretched her arms, trying not to think about how tight they'd be tomorrow—when she'd probably have to do all this over again.

CHAPTER 6

The strong scent of antiseptic burned Niko's nose. He hated the medical facility, but visiting McCade would be the highlight of his day. Later there would be a meeting with Anton, and he'd have to deal with Sophia, but at least he could start the morning with a friend.

His muscles ached and stretched from overuse. It had been a week since he'd taken the lead role in the unit, and six days of trying to wash her out. Somehow, she was still hanging on, and now other duties were calling.

He knocked before opening the door. Blinding-white light shone off even whiter walls, white sheets, and white beeping machines. He couldn't spend more than fifteen minutes in a room like this. How was anyone supposed to recuperate here?

McCade was resting in the bed in the center of the room, his leg in a sling that hung from the ceiling, and his green eyes were fixed on him. "I was wondering when I'd see you." Yellow shadows of bruising covered the whole right side of his face, purple spilled up from the neckline of his gown, and the visible portions of his leg looked like a bloody jigsaw puzzle. "Truthfully, I thought it'd be sooner."

He inched forward to take the chair next to McCade's bed. "I meant to come. How are you feeling, sir?"

McCade shifted in his bed. "I'm not your boss anymore. Call me Tobin."

Tobin. That sounded too weird. He was *Commander McCade.* He'd completed hundreds of missions. His tracking skills were legendary, and he was the only person Niko couldn't pin. He was born for black ops, but he was leaving it all behind for a woman.

He shook his head, not understanding at all. He wasn't at Guthrie's level, but he'd had his share of casual relationships. None of them could ever compete with the job, his purpose, or the unit. "Is she really worth it?"

McCade looked to the door, a quiet smile on his lips. "Yep."

Short, definitive answer. Steady gaze, relaxed features. How could someone like McCade—someone he thought was like him—be so ready to walk away? Were they really that different? A pang of loneliness throbbed, but there wasn't any point dwelling on it. McCade had made his choice. "The Tavians definitely got a couple good shots in, didn't they?"

McCade jutted a finger at his leg, fighting a smile. "Hit. A singular hit. And, yeah, it was bad. But all this?" He pointed to his neck and face. "All this is from where you broke my collarbone getting me out of there. And how *did* you manage to jack my face so bad?"

He held his arms out. "What were you expecting? They were still firing! It wasn't like I could wrap you in a down comforter and give you the white-glove service."

McCade laughed. "Yeah, I guess." The laughter died, and silence took over. "Seriously, though. Thanks."

"Any time." He said, glancing away from the sincerity in McCade's face. "What are the doctors saying?"

McCade sighed. "Apparently, they're working on some really cool stuff right now, some bonding agents for bones, muscles, even skin. Some day they hope to repair all of this with same-day surgery, but that day isn't today. I got an infection, so they're not sure how long I'll be here." He shrugged as if it wasn't that big of a deal. "How's the unit?"

"Good, for the most part." He couldn't help a small shrug at the thought of Sophia. "They sent a new recruit. She's a new L-1."

McCade's gaze bored right through him, the gray in his blond hair shimmered as he tilted his head. "What's the matter? She can't keep up?"

He shook his head, wishing it were that simple.

McCade frowned. "She doesn't want to be there?"

"That's not it either." He drew in a breath. A week's worth of hellish training, and she had never once complained.

"Then what's the issue?"

His eyes darted to McCade's. "Anton Cipriani sent her. He's grooming her for a *higher position.*"

McCade laughed and leaned back on his pillow. "From what I know of Cipriani, he would do something like that, but she sounds promising."

"Promising?" He raised his voice. It didn't matter if she could run longer than Guthrie or bench press more than Layla. "Anton sent her to make her look good. I can't kick her out, but I'm making sure she won't serve in the unit."

McCade's gaze pierced him, and he knew what he would say without him ever saying a word: *who cares as long as she's qualified?* He did. He'd get her to quit. He just needed to find her weakness.

McCade held up his hands. "You're the boss now."

Boss. The word sank in. Apparently, that didn't mean doing your job well or keeping the unit safe; all he had done this week was grant political favors, answer to clueless commanders, and waste his time with a stubborn recruit.

He checked the clock on his implant and stood. His meeting with Anton was fast approaching; he should check in with the unit first. "I should get going."

McCade grabbed his wrist. "I know you don't understand why I'm leaving. All I can say is that I know the unit is in capable hands with you, and…" He paused, flashing a crooked smile. "I really hope that you will understand my reasons for yourself someday."

He smiled, but the words slid off him like rain off Niotian marble. He felt nothing—no yearning, not even curiosity—about a pairing. The job came first, last, and everywhere in between. "Take care of yourself, sir," he called over his shoulder as he left.

"Call me Tobin!" McCade yelled.

~

NIKO GRABBED a coffee and checked the clock again. Anton would be expecting him soon, but he had to check in with the unit beforehand. He rounded the corner to the office, and Sophia launched herself from her chair, hands folded in front of her, gaze sweeping the room in no particular pattern. The others were chatting next to her at the table but stopped to watch the show.

She pressed her hands together in front of her. "You didn't come and get me this morning, so I—I just came here…sir."

He raised an eyebrow. Maybe it was his meeting with Anton, but he found all her little habits particularly annoying today. Why wouldn't she just quit? "Is it my job to come and get you every morning, L-1?"

"No…" She followed him into his office. "It's just that…well, you've come to get me every morning for a run. I thought that's what—" She shifted back and forth on her feet, and if she wrung her hands any harder, they might bleed. "Sir, I'm worried that you and I have started off on the wrong foot. Taking this assignment means a lot to me—"

He couldn't help but laugh at that one. "Do yourself a favor and stop right there. I know all about you. You're Anton's girl."

She froze, her brown eyes sparking. Her arms stiffened at her sides, and she balled her hands into fists. "No, I'm not."

There it is.

He beamed. Her weakness was Anton. Why bother hiding their relationship? He stopped himself. It didn't matter.

"All right, *Not-Anton's-Girl*, I have a meeting, but I'll be back in a bit and we can go on a run." *And I'm going to talk about Anton the whole time.*

She remained planted in her spot as he passed her. "Don't call me that."

"If you've got such a thin skin, quit. I'm sure Anton can get you a new choice assignment."

"*Shut up!*" Her voice filled the room. Even with five people in the office, it was dead silent.

Got her. The recruit from the last week had been skittish, hesitant, and polite even when he'd pushed too far—everything that made her wrong for black ops. Shouting at her commander in a room full of people meant she was finally breaking. He smiled and turned to her, but the smile dropped from his face. Her eyes had nearly ignited, and she stood tall. Was this the same person?

"I will go on a run even though it's pouring rain outside right now. I will do whatever crazy workout you want me to do. I'll even do it at four in the morning. But I volunteered for this assignment *despite* what my father, or Anton, or anybody else wanted, and I'm not quitting."

His eyebrows shot upward. Beneath that fidgety exterior was some serious ferocity he'd missed.

She took a pointed step toward him, and he took a step back. "You want to call me 'L-1,' or 'recruit,' or anything along that line, that's fine, but I am not Anton's girl. I never have been, and I never will be."

He could only stare while she took shallow tense breaths. He'd always been able to read people, but that was unexpected. Layla, Horacio, and Guthrie were as still as mannequins.

He looked her over. No *sir*, no fidgeting, a glare that made him shudder—and he wasn't intimidated by anyone. This was an entirely different person than the recruit of the last week, but which Sophia would come out when it mattered? He checked the clock from his implant; Anton would be expecting him in five minutes.

Anton could wait.

"Let's go over some close-hand combat." He waved her to the workout room. He could have had Layla or even Horacio spar with her, but he needed to see for himself. It was one thing to be able to run miles on end and another to stand and fight. He held up the pads and pretended not to notice the other three drift to the doorway to watch. "Let's see what you got."

She sank into her stance, no more jittery movements or hesitation, just sheer determination. The first punch landed hard—much harder than Layla hit. She followed it with a high kick that nearly took his head off, and he had to stop himself from smiling.

"Not bad." He dropped the pads and stood across from her, fists raised in a defensive position, but she showed no fear. Moments later, she struck first with a sweeping low kick. He jumped out of the way but couldn't hide his smile this time. "You know your best chance against someone my size is to knock them down."

She shrugged, her eyes darting to every move he made. "The bigger they are, the harder they fall."

He laughed. Somewhere underneath all that protocol and politeness, there really was a fighter in her. He stepped back with his hands up and palms out. If she had been anyone else—anyone not associated with Anton—he might have recruited her himself.

She stayed in the defensive position while he circled. How had he not seen this before. More importantly, had Anton misjudged her, too? Maybe their relationship wasn't what it had seemed at first.

Regardless, it would be stupid for him to forget Anton's insistence about her. If he knew anything about Anton, it was that he always had a reason for the things he did. "All right. That's enough for today. I have a meeting."

She narrowed her eyes, still honing in on every movement, and he grinned. Maybe he wouldn't try so hard to make her quit after this.

Maybe.

CHAPTER 7

*N*iko smiled the whole way upstairs, but as he approached Anton's office, the amusement wore off. Meeting with Anton was a lot like gearing up for a mission. He had to be prepared.

Guards in clean, pressed uniforms bustled around the front office of Combat Command, smiling and sipping coffee. The desks along the back wall were neat and organized, some were even decorated with picture frames and flower vases. If any of them had ever left the district on a mission, he would have been surprised.

"You're late," Gideon snapped from his unusually large desk, which sat in front of the row of division leaders' doors.

Just what he needed, a glorified secretary who thought his three bars of rank were enough to boss everyone around. The large desk made Gideon seem even smaller than he was, and he cowered as Niko approached. "Pardon me, L-3?"

Gideon leaned back in his chair. "It's just that, well, Captain Cipriani has a very busy schedule."

He smiled tightly. "Let's not keep him waiting, then." He had no patience for this peon.

He strode around Gideon and shoved Anton's office door open.

"No!" Gideon flew from his chair.

Anton, who had been asleep, startled awake.

Niko turned to Gideon. "You're right. I didn't want to interrupt naptime." He grinned at Anton, who wiped some drool from his face. "Are you feeling rested now, or should I come back later?"

"Knock it off, Kalos. I wouldn't have been sleeping if you had been on time."

He shrugged. "You know how it is, duties of the job and all. I'm so busy I don't have time for naps."

Anton rolled his eyes. "And how have your duties been going?"

"Fine. Nothing to report." He knew he had to disclose the activities of his unit, but the less information he had to give Anton, the better.

Anton narrowed his eyes. "How's Sophia?"

He flexed his jaw. She'd been part of the unit for a week, but Anton had made it sound like she was the most important part. He opened his mouth to let him know how little she mattered compared to everything else going on, but he paused. Those livid eyes, that high kick... He'd misjudged her, and he wanted to know more. "What's your deal with her? Are you and she..."

Anton's lips twitched. "Are you worried about my love life, Kalos?"

"Hardly."

"I assure you I'm not hurting in that department, but Sophia's different. She's like me. She graduated with honors. She's the daughter of two war heroes. She'd make a great match."

"So there's nothing between you two." He leaned forward with his elbows on his thighs. Anton was the type to brag if he could—with details whenever possible. Maybe there really wasn't anything between them.

Anton flashed a brilliantly white smile. "I'll get what I want. Pairing with her would be a great career move, and let's be honest, I think we all want to get her behind closed doors." He paused, his eyes glazing for a moment.

Was it possible to pity her more than McCade? At least McCade seemed happy and hopeful for the future. He wanted to be paired for the right reasons. Niko shook his head. "You're a real Prince Charming."

The smile dropped from Anton's face. "I'm not asking the head of black ops for relationship advice. There's a reason why they sent you to a unit where you can't be paired."

"The same unit where you sent Sophia?" He beamed.

He shrugged. "Until I'm ready for her."

He pictured her fists balled at her sides and pinched his lips together to stop himself from laughing. Anton wouldn't be paired any time soon—regardless of when he was ready for her.

He was liking her more every minute.

Anton lowered his voice. "You shouldn't underestimate me, Kalos. You'll regret it." He leaned back and straightened the front of his uniform. "Now, tell me about the raid where McCade got injured."

This idiot sat up here napping and plotting his own pairing as part of his career plan, but somehow he was entitled to know about their missions? He drew in a breath. The sooner he could get this over with, the better.

"There had been some reports of strange gunfire out of one of the rebel camps in Latin America. The damage sounded a little like it had been from a pulse gun—no bullets or casings were ever found, the power of a rifle with the spray of a shotgun. Anyway, we went down to investigate and picked up on some Tavian implant signatures. We followed them to a hideout but were ambushed by two units—approximately sixteen Tavian guards. With only the five of us, they were able to outflank us pretty easily. McCade broke through the Tavian line on the west side and laid down some cover fire so the rest of us could escape, but as he was retreating, they shot him in the leg."

"Why didn't you just teleport out the moment they started firing at you?"

Things weren't going to go well if he kept asking stupid questions. "When you go dark, it takes a little while for everyone to reboot their implants. The teleportation flash would have given away our position, and not a single person in the unit would have teleported out until we all were ready. Even a couple of seconds between teleportations could have left someone vulnerable. We all stay. We all protect each other."

Anton shrugged. "So what were the Tavians doing?"

"Best guess?" He glanced at the ceiling. He'd wondered the same thing. "They may be selling weapons to the rebel groups down there to strengthen their foothold in the area."

Anton frowned. "Why would they do that?"

He sighed, letting off pressure. When had it become his job to teach Anton about military strategy? "Because they don't accept that the war is over. Because if the war were to start again and they had the support of several rebel groups, we would have our hands full. Because they're violent and power hungry. Take your pick."

Anton leaned back. After a moment, he nodded. "I want you to go back down there."

He flew from his chair. "What? Didn't you hear me? We barely made it back last time. They're not stupid. They'll have more security now."

"Come on, Niko!" Anton inclined his head. "Have a little faith in the black ops unit. Satellite pictures are one thing, but if we could seize some pulse guns, the commendations would write themselves."

He needed to punch something. Anton was asking his unit of five people to walk into a hornet's nest of twenty— maybe thirty—Tavians, not to make the world a safer place, but for the commendations. "That's a stupid idea. You can't send a precision team in to take on a full platoon."

"If the Tavians are selling arms to a rebel group, it's a major violation of the treaty. We need proof, and that's why we keep you around."

"I'm not endangering the unit that way. It's too risky."

Anton shrugged. "If it's really that bad, teleport out, and I'll make the case for one of the larger combat platoons, but that requires me to go to the Panel of Seers."

The Seers were genetically engineered to process every detail of a situation and determine the most effective solution, making them invaluable in military strategy sessions. Both sides used Seers during the war, but it was the Niotians who had started targeting and killing Tavian Seers first, and the results for the Tavians had been devastating.

But why would Anton get them involved now? They lived in their own private complex in the heart of the Guard's Headquarters, but he'd never seen them. "They haven't been active in military affairs in years."

Anton smirked. "Oh, they're still active. You're just so far below their notice, you wouldn't know about it."

He turned to leave. "Then I'm not sure why I'm here. Sounds like you better use that shiny commander's eagle you have and go request a platoon."

"That's the beauty of this little reorganization plan," Anton called after him. "If I have to consult them, they'll ultimately get the credit for any seizures, but I don't need to consult them to send the black ops unit."

He stood frozen in the middle of the office. Half of him wanted to leave, and the other half wanted to make Anton bleed.

"It's an order." Anton rose from his seat, his blue eyes locked on him. "A direct order. Fail to comply, and I'll have you hauled in before a disciplinary panel. I'll make the case that you should be relieved of your duties."

He flinched. "Are you threatening me?"

"Yes." Anton closed the remaining distance between them slowly, casually until they were standing toe-to-toe. "The rules are clear. I'm your commander, and I have the grounds to make the order. Between you and me, I don't think you'd last very long in front of a panel."

His pulse pounded in his ears. This wasn't a game anymore. This wasn't Anton stealing the limelight like he had at the Academy, or prancing around the dog and pony show of Command. This mission was life and death.

He exhaled, but it sounded more like a growl. At some point, only one of them would walk away from one of their duels, but for now his options were few. Comply with the order, or Anton would replace him with someone who would. He liked the unit's chances better with him than without.

Anton watched him with a shrewdness he wanted to smack off his face. "Have I made myself clear?"

If he stayed a moment longer, he was going to hurt him. He nodded and stormed out the door. In the outer office, Gideon scurried out of his way with wide eyes—probably wise. He shoved the door to the stairs open, and it swung backward, hitting the wall behind it with a thunderous boom.

Cornered.

Not by the Tavians, but by a vain commander obsessed with commendations. By the time he reached the office, his anger could have propelled him through the wall. Every mission was dangerous, but this? It was crazy, and he still had an L-1 to deal with. The rules were clear. The unit had to have five members on mission, but what would Sophia do? He'd rather risk being shorthanded than having her freeze up.

Layla and Horacio stared at him with wide eyes. Guthrie smiled, but Layla elbowed him, and the smile dropped from his face with a cough. How could he explain to them that they'd have to go back? They were amazing guards, but they might not survive a confrontation like this. He might not be able to keep them safe.

Sophia sat next to them at the table, hands in her lap, with a sidelong gaze. As if he might miss her sitting there. "You," he growled. "My office. Now."

She crept behind him with barely audible steps compared to the resounding thuds of his footfalls. He slammed the door behind her, not even sure what he was going to say.

She wasn't as tied in with Anton as he had thought, but her nervous fidgeting had returned. Her gaze swept the office corners—not what he wanted to see.

"We've got a big mission coming. If I bring you, I can't babysit a skittish L-1 with textbook answers." He pointed to the workout room. "I need the Sophia who wasn't afraid to strike first and take out my legs."

The fidgeting melted away as he spoke. She stood tall. "It's a good thing I'm good at swing kicks."

He stepped closer to her. She didn't flinch or fidget. Her eyes met his, strong and sure. "Can I trust you?"

"Yes." Her answer was immediate and though her gaze softened, she didn't look away.

For now, it was enough.

CHAPTER 8

Sophia stepped over the steel door jamb to the launch room with shaky legs. Essentially the Guard's private teleportation zone, it was located next to the armory for rapid deployment during the war. She'd always thought of it as a relic. The Academy even sent her there on a field trip once.

The cold steel walls and armored door couldn't have felt more real now. Kalos's gaze was fixed on her, and she busied her hands, checking all the straps on her tactical vest so he couldn't tell how much she was shaking. She'd never been out of Nios before, and she had certainly never been in combat. Up until a week ago, she hadn't imagined herself in either situation.

Her fingers curled around the grip of her white pulse gun, getting used to the feel of reaching for it fast. The white weapons used air instead of bullets, so there was no need to reload, but that wouldn't do her any good if she fumbled it on the draw.

Guthrie secured one pulse gun pistol in his thigh holster, another in a hidden ankle holster, and slung a pulse rifle over his shoulder.

If he has to use all of those...

His eyes twinkled, and he flashed a grin when he noticed her watching. "What can I say? I like my toys."

"They're not toys, Guthrie." Kalos strapped his own pistol to his thigh holster.

"You ready to give us the final mission briefing on this little walk in the park we're about to take?" Horacio asked wryly.

"Huh?" Kalos's eyes widened, and he looked as close to surprised as she had ever seen. "Oh. Right. Okay. As you know, the rebel camp is approximately ten miles southwest of Santa Rita. We'll be teleporting into the municipal airport not too far from there. You should already have the coordinates to teleport there directly, and then we'll travel by car after that to avoid detection. Layla has secured a small flat above a bodega on the outskirts of town."

He clipped a twelve-inch hunting knife to his belt. "The objective is to seize one of the shipments they are selling to the rebels. The first twenty-four hours will be strictly surveillance, and we will be on an absolute implant blackout, no pinging, no thermal cams..." He looked pointedly at Guthrie. "No messaging girlfriends."

"That only happened once," Guthrie said as Layla and Horacio chuckled.

"All weapons and anything that may reveal who we are should be kept hidden at all times. If something doesn't smell right, we can expect the full weight of a Tavian platoon blowing down our door."

He stopped messing with his gear and glanced around the room with a grave expression. "You all know the stakes. We've already confirmed Tavian activity in the area, and we can expect stiff resistance. Mistakes will get someone killed, which brings me to the last rule. Teleportation isn't restricted to zones out there, but the Tavians will be able to trace the teleportation signature. No teleporting close to the operation unless we've been discovered, and nobody teleports out until I give the order."

"Yes, sir," Horacio murmured.

"Okay, put on the coats Layla has provided back there."

Sophia scrambled to find hers. There was no way the long, beige trench coat looked natural, but she wasn't about to speak up as she eyed the bulges from her vest and thigh holster.

"They don't have to look totally normal," Kalos said, his gaze on her. Couldn't he miss her reactions at least once? "They just have to conceal your weapons."

"Yes, sir," she mumbled, straightening it over and over to get it to fall more naturally.

"Prepare to teleport," Kalos announced.

Sophia's heart sped as her fingers fumbled with the tie. She pulled up the coordinates he'd sent to her.

"Three, two, one."

Static vined over her, and she shut her eyes as flashes of blue lit the steel room. When she opened them again, a massive tiled hall sprawled out before her—not the marble tiles of Nios but scuffed and dirty linoleum. People milled in every direction laden with bags, and the smell of cigarette smoke and a weird fuel she didn't recognize burned in her sinuses.

Horacio quickly scanned the area, his sharp gaze darting in a methodical pattern. "Clear."

A bell dinged over the intercom followed by someone speaking in a language she didn't understand. She scanned through the menu on her implant to find the translator, but Niko cleared his throat.

"All right, everyone, shut down your implants and let's head out."

Right. They were going dark... in the strangest place she'd ever been. With a tight breath, she turned it off.

"What's the matter?" Layla whispered as she fell in alongside her. "You never been to an airport before?"

"Um, no," she said, shuffling around a large group of people. "Is this normal for missions?"

"It is when we go dark. The Tavians are less likely to investigate teleportation traces this far from their operations, and both sides use airports to teleport in for leisure travel because they offer everything you'd need."

"You certainly know a lot about this," Sophia replied.

"My family was from Jordan. They didn't want us to lose our heritage, so we'd travel there incognito and visit family—they all thought my dad was a professor at a university." Layla shrugged. "It's not so bad once you get used to it."

Dad had never taken her out of Nios. Maybe he'd had too many bad memories out here, but right now, she was really wishing they'd travelled at least once. She slowed her pace as they approached a moving, metal staircase. Kalos hopped right on even though the deep tracks of each step looked like teeth.

"I know it looks bad, but just step on the closest step then bring your other foot to it," Horacio murmured. "Like this, see?" He stepped on as if the stair wasn't moving.

If I can't handle this, Kalos will never let me forget it.

She watched for the next step to emerge from the metal grate below and stepped on.

"Nothing to it." Horacio beamed—a real smile that made some of the jitters go away... some.

They crossed the threshold of the large sliding doors that led outside. They had sliding doors in Nios. At least there was something out here that seemed familiar.

The warmth hit her immediately, and she arched her back against the heat building in her coat. A horn blared, nearly sending her flailing into the air.

Cars.

She'd seen pictures of them. Some were quite pretty. Not these, though. At least fifty of them had lined up—loud, smelly, and dirty, some missing parts, some dented, and still others producing ridiculous amounts of thick gray exhaust.

"Our car's over there," Layla said, pointing, and they all followed to a small sedan.

Sophia slid in the back with Guthrie and Horacio, grateful Kalos was riding in the front seat. Maybe he wouldn't notice the horror that was surely written all over her face. She pressed herself into the back of the seat as Layla turned on the car and zipped into traffic.

"It'll go fast," Guthrie whispered. "Layla's a good driver."

It wasn't long before the roads turned to dirt, and she felt every single bump in her stomach. She just needed to make it to the flat. Guthrie had said they'd be there soon. She could handle this.

Swallowing hard she focused on the trees outside. Most things here made her feel like she was on an alien planet, but the plants hadn't changed much. The familiarity was a comfort.

It was midday when they finally reached the flat. Few people took notice of them as they sneaked inside to the small, dark room with one window and little else.

Better than the car.

Rain tapped on the roof. The wood planks below her feet warped and creaked, sounding like they would break altogether as Kalos swept the room.

She moved out of his way, bumping into the bureau behind her, which was coated in a thick layer of dust. The air was thick, humid, and heavy with the smell of onions.

In a little over an hour, they had set up the room as Kalos directed. The back corner had two spots for sleeping. Clothes were sorted into piles for each person. The backup weapons cache was along the back wall.

From now on, half the unit would always be awake. Nothing was by the window, and Kalos had made it clear that only the person on watch should be close to it.

He checked the gun holstered to his thigh. "Alright. I'm going for a preliminary patrol of the area to make sure we're clear. Guthrie, I want you with me to scout potential sniper nests. We should be back in an hour. Layla, you're in charge here."

Her chest lightened as he threw his coat back on and left. She sank to the floor, leaning on the wall. Silence set in as Horacio took the first watch by the window.

Layla sat next to her, a warm smile stretched across her face. "How are you feeling?"

Sophia stared at her hands, trying to find the words. An airport. Cars. Aging wood buildings and washed-out dirt roads. Where could she even begin?

"It's okay to be nervous. It happens to everyone. Horacio almost blew up the whole unit on his first mission."

He scoffed. "How was I supposed to know that warehouse was full of ammunition?"

"Anyway," Layla said with laughter in her voice. "My point is, it's normal."

"Thanks," Sophia whispered. She stretched her legs. The waiting was already driving her crazy.

"You got a casual at home?" Layla asked.

Sophia stared blankly.

"You know, a casual relationship?"

"That's all we're allowed to have," Horacio added, still scanning outside.

"Oh, no. I'd been dating someone before graduation, but things got busy." It was the first time she'd thought of Derick in a while. He'd been nice enough, but the chemistry hadn't been there. Too timid, maybe. She needed someone with passion, someone who put others before himself. Someone who would stand up and fight for what he wanted. Her cheeks reddened, and she hoped Layla couldn't see it in the remaining daylight. She was thinking of a fairy tale prince again.

"Yeah, I know how that is," Layla replied. "Come to think of it, 'casual' is a funny word for it. Horacio's been dating Genevieve forever. Then there was Captain McCade and Olivia."

"Genevieve is fine with not being paired. She knows how my job is."

"She's lying," Layla replied flatly, which earned her a scowl from Horacio. "I couldn't care for someone like you care about her and call it casual. We like to think of ourselves as so advanced, but there's still something about being paired, agreeing to raise kids together."

Horacio rolled his eyes. "You should know that Layla wants to get married like the rest of the world. She wants the whole thing—love, the wedding, babies..." He frowned, and his gaze shot outside. "Did you hear that?"

"Hear what?" Layla hopped up and drew her weapon. Sophia scrambled to follow. Except for the pattering of rain outside all was quiet. "You think Kalos is back already?"

Horacio held a finger to his mouth, his eyes bouncing around. "It's like a popping or crackle." He froze, a frown slowly appearing. Sophia grasped her pulse gun tighter.

His eyes bulged. "*Get dow—*"

Sophia was thrown backward into the wall, bluish-white light exploding around her with a thunderous crash. She clambered to the bureau to stand, shaking her head to get rid of the ringing in her ears. Horacio lay in the center of the room, glass from the window all around him. He gasped for air, and his hands were covered in blood.

The Tavians.

Her gun. Where was her gun?

She spun to the place where she had landed and dove for the white weapon as soon as she saw it. Gripping it tightly, she leaped to a stand and nearly hit something in the process. Her eyes trailed up the black pants and shirt to pale skin and cold black eyes.

A Tavian.

He leveled his weapon at her head with lightning speed while her mind still reeled. The Tavians were here. They'd hurt Horacio. One was about to kill her.

The Tavian jolted forward, and his arm went limp.

"Sophia, move!" Layla screamed as the Tavian teetered and then fell. It was like waking up from a dream. Her training took over. Two more Tavians appeared, and she fired her weapon at the teleportation flash closest to her before the Tavian's body even materialized. Direct hit. The Tavian, this time a woman with a long white ponytail, dropped to the floor and didn't stir.

"Cover me!" Sophia dove at Horacio in the center of the room. His whole shirt was soaked in blood. His hands shook. Not good. She pulled him toward Layla, trying to lug him on to her shoulders. "He's hurt! We need to take him to medical."

Layla nodded. "We're too exposed here. Take him into the hall to reboot your implant. I'll give you as much cover as I can."

Sophia trudged past her with Horacio's shaking body in tow. Pulse gunfire exploded in the wood paneling next to her, blowing shards into her face and eyes. Horacio tumbled off her shoulder with a groan. She couldn't see a thing, but the thick scent of wood burning wasn't a good sign.

She kicked the door open. The voices of frightened people echoed down the long hall. Smoke pooled above her head, and blazing heat stung her scalp. Her bleary gaze slid upward. Smoke wasn't pooling. It was streaming in from above. The fire was in the roof. She couldn't reboot here. The ceiling could collapse in seconds.

"Layla, the ceiling's going to collapse!" she shouted. "Let's go!" Holstering her weapon, she pulled Horacio down the hall with all her strength toward the stairs.

By the time she'd made it to the landing, she was choking on thick black smoke. She crouched to get the cleanest air possible and peeked back to the open door. It was barely visible, and Layla still hadn't emerged, but her orders had been clear: get Horacio to safety.

She allowed herself one last breath and tried to lift him to get him down the stairs. She clung to the sounds of pulse gunfire—as long as they were firing it meant that there was a battle and Layla was still holding her own.

Whether it was from the smoke, or the fact that Horacio was almost entirely limp now, she wobbled on the first step to keep her balance. Each step took three times as long as it should. Once she was halfway down the stairs, a figure appeared at the top, materializing from the smoke.

"Well, well, what do we have here." A tall Tavian, his white hair cropped short, bounced down the first couple steps, and Sophia reached for her weapon. The Tavian's weapon was trained on her in an instant. "Don't be stupid."

A set of footsteps thudded from the bottom of the stairs, and Sophia spun. Two more Tavians with weapons drawn. Her heart leaped into her throat.

"*Now!*" Kalos roared, invisible in the smoke.

Sophia dropped and covered Horacio as more pulse gunfire rang out. Two thunks from below were followed by clumsy falls.

Something heavy thudded on the stairs above her—someone, and there was no attempt to break the fall. A body collided with her as it rolled down the stairs, sending her head into the wall, but she held Horacio secure underneath her.

Silence.

Niko stormed out of the smoke from the hallway. "Sophia!"

Guthrie stepped over the three dead Tavians at the bottom of the stairs and raced up to meet them.

"Where's Layla?" Kalos asked.

"She was upstairs! There was an explosion, and Horacio got hurt. She ordered me to get him out."

"I just came from there." Kalos looked gravely at Guthrie, who nodded and ran back down the stairs. A joist above them creaked and a crash rumbled under her feet.

"Teleport out and get Horacio to medical." Kalos rose and hopped down the stairs after Guthrie. "Now!"

Sophia nodded, bringing her implant back to life. Moments later she appeared on the Guard's wing of Nios's medical facility, lugging Horacio behind her, his dark skin seemed drained to an eerie gray.

"Help!"

CHAPTER 9

*N*iko forced a breath from his tight chest.

"Look up for me?" The young doctor studied her stitch work along his eyebrow.

Down the hall, practically the entire medical staff tried to keep Horacio alive. And Layla had been captured. Fellow guards, friends.

There wasn't anyone he trusted more than Horacio during operations. His situational awareness was off the charts. He'd always known where to be and where the threat was coming from. And whether Niko wanted to admit it or not, Horacio was always the one to calm him down after something like this. The unit couldn't lose him.

Layla had advanced countless missions. There was no way she'd done something to give them away. She was one of the smartest people he knew. If she was still alive, he'd find her.

One hour, twenty-five minutes...

That was all it had taken. It didn't matter how good the Tavians were, no one could have that kind of power and speed in an ambush unless they were set up in advance. They had to have had people in position above and below. They'd known which flat the unit had rented and the escape routes. It could only mean one thing. The unit had been betrayed.

Even so, an attack like that used considerable resources. How could he have missed it? He'd searched the perimeter. He would have never left if he'd suspected anything, but there had been nothing—not an implant signature, not a civilian taking too much interest, nothing.

But there had to have been *something.* The enemy had been right there, and he'd left the unit vulnerable. His fingers curled into his palms.

"Please don't tense," the doctor said.

He shut his eyes, forcing himself to relax. The sooner this was done, the better. He would give his life for his unit, but he couldn't protect them and pay attention to all the extraneous factors. He'd been distracted before with Anton's whims, but that would change.

"Okay. That should do it. Anything else?"

There'd be a lot more when he got his hands on whoever had done this to the unit, but he forced a smile and stood up. "Nope."

As he reached the door, a nurse rushed by with four more packs of blood and hurried into Horacio's room. A breath rumbled in his chest. He'd make this right.

The after-action reports could tally up the mission losses in black and white, and Leadership could study it and come up with pragmatic and logical conclusions, but Niko knew the truth. The extraneous factors he'd been dealing with might cost Horacio his life. They'd led to Layla's capture. There was no block of text that could quantify that on a report.

He looked down the hall in one direction, then the other. Sophia sat in one of the curved alcoves along the hall between two tall, leafy plants, a doctor shining a flashlight in her eyes. Even covered with soot and grime, the beginning of a big, red bruise was forming above her eyebrow. Tiny cuts in a spatter pattern spread across her cheek, and Horacio's dried blood still coated her arms, tactical vest, and uniform shirt.

He'd seen that vacant look in her dark eyes before. What had he been thinking bringing her on this mission? Had Layla been forced to cover for her? Would Horacio have been able to avoid injury? Would the outcome have been any different if they hadn't had to worry about her? It wasn't like either of them could tell him, and he definitely couldn't rely on the reports.

Layla's capture alone would mean that the council would get involved now. They'd want to spend months poring over the reports from the security of their peaceful offices. They'd find a way to apply it to their agendas, and nothing meaningful would ever come of it.

Meanwhile, Horacio might die, and Layla could be tortured, starved, or worse. He needed *real* answers *now.* There had to be clues, and he'd find them. Niotian, Tavian, or civilian, it didn't matter. He was going to kill the person who had betrayed the unit. He stalked across the hall. Sophia was as good a place to start as any.

"Tell me what happened," he demanded in a low growl.

Her mouth dropped open, revealing a pretty nasty split in her lip. "I already—"

The doctor examining her held up a hand. "There will be plenty of time for debriefing later—"

"You can tell that to my *captured guard*," Niko said, keeping his focus on Sophia. "And as long as we're on the subject of debriefing, this is classified. You can go now."

The doctor stared at him with wide eyes. "I'm in the middle of an exam—"

"*I said you can go!*" Niko roared, and the doctor nearly fell over trying to clamber away.

"I—we…" She squeaked.

"Spit it out!" Lives were on the line. He couldn't deal with her jitters right now.

"We followed your orders. Horacio took the first watch," she said, her shoulders tensing upward. The shaking in her hands had spread over her whole body. "Layla and I sat against the back wall, away from the window. We barely made a sound."

"Well, something happened, didn't it?" he yelled, leaning over her.

"Kalos!"

It took a second, but he recognized the voice behind the harsh bark. McCade. He spun. McCade sat in a wheelchair with his leg propped out in front of him. The orderly who had been pushing him searched the ceiling.

"What are you doing?" McCade asked through a tight jaw.

"Just chatting with one of my guards." This wasn't his concern anymore. He'd left the unit.

McCade's green eyes burned right through him as he grabbed the doorknob to a hospital room and flung it open. "A word."

He drew in a deep breath. There wasn't time for this.

"Now." McCade said, and Niko strode into the empty room. The orderly pushed McCade in and quickly slipped back into the hall, shutting the door behind him.

He paced. "Say what you need to say. I've got a lot of stuff to do."

"I saw that."

Niko pointed out the window. "They were ready for us! I'm going to figure out how."

McCade raised his eyebrows. "And you think an L-1 with no combat experience is the best place to start?"

"She's the only lead I have, isn't she?"

McCade's gaze hardened. "Lead? She's part of the unit!"

Niko waved a hand. "Not really. Anton forced me to take her. She wasn't ready."

"Not—" McCade shook his head. "You're lucky I'm in this wheelchair. You don't deserve to lead this unit."

"You think you have the right to talk to me about leadership?"

"You want to blame me for this?" McCade jabbed a finger into his chest. "I should have stayed because you didn't want to step up and lead yourself?"

"I did everything I could. I'd give my life for the unit!"

"No. Not the whole unit," McCade replied so casually, it nearly sent him through the roof. "You only care about the ones who've earned your seal of approval."

"She's a pet project! I can't run missions and be a babysitter. She doesn't belong with us."

"Did she follow orders? Did she perform her duties to the best of her abilities?" McCade's voice thundered. "The most you can ask is that guards stick to their training and follow orders. I talked to Guthrie. She did all of that, and now you, *her commander*, have turned your back on her. You think guards are cut from some magical warrior cloth. You're wrong. She engaged the enemy. She got an injured guard to safety. She fits, Kalos. Maybe more than you do."

It was more complicated than that, and McCade knew it.

McCade pounded on the door, and the orderly opened it to take him away. As he was turned for the door he said over his shoulder, "What happened today was a tragedy, and it's not over. The unit needs you—all of them."

He skulked behind McCade into the hall. Sophia didn't need him. She had her textbooks, and Anton, and a fancy certificate that said she'd graduated with honors. He tried to avoid her as he emerged from the room, but his gaze quickly settled on her anyway. Scanning the floor in front of her, she sucked in her quivering lip and brushed a curl away from her face with bloody, sooty hands. He winced.

She had followed orders. She had gotten Horacio to safety, and Niko was grateful for that. He glanced at her again at the exact moment her eyes, red and brimming with tears, wandered to him. She rose from her chair and stalked away, almost running into a doctor on her way down the hall.

Niko drew in a deep breath, watching her as she left. Layla was gone. Horacio was still in surgery. Guthrie was already cataloging evidence. He'd do anything for any of them.

Sophia stared out a window at the end of the hall, clutching her arms in front of her. McCade had been right. Even if this job was only a bullet on her resume, she'd performed admirably today.

And he'd turned his back on her.

He trudged down the hall, approaching slowly. She wiped her tears, but it only smeared the grime across her cheeks.

"Go ahead," she said, her voice twisted. "Tell me I blew it, or that this is all my fault, or whatever it is you want to say."

As angry as he was, he couldn't say any of that. It wasn't true. McCade was right. She deserved better from him. "Are you okay?"

Her cold gaze darted to him—guarded, scornful. "Does it matter?"

He shifted from one foot to the other. Of course it mattered.

"I may have been the last person to see Layla alive." She covered her mouth and clamped her eyes shut as she heaved a sob. "I thought I was doing the right thing. She ordered me to get Horacio to safety. I thought she would be right behind me. I never meant to leave her alone."

She blamed herself? He reached out and placed a hand on her shoulder. "This is not your fault. You followed orders. You did exactly what you were supposed to do. Horacio might live because of you."

She shook her head. "Layla was captured because of me."

"No." He turned her to face him. "Listen to me. I'll find her. I'll bring her back."

She stopped crying and looked him square in the eye, and he shuddered at the intensity. He wouldn't have any reservations about fighting with her again.

"You mean *we.*"

No. He hadn't meant *we.* Even if he wanted her to stay with the unit, she'd be leaving as soon as Anton or her dad got news of all this. But staring at her now, he wouldn't dare contradict her. "Layla will come home."

She would. He'd start his search for answers tonight, and he'd go straight to the top.

~

THE MOONLIGHT SHONE off the swirls in the Niotian marble floor. The gossamer drapes floated silently on the breeze. Fireflies blinked from outside the floor-to-ceiling windows of the corner suite. Niko waited in the shadows.

This wasn't his brightest idea. Security had already come through twice. He'd had to go dark with his implant to avoid detection. But he needed information, and the Seers might be able to provide it.

Finally, the light padding of bare footsteps neared. A tall, black man entered in white robes, his smooth movements belying his age. He reached the center of the room before he froze. Minuscule head movements one way, then the other. "Please. Come out and have a seat."

Niko frowned. He'd searched the room beforehand, careful not to move anything. What was he picking up on?

"What's your name?" The Seer asked, no alarm in his voice.

Niko didn't answer. He'd hoped to sneak up on him. Fear was a powerful motivator, but this man seemed ready to have a friendly chat. What had given him away?

"I know you're here. This would be a lot easier if we could speak face to face," The Seer said before walking to a table in the center of the room with lithe steps. "I'm Royce Mensah, but please just call me Royce."

If he'd wanted to alert his security, he would have done it already. Niko stepped into the light.

Royce's gaze flickered over him, and the corners of his mouth curved upward, making his ears stick out all the more from his bald head. "You're not the typical guards who visit me."

"I'm probably nothing like the guards that typically visit you," he warned. He could easily kill him in seconds.

Royce shrugged his slim shoulders and pointed to the seat across from him. "What's this about?"

"A mission. Something went wrong. The Tavians knew we were coming."

"You think you've been betrayed."

Think? Niko bit down. "There isn't another explanation."

Royce sighed. "I'm afraid no one's consulted the Seers' Panel for a mission fitting that description in quite a while."

"I still need you to try. One of my guards was captured."

Royce's wrinkly face went slack. His gaze darted back and forth across the floor. "Captured? A direct confrontation without Panel approval? You're black ops."

Niko nodded once.

Royce pursed his lips. "I should have known. I'm afraid you and I are victims of the same system."

No. They weren't the victims. Horacio, Layla, and even Sophia were the victims. Niko's muscles started to tighten. "I need answers."

"Look around you. The very systems set up to ensure safety and peace now threaten us."

"I'm not here for an abstract conversation about society," Niko growled. "I'm here to get the proof I need to get my guard back."

"That's my point!" Royce let out a short laugh. "I'm locked in here for safety. You were sent out because it was probably too arduous to obtain approval for a more coordinated mission."

"This isn't some political debate," Niko snarled. "My guards were affected. People's lives are at stake." What had he expected by coming here? It had been a waste of time. "If you can't help me—"

"I didn't say that," Royce replied, his sharp gaze skewering Niko. The light-hearted humor disappeared from his face. "I think you and I may be of help to each other."

"How's that?"

"I haven't had a vision in years. Locked in here..." He paused, glancing around the suite. "The information the Panel receives is limited, but there's a shadow in my mind—something moving just beyond the perimeters of my abilities, using our own measures against us. It's created this disturbance, hiding everything. We're blind, and I can't help but suspect that someone wants it that way."

Niko grunted. "I've never been one for conspiracy theories."

"I propose an alliance." Royce slapped his knee with the tips of his fingers. "A back channel, if you will. You came to me, so you must know I need information to work. You give me all the information you have—after-action reports, data points, anything—and I'll help you save your unit."

"How will you do that?"

"A capture is messy business—worse than a casualty for the council. The Tavians will call for a highly public summit where they will hold the main bargaining chip. Nios will have no choice but to admit to the wrongdoing and make reparations. The council will be eager to end the hostility at as little of a cost to them as possible."

Niko's lips tightened. "I attended the Academy. I know how a summit works."

"Then you know that the council will be looking for a scapegoat, someone to flog in the public square to show we take this matter seriously and are handling it."

Niko propelled himself from his chair and towered over Royce. "I did nothing wrong."

Royce stared up at him, the deep lines on his face curving into a faint sympathetic smile. "Do you think that will matter?"

Niko paced away, his whole body bracing for a fight. He wouldn't go down for following Anton's order.

"The Guard will call a hearing soon to prepare for the summit. By law, the lead Seer must attend those hearings. I'll protect you in whatever way I can, but you have to give me as much information as possible. Do we have a deal?"

Niko stretched his neck. He'd come here for answers but had received few. Still, this was probably the best outcome he'd get. "Deal."

CHAPTER 10

Sophia smoothed the front of her starched button-down shirt and craned her neck to search the crowded room. The circular room's coffered dome seemed to amplify every noise.

Lighthearted greetings, friendly smiles from across the room, it all seemed casual... but she knew better. An intricate series of events was unfolding. Greetings were made in order of status. Decisions were being made in hushed tones around the edges of the room. Alliances were formed. Lines were drawn.

This was not a time for Kalos to be late.

She bit her lip and glanced at the door as Guthrie tapped a beat on his lap.

"He should be here by now," she whispered to him.

"He'll be here," Guthrie said calmly. He pulled at his collar. "I hate wearing these uniforms. No one would ever fight in these things. Why are they guard uniforms at all?"

A clerk walked in and took her place beside the podium. She smirked as her gaze slithered over Guthrie.

Sophia rolled her eyes. "How many casuals do you have?"

Guthrie beamed at the clerk and waved. "We're black ops. I might as well enjoy it, right?"

Sophia scowled at him and continued searching for Niko. Boisterous laughing drew her attention and off to the side, Anton stood with another captain—completely at ease. Dad was a captain. He'd never look that way if he'd given the order that led to all this. Then again, Anton wasn't nearly the man Dad was.

The armrest next to her jerked and Niko slipped into the chair. The muscles along his arms rippled as he grasped the armrests. He looked angry, defensive. Guilty. She winced.

"It'll be fine," she whispered. "Just tell them the truth. We have nothing to hide."

His brown eyes locked on hers, cold, hard.

"Let's call this meeting to order," the clerk announced as the remaining captains took their place in the front of the room. Dad walked in from a side door and sat in the middle of the panel. He glanced at her with a brief warm smile as the room quieted. Regardless of how things seemed, he'd be fair. He'd listen to Niko.

An elderly man in white robes took a seat at the end of the panel, a blissful smile stretched across his face. Was he in the wrong room? No way was he a guard.

Dad cleared his throat and spoke into his microphone. "As Captain of Personnel Command, it is normally my duty to preside over these hearings, however I must recuse myself, given my relation to one of the guards directly involved in the incident."

No. She sat up straight, her fingernails biting into her palms.

"Captain Ichiro, Captain of Drone Combat Command, will preside instead," he finished and sat back in his chair.

The captain next to him leaned forward. Silvering hair, broad shoulders— the same captain who had just been joking around with Anton moments ago.

"Let's get started, shall we?" he asked. "Lieutenant Kalos, please approach the microphone."

A low growl escaped Kalos before he rose and walked to the center of the room. Sophia pressed her fists into the rough wool fabric of her charcoal-gray uniform skirt.

"Why don't you start by telling us the mission objective?" Ichiro asked.

"The objective was to collect evidence of Tavian involvement with a rebel civilian group in Latin America. Tavian implant signatures and evidence of pulse gunfire had been found in the area on a previous mission."

Ichiro shuffled his papers. "I see. That was the mission where your former commander was injured, correct?"

Niko's shoulders flexed, pulling at the seams of his uniform jacket. "Yes."

"And yet you thought another mission was appropriate?"

The muscles along his jawline rippled. Sophia cringed. Just like the opening conversations, there were rules when testifying. Body language was just as important as what was actually said.

"I was against this mission due to the risks," Niko spat. "I was following orders."

The panel exchanged glances.

"An order?" Ichiro asked. "From whom?"

"Captain Cipriani." He leveled a harsh glare in Anton's direction.

"Okay. That will be all," Ichiro said, shuffling more papers.

Sophia frowned. That was it? They hadn't talked about what happened or how they'd been ambushed yet. That couldn't be it.

"Captain Cipriani?" Ichiro scanned the room. "Please approach the microphone."

Niko returned to his seat beside her, every muscle coiled.

"Good afternoon," Anton greeted the panel.

"Good afternoon, Captain Cipriani. It's Lieutenant Kalos's assertion that you ordered him to coordinate this mission. Is that correct?"

Anton never even twitched. "Absolutely not."

Sophia's mouth hung open.

"Kalos requested, and I authorized, an evidence-gathering mission after he'd greatly misrepresented the situation on the ground. I was not the commander during the previous mission and had no reason to believe Kalos would go to these lengths for approval," he continued.

He may have been the type to smile and work the crowd in the wake of a tragedy, but to lie? She'd been there when Niko had returned from his meeting with Anton. She'd seen the dread in his eyes as he'd planned the mission. There wasn't an ounce of her that believed Anton.

Niko launched himself from his chair. "You're a liar!"

Sophia grabbed his arm to pull him back down, but she could have hung from him and it wouldn't have mattered. He stared down Anton without moving. How could she quietly remind him that the truth of the mission wouldn't matter if he lost it now?

And the truth *did* matter. The whole Guard needed to know what Anton had ordered them to do. They'd been outnumbered and cornered, but Niko had fought his way in to save her and Horacio. She didn't have to go out on mission with Anton to know he would have abandoned her to the same fate as Layla.

"The blood of this mission is on your hands!" Kalos yelled, jutting a finger at Anton who stood with feigned wide-eyed surprise.

Sophia clamped her eyes shut. Niko didn't see what was happening. They'd never ask about the mission because this wasn't about the mission. This was about burying Niko, and he was playing into their hands.

"Order!" Ichiro called. "You had your turn to speak, Lieutenant. Captain Cipriani now has the floor. Please continue, Captain."

Anton's eyebrows pulled together for an award-winning performance in this sickening charade. "Given the initial after-action reports, Lieutenant Kalos either greatly underestimated or intentionally downplayed the Tavian presence in the area."

"That's not true!" Niko shouted.

"This was clearly a mission for a larger combat platoon," Anton said over Niko. "But I suspect he was eager to prove himself in his new role as unit leader."

"I wanted to prove *myself?*" Niko's voice thundered around the dome.

Not good. So not good. She jerked at his arm, trying to get his attention. He had to sit and wait this out, or he'd never get another chance to tell his side of the story.

"Lieutenant Kalos, if you cannot respect these proceedings, you will be escorted out," Ichiro warned.

Niko lowered himself to his chair but was so stiff he barely touched the seat.

"Captain Cipriani, you are Lieutenant Kalos's commander, correct?"

"That's correct, sir."

"What is your recommendation for disciplinary action?"

Disciplinary action? They couldn't ask that of a witness, could they?

Her father blinked several times and pinched the bridge of his nose. He knew what they were doing—everyone did—but he wasn't stopping it. Her pulse pounded in her ears.

Anton sighed. "I've known Niko a long time."

Niko's arm jerked, and Sophia clamped both hands around it to hold him in place.

Not now...

"It pains me to say this, but given his long disciplinary record..."

Niko's arm twitched.

"Stay put," she murmured.

"His highly volatile temper..."

Niko growled.

"And a clear pattern of impulsive behavior, I'm forced to conclude that he's not fit for service. The gravity of the incident necessitates a rapid and strong response. As the commander, I'm prepared to relieve Lieutenant Kalos of his duties, disband the black ops unit, and turn Kalos over to the legal system for full criminal prosecution for breach of the treaty."

The whole room sat in stunned silence. Niko's arm was rock hard. Even Sophia had to clamp her lips shut. The level of theatrics they'd been forced to endure was breathtaking, and good guards like Dad were allowing it to be taken seriously.

"You believe his actions to be criminal?" Ichiro clarified. "A breach of the treaty outside normal military authorization could mean exile."

"I'm aware, sir, but a strong condemnation of these actions before the summit will prove that this wasn't a sanctioned mission."

Ichiro nodded gravely. "Indeed. In the coming days, the panel will render its recommendation for the council—"

"Excuse me, sir. If I may," a small voice from the edge of the panel spoke up. The man in white robes held up a knobby finger.

Niko's arm relaxed. Ichiro winced. Even Dad raised an eyebrow. Who was he?

"Captain Cipriani, you said you believed you'd approved an evidence gathering mission."

"That's correct, sir."

"And the after-action report states that the black ops unit was ambushed shortly after arriving at the location."

"Yes, but no one was there when Lieutenant Ahmadi was captured. The evidence is still being analyzed," Anton replied as the smile faded from his face.

"Hmm." The man frowned. "As the commander of this unit, I'm surprised you'd be so quick to make a recommendation for disciplinary action."

Anton laughed, but it seemed a little too forced and condescending to be natural. "Well, as a commander, I have to think about the captured guard as well. The Tavians will soon call a summit to discuss reparations. Swift condemnation from our side may go a long way to negotiating Ahmadi's return."

"I understand you haven't been in command very long and appreciate your..." He looked around the room with a kind smile. "What did you call it? 'Eagerness' to prove yourself, but I would caution this entire panel against doing anything rash."

Anton cleared his throat. "The Tavians—"

"Pardon me, young man, but I know quite a bit about the Tavians. Many see me as the foremost expert on them." He kept his tone fatherly even though his words cut deep.

The foremost experts on the Tavians were the Seers—

Sophia's eyebrows jumped. No wonder she'd never seen him before. He was a Seer.

Ichiro's face tightened. "Royce, Nios owes you and all the Seers a debt of gratitude, but the rules of the summit are clear. The Tavians could make it appear as though we were guilty of the illegal activity in Santa Rita, and they're holding one of our guards as proof. We could have as little as thirty-six hours to prepare for the summit, and they could move forward with punitive action against her if we try to contest their accusations. Commander Mendoza, as well as the council, will be expecting this panel's recommendation."

Royce extended his hands outward with a wide grin. "The Magnolia Festival is coming. With all the ceremonies, we could easily claim scheduling conflicts until it's over. The Tavians will be confident in their leverage. They will give us the time to observe our traditions because they'll want to look reasonable when they demand steep reparations." Royce leaned forward, his gaze returning to Anton. "I'd rather take that time to investigate than be so eager to make concessions too early."

An awkward silence followed.

Ichiro cleared his throat. "It's not clear what the Tavians will do, but perhaps he has a point. I will postpone this hearing until either further evidence is gathered or a date is set for the summit. Until that point, Lieutenant Kalos will remain a part of the unit, but all leadership duties will be suspended. Full command and supervision will be given to Captain Cipriani."

Sophia shut her eyes and released a breath. Layla was being held prisoner, and Anton had somehow found a way to capitalize on it. All he'd had to do was to toss Niko aside.

She glared at the panel, glad-handing as if nothing had happened. How could Leadership do this to one of their own? No one stopped it—including Dad.

Dad.

This flew in the face of everything he'd taught her. He stood, speaking with another captain she didn't recognize, but she caught the subtle turn of his shoulders away from her. He was trying to avoid her. She didn't care what was on his schedule next, she'd be following him to his office.

"We should do lunch!" Anton's voice drifted over the crowd.

Niko launched himself from his chair. She leaped in front of him before he could get any closer.

"Now's not the time or place," she muttered. There was no sign he'd heard her through his cold glare. "You'll just give them what they want."

His gaze darted to her, hard, unrelenting. His lips curled, but he stormed from the room.

Sophia rubbed her forehead. What a mess.

A warm hand slid over her shoulder. Dad? She turned, and Anton smiled at her. She jumped away, scowling.

"How are you doing?" Anton asked, eyebrows drawn up together, a quiet smile. He'd lied about her unit leader, and he had the audacity to ask how she was doing? If she could have, she would've dropped him with a swing kick right now.

Now's not the time or the place.

She forced a smile but couldn't force out the words. He was a commanding officer. She might never be able to tell him exactly what she thought.

A moment passed.

"I don't want you to be worried about what will happen if we disband your unit. I will personally make sure you have your choice of assignments. I have a little time right now. Would you like to come back to my office? We can talk about it."

"I need to speak with my father right now," she said, unable to relax her glower.

"Okay. Maybe some other time." He smiled so easily, she would have never guessed what he'd just done.

Feeling more and more like Niko every second, she needed to get out of here before she said something she'd regret. She brushed past him without another word.

The corridor was crowded, but no one would stop a lowly L-1 to talk when there were captains around. She easily wove her way to her father's office.

His assistant, Fulton, rose from his desk as she strode past him. "Um, your father isn't back yet—"

"I'll wait." She plopped down in the chair in front of his desk. The longer she waited, the more her skin burned. How could he do this? He knew it was wrong.

Someone whispered in the lobby, and a tired sigh followed—Dad's tired sigh.

"I have a full schedule today, Sophia," he said, approaching her from behind.

"If you were so pressed for time, you could have canceled that hearing. Sounds like the panel has already made its decision," she snarled.

He shut his door and rounded his desk. His jade eyes narrowed as he sat. "Every guard has a right to a hearing."

Her skin reached a boil. "You missed a word. Every guard was supposed to be entitled to a *fair* hearing."

His fingers curled around a pen as his gaze hardened. "Watch the way you speak to me. You're an L-1, and I recused myself to ensure a fair hearing."

"Ensure? Anton was allowed to give false testimony that no one challenged, they gave *him* full command of the unit, and you think that was fair?"

He leaned over his desk. "There's no record of that order, and both Cipriani and Kalos's records speak for themselves. You expected the panel to simply believe Kalos?"

She sprang up. "No. I expected you to investigate instead of pinning this all on one person, who, might I remind you, saved me from the same fate as Layla."

Dad's lips pressed into a flat line.

"The facts are there, but everyone is in such a hurry to make this go away that you're willing to sacrifice a good guard."

"I recused myself!"

"You recused yourself to be fair!" she shouted. "You think that hearing was fair? Even as an observer on the panel, your word has power. You could have pushed them to do the right thing."

"Why are you doing this, Sophia?" he asked, eyes narrowing again. "The outcome will be the same. Even if we investigate down to the minutiae, mistakes were made. He was the unit leader. Whether he's relieved of command now or later, he will be held responsible. Everyone in the Guard knows that."

"Everyone in the Guard knows that they could be turned over to a criminal court to be exiled simply because they were forced to lead a bad mission?" She shook her head as he looked down at her.

He'd always taught her to stand up for what was right, and now he lectured her about how this was different—the exception to the rule.

"Maybe I'm not cut out to be a guard." She stormed to the door and yanked it open.

Dad heaved the same tired sigh just before she slammed it behind her.

CHAPTER 11

*N*iko rolled his eyes. Frayed threads blew across the ground of their workout room and floated through the air.

"I don't understand, though," Guthrie said, scratching his head. "How did you split the punching bag? That should be impossible."

"It was either the punching bag or Anton's face," Niko replied. Actually, if they exiled him, he'd probably still do this to Anton's face anyway. "Are you going to help me clean it up or not?"

Guthrie shrugged, still frowning. "Yeah, I guess."

"Kalos."

Niko rose with a handful of filling. Dark hair. Lean build. Eagle emblem. Captain Anuva. Just when he thought his day couldn't get any worse.

Guthrie jumped to attention.

"I'd like a word with you," Captain Anuva said, surveying the punching bag devastation.

"Right this way, *sir*," Niko said, trudging to the door. He led him into his office, where Captain Anuva's gaze bored into him as he shut the door. If he thought Niko would be intimidated, he was wrong. Niko plopped into his chair and leaned back to look at him.

"Tell me what happened in Santa Rita."

Niko shrugged. "I'm surprised you're asking me at all. Seems Captain Cipriani felt he had a strong understanding of what happened."

Captain Anuva planted both hands on the desk and leaned forward. "You want to whine and complain about the hearing today? Go do it to your casual.

I've got a full day of meetings and your disciplinary record memorized, but someone reminded me that even you deserve fairness."

Niko almost laughed. Fairness in the Guard? Who would demand that? They'd just taken away his leadership role on the word of a liar. Captain Anuva's green eyes sparked—just like Sophia's did when she was angry.

Sophia.

He sat up. Why would she help him? After everything he'd done to her? He swallowed hard.

He'd seen that hearing for what it was. That mission had disrupted the harmony at the top of the chain of command. A guard had been captured. Another had been grievously injured. They hated any reminder of the war being fought below them, but this? For a moment, they'd have to step away from their white-tie dinners and ceremonial summits, which were nothing more than lavish vacations. They'd have to do some real work, and they blamed him for that. Easy to do when he'd spent his career doing things they found distasteful but couldn't live without.

And never once had he played their game. He didn't talk about his missions often, but he'd never pretend they didn't happen, that his kills weren't necessary, that his unit's accomplishments weren't important. He'd already burnt his bridges, but her?

She'd just started her career. She had everything going for her, including powerful allies. She should've been looking for the first opportunity to get as far away from him, this incident, even the whole unit, if possible—but especially him.

She wasn't doing that.

Something flipped inside him. It wasn't nearly on the same level as when something didn't go as planned on a mission, but it was there. He'd missed something—something big. It had been staring him in the face all along—*she* had been staring him in the face, and he had misjudged her. Not just her skill, or aptitude for combat, *her*.

Captain Anuva raised his eyebrows.

"We were sent to collect evidence of the Tavians dealing directly with one of the rebel groups."

"What kind of evidence?"

"There have been reports of strange gunfire in the area for months. The mission with McCade showed us that not only were the Tavians there, they were willing to kill to hide whatever they were doing. Captain Cipriani wanted proof."

Captain Anuva nodded quietly for a moment. "He ordered you to go back."

Faint scarring webbed out from Captain Anuva's hairline on one side of his face, and he had an analytical gaze that seemed to take everything in without fear or repugnance. This was a man who had been in combat and had come out the other side. Maybe he could be trusted.

Niko had written off his commanders a long time ago, but just this once, he wanted them to believe him. Not for vindication, definitely not for a commendation, but because it was the truth. He would have never chosen to put his unit in danger that way.

"Yes," he replied.

Captain Anuva nodded again, studying the desk.

"I warned him of the dangers," Niko added. "From their reaction to our first mission, anyone could see they'd increase their presence in the area to protect their operation."

"Why not task a larger unit?"

He'd have to tread carefully here. It was territory that could never be proven, but the truth was the truth. "A larger unit tasking on a mission like this would require approval from the Seers Panel."

"Anton didn't want the Seers involved." Captain Anuva pursed his lips. "Did he say why?"

"He didn't want them to take the credit for this."

Captain Anuva let his head drop for a moment, but then his chin shot upward. "Royce—he's already involved in some way, isn't he?"

Niko winced. It was illegal to sneak into the Seers compound, but he'd rather go down for something he did do than something he didn't. "Yes."

Captain Anuva smirked. "How long have you been talking to him?"

Too late to turn back now. "The Tavians had surrounded us too quickly, and they knew our exact location, almost as if someone had warned them we were coming." Niko shrugged without an ounce of remorse. "I'd do anything for my unit, and I needed answers, so I sneaked into his suite the night after the attack. He said he'd help me in exchange for information."

Captain Anuva's smirk cracked into a full grin. "Royce would do that, wouldn't he?"

Niko opened his mouth to speak, but what could he say?

Captain Anuva backed away from the desk. "You've been in the Guard long enough. You know how this works. You, as the leader of this mission, will go down for this unless you can prove serious wrongdoing on someone else's part. Royce gave you a window of time to get your proof. Keep talking to him. If you're caught in the Seers compound, tell them you were following my orders. I'll cover for you, and I'll make sure you have as much time as possible, but the summit will come soon and only you can save yourself."

Frank, honest, even helpful. Niko had no idea how to respond to that.

Captain Anuva's gaze fell to his hands. For a moment, his stoic facade cracked. "And just in case I never get another chance to say this, thank you for saving my daughter."

Niko frowned. She was part of the unit. Even if she had been as inept as he'd feared, he would have still gone after her, but she hadn't been. He'd found her on the staircase with Horacio on her shoulders, trying to fight three Tavians by herself. "Sir—"

Captain Anuva held up a hand. "I've seen my fair share of combat. I know you'll say you were doing your job, and I understand that. But I'm a father, too, and even if she's furious with me now, I'll get to hug my daughter again. Thank you."

Niko pictured her, fists balled, big chestnut eyes gleaming, and couldn't help but smile. "She's a good guard, sir."

"She's a good person," he replied quietly, shuffling to the door. "Better than either of us."

He'd no sooner shut the door that Niko nodded in agreement.

CHAPTER 12

*N*iko sat at his desk. Even he couldn't make sense of the wall of reports and map overlays he'd projected in front of himself. He'd pulled out a piece of paper to make a flow chart, but that had been pointless, too. So many things had been crossed out that he could barely read it.

It had been a week since the Tavians had agreed to postpone the summit until after the Magnolia Festival. They'd even agreed to uphold the standards of the treaty for treatment of captives, which meant Layla was safe and unharmed. Captain Anuva had stuck to his word; no one in Leadership had bothered Niko. He'd met with Royce twice. He'd memorized the after-action reports.

But he wasn't any closer to the proof he'd need to exonerate himself.

He leaned back in his chair, rubbing his eyes. The Magnolia Festival would start tonight. Offices would be closed for days. It would be impossible to get anything done after this. He didn't have enough time. His allies were few. Despite the glimmer of hope, Captain Anuva had been right. Niko had been the unit leader. He'd take the fall—not because he was at fault, but because he couldn't prove who was.

He checked the clock on his implant. The Guard Ball would begin soon, and while he had no intention to attend, he wouldn't miss the hologram release that followed it. Meant to symbolize their discovery of light energy manipulation, golden holographic paper lanterns, butterflies, and just about anything else they could think of would rise from the cobblestones of the main square and float all the way up to the protective shield where they'd glimmer all night.

Tonight, kids would stay up late, all the stores would shut down, and Niotians of every specialty would gather in the main square. He'd never really bought into the overhyped festival spirit, but the hologram release was one thing he'd never miss.

The outer office door opened, and he leaned forward to see who it was. He'd given Guthrie and Sophia the night off for the ball. If he couldn't find anything, there certainly wasn't a point to them staying and staring at his flowchart of futility.

Sophia rounded the table in a red silk dress, and Niko's eyes nearly fell from his head. The dress clung to her hourglass frame down to her thighs, then flared. Her hair was pulled up on the sides and flowed down her back. And he couldn't be sure, but her brown eyes looked speckled with green flecks that he'd never noticed before. They stood out against her red lips.

"What are you still doing here?" she asked, but he barely heard her. She raised her eyebrows.

He blinked as if something had been caught in his eyes. "Nothing. Just... working on... stuff."

She planted a hand on her hip, showing the muscle tone in her arm. "The ball starts in an hour."

"I never go to that thing." He shook his head, regaining his composure. It didn't matter what she looked like in a dress, this was still Sophia. The L-1 spitfire who wouldn't wash out.

"Why not?" she asked.

"Really?"

She had to know his disdain for command at this point.

She folded her arms. "Sir, with all due respect—"

"Don't call me 'sir.' I'm not your boss anymore." He'd always been more comfortable as part of the team anyway, and she was probably more qualified to lead than him.

"I think it's a big mistake for you not to go."

"Niko," he insisted. He couldn't hear *sir* anymore, not right now—from the looks of his flow chart, probably never again. "I'm a unit member, just like you."

"Not if I can help it," she retorted. "You'll be unit leader again soon."

"We're equals, Sophia," he said with just a bit too much sincerity. He meant it more than she'd ever know. "Call me Niko."

She sighed. "Niko. Absence means guilt, and you've done nothing wrong."

He leaned back in his chair. "I know you're worried, but this investigation will stop with me. Your career won't be affected."

Her face contorted. "This isn't about me. You're a good commander, sir. What they're doing is wrong!"

It didn't change the truth. They were looking to make an example out of someone, and he was the most vulnerable.

"Sophia—" He paused.

The ball was about to begin, and she wasn't with some high-profile date or making the rounds with her dad. She was down here, trying to convince him to stand up to Leadership even though she gained nothing by convincing him to come.

She's a good person, her dad had said. *Better than either of us.*

Her gaze shifted around the room as it always did when she got nervous. "I know I'm only a Level-1, but I know this world. If you attend, it makes a statement that you have nothing to hide. It will make it harder for them to simply blame you and forget."

He raised an eyebrow. "They're going to blame me regardless."

She closed the distance between them—close enough to catch notes of vanilla, flowers, even a little apple—sweet and fresh like late summer. And he'd been right about her eyes. The green flecks danced against the red.

"Don't let them shame you into losing everything," she pleaded.

The ball was a nauseating display of status, where the captains tried to impress each other with their ribbons and everyone talked about themselves as if they were among the great military minds of the age. But part of him liked the idea of being the wrinkle in their perfect evening, their reminder that their job was more than telling everyone how important they were.

Earnestness shone from her beautiful eyes. How could he say no?

"I suppose I could go for a little while," he muttered, shuffling his papers.

She flashed a brilliant smile. "Great. You won't regret this, s-sssir—I mean, Niko."

AN HOUR LATER, he ran his fingers under the stiff collar of his formal military dress uniform. He was already sweating, and he'd barely arrived. He climbed the royal blue stairs to the main ballroom, scanning the crowd for Sophia.

Coming to the ball had been about standing up to command, right? He yanked at his collar again. She'd made a compelling case, and he trusted her judgment. That was all. It had been surprising to see her dressed up, but now that he knew what to expect, her looks would probably barely register with him.

He reached the top of the stairs, and there she was, talking with another guard in formal dress, just as stunning as before. He caught her eye, and she smiled before excusing herself and made her way over to him.

"Let's get this over with," he said, shrugging his shoulders to adjust his jacket.

She pressed her red lips together in a smile and reached out toward his neck. "May I?"

He nodded clumsily—as if he'd never been close to a woman before.

"I used to have to fix my dad's ties all the time," she said, pulling and tugging. She paused for a moment, her gaze flitting to his.

He swallowed hard.

She reached up to refold his collar, and he grabbed her hand.

"No," he murmured as a rush of warmth flooded his cheeks. "It'll show my tattoos."

"Everyone in command knows about your tattoos," she said. "You've never hidden them before. You have nothing to hide now, remember?"

She'd noticed his tattoos? What else had she noticed?

He stopped himself.

The early morning wake-up calls, the yelling, and the way he'd treated her at the hospital after the ambush. Not even she could overlook all that, but she had a point. He'd never hidden them before because it was a stupid rule. They didn't affect his ability to fight, and he didn't care what anyone thought of him...

Until she came along.

She was different than other guards. Loyal, braver than he could have possibly imagined, with a killer swing kick.

And beautiful.

With one last smoothing of the collar, her hands fell away, allowing him to think clearly again.

"Come on," she said over her shoulder, brushing away a curl. "Let's go find Guthrie."

They wove through the tables of stiff and stuffy guards, who eyed him as they sipped champagne. Gold eagles gleamed from too many chests to count. At any other time, he would have been clawing at the walls to get out of here. His gaze wandered over Sophia as she led the way to the floor-to-ceiling windows.

It was simple. She was a good guard, and it was an honor to serve with someone like her. In fact, he wished there were ten more guards just like her.

There could never be anyone like her.

He hissed. What was wrong with him? This investigation had him all messed up. He'd never had a problem attracting casuals. He didn't need to fall for someone he worked with—especially someone as capable as her. Attraction was irrelevant. She had what it took, and that was all that mattered.

"Sophia?" Anton's slick voice broke through his musings like a sledgehammer.

Every muscle in his body went rigid as Anton stood up from one of the tables they'd passed.

"You look amazing!" Anton said warmly.

He took a pointed step toward Anton. If he dared to touch her...

"Hello, Anton." She slipped around him, barely slowing. "We were just about to find Guthrie. Excuse us."

Short. Direct. Cold. Niko beamed as she continued on. The whole night had been worth it for that single moment. Anton's gaze iced over as he glared at Niko. For once, Anton was left speechless.

"Guess I better catch up with Sophia," Niko said, winking to plunge the insult ever deeper. "Enjoy your night."

They finally found Guthrie with a beautiful blonde on his arm, and despite the proverbial ax hanging over his head, he smiled more in the span of those few hours than he had in months. He'd almost forgotten the investigation entirely when the music slowed.

Guthrie's date curled into his chest and whispered something in his ear.

"We're going to dance." Guthrie glanced at them both. "You should join us."

Sophia's wide eyes darted to Niko.

He shook his head. "I don't dance."

Guthrie rolled his eyes as he stepped toward the dance floor. "You only live once. You're not even her commander right now."

"Guthrie!" Sophia scolded.

"What? I'm just saying he's got a rough road ahead of him. I don't know how you did it, Sophia, but you got him to come. He should enjoy tonight." With that he slid his arm around his date and moved to the dance floor.

Niko scoffed. "Guthrie's an idiot."

Sophia scowled, tapping her fingers on the cabaret table. "He makes it sound like this investigation is already over. You did nothing wrong."

Maybe not, but it didn't change reality. Guthrie was probably right—not that Niko would tell her.

She groaned. "Not you, too."

"What?" He held up his hands. "I didn't say anything."

"That's the problem. You think he's right." The green flecks in her eyes flared.

He sighed. "Look around you, Sophia. Every guard in this room knows about the ambush. Everyone here wants me to go away quietly so this whole thing will end."

"You don't have to do what they want," she insisted. "You have a choice."

"It's not like I can fight back." He yanked at his collar again. Was it getting hot in here?

She rounded the cabaret table. "I don't care if they have sworn testimony and the support of the Head of the Guard. You aren't responsible for any of this. You can still fight this. They want you to go away quietly?" she asked, her lips curving upward. She held out her hand. "Let's dance."

His mouth hung open. Beautiful. Courageous.

He blinked away the awe.

She's a guard—a respected guard.

"I don't dance," he mumbled.

She nudged her hand forward, undeterred. "Let's remind them you're still here."

He shook his head. How had she taken a room full of gleaming eagles as a challenge? Of course she'd be exasperatingly persistent.

He hid a smile and wrapped his hand around hers, trying to ignore the happiness radiating from her touch.

She led the way to the dance floor and turned to him, smiling with her chin held high. His fingers brushed along the smooth silk around her waist, but he kept his distance as they swayed—even if he desperately wanted to pull her close and savor her sweet scent.

Not that kind of dance, though.

To her, this was an act of protest. And to him? It didn't matter what it was to him, but he couldn't say no to her.

Besides, the Magnolia Festival had begun. This would all end soon. All he had was tonight and this dance, whatever it was.

"Are you smiling?" she asked, looking at him through thick eyelashes. "The great Niko Kalos is smiling! See! The ball isn't so bad."

He sniffed and looked anywhere but directly at those beautiful eyes. "I've always been more of a fan of the hologram release myself."

"You?"

"Yeah," he replied. "Why's that so strange?"

She shrugged. "An event where practically everyone in Nios packs into the main square doesn't seem like your thing."

She had a point there.

"I don't watch from the square."

She narrowed her eyes, but a smile crept across her face—the half smile that drove him crazy.

"I watch from the old bell tower," he admitted, looking away.

"The bell tower?" she asked, glancing out the window. "It's been closed down for a couple years now. How do you get in?"

He raised an eyebrow. "Are you really asking how someone in black ops could gain access to a locked tower?"

She bit her lip, still grinning. "I bet the view is amazing."

"Do you want to come?" He stiffened, eyes wide. Had he really just asked that out loud?

He hadn't meant anything by it, but it didn't sound that way. It didn't feel that way.

He wanted her to say yes.

"Um…" She glanced around the room, the green flecks dancing—taunting him, drawing him closer. He'd thought he could control his feelings—she was way more than a pretty face, and he could never reduce her to that.

But somehow in the midst of all this, thinking of her as just a good guard felt like a reduction, too. His mind was playing tricks on him. Best to get out of here fast.

He dropped his hands. "I'm sorry," he backpedaled. "That sounded…" He couldn't say it. "I didn't mean—"

"Yes." She bounced on her toes a little. "I want to see this."

CHAPTER 13

Sophia negotiated each rung of the ladder with the utmost care. Climbing the bell tower in heels and a mermaid-cut gown hadn't been the best idea, but she didn't regret it.

The ballroom had become stifling. Too much scheming, too many charades, and the life of an innocent guard—someone who had saved her—hung in the balance. Maybe Dad could tolerate that, but she couldn't. The arrogance, the laziness, the willingness to destroy one of their own still crept over her skin, making her itch.

Niko climbed onto the platform and offered her a hand, then easily pulled her through the opening. As one of the few structures in all of Nios that hadn't been computer generated, the bell tower bore the wear and tear of the real world. The aged wooden planks and wrought-iron railing were about the oldest things she'd ever seen in Nios. Somehow that was a comfort. It wasn't flawless, but nothing ever really was. At least this place felt real.

She crept to the railing, allowing the stiff breeze to blow through her curls and soothe her. The last rays of sunlight were fading on the horizon. People had already started to congregate in the square below. Children squealed and chased each other. Soft laughter and jovial voices drifted upward. Such happiness, but it had been marred by the investigation. She couldn't shut her eyes anymore to the downfalls and tragedies that had led to this perfection. It was bittersweet.

Niko stood beside her, warmth emanating from him. "Are you okay? I can help you back down—"

"No. It's not that," she replied, rubbing the corroded metal of the railing under her thumb. "How did I blindly enjoy things like this before? How did I miss all the sacrifices that go into..." She waved a hand at the square. "*This.* I feel like such an idiot."

"No." Niko's voice was low and comforting. Her gaze wandered to him, and he tightened his lips like he was holding back.

She didn't want him to.

She looked away, brushing her curls behind her shoulder.

"What we do is important. This," he said, pointing to the crowd below. "It's exactly why we fight. So this can be real. No matter what happens, I won't regret that."

She blinked. That's exactly why she fought, too—for her home, everything she loved. So children could giggle and stay up late, so families could focus on building memories like these rather than fearing for their safety. So no one else had to live without their mothers. He felt the same way?

"Very few people have seen what we've seen, and most people who do see it turn away. They pretend it's not there. You're different."

A laugh escaped from her tight throat. Maybe that was the problem. "I feel different, all right," she murmured.

He turned to face her, and she did the same before she even realized it.

"It's not a bad thing. You're genuine and brave. You're a great sparring partner." He shrugged, smirking. "You tried to take me out with a swing kick. I gotta say I didn't see that coming. You're the only person I know who doesn't seem to mind 4:00 a.m. wake up calls." He flashed a wide smile. "And you read paper books. Who does that?"

Her books.

Heat blazed in her cheeks. He'd noticed her fairytales on the shelves in her room. Her gaze dropped to the floor, and she couldn't pick it up. She nodded, keeping her head low. "After my mom died, my dad was still out in the field a lot. He would bring me fairytales when he would come home. I guess he wanted me to have an escape."

"I wasn't bringing up the books in a bad way." The urgency in his voice jarred her. "Don't change, Sophia—especially not for the Leadership. Promise me. No matter what happens with the investigation, no matter where you end up after all this, you won't change."

She rubbed her arms as another breeze blew by. She'd have to change, wouldn't she? Either she'd have to find a way to stomach the Guard's complacency, or she'd have to leave the Guard. She glanced out on the square as the crowd grew, remembering graduation. Even then, with her father assigned to black ops, she'd wanted to stand up and defend all this so badly. But it had turned out to be a lonely battle. Most people seemed obsessed with their own careers. And just when she'd found someone like herself, he might be taken away. "This is a far cry from a fairytale, Niko."

A twinge. Faint, but distinct in her core, like walking with a pebble in her shoe. A lie—she'd lied to him just now. It wasn't intentional, but even as she'd said the words, she'd known they weren't true.

There was more to fairytales than the end, and her heart had drawn the similarities the moment he'd mentioned her books. Leadership's betrayal, the battles waged, the losses they'd suffered, and yet here Niko stood. He'd been irascible when they'd met, but that wasn't who he was; he'd proven to be genuine and selfless.

He'd been there when she'd needed him most. He fought for good, and his passion—she smiled and allowed her gaze to wander over his broad shoulders to the tips of his tattoos. Even in the faint light, she could see the golden hue of his skin and feel the weight of his intensity. While she kind of preferred the tousled look he had when they were working out, the way he'd looked tonight in his formal dress uniform—the whole package... she drew in a breath.

Yep. She'd lied.

Regardless of what she felt, the idea of *them* was a fairytale. She was an L-1, barely noticeable to someone like him. And she'd seen the way women looked at him when they were out on runs; they practically threw themselves at him right then and there.

Yellow light shifted around them. The holograms. Hundreds of glowing images floated by, surrounding the tower in beautiful warmth and stealing her breath.

Perfection.

Not the facade she'd witnessed at the ball. Real, authentic beauty surrounded them. Darkness waited for them below. The cost of the beauty hadn't been fully paid, but for now it was here, with them. She peered at him only to find his gaze locked on her.

Turn away. Be professional.

She didn't. Instead, she took a step closer, unable to look away.

His hands drifted out toward her, then snapped to his side.

"You're right." He heaved a deep sigh. The yellow light on his face faded as the holograms rose beyond the tower. "This isn't a fairytale. Send me your reassignment request. I'll do what I can to get you a good assignment while I still can."

The moment shattered. The magic, gone. He thought she'd give up on him so she could get a good assignment?

"You think I care about assignments right now? They could hand you over for criminal prosecution."

His chest deflated with a heavy sigh. "Don't worry about me, Sophia."

"I know what really happened. You want me to forget and move on?" She raised her voice. "Look down on you from my cozy new office, think 'that's a shame,' and just move on?"

"Black ops is over," he said, his eyes too intense. "I've burnt too many bridges, but you can change things in the future."

"I want to change things now…"

For you…

She shook the thought away. Sure, he deserved to be cleared, but there was more to it than that. She couldn't leave *him* behind. All the things she'd seen without noticing, his selflessness, intelligence, sheer aptitude in combat—big brown eyes, his gleaming smile when he was happy, those tattoos.

"Listen to me. You don't have to be held back by this. You are an amazing guard."

Guard?

Her mind swelled with irrational disappointment.

Of course that's all he'd see when he looked at her. She'd fought for a spot on this unit. She'd earned it. That's what mattered.

"I want to stay on the unit," she insisted, backing away.

His massive shoulders sagged. "I appreciate everything you've done for me, but your dad is head of Personnel Command. You know how this ends."

She glared at him, pressing her lips together to hold back a multitude left unsaid. She didn't care how the Leadership wanted it to end. "I'm not giving up."

The sky gleamed gold, but he stood in the shadows, shaking his head. "It has been an honor to fight alongside you."

"Then keep fighting with me," she begged. "I know the odds, but that doesn't mean we can walk away. Until our very last breath, we have a choice."

"I will fight this to the end," he said, his voice low and solemn. Her hands ached to reach out and touch him. He cleared his throat, moving away. "You know you have a spot in the unit for as long as you want it, but for your sake, you should start thinking about your next step."

That might have been wise… if she could forget him. "I'm not interested in—"

"We'll fight this together under one condition," he continued.

She planted a hand on her hip. What would he ask now?

"I will fight, but I will *not* take you down with me—that's my choice. If there comes a time when I run out of choices, you'll have to accept it and find a new assignment far away from me."

She didn't want to think of a time when Leadership finally cornered Niko, but deep down she knew it was a possibility. He was an easy mark for them.

Regardless, she and Niko would be fighting this together for now. It was as good a deal as any. She nodded, even though inside she was gearing up for the battle that waited for them below.

CHAPTER 14

Niko dropped the barbell and shook out his hands. A couple more intervals of dead lifts, and he'd move to the box jumps or maybe just run until he hit exhaustion.

Sophia was good, bold, beautiful…

And totally off limits.

A group of guards passed by, eying the weight he was lifting. Maybe if they came to the gym to lift weights instead of gawk at people, they'd be able to lift more, too. He hated the main gym in the barracks, but it was his only option after breaking the punching bag. He lifted the bar again for slow, controlled reps.

Time was running out, but Sophia refused to acknowledge that. Leadership only needed one scapegoat, but if she stayed too long she'd get caught in the crossfire, and he didn't want that. She was a good guard—the kind of person who could actually change things at the highest levels. And she was risking all of it.

He shouldn't have even gone to the ball. He'd said too much—*felt* too much. And now the feel of her in his arms was in his head. At this point, he didn't even trust himself to tell her how much he respected her. Even a little bit of the truth would unravel the rest. She'd connect it all; she was too smart not to, and what would she do then?

He could still picture her in his office, feet planted, eyes glinting when he'd called her Anton's girl. Despite Niko's efforts to wash her out, nothing he'd done in the entire first month of knowing her had drawn her out quite like that. She definitely didn't need another guard falling for her. If she knew, would she resent him, too?

There'd been a light in her eyes last night, moments where she'd gotten close. His fingers curled, feeling empty. He'd wanted to wrap his arms around her, feel the warmth radiating through her silk dress, kiss her.

He gripped the barbell and started another interval, but it wasn't helping him forget—nothing had helped, but he needed to find something before he could face her again. Right now, he still wanted to throw that bar with all its weight through the window. Staying away from equipment that could be turned into projectiles was probably the best course of action.

Time for a run. He strode to the door.

"Going on a run by yourself?" Anton called from behind him.

Niko halted.

"I thought all those runs were to get Sophia alone. We both know how you like to parade around with her."

A veil of red clouded his vision, making it impossible to speak. It would be bad if he threw Anton through the window, right? Or would it be a favor to everyone? He turned around, glare settling on Anton's smug face as he strolled closer. "Some of us actually need physical training for our job, Anton—not that I'd expect you to understand."

"We'll see how much longer that's necessary," Anton replied, lips twitching upward.

He had to force the words from his tight chest. "Because of your order."

"You heard what you wanted to hear—because you're impulsive, violent, and dangerous."

Niko flinched. "I know I'm a monster, Cipriani. Do you know you're one, too?" He took a step closer, but Anton stood his ground. "I *never* wanted that mission. I told you it was too dangerous, and you ignored that. This is on you."

Anton held out his arms with a beaming grin. "My word against yours, I guess."

"I would never have put my unit in danger like that."

"*Your* unit? Last I checked, your leadership duties were suspended at the disciplinary panel. I'm the commander of the black ops unit now."

A breath rumbled out of Niko's chest, sounding like a growl. Defeated. Without so much as a fight. He needed to get out of here before he decided to dole out justice himself.

"Speaking of the unit," Anton said, tilting his head. "I'll be reassigning Sophia. As her commander, it's my job to make sure the best and brightest aren't mired by something like this."

Niko grinned. "Try it. She'll take your head off."

The smile dropped from Anton's face. Without throwing a punch, Niko had drawn blood.

"We'll see about that. You'll be gone soon. Then who will she be loyal to?"

A kick to the solar plexus would shut Anton up, but when he'd promised Sophia he'd fight—she hadn't meant like that. Instead, he shrugged. "We'll see where the investigation leads."

"The investigation is over," Anton spat. "Postponing the hearing got you nothing."

"There's still time," he said as casually as he could. "Maybe I'll go back to the scene and see what I can find."

"No, you won't." Anton's lips curled. "If you had come back with actionable intelligence, this might have been a different conversation, but you didn't, and now we need to bury this whole thing—and you with it. Stay away from Santa Rita. It's already going to be a nightmare to fix because of you. It's over. Accept it. That's an order."

Niko doubled over with laughter. "You make it sound like your orders mean something."

"You think I got to where I am without getting my hands dirty?" Anton stepped directly in front of him, features tight. "I don't need a pulse gun to kill you."

Niko's laughter faded. He stepped toe to toe with Anton, squared his shoulders, and met his glare. "I'm not scared of your threats."

"You should be. Imagine the commendations I'd get if I stopped a rogue guard from trying to restart the war with the Tavians."

"Restarting the war?" Niko rolled his eyes. "That's a stretch. Even for you."

"I thought you'd get it by now," Anton snickered. "It's all about what the evidence *suggests*."

Niko searched his face—wild eyes set in taut features with bulging jaw muscles. Two Level-1s lifted weights about ten yards away. Another Level-3 drank water off to the side. If he throttled Anton right now, he was pretty sure no one could stop him in time.

A flurry of white came to a stop in his periphery. Royce in his usual robes, but what was he doing in the Guard's gym? A small man who had to be about the same age as Royce straggled behind him. Royce's gaze fixed on Niko, and he inclined his head before walking out.

"As interesting as this is, I have to go," Niko said, stretching his neck and forcing the tension from his muscles. "Maybe you can tell me about your own magnificence some other time."

"Keep to your orders, Kalos!" Anton shouted after him.

You mean hurry up and die for your mistakes.

If Niko was going to burn for this, he'd figure out a way to take Anton with him. He stormed out of the gym and scanned the barracks' large lobby. It was nearly empty. Niko walked one way, then another, searching the many alcoves and corners used for meetings, friendly gatherings, and even the occasional casual hook up. He'd nearly gotten to the end of the space when someone cleared their throat from behind him. There, in the far corner, Royce smiled.

"Lieutenant Kalos, it's been too long." Royce's voice was as casual as it was serene.

"I've been a little busy," Niko said, rolling his shoulders to release the tension. "What are you doing here anyway? Aren't you supposed to be under constant protection in your compound?"

"Yes, but I'm a Seer." Royce shrugged. "Slipping through the security perimeter is one of my favorite games. Anyway, I simply hate unsolved riddles. I've mulled over your case for days, and it occurred to me I should introduce you to someone."

Niko raised an eyebrow, hoping this was going somewhere, but he never could tell with Royce.

"This is Edwin Harper. He's one of Nios's finest cyber engineers."

Edwin's eyes crinkled as he smiled, showing his age, and he extended his hand. "How do you do, Mister—I mean, Lieutenant Kalos."

Niko drew in a breath and forced a smile before shaking his hand. It was a wonder this man was still working at all.

"Edwin helps to manage many of the systems that integrate with our implants. In fact, he built quite a few of them before the war."

"Great. Can he monitor the Tavians, too? That's the only way I'm going to know how they found us," Niko snapped.

Royce pursed his lips. "No, but he often can find communications."

Niko's gaze shifted between the two men. "And you found someone who has been communicating with the Tavians?"

"Of course not," Royce replied.

Niko threw his head back. "I don't have time for this. The Magnolia Festival is almost over. I need to chase down real leads."

"Then you'll be interested to know that commanders often use the ancillary messaging system to communicate with their staff. I'm sorry to say your friend, Captain Cipriani, has developed quite a disliking for you."

Niko beamed, but it quickly faded. If Royce had actionable intelligence, he would have led with it, right? "Is there proof he issued the order?"

"Sadly, there's evidence he knew more than he let on at the hearing, but it wouldn't be enough to exonerate you." His gaze snapped to Niko. "Yet."

"Yet?" He would explain, wouldn't he?

Royce folded his hands across his stomach. "It's a common strategy we Seers use. When I can see the details clustering around something specific, but there's not enough to connect the dots, we set up a trap. I propose that's what we do for our dear friend to draw him out a bit."

Niko narrowed his eyes.

"It's really quite simple," Royce explained. "I barely had to focus to See the pattern in his behavior. It's quite consistent. He gets in an altercation with you, then spends hours speaking about it with his subordinate, Gideon Ravella. Much of the time, he gives specific details that could be considered a violation of commander confidentiality standards, which, as I've said, could sully his reputation, but it won't exonerate you."

Royce flipped a hand out. "That got me thinking. If you could bait him about the investigation—maybe float that you have a new theory but refuse to say what it is—he might discuss the investigation with his assistant, and then you'd have him."

A new theory. He could do that, and knowing Anton, that would infuriate him. He nodded. "Sure. Why not?"

"Fantastic." Royce bounced his shoulders. "This will be splendid fun."

"There he is!" Two guards ran down the hall in their direction, and all the joy fell from Royce's face.

"It appears my time is up for today," Royce said, then folded his hands and faced the guards. "Gentlemen! There you are. I do apologize for the miscommunication. I got turned around a bit, but what better place to find guards than the barracks, right?"

Niko's lips curved upward as he backed away, hoping he'd cause half the trouble Royce did at his age.

If I ever make it to that age...

Royce's plan could work. It was more than he'd had before he'd come to work out this morning, but the Magnolia Festival would end in three days. If they couldn't come up with anything by then, Niko could be arrested, maybe even exiled or executed.

All of this would end.

Dark curls pulled back into a loose bun bounced from the teleportation zone toward the gym. He'd know them anywhere. "Sophia!"

He clamped his lips shut. Why couldn't he just let her go? It wasn't right for either of them to look at his situation and have hope.

She spun, eyes wide. "Niko. Hi!"

His thoughts screamed at him. What should he say now? That he'd seen her and had to talk to her? That being around her made him feel like everything else could come crashing down, and he'd still be okay?

She pointed over her shoulder. "I was just about to work out." Her lip slid between her teeth, and she shrugged. "Care to join me? I was supposed to do my leg workout today, but I really just want to spar. I could use a partner."

"Spar with you?" He beamed. "Any time."

CHAPTER 15

Sophia sank into her stance on the red mats of the main gym and took a centering breath. She and Niko were just two guards, practicing their technique. It was simple—responsible, even. Launching herself forward, she hit Niko's pads with a jab, low-kick combination.

He quirked an eyebrow. "Not bad."

She blinked her gaze away to stop herself from grinning like an idiot and focused on the nearly constant clangs of weights around them.

Just her and another member of the unit. Being familiar with each other's fighting style could be really helpful on future missions.

Two jabs and a right cross.

"Try to put some more power behind your cross." He held the pad out.

She nodded, pulling her fists into the guard position, and focused on the black pad. There was nothing between them but mutual respect—

Giggles bubbled from the side of the mat. Her gaze slid to three female guards, standing there without a drop of sweat anywhere. Not on their way to another station, not stretching or cooling down—just standing there, ogling Niko.

Her skin simmered.

The woman in the center tossed a long, silky, dark lock of hair over her shoulder, scarlet highlights shimmering. The identical twin of one of the goddesses painted in the domed ceiling at headquarters, her deep-brown eyes wandered over Niko. Sophia's shoulders curved inward, and she brushed an unruly curl away from the sweat on her forehead.

"Sophia?" Niko stared at her blankly.

She shook out her arms. "Sorry."

She focused on the pad, but the goddess sauntered around the mat into Niko's line of sight and waited.

She launched herself into a hook, roundhouse kick combination.

"Whoa." Niko dodged the kick. "That was a little wild. Do you need a break?"

Right now? With *them* hanging around? She glanced at the goddess from the corner of her eye. "No, no. I'm fine."

His gaze followed hers.

Great...

He lowered the pads and stepped closer. "What's wrong?"

Her face felt like it was on fire, but there was no point in hiding it now. "It's *them*. That's so rude."

She could say that, right? She and Niko were trying to work. Those women were being disruptive.

His face twisted. "Who cares about them? They're just some other guards."

Her shoulders dropped. That's what he'd said about her last night. When she'd been ready to wrap her arms around his neck and kiss him, he'd probably been making the same face in his head as he was making right now. Because to him, she was *just a guard*, too.

She backed away. This had been an awful idea. She was fighting for him to be her boss again. And then what? Even if he did fall for her, black ops weren't allowed to have serious relationships, and a relationship with her boss would land them both in front of a disciplinary panel.

Maybe if she could get some space between them, her feelings would cool off and she could actually behave like an adult. "I should run."

"Wait." He followed her to the edge of the mat. "What's wrong?"

"Look at that, Kalos. You can actually be helpful!" Anton's voice grated over her like nails.

Speaking of roundhouse kicks.

The muscles in Niko's arms bulged as he glared at Anton.

"Sophia, we need to talk about your reassignment," Anton continued.

"I'm not ready to do that," she said through clenched teeth.

"Besides." Niko smirked. "I'm working on a new theory. It's big, Cipriani. Sophia may not have to go anywhere at all."

New theory? If her mind hadn't been such a mess, she might have been excited. But she couldn't hear about it now, not like this. Niko's shoulders were tensed and his eyes hard, but he never looked at her.

Slender fingers curved around his bicep from behind—the goddess. "Hi! I don't think we've ever met."

Her pulse whooshed in her ears. The goddess hadn't even waited until she'd left the gym to make her move.

"It's over, Kalos," Anton snarled.

"We'll see." He shrugged and winked. "I'm actually pretty excited about it."

"Oh, did I interrupt?" the goddess asked.

Yes. Sophia glowered at her.

Anton scoffed and reached out for Sophia. "This is a waste of my time. Sophia—"

She batted his hand away with a lot more force than she'd intended. "I'm not going anywhere with you."

"We really need to talk about this." Anton turned to face her, boxing out Niko, and the goddess pounced on the separation, sliding in front of Niko with a stunning smile.

"I've seen you around."

"Yeah. Nice to meet you," Niko said, his features still hard. "I'm kind of busy right now, working with one of my guards."

Guard? She shouted in her head.

She stormed around Anton for the door, ditzy giggles still tittering behind her. If she didn't get out of there soon, she'd say something she'd regret.

Anton chased after her. "Sophia, I'm trying to help you. I'm not sure what Niko has led you to believe—"

"I don't need Niko to explain to me what happened, and I don't want your help," she called over her shoulder. "I never will."

"Hey," he said. "I'm sensing a lot of anger. I know emotions are running high—"

"Sensing?" She stopped. That was it. "I'd thought I'd been clearer than that."

Somewhere inside, a more logical side was sighing. So much for keeping her feelings unsaid.

"I'm not sure what it is you see or want from me, Anton, but it's never going to happen."

Niko strode toward them. "Sophia."

"*No!*" she shouted, holding out a hand to stop him. "Not you, too. I have to go."

She nearly sprinted toward the teleportation zone, welcomed the prickling on her skin, and flashed away. In the safety of her barracks hall, she took a deep breath. What a mess. She'd told off a captain. He'd deserved it, but it wasn't smart.

And Niko. What had gotten into her?

She opened the door, and Emma smiled, but she walked right past her and fell face down into the cool, violet sheets of her bed. "I'm such an idiot," she said into her pillow.

"Uh oh," Emma said. "It sounds like we need chocolate. Hold on." She fumbled around and then tapped Sophia on the shoulder.

She reached out and grabbed the piece, rolling over to stare at the white ceiling. "I think I just broke about eighteen standards for guard conduct."

"You?" Emma hopped on the bed next to her, her big, brown eyes dancing. "I need to hear about this!"

Sophia paused for a moment, allowing the velvety milk chocolate with a hint of salted toffee melt in her mouth. "I yelled at Anton." She grimaced. "I think that was kind of inevitable, though."

"Girl, I will never understand that situation. He basically handed you a career on a golden platter, and look at him! He's not hard on the eyes."

Sophia's gaze curved with the crimson and violet brush strokes on the magnolia painting next to her bed. "I don't respect him."

Emma ran her fingers through her long blond ponytail and shook her head. "The only reason I'd turn down someone like that is if there were someone else—" She gasped.

Sophia covered her face with her elbow.

Emma squirmed next to her. "Is it that sniper you work with? Guthrie, was it?"

She cringed. "I could never go for Guthrie."

"Your boss?"

"He's not my boss... right now."

"You've fallen for *him*!" The beaming smile was evident in her voice.

"Yes! Can you see my problem now?" She waved her arms for emphasis.

Emma frowned. "Not really. I mean, you're black ops. *You* can't have a serious relationship. *He* can't have a serious relationship. It's not like anyone would have to know if something *just happened*."

Sophia sprang to sit up, kicking at the sheets. "I don't really agree with that, but it's not the point. I see the way other women look at him, and I *hate* it. I nearly lost it in the gym today all because some pretty girl had the guts to approach him—"

Emma shrugged with a mouthful of chocolate. "You should *approach* him."

"I don't want to just approach him!" she shouted. "I don't want to be just another one in the long line of women throwing themselves at him. I don't want to be just another one of his guards. I want..."

She couldn't say it. How could she even think about it? She wanted to be his *only one*. She wanted to drive him crazy, she didn't want to hide being with him, and when women ogled, she wanted to kiss him so they knew not to try.

She fell back onto her pillow and covered her eyes. "I've lost my mind. Tell me what I should do?"

Emma chuckled before popping another chocolate in her mouth. "You're normally the one to give me advice like this. What would you tell me?"

"That you're crazy. That there are plenty of other guys, so you should avoid becoming a pathetic cliché."

"Hey!" Emma said with feigned offense.

"I'm fighting for him to be my boss again, Emma. *My boss!* I need to get it together. With Layla still captive. Horacio in the hospital, and the disciplinary panel, he needs me right now. I can't fall apart over a stupid crush."

Emma pursed her lips and stared distantly at her shelf of books. "That's decent advice, I guess. I'd only add one more thing."

"What's that?"

"Don't be an idiot."

Sophia nodded. "Right. I just need to compose myself, go down there, and apologize—"

"No. Sophia, I've known you a long time. This feeling you're feeling? It's jealousy, and you're not a jealous person. You've never been this crazy about anyone. Don't let it pass you by unless you're sure you'd be able to find something like it again."

"This isn't just complicated. It can't happen."

"For now." Emma winked. "I gotta run. But I know you'll do the right thing."

Sophia rolled her eyes as the door shut.

For now...

The only way it wouldn't be against the rules is if they both got out of black ops and he wasn't her boss anymore. They'd both have to choose it—choose each other. Impossible.

But she still wanted it.

CHAPTER 16

Something thudded in the dark, and Niko jolted upright in his bed. He squinted around the familiar shadows of the contemporary, blackwood furniture in his bedroom, listening. Outside the window, everything was quiet. The moon cast a blue light over the white marble parkway below, and even at night, he could see the new dark splotches of blooming red magnolias along the vines.

He checked the clock on his implant: 2:02 AM. It was possible the noise had come from the hallway outside his apartment, but it sounded closer.

A faint sound, almost like shuffling, came from outside his closed bedroom door. He slipped from the bed and moved stealthily to the wall. The shuffling could have come from anything. It could have been from multiple intruders, but it seemed to be coming from his kitchen.

The second he opened the bedroom door, whoever was here would know he was awake. A swift, strong response was probably best. He rubbed his bare arms and neck to fully wake up.

Three, two, one.

He exploded into his living area, gaze set in the direction of the kitchen.

A short and slight silhouette, bald head, robes—he didn't even startle.

"Royce," he growled, bending over and putting his hands on his knees. "That's a really good way to get yourself killed."

"I'm sorry, but what I have couldn't wait," Royce said, sinking into one of Niko's two chairs at the breakfast table.

No eccentric greeting, no sense that he found humor in everything. He wanted to ask how Royce had gotten into his apartment in the first place, but it seemed like he wanted to get right to the point.

Niko took the chair next to him.

"How's your injured guard?" Royce folded his hands on the table.

Niko shrugged. "He's got a long road ahead of him, but he's healing well."

"I'm glad to hear it." Royce's gaze slid to the corner, distant.

He raised an eyebrow. "You didn't come here at 2:00 a.m. to ask me about Horacio. What's going on?"

Royce sighed. "It seems your bait worked with Captain Cipriani. You certainly got under his skin. He's been talking about you and another guard all night."

Sophia.

What had happened with her today? One minute, it had just been them—happy. And the next, she'd stormed away. He knew jealousy, and as much as he'd wanted to believe it had been that, he'd never been able to read her well.

Whatever it was, it had completely ruined any enjoyment he could have gleaned from the devastated rejection on Anton's face when she shot him down.

"What did you find?" he asked.

"Well, our friend loves to talk. I'll give him that." Royce adjusted his robes. "I had a glimpse from something he'd said about one of his previous missions. They'd consulted me about it years ago, but I remembered that it had been called off for high Tavian activity in the area. It didn't make sense. They were set up in a way that suggested they knew exactly how the unit would be entering the operation."

He leaned back in his chair. That sounded a lot like his own mission. The Tavians had to have been expecting them.

Royce trailed his finger along the grain of the wood table. "I believe the Tavians have access to Captain Cipriani's messages. There's been a number of instances that have suggested a pattern."

Niko had to snap his jaw shut.

"I'm not sure how they've gotten them—they could have found a way to hack his implant, I suppose. He could be passing information to them. Either way… this is catastrophic."

Catastrophic was right. He didn't think much of Anton, but this? Horacio, Layla, even McCade's injuries might have been preventable. This whole thing could have been avoided if Anton hadn't run his mouth.

He forced a rumbling breath from his chest. "Promise me I get to kill him after this."

Royce winced. "That's the other part of this."

"He pays for this, Royce," Niko said, his strained words low and raspy. "Any plan we have ends with that, understand?"

Royce pursed his lips. "I think that will happen. The main problem is the Magnolia Festival ends in two days. If we want to demand Layla's immediate release at the summit, we'll need proof of Tavian wrongdoing by then. Edwin, our cyber-engineering friend, thinks he might be able to get the evidence we need from a Tavian implant if he gets close enough, but he's not a guard. He can't walk into a Tavian hot zone without an escort."

Niko leaped from his chair. "No problems there. Just let me get dressed."

Royce held out his hands. "It's not quite that simple. Ichiro has authorized Captain Cipriani to track you. If he had reason to believe you were returning to the scene, he would most certainly message about it, and if I'm right, that message would land in the hands of the Tavians."

"Great. We can draw them out." Niko ducked into his room to grab a shirt.

"He can track you, Niko, and he has his sniper certification, but never mind that." Royce waved a hand. "We're essentially betting that he'll message about where you're headed and that he's concerned that you'll find something to exonerate yourself. We *want* that information to fall into the hands of the Tavians. They have to come looking for you if we want this to work, and I dare say they won't be happy to see you."

A weight came crashing down over him. "I'm not an escort. I'm bait."

Royce's thin eyebrows pulled together. "I'm so sorry. I can only give the information that I See. I wanted to give you the choice. I wish there was more time, but I've looked over everything I can find. We likely won't have another option before the summit with the Tavians."

Niko nodded absently, reality setting in. He glanced around the bare, white walls of his apartment. He'd never bothered to decorate because he'd always thought he'd have time to do it later. This was one of those missions where he wasn't sure he'd have the time anymore.

"The choice is yours. I can bring the evidence up through the normal Seer channels, but it will take some time to investigate. I'm positive nothing would be resolved before the summit."

Niko's gaze darted to him. "I don't want Layla in Tavian custody for a second longer than she has to be, and I've been on dangerous missions before." He sighed, rubbing his forehead. "I'll need a day to plan. The closing ceremony would probably be the best time to go. It will look like I'm trying to slip out without anyone noticing."

"That's a sound plan," Royce said with a somber smile. "I should get back to the compound before they figure out I'm missing, but please don't hesitate to come find me if you need anything."

He nodded as Royce slipped out of the room, gaze still fixed on the wall above his couch. So empty. Why hadn't he ever filled it? He could have easily found a painting or something from a mission, maybe even a flag. But he hadn't. His job took so much of his time, and he loved it, but suddenly he was left thinking about all the things he'd put off, and now might never happen.

McCade had told him that he hoped Niko would someday understand why he'd chosen to leave. It was 2 AM on the eve of an impossible mission, but there wasn't a doubt he understood now.

Visions of a life he might never have flashed before his eyes. He'd only been in Sophia's room a couple times to wake her up, but she'd had books and paintings. Pictures and purple sheets. He would have loved to bring her here, meld their lives together and see what this space would have looked like once it was *theirs*.

He stood up, locking his fingers behind his head, and strolled to the window.

A future I might never have...

Even if he stayed and could somehow convince her to take a chance on him, he was still under investigation. Without this mission, he could be handed over for exile. They'd try to take his memories, and he'd rather die than forget her.

He'd go on this mission. He'd get Layla back, and he'd help prove the Tavians were guilty of a major violation of the treaty. The unit would be exonerated. Nios would be safer. Maybe it would even stop the ambushes. Everyone would be better off...

He glanced back at the white wall. Everyone except him.

∽

THE NEXT MORNING, Niko sat at his desk and pulled up the ice-blue holographic map, then rotated it with the tips of his fingers to see the terrain better. He needed to find a cliff or rock formation close enough to the rebel camp where Edwin could hide.

The door to the outer office opened, and moments later, Sophia peeked in. "There you are. I just came from visiting Horacio."

Horacio. He'd need to visit him before he left. "How's he doing?"

She let out a small laugh. "He's going a little stir crazy in that medical facility room, but Genevieve hasn't left his side so it can't be all bad. Doctors are happy with his progress. They say they might be able to start thinking about discharging him soon." She squinted at the map. "Is that the Santa Rita rebel camp?"

"Yes." Niko said. Of course she'd remember.

She pulled the other chair closer to the desk and tilted her head. "What are you looking for?"

He sighed. "I've been looking for a place where I could hide someone."

She frowned but never took her gaze off the map. "Full concealment or cover for a sniper's nest?"

He hid a smile. Very few people would know to ask that. Could she be any more perfect? "Concealment. He won't need a vantage point at all."

A few moments later, she pointed. "What about that draw?"

Niko zoomed in on what appeared to be a dried-up creek bed.

"See that section right there?" she asked. "The steep ridges on either side would make it hard to see anything below, and it's pretty rocky, which could provide cover if they came under fire. The Tavians would probably have to go down there to actually find someone. The only downside is they may not be able to get out fast if they go dark on their implant."

He shrugged. "He can just teleport out as soon as he gets what he needs."

"That close to the rebel camp?" Her gaze darted from the map to him. "Teleportation would leave the rest of the unit vulnerable."

He sighed. There would never be a good time to tell her the truth. She wouldn't like it, but he'd warned her at the bell tower. He'd fight this until the very end, but he would not take her down with him. He turned off the map. "No unit. It's not even a mission. *We've* been ordered to stand down."

Her eyes narrowed. "Then what's all this about?"

"I need to get a cyber engineer close enough to get some evidence from Tavian implants."

"No mission."

He shook his head.

"Does Leadership even know?"

"Not yet," he said.

The green flecks in her eyes started to spark. "Just you and a cyber engineer? That's too dangerous."

"Agreed," he replied. "That's why no one else can come along."

Her features hardened, and he swallowed hard. She was always a little scary when she got angry—and really scary when she knew she was right.

"What's going on?" she asked, her voice sharp.

He sighed. "I've been talking to Royce."

"The Seer?" She leaned forward.

"It seems Anton likes to discuss missions on the ancillary messaging system, and those messages might have landed in the hands of the Tavians. It would be a major offense, one that would require serious reparations from the Tavians. We could probably get Layla back immediately." He allowed his gaze to settle on her, features tight. "But we'd have to prove it."

"And you think the best way to do that is to walk right up to a rebel camp without Guthrie and me?"

He tilted his head. "It's not ideal—"

"It's insane."

He raised an eyebrow at her. "There's no other option. We need the proof before we go to the summit. Anton is apparently tracking me now, so I have to be the one that goes. He'd know when I left and since I'd really be disobeying an order this time, he'd likely message about it—which is what would draw out the Tavians. This is the only way."

"I want Layla back as much as you do, and I would *love* to take Anton down for something this awful, but this isn't the way. You could be *killed*," she said, raising her voice.

"We could always die on mission. That's part of the job." He gritted his teeth as the tension grew. She didn't have to like it, but it wasn't her choice. He was going.

"This is different, and you know it." Her eyebrows pulled together. "Why not bring Guthrie and me? We can back you up—"

"No. It's too dangerous."

She flailed her arms. "We're black ops! Our entire job is dangerous."

"Sophia, we've talked about this. I told you I'd fight until the end. This is the end," he said, trying to keep calm. She wasn't going to change his mind. "Bringing two more guards won't make this any safer. It will only put you two in danger. I won't do that. Horacio was injured and Layla captured *on my watch*. I can fix this, and no one else will get hurt."

"You won't even—"

"No."

"Let's talk it out. We can look for other options. We can help!"

"Leadership's orders were clear." His muscles tightened.

She pleaded, "If you'd just listen—"

"No!" his voice boomed, and the light left her eyes. "If I wait any longer, I could miss my chance. The disciplinary panel could hand me over for prosecution. This is something I can do, and only one of us needs to go."

The office was suddenly deathly silent. It took everything he had to keep his voice strong as she iced over. Her eyes were harder than he'd ever seen them. She wouldn't even look at him.

"I swore to myself I'd do everything in my power to keep the unit safe. Please understand that—"

"No!" She leaped from her chair. "Guthrie and I are part of the unit, too. We want to fight with you."

"I'm just trying to do what I think is right—"

"You're wrong," she said, her disapproval ringing heavy. "So, you can run off on this insane operation by yourself, but I don't have to understand or respect it."

She stormed out of the office and slammed the door, leaving a bitter silence behind her.

CHAPTER 17

*S*ophia stared at the ceiling above her bed while Emma curled up in the high-backed velvet chair next to her, sipping her tea. "I cannot believe the Magnolia Festival will be over tomorrow. I'm not ready to go back to work."

Sophia nodded.

If there will be anything for me to return to...

Horacio was still in the hospital. Layla... and now Niko. She stretched her neck, trying to relax. It was getting dark now. It had been hours since she'd left the office. Niko could already be gone. He could be dying alone because he didn't think it was worthwhile to bring them along.

He could already be dead...

"Are you sure you're okay?" Emma asked in her high, concerned voice. "I know I've asked a couple of times, but whatever it is, you can talk about it with me. Was it Anton?"

"No!" she accidently shouted her response. "Actually, kind of. I swear he *ruins* everything."

Emma arched her slender eyebrows.

"I know that didn't make sense." She shook her head. "Just trust me when I say he's a real—"

Someone knocked on the door.

Frowning, Emma set her tea down and answered it.

"Hey, is Sophia here?" Niko asked.

She jolted upright. With how they'd ended things, and what he was about to do, she never thought she'd see him again. But maybe he'd changed his mind—he better have changed his mind.

"Umm." Emma spun so fast, her blond ponytail could have hit him in the face.

She took a calming breath. "I'm here," she said in a tone she hoped would convey he was on thin ice.

"I'm just going to…" Emma pointed at the door, scooting one way, then the other, trying to get around Niko's massive frame. "I'm just going to go grab a bite to eat in the cafeteria."

Sophia folded her arms. "It's 7:30. The cafeteria's closed."

Emma's brown eyes flashed. "Then it'll take me a lot longer to find something to eat. Excuse me." She slid past him, and moments later the hall flashed blue as she teleported away.

Sophia's gaze slid to Niko, still waiting in the hallway, deep-brown eyes soft, broken.

Be strong.

"Have you changed your mind?" she asked as evenly as she could.

His shoulders rose with a deep, somber breath. "No."

"Then there's nothing more to say." She reached for the door.

"No. Wait. Please, Sophia," he begged. "I can't leave things like this with you."

"You don't have to," she replied, her voice twisting. "Why are you doing this?"

He inched closer. "May I come in?"

She backed out of the way.

He shut the door behind himself. Not an ounce of the anger from earlier remained in his features. "I know you don't understand—"

She scoffed, a lump forming in her throat. "You're right about that. I don't understand this."

"It's something I have to do."

"I disagree, but you made that part clear."

He stared at his hands. "I didn't come here for this—" He took a step closer, and her heart flopped. "I…"

A moment passed. She could barely breathe. Standing before her was one of the best men she'd ever known. Her fingers ached to touch him, and her gaze was riveted to the curve of his lips. She wanted him to wrap his arms around her, to be held by him. Everything inside her demanded this moment be a beginning—even if it was really the end.

He glanced at the door, backing away.

This might be the last time I see him…

She grabbed his arm. He stopped and turned back to her.

"Help me understand, Niko," she said, her throat tightening. His gaze swept the ceiling. "Because right now, it feels like you're giving up, like you're walking away from me, and I can't stop it. I won't be able to help you."

"I'm not walking away from you." His voice low and tender.

She inched closer. "Please."

His gaze met hers, fierce, intense.

She didn't look away.

His arms closed around her, and he swept her up, pulling her to his lips. Smooth. Strong. But with a gentleness she'd known was there. His warmth surrounded her, and she pressed deeper into the kiss. How had she lived without this for so long? She never wanted to pull away.

His arms fell. "I'm sorry. I shouldn't have done that."

Keeping his gaze, she trailed her fingertips along his jaw. "I'm so glad you did."

She leaned in and pressed her lips to his, savoring his sandalwood scent. His arms tightened around the small of her back, and then his hand trailed upward, leaving a tingling path in its wake.

He ran a hand through her curls and pressed his forehead against hers. "Understand now?"

She wanted to shake her head and argue, but she wasn't willing to move an inch.

He reached behind his back and pulled something from his back pocket, then offered it to her. A royal-blue, leather-bound book.

A fairytale.

She gasped as she traced the gold-embossed rose on the cover. They'd talked about her fairytales in the bell tower. He'd remembered.

"I saw your bookshelf when I, um..." He sniffed. "When I came to pick you up for workouts."

She arched an eyebrow. That was one way to put it.

"Anyway, I wasn't sure which ones you had, but I was pretty sure I hadn't seen a blue one so..."

It wouldn't have mattered if she'd already had ten more just like it. This one was from him. She held it to her chest. "It's perfect, Niko."

He pressed his lips together in a faint smile and took a step backward—toward the door.

She grabbed his wrist. "Don't go. Please. We can figure this out together." She bit her lip, searching his soft eyes. "Stay here... with me."

He curled an arm around her, shutting his eyes. "You don't know how badly I want that. I've thought about it a million times, but there's no future for me here unless I fix this. Ichiro has already granted Anton the power to track me. In his mind, I'm guilty. I could be exiled, and I'd rather die than lose my memories."

He was being literal.

"Then, let me come with you. I can't lose you now."

"Nios will be a safer place with this mission." He brushed a curl away from her face. "Layla needs it, too, but the chances of surviving against a den of angry rebels and a platoon of Tavian guards aren't good, and you two wouldn't change that. I've made peace with it, but I couldn't do it unless I knew you'd be safe, that you could be happy someday." He looked deep into her eyes. "This might be it for me—"

"No." She shook her head and rested her forehead on his chest, his warmth, a harsh and temporary comfort. "I refuse to believe that. There has to be another way—"

"But this doesn't have to be the end for you," he continued with a slight quiver in his voice. "Go. Find your fairytale, Sophia—just not Anton, okay? I don't think I could handle that."

She wrapped her arms around him tighter, pressing her fingers into the firm muscles along his back, and fought a shudder. Anton wasn't even in the same realm as Niko. She wasn't sure anyone could compare.

He kissed the top of her head and ran a hand through her curls. "I should go."

She clamped her arms tighter. "No. Niko, don't do this."

He pulled away easily. "I have to. It's the only way."

"Stay." She reached for his wrist. "We can figure this out."

He twisted his hand in hers and brought her fingers to his lips, kissing them gently. "It's been an honor to serve with you. Goodbye, Sophia."

He strode for the door and was gone before she could say or do anything else. It felt like her heart had been ripped from her body. She dropped into her bed as the tears fell.

He was gone.

She hadn't been able to tell him how he was her last thought at night and first thought in the morning. How she loved the way she could see his thoughts in his eyes before he ever said a word and the way the tips of his tattoos stuck out from his neckline. He'd made her better, and he'd given her a reason to fight.

He *was* her fairytale.

THE NEXT MORNING, Sophia yawned as she trudged to the cafeteria. It had always bothered her that the Level-1 floors of the barracks didn't have kitchens, but she really hated it right now. She didn't want to be around anyone.

She got her usual breakfast of oatmeal, almonds, and berries, then found a table in the far corner where few people would see her.

"Hello," a sunny voice said from behind her. "Mind if I sit with you?"

Her eyes fell shut. Today, of all days, someone wanted to make friends. "I'm kind of in a hurry today. I probably won't be much company."

"That's okay." The old man in white robes slipped into the seat next to her with his tray of syrupy pancakes. The Seer. "I don't get many chances to chat with anyone, so I assure you this will be the highlight of my day. I'm Royce, by the way."

"I know who you are..." She flipped around, searching for a guard detail, but there was no one there. "Aren't you supposed to be under heavy security at all times?"

"I think the council prefers it that way—the minister definitely does. Most of the time, I try to oblige them." He shrugged. "But very few people come to visit me. The last was your colleague, Lieutenant Kalos."

Yes, about that...

She shut her eyes, forcing herself to remain calm. Niko had gone in search of Royce. It was the Seer's job to give information. She couldn't be mad that he'd made the connections they couldn't make on their own—even if it had been in the eleventh hour. But none of that changed the fact that she wished Niko had never gone to him in the first place. This might have been a very different morning if he hadn't.

He inclined his head toward her. "I remember you from the hearing."

She nodded absently. Not one of her fondest memories.

"You care for him."

She dropped her spoon and glared at him. Whether she did or not, it wasn't as if that would compute into his calculations of the situation.

"I'm sorry. I don't mean to pry."

"It's irrelevant," she replied icily. "He's out on mission now, by himself."

"I see." Royce frowned. "He must care a great deal about you, too, then."

She gritted her teeth. Leaving on a suicide mission by himself because he didn't want anyone else hurt wasn't a good excuse when Niko had used it, and she certainly didn't want to hear it from Royce. She sprang from her seat and snatched up her tray. "I don't think I'm all that hungry. Excuse me."

"You didn't know he cares for you?" He blinked his big brown eyes. "I thought it was obvious to everyone."

Her fingers tightened around the tray until it warped in her hands. "Why does it matter? He left on the mission *you* sent him on with no back up. We all know what that means."

Royce tilted his head with a gleam in his eye that made her want to throw her oatmeal against the wall. "But you know where he's going. Who's to say backup couldn't respond anyway?"

"*He did!*" she hissed. "He insisted on doing this alone."

He leaned forward with a sharp gaze. "I gave him the information he needed, just as I always do. And as usual, I anticipated how he'd interpret that information. It's not my place to interfere with how he chooses to execute the operation—even if I disagree—but that's what has brought me to you. Why are you still here?"

Her mouth dropped open. "I... Weren't you listening?'

"I watched you two at the hearing. Your concern, even then, was evident. And he yielded to you there, because he trusted your judgment about the situation."

"What good does it do to talk about that now?" she shouted.

"He trusts *your* judgment. And now you have actionable intelligence from the Head Seer that a Niotian guard is in imminent danger. If you want to save him, you won't have time to seek Leadership approval, but I'd say a rescue mission is in order."

Rescue mission...

"He made his choice. It's time for you to make yours."

Royce hadn't opened a door. In terms of justification, an urgent rescue mission was barely a cracked window. But for Niko, she'd take it.

"I have to go."

Royce grinned, his eyes crinkling. "I was hoping you'd say that."

She dumped the rest of her oatmeal and rushed to Guthrie's apartment on the Level-3 floor.

"Sophia," he said, answering the door without his shirt on.

"Get dressed," she said. "We have a mission."

CHAPTER 18

*I*t was 7:00 a.m. when Niko leaned on one of the Niotian marble pillars, scanning the main square. Red streamers and banners rippled in the breeze, and even though the magnolias had just started to bloom, their scent was heavy in the air.

He was supposed to be looking for Edwin—old, gray-haired Edwin—but his eye was drawn to every brunette in sight as the final preparations were being made for the closing ceremony.

He could live in that kiss with Sophia, he was happy that he'd been able to make her smile one last time with the book, but it had only made his misery worse. The way she'd asked him to stay with her, if there was any way, he would have. As it was, he'd probably never see her again.

He thumped the back of his head against the pillar. He couldn't go into this mission distracted. Right now, his focus should be on finding Edwin, who should have been here by now. None of this would work without him, but what would happen if he didn't show? Maybe if Niko went by himself, Royce could still somehow get the data he needed from Anton's implant. It wouldn't be the same as evidence directly from a Tavian, but if anyone could figure it out, it would be Royce.

Just off the stairs to headquarters, a flurry of motion caught his eye— Edwin waving both arms as if he was trying to get the attention of everyone in the square. A sigh rumbled from Niko's chest. At least they could get going.

"Do you have everything you need?" he muttered as Edwin got close enough.

"Yes, I think so. You said to make sure I had good hiking boots with ankle support. My partner wanted to make sure I had the best, so I think she went to every shoe shop in Nios." Edwin shrugged. "She's a little slow, nowadays."

That made sense. Edwin seemed seventy, maybe?

"She's due any day."

"Due?" Niko's eyebrows shot as high as they could go. "As in a child?"

"Yes!" Edwin grinned widely. "We're naming her after my mother, Leonora."

Edwin was about to have a child—even in their scientific society, that seemed rare. At twenty-seven, Niko had always thought he could have kids later, but he didn't mean *that late*. He would have really liked being a father—yet another thing he might never be able to do.

He stared at Edwin blankly for a moment before shaking off the mess of emotions. This mission was really messing with his head, but he needed to focus. "Let's go, so you can get back to your partner and baby."

They strode into headquarters and down one of the staircases toward the armory. "I'm almost positive the armory is closed for the ceremony, but as an L-5, I should still be able to get in and get to the launch room. That doesn't mean we can take our time. There are people who don't want us leaving," he said so low that only Edwin could hear.

Edwin nodded, his face paling.

"We'll be teleporting into a reserve section of the jungle. The Tavians may be able to detect our teleportation signature, but they'll have to move carefully to avoid the attention of the wardens. The rebels will refuse to go in there at all. We can use that to our advantage and hopefully evade them long enough to hide you."

"Sounds like a... wise plan," Edwin said, wringing his hands.

They rounded the corner of the white-brick hallway, and Niko stopped, turning to him. "I know you're nervous, but this is what I do. I will keep you safe. Just get whatever you need and teleport out. Getting that evidence to Royce is the most important thing."

Edwin's head bobbed. "I can do that. It shouldn't be too hard to retrieve it as long as they get close enough."

Niko placed a hand on his shoulder. "I'll make sure they do."

They continued on to the unmarked steel door at the end of the hall. Once Niko was in range of the door, the lock remotely released with a pressurized hiss.

Just as soon as they slipped inside, the door clanged shut behind them, and a heavy silence remained.

"Go stand over there." Niko pointed before rushing through the aisles of weapons and tactical instruments. He harnessed one pulse gun in his thigh holster and another in his vest. A rifle would have been great, but it was just the bare essentials for this trip.

Next, he fastened a belt of targeted explosives around his waist. Once activated, those blue-topaz marbles would detonate when a Tavian implant got within its range, yet they were stable enough to be crushed by a tank without a spark.

Finally he came to the bins of steel discs—beacons and scramblers. He took every single one he could fit in his vest and cargo pockets. Not much bigger than his fist, these little steel discs could confuse even the most skilled trackers by transmitting implant signatures and hiding which signals were human and which were inanimate objects like bombs or drones. He'd need all the confusion he could get today.

On the way back to Edwin, he grabbed the nasal antidote applicators and the provision pills—not great for long-term use, but the pills would give them all the hydration and calories they'd need on this mission. Actual food and water would be too heavy.

"Stick this in your nose and push the button at the bottom," he said.

"Why? What will this do?" Edwin asked, eying the tiny canister.

"This part of the world has everything from poisonous snakes and spiders to rabid bats," he replied, shooting his own antidotes up his nose and inhaling deeply. "These are the antidotes and vaccines you will be very happy to have if you need them."

"Right." Edwin scooped up the applicator and used it.

Niko shifted his shoulders against all the new weight in his tactical vest. "Since you can't turn off your implant, you'll need to be ready to scramble your signature the moment you arrive."

Edwin nodded. "I've already automated scrambling and pinging. As soon as a Tavian gets close enough, the download will begin."

"And you have the coordinates to get back?" Niko asked.

Edwin's head jittered up and down, the silence setting in again.

That was it. Everything was ready—as ready as it could be, anyway.

"Let's go."

They stepped into the launch room and pulled up the coordinates. As the static skittered up his arms, he glanced at the door one last time.

Be safe, Sophia. Be happy.

The heat and humidity pressed in on him even before he could open his eyes after the flash. Thick woody vines hung from ancient trees. A red parrot screeched as it flew overhead. The earthy smells of rain and soil mixed with the acidic smell of some animal's urine—probably a whole pack, from the smell of it.

"Oh my..." Edwin nearly fell over, bending back to see the treetops. "This is truly remarkable."

"We'll have to sightsee some other time," Niko muttered, changing his vision to binocular view from his implant. "From now on, we'll have to keep speaking to a minimum. Try to follow my path exactly. Don't bend or break too many branches, and if you can walk on rocks instead of mud, you should do it."

Niko spun, and while there was plenty of movement around them, he didn't see a single human form. He pulled up the map and searched it for the telltale glowing red dots of Tavian implant signatures. Nothing in the immediate area, although he could see quite a few a couple of miles away. They weren't even trying to hide anymore. Certainly brazen, but it was the best situation he'd probably get.

"We'll need to move fast," he whispered, stepping over a mammoth tree root, and then turned to help Edwin over it. "This creek down here dries up about a mile south of here. We're going to follow it for as long as we can, but be ready to hide at any moment."

He activated a beacon and tossed it behind them toward the ridgeline. The Tavians would already know someone had teleported in, and that person would likely either take the creek bed or the ridgeline—Niko would obscure both paths.

They reached the silty creek bed, and he lobbed two targeted explosives back in the direction they'd come. If they detonated, they'd know they were being followed.

The trek was slow but steady. He used the breaks he'd given Edwin to plant scramblers, beacons, and the occasional explosives along the ridgeline, the creek, and everywhere in between. His map now glowed white with the marks of all the beacons he'd placed, but nothing else had come into view.

Just before the border of the reserve, the sound of engines droned in the distance. Niko held out a hand to stop Edwin, who was now drenched in sweat and limp as a noodle.

They backed into the tree line, and he switched into binocular mode again. There weren't any roads for miles, but the engines sounded big like trucks.

They're using the creek bed.

His hand flew to his pocket, and he launched a handful of beacons and scramblers in every direction to give them as much cover as possible.

"Good news," he said. "You don't have to walk any farther. I think the Tavians are coming to you." He scanned the slope, pulling Edwin behind him. Finally, he spotted a large boulder with a crack running down its center.

Voices yelled in the distance.

"We need to hurry," he whispered.

"I know." Edwin's voice quivered. "The program has already started to download. They must be close."

Niko heaved him up on his shoulder and rushed toward the boulder. Just five hundred more feet, then Edwin would be concealed, and he could take up a defensive position.

Footsteps—too many to count—rustled through the underbrush in the distance. They were closing in.

He all but hurled Edwin into the crack, hoping there wasn't a jaguar inside, but it would still have been far preferable to the Tavians seeing him. "Get as far back in that crevice as you can, and don't come out for anything. They won't be able to get a clean shot on you back there, and at this point, their maps should be glowing white with all the beacons and scramblers. Get what you need and get out."

Edwin nodded, eyes wide, and scooted farther and farther back.

Niko sprinted for the ridgeline above, launching the rest of the beacons, scramblers, and targeted explosives he had. A knotted mess of roots rose just high enough to provide the kind of cover he was looking for. He paused only for a moment to make sure he wasn't diving into an ant mound and slid underneath it, sinking into the dead leaves and debris as an old pickup truck loaded with people wielding assault rifles bobbed its way up the creek bed.

He pulled up the map on his implant, and sure enough along the white network of beacons and scramblers were the red dots of Tavians, fanning out and flanking their position.

Niko drew his gun and pointed it out from his hiding spot in the roots.

Hurry up, Edwin.

CHAPTER 19

"*Y*ou're sure you can get us in?" Sophia asked Guthrie as they strode down the hall toward the armory.

"Yes." Guthrie chuckled. "I've been a sniper for a long time. With all the offices closed, this is actually one of those times where they'd expect us to get some target practice in, but since the ceremony is about to start, it'll probably be just us."

She still cringed as they neared the door. There was no backup plan. Wandering into a Tavian hot zone without weapons wouldn't work. When it unlocked, she released a breath.

Waggling his eyebrows, he made a show of opening the door.

She pursed her lips, trying not to smile as she passed him. "I owe you big."

"Oh, can I ask a favor, then?" Her gaze slid from the row of pulse guns back to him. His blue eyes were too bright. Something was up. "Introduce me to your roommate?"

She rolled her eyes and laughed. "She may be pretty, but she'd eat you alive."

"I'll be on my best behavior. Promise."

"Fine." She grabbed a pulse gun. "But just an introduction. After that, I'm staying out of it."

He nodded and disappeared into another aisle.

"When Niko was looking at the map, he'd been focusing on a creek bed that runs to the north and west of the rebel camp," she said loud enough for him to hear.

"He would have teleported into the reserve," Guthrie called from the next aisle over.

She paused to strap the pulse gun into her thigh holster, and then rushed to the belts of targeted explosives. "That makes sense, but how can you be so sure?"

"Really?" He peeked his head around the corner with a rifle slung over his shoulder. "This is my third time prepping for this mission. In the initial briefings, he'd said we should teleport into the reserve to exploit the tension between the rebels and the reserve wardens."

"Sounds like a great plan." She zipped up her tactical vest. "Do you have everything you need?"

He frowned. "Now that you mention it..." He wandered away, and she followed three aisles over.

"We might need these." He grabbed two machetes and handed her one before strapping the second to his belt. "And don't forget a med kit. There was this one reconnaissance mission, Horacio got bitten by this spider and his whole hand swelled up even with the nasal antidotes..." He splayed his fingers six inches apart. "About this big! And the pus!"

She writhed. "Okay! Let's just grab the antidote applicators and a med kit and go."

They used the applicators, and then she yanked a kit off the wall and chased after Guthrie into the launch room. Moments later, a hot wave of humidity rolled over her, and the ammonia smell made her eyes pop. A deafening guttural noise from the west had her backing into a tree.

"What was that?" she mouthed to Guthrie.

He pointed to the canopy. "Howler monkeys. Don't worry. They're really loud, but they're not aggressive. Probably just didn't like the flash."

She swallowed, trying to slow her heart rate. "I'll pull up the map if you sweep the area."

"Already on it," he said, slowly spinning. "I found your howler monkeys. Plenty of thermal signatures in the canopy over there." He shrugged. "They're really pretty cute."

"Guthrie." She glared. "Less monkeys and more about Tavians, please."

"All right, all right," he said, spinning again. "I'm not picking up anything big enough to be human on the ground."

"Okay." She pulled up the map and selected the option to project it in front of her. With any luck they'd see Niko's little white dot close by.

The icy-blue map flickered to life in front of them, and there was white glowing, all right. An indistinguishable mass of white—at least a square mile in size—hovered over everything to the south of them.

Guthrie's mouth dropped open. "How many beacons did he take?"

Sophia rubbed her forehead. Searching a square mile of jungle terrain could take days.

Guthrie shifted the map with his finger. "We got company."

Ringing the southern edge of the white blob were red Tavian signatures.

"What do we do?" she asked. "Should we start picking off Tavians or just try to hurry and find Niko?"

Guthrie scratched his head. "That's... I mean, if the Tavians are here, the rebels probably are, too. The only way we'd be able to see them is to wade right in to this mess and check for thermal signatures. Whatever we do, we're fighting blind."

"Well, we won't get anywhere by just sitting here. We can cover ground faster along the creek bed, so my vote—"

She caught the distinct flash of blue lightning in the distance followed by the sharp crackle moments later.

Guthrie jolted. "Did you see that?"

Sophia scoured the map for a new dot. "Look!" She pointed to the east of them. "Right there. It's white—Niotian."

The dot started moving right away toward the glowing white mass. No hesitation, very little variation in the path.

She frowned. "Who would rush into a mess like that without pausing to check the situation?"

Anton.

Her head dropped. It didn't matter how many beacons and scramblers Niko had used. He'd said Anton had been authorized to track his signature. "It's Anton."

"Cipriani?" Guthrie asked. "Nah. He wouldn't leave the safety of Nios, not without backup anyway."

"Trust me." She turned off the map. "He doesn't want anyone here to witness what he's about to do. We have to intercept him before it's too late."

And turnabout was fair play. She raced through the menu options. Tracking someone's implant in Nios without authorization was a violation of their right to privacy, but they weren't in Nios right now, were they? If she could analyze his signature in time, she'd be able to track him just like he was tracking Niko. The scramblers wouldn't hide him. Seconds passed.

C'mon, c'mon, c'mon!

Finally, just before he hit the edges of the white blob, Anton's dot blinked green.

"Got him!" She pumped her fist. "I think he'll lead us right to Niko."

"Nice," Guthrie said, grinning. He turned to face the creek bed. "All right. Should we do this?"

"Definitely."

They rushed into the white zone on the map, keeping their ears piqued for any sounds, but the jungle was a noisy place, even when the howler monkeys were quiet. Insects croaked, birds squawked, and rodents scurried through the dead leaves—at least she hoped they were just rodents.

Twenty minutes later, they were about halfway through Niko's web of beacons. She had to continually wipe the sweat from her face and neck, but everything from her hair to her clothes—even the air—stuck to her.

Something shifted on the western slope. They froze.

Another sound, rhythmic.

Hurried steps.

They dove into the protection of the trees along the bank. She drew her gun, pulling up her thermal vision and searched in the direction of the noise.

"Do you see anything?" Guthrie whispered.

She squinted, trying to see the subtle color and shape changes. "It's hard to tell when it's this hot."

"I tried binocular view, but maybe I'd have more luck with the scope on my rifle." He shifted to pull the rifle forward.

A pulse shot whizzed overhead and smashed into the wide trunk of a nearby tree.

She shot back with a volley of suppressive fire.

Three more pulse shots—all progressively closer—exploded into nearby trees.

"Do you see them?" she hissed.

"No!" he whispered back. "But they must have eyes on us. Let's get out of here."

They crawled up and around a wide tree and then clambered to the next. Pulling up the map, she followed him as they dove from tree to tree, gaining distance. Nothing but white. Anton's green dot was still ahead of them. The red dots were still along the ridge above.

"Nothing on the map," she called in a hushed tone. "It's either a Tavian who went dark or a rebel."

"The rebels haven't been the most skilled of fighters. Most of them are loud and horrible shots. I'll put my money on the Tavians." Guthrie peered out from behind his tree, but no other pulse shots came. "And if it is them, we should be careful. They might be trying to flush us toward a trap."

"I agree, but what should we do?" she asked. "It's not like we can stay—"

An explosion erupted from behind them, blowing leaves and debris past their trees.

Guthrie beamed. "Targeted explosive. I was right. It was a Tavian. Remind me to thank Niko for preparing the field."

She nodded, reaching into her own belt and launching the explosives in a rough line up and down the slope. They had enough to worry about in front of them without having to worry about Tavians from behind.

They climbed through the vines and roots as quickly and quietly as possible, creeping ever closer to Anton's green dot. In the distance, voices shouted and engines revved—the rebels. The red dots on the map never moved. She could only hope that meant they were content to let the rebels search the area.

They were nearly at the end of Niko's beacons when Anton's dot stopped. The rebels were close enough for her to smell the diesel exhaust from their trucks.

Sophia switched into binocular mode and could see the forms of several people down by the creek bed. "Go try to get eyes on Anton. I'll cover you from the rebels."

Guthrie slid the rifle off his shoulder. "Pull up your comm. I'll tell you what I find."

He stepped over a tree root and moved with surprising stealth while the rebels seemed content to simply mill about below.

"Found Anton," Guthrie said, but it sounded rushed—more urgent than she'd ever heard him. "He's already in the prone shooting position, but he's aimed forward—not at the ridge, not at the creek."

"At Niko," she whispered back.

Blue flashed from behind her with a loud crackle.

"I've got another teleportation here," she whispered, lunging behind a tree.

"Niotian or Tavian?" Guthrie asked.

"I…" She scoured the map, but beyond a slight aura from a teleportation, nothing new appeared. "I'm not sure. There's no new dots."

"Do you need me back there?"

"No," she insisted, searching the slope above. Nothing moved. "I'll check it out. You keep your eye on Anton. *Don't* let him take that shot."

She darted between the trees, nearing the aura on the map. It had appeared to come from a large cracked boulder. She approached slowly, as quietly as she could.

No one was there.

Her shoulders sank.

Could it have been a Tavian who had gone dark? Why would they leave when she and Guthrie were so close? Anton was probably aiming at Niko. The only other option was another Niotian.

The engineer.

"Guthrie, I think we're okay," she whispered into her comm. "Niko had said he'd brought another person who was supposed to teleport out. I think that's what—"

Three white flashes gleamed ahead of her with the distinct *thunk* of pulse gunfire.

Her heart stopped.

"Guthrie?" she whispered.

Another flash from a different angle, another *thunk*.

"Guthrie!" she hissed, leaping over a downed tree.

"Get over here as soon as you can, Sophia. Cipriani took a shot," he whispered back. "That burst of three was him, and his target is still unidentified. I never got a real clean shot on him, but I fired back, and I think I got him in the leg."

Her feet were moving before her mind could comprehend the rest. They'd made it all the way here. The engineer had gotten what he'd needed. Niko would be exonerated.

She could not lose him now.

"Cover me." She sprinted ahead, pausing only once in a thinner section of trees when a rebel spun to all the noises she was making.

Ducking under vines and hurtling through the underbrush, she closed in on Anton, who had propped himself up on a tree to check his leg. He'd have to check a whole lot more than that if he'd hurt Niko. She charged forward, and he jumped at the sounds, his gaze jittering around. He didn't see her yet. She picked up speed, leaping over a boulder, but he teleported away.

Racing to his spot, she scanned the area in front of him, looking for something—any indication of what he'd shot. Nothing. Silence. She clamped her lips shut to contain her scream, and then drew in a deep breath to calm herself. Niko needed her. She'd find him.

Switching to thermal view, she scoured the slope. He had to be there. Toward the top, a heated mass was huddled at the base of a tree. She crept up the slope, checking for the nearest red dots—they were definitely close enough to see her.

"Guthrie," she whispered. "I'm going to need some closer cover."

"I'm on it," he replied, his voice twisting as he started to move.

She switched into regular vision and stared at the tree. Nothing stirred, but a large root arched out from the base. She inched nearer.

"*Don't. Move,*" Guthrie ordered.

She froze.

"There's a Tavian at your ten. I don't think he sees you yet, but he hears you. His gun is drawn."

She lowered herself to the ground.

"I'm going to take this shot," Guthrie said. "But when I do, we'll be bringing the fury of the entire Tavian guard down on us. You won't have much time. Are you sure it's him?"

"No." In thermal view, there was clearly a warm spot, but it wasn't moving —at all. Had the sun created it somehow? It didn't seem like an area where sunlight could reach. She glanced down the slope, but there wasn't any other possibility for Niko that she'd seen. "Take the shot. I need to get up there and check it out. If it's him, he doesn't have much time."

"You got it."

She braced for the white flash, and the moment she saw it, she sprang through the air. Yells and other flashes burst from all angles. Pulse gunfire and bullets hailed over her head. She lunged at the tree root and thrust her arm into the dead leaves.

Her hand hit something warm, solid, and wet.

"Niko?" She curled her hand around an arm and yanked with all her strength.

"You've got another three Tavian guards headed toward you—I can handle them, but the rebels are advancing up the hill. I'd have to change position to get them. You're running out of time."

She planted a foot on the root and pulled harder. The leaves fell away from Niko's head and chest, eyes glazed and shaking.

"Niko, can you hear me?" She patted his cheek to get him to wake up, but he barely blinked. Leaves clung to his tactical vest and were dyed red.

Three quick *thunks* sounded from nearby.

"Tavians are gone, but the rebels are halfway up the slope. They'll be able to see you soon," Guthrie said.

"It's confirmed. It's Niko," she grunted, wrenching his body farther out of the hole. "He won't be able to teleport on his own."

"Get him out. You've got another five Tavians running at you now. I'll teleport once you're clear."

"We don't leave anyone!" she nearly screeched as she tried to get a better grip on Niko. "Layla told me to leave, too—"

"I have decent cover. I'll be right behind you. Trust me."

She dove headfirst into the leaves, trailing her hand down his leg until she felt the laces of his boot. She yanked it out and reached for his neck.

Bullets whizzed by.

"Get out, Sophia, now!" Guthrie warned.

"Teleporting in three, two, one..."

~

COLD. So cold. Niko couldn't stop shivering. Every breath felt like he was being stabbed, but the harder he tried to breathe, the less air he'd get. He tried to look around, but the light hurt his eyes. He'd been hurt on missions, but never quite like this.

"Help! We have a guard wounded in combat in need of immediate medical assistance!" Sophia yelled.

Sophia...

"Another one?" a female voice yelled.

Niko's thoughts began to drift. He couldn't concentrate on anything when he was this cold.

"Stay with me, Niko," she pleaded quietly. "We're almost there."

She ripped at the zipper of his tactical vest as the navy-blue scrubs of medical personnel started swarming around him.

"He's been shot in the chest," Sophia told them. "I think he's trying to breathe, but he's not getting any air."

"The shots probably went through his lungs," the woman said as he was hoisted onto a stretcher. "We're moving to OR 2. No time for prep. We need to stabilize his lungs now."

The lights overhead zoomed past, and he felt his body getting lighter and lighter. His eyes wouldn't open anymore.

"Don't leave me, Niko," Sophia said, running alongside him. "They're going to take you now, but I'll be right here." Her voice strained. "I love you."

His eyelids flew open, searching for her, but only doctors remained. He sucked in another excruciating breath and focused on keeping his heart rate as steady as he could. He wasn't going anywhere.

He'd stay for Sophia.

CHAPTER 20

*T*wo days later, Sophia stared at one of the pillars lining the circular room. Around her, people gathered for the usual political theater. Heads shaking, hushed tones. Warriors, skilled in combat, sharpening blades that couldn't be seen but were every bit as deadly. She pressed her palms into the rough wool of her uniform skirt to keep her hands from trembling. She'd just charged through a Tavian hot zone, but somehow this panel was worse. Much worse.

"Don't be worried," Guthrie whispered. "You've thought of everything. They won't be able to argue."

Her gaze slid to him, eyes bright blue and full of hope—as if none of this had ever happened. "I'm not so sure."

She opened the menu on her implant and replayed the footage from the map overlay. If she so much as stuttered when explaining everything, they could disregard her as a silly L-1, shocked by combat, who didn't know what she'd seen.

"Order," the clerk called from the podium, and people shuffled to take their seats. Royce emerged from one of the back doors, surrounded by guards. His face was twisted into a pouty frown, and she pinched her lips shut to keep from smiling. Rumor had it that the minister had assigned him his own security detail after she'd heard of all his trips outside the compound. From the looks of it, the rumors were true—much to Royce's chagrin.

Dad moved along the edges of the room toward the front, his gaze on her solemn but purposeful. Pressing his lips together, he nodded, and just like that, without ever saying a word, he'd told her what she needed to hear.

Give them everything they have coming to them.

He had faith that she could do it.

Ichiro took his seat, barely glancing up from the table in front of him. "We're reconvening this panel to discuss new evidence brought forward by the Panel of Seers. Since the summit with the Tavians is tomorrow, we are pressed for time, so we'll get right to the point. Royce, do you want to explain the nature of this evidence?"

"I'd love to, but I believe one of our fine cyber engineers is here, and he may be able to do a better job." Craning his neck, he waved at an old man in the back of the room.

The man hurried forward, then shifted on his feet. "Good morning, everyone—I mean, ladies and gentlemen—err, sirs and—"

"Please state your name," Ichiro interrupted.

"Edwin Harper, sir. I'm a cyber engineer, who primarily works with systems integration."

"And Royce believes you have come across something pertinent to this panel's investigation?"

"Yes, sir. Hold on just a second..." Edwin projected a row of screens in front of the panel. "These are copies of messages sent to and from Captain Cipriani on the ancillary messaging system. Some date back as far as two years—all are mission-sensitive."

Murmurs rolled through the crowd.

"Order," Ichiro warned with a wary glance toward the gallery. "If what you are saying is true—"

"And we have no reason to believe it isn't," Dad interrupted, his glare fixed on Ichiro.

Ichiro hesitated. "Regardless, discussing mission-sensitive material outside the proper channels is against the rules, but it's a private disciplinary matter that can be dealt with at a later date when we're not preparing for a summit."

So at some point in the distant future, they would deal with this behind closed doors? Anton would get little more than a slap on the wrist. Her blood boiled.

"Just—If I may, sir." Edwin extended a bony finger. "I didn't get these from Captain Cipriani. These were retrieved from a database I accessed through Tavian implants. The Tavians were using the information contained here."

Aside from the faint echo of Edwin's voice around the circular chamber, everything was silent. Not a single person in the gallery even moved. Sophia gripped her wooden armrests. Ichiro would be hard pressed to bring this matter behind closed doors now.

"Stealing Guard correspondence is a grave violation of the treaty." Royce's lips twitched upward. "It's very good you caught this, Mr. Harper. All of Nios owes you a debt of gratitude. Were you able to find anything pertinent to the incidents in Santa Rita?"

"Oh, yes, of course." One screen flew to the center of the room, and the others disappeared. "These messages pertain specifically to the operation in Santa Rita. The timestamps on these messages show the Tavians received them before Lieutenant Kalos and his unit started the... before they entered the, um, theater—however you say it, the Tavians knew they were coming and they knew where they'd be."

Anton sprang up from his chair across the chamber and propped himself up on his crutches. "I request permission to address the panel."

Niko never got that courtesy.

"If this is true, I'm just as shocked as all of you, and I want to know how it happened."

Dad's hard gaze slid from Anton to Ichiro and back, his head tilted forward slightly. She'd gotten that look before. Their charade wouldn't be tolerated.

"I'm a victim in this," Anton insisted.

Ichiro straightened in his chair. "I understand your eagerness, but it's not customary to offer a defense—"

Dad leaned forward. "Given that we're all here right now and the summit is tomorrow, the minister will want as much information as possible. If anyone here feels they may be able to provide a more complete picture of these serious events, they should be allowed to speak."

Anyone...

She tucked her chin to hide her smile. Anton could take his turn.

And then she'd take hers.

"Yes." Ichiro bobbed his head. "Captain Cipriani, please approach the podium."

Anton hobbled to the podium, his eyes tight and strained. "I want to assure you that I had nothing to do with this—"

She rolled her eyes.

"—and I will fully cooperate with the investigation, so we can determine how the Tavians hacked my implant."

"Mr. Harper, is that what the evidence suggests?" Dad asked. "That Captain Cipriani was hacked?"

"I can't tell how they obtained the messages," he replied.

"I would never give the Tavians my own messages." Anton raised his voice. "If I had, do you really think I would have followed Lieutenant Kalos into Santa Rita? The Tavians could have found and killed me."

Well, that was probably true. If anyone could be counted on for their strong sense of self-preservation, it would have been him. But whether he'd been hacked or he'd handed over the messages, it meant little to her. He still shot at Niko—nearly killed him. He'd face the full consequences for that.

"I would like to address the panel." She rose from her seat.

"Lieutenant Anuva." Ichiro drew in a tight breath. "We are under strict time constraints. Please send any and all information in a memorandum for commander through the proper channels for consideration."

"I have important evidence pertinent to this panel's investigation of the Santa Rita incidents." She waited, fingers curling into her palms. They didn't want to talk about it anymore—they'd always wanted this to go away, but she wasn't going to let them forget.

The captain next to Ichiro tilted her head. "We said that anyone who had evidence should be allowed to speak."

"Approach the podium, Lieutenant Anuva." Ichiro sighed with a dark look that all but screamed *this had better be good*.

Her heels clacked along the marble floor, bringing her closer to the most important battle she'd ever fight. Anton stepped aside, his smile not reaching his eyes.

She cleared her throat. "Two days ago, Lieutenant Kalos escorted Mr. Harper into an area known for high Tavian activity to retrieve the evidence from their implants."

Anton hopped forward on his crutches. "And in doing so, he disobeyed yet another direct order."

She spun. "You just said that you—his commander—were there as well. Why were you there if it wasn't a sanctioned mission?"

Anton's glare hardened. "I was trying to intercept Lieutenant Kalos before he could do anything stupid."

Got him. She could have leaped in the air.

"To that end, I'd like to present the map overlay for evidence." She blinked and projected the map. "The blue dot is where Lieutenant Kalos had sought cover, the green is Captain Cipriani, and the red dots around the perimeter are Tavians. As you can see, Captain Cipriani had a clear path to Kalos's position, if his goal had been to intercept him, but that wasn't what happened. Captain Cipriani stopped short and got into the prone position with his rifle pointed toward Kalos."

"This is all speculation!" Anton blustered.

She nodded at his leg. "If it's speculation, then how were you shot?"

"We all can see the web of beacons and scramblers." He waved a hand at all the white glowing on the map. "It would have been impossible to mark exactly where I was."

"I, too, will fully cooperate with the investigation." She talked over him. "And my implant logs will show that I locked on Captain Cipriani's implant signature the moment he teleported into the reserve. Additionally, I'm ready to testify to this, as is Lieutenant Guthrie Tejeda, who had a visual of Cipriani while he fired his rifle—"

Anton huffed. "They are loyal to their commander! Their testimony shouldn't be considered."

"Even if you'd prefer not to take our testimony, I request that you watch the full footage of the map overlay. Captain Cipriani takes a direct path to Lieutenant Kalos's position and then stops here." She pointed. "With a full line of sight—"

"The area was crawling with Tavians!"

"—and he waited in the prone position with his rifle pointed in the direction of Lieutenant Kalos." She pictured Niko's face as she'd pulled him from under the tree root, pale and unresponsive, and had to work at keeping her voice steady. "The first shots fired were from Captain Cipriani's vantage point, and no Tavians were in the area. He fired three shots, corresponding with the three wounds sustained by Lieutenant Kalos. This was no mistake."

Anton's whole body was rigid. "In the heat of combat, nothing is ever easy—"

Ichiro held up a hand, silencing Anton, while keeping his focus on Sophia. He raised his eyebrows. "Those are some very serious allegations."

"I don't make them lightly, but I urge the panel to consider the evidence," she said. "None of the Tavians in the area would have had a clear shot. Lieutenant Kalos's injuries could have only come from one person."

Ichiro eyed Dad. "If I recall correctly, the penalties for something like this could be prosecution for attempted murder."

Dad nodded gravely.

"We'll need some time to deliberate over the evidence and render a disciplinary decision," Ichiro continued. "But this is unprecedented. I have no choice but to recommend that Captain Cipriani is relieved of his command immediately while he awaits further disciplinary action."

"I want it on the record that I intend to appeal this." Anton jabbed a finger at the ground.

Ichiro's gaze darted to him. "That's certainly your right. I look forward to seeing how you could refute all this evidence."

"Sir." Sophia spoke up again. "In light of the proof that the Tavians possessed the messages that led to the ambush in Santa Rita and Captain Cipriani's actions in the field, I request that his testimony regarding Lieutenant Kalos be thrown out."

Ichiro nodded, shuffling his papers and already glancing at the door. "Yes. That seems reasonable. Lieutenant Kalos's leadership responsibilities are reinstated."

Her chest expanded with a breath but tightened just as quickly. It was the result she'd fought for, but now Niko would have to choose. Black ops guards weren't allowed to have serious relationships—especially true since he was her commander again. He deserved to be unit leader, but she couldn't help but hope he'd give it up to be with her.

"This panel is adjourned." Ichiro rose and left quickly. The entire chamber buzzed with the turn of events.

"See?" Guthrie approached the podium. "I told you."

She rolled her eyes. "I'm going to go see if Niko's awake, so I can tell him the news. Want to come?"

"Nah, I think you two will probably have a lot to talk about." He winked, and warmth rushed to her cheeks. He wasn't wrong. "Besides, I got a date with Emma tonight."

She let out a humorless laugh. "And so it begins."

"Sophia," Dad called from behind her.

"I'll catch you later," Guthrie said, backing away.

She turned as Dad approached.

"Nice job today." He hugged her, but his emerald eyes seemed distant.

"Not happy with the result?" she asked, lifting her head from his shoulder.

"What? No, it's not that at all," he said, his eyebrows pulling together. "In the few months you've been in the Guard, you've had to fight battles I'd hoped you'd never have to fight." He turned to face her. "But I couldn't be prouder of how you've handled it all. I'm amazed at the person you've become."

A lump rose in her throat. "Thanks, Dad. That means a lot."

"I have to run. I'm meeting with Commander Mendoza to help prepare for the summit, and she'll want recommendations for who should fill Cipriani's command role, but maybe you could come over for dinner soon?"

"I'd like that," she said, kissing his cheek.

He disappeared into the dwindling crowd, and she took a moment to let everything that had happened settle. She'd stopped them from making a scapegoat out of Niko. Anton would finally face the consequences of his actions. Horacio was set to be released from the hospital soon, and with any luck, Layla would be released after the summit tomorrow.

Only one thing left to do...

Her stomach squirmed. It was time to talk to Niko.

CHAPTER 21

*B*right sunlight lit up Niko's room—too bright. He wasn't ready to get up yet. He arched his back to turn over, and splitting pain shot through his chest.

Oh yeah...

Rolling onto his back, he groaned.

"Niko, are you awake?" Sophia whispered.

He opened his eyes. Sure enough, there she was, dark curls pulled back in a loose bun, eyes as gorgeous as ever, and her smile... He would have walked through fire just to see her again.

"You saved me," he croaked. The words ripped through his dry throat. How long had he been sleeping?

"Barely." Her eyebrows pulled together, and she smiled tightly. "It was touch and go for a little while. You were in surgery a long time, and you've been asleep for a week."

"Huh?" he grunted. How could he sleep that long and still be tired?

"A week. Your hourly scans for infection thankfully haven't come back positive, but your inflammatory markers were still high, so they kept you sedated."

A week. What happened in that time? He swallowed. "Edwin?"

She grinned, and for a moment all the tightness in her face disappeared. "He did it, Niko. He got everything he needed and more. The Tavians had all the messages between Anton and his assistant—including one where he said he was going after you. That was all the panel needed. He was immediately relieved of command, and it's possible he'll face attempted murder charges. You have been cleared of everything. You're unit leader again."

Cleared. He sucked in a breath, and even though it ached, his chest somehow felt lighter. Not an ounce of him wanted the unit leader position again—he couldn't be with Sophia and be her boss—but that could be dealt with later. Right now, there was too much he needed to say.

Her lips curved upward. "The Tavians showed up to the summit with their crazy list of demands, but when we showed them the evidence—213 counts of possession of Niotian correspondence—they backed off immediately."

The Tavians conceded. Did that mean... "Layla?"

"Released immediately. She's shaken up, of course, but physically, she looks good." Her smile faded. "She came by to see you when you were sleeping. She's really grateful for everything you did to get her back."

Niko let his head drop back into the pillow. Beams of amber sunlight shone on the ceiling and gave the white hospital room some color. All of this would have been worth it just to get Layla back—even if he hadn't been cleared.

But he had. Layla was free, and he was, too.

"So that's it?" Niko asked. "It's over."

She dropped her chin again and studied her hands. "Um, Royce has some concerns—something about the Tavians giving in too easily and how it might be a sign that they're covering something else up, a mole in our government. Commander Mendoza is taking that pretty seriously. She's leaving no stone unturned, but there's enough resolution to move forward. Gideon has been discharged from the Guard for his part in the messages. McCade was promoted to take over Anton's command, so it looks like he's your boss again."

Niko chuckled. "I bet he loves that." Truthfully, Niko did, too. There wasn't anyone better.

His hand drifted toward the edge of the bed, toward her. Even the small space between them felt like too much—not that she would have seen it. She was still frowning at her hands. He needed to tell her so much, but there was a massive wall between them. He ached to burst through. "But?"

"Hmm?" Her gaze popped up.

"This all sounds amazing, but you're fidgeting again." He pointed at her hands. "Something's wrong."

Her mouth opened, but she stayed quiet as her face tightened. It felt like his heart was being torn from his chest.

"I put in a request for reassignment," she finally said.

"What?" he belted out the question so forcefully, his chest heaved in a coughing fit.

"Niko!" She flew to his side and tried to steady him as he curled forward. If the coughs were any stronger, he might hack up his spleen, but she couldn't leave. Not after everything they'd been through. Only moments ago, the future had seemed so bright and hopeful, but without her?

She propped him up with pillows and grabbed some water from a nearby table. "Please try to take it easy."

He cleared his throat. "Is this about the unit leader thing? I won't take it. I don't even want it."

"No, no." She shook her head, still standing next to the bed with her hands out like she was ready to catch him. "Well, maybe a little bit, but that's not the whole problem."

"Then what is it? You're too good of a guard to just walk away."

Her gaze darted to him, strong and steady. The green flecks in her eyes glimmered, sending a wave of shivers over his skin. "*That's* the problem. I am a good guard, but that's not what I want to be to *you*."

"I..." Of course she was more than a guard to him. She was everything. She knew that, right?

She sighed and plopped into her chair. "You told me to go find my fairy-tale, so here it is." Scooting to the edge of her seat, she laced her fingers into his, sending his heart into his throat. "It's you. I don't need a pairing, but I don't want to be casual with you, either. If we stay in black ops, we'll always have to hide our relationship—pretend it's less than it is." She shook her head. "I *can't* hide my feelings for you. I'm not saying I want children tomorrow, but if I've learned anything about the Guard, it's that it can be a very lonely place." She shrugged. "I want a partner."

He was *her* fairytale? If it hadn't been for his stitches, he would have pulled her to his side. For her, it wasn't enough just to be together. She wanted it all.

Everything he wanted.

It was more than he would have dared to hope for. He'd been awful to her when they'd met. He could barely expect her forgiveness, and yet she'd seen right through him. She was beautiful, fearless, as fierce as anyone he'd ever fought with, yet gentle and kind, good—and she saw the good in him. Now that he'd seen her for who she was, he couldn't ever imagine wanting to leave her side.

He pulled her hand up to his lips and kissed it reverently. "You saved me, Sophia."

She huffed. "Let's not talk about that anymore."

"No." He shook his head. "You don't understand. You saved me twice."

Frowning, she searched his face.

"When we teleported here, I could feel myself dying. It actually wasn't so awful, kind of like drifting away with a tide, peaceful. I'd done what I'd needed to do."

She recoiled away from him, shaking her head. "I don't want to hear this. I can't—"

He tugged on her hand, pulling her back until she sat on his bed next to him. "Then you said, 'I love you.'"

Her gaze drifted to his, and he slid his arm around her waist.

"I didn't know if I'd make it, but I knew I wanted to try just to hear you say it again."

"I love you," she whispered, then dropped to his lips and kissed him, her sweet floral scent washing over him and every bit as lovely as it had been before. He ran a hand through her silky curls. Finally, McCade's decision to leave black ops made sense. A partnership, a love, a once-in-a-lifetime opportunity. He'd never regret leaving everything behind for her. Pressing his forehead to hers, he stared deeply into her eyes. Could he really look into those eyes for the rest of his life? Make her smile? Kiss her? Have children with her?

A smile tugged at the corners of his mouth. "McCade said this would happen, that I'd one day understand why he'd left black ops to be paired."

"So you're coming with me?" she asked, eyes bright.

"Yes, of course." He wrapped his arms around her, and she settled in next to him. "McCade will be sad that he can't boss me around anymore. He always loved doing that, but it'll make him happy that he was right."

She giggled and snuggled closer. Yep. He could get used to this. He'd have to find some way to thank McCade.

"I love you, Niko."

"I love you, too." He turned to her for another kiss.

THE END

ABOUT THE AUTHOR

Katherine is a military wife and mother of four kids, who loves all things sci-fi, fantasy, and action packed. Home is wherever the Air Force sends her family, and right now they're lucky to be in Colorado Springs.

She writes speculative fiction with strong characters and relatable struggles, but since she's always been inspired by the burst of creativity that happens when science, politics, and the human element collide, you can expect colossal adventures to ensue with a touch of romance to make the journey sweeter.

When she's not at her kids' school, church, or sporting events, you can find her either cozied up with her Kindle or writing on her laptop—always with a big cup of coffee.

To find out more, visit https://katherinebennet.com/

ALSO BY THE AUTHORS

MIRANDA HONFLEUR

"Winter Wren" (available on www.mirandahonfleur.com)

Blade & Rose (Book 1)

By Dark Deeds (Book 2)

Court of Shadows (Book 3)

Queen of the Shining Sea (Book 4) Available August 2018*

The Dragon King (Book 5) Available 2019*

Immortelle (Book 6) Available 2019*

RYAN MUREE

"What Blooms in the Dark" (available on www.ryanmuree.com)

The Last Elixir (Book 1)

What Rises From the Ashes (a prequel novella)

The Fallen Gate (Book 2)

The Shattered Core (a prequel novel)

EMILY ALLEN WEST

By Any Other Name (excerpt available on www.emilyallenwest.com)

EMERALD DODGE

"Ignite" (available on www.emeralddodge.com)

Battlecry (excerpt available on www.emeralddodge.com)

KATHERINE BENNET

Black Rose (prequel) (available on www.katherinebennet.com)

The Seers (Book 1)

95918864R00446

Made in the USA
Lexington, KY
15 August 2018